'Bring him over here,' Jeanne commanded. 'It is a he?'

'Oh, yes'm, Mrs Hamilton,' Henrietta said, and placed the boy in her mistress's arms. 'He is a big boy.'

'What shall we call him?' Jeanne looked at her husband.

'Well, Henry for a start,' Hamilton said. 'As he is Henrietta's child. As for a second name . . .'

'He'll be a playmate for Christopher,' Jeanne said. 'We'll call him Henry Christopher. How's that, Henrietta?'

'Why, mistress, that is very nice.' She gazed at Richard Hamilton. 'You ain't going sell he, Mr Hamilton? You ain't going sell he?'

'Not while I can afford to keep him, and you,' Hamilton agreed. 'As the mistress says, he'll be a playmate for Kit. Besides . . .' he placed Richilde in her mother's other arm. 'He's Richilde's twin. Well, almost.'

He stood back to look at them, the one so white, the other so black; the pair, so beautiful.

BLACK
MAJESTY

Christopher Nicole

THE SHERIDAN
BOOK COMPANY

This edition published in 1994 by
The Sheridan Book Company

First published in two volumes by
Severn House Publishers Ltd 1984, 1985
Book One – The Seeds of Rebellion
© F. Beermann BV 1984
Book Two – Wild Harvest
© F. Beermann BV 1985

Arrow edition 1986
Random House, Vauxhall Bridge Road, London SW1V 2SA

© F. Beermann BV 1984, 1985, 1986

Printed and bound in Great Britain by
Cox & Wyman Ltd, Reading, Berkshire

ISBN 1–85501–658–3

This is a novel, but the events it relates are history. Henry Christopher, born 1767, died 1820, whose name became Henri Christophe, was a Negro slave who fought his way to power as the Emperor Henri I of Haiti. With his great compatriots, Pierre Toussaint l'Ouverture and Jean-Jacques Dessalines, he created a black nation capable of matching itself against the two foremost countries in Europe, England and France.

The quotations in this book are taken from *The West Indies: Their People and History* by Christopher Nicole.

Christophe was every white man's conception of the noble savage. Over six feet tall and built to match, he had the natural grace that both Toussaint and Dessalines lacked. He was as intelligent a man and as brilliant a soldier as the one, and as illiterate and lion-hearted as the other. He was born in one of the British islands – both Grenada and St Kitts have been awarded the honour – and although sold to a Frenchman at an early age, he preferred to retain the English spelling of his first name until his coronation. His personality attracted legend, and there are many conflicting stories of his youth.

CONTENTS

Prologue

The rumble grew out of the still evening air, cascaded across the lush green of the sugar plantation, reached the heavy cedars of the forest beyond, echoed upwards into the foothills of the mountains which made a backbone to the island of Hispaniola and bounced back again across the quiet ocean. The sound might have been caused by a battle or by the first threatening groan of a coming earthquake; it might have been a volcano stretching or, more prosaically, the approach of a thunderstorm. But it was no more than the procession of three dozen barouches, gigs, phaetons, bounding behind their splendid horses, on the road to Plantation Vergée d'Or. It was 23rd March, 1765, and the Sieur de Mortmain was entertaining.

The Great House itself might have been on fire, so numerous and so brilliant were the candles and tapers, rushes and lanterns, which seemed to fill every window and flickered and swayed on every verandah. The polished floor in the great ballroom had been scattered with powder, the huge mahogany table in the enormous dining room sagged beneath the weight of countless dishes of food, West Indian – chicken and pork, smothered with peppers and cassereep, tuna fish and mackerel, caught off the coast of the plantation itself, avocado pear and eddo, sweet potato and roasted plantain – and European – sweetmeats and cheeses, best claret and finest brandies. The long row of portraits of previous Mortmains almost seemed to smack their lips as their severe gazes surveyed the scene beneath them.

Upstairs the bedchambers, each large enough to contain an average cottage, had been swept and polished, the beds overlaid with their pale covers decorated with the golden thread of the Mortmain emblem, the mailed fist, the snow-white mosquito nets withdrawn and secured to the high tents, ready to be released to protect those who would sleep from the countless insects which made up the Caribbean night, but for the moment not permitted to obscure for an instant the perfection they guarded.

And everywhere, in bedchamber and on gallery, on the main staircase and in the cavern-like entry hall, in the ballroom and in the dining room, in the study and on the verandahs, haunting the marble statues on the drive and the iron gates beyond, were the Mortmain servants. Every tall Negro – for Jacques de Mortmain recruited his domestic slaves rather as his idol, Frederick the Second of Prussia, recruited his guardsmen – was clad in a pale blue tailcoat, with gold thread at collar and cuff, white vest and breeches and stockings, and gilt-buckled black shoes, just as their female counterparts, hardly smaller, wore pale blue gowns with the Mortmain design, in golden thread, on their bodices, and white caps.

On the front verandah, waiting to greet the first carriage, were the three people who lived in this palace, and who owned everything, living or lifeless, on Vergée d'Or. Jacques de Mortmain, in a pale blue silk tailcoat with gold embroidery and buttons, a flowered silk waistcoat, with dark blue breeches, white stockings, and black shoes, the whole topped by a powdered and pommaded wig, suggested a gigantic bird of prey. He was above average height, but his sixty years made him stoop slightly, while his face was thin, dominated by the beak of a nose. His wife, some twenty years younger, revealed in her bloodless features the ravages of a lifetime in the tropics, the remnants of the bout of yellow fever which had once nearly killed her, and the continual malarial attacks which often sent her to bed with an ague. She wore a pink satin gown, carried away from her hips by enormous panniers embroidered in green and red silk; her wig, towering towards the ceiling, made her seem as tall as her husband, and winked with the sapphires which were her favourite stones, her malacca cane, which supported another enormous sapphire in its silver handle, reached her shoulder, and her fan was painted in the Mortmain colours of pale blue and gold.

Philippe, her only surviving son, stood behind his parents. He was twenty-two, and had but recently returned from Paris; the guests who were at this moment descending from their carriages would only remember him as a small boy, and he would remember them as very much his elders, or as grubby playmates. Now no one could doubt that he was a man, and more, that with his father clearly growing older and weaker every day he would soon be Seigneur of Vergée d'Or, owner of the greatest plantation in all St Domingue, grandest of *grand blancs*; not a man arriving tonight but would see in him a rival, not a woman but would see him either as a possible lover, if she was already married, or a possible husband, were she single. It was a thought at once exhilarating, and a little daunting to Philippe.

But he reminded himself that he would be a prize, even without his wealth. As tall as his father, and as slender, on his face the Mortmain nose fitted well between the high forehead and the wide mouth and big chin. He had refused to wear a wig, because it was absurd in the West Indian heat, certainly, but also because it would have concealed his own hair, which the Pompadour, on the one occasion he had met her, had remarked was the most beautiful she had ever seen, black and soft as night, a perfect match for his eyes. And for this of all occasions he preferred to dress quietly, a dark green coat over a gold-coloured waistcoat, and white breeches and stockings. If the ball was in celebration of the elevation of the eleven-year-old Prince Louis, grandson of King Louis XV, as Dauphin, there could be no doubt that Philippe was the true guest of honour.

The carriages were rolling to a halt before the marble staircase, and the first of the bejewelled and befanned ladies was being assisted down by white-gloved Negro footmen. Jacques de Mortmain's major domo snapped his fingers, and the orchestra struck up, while the maidservants hurried forward with goblets of iced sangaree.

Jacques de Mortmain kissed the hand extended towards him. 'Thérèse, how splendid to see you. You'll drink the health of His Highness?'

Thérèse de Milot raised her glass. 'And damnation to the English!'

Now the greetings, and the toasts, became general, and

the staircase became a long, glittering flow of people and comment, seeming the more brilliant because of the darkness which surrounded it.

Of varying shades. The overseers and their wives and children, whether *petit blancs* or mulattos, might be envious of their betters, but still were unable to resist the temptation to gather beyond the white palings of the gardens and watch the wealth from which they were forever excluded. Yet even they unthinkingly gathered into two groups. The meanest of the *petit blancs* would not allow himself to be a social acquaintance of the best mulatto, even if, under French law, any *café-au-lait* was born free. And the mulattos, of course, made sure they were nowhere near the *noirs*, who formed an even greater, and darker, concourse at the very end of the drive, from where they too, granted a holiday on this greatest of days, could stare and wonder, at beings as far above themselves, and as unaware of their existence as individuals, as was the very moon which was beginning to fill the sky and send a swathe of white light across the sea and the canefields and the forest.

And their numbers grew, constantly, as the maids and the coachmen of the guests, having discharged their immediate functions, left their carriages and joined the Vergée d'Or slaves. Opportunities for meeting those from other plantations, from the towns and the great houses of Cap François, were rare. Here was a chance to exchange gossip, to learn what was truly happening about them, in the world, no less than in St Domingue itself, to reunite with someone who had shared the horrors of the Middle Passage, or who had once been a slave on one's own plantation, perhaps to meet again a brother or a son, or even a husband, torn away for sale by the whim of his master.

And here too was an opportunity for plotting, for those who had at once the courage and the intelligence to suppose that the fact of their slavery was not an unalterable law of nature.

Into the crowd sidled one of the first of the coachmen to arrive, a little man, in his mid-thirties, who walked with a limp, but who was greeted with some affection by everyone he passed. His black eyes searched the black faces in front of him until they found the one he sought, a powerfully built Negro whose heavy shoulders made him seem about to overbalance, and whose face was angry, as if there were a fire burning inside his brain.

'Jean François,' remarked the coachman, and walked on.

The big Negro hesitated but a moment, glancing to and fro, and then followed. The coachman was already beyond the crowd of slaves, taking the road towards the Negro village. His visits to Vergée d'Or were not to be wasted. But Jean François sweated. He was a recent arrival in Hispaniola, was not sure whom he could trust, and who would betray him to the whip, or worse, the wheel. Yet he was already a man of power amongst his people, by the very force of his character, the dominant anger of his personality. And he had been told that only the young coachman would be his equal.

Toussaint walked down the lane between the Negro huts, found the one he sought. Now the noise and the laughter and the glittering lights were far behind him, almost lost in the whisper of the trees and the soughing of the gentle wind. A dog barked in the village and then another, but both fell silent again as the two black men ignored them.

'You know she will be there?' asked Jean François.

'She will be there,' Toussaint promised, and turned aside, to pause before the cane mat which made a doorway to one of the smallest of the huts, at the same time motioning his companion to be silent.

They waited for some minutes, and then a whisper seemed to come from the mat itself. 'Who waits to see Céleste?'

'Pierre Toussaint,' said the coachman.

'Jean François,' said the big man.

'You are expected,' said the whisper.

Toussaint nodded, and held the mat aside, then followed Jean François inside. The hut was dark, save for a single guttering candle set in the earthen floor, sending shadows racing into the corners. It was noisome, and at first sight it

13

seemed unfurnished. The two men knelt, hands on knees, facing the flame and the woman beyond.

If she was, indeed, a woman. She appeared as no more than a wisp of scarlet cloth, for this evening she had put on her red turban; her face, so lined and gnarled it was impossible to gauge her age, seemed but a cage for her eyes. And like her visitors, she knelt, her fists clenched in front of her.

'What do two such men seek of a poor *mamaloi*?' she whispered.

'We seek knowledge, Mama Céleste,' Toussaint said. 'We seek a sign.'

'The war is over,' Jean François said. 'Our masters have been defeated, it is said. But they are still our masters.'

'We wish to know when it will be time,' Toussaint said.

'Time,' Mama Céleste whispered, and peered into the flame.

'Time,' Jean François said, his great fingers opening and shutting.

'Not yet,' Mama Céleste said. 'Not yet, O mighty warrior. Aye, mighty you are, of limb and mind, but not yet mighty enough. You will do nothing without the aid of Damballah Oueddo, without the presence of Ogone Badagris. Without them, without those they will send, who will be mightier warriors even than you, you will perish, and all who support you.'

'Then where are they?' Jean François' voice grew louder, and Toussaint shook his head, warningly.

'Who knows?' Mama Céleste said. 'They are everywhere, at all times. But only they know when they will choose to reveal themselves. And then they will come, as warriors even mightier than yourselves, men even bigger, and stronger, and more terrible in battle. Such men are only now about to be born, yet will they live, and prosper, in your cause. I can but tell you to prepare and be patient. When the time comes, you will know it. The white people will talk amongst themselves, and argue, and quarrel, and then they will set to killing one another, and the mulattos as well. Then, and only then, will Damballah Oueddo make himself known to you.'

'And we will know him, when we see him?' Toussaint asked.

'There are many of our people, bigger than I,' Jean François said. And smiled, sceptically. 'Perhaps even mightier warriors, than I.'

'Black he will be,' Céleste said. 'Black as the night from whence he comes, and into which he will sweep the whites. And big he will be, a man of greatness apparent to all. Yet will his might be surrounded by beauty, and his blackness surrounded by light. By this beauty, by this light, shall you know him.'

PART ONE

The Slave

The West Indian planters and their families saw themselves as a race apart, creatures of unusual courage and ability, capable of creating vast fortunes under the most dangerous circumstances. They strode their verandahs like lion tamers, facing a horde of wild beasts kept in subjection only by terror. They placed their faith in the creation of an aura of personal ascendancy, of terrible omnipotence which permitted no opposition to, or even hesitation in, the carrying out of their slightest wish.

The symbol of this white supremacy was the whip.

Chapter I

THE CHILDREN

The Stamp Act, which aroused such a violent reaction in the North American colonies, evoked a similar response amongst the inhabitants of St Kitts, who not only destroyed all the stamped paper on their island, some two-thousand pounds worth, but sailed across to Nevis and repeated the deed there.

'Now then,' John Hamilton shouted. 'All together lads. All together. Charge.'

The men gave a whoop, and launched themselves against the iron-bound door, the log of wood they were using as a battering ram tucked under a dozen brawny arms. The wood crashed against the door, and the whole structure creaked.

'You'll cease this madness, Hamilton,' came the shout from within. 'I've muskets here. I'll blast you.'

'And hang for it,' Richard Hamilton shouted. 'Open up, Harley.'

'I'll see you damned first,' Harley shouted.

The men had paused, listening to the conversation, removing their tricorne hats to fan themselves and wipe their brows free of sweat as they awaited a signal from their leaders. The Hamiltons were cousins, their relationship immediately evident in the big, friendly features they each possessed, the wide mouth, too used to smiling for work of this nature, the thatch of curly brown hair, the lanky frame. It was in support of John Hamilton that Richard had brought his twenty men across the narrows from St Kitts to the much smaller island of Nevis. Here they had almost doubled the crowd; Nevis was one of the tiniest of the West Indian islands, hardly more than a huge mountain rising steeply from the sea to a height of more than three thousand feet. The village of Charlestown huddled at the foot of this immense extinct volcano, in the shelter of the only bay the island boasted, a collection of decrepit wooden shacks, of peeling paint and crumbling shingles, simmering in the afternoon heat. It contained hardly more than a few hundred people, and if most of them might have been expected to agree with their neighbours that the exactions of King George's government were rapidly becoming unbearable, they preferred to remain indoors, behind shuttered windows, and let others do their protesting for them.

'Break it down, Father. Break it down.' Little Alexander Hamilton, John's son, jumped up and down. The Customs House was one of the most solidly built structures in the town, yielding only to the church and the prison in the strength of its timber walls – but Richard Hamilton did not suppose it was going to withstand the efforts of a score of determined men.

'Again,' he shouted. 'Again.'

The men gave another roar, and ran forward. Once more the tree trunk struck the exact centre of the door and this time cracks appeared.

'Once more,' Richard shouted.

'There'll be a man-of-war here tomorrow,' Harley called. 'They'll have a yard-arm for you, Dick Hamilton. Oh, aye. And your people.'

Crash went the tree trunk and the door fell in. The men gave a whoop and swarmed over the shattered timbers, pausing only a moment at the sight of the Customs Agent, presenting a musket to them, then wisely throwing it to the floor in disgust.

'Just the paper, lads,' John Hamilton said. 'Just the paper. Don't touch a thing more. You'll send the account for this door to me, Ned.'

'Bah,' Harley said, sitting down at his desk and folding his arms. 'You'll not buy your way out of this.'

The men were carting great bales of stamped paper outside into the street, and now that the threat of bloodshed was averted, doors opened and people swelled the throng, chattering and sweating, sending nostril-tingling dust swirling upwards. It was a white crowd, although the people were as decrepit as their dwellings; their Negro slaves wisely looked on from a surreptitious distance.

'That is government property,' Harley said, coming to the broken door. 'And is worth two thousand pounds. I'll send you the bill for *that*, John Hamilton. And if it's not paid, you'll spend the rest of your life in a debtors' cell.'

'Twist his nose for him, Pa,' Alexander shouted. 'Twist his nose.'

'And your brood will starve,' Harley said, with some satisfaction.

'I'd not come outside if I were you, Ned Harley,' John Hamilton said. 'They might take to burning you along with the paper.'

The bonfire had already been lit in the very centre of the street, and the stamped paper was being hurled into the flames. Smoke drifted upwards into the still air; it would be seen by the watchers on St Kitts, who would know that the expedition had triumphed.

If that was the right word. 'What have we accomplished here, Dick?' John Hamilton asked his cousin, his exhilaration fading as the deed was done.

'An act of protest.'

'Will they not send more stamped paper? This time accompanied by soldiers?'

'I doubt the last. As for the stamped paper, why, we'll burn that, too.'

'We seek to defy the most powerful government in the world,' John Hamilton said. 'And that apart, have we not committed treason?'

Richard Hamilton watched the leaping flames, the cheering people. The entire white population seemed to have assembled now, and all were equally gleeful. He suspected that there was rum in the jugs being passed from hand to hand.

'Not of the hanging variety,' he said. 'Not even King George would consider hanging an entire colony.'

'But he will wish to make an example of the ringleaders,' John said. 'Harley will not forget. That is a certainty. And if there *is* a frigate due . . . here in Nevis, I suspect we lack your stomach.'

Richard Hamilton frowned. 'Well, then, abandon this desert island and come to St Kitts.'

John pulled his nose. 'I am considering that very point. But there is naught for me in St Kitts. I doubt there is much for you, Dick. I'm for Virginia. If you can arrange me a passage.'

'Do you not suppose King George's warrants are served in Virginia as well?'

'Maybe they are. But it is a big country. There is room for a man to flap his wings. And they share our point of view, from what I've heard.' He rubbed Alexander's head. 'There will be more opportunities there for Alex than clerking in his father's store. You'll accompany me, Dick?'

'Not I,' Richard Hamilton said. 'I like to see the sea, when I awake, and before I retire. Besides, Jeanne is about to deliver.'

'Then you should be there, rather than here.'

'Politics first, personal matters after,' Richard Hamilton said. 'Besides, Marguerite is with her.' He watched the fire begin to die, the ashes drifting with the wind. 'But now it is done, I'll send the boat back for your things, John. And arrange passage to the mainland. We'll have you out of here before Harley's frigate can drop anchor.' He grinned. 'Our slave woman is about to give birth as well. We're doubling our establishment!'

From the deck of the sloop St Kitts loomed to the north. A considerably larger island than Nevis, it too was dominated by a single peak, the massive bastion of Mount Misery, which rose out of the centre of the island like a huge finger pointing at the sky. Well below it, and only six hundred feet above the harbour, the equally massive natural strength of Brimstone Hill, jutting away from the rest of the mountain, with the setting sun gleaming from the brass cannon guarding the embrasures cut into the living rock, reminded the watchers that this island had had to fight for its existence, more than once.

St Kitts was the oldest of the British West Indian colonies. Here Thomas Warner had led his tiny band of adventurers ashore a hundred and fifty years earlier, and from here, after settling with the Carib Indians, the Warners and their descendants had spread over the entire Leewards. Not without competition from the French, who until the Treaty of Utrecht only fifty years before, had shared the island, as the name of the main town, Basseterre, indicated. And even now a considerable number of French planters and merchants remained, despite the inconvenience inflicted upon them by the recently ended Seven Years War. For which, Richard Hamilton thought with some pleasure, he should be sufficiently grateful.

For as the sloop dropped her sails and came into the little wooden dock there was his brother-in-law, Maurice de Mortmain, standing in the crowd to greet him.

'Is it done, then?' Mortmain called, reaching for his hand.

'Aye.' Richard looked back over his shoulder; Nevis was only two miles away, and the smoke could still be seen drifting on the afternoon breeze.

'And no violence?'

Richard grinned. 'It was necessary to break down Ned Harley's door.'

The crowd cheered, and fell to shaking hands and slapping backs. Here at least there were no doubts as to whether or not destruction of the stamped paper had been their right as free-born Englishmen. Only Mortmain failed to share the prevailing jollity. He was in any event a serious man, rendered more so by the beak of a nose and the thrusting chin which was his family's hallmark, and also, Richard sometimes thought, by the whim of fate which had left him merely a poor relation of his famous and wealthy cousin in St

Domingue.

Now he said, 'You English. Were this still a French colony, messieurs, I do assure you this would be a hanging matter.'

'But it ain't a French colony, now is it, monsieur?' somebody said. 'We've a habit of seeing to our own affairs, here.'

Mortmain sighed. 'Until the frigate comes. Ah, well, we'd best make haste, Richard.'

The two men hurried up the street towards the shipping agent's office, above which Richard Hamilton lived. 'Is all well?'

'She was just beginning labour when I left,' Mortmain said.

'My God!' Hamilton began to run.

Now at last Mortmain smiled. 'But she is in good hands, Richard. Marguerite is experienced in these matters.'

He had seven children, where the Hamiltons possessed but one, at this moment, and he was on the porch to greet his returning father. 'Papa,' Christopher Hamilton shouted. 'Mama is crying.'

He was three, and had been promised a little brother. Hamilton took the steps three at a time, threw open the door at the top, ran across the tiny living room, burst into the bedroom, checked, gazed at this smiling wife. 'Jeanne . . .'

'Here she is, Uncle Richard.' Madeleine de Mortmain, at eleven the eldest of the five Mortmain girls, was holding the babe in her arms.

'She?'

'A girl, Richard,' Marguerite de Mortmain said. The sisters were remarkably alike, with yellow hair and soft, liquid features, which in Marguerite were almost doelike. If Richard Hamilton could be said to have married above himself in securing one of the Desmoins girls, Marguerite could have no doubt that she had aspired to the stars. Her father had been a bankrupt planter, no matter how superior even that might have been to a shipping agent. Maurice de Mortmain might be only his cousin's attorney for the

23

Mortmain St Kitts plantation, but the wealth was *there*. Yet she had, Richard Hamilton thought, contributed more to the marriage than her husband; with her as a mother Madeleine, in her mass of pale yellow hair, her nose delicate rather than beaked, her chin pointed, already promised beauty, hard to find in a Mortmain, and undoubtedly her younger sisters would also in time catch the eye.

'I am sorry, Richard,' Jeanne said.

'Sorry?' he shouted. 'To have you safe . . . to have you both safe . . .' He held out his arms, and the babe was placed in them, somewhat reluctantly, by his niece.

'What will you call her?'

Jeanne Hamilton sighed. 'She was to be a boy, and called Richard.'

'There is an equivalent,' Marguerite said. 'Richilde.'

'Richilde Hamilton,' Richard said. 'I like that name.'

'Then Richilde it shall be,' his wife agreed.

'With Jeanne as a second name.'

'Richilde Jeanne. Yes, indeed.' He turned his head as a fresh wailing came from behind him. 'What the devil . . .'

'Is me own, Mr Richard,' Henrietta said. Not for her a bedchamber filled with anxious relatives. She had given birth alone, had severed her own umbilical cord, and was already on her feet. She knew she was fortunate, in being the slave of a shipping agent rather than a planter, even if, as the only slave the Hamiltons could afford, she had more than enough to do. But both the Hamiltons were indulgent owners, who treated the big black woman as a friend rather than a servant.

'Bring him over here,' Jeanne commanded. 'It is a he?'

'Oh, yes'm, Mrs Hamilton,' Henrietta said, and placed the boy in her mistress's arms. 'He is a big boy.'

'Big,' Jeanne said in wonderment. 'My God! He must weigh all of ten pounds. Did he not harm you?'

'Well, I did be bleeding just now,' Henrietta said. She raised her skirt to peep between her legs. 'But I thinking it is stop.'

'What shall we call him?' Jeanne looked at her husband.

'Well, Henry for a start,' Hamilton said. 'As he is Henrietta's child. As for a second name . . .'

'Who was the father?' Mortmain asked, with obvious amusement.

'Well, Mr Mortmain, sir. . .' Henrietta looked embarrassed. She was not only a large woman, and able to make her feelings felt, she was also extremely handsome.

'He'll be a playmate for Christopher,' Jeanne said. 'We'll call him Henry Christopher. How's that, Henrietta?'

'Why, mistress, that is very nice.' She gazed at Richard Hamilton. 'You ain't going sell he, Mr Hamilton? You ain't going sell he?'

'Not while I can afford to keep him, and you,' Hamilton agreed. 'As the mistress says, he'll be a playmate for Kit. Besides . . .' he placed Richilde in her mother's other arm. 'He's Richilde's twin. Well, almost.'

He stood back to look at them, the one so white, the other so black; the pair, so beautiful.

Richard Hamilton raised his eyes from the paper he had been studying, gazed across the desk at the man standing on the other side. 'This is madness, Troughton. You must know that.'

The Customs Agent sighed. 'No doubt what you did was madness, to others. Governments must govern.'

'At a distance of four thousand miles? Let them allow us a government of our own. Or at least representation in theirs.'

Troughton sighed again. 'I am not here to discuss politics, with you, Richard. I am here to present a simple fact.'

'Of my arrest? You'll have a riot on your hands.'

'Aye. What I am showing you there is merely the warrant. I am in possession of letters as well, instructing me not to force the matter until the frigate arrives.'

'The frigate,' Hamilton remarked contemptuously. 'Always the frigate.'

'She is really on her way this time, Richard. From Kingston, with a company of soldiers as well as her normal complement. She is, I quote, to restore the islands to their duty.'

'Their duty.' Hamilton got up, stared out of the window at the ships lying in the bay, loading sugar from lighters. He pointed. 'There is our duty, Troughton. To grow sugar, and to ship it, so that Farmer George can grow even richer. You will have a riot.'

'I am aware of it. But the frigate *is* coming. You will have some deaths on your conscience.'

Hamilton chewed his lip.

'Which is why,' Troughton went on, seeking to take advantage of his friend's doubt, 'I have come here at all. To give you time to consider.'

'What do you recommend?'

'Your cousin John seems content enough, in Jamestown.'

'You'd have me run? Anyway, Johnnie is a factor. He needs but a roof over his head and some goods to sell. I am a shipping agent.'

'Do they not have ships out of Virginia? Johnnie will provide you with introductions.'

'And the planters here?'

'Will find somebody else to organise their cargoes for them. They will have to. Believe me, Richard, it is the best way. It is the only way. You cannot defy King and Government, and Navy as well.'

'Ned Harley,' Hamilton growled. 'I should sail across to Nevis and wring his neck.'

'Then would you be wanted for murder as well. And he was only doing his duty when he lodged charges against you.'

'As you are only doing yours in arresting me.'

'I hope I am doing my duty as a friend, first, by giving you time to remove yourself.'

Richard Hamilton looked down into the yard, where the cradle waited in the coolness of the shade. It had been Jeanne's decision that the two babies should share it. In many ways she was treating the slave boy as if he were the son she felt she should have had. But Henry was such a smiling, happy child it was difficult to resent it, no matter what problems Hamilton might see looming in the future.

'I have a family,' he said. 'My daughter is still at the breast.'

'I know that,' Troughton said. 'Perhaps you should have considered them sooner.'

'You'd have me expose them to a sea voyage, and then a search for employment, and indeed, sustenance?'

'You'd have them starve, while you kick your heels in prison? Or even worse? It could come to that: you have defied His Majesty. You have a brother-in-law, Richard. Surely he could care for your wife and children until you have found your feet.'

Richard Hamilton sat behind his desk again. This was his home. It had been hard in the beginning, but he had done well, and been happy. And become a leader in the community, at least that of the Basseterre merchants. Nor had any of the planters, his social betters, either refused his company or attempted to dissuade him from leading their protest. But he knew them well enough, even Maurice de Mortmain – or especially Maurice de Mortmain, who lived in continual fear of his famous cousin's disapproval, which might leave *him* destitute – to be sure not one of them would raise a finger in his defence. And if the townspeople would be more faithful, as Troughton had pointed out, a few staves and pistols would hardly accomplish much against the cannon of a frigate, the muskets of a company of foot.

Did he regret what he had done, that sunlit day nearly a year ago? Only the consequences, not the deed. But how many men, he thought with wry humour, must have had an indentical reflection at some time in their lives? And did his ever restless spirit not thrill to the idea of once again adventuring, even without Jeanne? Or was the thought of being entirely his own man again the most exciting of all?

He raised his head. 'How long have I got?'

'A year,' Richard Hamilton said. 'Hardly more than that. You've my word.'

Jeanne Hamilton smiled through her tears. 'And I'll count

on that. I cannot help but feel once you set foot on that ship I will never see you again.'

'I'm not that easy to lose.' He kissed her again, then lifted his son from the floor. 'You're going to look after your mother for a season, Kit.'

'I want to come with you, Father,' Kit shouted. 'I want to fight the Indians.'

Richard Hamilton held him close. 'I'm not going to fight any Indians, Kit. I'm going to work. And you'll be coming soon enough.' He set the boy down again. 'Then you'll have to work, too. But meanwhile, you'll look after your mother, and you'll care for you sister, and you'll see to Henrietta and little Henry, and you'll help Uncle Maurice in everything he decides. You understand me?'

Kit was biting his lip, determined not to cry in front of his French cousins. But without success. Great tears rolled down his cheeks. Richard was glad to turn away. 'Marguerite.' A hug and a kiss.

'We'll look after them for you, Richard,' she said. 'It was a proud thing you did. It'll come right in the end. It must.'

'In the end.' He reached past her to shake Maurice's hand. ''Tis a heavy responsibility I load on to your shoulders, old friend.'

'A welcome one,' Mortmain promised him. 'They will prosper, as I prosper, until you are ready for them.' But his forced smile was sad, his thoughts easy to understand. Richard Hamilton was fleeing, to be a wanted felon. So John Hamilton, by report, had prospered. He was older, as his family had been older. He had always been more serious-minded than Richard.

But then, Richard thought, Maurice had always been a pessimistic man, so it was natural for him to view the future with concern. He squeezed the fingers a last time, looked over the seven children, who ranged from Etienne, at fourteen already almost a man, serious of face like his father, constantly putting on his brand new tricorne hat and then taking it off again to finger the braid at the brim, to little Annette, only two, waiting in the arms of her nurse. They were all blonde, all slender, all serious. He could never tell them apart.

He gave them a collective embarrassed smile, turned to Henrietta, who carried a babe in each arm.

'I too sad to see you going, Mr Richard,' Henrietta said. Her gaze drifted to Maurice de Mortmain, and then away again.

'Mr Mortmain is a good man,' Richard said. 'He will be a good master. You have naught to fear.'

'He ain't going sell we, Mr Richard? He ain't going sell my Henry?'

'No,' Richard said. 'He has promised me that. He won't sell you.' He smiled at her. 'You will be better off on the plantation than you are here.'

'But he going put Henry in the field,' Henrietta said dolefully.

'Now, that I cannot say,' Richard said. 'Henry will have to work. You do understand that, Henrietta?'

'Yes, sir, Mr Richard. I understanding that. But if he get put in the field he going get the lash. I knowing that.'

'He need never be whipped, if he works well. It is up to you to make sure he learns that.'

'Field slave must get the lash,' Henrietta said. 'I knowing that.'

'Not if you train him well,' Richard repeated. He chucked his daughter under the chin. 'He'll have Miss Richilde to care for.'

'Oh, he going do that,' Henrietta promised. 'I going train him to do *that*.'

'Well, then . . .' Richard Hamilton looked back at the people in the room, picked up the small carryall in which were his clothes. 'One year,' he said, and went outside.

There he paused to set his tricorne on his head and faced the people who waited to say goodbye.

'You don't have to go Richard,' said one of the men who had accompanied him to Nevis. 'Say the word and we'll fight that frigate. We've those guns up on Brimstone.'

'And become relvolutionaries?' Richard clapped him on

the shoulder. 'I'd not wish that on any man.' He went down the stairs, exchanging farewells as he did so.

'Only a year,' Marguerite de Mortmain said, and put her arm around her sister's shoulder. 'It will seem no time at all.'

'I shall never see him again,' Jeanne Hamilton said, her voice flat.

'Oh, come now,' Maurice de Mortmain said, glancing anxiously at his wife.

'I shall never see him again,' Jeanne repeated. 'I know it.' She touched her breast. 'Here. I shall never see him again.'

The children hurried through the long grass, panting, stumbling, sweating, effort oozing from every pore, trying to keep up with the General. Who now came to a halt, holding up his hand, so suddenly that Richilde Hamilton cannoned into Lucy de Mortmain, and Henry Christopher, bringing up the rear as usual, cannoned into Richilde.

'Here,' Kit Hamilton said; he spoke French, as the children were encouraged to do about the plantation. 'This is a good defensive position.'

The grass dissipated itself in a patch of bog, some twenty yards across, beyond which there was a stand of trees.

'I don't think it's good at all,' Lucy said, sitting down to peer at a scratch on her leg; a thorn had torn the stocking to get at the white flesh beneath. She was thirteen years old, actually a year older than the General, and was inclined to argue.

'They'll attempt to dislodge us with missiles,' Kit explained, his big, friendly Hamilton features expressing good-humoured patience. 'But we can sit here all day.'

'I don't see why we should sit here at all,' Lucy said, taking off her hat to fan herself, sending pale blonde hair tumbling. 'I want to go home.'

Kit sighed. 'We have to defend the stable,' he said. 'That is the whole object of the game.'

'I think it is a silly game,' Lucy declared. 'I don't see why we have to play soldiers all the time. I think we should play kings and queens. I think we should have a ball. I think you

30

should ask us to dance.'

Kit glanced at her in exasperation, and then looked at his sister and the black boy. Who stood together, as they always did. They were the youngest of the children, just eight, and always did exactly what Kit told them to. In many ways he was a father to them. They didn't have any other. Well, Richilde thought, Henry didn't, certainly. And if he did, it wouldn't matter. Henry was a slave, and belonged to Mama. She supposed *she* had a father. No one seemed to know for sure. Mama would never talk of him.

'We are playing soldiers,' Kit said. 'Because that is what Louis and I like to play. And you agreed to it, too, Lucy.'

'That was before it got so hot,' Lucy said, disagreeably. 'I want a glass of coconut water. If we go back to the house Henrietta will give us a glass of coconut water.'

'Ssssh,' Kit said. 'And lie down. They're here.'

Richilde immediately threw herself full length in the grass, regardless of the damage to her white dress. Henry lay beside her, panting. Lucy sighed, and also lay down, beside Kit. They peered through the grass, watched the other children coming out of the trees beyond the bog. Louis de Mortmain was first. He was fifteen, and dominated Kit, in their choice of games, much as Kit dominated the younger ones. With him were his other two young sisters, Annette, who was nine, and Françoise, who was eleven. With perfect symmetry, the Mortmains had had their children one every other year for seven births. Richilde thought it would be wonderful to have a lot of sisters, even if she was perfectly satisfied with a single brother; besides, Henry really acted as another brother. But sisters! Often Annette and Françoise and Lucy went into a huddle together, from which she was excluded, because she was too young, they would say, but she knew it was because she was only their cousin. And then there was Catherine, so dignified and aloof, at seventeen, and even more Madeleine, already married at nineteen, to whom they could turn for advice, or sympathy. Madeleine and Catherine were both perfectly willing to give Richilde advice or comfort as well, but it wasn't the same.

31

Besides, they all had a father, too. A real father.

'We'll let them know we're here,' Kit whispered, and stood up to wave his arms. Louis started forward immediately, but checked as his shoes slipped in the mud.

'You come back here,' Françoise shouted. 'You'll get all dirty.'

'Now then,' Kit said, crouching beside them again. 'While they're thinking about how to get across, we'll start a flanking movement. You and me, Lucy.'

'I thought we just had to stay here, and stop them from getting to the stable,' Lucy objected.

'If we don't outflank them, they'll outflank us, soon enough,' Kit pointed out. 'That is elementary military strategy. Besides, it's what Frederick would do. It's what he did at the Battle of Leuthen. He made a demonstration in front of the Austrians, and then marched more than half his army round their flank while they weren't looking, and beat them all up.'

'Frederick,' Lucy grumbled. 'Always Frederick. He's a *Prussian*. Why can't we fight like a French general?'

'Because the French generals always lose,' Kit said brutally. 'Now you two, listen. Show yourselves every so often, just to remind the enemy that we are still here. And when you hear me shout, launch a frontal attack. We'll catch them in the rear.'

'Across that bog?' Richilde squeaked.

'It's not as deep as it looks. You can take off your shoes and stockings. Now remember, wait for my shout. Come on, Lucy.' He crawled away to the left, and Lucy, after a moment's hesitation, followed him.

'If I get my legs all muddy,' Richilde said sadly, 'Mama will be so angry.' But she took off her shoes, pulled her skirt up to roll down her stockings. It did not really occur to her to disobey Kit.

Henry watched her with interest; as he wore only a pair of white cotton drawers he had nothing to take off. Nor did his presence embarrass her. He was her twin, Mama always said, which suggestion would send Henrietta into peals of laughter.

Besides, he was interested in other things. 'This Frederick,' he remarked. 'He is a real man?' He also spoke fluent French, overlaid with the soft West Indian brogue.

'Of course,' she said. 'He is the King of Prussia.'

'Kings ain't good,' Henry said. 'That is what I hear your mummy say.'

'You are talking about King George,' she said. 'He is King of England. He is a bad man, Mama says. But most kings are quite good. This new king of France, Louis the Sixteenth, he is a good king, Uncle Maurice says. And Frederick is a great king. He wins all his battles. And he builds lovely palaces. Miss Fitzgerald teaches us about him in the schoolroom.' She paused, her mouth a huge O, distorting her features which, like her Mortmain cousins, contained enough of her mother's looks to dilute the Hamilton strength – 'She'll never be beautiful,' Jeanne Hamilton would say. 'But she won't be ugly, either.'

The schoolroom was the one place Henry was not allowed to enter, their lessons the one amusement he never shared; it was against the law to teach a slave to read or write. And she wouldn't hurt Henry's feelings for all the world. 'Uncle Maurice has a book about him too,' she said. 'With pictures.'

Henry laughed, and leaned forward to ruffle her mane of curling light brown hair, making her flush. She adored his sudden, intimate gestures, so disconcerting when coming from a black boy. If the truth were told, Richilde was afraid of black people, the field hands, great big men and women who carried fearsome long knives called machetes, and stared at her with huge dark eyes. Louis had told them all horrible stories of a slave revolt only twelve years ago in a place called Berbice, a Dutch colony situated on the mainland of South America, when all the white people had been chopped up by the machetes, and, apparently worst of all, a Dutch girl named Miss George had been kept a prisoner by the blacks for several weeks before she had managed to escape. Richilde was not at all sure how being kept a prisoner could actually be worse than being chopped by a machete, but Louis assured her that it was, and Françoise had supported him, rolling her eyes and saying, 'It's horrible, you'll know when you grow up.' So presumably it was horrible.

But of course black people were not really the same as Henry, who with his friendly features and his wide grin *could* have been her brother, except for his colour. And who was her friend.

Now he said, 'You going show me those pictures, some time?'

'Some time,' she agreed, and turned away from him to peer through the grass. 'Are they still there, do you think?'

'I think they gone home,' he said. 'To drink coconut water.'

'Oh, they can't have,' she protested, and stood up, to kneel again as a clod of earth flew through the air towards her, followed by several others. 'They're still there.'

'Why they like to be soldiers, all the time?' Henry asked, lying beside her. 'Kit and Louis.'

'All boys like to be soldiers, all the time,' Richilde said, wisely. 'Don't you wish to be a soldier, all the time?'

'How can a slave be a soldier?' he asked.

She frowned at him, disconcerted by his sudden gravity. And by the realisation that he *was* a slave, which he had never actually put to her before. In any of its aspects.

Her thoughts were interrupted by a creaking of wheels, the stamp of hooves. She rolled over, on to her back, looked up at the pony and trap, at Etienne de Mortmain, coatless, sleeves rolled up his muscular arms and head shaded by an enormous straw hat, strong fingers tight on the reins. Beside him sat his sister Catherine, also sheltering beneath a straw hat, but looking much more elegant in a pale green gown, with a matching chiffon scarf round her neck and drifting behind her in the breeze set up by their progress.

Etienne brought the trap to a halt as the two children started out of the grass. 'Richilde?' he shouted. 'Whatever are you doing?'

'Just playing, 'Tienne,' she said.

His gaze shifted from her to Henry. 'You'd best get up,' he said. 'We'll drive you to the house.'

'Oh, but . . .' she looked across the bog at the trees.

'Do as 'Tienne says, dear,' Catherine said.

Richilde hesitated, then ran to the trap. Henry followed more slowly.

'You'll not ride, Henri,' Etienne said. 'I'll attend to you later.'

'I'm Henry,' Henry protested. 'Not Henri.'

'God damn you for being a mutinous black dog,' Etienne shouted, his hand flicking the whip to send the thong curling towards the little boy. 'You are anything I care to call you, boy. Now get yourself back to the house.' He jerked the reins, and the trap started to move. Richilde, just climbing into the back, nearly fell over, and had to hold on to both sides. Kneeling, she looked back at Henry. In avoiding the whip he had fallen over, and was only now getting up again, to gaze after the vehicle with smouldering black eyes.

The Mortmain plantation of Marigot was situated on the north eastern side of the island. Here was Windward, where the trade winds never ceased, and the great Atlantic rollers, hardly broken by the presence of the neighbouring island of Antigua, hull down upon the eastern horizon, constantly pounded the beach. It was a cool place, as compared to the more gentle living on the protected, Leeward, side. But Richilde loved the sea, the smell of it, the feel of it, the sound of it. She adored it when Miss Fitzgerald would allow them to walk on the sand, without their shoes and stockings, skirts held to their knees as they paddled on the edge of the waves. She dreamed of one day actually entering the tumbling waters, of feeling them pick her up and roll her over, of fighting with them. But that of course had to remain a dream. Miss Fitzgerland would never hear of it. If the slaves occasionally bathed in the sea, it was not something that a white person, and more especially a white lady, would ever consider doing.

The road from the orchard and the stream, where the

children played most of their games, skirted the top of the beach before turning inland towards the plantation house. Marigot was a large estate, by the standards of St Kitts; it covered some hundred and fifty acres and required over a thousand field slaves. The canefields stretched away to the north and west, under the very shadow of old Mount Misery, which seemed to hang directly above the trap as it entered the drive. Here on Windward the plantation house was the first building encountered, to make sure it remained upwind of all the smells and sounds from the slave village, as well as the plantation farm, and the factory, its red brick chimney a lone sentinel against the green of the fields and the trees carpeting the lower slopes of the mountain.

The factory was silent now, the plantation itself quiescent. It was the quietest part of the year, with the young cane, the ratoons – shoots taken from previously cut stalks and transplanted – all growing well, and with the grinding season still several months away. Richilde thought grinding almost as exciting as the sea. Then the plantation seemed to shake itself, and awake from a long sleep. The huge iron rollers would turn, crushing the canestalks, and screaming against each other almost as if the cane itself was crying out for mercy, the chimney would start belching black smoke, and a steady mound of glorious sweet brown sugar would accumulate in the storerooms, into which the children were often allowed to drive their fingers to consume whole handfuls of the delicious granules. While the scent of fermenting molasses would pervade the whole plantation, for the sugar which could not be properly crystallised, because of impurities, was not wasted, but converted into the plantation's other main product, rum. Sometimes, when Uncle Maurice was in a good mood, the children would be allowed mugs of the incredibly heady white liquid, which would send them into giggles and then a deep and dreamless sleep. Once the rum had been purified, and coloured, it was regarded as too strong for them.

Of course grinding had a dark side, too. Uncle Maurice was really quite an indulgent master. Today, for example, as she could see beyond the house, there were only four men occupying the stocks. This was sufficiently unpleasant, she supposed, as they were naked, and only given water once a day, and for the rest had to sit out in the sun, without even a hat, and unable to swat or scratch the insects which clustered on their skins, while the other slaves were encouraged to throw rotten fruit at them, which not only left an unpleasant smell but attracted even more insects. However, white people in Basseterre who had committed a breach of the peace were similarly incarcerated, save that they were allowed to retain their clothes for the sake of decency – which did not seem to matter in the punishment of the blacks – and unless one of the slaves had been especially wicked, such as insubordinate to an overseer, they would not actually be flogged. Uncle Maurice did not flog his slaves himself; like most planters he employed a professional, called a jumper, a man who went from plantation to plantation, offering his services. This was because the whip used to discipline the slaves was not an ordinary cat-o-nine-tails, but a cartwhip, a single long thong of leather, with a piece of steel embedded in its tip. Thus where the cat soon became matted with blood and flesh and dwindled into a single broad paddle – which no longer hurt, according to Etienne – the cartwhip went on cutting and hurting with every blow. Carelessly used, it could kill, very rapidly, and there was no planter who wished to destroy property he had paid good money for – none that Richilde had heard of, anyway.

But during grinding the overseers used their whips freely, and the slightest slackening of effort was rewarded with a flogging. Much as she loved the taste and smell of the sugar, the hustle and the bustle, she dreaded hearing the piteous screams of the wretches, men and women, strung up on the triangles to suffer; she would run to the bedroom she shared with Annette and Lucy and pull her pillows over her ears.

A sudden terrifying thought crossed her mind that Henry had been guilty of insubordination to Etienne. But Henry could not be flogged. He was her friend. Her twin. And he was only eight years old. And most important of all, he was a house, not a field slave. House slaves were only flogged if they actually attacked a master or mistress.

Yet he would certainly he punished.

'We were only playing soldiers,' she ventured.

'Alone, in the grass?' Catherine turned her head to look at her, not very severely, Richilde was happy to note, but frowning as she inspected her more closely. 'Where are your stockings and shoes?'

'I took them off.'

'You are getting too old to romp with slave boys,' Catherine said. 'And he is getting too old to be allowed to play games with you. He should be put out to work.'

'He is going to be put out to work, Etienne said, not turning his head, as he was concentrating on avoiding the ruts and pot holes in the drive. 'I intend to see to that.'

'Oh, but . . .' Richilde bit her lip. It really wasn't much good arguing with 'Tienne, who saw himself as very much the young master. Uncle Maurice would see her point of view. And certainly Aunt Marguerite. She wasn't at all sure about Mama any more. She was very moody; sometimes she would be quite kind and understanding and then at other times she would look at Richilde as if she really didn't know who she was.

The plantation house was the biggest building Richilde had ever been inside; it would have made two of even Government House in Basseterre. It gave the impression of being only a single storey with an attic, because the downstairs was a mass of large galleries, protected by a deep sloping roof, out of the centre of which the upstairs rose like an afterthought; but the upstairs, small in comparison with the rest of the building, contained six bedrooms. It was a happy place, where the sea breeze constantly soughed and the servants smiled, and of course, with so many children about the place there was always laughter or shouting or screaming or banging going on somewhere in the background. Richilde could not imagine living anywhere else. According to Kit, she *had* lived somewhere else once. She had been born in the little room above the Shipping

Agent's Office on the waterfront in Basseterre, because that was where Father and Mama had lived. She had seen the place, on one of their rare visits to town, and she found the thought quite incredible. Certainly she could remember nothing of it. Marigot was her home.

The trap pulled to a halt in front of the wide front stairs, and Richilde jumped down. She wanted to be first into the house, first to see Uncle Maurice, first to explain the situation. She ran up the steps, skirts clutched in front of her, only then realised that she had left her hat and shoes and stockings in the long grass. Mama would be furious. Uncle Maurice was very generous, but Mama could never forget that she and her children were nothing more than poor relations.

But surely they would still be there tomorrow.

'Uncle Maurice.' She burst into the office. Uncle Maurice only went aback – into the fields – once a day now that he was getting old, and spent the rest of his time working on the account books. Now he looked up with an expression that was at once tired and pleased; Richilde knew that he was very fond of her, where perhaps he found his own daughters rather tiresome – she never asked for anything.

Except today. 'Uncle Maurice,' she said. 'We were playing a game . . .'

'She was rolling about in the grass by the orchard, with that black boy,' Etienne interrupted, coming into the room and throwing the satchel he had been carrying into a chair. 'Half naked. It was quite disgusting.'

Maurice de Mortmain frowned at his niece. 'Were you doing that, Richilde?'

'It was a game.'

'Catherine saw it,' Etienne said.

Mortmain looked at his daughter, who waited in the doorway.

'Yes, papa,' she said. 'It really was quite disgusting.'

'It was a game,' Richilde shouted. 'All the others were there. They were hiding in the trees. We were playing soldiers.'

'That boy must be punished,' Etienne said. 'It is quite insufferable, allowing him to play with the children. And he was rude to me, answered me back. He should be whipped, and then put in the field.'

'You can't, Uncle Maurice,' Richilde begged.

Maurice de Mortmain looked at the tears gathering in her eyes, then at his son. 'Are there letters?' he asked, buying time.

'Several.' Etienne opened the satchel, placed the mail on the desk. 'About Henri Christophe . . .'

'His name is Henry,' Richilde said. 'He was christened Henry. He wants to be called Henry.'

'He wants?' Etienne sneered. 'A slave boy?'

'My God,' Maurice de Mortmain said, and held up the black-edged envelope. 'From St Domingue.'

Etienne frowned. 'Uncle Jacques?'

Mortmain slit the paper, took out the sheet inside, scanned it. 'Uncle Jacques is dead,' he said. 'Philippe says he never truly got over Tante Marie's death. We must . . .' he frowned as he continued to read. 'My God,' he said again.

'Papa?' Catherine came into the room.

Maurice de Mortmain stood up. 'Go and fetch your mother. And Aunt Jeanne. And find all the children. I wish to see them here. Immediately.'

'But what's happened, Papa?'

Maurice de Mortmain looked as if he had seen a ghost. 'Philippe wishes me, us, to go to St Domingue,' he said. 'To live at Vergée d'Or. Fetch your mother.'

'It seems that Philippe has decided to reorganise the estates,' Maurice de Mortmain said, surveying the family gathered in front of him. 'He has been studying our returns, and he is of the opinion that Marigot is no longer an economical proposition. Besides, he apparently does not like owning property on an English island. So I am to place the plantation on the market.'

They stared at him, unable to comprehend.

'Sell Marigot?' Marguerite de Mortmain asked at last.

'But . . . this is our home.'

'We are to make a new home, in St Domingue,' Mortmain explained. 'Philippe is very generous in what he says. He says he feels sure that I, with my great experience of planting, will be of tremendous assistance to him on Vergée d'Or. He also says that he looks forward to providing a home for all of you.'

'St Domingue,' Etienne said. 'The greatest colony in the entire West Indies. Oh, it will be marvellous.' He squeezed Catherine against him. 'You'll find a rich husband, in St Domingue.'

'Leave Marigot?' Marguerite de Mortmain said, half to herself. 'That is quite impossible. You must write Philippe, Maurice, and tell him that it is quite impossible.'

'My dear,' Maurice de Mortmain said, 'Philippe is now the head of the family. He *owns* Marigot, just as he now owns Vergée d'Or. If he has decided to sell, there is nothing I can do about it. Besides, there is sound economic sense in what he is saying. Only the big plantations are making the same profits they used to. Marigot is really too small.' He attempted a smile. 'And as Etienne says, in Cap François Catherine will be able to find a rich husband. Why, all the girls will be able to find rich husbands.'

'And Madeleine?' Marguerite demanded. Madeleine de Mortmain had done the best she could, in St Kitts, and married an English planter.

'Well . . . she will be able to come and visit us, from time to time.'

'Time to time?' Marguerite shouted. 'She will be hundreds of miles away. Hundreds.'

'I am sorry, Marguerite,' Maurice de Mortmain said. 'But we do not have any choice in the matter. If Philippe has made up his mind. . .'

'Philippe,' his wife sneered. 'Always Philippe. You would take orders from a man half your age?'

'Philippe is not half my age,' Maurice said, mildly. 'He is thirty-one. That is not half my age.'

'You are fifty-two. Are you going to take orders from a

41

man twenty years younger than yourself?'

'I am in no position to do otherwise, my love. Would you have us starve? All of us?'

Marguerite de Mortmain bit her lip, and flushed.

'I cannot go to St Domingue,' Jeanne Hamilton muttered.

'Why not?'

'Richard will not know where to find me.'

Maurice exchanged glances with his wife, who put her arm round her sister's shoulder.

'Richard will find you, my dear,' she said. 'If he ever comes to look. But you know that not even that nice boy Alexander has heard from him in five years. He went off into the West to seek his fortune, and has just disappeared. You must accept the fact that he is dead.' She raised her head, to look at Kit, almost defiantly, Richilde thought. But she was saying that Father was really dead. Richilde wanted to burst into tears, even though she had never seen the man. And yet she didn't, because of the excitement which bubbled through her. Of course they had to go to St Domingue, with Louis and Annette and Françoise and Lucy. Even with Etienne and Catherine. St Domingue was the greatest of all the West Indian colonies, whether English or French. Everyone said so.

'I think you children should run off and play,' Maurice de Mortmain said. 'Aunt Jeanne and Mama and I have things to discuss.'

Richilde raced through the drawing room and out to the back verandah. Henry Christopher sat here, fanning himself, with her hat. He had brought her shoes and stockings as well.

'Oh, you darling,' she cried. 'Thank you ever so much.' She sat beside him, kissed him on the cheek, held his hand. 'Henry, you'll never believe what has happened.'

'Your daddy has come home?' he asked, hopefully; his mother had brought him up to believe that he was still Richard Hamilton's slave, rather than a Mortmain.

'No.' Richilde's smile died. 'Aunt Marguerite says he is dead.'

'He ain't dead,' Henry declared. 'He can't be dead. Not Mr Hamilton.'

'I don't know. Oh, I wish I knew. But Henry, we are to go to St Domingue. All of us. We are leaving Marigot, to go and live with cousin Philippe at a place called Vergée d'Or. It is a most splendid place, Tante Marguerite says.'

'St Domingue?' He frowned at her. 'But that is French.'

'Well, I am half French.'

'I am English,' Henry said.

'Well, you will learn to be French,' she said. 'You will love it there, Henry. St Domingue is the place to be. It is the most wonderful place on earth. Everyone says so.'

Chapter 2

ST DOMINGUE

Only in the still young colony of St Domingue, with all
the hinterland of Hispaniola available for expansion,
were Frenchmen to be found who wished to become
West Indians.

'Cap François,' Louis de Mortmain told the children, 'is
the Paris of the Western Hemisphere.'

And even Richilde, prepared to be sceptical, was forced to
accept the suggestion that here was a city transported from
the very heart of European civilisation to grace the
magnificently lush green of the mountains and the forest
which had dominated the skyline for the past three days as
the sloop had skirted the coast. She had, of course, seen
pictures of European cities, without ever relating them to
reality; Basseterre had always seemed the ultimate in
civilised living for her. But, as they disembarked from the
boat on to the greenheart dock, it occurred to her for the first
time that Basseterre was in reality nothing better than a
fishing village.

The other children were no less impressed, and she could
tell that even Mama and Aunt Marguerite, and Miss
Fitzgerald, for all their pretence at sophistication, had had
their breaths taken away by the splendour about them. By
the buildings: every one seeming to be new and most
splendidly appointed; by the architecture, which cascaded
from turrets and high balconies to verandahs and patios, to
massed beds of multi-coloured flowers, to ornate and
voluptuous, and quite indecent – to Richilde's eyes – statues,

carved from the purest marble, to the tall trees leaning across the wide boulevards, their branches a glitter of crimson flowers. And then by the kaleidoscope of humanity which bustled everywhere, *grand blancs* displaying the latest in silk satin, ostrich feathers drooping and décolletages plunging; *café-au-laits* gossiping on street corners, brown faces animated, gowns like multicoloured firework explosions, heads bound up in no less brilliant bandannas; or *noirs* gleaming with sweat and endeavour working on the docks. And then by the variety of scents and aromas, almost every one pleasant, which arose from the perfumed gardens and the no less perfumed bodies of the population; by the accumulation of vast ships anchored in the harbour, and most of all by the deference paid to them as soon as it was learned that they were Mortmains, and bound for Vergée d'Or. Because waiting for them on the dock was an army of carriages and equipages, and several white men, supported by a regiment of slaves ... but no Seigneur de Mortmain for whom they had been waiting in a state of some apprehension.

'I am Fedon,' the first white man said. He looked every bit as well dressed as Uncle Maurice, who was wearing his best coat and a new pair of white stockings, and far more confident. 'I am the Sieur de Mortmain's attorney. Welcome to St Domingue. Ladies.' He kissed Aunt Marguerite's hand and then Mama's.

'My cousin is not in town?' Uncle Maurice asked.

'Ah, no. The Sieur de Mortmain seldom visits Cap François. And these are the children? How nice.' His eyebrows arched as he obviously counted, and arrived at eight. 'How nice,' he said again, and looked at the Negroes. 'There was no necessity to bring any blacks.'

'These are personal servants,' Aunt Marguerite explained.

'Ah,' he said again. 'Allow me to introduce these gentlemen.'

There were six more white men, all apparently overseers on the plantation, who were assigned one to each carriage. Richilde found herself in the last, with Annette and Kit and

Lucy, and a man named Morin. She wished to ask how the slaves, or at least Henry, would get out to the plantation, but she didn't dare. Instead she gazed out of the window as the carriage rolled through the streets, at the people who hastily moved out of the way the moment they saw the Mortmain crest, and saluted.

'Cousin Philippe must be very popular,' Lucy observed.

'Popular?' Monsieur Morin considered. 'He is very powerful. He is the richest man in St Domingue, and St Domingue is full of very rich men.'

'Are you very rich?' Kit asked, with that terrible directness of his which Richilde often found embarrassing.

Monsieur Morin merely looked at him. 'I work for the Sieur de Mortmain,' he said.

Now they had passed the last of the houses and were riding along a beaten earth road next to the beach, with the great rollers thundering on their left, and the huge mountains rising away to their right; in between there were cultivated fields, and in the distance dark forest.

'You will like it here,' Monsieur Morin said. 'It is the best place on earth.'

'Is the plantation far?' Lucy asked.

Monsieur Morin allowed himself a smile. 'You have been on the plantation for ten minutes.'

'Have we?' Richilde cried, speaking for the first time, and craning her neck to look out of the window. 'But there is no cane.'

'We grow other things on Vergée d'Or besides cane, mademoiselle,' Morin said. 'But you will see cane soon enough. Vergée d'Or is a large place. Look there.'

Canefields! Which stretched for as far as the eye could see. Just as the road stretched for as far as they could see, too; she realised that they had been travelling long enough to have ridden from Marigot into Basseterre, and they had been on the plantation all the time.

But then she saw what appeared to be a large town, although the houses were all low and small, and there were no church steeples.

'The Negro village,' Morin said.

'How many slaves do you have?' Kit asked.

'It is difficult to be precise,' Morin said. 'About seven thousand.'

'Seven *thousand*?'

'We have eight hundred white people too,' Morin said. 'Well, whites and mulattos. They live over there.'

Beyond the slave village there was a town of elegant houses and grassy lawns. Richilde found that she had taken off her hat and was scratching her head. She suddenly felt like a midget. Even the trees which lined the road seemed to be larger than any she had seen before, while the factory, which now came into view as the road at last turned away from the sea coast, made Marigot's seem no larger than a workshop.

Morin was smiling at their amazement. But now, like a good magician, he produced his *pièce de résistance*. 'If you look up there,' he said. 'You'll see the chateau.'

To begin with Richilde could only make out a stand of enormous trees, beneath which the carriage was now making its way. Then it stopped, and a blue-coated Negro footman was opening the door and another was waiting to help her down. Their wigs were powdered, their feet encased in brilliantly polished black leather shoes. Behind them was a regiment of blue and white clad Negresses, bowing and clapping their hands to welcome the guests, who gathered in a nervous huddle on the patio, all, even Uncle Maurice, looking up in amazement at the turrets which overhung them, at the balconies and the wings, at the brick patios which surrounded the lower floor and could only be insulted by being called verandahs, at the raised rose gardens which fringed the grand staircase, at the horde of servants which lined the walkway, at the mass of white people who waited beyond, and then at the man who was at this moment descending the staircase like a king.

Because he is a king, Richilde thought. Philippe de Mortmain has to be a king, to live like this.

Philippe de Mortmain looked surprisingly young. Richilde

remembered that he *was* much younger than either Uncle Maurice or Aunt Marguerite or even Mama, but still he was over twenty, which necessarily made him old, like Etienne or Madeleine. Yet the fact was that he did not look a great deal older than Etienne.

He possessed, of course, the Mortmain features, prominent and sharp, and the Mortmain height, with a breadth of shoulder which made him seem larger than he actually was. And surprisingly, amongst all the brilliantly dressed overseers and servants, he alone wore nothing but a shirt and breeches, tucked into black riding boots. But she observed, as he approached them, that the shirt was best cambric, and even that would have been unnecessary to delineate him as the master of Vergée d'Or. He moved with an unconscious arrogance, an utter certainty of his wealth and power, and of the lack of it in all those beneath him. Including his own relatives.

'Maurice,' he said, kissing Uncle Maurice on both cheeks. 'How splendid to see you. Marguerite.' He kissed Mama's hand. 'Jeanne? Yes, indeed. And these are the children?' He shook hands with Etienne and Louis, standing beside each other, paused in front of Catherine. 'But you are a beauty, dear cousin,' he said softly, and brought a rush of colour to her cheeks. 'You are all beauties,' he said, kissing Françoise and Lucy and Annette in turn, and arriving at Kit. 'And you?'

'Christopher Hamilton, monsieur,' Kit said.

'Ah. The English children. Then you will be Richilde.'

Her knees felt weak, and knocked together. She couldn't speak.

He smiled at her. 'Another beauty on its way,' he said. 'Vergée d'Or will glow. It has not glowed for too long. Now I know you will all wish to see your grandparents. Maurice, we'll talk when I return.'

He gave them a collective smile, went down the marble steps to where a horse was being held for him by a Negro groom, and where half a dozen other white horsemen, also dressed for the fields, were gathered, like military staff surrounding a general. Philippe de Mortmain raised his riding crop, and the little cavalcade moved off.

Marguerite de Mortmain said something in an undertone to her husband, who hastily frowned and shook his head. Clearly their cousin was not to be criticised, no matter how obviously he might treat them like his other myriad possessions.

'You going come with me, mademoiselle,' a voice said, and she discovered one of the Negresses at her elbow. She looked left and right, realised that each of them was being taken in hand, almost literally, by an attendant. And the others were already walking away, so that she was being left behind; even Kit was walking beside a Negress. She wanted to run, but the woman at her side was maintaining a most stately tread, and she made herself keep pace.

They climbed the stairs, past the white women and children, who smiled and bowed and greeted them; Richilde realised that they had to be the families of the overseers, who now started to drift away as the new arrivals reached the upper porch and were escorted through enormous double doors held wide by attentive black footmen in blue and gold liveries. Here was a gallery, big enough, she supposed, to contain the entire Marigot Plantation House, stretching almost out of sight in the distance, filled with a cool breeze coming in from windows at the far end, and circulated by fans which turned softly, suspended from the ceiling and worked by young black boys, all wearing the Mortmain livery. The walls of the gallery were hung with portraits of severe looking men with the pronounced Mortmain features, punctuated with women of varying attractiveness, but every one with an arrogant tilt to her head, a sneer of utter contempt on her lips as she looked down on the people below.

'We going this way,' the Negress said, and led Richilde through one of the many doors opening off the gallery. Once again she looked anxiously after her cousins, and more especially Kit, but he was being led through another of the doors. Now she found herself in a carpeted hallway; at the end of which was a staircase, leading down again, and then another hallway, this one with windows opening on to an interior garden, a place of lawns and flower beds, with a fountain in the centre, and entirely surrounded by the rest of the house, which she realised was built in the form of a gigantic hollow square.

Now they were ascending another staircase. She realised that she was quite lost, doubted that she could ever find her way back to the main part of the house. Except that she could always ask, because every doorway was guarded by a blue and gold liveried footman who bowed to her.

'This your bedroom,' the Negress said.

Double doors were being opened, and Richilde entered a cavern of a chamber, filled with exquisitely carved furniture, and containing a tester bed in the very centre of the floor; the drapes, needless to say, were pale blue and gold.

'But . . . where are Lucy and Annette?' she asked. On Marigot they had shared a room, and indeed a bed.

'They got room,' the Negress said. 'Not far from here. I will show you. When you done bathe.'

'Bathe?' But she was very hot and sticky. And the woman was already giving instructions to half a dozen maid servants who were bringing ewers of water, some hot and steaming, and others obviously cool, while two footmen were placing an ornately moulded tin tub in the centre of the floor. Others now bustled in with her box, containing her clothes and her dolls; it looked pitiable in the midst of so much elegance. As would her clothes, she realised; she had worn her best gown to land, on Mama's instructions, and it did not match the dress worn by the Negress. But then, she thought, even Mama would look like a poor relation in these surroundings. Because she *was* a poor relation.

The Negress smiled at her. 'You are sad,' she observed. 'There is nothing to be sad about. Vergée d'Or does be a happy place, for you. I am Amelia. I going look after you. You all get out,' she said to the maids and footmen, her tone suddenly brisk. 'The Mademoiselle going bathe.'

The bustled from the room, and Richilde allowed herself to be undressed and seated in the tub, to have Amelia scoop

50

water over her shoulders before applying a deliciously scented soap to her flesh.

'This is your home, now,' Amelia said. 'You going live here, and you going marry here, and you going die here. And you going be happy here. The master does like every-body to be happy. He does get very angry if somebody ain't happy. And you don't *ever* want to make the master angry. No, ma'am.' She straightened, stood almost to attention. 'Now Madame Jacqueline come.'

Richilde hastily wrapped herself in her towel, turned to face the woman who had just opened the door, and found herself staring in surprise. Madame Jacqueline clearly had Negro blood; Richilde could estimate at a glance that she was probably a quadroon, that is, one of her grandparents had been a Negro. Like so many women of her racial characteristics she was remarkably handsome, tall and strongly built, with almost perfect features, and glorious straight black hair, which clung, strand to strand, almost as if it were stuck together with glue. But the surprising thing about her was her gown, which was of dark green damask, the rings on her fingers, emeralds which winked at Richilde with incalculable value, her décolletage, and the utterly regal fashion in which she moved and carried herself. And spoke.

'You will be the English girl,' she said.

And the most surprising thing of all was that she was hardly older than Catherine, Richilde decided. She had to remind herself that whereas in the English colonies, people of colour, in whatever degree, were born slaves and remained slaves, unless manumitted by their masters, in the French colonies it was the reverse, and a single drop of white blood, sufficient to classify one as a *café-au-lait*, guaranteed freedom for oneself and one's dependents. Even more, in the French colonies mulattos could own property and accumulate wealth. As this girl had obviously done. Or someone had done for her.

'Yes, mademoiselle,' she said. I am Richilde.'

Jacqueline smiled. When she smiled she was quite beautiful. 'We shall be friends, you and I,' she said. 'Now get

51

dressed. Haste, Amelia.'

Amelia hurried, and Richilde found herself hurrying too, although, however wealthy she might be, this Jacqueline had to be her social inferior. But she was utterly ashamed of her gown; her best one was lying soiled on the floor, and this one had a darn where she had snagged it on a branch.

Jacqueline continued to smile, 'Dressmakers will be here first thing tomorrow morning,' she said. 'We must have you looking your best.' She took Richilde's hand. 'I will see to it personally.'

They walked through the galleries, passed the bowing footmen. 'Do you live here?' Richilde asked.

'But of course.'

'Oh,' Richilde said. Because she couldn't, however hard she tried, figure out what her new friend might do here. On the other hand, she was most certainly her friend; they had now regained the main gallery, and Jacqueline was introducing the people in the pictures. 'Pierre de Mortmain was the founder of the family fortune,' she said. 'He was a *boucanier*. A *matelot*. Do you know what that means?'

'I don't think so,' Richilde confessed.

'He and a boon companion, a *matelot*, lived right here in St Domingue when the whole island was owned by the Spaniards. They killed the wild cattle which used to roam these plains, and still do, in the interior. They smoked the meat, turned it into *boucan*, hence their name. And they fought against the Spaniards. Until eventually they found some small boats, with which they started attacking Spanish coasting vessels. They formed themselves into a sort of navy, the Brethren of the Coast. Pierre de Mortmain was one of the most successful. He eventually became a pirate, and was very famous. But he never forgot St Domingue, and his son created his plantation. There is no greater plantation in the entire Antilles, than Vergée d'Or.'

'Why is it called Vergée d'Or?' Richilde asked.

'A vergée is a measurement of land. Did you not know that?'

'I think so,' Richilde said, doubtfully.

'You are English,' Jacqueline said, with the faintest suggestion of contempt. 'You think in terms of acres. A vergée is about a third of an acre.'

'Oh, but . . .' they had reached a window, and Richilde looked out at the sweep of canefields in the distance.

Jacqueline laughed. 'Of course. There are thousands of vergées composing Vergée d'Or. But that is what Ranulf de Mortmain, old Pierre's son, called it. Because he began with just one vergée, but he called it the golden one, because he knew it would grow. He knew the wealth of this soil. And do you know that was only one hundred years ago? Ranulf de Mortmain was Philippe's great grandfather. No more.'

It was the first time that Richilde had heard anyone refer to the Seigneur by his Christian name, except for Uncle Maurice, and Uncle Maurice always used it with a great deal more respect than Jacqueline had just done.

'But what relation are you to the Seigneur?' she asked. Because white men did have mulatto relations, even in St Kitts, although they were not as a rule allowed around the house.

Jacqueline smiled. 'I am not a Mortmain. My name is Chavannes. I am merely Philippe's housekeeper.'

'Oh,' Richilde said, not understanding at all, either how someone so very young could possible be a housekeeper, or how a housekeeper could possibly refer to her employer in so familiar a fashion.

But if she was in a position both of knowledge and authority, and as she was being so very friendly . . .

'May I ask you a question?'

'Of course,' Jacqueline said.

'We brought some domestic slaves with us from St Kitts. Do you know if they have come out to the plantation?'

'I should think so,' Jacqueline said. 'It really wasn't necessary, you know. Indeed, I think Philippe may be rather displeased when he discovers that. He gave orders that Marigot was to be sold, together with its slaves.'

'Oh, but these are people we've always had. Especially Henry Christopher. Why . . .'

'Henry Christopher?'

'My twin,' Richilde said.

'Your what?'

'It's what Mama always says. It's a family joke, really. We were born on the same day. He's been my playmate ever since. Do you think we could go and find him? I really would like to know that he has settled in all right, and is being looked after.'

Jacqueline Chavannes had stopped walking, and was gazing at her in total amazement. Then she suddenly gave a peal of laughter. 'Why, yes,' she said. 'I think we *should* go and find this twin of yours.'

Jacqueline hurried Richilde along the gallery and on to the porch at the head of the great staircase. Here were Françoise and Lucy, standing together to admire the gardens and the trees.

'Oh, there you are, Richilde,' Lucy cried. 'Are you coming to explore?'

She glanced at Jacqueline.

'Mademoiselle Richilde is coming with me,' Jacqueline said. 'Come along, mademoiselle.'

Richilde gave her cousins an apologetic smile, hurried down the stairs behind her friend. 'Couldn't they come too?' she asked as they reached the bottom.

'Only if you wish them to,' Jacqueline said.

'Oh, but . . . well, they are the Mortmains, you know. I'm only a poor relation.'

Jacqueline gave another of her peals of splendid laughter. 'But that is why I like you, my dear girl. Because you are not a Mortmain. I am not a Mortmain either. That is why we are going to be friends, you and I.'

Richilde didn't understand her at all, but now she was again lost in wonderment as they entered the ground floor of the chateau, through an entry hall every bit as wide and as high as the great gallery, but this one hung with swords and muskets and pistols, and instead of windows or corridors leading off, here were great arches, those on the right giving into a magnificent withdrawing room, an expanse hardly less than a vergée itself of polished parquet flooring, littered with incidental tables made from carved wood and with equally splendidly moulded brass trays resting on top, containing a variety of ornaments, and comfortable chairs, arranged in groups, a spinet and, at the far end, a billiards table, while the whole was cooled by great glass doors which opened on to another patio behind which was yet another rose garden surrounded by a lawn as smooth as baize.

The arches on the left gave access to a dining room hardly smaller than the withdrawing room, where there was an enormous mahogany table, around which were some forty-eight chairs; the walls were lined with polished mahogany sideboards, laden with silver cutlery, with decanters of wine and brandy, while above them hung pictures of horses' heads.

'Philippe maintains a stud,' Jacqueline said, carelessly.

They had now walked the length of the hall, to where a red velvet curtain hung from the high ceiling. Jacqueline parted this curtain, to reveal that the corridor continued, with doors leading to pantries, where slaves were industriously cleaning silver, doors leading to storerooms, where other slaves were loading bottles or boxes, a door leading to a cool room, where the walls were lined with zinc and the floor was covered in sawdust, to keep the great blocks of ice from melting too quickly, and where whole carcasses of cows and pigs hung from the ceiling.

'Where does the ice come from?' Richilde asked in a whisper, fanning herself against the heat in the corridor.

'It is brought down from Newfoundland,' Jacqueline explained. 'Philippe maintains special ships for the purpose.'

They passed other doors leading to what were obviously cellars, and then at the end there was another curtain, and they entered an enormous kitchen, filled with wood burning ranges, with low tables at which slaves were cutting up pieces of pork for the evening meal, supervised by a large black man.

'This is Lucien,' Jacqueline explained. 'Lucien is the head cook. Mademoiselle Richilde is English, Lucien.'

Lucien kissed her hand, to her surprise. 'You going eat well here, mademoiselle,' he said. 'Everyone does eat well on Vergée d'Or.'

'We are seeking the black people from St Kitts,' Jacqueline said.

'Oh, yes, Madame Jacqueline,' Lucien said. 'They done been take to their place.'

'Then we shall find them. Come along, Richilde.' Once again she took Richilde's hand, and this time led her through the back door and on to another patio, fringed with fruit trees rather than flowers. While Richilde puzzled over another mystery; why her new friend was called madame, when she was clearly a mademoiselle, both by virtue of her age and because she wore no ring.

'The domestic slaves,' Jacqueline explained, 'do not live in the slave village. They have their own houses out the back, here. These houses are much nicer than slave barracoons. It is a great privilege to be a domestic. You must hope that your people will be able to retain their positions.'

'Oh, but they must,' Richilde cried. 'Henrietta and Henry Christopher must, anyway. Uncle Maurice promised.'

Jacqueline squeezed her hand. 'It is always a mistake to become too fond of servants,' she said. 'Just as it is a mistake to become too fond of animals. Pets. They always die, or get sick, or have to be put down. It is far better to remember, always, that they are just sent to please us.'

Richilde bit her lip. Even her cousins did not understand that Henry could be a friend, and not a servant. She could hardly expect this girl to understand. Except that this girl's grandfather, or more likely, her grandmother, must have bridged the gap between the races. She wondered if she dared ask her about that.

They walked down a smoothed earth avenue between coconut palms, with a stream bubbling on their left, and Richilde realised with a leap of her heart that they were only a few hundred yards from the sea. And once again an Atlantic facing beach, with rollers tumbling over the reef to come surging in as surf on to the sand itself. She wondered if it would be possible to swim here. Of course Miss Fitzgerald would forbid it here as much as in St Kitts, but this girl might allow it.

There were so many things she wanted to ask Jacqueline. So many things she felt she *could* ask her, where she had never felt that about a single human being before.

'Here we are,' Jacqueline said, as the avenue made a slight dogleg to the right, and they came upon another small village, a place of some elegance, where the cottages were separated by masses of pink-flowered oleanders, and the scent of jasmine was heavy in the air, while each cottage, Richilde observed, possessed a sizeable vegetable garden at the back. The place seemed deserted, as of course nearly all the domestics were up at the house, but there were one or two women with babies at their breasts, and several small children.

'We seek Henrietta, from St Kitts,' Jacqueline said.

The woman she addressed curtseyed. 'She does be just down the road, Madame Jacqueline.'

'Thank you,' Jacqueline said, courteously. 'Would that be your friend, Richilde?'

'Henry,' Richilde shouted, running forward. 'Henry!'

Henry Christopher's somewhat solemn face lit up, and he in turn left the little house and ran on to the street. 'Richilde,' he shouted. 'But I did wonder where you was. You are up at the Great House?'

'Oh, yes, Henry,' she said, like him speaking English without thinking. 'Henry, you must see it. It is like nothing you can ever have imagined.'

'Like something King Frederick must have built,' he said, grinning.

She squeezed his hands. 'Just like something he would have built. I can't wait to show it to you. I'll show it to you tomorrow morning.'

Henry's smile had faded. 'I don't know what I going be doing tomorrow, Richilde,' he said. 'These people say I got to go in the field.'

'Never,' she said. 'I'll speak to the Seigneur. We'll both

speak to the Seigneur, won't we, Jacqueline?'

'I think,' Jacqueline said, 'that to begin with you should make a habit of speaking French. The Seigneur does not like English, or anything about the English. And secondly, you, boy, Henri Christophe . . .'

'My name is Henry Christopher,' Henry said.

'Yes, boy. But it is Henri Christophe in French. Do you not speak French?'

'He speaks French,' Richilde explained. 'But he likes his name to be spoken in English.'

'He likes?' Jacqueline raised her eyebrows. 'Well,' she said, 'I think, if you mean to talk to the Sieur about your friend, Richilde, you should do so now.' She pointed, beyond the village, to a track which led back into the canefields, and up which the Sieur de Mortmain was at this moment riding, followed by his six overseers.

Philippe de Mortmain drew rein beside them. He did not frown, as he did not smile. His expression never altered at all. At yet Richilde suddenly felt as if someone had emptied a bucket of ice cold water over her.

'You, boy,' Philippe said to Henry, who was staring at him. 'You are from St Kitts?'

'Yes, sir,' Henry said, in French.

'Then you have much to learn. And the first thing you have to learn is that you do not look at me. Not ever. Do you understand me? When I am near, you stand with bowed head.' Philippe de Mortmain pointed with his riding crop at the women and children. 'Like those people are doing. Do not let me see your head raised in my presence again, or I shall be angry with you. Do you understand me, boy?' he asked, as Henry continued to stare.

'Yes, master,' Henry said, and hastily lowered his eyes to gaze at the dust. But Richilde could tell that he was angry, or afraid; his legs were trembling.

'Then you will do well here,' Philippe de Mortmain said. He turned to Jacqueline. 'And you, madame? What devilry are you up to now?'

Jacqueline did not appear to take offence. 'Mademoiselle

Richilde wished to discover if her slave had safely arrived, monsieur,' she said.

Richilde glanced at her in surprise; the quadroon had used the Seigneur's Christian name so freely up to this moment.

'And so I brought her down here to see,' Jacqueline said.

'This boy is your slave? Philippe de Mortmain enquired.

'He belongs to Mama, monsieur,' Richilde explained, 'But he is my friend.'

'Indeed?'

'Her twin,' Jacqueline observed with a smile.

'Explain.'

'We were born on the same day,' Richilde said. 'Almost the same minute, Mama says. So we are friends.' She was encouraged to be bold. 'You won't put him in the fields, monsieur? Say you won't. He is very good about the house.'

'Is he now? And what are you called, boy?'

'I am Henry Christopher,' Henry said.

'Henri Christophe. It has a certain ring to it.'

'Henry Christopher,' Richilde said. 'It is an English name.'

Philippe de Mortmain gazed at her for some seconds, then the grim face broke into a smile. 'Then Henry he shall be,' he agreed. 'How old would he be, if I may be so ungallant as to enquire a lady's age?'

'I am nine years old, monsieur,' Richilde said.

'The devil you are. He also looks older. He shall be my postilion. Will that please you?'

'I do not know what that is,' Richilde said.

'My groom,' Philippe de Mortmain said. 'He will stand on the step behind my carriage, and hold the door for me when I wish to get down. And for you, Mademoiselle Richilde, whenever you drive with me. Would you like to drive with me?'

'Oh, monsieur, could I?'

'You shall,' Philippe de Mortmain said. 'Beginning now. Now you shall ride with me.' He stooped from the saddle. 'Give me your arm.' She held up her right arm, had it seized in a powerful grip, and a moment later was seated behind him. 'Hold me round the waist,' he commanded. 'And you, boy, report to Jean François at the stables, and he will show you to your duties. Gentlemen.'

Once again, to Richilde's total surprise, he neither addressed nor looked at Jacqueline Chavannes, as the little cavalcade moved off towards the house. Richilde looked back at the girl, watched her trudging up the road behind them, with the dust from their hooves settling on her hair and her beautiful clothes and jewellery. And on her face, which was twisted in a mixture of anger and contempt.

The mystery deepened when Jacqueline was not present at supper. Indeed, Richilde did not see her again after she returned to the house, because it was time to join the rest of the children and exchange information and wonder at what they had discovered during their explorations, before they were called in to take their places at table. Philippe de Mortmain had arranged it so that they all sat at one end; he really was a much more friendly person than he appeared, even if he largely ignored them, preferring to talk with Uncle Maurice and Father Thomas, his chaplain, about all the unrest in the mainland British colonies.

'Madness,' Uncle Maurice asserted. 'I felt the same thing when poor Richard and his cousin stirred up all that trouble in the Leewards. And where has it got them?' He looked sympathetically at Jeanne. 'Now there is going to be a lot of trouble for the Americans.'

'I wonder,' Philippe said.

'Well, if the British have sent over an entire army . . .'

'Armies are all very well,' Philippe said. 'When there are other armies to oppose them, when there are garrison towns to be captured, with their stores of food and munitions. I have often thought, for example, that we here in St Domingue could declare our independence, and secure it, even against a French army.'

'But, my God,' Uncle Maurice said. 'That . . .'

Philippe smiled. 'Is treason? I do assure you, my dear Maurice, no one is going to arrest the Sieur de Mortmain for treason, nor anyone who is under his protection.' His gaze swept the table. 'But it is a point worth considering. Paris is often every bit as absurd as London. It will certainly be interesting to see how the Americans manage with their revolt. But that is sufficient politics for one night. Marguerite! Jeanne! Are you satisfied with your apartments?'

'They are magnificent,' Aunt Marguerite said. 'Quite beyond my expectations. I do not know how to thank you.'

'Then I suggest you do not try. I am but filling the house, with the right people. It is a crime for a house like this to be occupied only by a lonely bachelor.'

'None the less,' Marguerite insisted. 'Jeanne and I cannot just accept your hospitality. We must play our parts, as Maurice will play his. As you *are* a bachelor, Philippe, perhaps you will let us manage your household for you?'

'But monsieur already has a housekeeper,' Richilde said, without thinking, and blushed scarlet as every head turned to look at her.

'Go to your room, miss,' Mama said. 'How many times have I told you never to speak at table unless addressed?'

'Oh, but . . .' Richilde stood up, biting her lip to keep back the tears.

Philippe de Mortmain smiled at her. 'May I beg an amnesty, as this is her first night here, Jeanne? Sit down, child. She is right, you know. I do have a housekeeper, with whom Richilde has already become friends.'

'Oh,' Marguerite said. 'A . . .' she glanced at her husband. The word, and its various connotations, was not unknown in the English islands.

'I have, in fact, several housekeepers,' Philippe said, smiling at his cousins. 'Each of whom has certain duties to perform. I do assure you that there is no need to concern yourselves with any domestic matters. Rather would I have you rest and enjoy yourselves, and perhaps play the hostesses when we decide to entertain. There has been a sore lack, for both Papa and myself, since Mama's death.'

'I wonder you have not married,' Jeanne Hamilton ventured.

Philippe's gaze swept the table. 'I have never yet found

the woman with whom I would choose to spend the rest of my life,' he said. 'But now ... who knows. I suspect my quest may be coming to an end.'

Richilde discovered that he was looking at her.

'He's going to marry Catherine,' Louis de Mortmain said. 'No doubt about that.'

The meal was over, and the grown-ups, along with Etienne and Catherine, were seated on the outside patio while the younger children had been dismissed to the far end.

'Oh, that will be exciting,' Lucy said. 'We'll all be bridesmaids. Won't we all be bridesmaids, Françoise?'

'He can't marry Catherine,' Françoise declared.

'Why not?' Louis demanded.

'Because we're all cousins,' Françoise explained, triumphantly. 'You can't marry your own cousin.'

'But we're only second cousins,' Kit said. 'At least. Come to think of it, I don't suppose Richilde and I are related to him at all. But certainly he can marry Catherine, if he wants to.'

Why do they all think he wants to marry Catherine? Richilde wondered, her heart pounding. He was looking at me. And he likes me. That was obvious. And as Kit had just pointed out, they were not even related, except by marriage. Of course he was old enough to be her father, but many girls married men old enough to be their fathers. And marriage, to Philippe de Mortmain ... Why, it would mean that she would be mistress of all this. Françoise and Lucy and Annette, and even Catherine ... and even Etienne, the wretch, would have to call her madame, and be polite to her, and do what she said ... and then Jacqueline could be her housekeeper as well as Philippe's, and go on being her friend, as well. She felt so excited she thought she would burst.

But she hated it when the others kept talking about Catherine. The trouble was, Catherine was old enough to be married now, while she wouldn't be old enough for ages.

And perhaps Philippe did not want to wait very much longer; he was certainly very old. Her excitement was replaced by utter misery.

She was distracted by the arrival of several white men, with their wives, coming out of the candle-lit gloom of the patio.

"You'll have met Fedon, my attorney,' Phillipe de Mortmain said. 'His wife, Antoinette. And . . .' the names drifted into the darkness. Richilde was not really interested in them. She found herself wondering what Henry Christopher was doing, down in the domestics' village, whether he was thinking of her, and how he would take to his new duties, as a postilion. It sounded fearfully grand, and it suddenly occurred to her that when next she saw him he would be dressed in the Mortmain colours; undoubtedly the uniform would suit his already tall and muscular frame.

The evening filled with a vicious snarling, and she instinctively moved closer to Kit as she watched half a dozen large dogs being brought out of a gateway leading to the rear of the garden.

'They are only puppies, really,' Philippe explained. 'When papa died, I had his dogs put down. They were his. A dog can only have one master. So then I had to start from scratch with these pups. They are barely a year old. But they are good dogs, eh, Robert?'

The big Negro holding the leashes grinned at the white people. 'Oh, yes, sir, master, they are good dogs. They good and fierce. Nothing but red meat for them.'

Richilde watched the dogs' teeth as their lips drew back, and she clutched Kit's hand.

'Well, then,' Philippe de Mortmain said. 'I trust you have arranged a demonstration?'

'Yes, sir, master,' Robert said. 'They waiting now.' He gave a whistle, and once again the gate swung in to allow five men to enter, four of them dragging a fifth, who writhed and fought as he was pulled to the centre of the lawn beneath the patio. Richilde stared at him in horror, realising that he was naked, and smeared in blood, although she could see no sign of any injury.

'Master,' the man shouted. 'I begging you, master. Hang me, master. Hang me.'

'I am giving you the chance of life,' Philippe said, getting out of his chair to stand at the top of the steps. He snapped his fingers and the four men released their victim, immediately moving in front of him so that he could not climb the steps. 'That way,' Philippe said, pointing into the darkness. 'And you had best make haste.'

Jeanne Hamilton gave a gasp, and Maurice de Mortmain also got up. 'Philippe,' he said. 'You cannot be serious.'

'The fellow is due to be hanged for stealing,' Philippe said. 'As he well knows. This way his death will serve a purpose. And who knows, he has a sporting chance. Long odds, perhaps, but still a chance.'

'But Philippe . . .' Maurice grasped his cousin's arm. Philippe looked down at the hand on his sleeve, and Maurice slowly released it. 'Not in front of the women and children. I beg of you.'

'It will not be in front of the women and children,' Philippe said.

'Father Thomas,' Maurice de Mortmain appealed.

'It is the Seigneur's will,' the priest said. 'And the man is, in any event, condemned.'

Philippe was pointing at the black man. 'I told you to make haste.'

The man stared at the white man who was condemning him, then at those who sat or stood around him. Tears were rolling down his face. But he understood that further pleading was pointless. His tongue came out and circled his lips, and Richilde tried to imagine what thoughts must be going through his mind, whether he was considering an attempt to get up the stairs to attack his executioner, and realising that he would not make it. She felt sick.

The man turned, gave a despairing wail, and ran into the darkness.

'Count to ten,' Philippe said.

Jeanne Hamilton leapt to her feet, hurried across the

patio, grasped Richilde's arm. 'Bedtime,' she gasped. 'Come on, hurry.'

But I want to stay, Richilde thought. I want to watch, or at least hear. I want to feel some of the hate which has suddenly filled the evening. The hate and the fear and the bloodlust, all mingled together.

Chapter 3

THE MARCH
TO YORKTOWN

The fleet commanded by de Grasse recruited free men, of whatever colour, in Martinique and Guadeloupe and St Domingue and, as many of these volunteers were slave owners, there were also black servants on board the ships which dropped their anchors in Chesapeake Bay. Legend has it that amongst those who witnessed the surrender of Lord Cornwallis were a mulatto freeman named Chavannes and a Negro slave named Henri Christophe.

'Good morning, madamoiselle,' Phillipe de Mortmain said, smiling at Richilde. Who hesitated, like a thief caught in the very act, exposed in the centre of the great gallery. Because she did not even wish to see him, much less speak with him. Her confused emotions of last night had settled into the certainty that he was a monster. Mama had called him that, and for once Richilde had agreed entirely with her mother.

'I am going into Cap François,' Philippe said, coming closer. 'And I would like you to come. I promised you a ride in my carriage, remember? You will be able to see your friend Henry at work.'

'Oh, but . . .' She bit her lip.

'Madame Jacqueline is coming too,' Philippe said.

She so wanted to ride in the carriage. She so wanted to see

Henry. As if she could ever look Henry in the face again. Henry, all of the slaves, would know what had happened. Would know that she had been seated on the patio beside this man when he had ordered the destruction of one of them, in the most terrible fashion.

She looked past him, saw Kit, just appearing from his bedchamber. Oh, darling Kit. 'Can Kit come too? My brother,' she explained, as Philippe looked vaguely puzzled.

'But of course. The more the merrier, eh?' He threw his arm round her shoulders as he walked her towards the porch. 'We are riding into town,' he told Kit. 'Your sister and I. And she wishes you to accompany us. She does not wish to ride with me alone. She thinks I am cruel.' He gave her a squeeze. 'Do you not, Richilde?'

'Oh, I . . .' She was having difficulty breathing.

'It was a cruel thing to do, sir,' Kit said. 'It will make your people hate you.'

This time Richilde lost her breath altogether. But Philippe de Mortmain did not appear to take offence. Indeed, he smiled.

'My people hate me anyway, Christopher,' he said. 'And they hate you as well. Not for being cruel. Merely for having the complexion you possess.' He escorted them on to the porch, from where they could look down the great staircase, at the outside patio where they had sat last night, with the lawn beyond. Richilde expected it to be splattered with blood, or at least trampled and muddy – but it was as smoothly perfect as it had ever been, its borders patrolled by a platoon of slaves who knelt or squatted, each armed with a machete, chipping away at the weeds. Beyond, in the distance, they could make out other slave gangs heading into the fields: groups of fifty and sixty men and women, each similarly armed, each led by a single white man on a mule.

'They hate us,' Philippe observed. 'For being here, while they are there. Do you know how many slaves I own, Kit?'

'Monsieur Morin said about seven thousand,' Kit said.

'Give or take a hundred, yes. And I have seven hundred white or mulatto residents on the plantation as well, but of those, two thirds are women and children. Now what do you suppose stops that weeding gang down there from running up these steps and cutting the three of us to pieces? I assure you that they all know what happened last night.'

Richilde found that she was holding his hand, and his fingers gave her a reassuring squeeze.

'It is simply fear,' he said. 'It is a nameless, unconscious fear. I am the master. I possess the power of life and death over them. Were I to give an order now, I could have them all hanging in fifteen minutes. What is more, I could order that gang to hang one of their own number, and I would be obeyed without question. Because of their fear. And I will tell you this, Christopher Hamilton. The very moment those slaves, or perhaps even one of them, ceases to know absolute terror whenever I approach, then are all of our lives in danger. Remember that. The responsibility will soon be yours, no less than mine.' He pointed. 'The carriage.'

'Henry,' Richilde shouted, and ran down the stairs, only remembering to pause, and look over her shoulder at Philippe, as she reached the bottom.

Philippe smiled. 'Does he not look splendid?'

Henry Christopher stood beside the carriage, holding the door for them He wore a pale blue tail coat decorated with gold braid, pale blue stockings, and black leather shoes with gilt buckles. Kit realised that he had never seen Henry with shoes on before. Today he also wore a white powdered wig. And he carefully studied the ground as his master approached.

'You look splendid, Henry,' Richilde said.

'I thank you, mademoiselle,' he said. Always before he had called her Richilde.

'I entirely agree with mademoiselle,' Philippe de Mortmain said, giving Richilde a hand up into the carriage, where Jacqueline Chavannes was already seated, dressed as usual as if she was going to a ball. Kit sat beside her, and Henry closed the door on them. Then the driver, a very large black man named Jean François, flicked his whip and the carriage rolled down the drive. Kit looked out of the window to see

Louis standing on the porch, gazing after them, a puzzled expression on his face.

He glanced at Jacqueline. He and Louis had sat up talking for a long time last night; Louis had indeed advanced a similar reasoning to that of Philippe de Mortmain in explaining why his cousin had acted as he did. Kit had not agreed with him, as he did not agree with him now; Uncle Maurice, for instance, had maintained discipline on Marigot, where the proportions of white to black had been even more dangerously low, without ever descending to downright cruelty. But he and Louis had soon carried their discussion to more interesting topics. Louis had asserted that Madame Chavannes had to be Philippe's mistress. Both boys were just becoming old enough to understand the differences between the sexes, the delights which undoubtedly lay in front of them. Which, they both felt, were perhaps already available, when they looked around themselves at the scantily clad Negresses, many of them hardly older than themselves, and decidedly attractive in their slender, hard muscled and yet well breasted, bodies. Supposing their respective mothers would not be furious at the very idea. But none of the black girls in any way compared with this elegant and utterly composed creature, who now conversed with Philippe de Mortmain, calling him monsieur, but smiling and apparently content with her situation. To possess such a woman . . . Kit flushed as she suddenly turned her head and found him looking at her.

They were amongst houses, and people. The carriage pulled off the main thoroughfare into a side street, and came to a halt. Henry Christopher immediately opened the door, and Philippe de Mortmain got down. 'I shall not be long,' he said. 'You may visit your family, Jacqueline.'

'Thank you, monsieur.' She allowed Henry to take her hand, descended herself. 'Would you like to come for a walk, children?' she asked.

Did she really think he was a child, Kit thought angrily? But he climbed down and, with Richilde, followed her across the street and round the corner, into a small haberdashery, where the people serving behind the counter were clearly Jacqueline's relatives.

'This is my father's shop,' she explained. 'Papa, I would have you meet Monsieur Christopher Hamilton, and Mademoiselle Richilde.'

They shook hands with the old gentleman, whose features possessed many more Negro characteristics than those of his daughter.

'They are now living at Vergée d'Or Great House,' Jacqueline said. 'We are friends.'

'It is nice out there,' Monsieur Chavannes agreed. 'The Seigneur de Mortmain is a very kind man. He is very generous.'

Richilde looked at Kit, who raised his eyebrows. He wondered if this man knew the position his daughter occupied? Of course he would know. And was happy that it should be so, because to him Philippe de Mortmain was a kind and generous man. As no doubt he also knew of the inhumanity of which Philippe was capable, but which in no way affected him, or Jacqueline. Kit felt quite sick at the thought of ever possessing such power over other human beings. Not that he ever would, of course, as he was a Hamilton and not a Mortmain. And yet, in his remark this morning, Philippe had almost suggested . . .

'And this is my brother, Jacques,' Jacqueline was saying, introducing a young man who had just come from the back of the store. He was younger than his sister, certainly, not a great deal older than himself, Kit estimated, but lacked her open expression, and indeed, scowled at the visitors.

As Jacqueline observed. 'We must be getting back to the carriage,' she said, taking Richilde's hand. 'The Sieur de Mortmain was merely visiting his bankers. He will be ready for us soon.'

They emerged into the glare of the street, for the sun was by now high in the sky.

'Why doesn't he like us?' Richilde asked. 'Your brother?'

Jacqueline smiled, but it was one of her bitter smiles, this time. 'He envies you your white blood,' she said. 'He would

70

be as you.'

'Don't you want to be like us?'

She shrugged. 'I'm happy.'

'Mulattos are much better off in the French colonies than in the British,' Kit observed. And then glanced at her to see if he had offended her.

'That is quite true,' she said seriously. 'But it is also the cause of my brother's anger. Ten years ago, a mulatto had exactly equal rights with a white man, here in St Domingue. But my people became too wealthy, and too arrogant. And the whites grew to hate us. So they had laws passed against us, and now, why, we cannot wear clothes or jewellery of more than a certain value, and our menfolk cannot bear arms. We must know our proper place.' Her lips twisted.

'But you dress like any white woman,' Richilde said.

'Ah,' Jacqueline said. 'That is because I am under the protection of the Sieur de Mortmain.'

And despite what you say, Kit thought with a sudden flash of insight, you hate us just as much as your brother does.

'Why did the Sieur de Mortmain take us into town, instead of the Mortmains?' Richilde asked.

'Like I told you.' Jacqueline said. 'Because you aren't Mortmains. The Seigneur thinks very deeply. He plans all the time. You are, like me, nothing without him. This pleases him. And that is why we should be friends. Us three.'

Kit hadn't actually thought of it in that blunt fashion. But he supposed she had to be right. They of all people couldn't afford ever to quarrel with Philippe de Mortmain. Or even not to take his side.

Jacqueline paused on the street corner, gazed at the carriage. 'Like them,' she said, half to herself.

The children peered past her shoulder. Jean François had descended from his perch and was deep in conversation with another black man, obviously also a coachman, because he wore livery and a wig, although he was nothing like Jean François in appearance, but was small and narrow shouldered, and stood awkwardly, as if one leg was shorter than the other.

'Is he a Vergée d'Or slave?' Kit asked.

Jacqueline shook her head. 'But Toussaint and Jean François always seem to have much to discuss. If they are not careful they will both wind up on the wheel.' She jerked her head to where Henry Christopher waited, by the door, but obviously listening to what the two men were saying. 'Your friend too, Richilde. I should warn him against bad company, if I were you.'

Vast clouds of smoke rolled above Vergée d'Or, seeming to reach upwards into the heavens to mingle with the rain clouds which every noon gathered above the mountains. The plantation was grinding.

Grinding on Marigot had been a hectic affair, Kit Hamilton remembered. But it was nothing compared with here, where the concentrated efforts of nearly eight thousand people were dedicated to producing a new record crop. He had now experienced three of these annual cataclysms, and each one had left him more amazed, and emotionally drained, than the one before.

The smoke, rising in the air in a column for three hundred feet before spreading to obliterate the morning sky like some portent of inescapable doom. But rather was it a portent of inescapable wealth. It was a sweet-smelling smoke, which titillated the nostrils even as it filled the lungs. And beneath it, the furnace that was Vergée d'Or, the smell of the boiling sugar cane, and then the boiling sugar, and then the boiling molasses, filled the air, the mind, the body, even the soul. During the grinding season, a normal diet was impossible; everything tasted sweet. But then, during the grinding season, nothing was normal.

Gone were the lazy mornings spent riding the paths between the canefields, the huge lunches, the jolly evenings sitting on the patio drinking wine, the trips into Cap François, the fencing lessons and the shooting practice which Philippe de Mortmain regarded as an essential part of the daily routine of every white man on the estate. Gone even was the siesta considered so important to Europeans; even at two in the afternoon, when the sun ruled the heavens, the work went on. Although not even the sun, a Caribbean sun, huge and round and fiery and imperious, could penetrate the smoke blanket which covered the plantation. The sun could do no more than add its heat to the inferno below. Yet it was scarcely noticed.

The plantation made Kit think of the tales he had heard of the great slave revolt in Berbice, on the mainland of South America, sixteen years before, when the rampaging blacks had destroyed everything in their paths. For before grinding the canefields must be burned, to remove the possibility of snakes or poisonous insects attacking the cutters. Thus over a month earlier had the great smoke clouds first rolled across the landscape, and the brilliant white sheets in the Great House become dotted with black wisps of ash, which dissolved into filthy smudges whenever touched. The house servants had been the first to find their work doubled, as they washed and scrubbed and cleaned.

The fires smouldering, the fields had been assaulted with knife and machete. Philippe de Mortmain had himself led the van of the charge, supported by his overseers, by his cousins Etienne and Louis, and even, this year, by Kit himself, at last considered old enough, at thirteen, to control a work gang. Behind them the slaves had marched like an army advancing in extended order, shouting and cheering, driven always by the ear-splitting crack of the whip, and followed by the squealing axles of the carts on to which the cut stalks had been thrown.

Once this work had been properly commenced, Philippe left it in the care of Fedon, and attended to the factory. For the previous six weeks this had been made ready, with grease and polish, to take away the rust and the faults which would have accumulated during the growing season. Now it had been put to work. The selected slaves, great strong young fellows, had mounted the treadmill, the signal had been given, the whips had seared their backs, and the huge wheel had started its ponderous action.

Then it had been time to light the boiling fires. Special fuel had been stored for this purpose over the previous weeks, dried wood and straw. By now the first cartloads were bouncing down the tracks from the canefields, heaped with cut stalks, already turning from green to yellow, still showing the scorch marks from the flames; the casualties, Kit thought fancifully, despatched from the battlefield, where the dreadful work of execution went on and on.

The carts were drawn by mules bred specially for this purpose, up to the raised man-made mound behind the factory, where the giant chutes awaited. Here there also waited another regiment of slaves, controlled and marshalled by Maurice de Mortmain, and armed with spades and pitchforks. These dug into the canestalks and tumbled them down the chute, and thence into the first of the rollers, this one a system of interlocking iron teeth, which seized the cane and crushed it into splinters. The dreadful sound rose even above the whine of the treadmill and the gears, while every so often a stalk escaped, to fall over the side and arrest the process with an almost human scream of tortured metal. To discourage this were some forty picked hands, for time was not to be lost repairing machinery. Here was a dangerous job, and Kit could still remember, at last year's grinding, the truly inhuman scream which had followed the disappearance of a black man's hand and forearm, his fingers caught by the ceaselessly rolling drums.

That poor fellow had died from loss of blood and shock. But no one had had the time even to notice his passing. And he had soon been forgotten, as the mangled cane was thrown out the far side, on to another chute, before being forced through another set of rollers, these no more than barrels, touching each other as they rotated, which seized the shattered stalks and compressed them, causing the first drops of the precious liquid that would eventually be sugar to drip into the gutters beneath.

But still the cane's ordeal was unfinished, for there was yet another chute, and yet a third set of rollers to be negotiated, these so close and fine that their squealing creak against each other dominated all other sounds inside the factory. Here the last of the juice was squeezed free, and the stalks were left no more than wisps of useless wood.

Yet not so useless that they could not still be consumed. A sugar factory produced its own fuel, its own energy, whenever possible. Beneath the last of the rollers was an immense pit into which the stalks fell. But here again was a platoon of slaves with pitchforks and spades, for off the side of the pit there led a channel to the fires, and in this gully there were more carts and sweating labourers. The stalks were loaded on to the carts, and carried to the great furnaces.

This truly was the end of their journey, until they were belched forth to darken the sky as black smoke. But the juice had only just begun its travels. The gutters from beneath the rollers and the crushers ran down to the vats, huge iron tubs set exactly over the never cooling furnaces. Here the liquid bubbled and leapt, a witch's brew, constantly being combed through with nets at the end of long sticks held by the factory hands. Beyond were more gutters, more cauldrons, more furnaces, and not until Maurice de Mortmain was satisfied with the quality was the cane juice allowed to flow off into the cooling vats. These were also set over a pit, and had perforated bottoms. For as the liquid cooled, while the precious crystals would cling to the sides of the vats, the still molten molasses would slip through the sieves and into the fresh vats waiting beneath.

The manufacture, storage, and bunging of the hogsheads was a separate industry in itself, employing another horde of slaves under the supervision of Monsieur Huges, the head carpenter. And always there were the book-keepers, commanded by Monsieur Ferry, a dapper little fellow who wore spectacles, and was never to be discovered without a notepad in one hand and a pencil in the other, listing, evaluating, checking.

Nor was even the complete hogshead the end of the process, for the molasses in turn were drawn down yet another gutter, to yet more vats, and these were kept simmering, while the additives were carefully measured, for Vergée d'Or, like every other sugar plantation, manufactured its own rum. Here waited the head chemist, Monsieur d'Albret, a happy fellow who had to spend most of his day tasting the slowly fermenting liquid; there was more red in his nose then ever came from the sun.

But perhaps d'Albret was symptomatic of the whole, because, remarkably, Kit thought, grinding was a happy time, or at least a distracted time. There was not an able-bodied person on the plantation, from Philippe de Mortmain himself down to the smallest Negro boy or girl who did not work harder this month than throughout the rest of the year taken together. Only the white women and their children were exempt from labour. And yet, the change from the unending field work, the making and mending of roads, the back-breaking weeding, the repairs to houses, was itself pleasant, and during the grinding season there was no daily punishment parade. The whips cracked ceaselessly, and the men and women worked until they dropped, for the ships were coming, and would be in Cap François on the appointed days to load, and the life of a slave, valuable enough as part of the estate's assets, became trivial if set against any damage to the crop caused by a delay in shipment. Thus they remained too busy to be miserable.

Except perhaps those with too much intelligence for their own good. For as Kit walked his mule down the road from the factory, his spell of duty over for the day, towards the relative peace and sanity, and more important, the hot bath and the change of clothing, of the Great House, he encountered Henry Christopher.

Even the coachmen were required during grinding, to drive the largest of the carts. Henry, for all that he was only twelve years old, expertly controlled the two mules who drew his enormous load, a pile of canestalks which reached several feet above his head. No doubt he too was pleased to be doing something more than riding beside Jean François but he did not look happy. The laughing boy who had played with them on St Kitts might never have been. Henry already had the physique of a young man, taller than Kit himself, and quite as broad, and his face had assumed the grimly gaunt characteristics of so many slaves. Now he merely touched his forehead in respect as his old friend rode by. They were friends no longer. On Vergée d'Or there were masters, and there were slaves, and fate had decided that Kit should go one way and Henry the other. Which was a pity, Kit thought; he still liked the boy, still felt that they had the capacity for friendship. And Henry surely knew that it was due equally to Richilde and himself that he had been spared the torments of the field, the indignities of the slave compound.

But he seemed aware only that they had made their choice. And resented it. Kit somehow felt responsible for the black boy's future, because he was their slave. He certainly did not want Henry to be unhappy. That way led to irrational acts the consequences of which not even himself or Richilde would be able to save him.

And it wasn't as if there had ever been a choice. Philippe de Mortmain, for whatever reasons of his own, had given the Hamilton children the chance to escape their predestined role of permanent poor relations. The Mortmains had not liked the way in which their great cousin, over the past three years, had paid more attention to Richilde's progress on the spinet or with the needle, than any of Françoise or Lucy or Annette's efforts, had encouraged the marriage of Catherine to François the son of a neighbouring planter, Thomas de Milot, when she would obviously have made so perfect a wife for himself . . . But there was nothing they could do about it, either. What Philippe de Mortmain decreed, so it was.

Richilde had accepted this more easily than himself. But then, she came into less contact with the actual working of the plantation. For such was the fear that the very presence of Philippe de Mortmain inspired that there had never again been any necessity for him to reveal that mailed fist which was his treasured family emblem, at least before the ladies. Kit often wondered, indeed, if that first night, so shocking in its suddeness, had not been as carefully calculated as everything else the Seigneur did. In which case he was indeed a monster. A monster who intended to marry his sister.

But a monster who was also probably the wealthiest man in the West Indies, which in 1779 probably meant the world, and a monster who had never been anything less than unfailingly kind and generous to them both, and to Mama, for all that she daily seemed to fade as she dreamed more and more of her long lost husband who was only a distant memory to Kit.

So where did that leave him? A lifetime of security, as brother-in-law to the Sieur de Mortmain, provided that he stayed at the monster's shoulder, which would necessarily require him to become a monster himself? He really could see little alternative, however much he wanted one.

He approached the plantation from the western side, walking his horse beside the beach as he neared the domestics' village, drawing rein with a frown as he watched the woman walking on the sand, loose gown flowing in the constant sea breeze, hair drifting. She, like him, was still out of sight of the village, and she was utterly unaware of his presence, half hidden as he was by the trees. He watched in consternation as she stopped walking, lifted the gown over her head and threw it on the sand, revealing that it was her only garment, and then slowly walked down the beach towards the water. Because Jacqueline Chavannes was also spared the travails of grinding. Her labour was only to be performed in bed, beneath her master.

He became aware of a fresh rash of sweat, and of a sudden pounding of his heart, as he gazed at that body, so strangely light brown, so gleaming in the afternoon sunlight, so perfectly shaped, from high, pointed breast through softly curving buttock to gently muscled calf. And covered in such firm velvet flesh, to suggest that within was a volcano of passion, waiting to be released.

But it was the Sieur de Mortmain's passion. Jacqueline had, in fact, kept herself aloof from Kit over the past couple of years, where he had hoped their friendship would grow.

She and Richilde were still as thick as thieves. They sewed together and they walked together, and undoubtedly they talked together. About what he did not know and could not discover, for Richilde, as she entered puberty, was also less of an eager playmate than before, kept to herself, adopted a serious demeanour, except when in the company of her mulatto friend. Who was, he supposed, in many ways replacing the elder sister she had always wanted and never had. Which was just as well, because relations between her and the three younger Mortmain girls daily became more distant. They openly disdained Richilde's preference for a coloured girl, as they disparagingly put it. But there was nothing they could do about that either, save privately sneer over the peculiar etiquette that forbade the quadroon ever being allowed to join them for meals or entertaining, or in church. Richilde was the Seigneur's favourite cousin, and Jacqueline Chavannes was his favourite housekeeper. There was not anything even Uncle Maurice and Aunt Marguerite could do about that last, however much they obviously disapproved.

But the growing rift between the families was being extended to himself as well, and he had no older playmate. Save for Louis. Louis alone, with his relaxed approach to life, did not seem to find it uncongenial for the Hamiltons to have so advanced themselves. 'I tell you honestly, Kit,' he would say. 'I doubt I shall ever make a planter. I have not the stomach for it. You are welcome to my share.' Louis was a good fellow, but a frightful bore. It occurred to Kit for the first time in his life that he was lonely. And that his loneliness might be heading him into forbidden paths. For he had released the rein, and the mule was making its way forward, guided by his knees, on to the sand. And now the woman heard him, and turned sinking as she did so until only her head was exposed, frowning, and then smiling, as she recognised him.

'Why, Kit,' she said. 'Why do you not come in? The water is deliciously cool.'

He dismounted, wondering if he dared, wondering if it

might be possible, in the cool intimacy of the sea, just to brush against her velvet skin, to discover if she was indeed as delightful to touch as she was to observe.

But would she not be angry if he undressed before her? Even supposing he could bring himself to?

Yet she had invited him. And she had not been angry at his staring at her. Now she gave a low laugh and stood up. He supposed he would never forget that picture, of water dripping from hair and from chin, from nipple and from slowly uncovering pubic hair, as she waded towards him. 'Are you afraid of me?' she asked. 'I think you are.'

'I . . .' He licked his lips.

'I have seen you watching me,' she said. 'Just as I have watched you grow. I have known that one day you would seek me out.'

'I . . .' His tongue seemed stuck to his head.

She had come right up to him. Now she put her hands on his shoulders, drew him forward, kissed him gently on the lips. He could not stop himself. His hands closed on her ribs, and then slid down over her rounded hips. Her flesh was indeed like velvet, and seemed to glow beneath his touch. And her fingers were releasing the buttons on his shirt.

Her mouth turned up to his, and a moment later they were kneeling, and then lying, on the sand. He attempted to protest, to remind her that he had spent the day in the factory, that he was covered in grease as well as sweat, and smelled of smoke, but it really did not seem relevant. Here was the culmination of every vague stirring within him for the last three years, since he had first set eyes on her, and since he had first become aware of his own manhood. And in her arms all consideration of the past, the future, even the present, seemed irrelevant – until he had climaxed and rolled away from her, to lie on his back and gasp for breath, and become very aware indeed of who and what he was, and even more, what she was.

She knelt beside him and smiled at him. 'Fifteen years old,' she said. 'They are the best.'

He raised himself on his elbow. 'You . . . my cousin . . .'

'Oh, I shall not tell him. Unless I have to.'

'Eh?'

Again that liquid smile. 'You belong to me, now. You must never forget that. To me.' She shook her heavy wet hair in his face, scattered sand. 'And only me.'

He frowned at her. 'I don't understand.'

She sat on her heels. 'It is very simple. I do not find your cousin a very exciting man. Yet must I lie with him. He bought me as if I were a slave. He settled all my father's debts for him, if Papa would allow me to come out here. I was but sixteen. And should I leave, why, he would bankrupt Papa. But I do not want to leave. Why should I be poor? And yet, I may be forced to leave, when your sister grows up. Because she is what Philippe really wants. A wife whom he has trained from a very early age, to like the things he likes, to think as he does, to live as he wishes. Besides, she is what Mama Céleste promised him.'

Kit frowned at her. 'Mama Céleste? Promised?'

Jacqueline kissed him on the nose. 'You are too young to know of that. Yet Philippe will marry Richilde. And when that time comes, I may need someone to turn to.' She sighed. 'It will not be very long, now.'

'Me?' He sat up in alarm. 'You must be mad.'

'You,' she said. 'And you will not refuse me. The Seigneur will be amused to learn about us. Then. He would not be amused now. Were I to tell him what happened here this afternoon, he would beat me. But he would also send you from the plantation. He might even change his mind about Richilde. And he will certainly send your arrogant little black friend into the fields. And there would be the end of all your hopes and ambitions. So we will not tell him, and we will be friends, and we will be allies. And we will both be happy. I will make you very happy, Kit Hamilton.' Gently she pushed him back to the sand again. 'Oh, very happy.'

As if he could ever be happy again. That evening, and every evening for the rest of grinding, he seated himself as far as possible from Philippe de Mortmain, convinced that he would betray himself, his guilt, his surging desire. To which was now added the misery of jealousy. Because Jacqueline would be waiting, alone upstairs in the huge suite she shared with her master, to make him every bit as happy.

'Poor Kit is overtired,' Aunt Marguerite said, ruffling his hair. 'It is hard work.'

'But good work,' Maurice de Mortmain said. 'We have topped the record.'

'As we have done every year for the past three,' Philippe said. 'Since your arrival, indeed. I never doubted that with you here, Maurice, the plantation would go from strength to strength. But now it is all but done. You will be able to laze again, Kit.'

Kit joined in the laughter. Suddenly he was a conspirator. It was not something he had ever intended. He wondered if Henry was similarly unhappy because he too was a conspirator, remembered that day, so long ago now, that Jacqueline had pointed to the little lame coachman, Toussaint, whispering to Jean François. He had encountered Toussaint often since, when going into Cap François, had invariably been greeted with the utmost courtesy. Toussaint was, indeed, a most courteous and popular man, apparently amongst white people as much as black. Even Philippe de Mortmain always gave him a greeting. 'The most intelligent Negro I ever met,' he would say, and utter one of his short laughs. 'The only intelligent Negro I ever met.'

'I wonder you do not buy him for yourself,' Richilde had once remarked.

'I would,' Philippe had replied. 'But the scoundrel Milot will not sell. At least, dear Thérèse will not sell. She regards Toussaint as her prize possession. Mind you, I'm not sure it wouldn't be a mistake. One does not really want an intelligent Negro around the place, especially as coachman, where he can meet others. Look at Jean François, now. He is ideal. He has not a brain in his head. And the same goes for your young Henry. You can see that at a glance.'

Which was absolute nonsense, Kit reckoned. Henry had brains all right. It occurred to him that Henry was quite capable of conspiring. But conspiring to do what? Except perhaps run away, either to perish in the jungle, or be recaptured and flogged to death. Kit doubted even Richilde would be able to save him if he attempted anything as foolish as that. Supposing Richilde still wanted to look after him at all.

But it was his duty to look after both of them and, as Richilde clearly no longer needed his care, that left only Henry. He could not doubt that Jacqueline was probably right, and Henry would share in his disgrace, when it inevitably came.

'Now I have great news for you,' Philippe said, actually leaving his chair to stand before them. 'It arrived three days ago, but I have kept it to myself until today, until grinding had been completed. Because it will affect us all.'

'News?' Maurice de Mortmain frowned. 'From France?'

'Indeed, from France. You will hardly disagree, dear cousin, that the failure of Burgoyne's expedition against the Colonies from Canada, indeed, his surrender, has put an end to British hopes of reconquering America?'

'Well,' Maurice said. 'I wouldn't go so far as to say that. The British . . .'

'Bah,' Philippe said. 'The British. Always the British. This time they are going to receive a beating, I can promise you that.' He looked around him with a triumphant air. 'Because His Majesty had decided to throw the weight of France into the struggle.'

'What did you say?' Maurice shouted.

'I mean that, very shortly, France will be declaring war upon Great Britain,' Philippe said.

'War?' Aunt Marguerite cried. 'Oh, my God! Not again. The last time . . .'

'They had the better of things,' Philippe agreed. 'This time things will be entirely different.'

'War,' Jeanne Hamilton moaned. 'War.'

'War,' Etienne de Mortmain shouted. 'We shall lick them this time. I know it.'

'We all know it,' Philippe declared.

'But . . .' Maurice de Mortmain was obviously confused. 'You said, very shortly. Then how do you know of it?'

'We have been advised by fast sloop. A great fleet, commanded by the Admiral de Grasse himself, is on its way to Cap François. It is intended for America, to land an army to support the colonists. It is necessary for the fleet to be actually there when war is declared, or at least very close, or the Royal Navy may well intercept it. But the Governor-General was informed in advance, because it is de Grasse's hope to recruit here, and in the other French colonies.' He looked at the three young men.

'It seems madness,' Maurice de Mortmain said. 'For a monarchy to fight another monarchy in support of rebels. Suppose we here in St Domingue were to copy the Americans?'

'Well, now,' Philippe said. 'There would be quite a situation. But first we will fight for these other colonists. And make friends with them, eh, as we all share the same hemisphere. I have no doubt at all that several of them will volunteer for the colours. But I thought that one of you might like to lead the way. Etienne?'

'Eh?' Etienne twisted in his seat. 'Well . . .'

'Not 'Tienne,' Aunt Marguerite declared. 'It can never be 'Tienne. Why, Philippe, he is your heir.'

'Yes,' Philippe said, somewhat drily. 'As you say, not Etienne.'

'I will volunteer, monsieur,' Louis said, getting up.

'You, boy?'

'I am seventeen, monsieur. Quite capable of bearing a musket.'

'It will hardly come to that,' Philippe promised. 'I will get you a commission, I promise you. But I am proud of you, boy. Proud of you.'

War, Kit thought. Against the British. But he was British himself. No, he wasn't; he had been born in St Kitts and was French by adoption. The British had driven his father into exile and probably death. His every instinct cried out to him to support the Americans.

Just as his every instinct cried out to him to escape Vergée d'Or, at least for a while, to think, and to avoid the baleful influence of Jacqueline Chavannes.

'I would like to volunteer also, monsieur,' he said.

'You?' Philippe looked amazed.

'You?' Jeanne Hamilton shouted. 'My God, not you.'

'You, Kit?' Richilde asked. 'Why you?'

'Because . . . because Father is in America, somewhere,' Kit said. 'I know it. And cousin Alex is certainly there. My family, all fighting against the British. I should be there too.'

'Spoken like a man,' Philippe said. 'But do you not suppose that you are rather young?'

'I am fifteen,' Kit insisted. 'And I am as tall as Louis. I am a man.' If you only knew how much of a man, dear Philippe, he thought. He looked from left to right, defiantly. 'It is more my fight than any of yours.' He smiled at his mother. 'Who knows, I might find Papa for you.'

'But who'll look after you?' Jeanne wailed. 'Out there, all on your own?'

'That is an important point,' Philippe agreed. 'You will both need servants.'

'Why . . .' Kit grinned at them, all of his problems suddenly falling into place. 'We'll take Henry Christopher. Who could ask for a better servant than that?'

'The column will advance.' The colonel spoke quietly, hardly seeming to be addressing more than his immediate subordinates, his voice certainly not carrying to the mass of white clad infantry standing rigidly to attention behind him. But now those subordinate officers drew their swords and pointed them at the distant earthworks which guarded the town of Savannah, the drums began to roll, and the soldiers marched forward.

Kit's stomach rolled with the drums, and his mouth was dry. It was only just past dawn, and he had been unable to digest any breakfast. He glanced quickly to the left, saw Louis also advancing, fifteen yards away, sword pointed at the British position, face grim with determination. Then he looked forward again. It had been impressed upon the volunteer officers that they must always look to the front.

Yet he was continuously aware of Jacques Chavannes' eyes, fixed on his back. He did not suppose it was at all coincidental, really, that the mulatto should have volunteered for the American expedition; half the mulattos in Cap François had taken the opportunity to fight alongside the whites. Nor could he suppose it strange that the young man should be in his regiment, his company; there were only two regiments of volunteers from St Domingue, one from Cap François in the north, and one from Port-au-Prince in the south, and they both came from Cap François. And presumably he was not even the only officer in this army who had made a mistress of the sister of one of the enlisted men. But he was certainly the one with the guiltiest conscience.

Made a mistress of Jacqueline Chavannes. There was humour. She had taken him, because she had felt like it, because she was bored with Philippe, and because she had surmised that he might one day be useful to her. He was the one to be pitied, not her.

What thoughts to be taking into battle. Because now the active army was advancing, towards the little balls of white smoke which broke into spreading cloud above the British lines. Undoubtedly, early as it was, the defenders were fully aware of the French and American plans, no doubt because the fleet had wasted hours yesterday, and a great deal of powder and shot, in a futile bombardment of the defences.

A cannonball bounced over the ground towards him. He had the greatest urge to jump to one side, but dared not. Instead he watched it pass him, and listened to screams from behind. But he dared not turn, not even to see if Jacques Chavannes had been hit. He must always look towards the enemy.

The pace was quickening, and remarkably he had not been wounded. Now he could see soldiers manning the redoubts, mustachioed fellows in very dark blue coats with bright yellow waistcoats, and huge, braided grenadier bonnets, obviously Hessians, the mercenary Germans hired by King George to fight his colonial war for him. They were preparing to fire a volley, as soon as the French and Americans came within range. Kit almost hesitated, then forced himself onwards, watched the ripple of smoke, felt the rush of hot air, and still remained standing. But standing, now; not advancing. From behind and to either side there came cries of dismay, and he realised that the other officers were retiring. He looked to his right, watched Louis run back towards the men he had been leading.

Kit turned right around, his whole being consumed with an angry frustration, an immense desire to rush forward all by himself, to conquer the hated Germans or die in the attempt. But his own column had also dissolved, and was retreating out of range, leaving several of their comrades tossed about the meadow like so many white sacks, bicorne hats rolled away, muskets and bayonets useless toys, blood already coagulating as the sun rose.

And now too he could smell the death, mingling with the powder which hung in the still air, mingling too with the sweat and the fear, as he found himself also running after the defeated Frenchmen. He wanted to catch them up, to belabour them with the flat of his untried sword, to drive them once again into the assault. But when he reached them he did nothing. He had run away as well, and besides, there was a senior officer, mounted, telling them to fall in and march back to their cantonments. There would be no more fighting today. Or ever, perhaps. Watching the conflict had been the Admiral, as well as the army commanders, and now the Admiral turned away in disgust; the dawn assault had been his idea, as had been the preliminary bombardment.

He found himself amidst the tents of the regimental camp, already being stowed. 'We are to leave,' Louis de Mortmain said. 'Savannah is too strongly defended.'

Kit stopped in front of Jacques Chavannes. 'Why did you not follow me?' he asked. 'We could have won, had you followed me.'

'I ran because the others ran, monsieur,' Chavannes said.

'I would have followed you, master,' Henry Christopher said. His face was as grimly stern as ever. 'Why do you not give me a musket?'

'Now you know that is nonsense, Henri,' Louis said. 'We cannot arm our slaves.'

Henri opened his mouth to protest against the misuse of his name, caught Kit's eye, and shrugged. 'Yet these Americans fight to avoid being slaves themselves,' he said.

'You talk too much, boy,' Louis snapped. 'And think too much. Watch yourself.' He stalked away.

'He is right, Henry,' Kit said. 'About talking. And even perhaps thinking. There is a time for everything.'

'And now is not the time for me,' Henry said thoughtfully. 'But I am thinking only on military matters, master. As you have taught me to do.'

'Military matters,' Kit said bitterly. 'The ease with which an army can be routed?'

'The ease with which an army can lose heart, certainly,' Henry agreed. 'But even more important, the strength of a defensive position, well held. Even Frederick the Great would have found Savannah difficult. That is something to remember, master.'

Even inside the tent ice formed beneath the ground sheets, crackled as they moved; outside the snow clouded down in a constant blizzard, driven by unceasing winds. This winter of 1780 was even worse than the last, and that had been bad enough. Kit huddled in his greatcoat and shivered, watched Louis de Mortmain attempting to light a pipe, listened to Henry's teeth chattering; the black boy felt the cold more than any of them.

On Vergée d'Or they would still be celebrating Christmas. Certainly they would drink a toast to absent friends, and Mama and Richilde would shed a tear for him, as no doubt Aunt Marguerite would shed a tear for Louis, and Henrietta for her Henry. But they could hardly drink a toast to the coming victory.

It had been the Admiral's decision to move the French

army north after the abortive onslaught on Savannah. It was still supposed by the Americans that the main British effort would eventually rise out of New York, where General Sir Henry Clinton was in overall command of the British forces in North America. Thus they had sat around their various encampments and occasionally engaged in a skirmish with the redcoats while the British had been allowed to overrun Virginia and Georgia and the entire southern half of the country. It had hardly seemed an adequate strategy to Kit, brought up on the aggressive notions of the great Frederick, but then there did not seem any coherent strategy evident in any of the Americans' plans; they did not even allow their commander in chief, a Virginia farmer named George Washington, a free hand in whatever he might attempt to do, but subjected him to long-distance control by a committee of civilians.

The French soldiers had at the least been cheered by the arrival of a general officer to command them, Jean Baptiste Donatien de Vimeur, Count de Rochambeau, a veteran of both the War of the Austrian Succession and that Seven Years' War in which Frederick of Prussia had earned his reputation as the greatest soldier of all time. Kit had felt rather ashamed as he remembered their childhood games when he had teased the Mortmains with the fact that the French generals had always lost their battles; Rochambeau had been one of those generals. But he was at least a professional. And yet his arrival had made very little difference either to their success or lack of it. They had merely spent more time during the summer drilling. And even that had been preferable to sitting around their tents in the deadening cold, waiting for something to relieve their boredom.

'I wonder you do not take a pipe,' Louis said, at last puffing happily. 'It is a great solace.'

'I suspect it would freeze to my lips,' Kit said.

'You are a sad fellow,' Louis commented. 'Well, I shall go for a walk. There are some women down by the canteen. I saw them there this morning.' He winked. 'A fellow must endeavour to keep from freezing.'

'Good luck,' Kit said, and pulled his greatcoat tighter yet.

Louis regarded him for some seconds. 'I think your master is sickening, Henri,' he said. 'You'd best see to him.' He lifted the tent flap and stepped into the snow.

'It is a fact,' Henry remarked. 'A woman would be good for you, Master Kit.'

'What do you know about women?' Kit sneered, instantly regretting his mood.

But Henry did not take offence. Henry never took offence, no matter how Louis might treat him. Although he could no doubt, even at thirteen years of age, take Louis in one hand and break his neck. Kit wondered if he realised that. If slaves ever dared have thoughts like that.

'I know nothing about women,' Henry said. 'Save that they are soft, and good for men.'

'Have you ever had one?' Kit asked, with genuine interest. Here was a possible way of getting inside that massive black head.

'How I am going to have a woman, Master Kit?' Henry asked.

'Oh, I had supposed, down in the slave village . . .'

'Nobody ain't having any young woman without the Seigneur saying so,' Henry pointed out. 'He does like to select. And the old ones, what they are going want with me?'

You might be suprised, Kit thought, but he did not say it. 'You will have a woman, soon enough,' he said.

'Oh, yes,' Henry agreed. 'I have been told this. By the time we return to St Domingue I shall be a man, and right for being a father.' He gave one of his very rare smiles. 'Unless I am a very old man by the time we return.'

'Yes,' Kit said, thoughtfully. 'Have you ever thought, Henry, of *not* returning to St Domingue?'

The black boy stared at him.

And Kit flushed; he had uttered an only half-formed thought. 'It is that . . . well, I doubt the Seigneur is doing me, or anyone, a favour by attempting to turn me into one of his family. I am not, and never shall be. And I doubt I really wish to be a planter.'

'You have too kindly a nature, to be a planter,' Henry observed.

Kit's flush deepened. 'I . . .' he groped for words. 'I would like to see the world different, to be sure. Were it possible. But as it is not . . .'

'You going to stay here?' Henry was incredulous. 'Them British will hang you.'

'It's a big country,' Kit said. 'We could go west, into the wilderness.'

'We?'

'I should take you with me, of course,' Kit said. 'You are my slave. You are my responsibility.'

Henry looked at him for several seconds. Then he said, 'I am your mummy slave, Master Kit. Just like I am my mummy son. I must go home to St Domingue.'

'Oh, but . . .' Kit looked up as the tent flap was raised, and a man stepped inside. The visitor wore the blue coat and tan breeches of an American soldier, but also the red waistcoat of one of General Washington's guard, just as his sword and epaulettes denoted an officer. He was no one Kit had even seen before, although there was something familiar about his big, handsome, good-humoured face.

He looked at Henry first, frowned, and then at Kit, and smiled. 'I seek a certain Christopher Hamilton, serving with the Touraine infantry regiment.'

Kit scrambled to his feet, saluted. 'I have that honour, sir.'

'I knew it.' The officer held out his hand, then spoke in English. 'I have the honour to bear that name also, sir. Your cousin, Alexander Hamilton, at your service.'

'Alex?' Kit allowed himself to be embraced. He had heard so much about this man, from Mama, without ever having seen him before, to his memory. 'But . . . how did you know I was here?'

'I was speaking with the general,' Alexander Hamilton said. 'Your general, who told me there were several young men from St Domingue in his force, and I knew that was where you had gone, so I examined the lists. But it is good to see you, I can tell you that. I remember you, you know, when you were just a child. And you had a sister, just born.'

'Richilde?' Kit said.

'That is right. The prettiest babe I ever saw. That was just before I left the island for Virginia. Why, she must be a big girl now.'

'Thirteen years old,' Kit said. 'This is Henry Christopher.'

Hamilton glanced at the Negro boy, without interest.

'He was born in St Kitts, also,' Kit explained. 'The same day as Richilde.'

'Indeed, I remember your father telling mine of the event,' Hamilton agreed.

'As no doubt you remember my father also,' Kit said.

'Why, yes, boy, so I do.' Hamilton's face became grave. 'As you do not. That is sad. He stayed with us, for a season, when he first came from St Kitts, and then he went west. There are great forests to the west, Kit. No man knows for sure how far they stretch. But that was twelve years ago. He would have returned by now, were he coming back.'

Kit nodded. 'It is something we have learned to face. But you . . . you have prospered?'

'I am a captain,' Hamilton said proudly. 'In the Continental Army. And more . . .'

'And an outlaw when this rebellion finally collapses,' Kit said.

Hamilton frowned. 'It is not a rebellion, Kit. It is a war. A war of independence. And it will not collapse We shall win it, if we have to fight for fifty years.'

'We shall not win it by sitting here freezing,' Kit said.

'This is hardly the season for campaigning,' Hamilton pointed out. 'Although General Washington has campaigned in the winter, certainly. Four years ago he crossed the Delaware on the ice to defeat the Hessians at Trenton. But now he thinks of larger victories. Come. I would have you meet him.'

'Meet General Washington?'

'Of course. That is what I have been trying to tell you. I am his military secretary. Come along.'

'But . . . my God,' Kit hastily straightened his tunic, attempted to smooth his breeches. Henry held a mirror for him.

'The general has spent five winters at this war, Kit,' Hamilton said. 'He will be glad to see you clothed and shod, no more. But wear your sword. You are a soldier.'

'Of course.' Kit buckled on his belt, placed his tricorne on his head. 'Henry . . .'

'I will have supper ready for your return, master,' Henry said, bowing.

'He will make a good worker,' Hamilton said, as they hurried through the snow. 'If he is but thirteen, he will be a big fellow. But you are a shade too friendly with him, Kit. Believe me, black bucks understand only the lash, the discipline of fear.'

Kit opened his mouth to argue, then thought better of it. It was difficult to explain to anyone the exact relationship he had with Henry. It was not something he was sure he could explain to himself. And he certainly did not wish to quarrel with this long lost cousin, so strangely and happily reappeared.

Now they were being challenged and then saluted by sentries, and in place of tents there were huts of logs, with proper roofs, and welcoming wisps of smoke rising into the still air. And finally, a doorway, guarded by a private soldier dressed much as Hamilton, who in turn presented arms. Hamilton opened the door and ushered Kit inside, into a delightful warmth and a surprising amount of light. To the left was a small table on which were the remains of a sparse supper; to the right was a much larger table covered in maps; both supported several candles. At the rear of the one room hut there were two cot beds, separated by a grate in which there was a roaring fire, and on one of these there sat a man, coatless, gazing at the roof with both hands apparently attempting to fit inside his opened mouth.

Kit paused in surprise, uncertain whether or not to salute, then took his cue from Hamilton, who merely came to attention.

'My cousin, sir,' he said. 'Lieutenant Christopher Hamilton, of the Touraine regiment.'

George Washington slowly straightened, dried his hand on a towel. 'Have you sound teeth, lad?' he asked.

'Sir?'

'Because if you have, you are a lucky fellow. Preserve them, Christopher Hamilton. Perserve them as if they were gold.' He gave a brief smile. 'Or they soon will be, and will hurt the more for that!' He stood up, well built without being tall, face dominated by a massive jaw and a pronounced nose, and by the clearest eyes Kit could remember. 'Welcome.' He held out his hand, and after a glance at Hamilton, Kit took the proffered fingers. 'Sit down, Lieutenant,' Washington said. 'Alex, pour us a glass of wine. It is a chilly night. Your name is not French, sir.'

'Indeed not, sir. I was born on the island of St Kitts. My father was a cousin of Captain Hamilton's.'

'But you were recruited in Cap François.' Washington's gaze played up and down him, taking him in.

'I live with another cousin, sir. A French planter, in St Domingue.'

'And volunteered,' Washington said, raising his glass. 'I drink your health. And now you wonder what you have done, to be sitting here in the cold and the damp, fearing a British onslaught.'

'Well, sir . . .' Kit flushed with embarrassment.

'Believe me, Mr Hamilton, so do I, from time to time,' the general said. 'War is often a frustrating business. Have you studied it?'

'Indeed, sir, I have spent much time on the campaigns of Frederick the Great.'

'And you fight for the French?' Washington raised his eyebrows. 'But you could hardly have found a better teacher. Tell me what you consider the secret of his success.'

'Concentration, sir,' Kit said, his eyes sparkling as they always did when he thought of Frederick. 'Concentration, on the battlefield, against a portion of the enemy, by skilful use of the ground to disguise his movements.'

94

'Admirably put. And that, Mr Hamilton, is the most difficult of all the martial arts. Concentration on the battlefield. Yet the concentration of forces against an enemy weak point is the whole secret of victory.' He finished his drink, stood up. 'We shall have to find somewhere for us to concentrate, Mr Hamilton, your French and my Continentals. Then we also might gain a victory. It has been a pleasure, lad.' Once again he held out his hand.

The armies marched south. Long forgotten now where the freezing winds of the winter. Now it was high summer, and they knew only the heat and the dust. When they halted for the nights, Kit thought he would have given a great deal for a blast of cold air. But always there was Henry, waiting with a cooling drink, preparing their bivouac – they no longer possessed a tent. Henry was happiest in the heat. Besides, he, in common with everyone else, was happy to be on the move, with a purpose. Supposing they knew what it was.

There were a great number of soldiers; this was by some way the largest army Kit had ever seen, perhaps ten thousand Continentals and some seven thousand French. Their uniforms were new, their muskets were clean, they had ample supplies of powder and shot. They were accompanied by a train of the new Gribeauval artillery, reputed the finest in the world. He supposed they must be one of the best equipped armies ever in existence, a far cry from the tales Alex had told him of the early days of the war, when the men had barely had sufficient powder to fire a volley, or shoes to cover their feet, of that winter in Valley Forge when the army had all but distintegrated, had only been kept in being by the indomitable spirit of its commander.

But more important, now, they were all professionals. The Americans by five years of warfare, the French either because they had always been regulars, or because, like Louis and himself, and Jacques Chavannes and all the other colonial volunteers, they had been trained to perfection over the past year.

Only their destination remained a mystery, locked in the minds and hearts of Washington and Rochambeau. And their immediate aides. Alex undoubtedly knew of it, in his demeanour, his cheerful confidence, but he knew how to keep his general's secrets. In the beginning it had been supposed, with much grumbling, that they were again retreating. This was because in the early summer the allied armies had taken up a position before New York, where the main British armament, and Sir Henry Clinton, lay. The expectations of a battle, perhaps the battle which would decide the war, had been high. For the first time the Continentals, with French support, were preparing to take on the British veterans in an open field, with some prospect of victory.

But once again nothing had happened. The armies had faced each other, and drilled, and skirmished, - and exchanged cannon fire, as each long, lazy day had succeeded the other. Kit's sword had still never been contaminated by blood. If this was warfare, he had supposed, then it was a remarkably wasteful way of spending one's life. Louis had enjoyed it. Louis just enjoyed being in uniform, and he did very well with the women who always hung around the encampment. But women were not for Kit Hamilton; he had no intention of catching his feet in another snare such as Jacqueline Chavannes, however often he wanted, and envied, his cousin's easy facility.

Henry had fretted too. He considered himself a part of this army, even if he possessed no uniform, carried no weapon. Their success was his cause for joy, their failure cast him down as much as any white man. In this attitude he was unique. The other black servants – and there was a considerable number, including quite a few from St Domingue and even one or two others from Vergée d'Or, accompanying those overseers who had also volunteered – were content to enjoy life. However much leather they had to polish, however often they had to erect and then dismantle tents, however long they marched behind their masters, inhaling dust, this life had to be better than that on a plantation. They would be happy if the war should never end. Henry seldom mingled with them, spent his leisure moments in solitary contemplation, staring at the drilling soldiers, gazing at the brilliant uniforms with obvious envy, polished Kit's sword with loving care. This was an experience he would remember all of his life, Kit knew. It would, no doubt, be the great experience of his life, the only experience of his life worth remembering. Certainly if he intended to go back to St Domingue.

But that must wait on the end of the war. Which did not seem any closer. Except for the excitement in the air. It had begun the night, only a week ago, when their colonel had come round, very quietly, and told them to prepare to move out before dawn, speaking with each officer in turn, and reminding them that they must leave their tents standing, their camp fires burning. Certainly it had seemed that they were running away, from an as yet untried enemy – save that some two thousand men under Colonel Heath had remained behind, to keep those camp fires burning, to convince General Clinton, and his seventeen thousand men, that the entire allied army was still waiting for him to come out.

It had seemed an elementary manoeuvre, but it was none the less apparently successful for that. They did not know if the British had as yet discovered their departure, but in any event the enemy had to be several days behind in the race to wherever they were going.

'Except,' Henry said, 'that the British have the Navy. They can move by sea.' Because they marched close by the coast, and every so often saw the rippling waters.

'God damn you for a pessimistic black boy,' Louis grumbled. But the fact was undeniable, and a couple of days later they saw the fleet, a huge array of yellow-varnished three deckers, moving slowly south with all their canvas spread before the light northerly breeze. Kit thought it the most beautiful sight he had ever seen, even as he hated them.

'They *are* beautiful, lad,' said Colonel Dufour, sitting astride his horse to watch them.

97

'And they carry the end of all our hopes, sir,' Kit said.

Dufour laughed. 'You mistake the situation, boy. Those ships fly the fleur de lys. That is Admiral de Grasse's fleet. We have caught Admiral Graves napping.'

A fleet, and an army, moving together. Concentrating. This then was the campaign on which General Washington had been brooding, last December. The next day they arrived at the promontory called Head of Elk, gazed at the huge, slow-moving Chesapeake Bay, at the forests and streams which surrounded it, the occasional hamlets which dotted the shore – and the French fleet, waiting at anchor, to transport them further south.

'There is a town at the bottom of this bay,' Alex said. 'Called Yorktown. It is garrisoned by the British Army of Virginia. That is our destination.'

The guns roared, continuously, and from their positions the soldiers could watch the bursting plumes of smoke and masonry, no doubt mingling with arms and legs, flying into the air as each shot struck home. It was horrifying, and yet it was magnificent.

The British were entirely surrounded, by the French and Americans on two sides, by the James river on the other two sides. yet the river would have been sufficient to make Yorktown impregnable, with the support of the Royal Navy. This was the fear of both Washington and Rochambeau. They knew that Admirals Hood and Graves were hurrying to the rescue of their beleaguered countrymen, and they knew too that while the Compte de Grasse still patrolled Chesapeake Bay, where the River James debouched into the sea, the British had won too many naval victories over the French to say what would happen when the two fleets met.

Thus the reason for haste. There were eight thousand redcoats inside the town, commanded by Lord Cornwallis. Could they be forced to surrender, coming after Burgoyne's disaster at Saratoga four years ago, and with Clinton unable to make any headway in the north, then no one could doubt that the British position would be incalculably weakened.

'The regiment will advance,' Colonel Dufour said, and Kit drew his sword. Once again he was aware of the stomach-churning excitement of going into battle. But this time there were no doubts, and he did not suppose there were any doubts behind him, either. He was a professional, as were his men. They knew what they were about. The assault would be costly, but if they could dislodge the British, drive them back into the town proper, enable the great guns to be advanced to a position from whence they could fire into the houses themselves, then Cornwallis's position would become untenable. Normally such a manoeuvre would be accomplished by means of parallel trenches, which would slowly approach the enemy while enabling the besiegers to remain under cover. This was the art of siegecraft. But there was no time for siegecraft, with the Royal Navy at sea.

The drums began, the boys marching immediately behind the officers, their sticks thumping the *ra-ta-tat* which enabled the men to keep step. And now the guns from the redoubts were firing back, those that remained; most had been overturned by the French fire. And yet there were sufficient. Once again a cannonball bounced across the uneven ground towards Kit, and once again he heard yells and moans from behind him. But his gaze was fixed on the parapet in front of him, and the men who waited there. Not Germans, now. These were truly men in red coats and white breeches, his own countrymen, and the Union Jack waved above their heads. No doubt there was even someone in that trench named Hamilton. But they were fighting for tyranny, and he was fighting for freedom.

He had the strangest thought: would Henry Christopher consider he was fighting for freedom?

A man stood on the parapet, his musket levelled. Kit could do nothing about him, save keep on walking. This was his duty, as an officer. He watched the musket move, watched the puff of smoke, and felt nothing. He had been told that he would feel nothing, when he was hit. At least for a while. And he was till walking forward, while the man had lowered his musket and was presenting it like a pike, with his sixteen inch bayonet thrusting from the muzzle. It came at Kit's chest, and he knocked it aside with his sword, prepared for a thrust, and watched the man fall backwards, arms and legs suddenly scattered. He glanced to his left, and Jacques Chavannes grinned at him; smoke still drifted from his gun muzzle.

'We fight together, monsieur,' the mulatto said.

'Together,' Kit agreed, and dashed forward again, realising that he had never actually looked into the Englishman's face. But the man before him now wore a moustache and a sneer and carried a sword. Their blades clashed and Kit whipped his to and fro, forgetting much of the fencing he had been taught at Vergée d'Or in his anxious haste to beat down his assailant. The Englishman slipped and fell, and Kit felt a crunching beneath his blade. He looked down in horror, at the blood spurting upwards, at the expression on the man's face, of surprise and dismay, as he died.

Slowly he withdrew the sword, stared at the dripping blood, so bright for the moment, only then recalled that he was in the middle of a battle, jerked his head so hard his bicorne fell off, gazed forward, and watched the redcoats hurrying back to the next line of defences, several hundred yards away. Some of the French sent bullets after them, most just stood and cheered, and the cheering spread right round the line of redoubts to signify that they had all been captured.

'You are hurt.' Henry handed him a water bottle, began feeling his arms and legs and chest; the white uniform was splattered with blood.

Kit drank deeply, gave the bottle to Louis, who was panting at his elbow. 'Not my blood,' he said. 'But Henry, you should not be here.'

'I followed the advance,' Henry said. 'I ain't never seen anything like that.' He took the sword from Kit's nerveless fingers, knelt to clean the blood away, using the dead arm of the English officer. 'Now you are a proper soldier, Master

Kit.' He raised his head, his expression filled with admiration, and envy. He would like to be able to kill, Kit thought. But who?

'A great day.' Alexander Hamilton pulled his horse to a halt, leapt from the saddle to shake Kit's hand. 'A brave assault. The general is delighted. Look there.'

He pointed to where the cannon were already being dragged forward, careless of dead and wounded they might crush in their gunners' haste to get them in position and resume the bombardment before the British could launch a counter attack.

'Then we have them,' Henry shouted, slapping his hands together in glee.

Hamilton gave him a curious glance, then turned back to Kit. 'All depends on the navy, now. Listen.' Even above the shouting of the excited French, the bugle calls and the rattle of hooves, they could hear the deeper booms of the heavy cannonades, thudding out of the bay. 'They have joined battle, Graves and de Grasse.'

The tune played by the band, appropriately enough, was called *The World Turned Upside Down*. But apart from the music, there was no movement amongst the watching men, and had the drums and bugles ceased, Kit supposed there would not have been a sound, either.

The French, no less than the Americans, were too conscious of the immensity of what had happened. They had not believed it, six weeks ago, when after an ineffectual cannonade, the British fleet had hauled away again and left de Grasse master of the Chesapeake. Such a thing had never happened before in all the annals of the interminable conflict between English and French. They had not believed it as their heavy cannon, moving ever closer, had pounded Yorktown, and all within it, to pieces. Here too was a unique mishap for the British military machine which less than twenty years before had rampaged the length and breadth of the world, never tasting defeat. And the culmination of their disbelief had come only two days ago, when a red-coated

101

drummer had mounted the parapet outside battered Yorktown, and beaten a parley.

Now they were left with a feeling of utter exhaustion, as the redcoats marched out of the surrendered town, rank upon rank of them, and slowly piled their arms before Generals Washington and Rochambeau, Lafayette and Greene. There could not be a man present, Kit supposed, who did not know that he was stepping into history. Yorktown had to rank as the day the Thirteen Colonies secured that independence they had so rashly declared five years before, just as for the men whose ancestors had gained Agincourt, Crecy and Poitiers, it had to be the most disastrous defeat since they had fled from Hastings before the Norman invaders.

He glanced at Louis, to see what his feelings were. But Louis was merely looking hot and bothered at having to stand so long in the sun. His imagination could not soar above the commonplace, the obvious, that this campaign had at last been successful, that tonight there would be more wine than usual to drink, and that the women of Yorktown would undoubtedly be most accommodating to an officer in the conquering army, especially one with money in his pockets.

Henry knew what had been accomplished. His eyes shone as he gazed at the sight, and his hand and arm twitched as Kit returned to the encampment. Kit could tell what he was thinking, held out his own hand, had the fingers seized in that strong grip.

'I have seen history, Master Kit,' Henry said.

'My own thoughts,' Kit agreed. And smiled. 'So you see, Henry, that even strongly defended fortresses can be taken.'

Henry watched the British, now forming lines, an army without its weapons, awaiting the will of its conqueror. 'Them boys say eight thousand surrendered,' he observed.

'Something like that.'

'Then they should not have been taken,' he said. 'Not by seventeen thousand.'

Kit frowned at him. 'They were outnumbered by two to one.'

'Armies have fought before, at greater odds,' Henry said. 'Frederick has done so. You have told me that, Master Kit.'

'Well, yes,' Kit said. 'Perhaps the British were badly led. Perhaps their mistake was to allow themselves to be bottled up in the first place. But once they were there . . .'

'They let the guns get too close,' Henry said. 'Had they stopped the guns getting too close, even if they had had to die doing it, they would have held the town. Those men did not wish to die for their King. What is the point in going to war for a King, Master Kit, if you are not prepared to die for him?'

Kit scratched his head. 'You do think too much, Henry,' he said. 'I shall have to consider that one. Alex!'

Once again a handshake and an embrace. 'It is over, Kit. Thanks as much to your good fellows as to ours. Over. The General is sure of it. You will be going home.'

'Home,' Kit said, thoughtfully. Home to Vergée d'Or, to having to treat Henry like the dirt beneath his feet, to the futile amusements of the plantocracy, the unchanging rhythm of the planting seasons. Home to Jacqueline Chavannes, and Philippe. Home to conspiracy, to an awareness that he did not belong, and could never belong. The Hamiltons were not planters, and had never been planters.

'The thought does not seem to please you,' Alex said.

Kit flushed. 'Perhaps I have too much enjoyed being able to speak my own language, these last two years.'

Hamilton studied him for a few minutes. Then he said, 'Then why not continue to do so?'

Kit's heart leapt. 'Is it possible?'

'If you will swear allegiance to the Stars and Stripes. You have fought for it.'

'Willingly,' Kit cried. 'Oh, willingly. But . . . Mama? Richilde?'

'I will have you transferred to an American regiment,' Hamilton said. 'The general will attend to it himself. You are one of us, far more than a Frenchman. Then, when the war is over, we will set up in business, you and I, and then you may

103

send for your mother. And Richilde.'

'If she will come,' Kit said thoughtfully. 'She is by way of being betrothed.'

'At thirteen? She must be quite a lady. Well then, you have naught to worry about, there.' He clapped his cousin on the shoulder. 'You will visit her, I promise you. But you are right, this is the land of the future, the place to make your home and your fortune. I have never regretted a moment since I landed here. Will you give me your hand on it?'

'Willingly.' Kit held out his hand, and glanced at Henry. 'And Henry?'

'You may keep your slave, of course. He also will do well in America, if he will but work. And you have never criticised him for lack of that.'

'Well, Henry, how about that for a future?' Kit asked.

Henry's face was sad. 'I am your mummy slave, Master Kit,' he said. 'And St Domingue is my home, now. It is there I have to go. I will return with Master Louis.'

Kit opened his mouth, glanced at Alex, who was regarding the pair of them with a puzzled expression on his face.

'Besides,' Henry said. 'You will need someone to tell your mummy that you are well, and will be better. I will tell her that, Master Kit. And Miss Richilde.'

Chapter 4

THE COACHMAN

In an age of exceptional military commanders, Toussaint must rank as the most remarkable. Napoleon had at least spent his youth at a military college; Toussaint had spent his driving a coach. In everything he was self-taught, but so successfully had he accomplished his own education that long before the first disturbances he was highly regarded by his owner and his fellow Negroes alike.

'Wake up, sleepy head,' Jeanne Hamilton said. 'And many happy returns.'

Richilde sat up, pulling straying hair from her eyes. The room seemed crowded, with Mama, of course, and Aunt Marguerite, with Françoise and Lucy and Annette, with Miss Fitzgerald and Amelia.

'How does it feel to be fifteen?' Aunt Marguerite asked, and kissed her on the forehead. Aunt Marguerite was being very generous about the whole thing, although Jacqueline was positive that she must have prayed for Richilde's death a hundred times. Richilde had not believed that for a moment, but at the same time she knew that Aunt Marguerite had to be thinking that were she *not* here, then one of her own daughters might be in this happy position – as both Lucy and Françoise were past sixteen – might already be the mistress of Vergée d'Or.

She was so excited she wanted to burst, as she accepted their presents, hugged and kissed them one after the other. Miss Ftizgerald was last. Today even her habitually stern face was relaxed; indeed, she appeared on the verge of tears.

'I will bid you goodbye now,' she said. 'I would not spoil your betrothal.'

'But . . . you're not leaving today?' Richilde cried.

'I am leaving Vergée d'Or today,' Miss Fitzgerald said. 'I will remain in Cap François until my ship is ready to sail. That will be next week.'

'But . . . why are you leaving at all?'

Miss Fitzgerald smiled through her sadness. 'Because my task is finished here, Richilde. You are the last of the children. And today you are no longer a child.'

'But . . . the wedding . . .'

'Will not take place for another year, my dear girl. I have things to do with my own life.'

She was lying, Richilde knew instinctively. She had indeed developed the art of knowing most things instinctively, because she was never told anything, never actually instructed in what was about to happen, or what was not about to happen. The plantation, no doubt from years of often frightful experience, responded instinctively to the Seigneur's wishes, and over the past six years of her stay here Richilde had become an extension of those wishes.

She did not know why, or how. Her life seemed to have been taken over from the day she had set foot in St Domingue. Sometimes she felt vaguely resentful about that. But only sometimes.

She leaned back in her bath to allow Amelia to soap her, feeling vaguely surprised that Jacqueline had not yet come in to congratulate her. But Jacqueline was a law unto herself. She would be along.

She had come here, *expecting* her life to be taken over. There it was. They all had, summoned by the great man to do his bidding, and that first day she had been overwhelmed by the splendour with which they had suddenly been surrounded, by the personality of Philippe himself, and by the shocking evidence of his cruelty that first evening. Richilde thought that only Kit had ever been able to stand back and look at the plantation, and their new life, with any detachment. Which probably accounted for the haste with which he had wanted to get away from it, at the first opportunity. Dear Kit. They had received only a handful of letters, but even Mama was reassured; the French army did not appear to be doing sufficient fighting for his life to be in any danger. According to Kit, both Henry and himself, and even Louis, were having the times of their lives. Dear Henry. It was impossible to confess that she missed him even more than she missed her brother. But she did. And yet at the same time was happy that he wasn't here, exposed to the risks of being a plantation slave, the whims of her future husband.

Because she knew now that not even she would be able to protect him should he fall foul of the Seigneur. Philippe de Mortmain could be, as she had observed that first night, a monster. She saw little of his ice cold rages. Vergée d'Or was so enormous that everything to do with the field slaves was more than a mile away from the chateau, and the young ladies were not encouraged to visit the factory or the barracoons. She had not seen a slave flogged since coming here, much less heard one wailing his misery. Yet these things did happen and, according to Jacqueline, they happened much more regularly than ever on Marigot. Philippe de Mortmain did not employ a jumper; he required his own overseers to be experts in handling the cartwhip, by constant practice, just as he himself was an expert, by constant practice. According to Jacqueline, he ruled his plantation like the most omnipotent of Asian despots, and even to look him in the eye was, for a black person, an immediate reason for punishment, as she remembered his threat to Henry, again on that unforgettable first day. Nor could she doubt that Jacqueline, for all her tendency to exaggerate, was telling the truth. She had observed a fraction of his true demeanour on that day, and she often enough saw Uncle Maurice come in from the factory, trembling and sweating, reaching for the wine bottle in an attempt to blot out the dreadful scene he had just witnessed.

And this was the man she was going to marry. The man to whom, today, she was about to be formally betrothed. This too had been decided that first night. She had known it then, without understanding it, any more than she truly understood it now. Once again Jacqueline had an answer. 'He has chosen you because from the start he could see that you would be more beautiful and have more character than any of your cousins, and because, more important, the others are *his* cousins, too. His father married a cousin, and out of nine children, only Philippe survived. He fears for the future, and with more reason than most,' she would say, enigmatically. 'He wants a wife who will be everything to him.'

As Richilde had been groomed to be. She played the spinet, because he enjoyed hearing the music. She had not been taught embroidery since the age of thirteen, because Philippe did not consider it a necessary accomplishment for a lady, surrounded as she was by servants. He wished her to be able to converse like a man and so, where her cousins had been provided with needles, she had been provided with books. Mama had been scandalised. But undoubtedly books were far more interesting than tapestry.

But was she not scandalised by the whole thing? Without knowing what to do about it, or even if she wanted to do anything about it. She had not been less overwhelmed, from her first moment on the plantation, than any of the others. And she had been more overwhelmed by his kindess to her. She had known him as a monster, that first night – but as a handsome, gay, enormously wealthy and powerful monster, who was offering to share all of that power, all of that wealth, with her. Well, she did not suppose he actually intended to share it. But providing she did as he required, was all that he required, she would have the use of it.

She chewed her lips and Amelia, now patting her dry, clucked her tongue disapprovingly. Amelia, terrified that the slightest blemish would form on her skin, trailed behind her with a parasol whenever she would go walking abroad. She had never dared broach the subject of a swim in the sea to her maid. She was more afraid of Amelia's disapproval than of Miss Fitzgerald's. Besides, it would be different when she was married.

To a monster. To the most exciting man in the world. Besides, he had explained and she could understand the reasoning behind his deliberate harshness. He was protecting her as much as himself, as much as his plantation. And he was acting no differently from any other planter. If she doubted, if she feared, if she hated what he had to do, it was surely because she did not come from planting stock. She would have to learn. She *was* learning. Philippe de Mortmain was her gateway to the stars. She would not find another.

The Seigneur stopped speaking, the crowd of whites and mulattos politely applauded. Do they envy me, Richilde wondered? She stood beside her future husband on the upstairs porch, looking down the sweep of the great staircase at the people gathered below. Or did they not envy her as she had never envied, for example, the Queen of England, because hers was a rank and a position beyond envy? But what of those gathered behind her? Even Etienne was forced to stand there today, his Milot bride at his side. Claudette de Mortmain was a lovely and charming girl; Etienne had done well for himself, even if his marrying the sister of Catherine's husband was but another example of the inbreeding which was apparently practised by all the *grand blancs*. But even the wife of the heir must necessarily stand behind the future mistress of Vergée d'Or; because, Richilde realised, once she was married and had given Philippe a son, Etienne would no longer be the heir.

Philippe was smiling at her and lowering his head for a kiss. It came as something of a shock for her to realise that her mouth was the first part of her body he had ever touched, save for her hand and her cheek. In six years. Six years in which he had watched her grow from a child into a girl. She did not suppose she was yet a woman. Her legs were too long for the rest of her body and she had very little bosom. Even Annette, a year her elder, had more. While her hips were so slender it was impossible to suppose she could ever be a mother.

But she was prepared to wait, because he knew what she would be at the end of it. Thus Jacqueline. Only another year.

His lips brushed hers, and she could no longer hold her breath. But his breath was sweet, and he was smiling into her mouth. She wondered what he was actually thinking about her. Did he love her? Was it possible to love someone more than twenty years younger? And if it was possible to love her, was it possible to love her and not wish to touch her?

But then, did she love him? It was not something she had ever considered before. One was not expected to love one's husband, only to serve him and obey him and bear him children. Thus Mama.

But it seemed such a waste, not to love a man like Philippe de Mortmain.

Philippe raised his head, holding her hand now to slip the huge sapphire ring over her finger. The ring had belonged to his mother, and was quite the most magnificent thing she had ever seen. She was afraid to look at it, much less touch it. The overseers and their wives and children cheered again. Then it was time for more congratulations from the family, more presents and glasses of ice-cold sangaree. At dinner, for the first time she sat at his right hand, turning her head to look down the sweep of the table at Aunt Marguerite, seated at the far end, some thirty feet away. From this day next year, *she* would be seated there not her aunt.

She suddenly wondered who would then sit at Philippe's right hand. And immediately, where Jacqueline might be, as she had not appeared all day.

'Why did you send Miss Fitzgerald away?' she asked.

He turned to her. 'Because you are no longer a girl,' he explained. 'To trail behind a governess. Even an Irish governess. Or to be influenced by her points of view. And now, I think you should retire early, my dear. It has been a long and exciting day for you, has it not?'

She really did not like it when he spoke like that, almost as Mama might have done, or her own father. And yet there was no question of disobeying him. She rose immediately, curtsied to the table, and left the room. Was he angry with her? He had answered her question good humouredly enough., Perhaps she had not measured up to his expectations, this of all days. Did he not like her gown? But he had chosen the material himself, according to Jacqueline. It was made of straw coloured satin, with a white fichu and sleeve frills. Jacqueline had said that it should, of course, be worn with a wig, but she was too young and her own rich brown hair had been curled into ringlets which lay on her shoulders and on her bosom, because the gown carried the most daring décolletage she had ever worn – she could just imagine Lucy whispering to Françoise, 'What a waste for such a flat-chested child.'

She·had supposed she looked perfectly elegant, and the ring set off the whole thing. Now she was out of the room she could hold it, and slip it up and down her finger, and take it off to look at the flickering candlelight through the translucent stone. And she was being sent to bed before anyone else. She wanted to weep.

'Well, mademoiselle?'

She checked, her foot on the first step of the great staircase, gazed at Jacqueline. A strange looking Jacqueline, for she wore a cloak with a hood, which effectively concealed her clothes, and carried another such garment over her arm. And she had never addressed her as mademoiselle before, Richilde realised.

'Jacqueline!' She ran forward, was embraced, kissed on both cheeks and then the mouth. And felt a tremendous rush of happiness. This was her friend. Perhaps her only friend, now that Henry was away across the sea. And certainly her best friend. Of course she now knew exactly what function the mulatto girl filled in the house, but she thought that only brought them closer together, in that it was a function she also would be fulfilling before too long. She had questioned Jacqueline about the duties of a mistress, which to a certain extent had to be those of a wife, and never obtained any answer other than a smile, just as Mama had always answered such queries with a frown and an admonishment that all would be revealed to her in good time. She had also asked Jacqueline what would happen to *her* after the wedding. Not that she was in any degree jealous. Rather would she have liked to think her friend would be there with her always, guiding her and advising her. And again Jacqueline had just smiled, and said, 'That must depend on how well you please the Seigneur. But you will always be my friend, won't you, Richilde?'

A promise she had been happy to make, without reservation.

Now Jacqueline gave her another squeeze. 'The day of your life. At least up to now. And I have not congratulated you.'

Richilde held her away. 'I have been sent to bed.'

'What nonsense. You have been sent to look at a bed. Today your education as a girl ends, and your education as a woman begins. But it is not something that the Seigneur would discuss before your mother or your cousins. Come.'

She held Richilde's hand. My left hand, Richilde thought, and thus she is also holding my ring, crushed against her fingers as it is crushed against mine. But she has not commented on it. No doubt she has seen it too often before. And besides, they were hurrying up the stairs and along the great gallery to the very end, then up another flight of stairs. The flight of stairs to the Seigneur's private apartments, where none of the children had ever been allowed.

Footmen opened the double doors and she entered a small withdrawing room. She was past wonder, she supposed. Because everything on Vergée d'Or was wonderful. But this was to be her very own. It adjoined a huge dressing room, and then a boudoir, looking out over the trees at the sea. And then the bedroom. It was the largest she had ever seen, just as the bed was the largest she had ever seen. She glanced at Jacqueline. Would she sleep here tonight?

Jacqueline smiled at her, able to read her thoughts. 'Come, we have a visit to make.'

'A visit?' Richilde glanced through the window; it was quite dark outside.

'There is someone I want you to meet,' Jacqueline said. 'Someone Philippe wants you to meet, although you must never tell him that you have done so.' She held out the cloak, wrapped Richilde in it. 'There is a private entrance at the back of the house,' she said, and smiled. 'It is the one that I use.'

Richilde's heart started to pound, even if she had no idea what she was doing, what to expect. But Jacqueline was also excited. She opened a door in the boudoir, which led into a closet, at the back of which there was another door, and this led down a staircase, unusually narrow for this vast house, and both unlit and unguarded by any blue and gold clad sentries. Jacqueline had armed herself with a candle, however, and with this she led them down the curving steps, their reflections sending great shadows guttering up the walls.

'You aren't afraid?' Jacqueline asked.

'Of course not,' Richilde said, unsure whether or not she was lying.

'There is nothing to be afraid of,' Jacqueline said, reassuringly. 'Not even Mama Céleste.'

'Mama Céleste?'

They had reached the foot of the stairs, and Jacqueline doused her candle. Now it was utterly dark and Richilde gave a little shiver. But Jacqueline knew exactly where to put her hand on the lock, and a moment later the door swung outwards to admit them into one of the exterior rose gardens. 'Quiet now,' she said. 'The white folk will still be up.'

Richilde glanced at her curiously; there was no moon but there was also no cloud; the stars were bright and she could see her friend's face. And never before had Jacqueline used such a term. Had she forgotten that she was with a white girl?

'Who is Mama Céleste?' she asked again, whispering.

Jacqueline held her hand, led her round the flower beds towards a wicket gate set in the white paling. Now the house was a blaze of light to her left, and indeed Richilde could

113

hear the voices of her cousins raised in animated conversation, coming from one of the verandahs.

They went through the gate, Jacqueline carefully closing it behind them, and then walked away from the chateau itself, towards, Richilde realised, the factory. She had never been down this path, although she had been taken for a ride round the factory in Philippe's coach.

'Mama Céleste,' Jacqueline said, speaking normally now they were away from the house. 'Is a *mamaloi*. Do you know what that means?'

Richilde frowned. 'She is a witch.'

'Not at all,' Jacqueline said, quite sharply. 'Voodoo is not witchcraft. It is a religion, just like Christianity. Mama Céleste is a priestess.'

Richilde was more confused than ever. 'You mean she lives on Vergée d'Or?'

'Of course.'

'And Philippe doesn't drive her away?'

'He doesn't drive Father Thomas away,' Jacqueline pointed out.

'Yes, but . . .'

'Black people also have their gods,' Jacqueline said. 'Their beliefs. Philippe knows that Mama Céleste is good for the plantation. She is a famous *mamaloi*, revered all over the island. Even if they have never met, he also knows that she helps him to keep his slaves in subjection.'

'They have never met?' Richilde glanced left and right, at the great trees beneath which they were hurrying. The path they were taking skirted the factory and the slave village, she realised, and headed ever inwards, towards the canefields, and beyond, the jungle.

'He cannot afford to recognise her presence,' Jacqueline explained. 'Voodoo is regarded as heresy by the Church, and is officially condemned. The practice of it is a crime. But of course everyone knows that it exists, and that without it the black people would not be so docile. So it is there, but it is not there. Do you understand?'

'Yes,' Richilde said, doubtfully. What she could not

understand was the idea of Philippe, so masterful, so omnipotent and so ruthlessly his own man, being bound by a situation which not even he could control.

'That is why you must never admit to him that you have visited Mama Céleste,' Jacqueline went on. 'Even though he knows that is where you are going tonight.'

'But why?' Richilde asked. 'I do not believe in voodoo. I know nothing about it. I will have to confess this visit to Father Thomas, if it is wrong.'

'You will not,' Jacqueline snapped, her voice again sharp.

'Then I must go home,' Richilde said, stopping.

Jacqueline looked at her. 'Would you disobey Philippe?'

'How can I be disobeying Philippe, when you say he will not recognise that this creature exists? I cannot believe that he does know where we are going, or that he would approve.'

'Listen to me,' Jacqueline said. 'I have not told you this before, and I would prefer not to have to tell you now. I was going to keep it until after you had met Mama Céleste. But your Philippe is not the man you think he is.'

'What are you saying?' Richilde demanded angrily.

'Listen to me. All his life he has had too much wealth, too much power, too little restraint. All his life he has been able to do exactly what he wished, as he wished it. And as a youth, perhaps, he was equally blessed with too much health, too much vigour. Thus now that he is nearing forty, he is in many ways already an old man.'

'Philippe? What nonsense. Why, he is . . .'

'Why do you suppose there are no direct heirs to the plantation?' Jacqueline asked. 'Why do you suppose he has never married? He has slept with me in his arms for the last seven years, every night, and I have never become pregnant. Can you answer that?'

Richilde stared at her. She had no real conception of what they were discussing. As Jacqueline realised.

'A man has an organ,' she said. 'With which it is necessary for him to enter the female, for the gratification of them both, and for fertilisation. But his organ must be hard, or

115

entry cannot be attempted. You have seen them, on the slaves.'

Richilde gasped for breath; somehow she had not associated anything like that with Philippe.

'For most men, it is a simple matter,' Jacqueline continued. 'The sight of a pretty naked woman, sometimes even the thought of one, and they are ready. Poor Philippe can manage it but once a week, if then. And pleasure, the real pleasure, which they say is essential to impregnation, much less often than that. I have had him weep in my arms, because of his impotence.'

'Philippe? Weep? Now I know you are lying.'

'It is something you will see soon enough,' Jacqueline said. 'If you are unfortunate. And when he has finished weeping, his anger is terrible to behold. This is why he looks to you, of his house, but not of his blood, young enough to be his daughter, and utterly pure and sweet. He dreams, and hopes, and even prays, that with you in his bed he will find the happiness only I have ever been able to grant him. But even more, he prays that you will be able to give him the son he has always wanted. He is so desperate that he will leave no stone unturned. And he knows that someone like Mama Céleste, with the aid of her gods, will help you to be everything of which he dreams. Can you refuse to honour such a wish?'

Richilde chewed her lip. But she was already resuming her walk, reminding herself not to be afraid, or even repelled by what she had just heard. Today she was no longer a little girl, but a woman. And thus, from today, she had to act the woman's part. She followed Jacqueline down the path, round behind the negro village. A dog barked at them, and then was quiet. The breeze off the Atlantic soughed through the trees to muffle the sound of their footsteps. And the stars, gleaming through the trees wherever there was a break in the foliage, seemed to provide sufficient light for Jacqueline to know exactly where she was going.

And to raise a question which had not previously occurred to Richilde. 'Jacqueline,' she said. 'Do *you* believe in voodoo?'

Jacqueline glanced at her. 'I pray to Jesus Christ every night,' she said. 'But I pray to Ogone Badagris as well. Who is to say which of them answers my prayer?' She pointed. 'There is Mama Céleste.'

Richilde saw a little hut, snuggled in the trees. She looked over her shoulder; the negro village was perhaps half a mile away behind her, the chateau more than two miles distant. Here she was in the foreign land.

But with Jacqueline at her elbow, there was surely no cause for fear. She followed her friend forward, to stand before the hanging mat which made a door. When she would have spoken, Jacqueline shook her head, and gestured her to be quiet.

'Who seeks Céleste?' came the whisper.

'Jacqueline Chavannes,' Jacqueline said, and nodded to Richilde.

'Richilde Hamilton,' Richilde said, and wondered why she was taking part in this farce at all.

'You are expected,' said the whisper, and Jacqueline raised the mat.

Because it was a farce, Richilde reminded herself, fiercely. It had to be a farce. Of course this Céleste person would say they had been expected. Of course . . . Her breath was taken away by the stench inside the hut, a mixture of every unpleasant odour she had ever known; from human excreta to rotten meat, overlaid with the most delicious perfumes, to make her senses reel, just as the utter darkness, disturbed only by the guttering candle set in the floor, made her lose her sense of balance. She was quite happy to follow Jacqueline's example and fall to her knees, blinking, aware of the mosquitoes, where outside in the breeze they had not troubled her, and slowly identifying the crimson robe beyond the candle. But the woman had to be wearing a mask; no face could be so ancient, so gnarled, so inhuman.

'You are the one who would be mistress of Vergée d'Or?' Céleste said.

Again farce; everyone on the plantation knew that. 'I am

117

she,' Richilde said.

'And you would have your husband love you,' Céleste said, 'and be fruitful, through you?'

'I am to be his wife,' Richilde said.

'Do you suppose that alone is sufficient?' Céleste asked. 'Have you not come to me, for help?'

'I . . .' Richilde glanced at Jacqueline. But the mulatto's eyes were closed; she hardly seemed to be breathing. 'Can you help me?' Richilde asked.

'I can teach you to be a woman, such as your husband will never have known.'

'Did you not teach Jacqueline the same thing?' Richilde asked.

'Jacqueline Chavannes is one of us,' Céleste said. 'Her ability to love, through self knowledge, is expected. It is not expected in a white woman. Would you learn these things, white girl?'

Once again Richilde glanced at Jacqueline. If only her friend would wake up and come to her rescue. 'I . . . if it will make my husband love me.'

'He will love you, white girl,' Céleste said. 'If you know yourself, he will prize you above all others. He will prize you even above the brown girl. Does she know this?'

'I know this,' Jacqueline said, without opening her eyes.

'And you wish this?'

'I wish this,' Jacqueline said.

'Then it shall be so,' Céleste said. 'Stand, white girl, and take off your robe.'

Richilde stood, heart thumping, and removed her robe. She hesitated, then let it fall to the ground.

'And now your gown,' Céleste whispered.

Richilde gazed at her. She had no real objection to undressing before a black woman; she undressed before Amelia every day. But she had never undressed before Jacqueline. Besides, she did not know what would happen after that.

'Show her the way,' Céleste said.

Jacqueline also stood, shrugged her robe from her shoulders, and Richilde discovered to her consternation that beneath the single garment her friend had been naked.

'If you will not obey me, white girl, then do you waste our time,' Céleste said.

Richilde unfastened her gown, allowed it, too, to lie on the noisome earth of the hut. Once again she seemed to have lost her mental balance, her ability to reason, before the odours with which she was surrounded, before the softly insistent whispering of the *mamaloi*.

'Now come to me,' Céleste said.

Richilde opened her eyes, stretched, sat up in utter alarm.

But she was in her own bed. She had been doing nothing more than dream. Except that her hair was still wet. With salt water. Because last night she had bathed in the sea. It had seemed the most natural thing in the world, as they had made their way home, she and Jacqueline. There had been nothing she could not do, could not say, no demand of her throbbing body she had even considered refusing. Thus to plunge into the tumbling rollers, to be knocked down by them and regain her feet in the shallows, gasping for breath and laughing, while the next wave thundered up to her and sought her out again, like an embrace, reaching into the most private recesses of her body, caressing her as she had never been caressed before. That had been no dream.

Slowly she lay down again, feather pillow clutched to her chest. Therefore nothing else had been a dream, either. She had been ... she could find no words to express her thoughts. Stroked? Manipulated? *Loved*? By a *mamaloi*. A woman of incredible age, and ugliness. But a woman who had *known*, everything there was to know, about woman.

She rolled over, on to her face, afraid to look at the light, afraid to admit what her eyes might see. Had Philippe known what would happen? According to Jacqueiine he had not. But he had known what he wanted in a woman. Someone who could love, who could move, who could feel, with the rhythmic passion of a black girl, who would fear no centuries old Bible-induced inhibitions, who would understand that when a woman went to a man it was not merely for the procreation of children, not merely a duty to be performed by a wife for the gratification of her husband, but a tremendous upsurge of physical joy, of sensation, of ecstacy.

Had Mama ever known such joy, with Papa? Aunt Marguerite, with Uncle Maurice? Madeleine, with her po-faced Englishman? Catherine, with François de Milot? Or Claudette, with Etienne? She could not believe it. Nor did it necessarily follow, as none of them would have known a *mamaloi*, first. And yet . . . she seized the mirror which lay on the table beside her bed, studied her face. It had not changed. No one looking at her could tell that she knew the secret of all human pleasure.

But, oh yes, they would. Because when she remembered, her nostrils dilated as she could never recall them doing before, and her lips parted, and her eyes sparkled, and she realised she was beautiful.

And her nipples ached, no less than her vagina.

Another sprawl across the bed, the mirror thrown from her hand. It was not to be confessed. Mama Céleste had insisted upon that. Not only would the priest not understand, but Ogone Badagris would be angry. Ogone Badagris was no less jealous a god than the Almighty.

But then, she had sinned. She had blasphemed, for a start. And she had worshipped a false god, momentarily, but with her entire being. And if she did not confess, she would be but compounding crime upon crime.

Jacqueline had laughed at her fears. Jacqueline found it simple, in her mixture of races, to mix her gods with a similar facility. Jacqueline was a devil from hell. Or the most adorable creature on the face of the earth. It was entirely a point of view.

But not to confess . . .? Because in her ecstacy, and at Mama Céleste's behest, she had even prayed to the Snake God, without knowing whom she sought. But she had prayed, as she prayed to God . . . for the safe homecoming of Kit and Henry, for their preservation from all the dangers implicit in being soldiers, in time of war. And for their speedy and safe return. But now . . .

She burrowed into the sheets. Did she want them to return, at least, before she was married? Kit, with that pentrating gaze of his, his analytical mind, would certainly know that she had changed. And Henry . . . could she doubt that Henry knew of Ogone Badagris, had even worshipped him? And if the Snake God could do so much for a woman, what might he not be able to do for a man? Might that not explain Henry's remoteness, these past few years, even before he had departed for America? His ability to be there, and yet obviously not be there? It was a characteristic he shared with most of the blacks. It was obviously the only way they could survive their slavery and their mistreatment. But never before had she realised that they were all probably praying to their god.

She listened to an immense noise in the distance, a shouting and a cheering coupled with the rattle of hooves. Even the great gong in the downstairs hall which summoned them to dinner was being beaten. At six o'clock in the morning?

She sat up again, looked at Amelia, who was hurrying through the door, and wanted to lie down and bury her face once more. How could she look Amelia in the eye, or any black person ever again, after having knelt, naked before the shrine of Ogone Badagris and given over her body to the ministrations of his priestess?

'Mistress, mistress,' Amelia shouted. 'Mistress, them boys come home.'

'Who?' Richilde got out of bed without meaning to. 'Who has come home?'

Amelia gazed at her in surprise; her mistress had never slept naked before, to her knowlege. But she was too excited to care. She wrapped Richilde in her robe. 'Them soldier boys, mistress,' she cried. 'The war done. Them English people done beat, and the soldiers come home. Master Louis is downstairs, and . . .'

'Louis,' Richilde shrieked. She forgot her slippers, threw open the door and raced along the corridor, into the great gallery, and on to the porch, where the rest of the family was already assembled, incongruous in dressing robes and night caps – even Phillippe – while at the foot of the stairs the overseers and their wives and children were gathered to greet the men who were disembarking from the coach.

'Louis!' Marguerite de Mortmain shouted, and ran down the stairs to embrace her son. 'Oh, Louis, thank God you are home.'

'Louis.' Uncle Maurice shook his head, stood back to gaze at the white uniform. 'But you look well. Well.'

'Home the victor,' Philippe said. 'You are to be congratulated boy. Boy? You are a man.' He embraced his cousin. 'You are a hero.'

'But Louis . . .' Jeanne Hamilton felt her way forward. 'Louis? Where is Kit?'

'Kit?' Louis looked embarrassed. 'Well, Aunt Jeanne . . .'

'Henry!' Richilde cried, almost tumbling down the stairs to reach the bottom, and dart into the knot of slaves to seize Henry's hand, only just stopping herself from throwing both arms about his neck. 'Henry! You're safe.'

Henry looked embarrassed and gave a hasty glance at Philippe de Mortmain. But this morning even the Seigneur was smiling.

'Yes, mistress,' Henry said. 'I am safe.'

Her prayers were answered, Richilde thought. Her prayers to whom?

'But Kit,' Jeanne Hamilton wailed. 'Where is Kit?'

'Well, Aunt Jeanne,' Louis said, going very red in the face. 'Kit decided not to come back. He has stayed in America.'

Jeanne Hamilton gave a moan of horror, and had to be supported by her sister.

'He gave me this letter,' Louis said. 'Well, it seemed the right thing to do. For him. We met his cousin, Alexander. He is doing very well for himself. He is aide-de-camp to General Washington. And he and Kit plan to go into business together. There is much business to be done in America.' He realised he was gabbling, but he could not bear to see his aunt so distressed. 'I mean, the war isn't really over, yet. We are still fighting the English. But there is a truce in North

America. The British realise that they have lost there. And Kit, well, he knows that he is not French. He has chosen to become an American, Aunt Jeanne.'

'My husband,' Jeanne Hamilton sobbed. 'And now son . . .' she gazed at Richilde as if expecting her to disappear before her eyes.

Philippe de Mortmain decided there had been enough excitement for one morning. 'I am sure Kit has made the right decision,' he said. 'As I know you will appreciate when you have read his letter, Jeanne. Marguerite, you will put Jeanne to bed, and give her a sedative, and when she awakes again she will be much happier. Louis . . .' he clapped his cousin on the shoulder. 'I am pround of you, proud to have you back. Now tell me, was Henry Christopher a good servant?'

'Indeed he was, Philippe,' Louis said, his facing shining with pride. 'Do you know, Kit invited him to stay in America, and he refused. He said his home was here.'

Philippe de Mortmain shrouded the black boy in his gaze. 'There is loyalty for you,' he remarked. 'Welcome home, Henry Christopher. Now come, gentlemen, ladies, I am sure we have displayed ourselves in our nightclothes long enough!' He turned, to Richilde 'A word with you, mademoiselle.'

She followed him, her heart pounding. Was he angry with her? It was so difficult to tell. But he was leading her into his upstairs study, while the rest of the family departed to their apartments, casting curious glances behind her. But she was his betrothed now. Would he treat her like a schoolgirl after they were married? After she was a mother?

Philippe sat behind his desk, gestured her to a chair. 'How beautiful you are,' he remarked. 'Even in déshabillé. Always so beautiful, my Richilde.'

She opened her mouth, and then closed it again. She didn't know what to say, felt the heat of her flush.

'Did you have a talk, last night, with Jacqueline?' he asked.

'Yes, monsieur.'

He gazed at her. 'Thus today you are a woman.'

Once again she did not know how to reply. How much did he know?

'I do not know what Jacqueline has told you,' he said, 'about me. Yet my plight is plain to see. I am cursed in my inability to procreate.'

Richilde waited, her heart pounding.

'Thus I must expose you to witchcraft,' he said, bitterly. 'Yet must I have an heir. Of my loins.' He smiled. 'And yours. Do you understand me, Richilde?'

'I can promise nothing, monsieur,' she said. 'Except to be your wife to the best of my ability.'

'That I understand. And that I seek. Thus I sent you to that witch. You understand that she is a witch?'

'I understand that she practises a religion at variance with our own, monsieur.'

'Yes,' he said. 'What did . . . no, I do not want to know. You must never tell me, Richilde, as you must never tell anyone, what she said to you.'

He does not know, she thought. He does not even suspect. Or he would have said, what she *did* to you.

'But you must never forget,' he went on, 'that it is a strange and different religion. It is the religion of the West African demons, and it carries with it the taint of *obeah*, and even the Africans agree that is witchcraft. It is an evil thing, by our standards. Yet do I permit it on my plantation, as it is tacitly permitted all over St Domingue, because without their religion the blacks would not be so peaceful.' He half smiled. 'That is the theory, at least. It was held by my father. Have you heard the drums?'

Richilde frowned at him. Because she had, from time to time, thought she had heard drums in the night, and rolled over with her pillows across her ears; the cadence, so regular it seemed to drive all thought from her head, to send her mind spinning through a kaleidoscope of remarkable and unspeakable dreams and desires, had been terrifying.

Then she stared at him, her mouth open. Because she realised that, after last night, her dreams could never be either remarkable or unspeakable again.

'You have,' Philippe said. 'I can see it in your face. They meet, in the bush at the rear of the plantation, and they offer the blood of a cockerel to their Snake God, and they indulge in obscene dancing and even more obscene ritual. I know of these things. I send my spies to their meetings often enough. And the Snake God tells them to fear the white man, and especially me.' Another smile. 'So we are all happy.'

Richilde's mouth slowly closed, tightly. Suddenly she understood that Philippe de Mortmain was as afraid of the black people as he claimed they were of him. Her future husband.

'So,' he said. 'We know these things, but we do not acknowledge them. Black people are creatures apart, creatures of the night, perhaps, as that is their colour. And you are now seen by all as the next mistress of Vergée d'Or. There will be no more familiarity with them. Your greeting of Henry Christopher just now was too effusive. Remember that he is your slave, not your friend. A slave cannot be your friend.'

Richilde drew a long breath; his disapproval was less severe than she had feared. 'Am I to see Mama Céleste again?'

'No. Once is sufficient. I do not know if I should have allowed it at all. But Jacqueline promised . . . once is sufficient. I would have you spend your next year preparing yourself entirely for my bed. As I will do the same. There, you have my word, and you have a pact.'

'But . . . Jacqueline . . ?'

'Has she discussed my bed with you?'

'No.' Richilde lied instinctively. 'But . . . everyone knows that . . .'

'Jacqueline has fulfilled her role.'

'You'll not send her away?' Richilde cried.

'Indeed I shall not, unless you wish it. But I swear to you that I shall not touch her again.' He got up, came round the desk, held her hands. 'From this moment, I wish to love only you, sweet Richilde.' He kissed her on the mouth.

It occurred to Richilde that he was not quite sane. A thought she immediately rejected. But that he was as confused and uncertain as herself, or as anyone else for that matter, seemed plain. Philippe de Mortmain, the most feared and respected *grand blanc* in all St Domingue. Why, as he had sent her out to learn from Mama Céleste, as he had turned her into a woman, had he not taken her, there and then? Why wait a whole year, and make her wait as well? If she was ever going to be a wife to him, she wanted it to be now.

Suddenly she was afraid herself, did not know what to do, only that she must find Jacqueline, and talk with her. Only Jacqueline knew her secrets as she knew Philippe's. Only Jacqueline seemed to understand them both. And only Jacqueline would know which god had answered her prayer.

As if she did not know that already. Only Christopher had come home. Kit, like Father, had gone. She supposed she would not see him again. Jacqueline would be able to tell her about these things. It did not cross her mind for a moment that Jacqueline might be angry or concerned at Philippe's vow to exclude even her from his bed, from this moment forth – from what she had said last night, the mulatto would regard that as a blessing. But Jacqueline was not to be found. 'She has gone into Cap François,' her maid said. 'Her brother has also returned from the wars. She has gone to welcome him.'

The scowling young man, Richilde remembered. How odd to think that he had spent the last three years fighting shoulder to shoulder with Kit, and with Henry Christopher, just as she had spent the last three years shoulder to shoulder with Jacqueline. She wondered how much more closely would their lives be intertwined.

'An invitation,' Françoise said. 'From Thérèse de Milot, for tea.'

Françoise sniffed, and held the envelope as if it were burning. Now indeed was the metamorphosis complete. The Mortmain girls had been invited to Rio Negro for tea often before. Never Richilde Hamilton. But now she was the be-trothed of Philippe de Mortmain. She hurried off to get dres-sed, wildly excited. But not at the thought of sitting down to tea with Madame de Milot and Catherine. That was a bore. But to get there, she would have to ride in the carriage, with Henry Christopher. Of course Jean François would be there as well, but still, it would be an opportunity to talk ... to disobey Philippe right away. But surely she could be per-mitted to ask Henry about Kit, and about America, and ...

'Tea with Thérèse,' Philippe said, smiling at her, as she emerged on to the porch, carrying her parasol, Amelia hur-rying behind. 'That is good of her. Remember that she has an aunt who is a fourth cousin of His Majesty, by marriage, and therefore regards all other human beings as inferior creatures.' He winked, his strange indecision of earlier quite vanished. 'But remember too that you are the future mis-tress of Vergée d'Or, and could buy her out three times over. Toussaint,' he shouted, descending the staircase beside her. 'You'll watch the weather. Those are rain clouds.'

'I will do that, monsieur,' Toussaint agreed, climbing down from his seat himself to open the door for Richilde. Because Madame de Milot had paid her the ultimate com-pliment of sending her own coach for her. Oh, confound it, she thought. She got in, and Philippe closed the door. Ame-lia climbed on to the box to sit beside Toussaint. Philippe waved. How splendid he looked, standing on the steps of his palace, lord of all he surveyed. If only she could understand. Anything, of what was happening around her.

Even the weather. They had left the plantation, heading south west, now, for Rio Negro. The Milot Plantation, was several miles further inland, away from Cap François. Thus they seemed to be moving into the shade of the huge moun-tains which formed a backbone to the island, each gigantic peak bigger than Mount Misery, reaching up until they seemed almost to touch the sky. Those mountains were still many miles away; no one ever went there, or knew what really existed there. They were truly the homes of devils and monsters, their lower slopes wrapped in impenetrable forest,

127

their upper peaks always lost in cloud. And today the clouds were lower than usual, forming a dense grey blanket just at the tree level, spreading across the island. As Philippe had said, it was going to rain. She hoped it would not start until after they had reached Rio Negro; she was wearing her newest silk gown, and she did not wish it to get wet.

The first drops fell, splattering on to the dust of the road almost like bullets, pounding on the roof of the coach. Suddenly the entire afternoon was dark. This was going to be a heavy storm. She tapped on the roof, recoiled as Toussaint opened the hatch and peered in; a flurry of raindrops came with him.

'Send Amelia down,' she said.

The coach pulled to a halt, and Amelia scrambled through the door, panting and already soaked. 'I thanking you, mistress,' she said. 'Aiee, but it wet.'

Now there was wind, pushing the rain before it, and the pouring water was so thick it was almost impossible to see fifty yards. The entire day smelt damp, as the overdry grass and shrubs sucked at the moisture in gratitude.

'Toussaint,' Richilde shouted, through the trap. 'Can you see?'

'I can see, mademoiselle.'

'But you must be very wet.'

'Well, I am wet, mademoiselle.'

'Then don't you think we should stop? You and the postilion can sit in here until the rain stops. It can't last long, this heavy.'

'I am thinking we should go on, mademoiselle,' Toussaint said. 'I am thinking . . . whoa, whoa.'

A jagged flash of lightning had cut across the sky, accompanied almost immediately by a roaring crash of thunder, and the horses had started to rear. Richilde hung on to the window as she listened to the crack of the whip and could imagine Toussaint slashing and straining to control the animals, even as she felt the carriage swinging sideways.

'We going capsize,' Amelia shrieked. 'I knowing this. We going capsize.'

'Nonsense,' Richilde snapped. 'Nonsense . . .' The carriage left the road, went bumping into the ditch, came to a sudden jolting stop, with a thump that threw Richilde off her seat and into Amelia's arms. They fell to the floor together, sat there for a moment, only dimly realising that the floor was covered with water which was soaking their gowns.

The door was pulled open. 'The horses have broken out,' Toussaint said. He looked like a large drowned rat. But Richilde was more concerned with what was happening behind him; the ditch had turned into a river of fast flowing water, which seemed to be rising as she looked at it.

Toussaint saw her expression. 'We can't stay here,' he agreed. 'Too much rain, too quick. You will come out, mademoiselle. It is damp.'

An understatement, she thought, as she eased herself forward, held his arm, and jumped down; the water immediately rose to her waist, even soaking the bottom of her corset.

'Ow, me God,' Amelia shrieked. She did not specify to which god she was appealing. 'Ow, me God.'

'You have to get up,' Toussaint explained.

'I'm trying,' Richilde gasped, having her legs knocked from beneath her by the force of the water, and having to clutch him to remain upright. 'On top of the coach?'

'The coach may get swept away,' Toussaint said. 'Up the hill. Come. Racine, you helping the girl?'

He clutched Richilde's arm, pushed at her thighs, got her climbing up the slope and out of the water. It was terribly difficult work with her sodden skirts wrapping themselves round and round her legs, and now one of her shoes came off; she had not worn boots but light slippers, as she had not anticipated having to do any walking, much less climbing. While the rain continued to pound on her head, plastering her hair to her scalp, cutting through the flimsy bodice of her gown to sting her back and shoulders.

'Trees,' she shouted. 'Over there.'

'No, mademoiselle,' Toussaint said.

'But . . .' she watched another vivid flash of forked lightning cut across the afternoon.

'The trees will be struck,' Toussaint said. 'This is best.' He found her a place to sit, half sheltered by an outcrop of rock, some fifteen feet above the rushing water; even as she watched, the coach trembled then fell over onto its side, the splashing crash bringing another scream from Amelia. But now she too had reached comparative safety, sitting like a rag doll with her legs thrust out in front of her, and still clutching the collapsed remains of her mistress's parasol. Racine, the postilion, sat beside her, while Toussaint stayed close to Richilde.

'Toussaint,' she said. 'Are we in any danger?'

He gave one of his quick, crooked smiles. 'You may catch cold, mademoiselle.'

'I mean really.'

'The Seigneur will send someone, soon enough,' he said.

She watched the pouring rain, still limiting visibility to less than a hundred yards, blinked at the vivid streaks of lightning, shuddered at the rumbles of thunder. Yet where she would normally have been terrified, she was reassured by the presence of the little coachman, by his own lack of fear. She glanced at him. Pierre Toussaint. A strange name, for a slave.

'Toussaint,' she said. 'May I ask you a question?'

'Mademoiselle?' He was obviously astonished that she should require permission.

'Why are you called Toussaint?'

'It is my name, mademoiselle. It was the name of the master who first owned me.'

'Yes,' she said. 'But to have a surname . . . none of the slaves on Vergée d'Or has a surname.'

'Well, mademoiselle, not many on Rio Negro either. But Madame de Milot, well, she is proud of me.' He looked embarrassed. 'I can read. My first master taught me to read. I read well, mademoiselle. So Madame de Milot lets me read all the books in her library, and then she has me read to her guests.' The embarrassed look faded into a sudden hardness. 'They find it amusing, mademoiselle, to be read to by a slave. But you see, I have to have a proper name, to recite.'

'Yes,' she said. 'Do you hate her? Madame de Milot?'

'Mademoiselle?' He looked positively alarmed.

'And me. Us. White people. For being the masters. If you are allowed to read, you must know that it was not always so.'

Toussaint brushed water from his face and hair; the dye of his green coat was starting to run beneath the flood of water rushing down his neck. She wondered if he was as aware of the absurdity of the situation as she was.

'Tell me,' she said. 'I will not repeat it. But I would like to know.'

A sidelong glance. 'Well, mademoiselle,' he said. 'As you say, when you read history, you know that things always change.'

'It is often possible to make them change,' she said, 'Would you like to do that?'

'Me? Mademoiselle, I drive a coach. And I have one leg shorter than the other. How can I make anything change?'

'You can pray to your god,' she said. 'To Ogone Badagris. Even to the god of war, Damballah Oueddo, to change them for you.'

Now he gazed straight at her.

'I know of these things,' she said. 'I have talked with Mama Céleste. Do you know Mama Céleste?'

Toussaint's face seemed to close. But she would not be distracted by his withdrawal. The rain, which had by now completely saturated her gown and was in any event pouring down her neck to leave her as wet as if she had been sitting in a bath, gave her a curious feeling of personal intimacy, awoke some of the responses that Mama Céleste had achieved, while it also seemed to isolate the pair of them from the rest of the world – even from Amelia and Racine, huddled together beneath them.

'I know you have,' she said. 'I would understand about these gods of yours. I would understand about your people.'

'Why, mademoiselle?' he asked.

'Because . . .' for the first time she was grateful to the rain, which hid any suggestion of a flush. 'Because we share the same country. And because we may well still be sharing it, if there ever is a change.'

'And do you understand, mademoiselle,' he said, 'that there can only be a change, in St Domingue, by means of a war? That it would be a terrible war? The most terrible war ever fought? Because my people do hate yours.'

'I understand that,' she said. 'But I believe it is because not enough of my people care about your people, that this hatred exists.'

'And you would change that,' Toussaint said thoughtfully. 'Then would you be blessed, by Ogone Badagris. But hated by your own people. Do not share your thoughts, mademoiselle.' He half smiled. 'Do not share this conversation, either. Or they will stretch me on the wheel.'

'Did you suppose I would do that?' she asked.

He considered her for several seconds. 'No,' he said at last. 'I did not think that.'

'And when the change comes, Toussaint, and you are a great man among your people, for you will be, as you are the most learned of them, what will become of me?'

Now his eyes were fathomless pits. 'For that, mademoiselle, must you truly pray. For any promise I might make you would be meaningless. Listen.' She could hear the sound of bugles, the shouting of men. 'The Seigneur comes to find you,' Toussaint said. 'Give me your hand, mademoiselle.'

She held his hand to stand up, and for a moment his fingers squeezed hers.

But, she suddenly realised, he had not told her which god to pray to, his, or hers.

Chapter 5

THE PAPALOI

Bokman was an obeah man who appealed to all the darkest characteristics of the superstitious slaves, and [would lead] them into battle smeared with the blood of the cockerel he had just sacrificed.

'I cannot leave you for a moment,' Jacqueline said. 'And you attempt to drown yourself.' But she smiled as she spoke, smoothed the pillows beneath Richilde's head. She was the best friend in all the world, and the most reliable. Where Mama had merely thrown up her arms and swooned when the half drowned rat that was her daughter had been brought in, Jacqueline, only just returned from town and herself soaked by the sudden downpour, had taken immediate command, wrapped Richilde in blankets and had then insisted she go to bed with a glass of hot buttered rum. It was the strongest drink Richilde had ever tasted, causing the room to rotate gently around her head.

'I was in no danger,' she said, drowsily. 'Toussaint was there.'

'Toussaint?' Jacqueline was contemptuous.

'He knew exactly what to do,' Richilde said. 'And he wasn't afraid.'

'I have told you before,' Jacqueline said severely. 'Do not become involved with Toussaint. He is an evil man.'

'Toussaint?' Richilde was incredulous. 'I cannot believe that. He is unlike any other Negro I have ever met.'

'Which is why he is dangerous,' Jacqueline said. 'He dreams of freedom. That is dangerous for a slave. Madame de Milot made a mistake in allowing him the use of her library. What can he do with such knowledge, save dream? And how may he make his dreams come true, save by causing a great deal of trouble?'

Richilde attempted to think. Because undoubtedly what Jacqueline was saying was very true. And there had certainly been a hint of menace in what Toussaint had said to her. But as Jacqueline said, his dreams had to be only dreams.

And she had more important things on her mind. 'Is your brother well?' she asked, to change the subject.

'Oh, yes. He has grown up.' Jacqueline pulled a face. 'Badly. He also dreams. He always did. Just like Toussaint. But he is even more dangerous than Toussaint.' She sighed. 'Why do men have to dream about things they cannot have? Why can they not be content?'

'Jacqueline,' Richilde said. 'I must talk with you. You must explain what is happening to me.'

Jacqueline gazed at her for a moment, then she got up and shut the door which had been left open to allow the maids to pass in and out with dry towels; Amelia had also been put to bed. 'You are confused by Philippe's vow,' she said. 'You think I may be upset.'

'But . . . you know of the vow? He made it only yesterday morning.'

'I know everything about Philippe.'

'And you are not upset?'

'Why should I be? I knew it would happen. And besides,' she sat on the bed and kissed Richilde on the forehead. 'I am not terribly sorry. I have told you, he is not an easy man. Now he is your problem. But if everything happens as it should, as it must, you will be all right. I know this.'

'As it must? As you knew would happen?' Richilde clutched her friend's hand. 'That is what you must explain to me. Everyone knows what is going to happen, apparently. Except me. You must tell me how they know, and why I do not know.'

Once again Jacqueline gazed at her for some seconds. Then she said, half to herself. 'It is right that you should know, I suppose. But it is a deadly secret. It is known only to three people, and none of them, except me, of course, must ever know that I have told you. Will you swear that to me?'

'Of course.' But a great light seemed to be shining in her mind. 'And the other two people are Philippe and Mama Céleste.'

'You have a brain, behind those big amber eyes,' Jacqueline said.

'Tell me.'

Jacqueline shrugged. 'As I *have* told you, Philippe has not only never had children, he finds even the sexual act difficult, nowadays. This despite the fact that he is healthy, and certainly fond of women. That is why he took me from my father. He thought that with me . . . I do not boast, when I say there is no one more beautiful in St Domingue.'

'I know that,' Richilde said.

'Well, even with me he found it difficult. And he came close to despair. I thought he might even blow out his own brains, such was his anguish. So I took him to Mama Céleste.'

'You took Philippe de Mortmain to Mama Céleste?'

'It was his only hope.'

'But . . . you said he had never met her.'

'Well, as I have just told you, it is a secret shared only by us three. And now by us four. And Mama Céleste certainly saved his reason. She told him of you.'

'Of me?'

'Not by name. She told him that a girl would come to him, a white girl, just a child, from across the sea. Of his house, but not of his blood; of his nation but not of his nation, and that this child would make him whole again, and bear him children, and be a perfect wife to him.'

'My god,' Richilde said at last understanding everything that had happened from her very first day on the Plantation.

'But she also said that he must not touch this child until her sixteenth birthday, and that for a year before that day, he was not to touch any woman.' She smiled. 'I cannot tell you how delighted he was when you came to Vergée d'Or, when I convinced him that you had to be the girl of the prophecy. That night he took me twice. He had never managed that before. Or since.' She kissed Richilde again. 'Mama Céleste is a great *mamaloi*. In her care, you have nothing to fear.'

'Jacqueline,' Richilde said. 'Have you ever been to the drums?'

Jacqueline's head turned, sharply.

'Because I would like to go,' Richilde said. 'I would like to see the ceremony. After all . . .' she attempted a smile, 'I am under their influence now, am I not? If I am ruled by Mama Céleste.'

'The drums are not for you, child,' Jacqueline said. 'They are black people's drums. For you, they would be dangerous.'

'And not for you?' Richilde asked. 'You are not black.'

'I am not white, either,' Jacqueline said. 'But you . . . the drums would consume you, white girl. They are not for you.'

On fine days, when the sun scorched down, it was difficult to accept that there were ever hurricanes, or even rainstorms for that matter. Richilde had never experienced a hurricane, although she had heard sufficient tales about the tremendous damage the winds could cause. Not that she supposed there was any force on earth could harm Vergée d'Or chateau. Because all of its old security had returned for her, and the doubts she had known for that unforgettable week had disappeared. She was a part of it, at last, a figure in a prophecy. Now she could understand Philippe, his moods and his fears, because she knew them herself. Together they trod a narrow and terrifying line between the Christianity in which they had been born and educated and in which they would be married, and the dark forces which surrounded them, physically and supernaturally, and which could not be ignored or gainsaid. But the knowledge that they shared that narrow path was all that mattered, even if she dared not tell him that she knew, could only watch him when, as she alone seemed able to discern, one of this moods of uncertainty was sweeping over him.

Yet she knew that there was more to be discovered, and perhaps even more to be shared. She put down Jacqueline's lack of co-operation to a form of jealousy. The mulatto did not mind sharing Philippe, whom she obviously loathed and feared in any event, as her owner rather than her lover; but she would not share her prerogative of being the intermediary between the white people and the black priestess – there was the source of her power. Richilde begrudged her none of it, had every intention of maintaining Jacqueline at her side for the rest of her life – she could not imagine life without the quadroon's calm presence and gentle smile, or without the utter intimacy she provided – but she also saw no reason why she should not attempt to get closer, and therefore understand more, about this strange belief that seemed to be taking over her life. And there were other roads to Rome.

She walked down by the stables, shading herself beneath her new parasol, looking in the doorway, inhaling the scent of the horses, watching Jean François standing by the forge, huge muscles rippling in his arms and shoulders as he beat at the iron horse shoes – he was naked from the waist up.

'Good morning, Jean François,' she said.

He turned his head, and a strange look flitted across his face to suggest she had interrupted some deep train of thought, but it was gone so quickly she could not decide what it was. Then he laid down his hammer.
'Mademoiselle?'

'Is Henry around?'

'I am here, mistress.' Henry had been polishing the coachwork, and now stepped round the vehicle.

'I am sure Jean François can spare you for a moment, Henry,' Richilde said, and went outside. A moment later Henry joined her. He too was naked from the waist up; his physique, for all his youth, was not greatly inferior to the big black man's. 'Yes, mistress?'

'You have not told me about the war,' she said. 'About America. About Kit.'

He grinned, his face for a moment almost recapturing the careless excitement of their games together as children. 'It was playing soldiers,' he said. 'Only with real muskets, and real bullets.'

'You have seen men killed?'

'Many men.'

'Was it not horrifying?'

He shook his head. 'I did not think so, mistress. But the uniforms, the numbers . . . There is no sight on earth like ten thousand men on 'the march, all wearing uniforms. That is the most beautiful thing I have ever seen, Mistress Richilde.'

She made a face. 'You should be a soldier. Henry, why did you not stay, with my brother? You might have been able to become a soldier, and wear a uniform.'

'A slave cannot be a soldier, mistress,' he said. 'And St Domingue is my home.'

'As it is the home of your gods?' she asked, her breath quickening.

His eyes narrowed.

'Henry,' she said. 'I know of them. And I have heard the drums. Henry, I wish to attend one of your prayer meetings. Will you take me?'

'I?'

'I know you believe in Ogone Badagris,' Richilde said. 'All black people do. I know you pray to him. And I know you must attend the drums. I wish you to take me with you. Just once. I shall tell no one about it. I promise you. And I shall wrap myself in my cloak, and no one will know it is me. Please, Henry, will you take me?'

'I came back,' Henry said. 'Because St Domingue is my home. And because my mummy has told me, often, that Mr Hamilton told her to raise me, to be big and strong, to take care of you, Mistress Richilde. That is my duty, she has always said. To take care of you. And I am failing in that duty. You are marrying a bad man.' He bit his lip, as if realising the enormity of what he had just said. But he would not lower his gaze. 'Now you would have me fail again. The black man's gods are not for you, Richilde. They would frighten you.' He turned, and went back into the stable.

Henry's refusal distressed her where Jacqueline's had not. She had been so sure of him. The old Henry would never have refused her anything. But Henry had changed, during his years away. He was growing up, developing a mind of his own.

And his remark about her marriage was disturbing, even if it was entirely predictable. She did not suppose there was a single black person, certainly not on Vergée d'Or, and unaware of the prophecy, who supposed she, or anyone, could possibly be happy married to Philippe de Mortmain. And to Henry there would be a deeper and more disturbing aspect of the situation; it would mean the final and irrevocable break between them. As Madame de Mortmain, mistress of Vergée d'Or, she would be required to stand always at her husband's right arm, to support him in everything he did. Henry could not see that she might hope to use that position to improve his lot, and the lot of everyone on the plantation. Certainly that she would use it to dilute her husband's more savage moods. Henry knew only that Philippe de Mortmain was the master, who ruled his empire by fear alone.

But there was nothing that either Henry, or herself, or even, she supposed, Ogone Badagris himself, could do about it now. For suddenly the wedding was rushing upon them all. It would be the greatest event to take place on Vergée d'Or within the memories of any of them, even the oldest slave: Jacques de Mortmain had married his wife in Paris. Thus the preparations – the accumulation of innumerable cases of wine, shipped especially from Bordeaux to supplement the vast stock in the chateau's cellars; but also the preparation of entire vats of sangaree and rum punch, for the celebrations would last all day; the selected breeding of all the turkeys and hens and sucking pigs which would be slaughtered for the wedding dinner; the arrangement by Lucien of all the species and herbs he would use to produce this, the greatest meal of his life; the redecoration of every inch of the chateau, the laundering of all the sheets and pillow cases in the spare bedrooms; and above all, the making of the gowns – all began to dominate the life of the plantation from the moment the 1782 grinding season was completed.

It was decided, by Mama and Aunt Marguerite, and Claudette, and Catherine, and of course, Thérèse de Milot, sitting in conference, that the three younger Mortmain girls would be the bridesmaids, with Lucy the maid of honour. This was what Richilde had always assumed would happen, and she would not understand the long discussions which preceded the decision. Granted that she and her old playmates hardly ever spoke to each other nowadays, and that Françoise was herself betrothed to a planter named de Beaudierre – a liberal, it was whispered disparagingly, whatever that meant – and that Lucy was clearly well on the way to being an old maid, and that Annette, by some way the prettiest of all the Mortmain girls, did not seem interested in any of the unmarried planters, or army officers, that her mother from time to time suggested as suitable husbands, but they were all three of them unable to resist the lure of the wedding, of the preparations, of the new clothes which would be theirs.

Even if they had to play second fiddle to their hated cousin. It took seven dressmakers, supervised and constantly scolded by Jacqueline, to make Richilde's trousseau. For however generous Philippe might have been over the past years, those were all, as Jacqueline remarked contemptuously, children's things, and now Richilde was to be a woman in every sense of the word. If the cumbersome pannier had at last gone out of fashion, much to her relief, there were sufficient other accessories to fill an entire spare room, powdered wigs, so absurd when intended to conceal her own splendid brown hair, straw hats and felt hats and silk hats, each with their accompanying ribbons and bows, ostrich feathers of frightening value, canes for walking and sticks for just holding, all inlaid with precious stones and strips of jade or ebony, boxes of rouge for her cheeks and lips, gloves and parasols, underskirts and corsets, shoes and boots, even stockings, although they were rarely used in this climate.

And of course, gowns. Satin gowns and silk gowns, taffeta gowns and linen house gowns, all dominated by the slowly maturing wedding gown of white satin, lined with white silk, and decorated with white lace ruffles. Her train was of white silk, and would lie several feet on the floor behind her, and Philippe gave her a magnificent necklace of enormous pearls, which, with her sapphire betrothal ring, was to be her only jewellery. While amazingly, she discovered, she was to be allowed to wear her own hair, as she was a bride. It would of course be powdered, and presumably it would be very difficult for anyone to tell the difference. But she would know. She was delighted.

'You are beautiful. Quite beautiful,' Aunt Marguerite said, two days before the wedding, which was to take place on Richilde's sixteenth birthday, when for the first time she was allowed to try on the complete ensemble. Because whatever her feelings on the matter, that Richilde should have gained the prize she must have felt belonged by right to one of her own, Marguerite de Mortmain knew where her prosperity, and that of her sons, lay, and was determinedly enthusiastic.

'Quite beautiful,' Mama agreed. 'Oh, if only Kit could be here to see you, my dear child. If only.'

'Kit!' Richilde cried, looking through the opened dressing room door. Because there he was.

Could it really be Kit, this tall, powerfully built, sunbrowned man, who looked much older than his nineteen years? But it had to be Kit, in his smile, his walk, the way he opened his arms for her. She gathered her skirts and raced forward, ignoring the shrieks of her aunt and the dressmakers.

Aunt Maguerite ran behind her. 'Richilde,' she shouted. 'You cannot wear that gown outside this room until the day. If Philippe were to see you it would mean terrible bad luck. Jeanne, you must stop her.'

But Jeanne Hamilton had left the rocking chair in which she spent most of her time – she had abandoned the fitting

141

and the stitching to her sister and the seamstresses – and was also rushing towards her son. Kit hugged them together.

'Oh, Kit,' Jeanne murmured, kissing his cheek. 'Oh, Kit. To have you back. You never told us you were coming.'

'I'd not let the wedding of my little sister go by,' he said. 'And as I was on passage to Kingston, in any event . . .'

'Is your ship in the harbour?' Richilde cried. Because of course he had written to tell them how his cousin Alexander had become the owner of a trading vessel, and had found Kit a berth as mate, with a master's ticket to follow just as soon as he had gained sufficient experience. 'You must take me down to see it.'

'I shall,' he promised. 'Whenever you can spare the time.'

'Oh, Kit,' Jeanne said again. 'To have you back. If only papa could be here too. What a happy family we would be.'

Kit hugged his mother closer, gazed above her head at Richilde with sombre eyes. 'Mama,' he said. 'Papa isn't coming back.'

'Of course he is,' Jeanne said. 'As soon as he has made his fortune. Now that the war is over, and like you, he can become an American, and stop being an outlaw, why, he may even get back for the wedding.'

'Mama,' Kit said. 'Papa is dead. I have spoken with a man who knew him, twenty years ago, in the Mississippi country. They lived together for a while, trapping. And this man was there when Father died, Mama. Of a fever.'

Jeanne's head jerked backwards as she stared at her son. 'I don't believe you,' she said. 'You are lying,' she shouted. 'You are a nasty, deceitful boy, and a horrid one, coming back here to spoil your sister's wedding. Go back to America, and tell your lies there. I hate you.' She pulled herself free and ran from the room.

'Your mother is not herself,' Philippe de Mortmain said. 'She is seldom herself.'

'Philippe!' Richilde squealed, gathering her gown; she hated his habit of being able to approach so quietly.

'You look simply superb, Richilde,' he said.

'Do not look at her,' Aunt Marguerite begged. 'It is ill

142

fortune. Do not look at her, Philippe.'

Philippe looked at her.

And she returned his gaze, allowing the gown to fall back into place. Because were not they superior to everyday superstitions, safe beneath the protection of their heathen gods?

'Do we believe in luck Philippe?' she asked. 'Or do we make our own.'

He laughed, and seized her fingers to kiss them. 'We make our own, sweet girl. We make our own.' He gripped Kit's hand. 'Welcome home, boy. Welcome home, brother-in-law-to-be. Now let us leave these ladies to their needles, and walk together, and you will tell me of America. Besides,' he added, 'here is Jacqueline. Who do you suppose has come home, Jacqueline? The bad penny himself.'

'Why, Kit,' Jacqueline Chavannes said. 'How splendid you look. Will you not give me a kiss? When you ran away, four years ago, without even saying goodbye, I thought you hated me.'

Kit glanced at Philippe, who did not seem to find anything exceptional in his mistress's choice of words, then kissed the quadroon on each cheek. She had not changed at all, remained exactly as he remembered her – and he had thought about her a great deal – even wore the same perfume he remembered. But, he realised, *he* had changed. He saw her differently. Still beautiful, certainly, still alluring, but with a brittle hardness in her eyes and lurking at the corners of her mouth which almost turned her beauty into ugliness.

'You have grown,' Jacqueline said, kissing him in turn. 'Why, you are a man. You must come and sit with me, and tell me of your adventures. When you can spare the time.' She stepped past him, closed the dressing room door.

'Poor Jacqueline,' Philippe de Mortmain said. 'She is about to become redundant.' He winked. 'As of the day after tomorrow. But actually, she had been so for some time now. I approach your sister as recently chaste as she herself.'

'I wonder she remains here,' Kit said. 'Madame Jacqueline, I mean.'

Philippe laughed. 'Mainly because she has nowhere else to go. What, return to that miserable shop in Cap François? Certainly she is welcome here, for as long as Richilde is content that it should be so. I would not return so old a friend to poverty, unless forced to it.'

So, Kit thought, as they walked, as he told his future brother-in-law of America, what she has feared has come to pass. And instead of being here to stand by her side, as she always hoped and intended should happen, I have taken myself off to a new life. No wonder she was angry with me.

But did that mean she was not his for the taking? If he wanted her? Because of course he did want her, at least with a part of himself. She was the only woman to whom he had ever made love, and she remained the most beautiful woman he had ever seen. He wondered what cousin Alexander, with his somewhat rigid views on colour, would say were he to appear in Virginia with a quadroon in tow. Alex would certainly disapprove. But that was something he would be prepared to face, were he sure that Jacqueline Chavannes was truly what he wanted, could be sure that she would love him, and not herself, not subject everything he might want to her own plans, her own ambitions.

'Why, Annette,' Philippe said. 'You remember Kit?'

'Of course I remember Kit,' Annette de Mortmain said. They had wandered into one of the rose gardens, and disturbed the girl, who was seated on a bench in the shade, reading a book. 'How splendid you look, Kit.'

'As do you, Annette,' he said. She had always been the prettiest of the sisters, – save only perhaps for Madeleine who was due here later on this afternoon, though her English husband had decided against making the journey – but he had never taken much notice of her before; she was only a year older than Richilde. But now she was seventeen, with long yellow hair and dark eyes, and a perfectly white complexion, and with a figure which suggested she was already a woman. He flushed at his thoughts. 'You are quite a beauty.'

'Then I will leave her to entertain you,' Philippe said, and hurried off. Clearly he had been bored, had been doing nothing more than his duty by Richilde's brother.

'Why do you not sit down,' Annette suggested, and he obeyed. 'Are you really a sailor now?' she asked.

'Indeed I am. I've always loved the sea.'

'I remember,' she said. 'I wish I could be a sailor.' Her turn to flush. 'I mean, were I a man. Sometimes I wish I *were* a man, and able to travel, as I wished, and adventure, as I wished. Instead of just sitting here on Vergée d'Or, waiting to die.'

'There's a sombre thought, for a young lady,' he remarked. 'Waiting to be married, you mean.'

She shrugged and smiled. 'If you could see some of the gentlemen Mama has produced for me to marry, you would agree with me that the two eventualities are too similar for comfort. But if I cannot adventure myself, at least I can do so at second hand.' She showed him her book, a French edition of *Hakluyt*, then laid it down and held his hand instead. 'Tell me of America, Kit. Everything you can think of.'

Kit supposed that never in the history of Vergée d'Or, perhaps even in the history of St Domingue, had there been such a glittering assembly of notables in one place, from the Governor-General, Monsieur Peynier, and all his principal officers and their wives, through almost every planter in the north of the island, and even one or two from the south, and all the leading merchants of Cap François. It was strictly a *grands blanc* gathering; he estimated he was by many degrees the lowest person present, either regarded from a financial point of view or from his birth.

But whatever his stature, he was the bride's brother, and therefore exalted. Because dominating even this magnificent assembly, dominating even the glittering wealth displayed by the Milots, was the Mortmain clan. Etienne, wearing a moustache nowadays, and somewhat plump, with his superbly lovely, auburn-haired Claudette on his arm, her babe carried behind her by a white nurse; Louis, also wearing a moustache, which grew but slowly and required continual stroking, apparently – but genuinely pleased to see again his old comrade in arms; Uncle Maurice and Aunt Marguerite, better dressed than he had ever seen them, smiling and bowing as if they were the hosts; Madeleine, tall and slender despite the three children who clung to her skirts, two of whom, the eldest boy and girl, had acted as attendants for Richilde and were clearly overwhelmed by the whole occasion; Catherine, who had allowed herself to put on weight, no doubt, he surmised, to match her husband François de Milot, who was decidedly fat; Françoise, eager to display her Ferrand de Beaudierre, a small planter whose eyes burned with some inner fire, and who seemed anxious to tell everyone how things could not continue as they were at present – without actually specifying which things he was referring to – and Lucy and Annette, splendid in pale blue and gold gowns, as they were the principal attendants of the bride. Annette had never looked lovelier, he thought. But, he had realised over the past twenty-four hours, he had been allowing himself some dangerously immoral thoughts. Annette was his first cousin.

And then, Mama, for this evening also dressed with an elegance he had never seen in her before, but catastrophically and obviously revealing her dementia for all to understand, as she wandered from guest to guest, telling each one that her husband was but delayed, and would be arriving at any moment, to give away his daughter in marriage. His fault, Kit thought, with desperate self bitterness. Better he had not returned at all.

An emotion he experienced even when he regarded the bride and groom, standing together, flanked by the Bishop and Father Thomas, as they raised their glasses and prepared to cut into the many-tiered cake. Richilde looked radiantly happy, and in her happiness she was the loveliest woman in the room. Philippe de Mortmain merely looked alert, watching always to make sure that every guest had everything he or she desired, only smiling when he caught the eye of someone who was smiling at him. But that he was more than twice Richilde's age, that he was in every sense a very mature man where she was equally in every sense a totally innocent young girl, was disturbingly obvious. And presumably not everyone present knew of the blackness which could consume him. From this moment Richilde would be at the mercy of that.

Which was a totally irrational consideration; had she not in reality been at the mercy of that for the past eight years?

The toasts were drunk, and he could legitimately leave the drawing room and wander among the servants, gathered in the great hall to watch their masters and mistresses disporting themselves. Most of them remembered him, as he remembered them, and he had not yet had the time to greet more than a few. This he now rectified as he made his way slowly to the kitchens, to congratulate Lucien on the splendour of his meal, while all the time he searched the throng . . . and at last found Henry, sitting by himself on the wall of the back patio, gazing out towards the distant beach, and the sea.

He had, of course, seen Henry earlier. But only for a brief greeting.

'Well, old friend,' he said. 'A milestone in our lives would you not say?'

'A milestone for Miss Richilde, Master Kit,' Henry said.

'Do you not feel a sense of loss?' Kit asked. 'She is your twin.'

'I lost Miss Richilde many years ago,' Henry said. 'When we came to this place, I think.'

He'd been brooding again, Kit realised. And Henry Christopher was too intelligent to be allowed to brood. Besides . . . perhaps it was un unthinkable thought, but it occurred to Kit that perhaps Henry felt more for Richilde than a slave should feel for his mistress.

'Henry,' he said. 'You know, if ever you change your mind about living here, my offer remains. You can come away with me. And I am not living in America itself, you know. Well, I suppose I am. But I have adopted the sea as a livelihood. In a year or two I shall have a master's ticket and, in any event, I sail on a vessel owned by my cousin. You remember Alexander Hamilton?'

'I remember Mr Hamilton,' Henry said.

'Well, you could sail with me. It's a good life, Henry. A free life. Even for a slave.'

Henry gazed at him.

'And then,' Kit went on, somewhat lamely. 'Well . . . I do not think you are really happy here.'

'I must stay here,' Henry said.

'Why? Because of your mother? She is old, just as my mother is old. They are going to die some time soon. And then, what will you have stayed for? While Richilde . . . Well, as of tonight, Richilde will have no more need of either of us. Not ever.'

'She will need, Master Kit,' Henry said. 'She will need, more than ever. One day.' He slipped down from the wall. 'It is for that day I must be here.'

He walked into the gloom. Kit looked past him, saw the massive figure of Jean François standing by the gate. With the big man, he could make out the smaller shape of the lame Milot coachman, Jean Pierre Toussaint. When Henry joined them, the three men walked into the darkness together.

The women clustered round the bed, smoothing pillows here, straightening the sheet here, clucking and laughing, joking and even weeping. There was an awful number of them, many people Richilde had hardly seen before this evening, but all anxious to assist the bride in preparing for the most important night of her life.

She sat up in bed, her back against the pillows, her satin and lace nightgown half concealed by the sheet which had been folded across her stomach. Her hair had been released from its various pins and curls, and was loose on her shoulders – it had been brushed time and again to rid it of most of the cloying powder. And remarkably, she was not aware of the slightest feeling of fear. She estimated that she was by some distance the calmest person in the room. The amount of wine she had drunk had certainly helped, but she was more aware that she had been waiting, and preparing, for this night for seven years; that thanks to Mama Céleste, and to Jacqueline, she was in every way ready, and indeed eager, to belong to her husband, to know if, as was promised her, the touch, the feel, the love of a man was superior to any other physical sensation.

So no doubt she was the greatest sinner on the face of the earth, the most utter heretic. She was a sinner in never having confessed one part of her secret life to Father Thomas. And she was a heretic in having reserved that secret part of her life to Ogone Badagris. And she was a depraved woman, by any Christian standards, in having, so often during the past year, reawakened with her own fingers the enormous sensual pleasure first revealed to her by Mama Céleste, in having, so often, left her bedchamber in the middle of the night to walk, all by herself, on the empty beach, and plunge into the rollers, and be loved by them, because that too had been undertaken in a spirit of pure self gratification.

Thus Christian ethics. But she could always reassure herself that such behaviour was approved by the Snake God, more, was demanded by him.

And all would be expiated tonight. In the love of her husband, in her ability to welcome him, without fear and without restraint, would she atone for all of her crimes. She told herself that after tonight she would no longer even need Ogone Badagris. He would have done his duty by her, and could then be allowed to revert to his more important duties, of caring for the black people.

Why, after tonight, tomorrow morning, in fact, she could even confess the whole thing to Father Thomas. There would be nothing he could do about it then. Tomorrow morning she would awaken as Madame de Mortmain, Mistress of Vergée d'Or, and would hold his livelihood in the palm of her hand. Oh, she was a depraved creature.

'Well, my child . . .' Aunt Marguerite bent over the bed to kiss her on the forehead – her mother had long been put to

149

bed. 'I think the time has come to leave you.' She smiled. 'In my day, the ladies of the family, at least, remained to witness the consummation. But Philippe will have none of it. So you must face him alone.'

'It will be well, Aunt Marguerite,' Richilde assured her. 'All will be well. And I must thank you, for everything.'

Marguerite ushered her daughters and all the other women through the door, turned and curtsied. 'It is we who should thank you, Madame de Mortmain,' she said. 'I will wish you a good night.'

A good night, Richilde thought. And a happy one. Because she could hear the noise now, the shouting and the laughter, the approach of the men. She hoped he would keep them outside. She had no desire to share this evening with anyone but Philippe. And perhaps . . . She turned her head as the inner door opened.

'Jacqueline,' she cried. 'Listen . . .'

'I know,' Jacqueline said. 'Those women stayed so long.' She ran across the room, took Richilde in her arms. 'Remember everything.'

Richilde nodded.

'Then be happy,' Jacqueline commanded. 'And make him happy, too.'

A quick kiss, and she ran from the room again, just as the noise reached the door. The men shouted advice and congratulations and a variety of lewd jokes, and Richilde sank beneath the covers until just her head was visible. But only Philippe came through the door, laughing and replying to the repartee, but with a touch of impatience in his voice. Then he closed the door and shot the bolt, turned to face her.

'I suppose they must have their little games,' he said.

'Perhaps they are envious of you,' she said, sitting up.

'Envious? Yes, they should be that.' He wore a nightshirt, and a cap, but this last he now threw on the floor. 'Richilde, my Richilde,' he said, sitting on the bed to take her in his arms and kiss her, again and again, sending his tongue questing into her opened mouth as she attempted to match it with her own – for how long had she dreamed of doing this – moving her body against his.

'Oh, Richilde,' he said, and at last released her, only immediately to hug her close again. 'You are everything I have dreamed of, everything I have waited for. Oh, Richilde . . .' he half threw her away from him, stood up, took off his nightshirt. Here at last was a man, a white man. She had of course during her life seen many naked slaves, of both sexes, but that had been before her awakening of this last year, and she had hardly looked at them closely any more than she ever looked closely at horses or donkeys or dogs in a state of arousal. But here was a man, and her husband, huge, magnificent, and so ready for her. Truly she had to suppose that the tales Jacqueline had told her of his impotence were no more than figments of the quadroon's imagination.

'Do I frighten you?' he asked.

'Frighten me? Oh, Philippe . . .' she reached for him, slipped her hands round his naked buttocks, brought him against her, smothered him in her embrace. She tilted her head back. 'Do you wish me to undress also?'

'Yes,' he said. 'Yes, I would look upon you, too.'

She released him, rose to her knees, lifted the nightdress over her head and threw it on the floor.

'Richilde,' he said. 'My Richilde. My marvellous little girl.'

She was on her back, with him on top of her. It was quicker than she had either expected or hoped, and certainly she was not aroused as she wanted to be, and as she was sure she would be. But of course tonight the important thing was Philippe. That he should possess her and be happy. And there it was, inside her, hard as a bone, with an ease she would not have supposed possible.

She felt almost no pain, only a delightful sensation spreading away from her groin, even as she reached for his mouth again, sent her fingers scouring up and down his back in her anxiety to hold him against her . . . and was taken completely by surprise when he suddenly pushed himself up and rolled away from her, rising to his knees at the edge of

151

the bed.

'Philippe?' She raised herself on her elbow.

'Soft,' he muttered. 'Two thrusts and then soft. Soft,' he suddenly shrieked.

She gazed at him. He was certainly incapable of entering her again, at this moment.

'Let me help you,' she said, reaching for him.

'No,' he snapped, leaping from the bed. 'It would do no good. It is the same as always. I have been betrayed. Betrayed,' he screamed, his entire body seeming to swell with fury.

She bit her lip, uncertain what he meant. 'Philippe,' she said. 'If I have in any way . . .'

'Not you' He gave her a glance then reached for his nightshirt. 'Never you, poor child. You are but an innocent pawn in this game. But that Jacqueline . . . by Christ she shall pay for this.' He picked up his riding crop, crossed the room and opened the inner door before she fully grasped his intentions. Then she leapt from the bed herself, ignoring her robe in her haste.

'Philippe,' she shouted. 'Philippe . . .'

He had already crossed the inner room, which was his own private dressing room, she realised. Somewhere she had never entered before. But now she was exploring entirely new territory, as she followed him down a brief corridor, at the end of which he threw open another door.

Jacqueline's bedroom. A place of heavy dark drapes and equally heavy perfume. And Jacqueline, sitting up in bed to stare at her master; she had not yet been to sleep – the candles still burned.

'Philippe?' she asked, and saw the riding crop. 'Philippe?'

'Bitch,' he shouted. 'Whore from the pit of hell. You and your black magic. You and your obeah.' He swung the crop, and the quadroon gave a shriek and rolled across the bed, but the leather thong caught her on the shoulder, with such force that a red weal immediately appeared, and her scream ended in a gasp of pain as she fell to the floor on the far side.

'Philippe!' Richilde shouted, trying to catch his arm, and

being thrown away by the violence of his next movement, as he stamped over the bed itself to reach his erstwhile mistress.

'I'll take the skin from your back,' he growled. 'By God, I'll see the colour of your blood. I should have done so long ago. I should have . . .'

Jacqueline gave a moan and attempted to protect her head with her arms as the whip again slashed across her shoulders.

With desperate urgency Richilde threw both arms around Philippe's right arm, hung on to it as he tried to throw her off, cut her lip on his elbow, but delayed the next blow long enough for Jacqueline to crawl to the door.

'Philippe,' she said. 'Please! It will be all right, I know it will.'

'It can never be all right as long as that witch lives in this house,' he said. 'It is she has bewitched me these past six years, all for her own purposes.' He pointed, his chest heaving. 'Get out,' he said. 'Get yourself from Vergée d'Or. So help me God, if you are seen here I again I will set the dogs on you.'

Jacqueline stared at him, then at Richilde. Richilde gave a quick nod, to try to convey to her that it would certainly be best at this moment. Slowly Jacqueline held on to the door and dragged herself to her feet, made as if to stroke her burning back, then shrugged her shoulders and tossed hair from her face – it was the first time that Richilde had ever seen her hair disordered.

Jacqueline reached into the cupboard for a valise.

'What are you doing?' Philippe demanded.

'You told me to leave, *master*,' she said.

'I did not tell you to rob me.' he said. 'Get out.'

Jacqueline hesitated.

'Please, Philippe,' Richilde begged. 'You cannot send her away, naked.'

'She came to me naked,' Philippe said. 'Let her go naked.'

Jacqueline gazed at him, her eyes black pits from the very depths of hell. Then she turned and walked through the door.

'Philippe,' Richilde said. 'That was cruel of you.'

'You do not know her as I do,' Philippe said. 'She is an evil creature. And I let her have the education of you.' He turned, his eyes hardly less fearful than had been Jacqueline's.

But he was her husband, and this was their wedding night. Time enough to do something about Jacqueline tomorrow.

'We will not think of her,' she promised. 'Come back to bed, Philippe. Come back to bed, and all will be well. I will make it so.'

He shook his head. 'Nothing can be all right, tonight. Perhaps never, now. I am cursed. She has cursed me. By God, I should have hanged her, rather than let her walk away from here.'

Richilde sighed, and fought to restrain the tears, the utter despair, that was threatening to overwhelm her. 'At least then, let us retire to sleep,' she said. And forced a smile. 'It has been a tiring day.'

'Aye,' he said. 'Do you go to sleep, Richilde. I will remain in here.'

'In here? But . . .' she stared at him with her mouth open.

'I will come to you when I can,' he said. 'But for this night you must sleep alone. Now leave me.'

'Madame de Mortmain,' Monsieur Chavannes said, twisting his fingers together. 'Good morning, Madame de Mortmain. What can we do for you? Some cloth? See this fine linen? May I say what a great pleasure, and an honour, it is for us to receive you in our humble shop, madame.'

You miserable old hypocrite, Richilde thought. How you must hate me, and all I stand for, yet you stand there like some obsequious eunuch, terrified of causing offence.

'I wish to speak with Jacqueline, monsieur,' she said.

'Jacqueline. Ah.' Monsieur Chavannes' eyes became opaque. 'She is not well, you understand. That is why she has returned from the plantation to stay with us. Only for a while, you understand. But of course, you know all of this.'

'Yes,' Richilde said. 'I would still like to speak with her.'

'Well, of course, madame, if that is what you wish. Will you excuse me? I will fetch her.'

He bustled out of the shop. Richilde turned, surveyed the stacked bales of cloth, twirled her parasol, looked through the outer door at the waiting carriage, and Jean François and Henry Christopher and Amelia, conferring – none of them approved of this visit, obviously, although only Amelia had ventured actually to say so.

'What, do you mean to torment her?' Jacques Chavannes asked.

She had not known he was there, concealed behind a mound of drapery at the far end of the shop. Now she could feel his dislike coming at her in waves. It was a feeling she had known the first time she had ever met him, seven years before. And if anything it had grown since his return from America. Yet Kit had told her how this man had once saved his life.

'No, monsieur,' she said. 'I do not mean to torment her. We are friends, your sister and I.'

'Bah,' he said. 'How can a mulatto be the friend of a white person? You are asking the snake and the mongoose to lie down together, madame.' He flushed, as if realising that he might have said a great deal too much, and withdrew to the far corner of the shop, as Jacqueline came through the inner door. She did not appear to have slept for the three nights since she had left Vergée d'Or – her face was drawn, and there were shadows under her eyes.

'You wish to speak with me, madame?' she asked.

'Jacqueline . . .' Richilde glanced from left to right. 'Is there somewhere we can talk in private?'

'There is here, madame.' Jacqueline said.

Richilde hesitated. But to be angry herself was utterly futile. 'I . . . I could not come before,' she explained. 'I had our guests to entertain, and to come into Cap François might have been too obvious. Philippe is very insistent that no one should know of what happened.'

'No one will know,' Jacqueline said. 'No one ever has.'

'Yes.' Richilde bit her lip. 'He still has not . . . I am not yet

155

truly his wife.'

Jacqueline shrugged. 'Then you must pray.'

'To whom should I pray, Jacqueline?'

The quadroon's eyes were dark. 'That decision you must make for yourself, madame.'

'Will you not call me Richilde? I had supposed we were friends. You knew of Philippe's moods, long before I. You will know I cannot gainsay them. At least, not until I can be a wife to him. But I can still be your friend, Jacqueline. You have but to tell me what you require, anything you require, and I shall obtain it for you. And I would be your friend, always.'

'We cannot be friends, madame,' Jacqueline said. 'Our blood makes it impossible. The mistake was mine, to suppose such a thing might be possible. Now you must go to your life, and do with it what you can. Leave me to mine.'

Richilde gazed at her. 'Hate,' she said. 'However justified you may feel it at this moment, is a wasting, hopeless, consuming emotion, Jacqueline,' she said. 'Do not waste your life hating.'

Jacqueline's smile was twisted. 'Yet is it an emotion, madame,' she said. 'And it is the only one I know. Now go to your husband, to your god, and leave me in peace.'

'Well,' Kit Hamilton said. 'I must be on my way.' He held Richilde close. 'Take care, little sister.'

And can you see into my mind, dear brother? she wondered. Can you make out the misery there?

But she smiled, and kissed him on the cheek. 'It is you who should take care, out there on the ocean. But you will remember that Vergée d'Or is always here, waiting for you, if you should choose to visit us.'

'Be sure that that will be as often as I can manage it,' he promised, and shook hands with Philippe. 'I know that Richilde is in good hands, Philippe,' he said. 'You will keep me informed as to Mama's health?'

'I shall do that, Kit,' Philippe promised. 'As I shall treasure Richilde's love above all other things.'

'I am sure of that,' Kit said, meeting his brother-in-law's gaze, before passing on to say farewell to the rest of the family.

And at the end of the row, Annette. 'I shall write to you, with your permission,' he said. 'And tell you of my adventures, supposing I have any.'

'Will you, Kit?' she asked. Her eyes shone. 'I should so like you to do that.' She blushed. 'And will you truly come to see us, often?'

'As often as I can,' he said, and bent his head to kiss her on the cheek. She wore a voluminous bonnet, and for just a moment their faces were lost to view. In that moment she half turned her head so that her lips brushed his.

Philippe watched him going down the stairs to the waiting carriage. 'I hope he does come to visit us, regularly,' he said. 'I think he may well do so.'

'Indeed?' Richilde asked.

'Have you not seen the way he looks at Annette? The warmth, indeed, with which he has just kissed her goodbye?'

'That would be impossible,' Richilde said. 'They are first cousins.'

'Who can tell what is impossible?' Philippe mused. He held her arm as they mounted the great staircase together. 'I wish to thank you, for so dissembling before him. Before everyone. It would have done credit to someone twice your age.'

She checked at the upper porch. 'But you will not remove the reason.'

His eyes gloomed at her. 'I will come to your bed, Richilde, as soon as I feel able. It . . . it is a terrible thing, for a man to admit, even to himself, such a weakness as mine.'

'I do not care for your weaknesses,' she said. 'I care only for your love. I wish to sleep beside you, nothing more than that.'

'Dear Richilde,' he said, and bent his head to kiss her. 'You shall, sleep beside me, in time. But now . . . now, when I wish to take you, and love you, and cannot, my anger grows . . . and I am afraid of harming you. I would not harm you for all the world, my Richilde.'

But you will not sleep with me, she thought bitterly, lying by herself in the centre of the huge bed. I am a bride of more than a week, and I am as virgin as the day I was born. Do you not know, you silly, proud man, so strong and imperious, that I would cheerfully exchange a few bruises to be made into your wife? Have I really lived and waited and anticipated for eight years, just to lie here all alone?

She slept, an angry, frustrated sleep, and awoke suddenly, disturbed by the silence of the night. And then realised that there was, after all, sound. The steady, distant throb of a drum. Or perhaps there was more than one, seething across the night, in their incessant rhythm dulling the senses, but beckoning at the same time. Come to me, come to me, come to me.

She got out of bed, opened the door, and listened. The house was silent. She went to the window, looked out at the ocean. There was no moon; the night was dark. And still – there was no wind to mask the throbbing of the drums.

She discovered her heart was pounding and sweat was gathering on her neck. The drums were obliterating her senses, driving the lonely resentment from her mind. Before she could reason, allow common sense and caution to come to her rescue, she had gathered her hair into a bandanna, and wrapped herself in her robe. She went down the private staircase, stood in the garden, listening. Where the drum was, there she would find Mama Céleste, surely. Hitherto she had not dared return to the *mamaloi*, however much she needed her. But tonight she could wait no longer. Not when she was being summoned by the drums.

Her bare feet scuffed the dust of the drive; she skirted the overseer's town, dark and silent, and reached the back of the slave village, heart still pounding, afraid, but determined. The throb of the drums caressed her mind, reached her belly and beyond, demanding, urging, calling. And then she discovered that she was not alone. As she approached the slave town she saw white clad figures leaving the barracoons and disappearing into the trees that lay beyond. She took her place with them. No one gave her even a glance. It could not occur to a slave that a white woman, who was also the mistress of the plantation, would wish to join in their nocturnal service.

Now the darkness increased, as they entered the shade of the huge branches, and twisted vines snatched at her feet, together with scurrying lizards and the thousand and one other things that made up the night in the tropical forest. She felt no fear. She had explored the woods of St Kitts often enough as a girl, knew that the most vicious creatures in them were stinging ants, and did not suppose St Domingue was greatly different. But even had she been afraid she could not now have resisted the power of the drums.

The trees were parting again, and the white-clad figures were moving to their right around a clearing. And here there was light, provided by emptied coconut shells, cut in half and filled with oil, to burn with an eerie glow, guttering even in the windless night. And here too were six fowl cocks, tethered by their legs to sticks, eyes darting to and fro, heads jerking at the stealthy sounds around them. For the moment they occupied the clearing alone, but beginning to surround them were more and more people, kneeling and crouching in the tree fringe, men and women, and even children. Richilde knelt, well to the back of the throng, to stare at the flames and the cocks, and identifying, in the gloom beyond the helpless birds, the forms of the drummers, three of them, each controlling a different shaped instrument, each sending forth a different note, over and over again, echoing through the trees, and up and down the mountains.

She was one of the last to arrive. Only a handful of white-clad figures came behind her, to take their places in the silent assembly. But as her eyes grew accustomed to the gloom she realised that there were several thousand people present, an immense gathering. She wondered if Philippe, who claimed to know all this, had an inkling of the size of the meetings he so contemptuously permitted.

Her attention was drawn to the flickering lights in front of her, where suddenly a figure appeared beside the fowl cocks, a young man, tall and strong and gleaming in the darkness, sitting cross legged before the drummers, shoulders square and head erect. On either side of him waited a young woman, each holding a palm leaf, faces and bodies rigid with tense expectation. And the drum beat had altered, reaching ever deeper into the senses, summoning all the powers of belief it could induce.

She saw the flicker of a red robe, and raised her head expectantly: Mama Céleste. But this was not Mama Céleste. This was a man, as tall and as powerful as any Negro she had ever seen. More than that she could not tell, for the robe was across his head as well, and half concealed him. Her heart constricted. She had no idea what was about to happen. But she knew that if it was so important that it required the offices of a *papaloi* – a priest – rather than a woman, then it would be terrible indeed. And she suspected that this was no mere *papaloi*, but rather a *hougan*, a high priest of the voodoo religion.

The red robed man walked into the centre of the circle, stood next to the young man, threw his arms to the skies, and shouted, 'Hear me. O mighty one. Hear me, O Serpent, Damballah Oueddo. Hear my prayer, and promise me deliverance for my people.' He paused, and inhaled, while a moaning chant arose from the watching multitude. 'How long, great Ogone, master of all the Oceans of the World, must we wait? Hear me, O mighty lord. Speak to me, great Loco, Lord of the Trees. Grant me and my people thy sin of deliverance. Come to me gentle Ezilee, sweet *maîtresse*, and take from my mind, from my body, the very last human weakness.'

Once again he paused, and now the chant had grown louder. Richilde discovered that sweat was pouring from her body.

'Come to me, O mighty Ogone Badagris. Come to my people, O Dreadful One. Lead us to war, as is thy purpose. Grant us an end to all the white people. Grant us the mood of hate and cruelty, that their destruction may be known throughout the world, and forever. Grant us revenge, O

160

Dreadful One, for the wrongs that are daily committed upon us. Grant us now a sign, my lords, that our prayers are heeded.'

He stood still, his body trembling, and Richilde watched a man get up from the crowd, and hold out a machete, which the *hougan* took, slowly and reverently, testing the sharpness of the blade with his thumb. She wanted to scream. She wanted to get up and run away. But like everyone else she merely stared in horror, as the priest stood before the motionless young man, neither of them even blinking their eyes as they gazed at each other. Then the priest threw back his head and screamed to his gods in an unknown tongue, as he whirled the cutlass around his own head, and with a single unbelievable sweep of the razor sharp sword swept through the neck of his victim.

The head fell forward, and the machete had been dropped. The priest caught the head, his great hands immediately smeared with blood, while the two girls hastily fanned the still upright, blood-spouting neck with vigorous anxiety, determined to prevent a speck of dirt, a single insect from settling on the tortured flesh.

Richilde forced herself to watch. Because I am not seeing, she told herself. I am not even here. I am lying in my own bed, and dreaming. I have got to be dreaming. But the blood spurting from the severed arteries held her spellbound.

And now the *hougan* was advancing again, having held the dripping head high to present it to the worshippers. Slowly he paraded his ghastly trophy, and equally slowly he replaced the head, carefully, exactly, while in that moment another young woman threw a large piece of red cloth over the dead man.

The dead man? Within seconds his feet began to move, and then his arms, and the throbbing of the drums had resumed command over all of their senses. The young man's mask was taken away, and he was unchanged, but standing now, shuffling and posturing, exuding all the immense manhood of his naked body. Then he reached for the nearest fowl cock, and with a twist of his powerful fingers tore its head from its neck.

There was a shriek from the people around Richilde, and they surged forward, holding up their hands to catch the flying blood, reaching for the quivering body to grasp it and shred it into pieces, cramming raw flesh and blood and bone into their mouths, seizing the other birds to destroy them in turn. And as they did so, the beat of the drums changed, slightly and perhaps insensibly to all but a detached observer, but the rhythm had increased, and the slaves danced, sinuously and even gracefully at first, but rapidly becoming more vigorous and forceful, while the drumbeat gradually quickened its tempo ever more. Now passion and desire and hate and fear and lust came bubbling to the surface, and turbans and gowns, cotton drawers and straw hats were discarded, flung to the edges of the clearing, while the night became a seething delirium of aroused sexuality.

Richilde knew that she must get away, if only because she was suddenly isolated, standing on the edge of the clearing. She ran into the trees, checked in horror as she came up against a large black man, gasped for breath as she recognised Jean François.

He was equally surprised, as he pulled the bandanna from her head and looked at his mistress. Immediately he drew her further into the privacy of the trees. Yet he still held her, and she felt his hands slip up to her neck, stroking across her breast as he did so, bringing her out in a rash of shivering.

'No,' Henry Christoper said.

The big man looked at him. Even at sixteen Henry was already the taller, and the broader.

'She has seen all. She will tell all,' Jean François said. 'And she must die . . .' Again his hand moved over her breast.

'You cannot kill her,' Henry said. 'And you must not touch her.'

Jean François hesitated, and Toussaint spoke. He had approached them unheard, as the four of them were quite ignored by the frenzied dancers. 'She will not betray us,' he said. 'Will you, Madame de Mortmain?'

Jean François had released her, and she could draw an

unhindered breath. She slipped from his grasp. 'No,' she gasped, 'No, I will not betray you.'

She looked to Henry, reached for him, felt his arm go round her shoulder.

'You can believe her?' Jean François asked. 'Married to that man?'

Toussaint looked at her, then at Jean François. 'Are you not looking at the prophecy?' he asked.

Richilde looked down at Henry's black arm resting across her white one.

'Go,' Toussaint said. 'Make haste, Madame Richilde. You should not have come here. This night your eyes have seen what no white person should ever see. Go.'

'Toussaint,' she gasped. '*Did* I see? Was that boy really ...?' she bit her lip.

Toussaint's face was as remote as that of a god itself. 'You saw, what you saw, madame,' he said. 'What your brain told you was there, was there. Now go. Henry Christopher will take you back to the chateau.'

He seized Jean François' arm, and hurried him back to the dance, speaking urgently in his ear.

'Come,' Henry said.

She realised for the first time that he was naked. She had not seen him naked before, at least since he and she had been small children together. Now she realised he was the handsomest man she had ever beheld. 'Henry ...'

He held her arm, hurried her though the trees.

'Henry,' she begged, uncertain what she was begging for, knowing only that she could still feel the touch of Jean François' hand, that she could never be the same, after this night. And that therefore he could never be the same either? Then what of all the other people? The thousands of other people who had attended the ceremony. 'Henry!'

Still he forced her on. 'What you did was madness,' he said. 'Madness, Richilde.' It was the first time he had not addressed her as mistress or madame since the day at Jean François' forge. 'And dangerous. Had you been discovered ...'

She dug her heels into the earth and made them stop; the lights of the chateau were in the distance. 'Henry,' she said. 'What did I see?'

'As Toussaint has said, what you think you saw, you saw.'

'Henry,' she said. 'Tell me the truth. That could not have happened. It could not.'

He looked down at her. 'The drums have a strange power over the human mind,' he agreed.

'Do you believe it?'

He hestitated. 'No,' he said. 'But I saw it. And those people back there believe it.'

'And the *papaloi*?' she said. 'Who was he?'

'So that he can be hanged?'

'Do you believe that of me, Henry?'

Another hesitation. 'No,' he said at last. 'His name is Boukman. He is a great *hougan* amongst my people.'

'He lives on Vergée d'Or?'

He shook his head. 'He has come from far away.'

'Then this was a special occasion. Why, Henry? Why? Was it to do with my marriage?'

For the first time he looked genuinely puzzled; the thought had obviously not occurred to him. 'I do not know,' he said. 'Boukman said it must be tonight. Boukman knows all things.'

'And you believe *that*?'

'It is my business to believe, for now, Madame Richilde,' he said.

For now, she thought. He was too intelligent to believe with all of his mind. Just as he was too self-possessed to continue calling her Richilde, treating her as an equal. That brief moment was past.

But she did not wish it to pass. She could not allow it to pass.

'Henry?' she asked. 'What did Toussaint mean, about a prophecy?'

'He was told a prophecy, once,' Henry said. 'He and Jean François.'

'To do with your people becoming free?'

He gazed at her.

'And it was to do with me? Or a white woman?'

'Who can tell, with a prophecy, Madame Richilde?'

'But it is to do with your freedom,' she insisted.

'A people must dream, Madame Richilde. If they cannot dream, then they are animals.' Almost he smiled. 'We are not animals, no matter what your husband may suppose. But Madame Richilde, remember your promise. If you were to break it, there would be much misery, many of us would die.'

'I will keep my promise,' she said. 'But Henry, if the prophecy were to come true, will there not be much misery then, and many deaths?'

'Prophecies are like dreams,' he said. 'They fade, when daylight comes.'

'But Henry, as we are a part of the prophecy . . .' she looked him slowly up and down. She did not wish ever to forget what he looked like. As she wished him to remember her, this night. Her fingers released the tie for her gown.

But he caught her hand. 'Tonight is also just a dream, Richilde,' he said. 'If you return to your bed now, it will not become a nightmare.'

He squeezed her hand, and disappeared into the trees, and the darkness, and the distant throb of the drums. She remained staring after him for several seconds, aware that she was till panting, that her body was still alive. Then she turned, and hurried across the lawns and up the private staircase, and into her bedroom. Her empty bedroom.

But sleeping alone, this night, was not possible. She threw her robe on the floor, made her way along the corridor into the other room. At the sound of her entry the glare of the candle, Philippe de Mortmain sat up, stared at her in total amazement. 'What the devil . . .'

Richilde knelt on the bed beside him. 'I have come,' she said. 'To make you a man. And to make me your wife.'

PART TWO
The Soldier

Caught up in the enthusiasm of Boukman's rebellion, [Toussaint] was at first employed as a doctor: already middle-aged, and wizened in appearance, he never sought to command, but before long his ability as a tactician began to be noticed and envied. He made an enemy of Jean François himself, and found it necessary to take service with the Spaniards in the other half of the island. The British invasion and the death of Jean François combined to attract him back to his native country. He took command of the black army of the north and brought men like Dessalines and Christophe out of the slave mobs and into positions of authority. He developed his own strategy to suit his brilliant tactics, and if never able to meet the British regulars on a set battlefield, he harried and outwitted them. It was during these years that he earned the nickname of L'Ouverture, from the manner in which he opened gaps in the opposing forces.

Chapter 1

THE FAILURE

The pronouncement [of 26th August 1789, 'that all men are born and continue free and equal as to their rights.'] encouraged the mulattos' wildest hopes ... and in St Domingue, both to defend their persons and to prove their re-established rights, they appeared in arms. This could be interpreted as rebellion, and they were immediately dispersed by the troops, on this occasion without undue violence. But the temper of the frightened white population was revealed by the fate of Ferrand de Beaudierre, a white man who sided with the mulattos and had the temerity to draw up a memorial claiming for his friends the full benefits of the declaration of rights. The authorities regarded this as a seditious document, and de Beaudierre was imprisoned; a white mob burst open the cell and tore him to pieces.

'Her life was not easy,' Father Thomas said. 'She had more than her share of tragedy. And her later days were clouded. And yet, in the health and prosperity of her children, the brightness of the future of her family, she must have known happiness. And now she knows the greatest happiness of all, that of being reunited with her husband, kneeling before the Lord God our Master. Jeanne Hamilton, rest in peace.'

The first clod of earth fell on the coffin with a dull thud, while the mourners waited. Only the immediate family had attended this last ceremony – Jeanne Hamilton had been socially important in St Domingue only as the mother of

Madame de Mortmain. But it was a large family, even if Kit was not here – probably did not yet know of his mother's death. Maurice de Mortmain, grey haired and stooped, was here, Marguerite at his side, also grey and old, mourning a sister who had died in truth long ago. Etienne was here, fat and florid, with his magnificent pink and white Milot wife – even after four children Claudette de Mortmain remained the most beautiful woman in St Domingue, and she had certainly assured the succession. Louis de Mortmain was here, slender and serious as ever. Catherine de Milot was here, her husband François at her side – her parents-in-law could not really be expected to attend the funeral of a woman they had despised – Catherine apparently suffered the Mortmain curse, and was childless, although she remained tall and willowy and attractively severe. Françoise de Beaudierre was here, apeing her brother Etienne in the roles of fat which she had allowed to develop, as – unlike her sister – she aped his wife in the regularity with which she produced her children, one every other year with the same precision as her parents had managed their own lives; her husband, Ferrand de Beaudierre, was as usual restless at her side, burning with an inner fire which made him wish to argue even with his illustrious host. And the unmarried girls were here: Lucy, already set to be an old maid in the tightness of her features, the way her pale hair was screwed into a chignon and her gown, even on a warm afternoon, was buttoned to the neck; and Annette, at twenty-three still in the bloom of youth and even beauty, as she was the prettiest of all the girls, and the most vivacious, when she chose to be; Annette was the toast of Cap François, but she remained a spinster. Today she had the saddest face of any of the Mortmain women. Because Kit was not here? Everyone knew they corresponded regularly, and that whenever his ship dropped anchor in Cap François he enjoyed her company more than anyone else's. Forbidden fruit, doomed to wither on the vine. However much it might amuse Philippe de Mortmain.

Who stood with his wife at the foot of the grave. The most

splendid, the most regal, the most envied couple in all St Domingue. The Seigneur in his early forties, in the very prime of his health and power. And the Madame, at twenty-two the youngest adult woman present, perhaps yielding to her cousin-in-law Claudette in sheer beauty, but still the most striking of the women, in the silk of her gown, the sparkle of her jewellery, the purity of her pearl necklace, the sheen of her golden brown hair, and above all, in the utter confidence with which she surveyed her surroundings, and with which she alone allowed herself to weep unashamedly as she watched her mother's coffin disappear.

Because I am Richilde de Mortmain, she thought. Nothing more than that need be said, or thought. I have been tried in the crucible, and not been found wanting. I have made my husband happy, which no other woman has ever accomplished. He remained cursed in his inability to have children, and that curse had naturally encompassed her. But at least they slept together, and more often than not, they made love.

What she might have to do to inspire and then consummate that love was their secret, and made their life together the more intimate, the more precious. But then, she was a woman of many secrets, as even her husband recognised, although he would never acknowledge the fact. Perhaps he even knew – certainly he suspected – where she had gone on that never to be forgotten night six years ago, when she had placed her body on his and seduced him with all the power and certainty of a *mamaloi*. But it was not a question he dared ask. As it was not a medicine she had ever dared reach for again. Now, as she looked around the mass of slaves who had also attended the funeral, she could make out the huge figures of Henry Christopher and Jean François, standing side by side, close friends these, as they worked in harness. Men who knew her secret, as she knew theirs. That had not made for intimacy. Her days for intimacy with Henry were gone forever. The intimacy that had swelled into a mad desire on that night. It had been he who had had the sense to realise the catastrophe which awaited them. So he was as responsible for her marital bliss as anyone. Had he waited but a moment longer . . . but that was in the past, and she was no longer a sixteen-year-old girl. She had learned that he, like Jean François and Pierre Toussaint, and all their fellows, had their own lives to live, as she had hers. To attempt to bridge the gap between them, to consider their aspirations as a threat to herself and the society she ruled, to remember the death and rebirth of the young man as anything more than superb sleight of hand and mass delusion, could lead only to disaster, as it so nearly had done six years before. There were things which could not be explained, just as there were dreams which could never be anything more than dreams. Henry, the memory of him standing there in his naked glory beside her, was for her midnight dreams. And again, after such a dream, Philippe was the one who gained.

How incredible, she thought, that I, Richilde Hamilton, the daughter of a shipping clerk and outlaw, should have come to dominate a man like Philippe de Mortmain. And through him, perhaps, all of St Domingue. Had she been able to have a child, then her triumph would have been complete. But in that failure, and in Philippe's increasingly morose moods, was all her life at risk, all her confidence a sham.

She watched the headstone being set. It wore a very simple inscription:

JEANNE HAMILTON
WIDOW OF
RICHARD HAMILTON
1740–1789
RIP

There was really nothing else to be said about Jeanne Hamilton.

The family was already walking back towards the house. Philippe had gone with them, knowing that she would wish these five minutes alone; the slaves too, had melted away.

171

Except for Henry. He did not approach but remained on the far side of the grave.

'She was my mistress,' he said.

'Now I am your mistress, Henry,' she said.

He nodded, thoughtfully. 'She going see my mummy, in heaven, madame?'

It was the first time such a subject had been broached between them for six years.

'If there is but one heaven, Henry,' Richilde said. 'As I am sure there is, then they will see each other.' she gazed at him for a moment, but he had nothing more to say. So she turned away, and walked after her family.

The horses swept up to the grandstand. There were six of them in the race, but only the two Mortmain stallions were in the running – Diable and Vitesse. Each of the Mortmains had his favourite and shouted vociferously. And now the roars of the competing parties seemed to raise the very heavens. It was four in the afternoon, and this was the last event of the Cap François races, as it was the main event of the day, and the very sun, now beginning its stately decline in the west, seemed to be gathering itself for a last burning effort, as it bore down on the flying dust, the sweating horses, the straining Negro jockeys and their vari-coloured silk shirts, the stand, crowded with everyone who was anyone in either Cap François or Port-au-Prince, a kaleidoscope of pale greens, pinks and blues of the ladies, the sombre browns and blacks of the gentlemen's coats, dotted with the brilliant blue of the officers of the garrison, and then the slaves themselves, for race day at Cap François was a holiday, gathered in a vast crowd, several thousand strong, all in clean white cottons, in the cleared area beyond the paddock.

And now the horses were past, and the dust filtered slowly through the still air, coating faces and arms and expensive gowns, causing the onlookers to cough and sneeze.

'Diable,' Philippe said. 'Now there, Maurice, is a horse for you.'

Etienne de Mortmain nodded. 'Only a short head, though.'

'Enough,' Louis grumbled. 'That is fifteen hundred livres.'

'My God,' Etienne said. 'I shall have to whip that jockey.'

'You may owe it to me,' Philippe said, magnanimously. 'Now let us get home before the crowd blocks the roads. Ah, Ferrand. I trust you backed Diable?'

Ferrand de Beaudierre had Françoise clinging to his arm, as usual, and looked wildly angry, as usual. 'Horse races,' he said. 'At a time like this.'

'My dear Ferrand,' Robert said. 'The Cap François Races have been held every year for the past fifty, to my certain knowledge. Even in time of war. Do you suppose we are going to cancel them because of some absurd upheaval in Paris? There are always being absurd upheavals in Paris.'

'This, monsieur, is not an upheaval,' Beaudierre insisted. 'It is the dawn of a new age.'

'Then I tell you what we shall do,' Philippe said. 'As I have just had a most successful day, I invite you and Françoise to return to Vergée d'Or with us, and we will drink to this new day. Is that not to your taste?'

'Oh, yes, Philippe,' Françoise said. 'Come along, do, Ferrand.'

But he suspected he was being made a fool of, arrived at the château even more excited than usual; took his place in the centre of the downstairs drawing room, left hand thrust into the front of his vest, like an orator.

'I tell you, messieurs, mesdames,' he proclaimed. 'That the Third Estate is the true voice of France.'

Philippe smiled at Richilde, lazily. 'You do not suppose that the Paris scum should have been greeted by cannon and bayonets, instead of abject surrender? They would have been met differently had I been there and in command.'

Beaudierre was not to be browbeaten, even by his wealthy cousin-in-law. 'Then would you have been wrong, Philippe,' he insisted. 'You would have been attempting to hold back the tide of history. And you would suffer the inevitable fate of the royal party.'

'We'll have no treason spoken here, Ferrand,' Maurice de Mortmain said.

'Nor do I intend any, father-in-law. I spoke of a party, not a king. But the King, God bless him, has for too long been pulled and prodded by this faction or that, by Necker and Calonne. Were he but to commence to rule, with the aid of the people, the true people of France, then things would be different. The Fall of the Bastille will go down in history as the moment the French people asserted themselves, and became a nation of free men.'

'I hope you are right, Ferrand.' Philippe said, drily. 'I can but see it as a lot of louts seizing the opportunity to wreak a bit of mayhem. And what of the crew of the *Leopard* in Cap François, declaring for Liberty, Equality and Fraternity, and refusing to obey their officers?'

'Monsieur Peynier has managed to settle that matter,' Beaudierre said.

'Oh, indeed, by turning the guns of the fort on them. As I have said, there was the way to settle the entire matter. Had the King sufficient gumption.'

'That would lead to civil war if it were practised against a lawful assembly,' Beaudierre pointed out.

'Which I think is an extremely likely outcome of this business in any event,' Philippe said.

'What disgusts me,' Claudette de Mortmain said, 'is the way all the people here, and in Guadeloupe and Martinique, are so anxious to crawl to this ridiculous National Assembly. Sending deputies back to France, indeed.'

'They were invited to do so, Claudette,' Françoise pointed out, deciding to take her husband's side.

'They were invited to send six deputies,' Annette said, making the discussion general. 'Not more than twenty. And making some of them mulattos! They have made the entire French Antilles look ridiculous.'

'On the contrary,' Beaudierre said. 'It will show those in Paris that we, too, are anxious to play our part in making France a nation more worthy of her great traditions. A country where all men can be free, and equal before the law.

A place . . .'

'Now that sort of statement is typical of you political dreamers,' Philippe said. 'A country where all men can be free, indeed. And equal. That is exactly what those madmen in Paris are preaching. How can all men be equal, when they are manifestly unequal? And how can all men be free, when it is obviously necessary for some of them to be enslaved? ·What do you suppose would happen to St Domingue were all men declared free and equal, regardless of colour?'

'Well . . .' Beaudierre flushed. 'Obviously there would have to be exceptions. Black people, well, they are slaves, and there is an end to the matter. I am sure the Third Estate did not mean to deprive us of our slaves. But that apart . . .'

'You'll be giving the mulattos equal rights, next,' Etienne said.

'That, monsieur, is certainly something to be accomplished.'

'What?'

'Why else should the National Assembly have insisted that our representatives be drawn from all sections of the free community, regardless of colour? It is grossly unfair that because of a touch of black blood a man should forever be regarded as an inferior being,' Beaudierre declared. 'Or a woman. I am sure you agree with me, Philippe?'

Philippe de Mortmain stared at him for several seconds, then he got up. 'I agree with Etienne,' he said. 'That you are talking the most absolute rubbish, Beaudierre. And the most dangerous, seditious rubbish. You would do well to watch your tongue.' He stalked from the room.

Saturday morning was market day in Cap François. It was thus a slave holiday, in order that the more industrious of them could go into the town and sell the produce of their vegetable gardens and, with the proceeds, buy small luxuries for themselves. It was a great occasion, when the city seemed to boil with colourful, excited humanity; naturally it was most certainly not a holiday for the garrison, who were on duty on every street corner, not in anticipation of any

175

violence, but to arrest any black man, or woman, who had the temerity to purchase alcohol with their profits.

It was a day when most white women stayed away, but Richilde always went into town on a Saturday morning. She enjoyed being a part of the bustle and the enthusiasm, she enjoyed being able to smile at Toussaint across a crowded square, and receive in reply his grave nod, and she enjoyed being able to walk through the market stalls, Jean François and Amelia attentive at her heels, shaded beneath an enormous parasol held by Henry Christopher, to see and to purchase some of the Negro goods – for they not only sold market produce, but also carved wooden ornaments, some knives and bows or canoes filled with surprisingly accurately delineated figures, and some strange gods and enormous curving snakes. She flattered herself that she was the only white woman in St Domingue who understood what these images really represented, and had already bought several for her boudoir. Philippe was quite prepared to indulge her in what he described as her hobby of exploring the Negro 'culture', just as he indulged her visits to town, although he seldom accompanied her.

Today she was officially in the care of Etienne, because a slave ship was due in from the Benin coast, and Etienne was the slave master of the plantation.

Thus, when her basket was sufficiently full, she walked down to the docks to watch a different sort of hustle and bustle, for there were two ships apparently just making port from the blue wastes of the Atlantic, and being warped alongside the docks.

The slave ship was secured first, her gangway run out, and the cargo led ashore. Richilde had witnessed the landing of slaves before, and reached into her reticule to hold a perfume soaked handkerchief to her nostrils; the ship had spent several months at sea. As could be seen by the men and women who stumbled on to the shore, many falling over from lack of balance, combined with weakness, for they were all terribly emaciated, while their uncertainty was aided by inebriation, for again as she knew, they would all

176

have been given a tot of rum to inspire them with some animation as they landed – the auction normally took place almost the moment they came ashore.

She glanced at her slaves to see what they thought. Both Henry and Amelia had been born in the West Indies, but they would have heard sufficient tales of the horrors of the Middle Passage. Jean François had actually made such a passage, as a boy, some twenty years before. Now his face remained expressionless, however much the sight of the new arrivals must have evoked memories of his boyhood in Africa, of the Arab slaving gangs who had blown his tribal armies to pieces with their gunpowder and then shackled the surviving men and women together for the march to the coast, of the steaming hot weeks spent in the Gulf of Guinea, trapped in the foetid bowels of the slave ship, until her complement was full, of the endless days crossing an ocean not knowing if there was another side, with the bodies of his comrades in distress being fed to the sharks as they daily died, until he had arrived in St Domingue, and been delivered over to the tender mercies of Jacques de Mortmain, who from all accounts had had his son's sternness, and none of his self doubts.

But Jean François had survived and prospered. And so, she supposed, like most human beings, he was prepared merely to be contemptuous of those who had not yet succeeded in achieving his stature.

'By God, what a sorry looking lot.' Etienne strolled along the dock, accompanied by Monsieur Dessalines, another planter, tall, lean and malaria-visaged, who raised his hat to Richilde.

'Madame de Mortmain, your cousin is in a pessimistic mood.'

'Bah,' Etienne said. 'Who would not be pessimistic at the news from France? No one there appears to be capable of taking control. This Mirabeau seems an utter charlatan. Come along, Richilde, let us go home. To buy one of that lot would be to insult Philippe.

'Oh, come now, Etienne,' Dessalines objected. 'You do

not look closely enough. What of that fellow?'

He pointed with his cane, where a yoke of Negroes had just reached the dock. Three of the men staggered and all but fell, but were kept from doing so by the strength and balance of the fourth. This man was not tall, but was built like a bull, with immense strength of shoulder and thigh, rippling muscles in his chest and abdomen and down his legs.

And he was neither dejected nor afraid, but looked around like an angry bull, meeting the eye of anyone, black, brown and even white.

'A good investment, I think,' Dessalines remarked.

'A very bad investment, monsieur,' Etienne objected. 'The fellow has scoundrel written all over him. You'll get nothing but mutiny from such a rogue.'

Monsieur Dessalines smiled. 'There is no such thing as a slave which cannot be broken, Etienne,' he said. 'I shall have that fellow. And some of these others.'

'And we shall go home.' Etienne took Richilde's arm, and they strolled further along the dock towards the waiting carriage, escaping the stench of the slave ship, and watching the second vessel being made fast in her berth. She was direct from Nantes, and her decks were filled with excited male passengers, who could hardly wait for the gangway to be run out before hurrying down. They were dressed in the height of fashion, wore swords on their hips and tricolour cockades in their bicorne hats. But their skins were brown.

Richilde caught her breath, and looked at Etienne, who was frowning. And then back at the men again, one of whom had stepped away from his fellows, thumbs tucked into the lapels of his vest. 'Friends,' he shouted. 'Citizens. We are returned. Back, from the National Assembly. Back to tell you . . .'

'James Ogé,' Etienne muttered. 'James Ogé, by God,' he shouted, and hurried forward.

'Etienne,' Richilde begged. 'Please. There will surely be a scene . . .'

'You, wretch,' Etienne shouted. 'Ogé. Discard that sword,

monsieur. You are not fit to wear it.'

Ogé turned, and also frowned. 'Are you addressing me, monsieur?' he demanded, his hand dropping to his sword hilt. 'Why,' he said with mock alarm. 'It is Monsieur de Mortmain. One of the Citizens Mortmain, my friends. See how he struts? He thinks himself better than us. He thinks . . .' His words ended in a gasp as Etienne struck him across the face with his cane, so hard he almost fell.

'Oh, my God,' Richilde cried. 'Henry, stop them.'

Henry hurried forward, and just in time, for Ogé had recovered himself and drawn his sword.

'There,' Etienne shouted. 'A mulatto, by God, and drawing on me. Soldiers, seize that fellow. Seize them all.'

For the soldiers on duty at the docks had drawn closer to discover the cause of the tumult.

'Master,' Henry said, touching Etienne on the shoulder.

'Attacked,' Etienne shouted, and turned, cane slicing through the air again, catching Henry across the face and sending him staggering.

''Tienne!' Richilde screamed, being jostled sideways by the crowd of people which was suddenly rushing forward.

And pausing in horror as she realised that Henry, in falling, had instinctively swept his hand round and torn the cane from Etienne's grasp.

Instantly armed guards surrounded the black man, pulling him to his feet.

'It is all right,' Richilde said. 'Henry is my personal slave.'

'It is not all right,' Etienne said, apparently very angry. 'He assaulted me. For too long he has been an arrogant scoundrel. I will make an example of him, by God. Bind him and put him in my slave cart. As for Ogé . . .' he swung round to face the mulatto and his friends, who were entirely surrounded by soldiers.

'You cannot arrest us,' Ogé was protesting. 'We come from the National Assembly. We come . . .'

'Bearing arms,' the captain of the guard said. 'That is against the law for you, Monsieur Ogé, and you know that.'

'Law,' the young man shouted. 'There are new laws, my

friend. Laws you break at your peril.'

'There are no new laws in Cap François, monsieur,' the soldier said. 'You are under arrest.'

Richilde grasped Etienne's arm. ''Tienne,' she said. 'You cannot be serious about Henry.'

'Would you quarrel with me in public?' he demanded. 'And over a slave?'

She bit her lip, looked around at the interested watchers and listeners. Here was source for next week's gossip, quite apart from the excitement of Ogé's arrest. Still shouting, the mulatto was being marched down the street.

In a turmoil of uncertainty, she looked the other way, to find Henry. He was being loaded into the slave cart, his wrists bound behind his back. He made no effort to resist his captors, but he turned his head to look at her, expectantly. He had no fear, while she protected him.

'Philippe,' she said, bursting into his office. 'Philippe. 'Tienne has quite lost his head . . .'

'I have heard,' Philippe said, putting down his pen and leaning back. 'And I do not think he lost his head at all. I have never doubted that these mulattos were going to cause us trouble, one day. The sooner their ideas of equality are nipped in the bud the better. They are conspirators, all of them. And filled with heady ideas, inspired by people like Beaudierre.'

'I am not talking about Ogé's arrest,' she said. 'I know nothing of politics. But I feared for 'Tienne, as he was unarmed, and sent Henry to stop the fight. And 'Tienne thought Henry was assaulting him, and had him bound and returned here. He has ordered a flogging. That is quite absurd.'

Philippe gazed at her. 'Because you choose to call him your twin?'

She flushed. 'Of course not. Because he was doing what I had told him to. Philippe, you must order his release.'

'You are asking me to override an order given by my own slave master, who also happens to be my cousin and my

180

heir? Do you suppose, if I were to do that, 'Tienne could ever expect to be obeyed again?'

She stared at him in horror. 'You . . . you will let the punishment stand?'

'I must. As you must understand.'

'You . . . you have been waiting for an opportunity to flog Henry,' she accused. 'Ever since he came to Vergée d'Or.'

'Now you are being childish. Do you really suppose I would not have had him flogged, whenever I chose?'

'You . . . you are playing the tyrant,' she stormed at him.

'Well, I . . .'

'Will do nothing,' he said. 'Understand me well, Richilde. I have never failed to humour all of your eccentricities, from the day of your arrival here, and I am more aware of them than you suppose. This absurd friendship for a nigger boy is but one of them. But I will not have you, or anyone, interfering in the management of my plantation, the authority of my overseers. I will have a word with Etienne, as you are so upset, but as the punishment was ordered in public, so it will stand.'

She stared at him, feeling the anger burning red spots in her cheeks. It was the first time they had ever really quarrelled, and the dispute had arisen over the subject she had always known it must, one day.

'I should go to you room,' Philippe suggested. 'And lie down for a while. When you awake, it will all be over, and forgotten. Believe me, a few strokes of the lash are not going to hurt a great buck nigger like Henry.'

She left the office, climbed the stairs to her room, threw herself across the bed. How she wanted to get up again, and storm down to the compound, and command Henry's release. She was Madame de Mortmain. These people were bound to do her will . . . but only as long as that will coincided with that of the Seigneur.

Amelia brought her a glass of coconut water. 'You going change for dinner, mistress?'

'No,' Richilde said. 'No, I will not come down to dinner. Amelia . . .'

'It done finish, mistress,' Amelia said. 'He is take down.'

'How . . . how many?'

'Well, I think it is twenty-five, mistress.'

'Twenty-five lashes?' Richilde sat up. 'Oh, my God! Is he badly hurt?'

'Well, I ain't see he,' Amelia said. 'But he must be cut up. Twenty-five lashes . . . oh, he must be going cut up.'

Richilde got out of bed. 'I must go to him.'

'You, mistress?'

'Yes.' Richilde pulled on her pelisse. 'You will accompany me.'

'Me, mistress? But the master . . .'

'You are my maid, Amelia,' Richilde pointed out. 'Where I go, you go. You will come with me to see Henry Christopher. Now.'

Amelia rolled her eyes, but there was no way she could refuse a direct command. 'He does be in the dispensary,' she said, sadly.

Richilde possessed her own pony and trap for riding about the estate, and this they used, and for the first time in her life she directed it towards the slave compound. It was now late in the afternoon, and the work gangs were on their way back from the fields. They stopped to stare in amazement at the Seigneur's wife driving towards their village, while the white overseers accompanying them scratched their heads in equal surprise, and one at least hastily rode off towards the chateau.

She flicked her whip in the air to increase the pony's speed, rode past the now empty triangles with a shudder and through the gate to the slave compound. 'Where is the dispensary?'

Amelia pointed, looking about her with terrified eyes. Like most of the domestic slaves, she was as afraid of the field slaves as any white person.

'You,' Richilde said to one of the crowd of young black men who had gathered round the trap. 'Hold the reins.' She tossed them to him, stepped down, and went towards the large building which was apparently the sickhouse.

'Mistress?' An elderly black man stood in the doorway.

'Who are you?' she asked.

'My name is Oliver, mistress,' he said.

'And you are the doctor?'

'I does dispense the medicine,' he said.

'I wish to see Henry Christopher.'

'He is inside, mistress.'

She felt like stamping her foot with impatience. 'I know that, Oliver. Open the door.'

He hesitated, looked past her at the spectators, steadily growing in numbers, then opened the door, and she stepped into the gloom. It was a noisome gloom, for although the interior of the hut had been carefully washed with lime, the smell of human sweat, and human excrement, and human suffering, could not be excluded. As her eyes became accustomed to the sudden absence of sunshine, she could see that there were perhaps a score of people in here, men and women, lying on pallets of straw on the floor, most trying to raise themselves on their elbows as their mistress came in, but several unable to muster even that much strength.

'What . . . what do they suffer from?' she asked Oliver.

The dispenser shrugged. 'They got many things, mistress. Some get bite in the fields, by insect and things. Some cut theyselves with their machete. Others got the fever. And some . . . they just swell up.'

He indicated one young man, hardly more than a boy, whose right leg was swollen to twice the size of his left.

Hastily she looked away. 'And they lie here . . .' she was going to say, in this airless filth, but changed her mind. 'Until they get better?'

'Or until they die, mistress.'

My God, she thought, carefully making her way down the row of bodies to the pallet at the end, and Henry Christopher. He lay on his face, his back a criss-cross of cuts and gashes. These had been smothered in some white substance, but they still oozed blood.

'Is he all right?' she asked, in a whisper.

'Oh, he will be all right, mistress,' Oliver said.

'But . . . what is that you have put on the cuts?'

'Salt, mistress.'

'Salt?' she could not stop her voice from rising.

'It is the best thing, mistress. That way the cuts do heal up quick.'

'But . . . was it not agony for him?'

Oliver grinned. 'You don't feel no agony, mistress, after the lash.'

She stared at him, then realised that Henry had raised his head.

'Henry,' she said, stooping beside him. 'I am sorry. Very, very sorry. Do you believe me?'

His eyes were dark pits of hell. 'I know you are sorry, Mistress Richilde,' he said.

'Can you ever forgive me?'

He gazed at her for several seconds. 'I can forgive *you*, mistress,' he said.

She stopped the trap at the foot of the great staircase, threw the reins to the waiting groom. It was already quite dark, and she frowned with impatience at the sight of the carriage waiting further down the drive. It belonged to Ferrand de Beaudierre, and undoubtedly meant that Françoise had come to call. She really was not in the mood for Françoise this evening.

'You'll draw me a bath, Amelia,' she commanded, and went up the stairs.

'Madame.'

She checked, half turned her head. Philippe stood on the lower verandah.

Amelia hastily scuttled into the gloom.

'Can you spare me a moment?' Philippe asked.

She hesitated, then turned and went back down the stairs.

'Does he live?' Philippe asked.

'Yes,' she said.

'You know, of course, that the slave compound is not the place for any white woman to visit, much less the mistress of the plantation. As for the dispensary . . .'

Richilde tossed her head. 'I do not agree with you, monsieur. If I am your wife, then your slaves are as much my concern as they are yours. I do not seek to interfere, believe me, only to complement your authority. I should have visited the slave compound long ago. I would say that I have grievously neglected my duties and my responsibilities. As for the dispensary, it is quite the most disgusting place I have ever seen.'

'Which is why it is no place for a white woman.'

'It is no place for a black woman, either,' she said. 'Or a black man. I am not speaking of their illnesses, which for God's sake are ghastly enough. I am speaking of the conditions in which you force them to exist. For heaven's sake, Philippe, these people represent a large part of your wealth. Are they not worth caring for? You care more for your dogs and horses than for your slaves.'

He stared at her, a frown gathering between his eyes.

'I would like your permission,' she said. 'To visit your slave compound as and when I choose.'

He continued to study her for several seconds longer. Then he said, 'I shall not give you my *permission*, Richilde. As you are so concerned, and as undoubtedly there is some truth in what you say, I shall give you my express *command*, as of this moment, that you will visit the slave compound at least twice a week, to see to the needs of your black-skinned friends.'

'Thank you,' she said. 'I would also like to rebuild the dispensary.'

'Rebuild whatever you like,' he said. 'Now come inside, and attempt to do something with your cousin. She is having hysterics.'

Richilde's turn to frown, as she gathered her skirts and hurried behind him. 'Whatever is the matter?'

'Her irrational husband appears to have got himself into some sort of trouble,' Philippe said. 'I knew it had to happen, with that hothead. She is in the small drawing room.'

Richilde went in, found Françoise seated on the sofa

Lucy on one side of her and Aunt Marguerite on the other. Françoise was weeping noisily, and at the sight of Richilde gave another great shriek. 'Richilde, oh Richilde . . .'

'Whatever is the matter?' Richilde demanded, somewhat irritably.

'Oh, Richilde. Oh . . .'

'Ferrand has been arrested,' Lucy said.

'Ferrand? Whatever for?'

'He was so angry,' Françoise wailed. 'When he heard that those coloured men had been locked up. He wrote out a denunciation of what Etienne and the soldiers had done, and went into town to nail it to the door of the Hotel de Ville. And they arrested him, and locked him up too. Oh, the disgrace of it. They say he will be tried for sedition and conspiracy. He could be hanged.'

'And quite right, too,' Philippe said

Françoise gave another shriek, and once more collapsed into tears.

'You must help him, Philippe,' Richilde said.

'Me? I think he has at last got his just deserts.'

'Nevertheless, we cannot leave one of the family locked up in the common jail. You must get him out. And for God's sake stop that snivelling, Françoise. Of course he is not going to be hanged. How can anyone hang Philippe de Mortmain's cousin-in-law? Philippe . . .'

'You have become quite the little avenging angel,' he remarked.

'You made me understand, this afternoon, the importance of the family. Whether you like him or not, Ferrand is now a member of the family. If you will not help him, then I will.'

He gazed at her for a moment, then to her surprise, picked up her hand and kissed it. 'I like avenging angels,' he said. 'We will go together, and assail Peynier, and return in triumph, with Beaudierre. Françoise, have yourself a glass of wine, and do try to stop crying.' He rang the bell. 'Have Jean François bring round the carriage,' he told Bartholemew the butler. 'Marguerite, supper may be a little late tonight, but it will be a celebratory occasion, I do promise you.'

186

He himself fetched Richilde's wrap, sat beside her and squeezed her hand as the carriage rumbled down the road towards Cap François; she had not dared look Jean François in the face. But Jean François would undoubtedly regard Henry's flogging as he regarded everything else – with contempt so long as he was not involved.

'I did not mean to upset you, Philippe,' she said. 'But I really cannot consider poor Ferrand left in jail all night, with a lot of coloured men.'

'Who are his friends,' he reminded her. 'But I agree with you. And you did not upset me. Rather did you excite me. As you have not excited me for years.'

She turned her head to peer at him in the gloom.

'I had forgot,' he said. 'That I had you trained, and educated, to be my wife.'

'Then the fault is surely mine, monsieur,' she said. 'For not having played the part sooner.'

'But you will play it now,' he said. 'To have a woman, strong and forceful, ever at my side, ever in my bed . . . will you do me the honour this night, madame?'

She laughed with pleasure at their little game. 'I shall be happy to do so, monsieur.'

'Then let us make all possible haste.' He opened the trap. 'Can you drive no faster, you black devil?'

'Is a fact there does be crowds, master,' Jean Francois said.

Philippe peered from his window, Richilde from the other. They were amongst the houses of Cap François by now, and undoubtedly there were a great number of people on the streets, standing in groups on street corners, muttering to each other, and insensibly moving towards the town centre, where the jail was situated. And from where there was coming a great deal of noise.

'Use your whip,' Philippe commanded. 'Drive through them if you have to. Take me to the Governor-General's house.'

Jean François cracked his whip over the horses' heads, but their progress was still very slow. Most of the crowd recognised the Mortmain crest, and the carriage attracted a considerable amount of comment, but it was difficult to decide whether it was mainly good or bad.

'I doubt you should have come,' Philippe said. 'This has the makings of a mob.'

'Nonsense,' she said. 'The soldiers will disperse these people if they get out of hand.'

'Then where are they?' he muttered.

'There,' she said, as they debouched into the square to find themselves upon the outskirts of an enormous crowd, which constantly swelled. But these were mainly white people – *petit blancs* rather than planters, with a scattering of mulattos. She wondered if the Chavannes were here. How could they not be? She had not laid eyes on Jacqueline for seven years. She had ceased to patronise Monsieur Chavannes' shop, at Philippe's request.

The soldiers, and there was a large number of them, were grouped on the far side of the square, before the Hotel de Ville, watching the mob, but making no attempt to interfere with it.

'They should be at the prison,' Philippe muttered, half to himself.

'At the prison?' Richilde looked through the window again. The carriage had by now been brought to a complete stop, so dense was the crowd. But they were not more than a hundred yards from the prison. It was there that the greatest number of people were congregated, surging against the door, and chanting. And now she could hear what they were saying.

'We want Beaudierre,' they were shouting. 'Give us Beaudierre.'

'They will have him out of there for us,' she said.

Philippe glanced at her. 'I do not think they mean to rescue him, Richilde.'

'Not to . . .' she stared at him, her belly seeming to fill with lead.

'There is no time to see Peynier,' he decided. 'I must get to those soldiers. You stay here. Jean François, you will take care of your mistress.'

'But Philippe,' she protested, too late, He had already opened the door and stepped down, to vanish into the mob.

'Jean François,' she called through the trap.

'Nobody is going trouble you, mistress,' the big coachman said.

'I must get to the prison,' she said.

'But mistress . . .'

'Come with me,' she opened the door, and stepped down, was instantly surrounded by people, odorous bodies pressing close. Hands slapped her shoulders and pummelled her back, and she lost her hat together with her breath. But she pushed forward with determination, aware that Jean François was immediately behind her, having the utmost confidence in his ability to protect her from assault. Because he loved her. All the slaves did. But he more than any other, because he had once, briefly, held her in his arms. She was aware of a remarkable feeling of exhilaration, which rose above even her apprehension, at being able to stand astride two such different worlds, at thus being able to rely on Jean François' strength and loyalty against these people, as she would be able to rely on these people against the blacks, should the occasion ever arise, should the dream shared by Jean François, and Toussaint, and Henry Christopher, ever come true.

'Richilde!' Louis de Mortmain struggled towards her. 'What are you doing here?'

'I wish to rescue Ferrand from this mob,' she gasped.

'You?' Louis looked past her at Jean François. 'And him?'

'Oh, Philippe is here somewhere. He is trying to arouse the gendarmerie. Louis . . .' her head twisted at the sound of splintering wood. Now the crowd had at last surged against the doors of the prison itself, and were hacking at the lock. A jailer's terrified face appeared at the barred window for a moment, and then disappeared again. 'Come on,' Richilde shouted.

She pushed her way forward, and was knocked from her feet by the surging bodies, who seemed unaware of who she was, or even that she was a woman. For a moment she debated identifying herself as the mistress of Vergée d'Or, and then decided against it – these people would know that she was related to Beaudierre. She thought she would be trampled, and discovered she did not even have the breath to scream, then Louis seized one arm and Jean François the other, and between them they set her on her feet again.

'We must get she out of here, master,' Jean François said.

'Yes,' Louis agreed. 'Yes, you are right. You will be hurt, Richilde. And there is nothing we can do. Philippe, and the soldiers . . .'

The crowd began to bay, and Richilde almost climbed into Jean François' arms to see what was happening. The prison doors had now been torn from their hinges, and the crowd were penetrating the interior, urged on by the yells of their supporters in the square. Dimly Richilde became aware that Louis and Jean François were pulling her back towards the waiting carriage. She tried to fight them, but remained staring at the shattered doorway, watched Ferrand de Beaudierre appear there, his arms held by two of the mob, being pushed forward, his face flushed, but his eyes blazing with anger rather than fear.

'Scum,' he bawled, his voice rising even above the hubbub. 'Would you defy your government? Your lawful government? Those men in there are free. They bring a message from France. They . . .' he gasped as he was pushed forward and tripped and fell down the steps. Instantly the mob surged over him, yelling and screaming.

'Oh, God,' Richilde said. 'Oh, God!'

She realised that Louis was no longer holding her arm. He, too, was overcome by the horror in front of him.

They saw Ferrand de Beaudierre once more, being raised in the air, arms and legs flying, face already a bloodied mass, mouth opening for a last scream of pain and terror, and despair, as he realised what was happening to him, and then he disappeared again, and the mob roared.

'You must come away, mistress,' Jean François said, and dragged her to the carriage. She realised tears were streaming down her face and she knew she was going to be sick. She fell to her knees beside the carriage and vomited, while Jean François stood beside her, unsure what to do. She saw other feet, and raised her head, looked at Pierre Toussaint.

She sucked air into her lungs. 'Is this a part of your prophesy, also, Toussaint?' she asked.

He gazed at her for a moment, then at Jean François, and turned, and vanished into the crowd.

Chapter 2

THE DAY

The opposing sides had now for two years confounded the colony with their disputes, while the slaves, in whose future neither whites nor browns had shown the slightest interest, had continued to perform their duties. Now, on 23rd August 1791, the Negroes in the northern half of the island revolted. The planters and their families and their overseers, and those of their servants who remained loyal, were murdered, not in their scores, but in their hundreds. Women were violated and disembowelled; men were sawn in half; the glare from hundreds of burning plantations and the incoherent gasps of the first refugees to stagger into the towns spread the panic like the plague itself – over-night a country the size of Ireland became a no-man's land of hatred and violence.

'No, no, no,' Richilde saud. 'I want the walls green, the roof white. You will have to change that, Oliver.'

'Yes, mistress,' Oliver said with a happy smile. He didn't mind having his people scrape off all the white paint they had inadvertently put on the walls. Painting, and scraping the paint off again, was a game. Compared with working in the fields.

While Richilde sighed; unless she was down here every moment of the day something always went wrong. But it was an artificial sigh. She enjoyed being down here every moment of the day, even if it was merely to see her slaves happy. They liked working for the mistress, because her work was so different, and interesting. They had fallen to with a will to destroy the old dispensary, while she had transferred the sick up to one of the stables by the chateau, over the frowns and mutterings of Lucien the cook and Bartholemew the butler, and of Jean François, the head coachman, who had growled about his clean horses being messed up with a load of sick people. While Henry Christopher had stood and watched in amazement. But he had found time to say, 'Now you are an angel, madame.' Which was the most important praise she had received, far better than Philippe's pat on the back. It made her feel that one day, perhaps, she and Henry could again be friends, despite the flogging. When they were old together.

But now the new dispensary was almost complete, four times the size of the old building, with jalousie windows to let in the air while keeping out the glare, with clean straw on the floor, and orders that it was to be renewed every day, with fresh paint being lavished everywhere ... a colossal preoccupation of so many field hands, Fedon grumbled. But Philippe merely smiled and let her have her own way. He was a far more sensitive man than he sometimes appeared, and he could understand just how difficult she had found it ever to regard the chateau as her own. She had come to it as a little girl, had grown up in it, surrounded by the housekeepers – the genuine housekeepers – Negresses who had spent their lives in domestic service with the Mortmains, who knew every sheet and every pillowcase amongst all the hundreds that were laundered every week, and who would have been amazed and distressed had their new mistress attempted to interfere with their management of the house and the staff, just as Lucien would have been had she suddenly announced that she wished to cook a meal – or even plan a menu.

But the new dispensary was hers, her concept and her design and her ambition. Besides, its construction was occupying the minds of the blacks, and that was very important right now, with all of St Domingue a seething mass of incipient revolt.

It was difficult to grasp, Richilde thought, as she turned

the trap and walked the pony through the slave compound gateway and on to the drive leading up to the chateau, greeted as always by the black women she passed on their way to the fields. Certainly here on Vergée d'Or, and she had not been off Vergée d'Or for several months, not since that fiery young man James Ogé, on his release from jail following the tragedy of Ferrand de Beaudierre – and while Monsieur Peynier had written post haste to Paris to discover whether or not the mulattos *had* been granted full equality with the whites – had promptly raised the flag of revolt in the name of the National Assembly. He had, apparently, been widely supported, and had formed an armed camp outside Cap François, from whence his followers had fired upon and killed an emissary sent by the Governor-General to parley. Naturally such an act of open rebellion had not been countenanced. Peynier had called up the troops – who were white and certainly prepared to obey him against coloured rebels – and the mulattos had been dispersed. Ogé had fled across the border into the Spanish half of the island. But the whole colony remained in such a ferment it had not been considered safe for ladies to ride abroad, except under considerable escort.

Not that she had any desire to ride abroad in any event. That night in Cap François had been the most terrible she had ever known. The city she had always loved, the people she had always delighted to be amongst, had suddenly revealed a very ugly face, had discovered a savagery she would not have supposed any Frenchmen capable of possessing, and especially those who prided themselves on inhabiting the Paris of the Western Hemisphere, Vergée d'Or had become the only truly secure place on the island, just as the vast mass of the black people, proceeding about their appointed tasks, smiling at her and touching their foreheads as she rode by, had become the most reassuring of human factors. She wondered what they thought of it all, whether they understood anything of the immense upheaval which was taking place in France itself, and which was sending its blood-streaked tentacles all the way across the

194

ocean to affect their lives. Probably only a very few of them, like Toussaint, thought of it at all.

The white gate to the chateau paddock was opened for her by a waiting slave, and she threw Henry her reins as she stepped down. 'He is thirsty,' she said. 'Make sure he gets a good drink, Henry.'

'Yes, mistress,' he said.

She smiled at him, was disappointed not to receive a smile in return. But he had his moods. He had always had his moods of introspection, suggesting some apparently inner conflict. She blamed his gods. In their gloomy possession of all the bestial instincts in humanity she thought they were responsible for many of the ills suffered by the black people, though they might also grant them the occasional relief of orgy. She was happy to be done with them. They had served her well, when she had needed them. Now she no longer did so. She could only hope their worship would never lead Henry into an absurdity, like conceiving it might be possible to escape to the forests and mountains, to starve if he was not hunted down like a wild beast.

She walked towards the house itself, long strides fluttering the divided skirt of her habit, taking off her tricorne to fan herself, looking forward to an ice cold glass of sangaree. Despite all the tragedy which seemed to have filled these last two years, she supposed that she had never been so happy. She was growing into her role. It had taken a long time. Eight years. In the beginning she had required all her mental energy, her physical strength, just to maintain herself as Philippe's wife, and even after she had become sure of her success there, she had then devoted herself to becoming pregnant, while the constant worry for, and care of, her mother had further encroached upon her personality. In many ways Mama's death had been a release. As in many ways Henry's flogging, that dreadful day last year, had jerked her to her senses. She had at last realised that she could not spend her life merely moving from Philippe's bed to his table and back again, and expect to have any part in the life of her people. Because they were her people. Only

195

by making sure everyone, from Philippe down, understood that all the time, could she ever hope to control events, to help the black people achieve some measure of contentment.

As she had obviously developed herself. Kit had noticed it, when he had arrived for Christmas, and to look at Mama's grave. 'You have become a woman, Richilde,' he said. 'But more than that, you have become Madame de Mortmain.'

Poor Kit. He had come, also, to see Annette. Because now that their cousin Alexander was high in the United States Government – he had recently been made Secretary of the Treasury by his friend George Washington, who had been chosen president of the fledgling republic – the shipping line had prospered, and Kit with it. He was now the master of their finest vessel, and could call on Cap François whenever he wished. Thus he was also ready for marriage, and had broached the subject with Uncle Maurice.

And been turned away. There was no one in the world that Maurice de Mortmain would rather have had his youngest daughter marry – had Kit not been her first cousin. But there it was. And having come out into the open, Kit had had no alternative but to leave – their surreptitious but well-known meetings and loving handclasps were no longer possible. Annette had wept for two days, and had then declared that she would never marry, but would join Lucy in her steadfast chastity. While Richilde had accepted the fact that she might not see her brother again for years.

But, she thought as she approached the house, perhaps Annette was the lucky one, at that, in avoiding the tragedies as well as with the triumphs of matrimony. For on the lower verandah, Françoise de Beaudierre slowly rocked herself to and fro. Her hair was uncombed, and although it was nearly lunchtime she still wore her undressing robe. Françoise had not dressed in six months, since Ferrand's death, just as she had hardly spoken in that time, even to her children. She merely sat, and rocked, and stared into space, and occasionally wept, silently and copiously. And she hated. That much was very evident. She hated all humanity. But she hated Richilde and Philippe the most of any, because they had set off so confidently to bring Ferrand home, and had failed. Besides, undoubtedly the lynch mob, a white mob, had been whipped up by the planters' agents. Françoise could not be convinced of Philippe's innocence in the matter, however much the rest of the family assured her of it.

That he had not been involved was as certain as anything on earth, Richilde knew, but she could not blame her cousin for feeling so bitter; she avoided the front verandah, went to the back of the house, and the private staircase to her apartment, where Amelia would have her bath waiting for her.

'Madame.'

She checked, and turned, frowning even as her heart did a surge up and down her chest. It was nearly eight years since she had heard that voice. 'Jacqueline? Jacqueline Chavannes?'

The quadroon stepped from the rose bushes, pulled her cloak back from her head. Certainly it was Jacqueline Chavannes, and certainly Jacqueline had to be about thirty years of age. But this woman looked much older than that. And she too had recently been weeping. There was a complete absence of the elegant demoiselle Richilde remembered, in the shabby clothes and undressed hair of this distraught creature.

'Whatever are you doing here?' Richilde asked.

'I wish to speak with you, madame.'

Richilde hesitated. 'Then you'd best come upstairs,' she said. 'If Philippe were to discover you . . .' She opened the door, led her old friend inside. 'You'll see I use the private staircase just as often as you ever did,' she said, attempting to lighten the atmosphere.

'Yes, madame,' Jacqueline said.

They reached the top, and Richilde showed her into the bedroom. Amelia was already there, with the tub, but Richilde dismissed her with a wave of the hand. Amelia cast a curious and disapproving glance at the mulatto woman as

197

she left the room.

'Will she not tell . . . your husband, that I am here?' Jacqueline asked.

'She is my servant, not his,' Richilde said. 'She is not likely to forget that.'

Jacqueline sat down, head bowed, hands on lap. 'You have succeeded in everything, where I failed.'

'I am not yet a mother.' Richilde sat down beside her. 'What has happened? What do you wish of me?'

'I need your help, madame,' Jacqueline said. 'I know that it is presumptuous of me, after all that has passed between us, but . . .'

'If you need my help, Jacqueline, then you must call me Richilde.'

Jacqueline raised her head. Her eyes were filled with tears. 'You mean you *will* help me?'

'If it is in my power to do so, certainly. And if you will tell me what it is you require.'

Suddenly the huge dark eyes overflowed, and the tears rolled freely down those once lovely cheeks. Jacqueline slipped from the bed and knelt before Richilde. 'It is my brother . . .'

'Jacques? He is in trouble?'

'He was with Ogé.'

'My God,' Richilde exclaimed

'And now they have been captured together. But you must know of this.'

'No,' Richilde said. 'No. I did not know. I understood the rebels had fled into the Spanish colony.'

'They did so, Richilde. But the Spanish authorities have arrested them and returned them to Cap François. How can you not know of this?'

'I suppose because I did not enquire,' Richilde said. 'Go on.'

'They arrived two days ago, and were tried immediately, and sentenced to death.'

'Oh, my God,' Richilde said. 'But . . . can Monsieur Peynier *do* that?'

'He has done it, madame. Richilde. Twenty-two of them. Not one of them older than I.'

Richilde stared at her, aghast.

'They are to be executed the day after tomorrow,' Jacqueline said.

'But ... if he *was* rebelling, and Monsieur Peynier supposes that he has the power ... I will do what I can, of course, Jacqueline. Believe me. But I cannot promise anything.'

'I do not expect you to intercede for my brother's life, Richilde,' Jacqueline said. 'I know that is forfeit, by the reason of his rebellion. I am here to beg for your help in securing him a decent death.'

Richilde frowned at her. 'I do not understand you. A decent death? What is to happen to him?'

'Twenty of them are to be hanged, as rebels,' Jacqueline said, her voice faltering. 'But the Governor General is determined to make an example of Ogé, and his closest associate. Because Jacques was taken when in Ogé's company, it is supposed he shares the responsibility for the revolt with him. Richilde, they are to be broken on the wheel.'

Richilde stood before her husband's desk. 'You did not tell me Ogé had been taken.'

He raised his eyebrows. 'I did not know that you were interested.'

'And with him, Jacques Chavannes?'

He frowned. 'Now, who told you that? Louis? I told him not to speak of it, the wretch. I knew it would upset you.'

She sat down. 'Does it matter who told me? Philippe ... is it true they have been sentenced to death?'

'They are rebels in arms against the government of the colony, Richilde. There can only be one punishment for such as them.'

'But ... the National Assembly ...'

'Has turned out to be a more sensible body than we had hoped it could possibly be. Peynier has received a letter from it informing us that it was never intended that any resolution passed in Paris should alter the laws or the way of life we have practised here for centuries, and which may be regarded as essential to our security. That in effect gave us carte blanche to deal with these upstarts as we thought fit.'

'We?'

'I am consulted by the Governor-General in matters of security, as you well know.'

'And you approve of sentencing twenty-two young men to death?'

'You speak as if they were young gentlemen. They are young scoundrels. Besides, these are unusual circumstances. You must understand, Richilde. Whatever is truly happening in France, whatever is the eventual outcome of all these meetings and assemblies and speeches and pronunciamentos and riots, it is obvious that there is a great upheaval going on over there, and that Paris, all of France, is going to be entirely preoccupied with its own affairs for some time to come. Thus we are left entirely to our own resources. We, no more than a few thousand whites, with a few hundred soldiers, must hold down several hundred thousand blacks and, alas, because of our parents' casual lusts, several thousand mulattos, without the supporting power of France. Thus it is absolutely essential that we show the people of St Domingue, of whatever colour, that we mean to continue our rule – we, the planters – and that we will make a most condign example of those who attempt to rebel against us.'

She supposed he had just repeated part of the speech he had made to the Governor-General, and sighed. 'An example. To be hanged, in public. But Philippe . . . I am told that Ogé and Chavannes are to be broken on the wheel.'

'They were the ringleaders. It is fitting that they should suffer the most severely.'

'I don't even know what breaking on the wheel means. Is it very painful?'

'Painful?' he smiled. 'I would describe it as the most terrible form of execution ever devised. It is far worse than being burned alive. The culprit is stripped and then spreadeagled on a carriage wheel, arranged so that everyone watching can see his suffering. The executioner, using an iron bar, then taps his bones, one after the other, starting with the smallest of course. Each tap breaks a bone.'

Richilde clasped both hands around her throat.

'Obviously,' Philippe went on, 'no one dies from merely breaking a bone, especially wrists and ankles and ribs and such like. Or even all of those. A skilful executioner can reduce his victim to an absolute jelly before he permits death. Of course, no one knows for sure whether or not Pallot is skilful – he has never done it before.' He smiled again. 'But I am told that he is feverishly reading books on anatomy.'

'You . . . you can sit there, and discuss something so . . . so barbaric, with a smile?'

'They will suffer horribly,' he acknowledged. 'But that is necessary, don't you see? We want their deaths never to be forgotten, so that every scoundrel who considers rebellion will have to stop and think that he too might wind up on the wheel, like Ogé and Chavannes. You must understand that, Richilde.'

'I don't know,' she said. 'I wish I did understand why it is necessary to make a man suffer when he is going to die anyway. But Philippe, Ogé led the revolt. Jacques Chavannes didn't.'

'We can't make an example of just the leader. Believe me, there were those wished to have them all die on the wheel. I argued against that. I do not think the spectators would have been able to accept that.'

'The spectators . . . my God. But Philippe, you know Jacques. He's just a confused young man. Surely one of the other twenty is more guilty than he.'

He frowned at her. 'Who have you been talking to?'

'Nobody. But . . . he saved Kit's life, once, in America.'

'Perhaps he did. But it was the sort of instinctive thing that soldiers do. And it was a long time ago.'

'Philippe, please. I'm not asking for his life. I know that

isn't possible. But let him be hanged, like the other men. Please, Philippe. If you were to speak with Peynier . . .'

His frown deepened. 'You've seen Jacqueline.'

'Well . . .' She flushed.

'And I know you haven't been off the plantation in weeks. You mean she came here?'

'Well . . .'

'After I told her never to set foot on Vergée d'Or again? You should have thrown her out.'

'She was distraught, Philippe. This is her brother, we're talking about. Her only brother.'

'The sentence cannot be changed now.'

'Because it would show weakness,' she said bitterly. 'I know. Or do you just hate him, that much. Because of her?'

'Yes,' he said. 'I hate him. Because of her. Because of all the humiliation she caused me, for so long, when I thought I could not do without her. But that has nothing to do with his fate. He has committed armed rebellion against the government of the colony. He has to die. And he has been chosen as one of those of whom an example will be made. There is an end of the matter.' He leaned back. 'Would you like to attend the execution?'

'Me?'

'Don't sound so shocked. It will be quite an occasion. Claudette is going. And Catherine, and Thérèse de Milot.'

'To watch two young men being broken into pieces?'

'I am told it is a sight never to be forgotten. I have never seen a proper execution. I was in Paris when they executed Damiens for attempting the life of Louis XV, but Aunt Aimée would not let me go. She went. They tore him into four pieces with horses. She never tired of telling me of it. One should try to experience most things in this brief life of ours. I think you should come. Madame Peynier is attending. And so will most of the ladies in Cap François.'

He was being his most hateful, arrogant, baiting self. But she was not going to lose her temper. 'I think that is too horrible for words,' she said, quietly. And raised her head.

'Are you going?'

'Of course.'

She stood up. 'I'm sure you will enjoy yourself,' she said, and left the room.

Rio Negro Great House blazed with light. It was a small party – for their thirtieth wedding anniversary Thomas and Thérèse de Milot chose to entertain only their immediate family. But it was a large family, for now it included the Mortmain clan, even if only half of them had actually decided to attend.

But like all Milot parties, it was a lavish affair. They played at bowls on the lawn, and drank iced sangaree. They dined on turtle steaks and crayfish tails, fresh salads and ripe fruits, and drank claret. They sat on the patio to watch the August sun disappearing into the mountains, to fan themselves even as they felt the sweat trickling down their backs and soaking their corsets, and drank iced champagne.

'I think we will have a hurricane this year,' Thérèse de Milot declared. 'I can feel it in the air.'

'You can always feel hurricanes in the air, in the summer,' Etienne said. 'But they never actually happen.'

Thérèse gave her son-in-law a disapproving look. 'They do. These things go in cycles. When I was a girl we had hurricanes here three years in succession. Do you remember that, Thomas? We were newly weds.'

'Too long ago,' Thomas de Milot said, and raised a laugh. 'Richilde, my dear girl, you were not at the execution.'

Richilde caught her breath. She had made Philippe promise not to mention the execution. But in her heart she had known there was no way it could be avoided. It remained the most exciting thing that had happened in Cap François for years – and at least, she supposed, it meant that everyone no longer discussed poor Ferrand de Beaudierre.

'No,' she said. 'I do not find executions my favourite form of entertainment.'

'But it was splendid, Richilde,' Catherine de Milot said. 'So dramatic. There is something utterly memorable, about twenty-two young men, being led out to die. Oh, I nearly wept.'

'They were weeping too,' Etienne said, with a laugh.

François de Milot pulled his moustache. "Tienne and I were having a wager on which of them would break down completely. I must say, I never expected it to be Ogée himself. The confounded fellow cost me twelve crowns.'

'That really was quite disgusting,' Thérèse de Milot declared. 'He is supposed to have been the leader of these people. And then to start screaming and shouting and begging. Really!'

'He actually offered to give us lists of everyone else who had been a party to his revolt, if we'd let him be hanged,' Philippe said.

'And did you see ... well ...' Claudette de Mortmain flushed.

Etienne gave a shout of laughter. 'I thought that was what you were looking at. Anatomical studies. Did you know, dear Mama, that fright can make a fellow ... well, I mean ... talk about ramrods.'

'I really think that is unsuitable conversation for mixed company,' Marguerite de Mortmain protested mildly.

'I don't think this entire conversation is suitable for any occasion or company,' Richilde declared. 'I think the whole thing was too horrible for words. And actually to go and watch it ...'

They looked at her in amazement.

'You don't have to get upset, Richilde,' Etienne said. 'Your friend Chavannes died like a gentleman. Do you know, he never uttered a sound? And it took him over two hours to die. I thought he was never going to make it. I had visions of this dreadful jellylike creature rolling about the streets of Cap François, making himself a general nuisance.'

Richilde glared at him, trying to convey her utter loathing in her expression.

'Everyone is soft, nowadays,' Thomas de Milot said, into his champagne. And belched. 'When I was a boy ...'

His son raised his eyebrows, and sighed, loudly. But his

father ignored him.

'We had executions like that every week. We were used to them. And here on the plantations, too. Do you remember that time a dozen Negroes escaped Rio Negro, and went into the hills? Philippe? No, I suppose you were too young.'

'I remember, Thomas,' Philippe said. 'Even though I was only a boy.'

'And we went after them. Your father, and mine, and myself, and about twenty overseers. We caught them, too, and brought them back. And papa decided to make an example of *them*. Do you know what he did, Richilde?'

'I don't want to know,' she said, hopelessly.

'It was that very lawn out there,' Thomas de Milot said. 'Where we played bowls before supper. We played bowls then, too. Only Papa had pits dug, into which he placed these scoundrels, buried them up to their necks so that only their heads were showing, and *then* we played bowls. Only instead of knocking over a pin, you see, you had actually to kill a man. Or knock out his eye, or something. Papa worked it all out. A very complicated set of rules. But he was good at that sort of thing. I won, as I remember.' He sighed. 'I was much stronger then.'

Richilde got up. 'If you'll excuse me, Thérèse, I really think I must be going.'

'Going, Richilde? It's not yet midnight.'

'I'm sorry. I don't feel very well.'

Thérêsè looked at Philippe, who also got up.

'I must apologise for spoiling your party,' he said. 'But if Richilde isn't well . . .'

'Weak stomachs,' Thomas de Milot said. 'People nowadays have weak stomachs.'

'Ring for Charles, will you, Catherine?' Thérèse' said.

Catherine got up, slowly and resentfully; her mother-in-law had this habit of using her as an extra maid.

'I shall say goodnight, Thérèse, Thomas,' Richilde said. 'Thank you for a most delicious meal.' She looked past them, over the gardens and the stables, in the direction of the white township. 'Where is that fire, do you suppose?'

Thomas de Milot merely turned his head, but François got up. 'Must be a canefield,' he said. 'When the weather gets this hot fires are liable to start anywhere. Would you like me to ride out there, Papa?'

'The butler can see to it,' Thomas said. 'Sit down and have some more champagne.'

'Where the devil is that Romerre?' Thérèse de Milot enquired. 'Catherine, did you ring the bell?'

'Of course I did, Mama,' Catherine said.

'No doubt he will be along directly,' Richilde said. 'Good night.'

She went through the open glass doors into the large drawing room, and thence into the hall. Philippe hurried behind her. 'Richilde,' he said. 'You really are being rude.'

'I consider they were rude to me,' she said. 'Teasing me like that, and about something so ghastly!'

'Old Thomas is right. You really should not be so soft centred. Life is a cruel business.' He stood in the great hall, hands on hips, looking right and left. The hall was deserted. 'I must say, though, Milot seems to be losing his grip. This place is going downhill.'

Richilde went to the huge front doors, made of cedar reinforced with iron bars, and thence on to the front porch. Normally there would always be half-a-dozen liveried grooms waiting here, as well as their own coachmen. The coaches waited in a line, horses patiently munching at their nosebags. But there was no one in sight.

'The scoundrels have run off to see what's happening,' Philippe said. 'My God, I'll have them at the end of a whip.'

'How very odd,' Richilde said. 'Listen.'

Because suddenly she heard the sound of drums, and conch shells, and then a great deal of confused sound, punctuated by a pistol shot. While the whole night sky to the west had started to glow.

She gazed at Philippe with her mouth open.

'By Christ,' he said, and left her to run back into the house.

'Etienne,' he bellowed. 'Louis. Get up. Get to the

coaches. Thomas, there is trouble out there. You have a slave revolt on your hands.'

Richilde stood alone on the front porch, staring into the darkness. A slave revolt? That was impossible. There had never been a slave revolt in St Domingue. At least, not for a hundred years. There had not been a slave revolt anywhere this century, save for the Dutch colony of Berbice, and that was nearly thirty years ago. And everyone agreed that that had been caused by a panic on the part of the planters.

And Henry Christopher and Jean François had run off to join it? Oh, my God, she thought. Henry, broken on the wheel. Oh, my God!

'Hurry.' Louis ran outside, catching her arm as he did so. He was herding his mother and Claudette as well. 'Philippe wants us back to Vergée d'Or as rapidly as possible.'

'But . . . Philippe . . .?'

'He will follow on horseback, as soon as he has discovered what is happening here.' Louis half pushed her down the steps, and into the first coach, where Marguerite and Claudette were already seated; the three younger Mortmain girls had remained at home.

'Wait for your father,' Marguerite said, as Maurice de Mortmain appeared in the doorway. 'Do hurry, Maurice.'

Thérèse de Milot and Catherine stood above them. 'Take care, Louis,' Thérèse shouted. 'Do not stop for *anything*.'

'Why do you not come with us?' Marguerite asked.

'Come with you?' Thérèse enquired.

'Oh, yes, Mama. I think that would be a very good idea,' Catherine said. 'If you will wait just five minutes I will fetch the children, and . . .'

'Stuff and nonsense,' Thérèse de Milot declared. 'This is my home. *Your* home, Catherine. And you wish to abandon it? Shame on you, girl. Shame on you. Now come and help me, and we will close these doors.'

'Wait for your father,' Marguerite said, as Maurice de Mortmain on the box, the three women inside, peering out of their windows at the darkness, looking back at the flames.

'It will be nothing,' Marguerite de Mortmain said,

reassuringly. 'It will have been some kind of a riot, caused by the fire. The overseers will stamp it out.'

'No one will ever riot on Vergée d'Or, anyway,' Claudette said.

Richilde chewed her lip. She did not suppose they would ever riot on Vergée d'Or either. But Henry and Jean François had run off. Of course they would not wish to take part in anything so dangerously stupid as a slave revolt, it must have been sheer curiosity. But at the very least it would mean another flogging for Henry and, as Philippe himself was involved, it would be a far more serious one than the first. She blamed Toussaint. They were too friendly with the lame old coachman, and undoubtedly had gone to find him, and discover what was happening. Oh, if only she had not decided to go home early, their absence might not have been discovered.

Vergée d'Or lay bathed in moonlight, silent and quiet. It was not quite two in the morning.

The carriage rumbled up to the front porch, and sleepy grooms hurried forward to take the bridles – but how reassuring their presence was.

'I will rouse Fedon, and the town,' Louis said, jumping down and running to the stables for a horse. 'I will send the messenger to Cap François, as well.'

'Fedon? Cap François?' Marguerite asked.

'This is what Philippe has instructed us to do,' Maurice de Mortmain said, handing them down himself. 'Ah, Bartholemew. I wish the doors closed and the shutters raised. Haste, man.'

The Negro butler stared at the old man in amazement, then looked past him for Henry Christopher and Jean François. He scratched his head. 'They got hurricane, master?'

'Just do as I say.'

Richilde followed them up the stairs. 'I'm sure that if we were just to go to bed it would be best,' she said. 'This way we are creating a crisis where there may not be one.'

'I am doing what Philippe told me to do,' Maurice

explained, patiently.

'Well, I think the storm shutters are a good idea,' Claudette said. 'My God, the children. I must wake the children.'

'But why?' Richilde asked.

'Because . . . because I must.'

Richilde went up the inner staircase, encountered a sleepy Amelia.

'Eh-eh, mistress, but you home early. Them boys saying we got storm.'

'Yes,' Richilde said. 'There is a rumour of one.'

'You going to bed, mistress?'

Richilde stood at the foot of the staircase to her apartment, biting her lip irresolutely. Of course she could not just go to bed, if everyone else was staying up. She turned her head, as there came a hubbub from the front drive, and her heart gave a curious leap. But those weren't black voices. She hurried back along the great gallery, stood at the top of the stairs, watched the white women and children flooding into the downstairs hall. 'What on earth is . . .?'

'Orders from Monsieur Louis,' explained old d'Albret the chemist, who appeared to be in charge of them. 'We are truly sorry to invade your home, madame, but Monsieur Louis said we must all come up here.'

'Yes,' Richilde said, absently. 'Yes, Amelia, find Rosamund and tell her I wish bedding brought downstairs. Everything we have, for these people. You are welcome, to be sure, Monsieur d'Albret. Perhaps you will arrange them in families.' She gathered her skirts and went down the stairs, watched Fedon and Maurice de Mortmain organising the white men, handing out muskets and pistols, barricading the windows and doors and making loopholes for their weapons, while Bartholemew and the footmen stared at them in bemusement. 'Uncle Maurice,' she said urgently. 'I am sure we are doing the wrong thing, anticipating trouble where there is none.'

He ignored her. She felt like stamping her foot, and shouting at them all to listen to her. Instead she went outside on to the front verandah, stood in the cool of the dawn, gazing down the drive. The white township was alive with lights as the last of the overseers gathered their families and their most precious belongings to take to the safety of the chateau. But now the slave village was awake too; she could see lights flickering down there. And they were being treated as enemies already, while they still obviously knew nothing of what was happening. Equally obviously, they had to be told something to reassure them and to keep them quiet.

She went down the steps, turned towards the stables and her pony and trap, and paused in horror – almost the entire western sky had turned brilliant red with the blaze – clearly all of Rio Negro's canefields were burning. But was it just the canefields?

While she hesitated, there was a drumming of hooves, and a horse dashed up the drive, to come to a steaming halt beside her, while Etienne de Mortmain half fell from the saddle. 'A drink,' he gasped. 'For God's sake get me a drink.'

'Bartholemew,' Richilde snapped, and the butler hurried off to his pantry.

''Tienne, you're hurt.' Claudette almost tumbled down the stairs, her eldest child, Felicité, a girl of nine, running at her heels.

He shook his head, drank the brandy brought to him by Bartholemew. 'Not me. But it is hell out there. Thousands of them. They tried to stop me on the road, but I got through. You're barricaded here? That is good. Have you sent into Cap François for troops?'

'Yes,' Louis said. 'I have sent a messenger.'

'One messenger?' Etienne shook his head at his brother. 'Not sufficient. They are on the roads, I tell you. I will go myself. Fetch me a fresh horse, Bartholemew.'

'Into Cap François?' Claudette cried. 'Oh, 'Tienne, take me with you. I'm so afraid.'

Etienne hesitated, glanced from face to face. 'It would not

be safe for you,' he said. 'The roads are dangerous. Can't you understand that? You are better off here.'

His terror was frightening to watch.

'Where is Philippe,' Richilde asked, trying to keep her voice calm.

'I don't know. I know nothing, save that the overseers were routed by a charge of the blacks; the fools would try to fight them in the open. Then they retreated to the chateau. I happened to be mounted, and thought I had best ride over here to warn you. Now I will go to Cap François. They must be told.'

'You rode off and left Philippe?'

'And your sister? And the little ones?' Marguerite de Mortmain cried.

'For God's sake, did you wish me to stay and be killed?' he shouted. 'I did not know where they were. Anyway, Catherine is a Milot now. It was her business to stay. Mine was . . . to come here,' he said lamely, obviously deciding against proclaiming that his place was with his family. 'And now I must warn Cap François. That is my duty. I will be back in the morning, with the soldiers.' He mounted the fresh horse, kicked it in the ribs, and galloped down the drive.

Claudette burst into tears. The Mortmains looked at each other. Then they looked at Richilde.

Because, she realised, in Philippe's absence, she was the one to whom they had to turn. She was the mistress of Vergée d'Or.

'Well,' she said. 'I am sure he is doing the right thing. As he says, he will be back in the morning, with the soldiers. It really would be far too exhausting and dangerous a ride for you, Claudette. Now, let me see . . .' She went back up the stairs, her intended mission to the black people forgotten, looked at the huge grandfather clock in the hall. The time was just past three. 'I think,' she decided, 'as obviously no one is going to sleep tonight, that we shall all have a cup of chocolate. Batholemew . . .' she looked left and right, but after delivering the horse for Etienne, the butler had disappeared. 'Do ring the bell, would you, Lucy.' She frowned at her cousin, who was just coming down the stairs, followed by Annette – both wore their nightclothes. 'And then,' she said. 'I think it would be a good idea for you to get dressed. We have guests in the hall.' She paused, uncertainly, amazed at the way they were hanging on her every word. Because they were terrified, needed to be reassured, and told what to do. And did she not need to be told what to do?

Fedon came hurrying through from the back of the house. 'Those black bastards have gone.' He checked, and flushed, at the sight of the group of gentlewomen. 'I beg your pardon, madame, mademoiselles But your servants appear to have fled the house. Even Bartholemew. They left the back doors open, too.'

'Then have them closed,' Richilde said, and tried to ignore the dreadful pounding of her heart, the sick feeling which was spreading away from her stomach. 'Please attend to that, Monsieur Fedon. And we shall have to make our own chocolate. Aunt Marguerite, will you take charge of that? I'm sure some of the ladies from the township will wish to help you. Lucy, perhaps you would help Aunt Marguerite too. Annette, be a dear and wake Françoise, and help her to dress. Claudette, as you suggested earlier, you had better get up the other little ones, Françoise's as well, and make sure they are dressed.' She rubbed Felicité's head. 'You can help your mama. Uncle Maurice, Louis . . .' she walked away from the throng, was joined by the two men.

'I can only apologise for my son,' Maurice de Mortmain said.

'He was always a coward,' Louis said, bitterly.

'If he brings the soldiers,' Richilde said. 'I will forgive him everything.' Even having Henry Christopher flogged, she thought. Or sneering at Jacques Chavannes dying. All factors in causing tonight's horror, surely.

'But if he is right about what is happening at Rio Negro,' she said in a low voice. 'Then it may well be that we shall have to fight here on Vergée d'Or. I would have liked to have spoken to our blacks, have reassured them. But if the

212

domestics have gone down there it may be too late. So we must prepare to stand a siege, at least until the soldiers get here. How long will that be, Louis, do you think?'

'They should be here by lunch time, Richilde,' Louis said. 'But . . .'

'If only Philippe were here,' Maurice de Mortmain muttered. 'If only.'

'He will be here,' Richilde said, almost angrily. 'And when he arrives he must find that we have anticipated his dispositions, as far as we can. Now then, Louis, will you take command of the front of the house, with half of the men? Appoint Monsieur Fedon to command the rear, with the other half. Less twenty. Uncle Maurice, I would like you to take twenty men, and maintain a sort of mobile reserve, able to go to the assistance of whichever part of the house is most threatened.'

They stared at her.

'It's what Frederick the Great would have done,' she insisted. 'Or Kit, had he been here.' Oh, God, she thought, to have Kit here, with his confidence and his decision, and his courage. 'And it is what Philippe certainly would wish.'

'Of course you are right,' Louis said. 'I am a fool not to have considered the situation from a military point of view.' He smiled, and kissed Richilde on the cheek. 'Don't worry, Richilde. No one is going to burn *your* house.'

My house, she thought, retreating to the stairs the better to survey the ordered chaos which was spreading about her. She had never thought of it as *her* house, before. Oh, God she thought, let Philippe come. Please let him come.

She went upstairs, hunted through the various bedrooms, gathered Annette and a sleepy, complaining Françoise and the various children together, and made them go up to the master apartments at the top of the house.

'If the blacks have overrun Rio Negro,' Annette said, thoughtfully. 'What has happened to Catherine and the children?'

Richilde caught her breath. No one had up to now dared put that question into words. 'We do not know that the blacks have overrun Rio Negro,' she pointed out. 'Only that the overseers have retreated to the chateau, which they are undoubtedly holding, as we shall hold Vergée d'Or, if we have to. Anyway, if there was to be a disaster there, you may be quite sure the women would have been got away. Philippe would have seen to that. Now, children, I want you to stay in here with Tante Françoise and Tante Annette.'

'Here?' Annette whispered. 'But suppose the house catches fire? We will be trapped.'

'Here you will be safe from bullets,' Richilde said. 'And Annette, if the house catches fire it will be because it has fallen. Would you not rather die of suffocation, or even burning, than fall into the hands of the slaves, alive?'

Annette stared at her, mouth slowly sagging, tales of what had happened in Berbice filtering back to her through the mists of memory.

Where, oh where, was Philippe?

She encountered Aunt Marguerite in the great gallery. 'All the woman must have pistols, Richilde,' Marguerite said. 'And an extra charge for each of the children, so that they may . . .' she hesitated, unable to speak the dread words.

'Of course, Aunt Marguerite,' Richilde said. 'Will you see to that?' She opened the door, went out on to the upper porch. Here four men had been stationed, clutching their muskets, peering into the gloom. Because it was no more than a gloom now, with the western sky such a sheet of pink flame, and the dawn rapidly approaching. The dawn, she thought. Everything would be better in daylight. And by dawn the troops would have left Cap François, and be marching to their help.

'There they go,' one of the men said.

She stared down the hill at the slave village, at the flaring torches, listened to the hubbub, the raised voices. Still enquiring. Still wanting to know what had happened. It could have been averted, she thought. If we had just come back here, sent a messenger into town, certainly, but had not panicked, like those Dutchmen in Berbice, not . . .

214

'Listen,' said another man.

A huge noise was swelling towards them, a shouting and screaming, a whistling of conch shells, coming out of the west.

Louis stood beside her. 'They will be here in half an hour,' he said. 'You will retire inside and barricade this door if they appear on the drive,' he told the men.

They nodded.

'Louis . . .' she bit her lip; her voice had trembled.

'Yes, I'm afraid,' he said. 'You're always afraid, just before a battle, Richilde. But when it actually starts you don't have time.'

'A battle?' she asked. 'Or a massacre?'

He shrugged. 'Battles have been won at greater odds, eh? I remember my Frederick too. Do you think Henry is out there?'

'I don't know where he is,' she said.

He smiled at her. 'Because I was wondering if he remembers his Frederick as well.' He squeezed her hand. 'We'll hold them, Richilde. I promise you.'

'If only Philippe were here,' she said, and gazed down the drive, into the first pale fingers of the dawn, suddenly rendered brighter than she had ever known it by a myriad flood of torches, held high and waving to and fro. Held by people. More people than she had ever seen before in one place in her life, thousand upon thousand of them, and they were all black, and constantly being reinforced as she saw men and women pouring from the slave village to swell their ranks, to join the thunderous clamour as they poured up the drive. Some had already diverted to the white township, in search of liquor or loot, and she could see flashes of flame rising from there as well to indicate that that too would soon be reduced to ashes.

But her attention was taken by the mass coming up the drive, headed by a huge figure, who did not march so much as leap and twist, dance and jump, his red robe swirling through the air.

'Boukman,' she muttered. 'Boukman. Oh, if you can bring

him down, the day is ours.'

She bit her lip. Never before had she asked for the life of a man.

And would his death make any difference, to those shrieking legions behind him, advancing towards her, their banners streaming in the dawn breeze ... their banners? Her stomach did a complete roll as she blinked to clear her eyes, saw the ghastly, hate and pain and terror filled features of Thérèse de Milot and Catherine de Milot, and at least two of Catherine's little girls, their heads stuck on the end of poles, their long hair straggling behind them, while there was a fifth pole, carried in the centre, on which the lower half of a woman's body was impaled, the legs flopping to either side. The lower half?

She had a sudden, irrelevant ghastly thought: Thérèse's dead mouth was frozen open. Had she, like poor Ogé screamed and begged, or had she died as a Milot should, with stoic courage?

And how should a Mortmain die?

'Don't look, madame,' one of the men begged, and another grasped her arm to urge her inside. 'Don't look.'

But Richilde resisted him, checked herself in the doorway, to look. Because Philippe de Mortmain had, at last, returned to his plantation.

Amazingly, he appeared to be unhurt, although he had been stripped of all his clothing save for his boots. He was being half marched, half carried in the front ranks of the slaves, and these now halted, just beyond musket shot from the chateau, while Boukman in turn stopped his gyrations. Even the noise seemed to settle, as they gazed at their prey.

Richilde stared at her husband. He was attempting to move, and she was sure he was shouting something. Was he afraid? Who could not be afraid, in such a situation? And Philippe could be in no doubt as to how much he was hated by his slaves. It was a hatred he had arrogantly cultivated.

Just as she was in no doubt that he had always been afraid of them. And now they were about to kill him. She knew that, and he undoubtedly knew that too, just as he must

216

know that she was looking at him now.

Did she love him? Had she ever loved him? Or had she just always envied his power and his wealth, even as she had feared them, had wanted to share in them, had never hesitated for a moment when offered that prize?

Just as now she must share in the terrible agony of having it ripped from her grasp.

Fedon panted up the stairs to stand beside her. 'They want to parley, I should say,' he said. 'Don't you think they want to parley, madame?'

Louis de Mortmain stood beside him, his face grim, because he too had recognised the remains of his sister, and his nieces. 'Of course they wish to parley,' he said. 'They are offering Philippe's life, against our surrender.'

'It is a chance, madame,' Fedon said. 'If they would agree to let us go into Cap François . . . Say the word, madame, and I will speak with them myself.'

Richilde was hardly breathing, as she watched her husband being marched out in front of the procession by four of the black men. One of them she recognised: Jean François. She could not make out Henry Christopher. To parley she remembered what they had heard of the slave revolt in Berbice. The planters had all congregated with their wives and families, in one strong house, and there they had resisted all the efforts of the slaves to break in. Until, after twenty-four hours, water had run short, and the slaves had offered to parley, offered to let the white people gain their boats and go down river to safety. The white people had agreed, and had left the security of their fortress – and had been cut to pieces. The lucky ones, that is.

'He is saying something,' Lucy de Mortmain had come to stand with them. 'Oh, my God, poor Philippe. The humiliation of it.'

Richilde continued to gaze at him. He had been forced to his knees by the men holding him, his body grotesquely white in the dawn, while Jean François stood beside him, a sharp-bladed knife in his hands. The humiliation of it. But Lucy had put her finger on the truth. Philippe de Mortmain was already dead. After today, he would never be able to look a black man in the face again.

'We cannot parley,' she said.

'But madame . . .' Fedon protested.

'Philippe knows that as well as we do,' she said. 'If he is speaking, he is begging us not to be tricked. We cannot parley.'

Louis stared at her in horror.

'My God,' one of the men whispered. 'Do not look, madame, I beg of you.'

Richilde's nostrils dilated. Because they had not meant to parley, after all. They had only, with demoniac patience, wished to save their master's ultimate degradation until it could be overlooked by the whites. For now Philippe was stretched on his back on the earth, and they could hear his shriek of pain and misery and shame even above the chanting of the crowd, and a moment later Jean François held aloft his bleeding trophy, waving it at the horror stricken defenders of the chateau.

Jean François. The man she had thought she could trust with her life. The man who had once held her in his arms. The man who *loved* her.

Lucy fell to her knees, and began to pray. Richilde realised she was in pain; her fists were so tightly clenched the nails had bitten into her palms.

Because, she thought, she *could* have loved Philippe, given only a few more years.

The only sound in the chateau was that of Marguerite de Mortmain weeping, from the downstairs hall.

'Now we know we have to fight, or die,' she said, in a low voice, and watched her husband being dragged away, writhing and screaming while blood streamed down his legs. Surely he would soon be dead and out of his agony. 'Go to your posts, messieurs,' she said.

She wanted to be sick. She did not seem to have any control over her stomach. But she was the mistress of Vergée d'Or, and, she realised, her determination was the only thing that stood between them all and a similar fate,

218

just as the constant awareness of her position was the only thing that stopped her from collapsing on the floor in screaming hysterics. She walked through the house, speaking with every man, making sure they had sufficient ammunition, smiling at the women, reminding them of the strength of the chateau, pausing to stand by the weeping Marguerite de Mortmain, unable to say a word of comfort to her, and being brought to a horrified stop by a scream which came up the hill, the most unearthly wail she had ever heard.

She ran to the window, stood beside Louis. The wind had dropped, and the night was still. The scream had come from a long way off, and now, too, seeping up the hill, they could hear the slow clank of machinery.

'Oh, my God,' Louis said. 'Oh, my God.'

Richilde understood that the slaves were feeding Philippe through his own cane crushers. Her knees seemed to have lost their strength and she all but fell. But there had been only one scream. He was dead, or beyond feeling. Now he had to be forgotten, as she concentrated upon saving the lives of the living. If she could.

'They are coming, madame,' Fedon said.

She looked in the direction of his pointing finger, saw the dark mass moving once again up the drive, Boukman to the fore.

'That man,' she said. 'Wearing the red robe. He is their leader. Bring him down, and they may well withdraw.'

'You hear that?' Fedon told his overseers. 'Bring down the *hougan*.'

Once again the slaves halted, perhaps two hundred yards from the chateau, and Boukman harangued them. She could not make out what he was saying. But she recognised Jean François at his side. Jean François. He at the least had to be killed, and Philippe's death avenged.

She was amazed at the intensity of her own thoughts, how filled with hatred, when for so long she had been sympathetic towards these people, had endeavoured to understand them, had wanted only to improve their lot.

And had the evidence of her own ears and eyes that

219

nothing they could do could truly atone for the hundred years and more that the planters had tortured and exploited them.

Boukman waved his stick, and the mass moved forward.

'Steady now,' Fedon said.

'Take aim,' Louis said, walking up and down behind the men at the windows. 'Choose your targets carefully. Wait for the command.'

'Fire,' Fedon shouted, and the sound of muskets ripped through the rooms and along the corridors of the huge house, while the air became filled with acrid white smoke. From the downstairs hall a woman started screaming in a high-pitched wail, but the men were cheering, for the Negroes had been halted, and were indeed in full retreat down the drive.

'Well done, lads, oh, well done,' Louis de Mortmain shouted.

'Recharge your pieces,' Fedon command. 'Quickly now, they may come again.'

'Not them,' Louis said. 'Not for an hour at the least. By then the soldiers will be nearly here. We'll hold them, Richilde. We'll hold them.'

Richilde looked down the drive. The sun had risen now, and its first beams were playing over the plantation, shining upon the score or so of bodies which lay scattered on the drive and in the flower beds, some lying still, other writhing in agony. And then upon the black mass gathered further down the hill, sullenly waving machetes and home-made spears, and even some muskets they had obviously obtained at Rio Negro, and which they did not know how to use.

And still, miraculously, Boukman stood before them, unhurt. Once again he was gesticulating and shouting, but this time without any immediate response – Jean François was no longer to be seen. Perhaps, she thought, he is amongst the dead.

She did not wish to think of Henry Christopher. And it was terribly important not to think of Philippe, of the way he had died, or of what tomorrow might bring. Tomorrow had first to be reached.

'Lucy,' she said. 'While there is a lull in the fighting, I think we should prepare some breakfast. We may be here for some hours yet. Madame Fedon, will you help us? Madame d'Albret?' She led the ladies into the kitchen. 'I'm sure the men would appreciate something to eat,' she said, smiling at them reassuringly. And then left them and went to find her uncle. He sat on the bottom step of the great staircase, shoulders bowed, overwhelmed by the catastrophe of his daughter.

'Uncle Maurice,' she said, and sat beside him. 'I think you should take Aunt Marguerite upstairs and put her to bed.'

He raised his head. 'Yes,' he said. 'Yes, I must do that. I . . .' he just ceased speaking. His eyes had a faraway look. She kissed him on the cheek and hurried off to speak with Father Thomas.

'Perhaps you could lead the ladies in morning prayer, Father,' she said. 'I'm afraid the men will have to stay at their posts, but it will be a great comfort to them all, surely.'

'Of course, madame. Madame . . .' he was interrupted in his attempt to offer sympathy.

'Here they come again,' someone shouted from the front of the house. Richilde gathered her skirts and ran through the hall to stand beside Louis, and watch the dark mass again surging up the hill, led this time not by Boukman but by a single huge man, young and strong, and brave, as he ran with his machete pointed straight at the front door of the chateau.

Henry Christopher.

'Him, at the least,' Louis muttered, and levelled his musket. Richilde opened her mouth and then closed it again. Of course he had to die. He and all the others had to die, that *they* might live. There was no alternative.

But she closed her eyes as the musket exploded, opened them again, and saw Henry still running, and now at the very foot of the patio steps, while behind him the huge mass had also surged across the lawns and flowerbeds, not checking this time as the musket balls tore through them, yelling their paean of hate and revenge.

She looked left and right, at the men feverishly reloading their pieces, listened to the splintering of glass and the crashing of timbers, from the library. 'Uncle Maurice,' she shouted. 'Your reserve. To the west wing.'

But Maucice de Mortmain had gone upstairs with his wife; the men he had been appointed to command were standing around irresolutely.

'In there,' she shouted, pointing – and then watching the defenders of the west wing come retreating through the hallway, several having discarded their weapons.

'Don't retreat,' she shrieked. 'Stand and fight. For God's sake . . .'

There were black men in the library, and swarming through the small drawing room. At the sound of their shouts the white men at the eastern windows turned back from their posts to face this new threat. Richilde watched in horror as Fedon himself turned, and was struck down from behind by a machete thrust through a broken window. She realised in that instant that the house had fallen. The unimaginable had happened, and they were all going to die.

She stood on the bottom step of the great staircase, and stared at the white women and children, huddled in front of her, at Father Thomas, looking utterly bewildered as he held his crucifix above his head, obviously unable to understand why his payers were not being answered. She looked beyond them, at Lucy, running in from the kitchen, a black man behind her, reaching out to catch her by the hair and bring her tumbling to the floor, screaming her terror in heart-breaking shrieks. And remembered that she held a pistol in her hand. She levelled it, as the man bent over her cousin, tearing the clothes from her back, and squeezed the trigger. She did not suppose she hit him – she was blinded by the powder smoke – but he jerked away, and Lucy, her gown in ribbons, regained her feet and came staggering towards the stairs.

Then the entire hallway was filled with black men, and machetes. An enormous wail arose from the white women and children, as an enormous snarl rose from the black throats. Lucy brushed past Richilde and ran up the stairs, panting and screaming, a horrifying sound. Richilde reached for breath, and then ran behind her, hating herself for a coward, for seeking just a final few minutes of life, her ears filled with the ghastly sounds coming from behind her.

She gained the great gallery, an utterly empty great gallery at the moment; the little knot of men on the upper porch still fired down into the mass below them, unaware that their battle was lost. But there was nothing she could do about them. There was nothing she could do about anything. Like them, she could only prepare to die. She looked at the portraits of all the past Mortmains staring down at her from the wall, at her own portrait, added there four years before, the alert amber eyes, the half smile, so confident, the pointed chin, the wealth of golden brown hair . . . That was what the man who killed her would see, just before he cut off her head to mount on a stick, save that the mouth would be wide open, screaming its terror. Unless she anticipated them.

She looked down at the pistol in her hand. But it was empty. She dropped it and ran along the corridor, gasping for breath, thence up the stairs to her bedroom, burst open the door, stopped in consternation. She had forgotten her earlier dispositions. But here were Françoise, lying on the bed and howling, Felicité, staring at her with wide eyes, Claudette, seated on the bed with her arm round her daughter's shoulders, Annette, standing by the window to look out, but turning to gaze at her cousin, the other six children huddled in a corner in mutual terror – and Lucy, sprawled on the floor, still shrieking between repulsive gulps for air.

'They are inside,' Richilde said. 'They are inside. Oh, God, they are inside.'

Annette pushed past her, closed the door, turned the key. 'Where is Mama?'

'I don't know, Richilde said. 'She went to her room, with your father. Oh, my God.' She leaned against the door, listened to the screams and the howls from outside, the bestial baying of men who were avenging every terrible ill done them for so long.

'We must kill ourselves,' Annette said.

They gazed at her.

'We must,' she shouted. 'Have you any *idea*? Didn't you see Catherine . . .' Great tears rolled out of her eyes and down her cheeks. 'At least the children,' she begged. 'Claudette . . .'

Claudette held Felicité tighter, while one of the smaller children began to cry.

'Wait,' Richilde said, heart pounding at the thought of escape. 'The private staircase. If we can reach the garden . . .' She ran into her dressing room, pulled open the door, the others crowding behind her, gazed down the stairwell in stupefaction at the black men coming up towards her, turned to push her cousins back into the bedroom, watched the door come crashing down, gazed at Henry Christopher.

He was naked from the waist up, and there was blood staining his machete and his right arm, and also splashed across his chest. But it was not his blood, from the vigour of his movements. Behind him was a crowd of eager slaves.

Annette fell to her knees. 'Henry,' she begged.

For a moment he filled the doorway, taking long breaths, discovering just who had so far survived. 'I can save one,' he said, speaking English.

They stared at him, and then Claudette, without speaking, held up Felicité.

But Henry had found the one he wanted. Richilde thought she was going to choke, with relief, with self horror that she might survive where her cousins could not, with an utterly breathless feeling of helplessness as she understood that her life could only be saved in one fashion.

Henry pushed Annette out of the way, stepped towards her. 'No, Henry,' she gasped. 'Not me. One of the others. The child . . .'

He lowered his shoulder, and thrust it into her midriff, closed his hands on her thighs, one of them still grasping the

224

machete, and lifted her bodily from the floor, draped across him like a sack. The impact knocked all the breath from her body, and before she could regain it her head was hit a sickening blow on the door frame as she was carried through, and down the corridor, and into Jacqueline Chavannes' old room, there to be thrown across the bed.

She raised herself on her elbow as he dropped his pants. 'Henry,' she said. 'One of the children. Please . . .'

'You are my twin,' he said.

She watched the door open, other people come in. They had come to watch their mistress being raped. The ultimate humiliation. But nothing she could suffer could equal what Philippe had suffered. She fell backwards as he knelt above her, huge and demanding, his face twisted with a mixture of passion and lust – and also distress and even tenderness. She was suddenly no longer aware of fear, because he would save her, and because she had always known that what was about to happen would happen, one day. She had known that from her very earliest childhood, without being prepared to accept the fact.

He split her gown from her bodice to her knees in a single tear, ripped her petticoats with no more effort, paused in amazement at her corset – she realised that he knew nothing of white women's clothes. She brought her arms around in front, thinking vaguely that she might assist him, and he supposed she was fighting him, thrust them back again, and pinned them there with his own as he lowered his body on to hers, was inside her with a gigantic thrust which seemed to impale her against the bed. Her ears were filled with a tremendous drumming, above which she could hear the most heart rending screams. Her own screams? But they were coming from the next room.

He lay on her, crushing her with his weight, while dark faces surged about her, pulled at her legs and her hair, tried to thrust hands between their heaving bodies to reach her breasts and her crotch. Presumably they were people she knew, people who had helped her build the new dispensary, who had touched their hats as she had passed them yester-

225

day morning, had smiled at her and pretended she was their friend. She did not wish to look at them, but she could not move, pinned as she was to the bed by Henry's weight, while he lay still. She could feel him breathing, against her neck, but he would not raise his head. Out of remorse, inability to meet her eyes – or because he knew that to move would be to relinquish possession of her, mean that he would have to hand her over to the eager mob?

She wondered if he was still inside her. She could feel nothing. It occurred to her that she had felt nothing after the entry. She had been too numbed, her brain too dull with shock after shock, too unable to contemplate what was actually happening about her . . . and she was obsessed with a sense of utter failure. Madame de Mortmain, who had been going to defend her chateau to the last, or at least die in the breach.

She stared past Henry at Jean François, standing above the bed, huge and bloodstained. Some of that blood would be Philippe's. And smiling at her, mouth a wide cavern of dark desire.

'There she is,' he said. 'Man, Henry, if you knew how I been looking for this one.'

Richilde realised that her ams had folded themselves over Henry's back, holding him tightly, crushing him against her. He was her shield. Her only possible shield.

But now he was pushing himself up, rolling away from her to sit beside her. Jean François dropped his pants. 'I knew you would be having her,' he said. 'But she is sweetness, eh?' he knelt above her, reached for her sweat wet hair, while she shivered, desperate to bring up her knees and curl herself into a ball, too afraid to move.

'No,' Henry said.

Jean François turned his head, looked at the machete. 'You gone mad, boy, or what?'

'She is mine,' Henry said. 'She has always been mine. You know that, Jean.'

Jean François laughed, and seemed to pick up one of Richilde's breasts, pulling her from the bed. 'I know you did always dream of she,' he said. 'But I did dream too. you know I ain't never think she had bubbies like this? How we going get this thing off?' He thrust his fingers into the top of the corset and attempted, futilely, to peal it down. Richilde's head flopped backwards and she stared at the ceiling. Let him lose his temper and kill me, she prayed. Oh, let him.

'She is mine,' Henry said again, standing above his friend. 'I led the assault. Without me, you wouldn't be here now. She is my reward.'

Jean François let her go; she hit the bed with a thump. He turned to face the younger man. 'You want a reward? I am the general. We agreed so.'

'Boukman is the general,' Henry said.

They stared at each other, and Richilde held her breath, unable to decide what she really wanted to happen . . . and had her nostrils suddenly assailed by the acrid smell of burning wood.

'Fire,' came the yell from outside.

'Fire!' It was taken up from down the stairs.

'We are at the top,' Jean François ran for the door.

'Henry,' Richilde gasped, unsure whether she was asking to be saved, at least temporarily, or whether she was asking him to leave her to die.

He picked her up as if she had been a toy, hesitated for a moment, and then plucked the sheet also from the bed and wrapped her in it, ran through the door. Dimly she could see that they were passing through her bedroom, a place of blood and scattered bodies, then they were running down the stairs, to pause at the head of the great gallery, watching the flames sweeping up the grand staircase, sending billowing clouds of smoke in front of them.

Henry hesitated; he had never been inside the chateau before.

'Down there,' she gasped.

He ran in the direction she had indicated, while she hated herself for having spoken. They would have died instantly if they had waited a moment longer, and inhaled the smoke. But now they were hurrying towards the back of the house, and survival. Brushing shoulders with other Negroes now, all fleeing the holocaust they had ignited, bursting into the morning. She had forgotten it was broad daylight. She twisted her head as they ran towards the stables, looked back at the chateau, at the flames billowing from the upstairs windows, listened to them crackling and to the boom of collapsing timbers. It would be destroyed, together with its ghastly secrets.

The black people stared too, unable to believe that such a symbol of white supremacy was crumbling into dust before their eyes. Why, Richilde thought, that smoke, reaching higher than the factory smoke had ever done during grinding, must be visible in Cap François itself.

Conch shells were wailing, and her heart constricted as she saw the leaping figure of Boukman, red robe flapping, coming down the drive, waving his stick. 'You all stand here,' he shouted. 'You think it is done? It ain't yet begun. We have to fight the soldiers. We have to beat the soldiers. We have to march on Cap François . . . It ain't done until Cap François burning just like that. Follow me. To Cap François.'

She looked up at Henry. And he looked down at her. It was the first time he had looked at her since the rape.

'I must go,' he said.

She waited, afraid to think, and he licked his lips. 'Nobody ain't looking at you now,' he said. 'Crawl into them bushes, and wait, until they is all gone. It ain't going be long. Then . . .' he faltered, drew a long breath. 'There got to be somewhere you can go, Richilde. Somewhere.'

He set her on the ground, rolled her into the bushes. Still wrapped in her sheet, she looked like a corpse, she supposed. Then he turned his back on her, and strode off behind the black army.

228

Chapter 3

THE TERROR

The mulattos hesitated but an instant, and then joined the blacks, hoping no doubt to be able to control events. They were mistaken. Boukman himself was taken in one of the early skirmishes with the regular soldiers, and promptly executed, but a new general was found in the Negro Jean François, and as the National Assembly had appeared to favour the planters, the Negro army marched into battle wearing the white cockade of the royalist party.

Richilde was aware of tremendous thirst. But no hunger. She did not suppose she would ever wish to eat again. She realised she was still lying where Henry had left her, behind the wall of the stable, still half wrapped in her sheet, with the whalebone of her corset eating into her thighs and ribs, and bathed in a most tremendous heat, partly from the still burning building, and partly from the sun, which was low in the western sky, and shining full upon her. She supposed it must be about five in the afternoon. Only twenty-four hours ago she had been dressing to attend the Milots' wedding anniversary party, afraid, rightly, that the conversation might be too disgusting to stomach. The conversation!

The chateau still glowed. The upper storey had by now completely fallen in, but the lower floor had accepted the blazing timbers early, while every so often a wine barrel in the cellars flared up, to send flames leaping up the stairwells, following the undispersed immense smoke cloud which hung above the plantation.

She had to have water, and she remembered that there was a pump behind the stable. Once she had drunk, she would be able to decide what to do. Henry had said there must be somewhere she could go. But the only place she could think of was Cap François, and presumably the blacks lay between her and the city.

And anyway, how could she, Richilde de Mortmain, consider walking to Cap François – much less walking there when wearing only a sheet and a corset?

But first, water. It was very necessary to plan, to proceed step by step, and not to think about last night, about any member of her family, about Philippe. Or about herself.

She dragged herself to her feet, let the sheet fall. It did not seem particularly relevant. She walked around the building – the horses had all been released and it was empty. She worked the pump, allowed the stream of water to flood over her hair and shoulders while she lapped at it like a dog, and seemed to freeze as she heard voices.

'Eh-eh,' Amelia said. 'But look at she.'

Richilde turned, slowly, gazed at the women. There were perhaps a dozen of them, and behind them there were others again. And children, and dogs. The inhabitants of the slave compound, come up the hill to gaze at what was left of the chateau.

'Amelia,' she gasped. 'Oh, thank God, Amelia.'

'Man, mistress,' one of the other women said. 'You ain't know your tail is bare?'

'Mistress?' Amelia gave a shriek of laughter. 'She ain't no mistress no more. She is a slave, now. We are the mistress.'

Richilde knew her lips were trembling; they had always been friends. Such intimates, in their shared experiences. 'Amelia,' she said.

'You call me mistress, girl,' Amelia said. 'Mistress. And you ain't looking at me when you speak.'

'Why should you hate me?' Richilde asked. 'I have always been kind to you.'

'She ain't calling you mistress,' one of the women pointed

out.

Amelia thrust her forefinger at Richilde. 'You,' she said. 'I sentencing you.'

'Let we cut off her bubbies,' said another of the women. 'Like we did with that red hair one. I ain't never hear screeching like that. And she fighting so. That was sport.'

Richilde's stomach did a complete roll, and her knees gave way. To her horror she discovered herself kneeling before them.

'We going do that later,' Amelia decided. 'But first we going play with she a little. I sentencing you,' she said again. 'To twenty-five lashes. Take she down to the triangle.'

They gave a shriek of delighted approbation, and surged forward. Richilde turned on her knees, reached her feet in an endeavour to flee, and had her arms gripped. She tried to fight them, and was kicked and punched, her hair seized to pull her head backwards until she thought her neck would break and her eyes start from her head. Now quite a crowd had gathered, everyone seeking to grasp some part of her body, and she was being thrust forward, facing Amelia, who was walking backwards, laughing at her, and snapping her fingers in her face. Then she tripped over a dead body, realised with a gasp of horror that it had been a white man. She half fell, was pulled back to her feet, and again forced on her way. Her head sagged, and she stopped fighting, understanding something of the terrifying horror that Philippe must have known this morning. But would her fate be any different? Only in degree.

Her bare toes were paining and bleeding from being dragged over the stones. Her flesh was burning from exposure to the sun and aching with the many fingers tearing at it. She only dimly understood where she was when they halted, and her head was jerked back, so that she could look up at the triangle above her head. Oh, Christ, she thought. But she could not possibly survive twenty-five lashes. She did not think she could survive one.

A rope was looped round her wrists, suspended from the apex of the triangle, and she was pulled upright, while the crowd of women and children leapt and laughed about her, poking her body with sticks to see it writhe, tugging her hair. Then other ropes were brought out from the uprights, and secured to her ankles and drawn tight, until she was held fast, her feet a few inches from the ground, all her weight being taken on her already agonisingly painful wrists, trussed as she had seen many a black man, or woman, trussed in her time, with never more than a faint awareness of revulsion.

Fingers were dragging at the cords for her corset, and a moment later it fell from her body. That at least was some relief. But only momentarily.

She found herself staring at Oliver the dispenser. 'Oliver,' she begged. 'Oh, Oliver . . .' because he surely had to be on her side.

'Well, is a fact I ain't never know white woman had legs,' he remarked. 'And hams. And . . .' he put his hand between her thighs, and she could not even squirm. 'You all give her to me,' he said. 'I got for study this.'

'You go study one of them dead ones,' Amelia said. 'They is all the same, old man. This one getting flog.'

'But he can have she after,' said someone else.

'After,' Oliver agreed eagerly. 'Make haste with that whip.'

Richilde opened her mouth to speak to him again, to remind him of the way they had built the dispensary together, had laughed and talked together . . . and felt herself cut in two, from right shoulder to left buttock. For a moment that was all the feeling she possessed, that her legs had no relation to the rest of her body, then the searing agony raced through her system to expel a voice cracking scream from her lungs. Dimly she was aware that she was twisting and attempting to kick even when the ropes would not let her move an inch, that she could not breathe, that she could not see, that her tongue was lolling out of her mouth and in danger of being bitten . . . and that there were twenty-four more such agonising blows to be survived, before her real death could commence.

Just as she thought she would choke, she managed to get some air into her lungs. Her eyes flopped open, even as she endeavoured to tense herself against the next blow . . . and she gazed at Pierre Toussaint.

'Move, nuh,' Amelia shouted. 'Move, old man. You want to get strike by the lash?'

'Toussaint,' Richilde begged. 'Please kill me. *Please*.'

'You all crazy?' Toussaint demanded, and stepped round her.

'You moving?' Amelia shouted.

'I am moving *you*,' he said. 'This is all you have to do?'

They backed away from him, cowed by his utter confidence in his own authority.

'She white,' someone said. 'You ain't seeing that, old man? Boukman say all the white people must die, and must holler while they doing it.'

'Boukman is a madman,' Toussaint said.

'He is a god,' they insisted. 'You ain't see he walking against them white people musket, and nothing hitting he? He is a god.'

'Then I am his prophet,' Toussaint said. 'Them boys will return here soon enough, and they ain't going be happy with what they find. They going want food, and drink, not dead bodies and chopped up women. You had best prepare those things, or *you* will be flogged.'

Richilde heard them muttering, but the sound was fading. She could not believe it. Nor did she want it to happen. A few more blows of the whip and she would have died. She knew this. Toussaint could only wish her in order to inflict some other terrible torment on her. His skin was black.

'You help me,' Toussaint commanded.

She felt hands on her legs, and tensed her muscles for some fresh outrage, but the hands were only releasing her ankles.

'She is one good-looking woman,' Oliver said. 'You know I never realise that before, Toussaint, what with all them clothes and thing? When you done with she, I can have she?'

'Hold her,' Toussaint commanded, and she felt Oliver's

arms go around her waist. Her back was against him, and she moaned in agony, and then cried out as a moment later Toussaint cut the bonds suspending her wrists and she slid down the dispenser's body.

'I said, hold her,' Toussaint snapped, and pulled her away from Oliver, lowering his left shoulder to catch her as Henry had done. She was surprised by his strength, even as she lost her breath. Her head flopped against his back, and she realised she was being carried into the slave compound. There were people all around her, talking and laughing, one or two grabbing at her trailing hair, but she could not hear what they were saying because of the drumming in her ears.

Then she entered gloom, realised she was inside the dispensary. Her dispensary. And being laid on straw on the floor, very carefully, on her face. But it could only be because he wanted her body.

'I got salt,' Oliver said.

'You mad, or what?' Toussaint asked. 'This is a white woman. Salt would kill her. I will use ointment.'

A finger touched her cut, and her head jerked in agony.

'Easy, madame, easy,' Toussaint said. And she realised the pain was starting to fade. 'There is only one cut,' he said. 'It will soon heal. In six months time you will not even have a scar.'

Six months time? How could anyone consider so long a period of time, without going mad? But incredibly, she felt her muscles starting to relax beneath his gentle massaging. Yet was it not equally incredible that she, Richilde de Mortmain, mistress of Vergée d'Or, should be lying on a wooden floor, beneath a black man, and not fighting or screaming, or wishing to die? Because that urge, too, was fading with her fear.

'She will be thirsty,' Toussaint said. 'Fetch some water, old man.'

The fingers were gone. She raised herself on her elbow, and Oliver held a cup of water to her lips. It was lukewarm, but tasted like nectar.

'How long them boys gone?' Toussaint asked, slipping

naturally into the careless grammar of the slaves.

'Nine, ten hours,' Oliver said.

'To fight the soldiers,' Toussaint said, contemptuously. 'They will soon be back.'

'They going burn Cap François,' Oliver said. 'That is what Boukman tell them they must do.'

'Burn Cap Francois?' Toussaint's contempt grew.

'They done burn here,' Oliver reminded him. 'And they burn Rio Negro. At least, they saying so.'

Toussaint nodded. 'I was there. Tell me how they took this place.'

Oliver shrugged. 'They rush it, Toussaint. That crazy boy, Henry, he just rush it.'

'Henry Christopher,' Toussaint said, thoughtfully, and looked at Richilde. 'You couldn't stop them, madame? There must have been more than a hundred men at your command. With muskets.'

She inhaled. 'I did not know how to command them. They were afraid.'

Toussaint studied her for several seconds. Then he nodded. 'And now they think they can just rush an army, a walled town, and still win. As I say, they will soon be back. Maybe with the soldiers behind them. He smiled at her. 'You will be rescued, madame. If we can keep you alive that long.'

'You . . . you wish to help me? Don't you want to beat the soldiers?'

'I have to want that, madame. But this is a business for men, and guns, and swords. It is not a business for torturing and killing women. Especially you, madame. Of all white women, my people should least wish to kill you. They will understand that, soon enough.'

She did not understand. Despite their conversations together, despite her belief that he was basically a good and honest man . . . 'You were at Rio Negro,' she said.

He nodded. 'They followed Boukman there, as here. And men, who are roused as he can rouse them, are capable of any atrocity. White men can be roused too, madame. You saw them once, in Cap François. It must be my job to remind my people that they *are* men, and not animals.' Again the smile, but this time it was sad. 'If Boukman will ever let them stay still long enough for my lame leg to catch up with them. But Henry ... he was splendid, eh? Are you not proud of him, madame, even if he is now an enemy?'

She frowned. Proud of Henry? But it had been a proud thing. 'He ...' she bit her lip.

Toussaint nodded his understanding of what she could not put into words. 'He is a man. And he loves you, madame. He has often said so. Had he *not* taken you, there would have been the unnatural act. And you are a beautiful woman.'

Henry, loving her? But she had always known that. And now Toussaint ... she looked down at herself, and then at the little old man.

This time Toussaint laughed. 'Me? I have not just fought a battle, madame. Nor do I think I would wish to, even if I had. I have a wife, madame, and children. I am content.'

She wanted to scratch her head, to try to arrange her thoughts, which were suddenly so calm, where only a few minutes ago they had been tortured emissions of emotion. And then she heard a scream, and her head jerked. The terror was beginning all over again, somewhere close.

'Oh, please,' the voice wailed. 'Please don't hurt me. *Please*.'

'Annette,' she gasped. 'Oh, Annette.'

Toussaint got up, and ran outside. 'What you doing?' It was amazing how his voice could change from a gentle monotone into a brittle rasp.

'You ain't wanting this one as well?' a woman demanded. 'Man, you too old. You can't manage more than one.'

'Please,' Annette begged. 'Oh, please.'

'Give her here,' Toussaint commanded.

'Man, you spoiling all our sweetness.'

'Go play with the dead,' Toussaint said, and a moment later emerged into the dispensary, Annette half draped across his arm. Like herself, Richilde realised, Annette was naked, and smeared in dust, her golden hair plastered to her shoulders, her eyes dull with horror.

'Richilde,' she whispered. 'Oh, Richilde.'

Richilde took her in her arms, winced when one of Annette's hands flopped over her shoulder to touch her weal.

Toussaint held a cup of water, but the French girl shrank away from him.

'He wishes to help us,' Richilde said. 'Drink.'

Annette gulped, greedily. 'They will kill us,' she said. 'I know they will. They will cut us, like they did Claudette.'

Richilde stroked her hair. She felt like a grandmother, although Annette was a year the elder. 'How did you escape the house?' she asked.

'They held me down,' Annette said. 'Twelve of them, one after the other. They held me down, and . . .'

'They are gone now,' Richilde said, staring at Toussaint with tragic eyes. 'Tell me how you escaped.'

Annette sucked air into her lungs noisily. 'I got down the private stairs, when they ran out because of the fire. Claudette came with me, and Felicité. They had . . . they had assaulted them too. Even Felicité. A child of nine. But they came with me. Only at the bottom, there were more of them, waiting for us. They dragged us into the bushes. They cut off Felicité's head. Her head,' she screamed.

Richilde held her closer.

'Let her speak of it,' Toussaint said. 'It will be better.'

'And then they took Claudette,' Annette said. 'And they cut off her breasts. Before her own eyes, they cut off . . . she screamed . . . oh, God, how she screamed.' She began to weep.

'That is best,' Toussaint said.

'But you got away,' Richilde said, stroking her hair.

'They forgot about me,' Annette whispered. 'I crawled into the bushes and lay down. But then they found me again, just now. They were going to feed me through the rollers. They took me to the factory, to show me Philippe. Oh, God, they showed me Philippe.'

Richilde gazed at Toussaint. 'Can you defend them?' she

asked. 'Can you possibly defend them?'

His eyes were solemn. 'Look at the history of your own people, madame,' he said. 'Not just here in the Antilles. Everywhere. And then you defend *them*.'

They stared at each other, and turned their heads together, to look at the doorway, and listen to the noise. The Negro army was returning.

'Oh, God,' Annette whimpered. 'They'll kill us. I know they will. They'll kill us, Richilde. They'll cut us up, as they did Claudette.'

Richilde hugged her close, and gazed at Toussaint. And then at the doorway, and Jean François.

A weary Jean François, droping with exhaustion. And more than that. A dispirited and wounded Jean François – blood trickled down his right arm.

'You were beaten,' Toussaint said.

'We didn't take the town,' Jean François said, and sat against the wall. 'You going treat this arm?'

Toussaint snapped his fingers at Oliver. 'Bring water.' He knelt beside the big man. 'You reached the town?' he asked. 'So what happen to the soldiers?'

Jean François shrugged his massive shoulders. 'They were in the town. They waited for us, in the town.'

'In the town?' Richilde cried, without meaning to. 'They weren't coming?'

Jean François turned his head, to grin at her. 'They weren't coming,' he said. 'They more afraid of we than we of them. Ow, man, what you doing?'

Toussaint removed a sliver of lead, cleaned the gash. 'You won't die,' he said, perhaps regretfully. 'So you just walked up to the walls and charged them.'

Oliver had brought water, and Jean François drank deeply. 'What else we going do?' he asked.

'You could think,' Toussaint suggested. 'You got brains? Boukman got brains?

Another grin . . . 'Not any more.'

'He is dead?'

'They took he. He fell, and they dragged him in through

238

the gate. He must be dead by now.'

'So they stopped believing he is immortal,' Toussaint said. 'And you ran away.' He applied some of his ointment to the wound to stop the bleeding.

Jean François scowled at him. 'We come home, to rest, and eat. And get some sweetness.' He rose to his knees. 'That one.'

Toussaint stood in front of him. 'Who told them to come home?'

Jean François got up. He towered above the little man. 'Me,' he shouted. 'Me, nuh? I is the general. Everyone does know that. Boukman was the *hougan*. I is the general. I saying, go home, and rest, and eat, and sleep. We can go back tomorrow. We can't fight in the dark.'

'You think the white men sleeping?' Toussaint asked.

Jean François' scowl deepened.

'You are the general,' Toussaint said. 'And you have been beaten. You watch, by tomorrow morning you ain't even going have an army. Them boys ain't going stop around here until the white soldiers come. And what of them other boys? You knowing anything about them? All the other plantations? You knowing what is happening there?'

'How I going know that?' Jean François demanded. 'I got eyes can see a hundred miles? And how I going keep them boys here, if they wanting to leave?'

'You are the general,' Toussaint said. 'Then be like a general. Send messengers. Send men to all the plantations, and where those boys have got free. Put your men on horseback, and tell them ride hard, to tell all the black people to concentrate, here on Vergée d'Or.'

'Concentrate?'

Toussaint sighed. 'Gather. Here. Tell them you will organise them into an army, and lead them against the white men. And then you must tell your own people the same thing. Tell them tomorrow you will attack Cap François again.'

Jean François shook his head. 'We can't take Cap François,' he said.

'You will take it,' Toussaint said. 'Or you will chase the white people out, which is the same thing. But you must *make* these things happen. You must lead, if you are the general.'

Jean François grinned. 'You right. I am the general. I going lead. After I have had that woman, and after I have slept.'

Toussaint shook his head. 'Generals have no time for women, or for sleep. You must lead now, while your people resting. Or you ain't never going to lead at all.'

Jean François chewed his lip, gazed at Richilde, and then stepped outside. Toussaint also gazed at Richilde, and she almost thought he winked. Then he followed his general.

'He going come back,' Oliver said. 'But I going have you first.'

'You and who else, old man?' Henry Christopher asked.

Richilde's heart leapt. She had been afraid to ask after him, had expected him to have been killed, like Boukman. Because he would have led the charge. But now he filled the doorway, as he had filled her bedroom doorway this morning, tall, and strong – and unharmed.

'Outside,' he ordered Oliver, and knelt beside them.

'He's going to kill us,' Annette whispered, nails biting into Richilde's shoulders.

'I told you to get away,' Henry said.

'I was captured by the women.'

He frowned at her, moved Annette, gently, looked at her back. 'Who did this? Which one?'

'It does not matter,' she said. 'Toussaint took care of me. Henry . . .'

'You heard Jean François,' he said. 'We got beat.'

'But you will go on fighting?'

'We have to do that, now,' he said. 'Or the white people will kill us all. You hungry?'

She shook her head. 'Henry, could I have some water, to wash?'

He frowned at her. 'You think you can wash me away?'

'I didn't mean that.'

His shoulders slumped. 'You should. You can bathe in the sea.'

'Could I?' she scrambled to her feet. 'Annette . . .'

'They'll kill us,' Annette said. 'If we go out there they'll cut us up, like they cut Claudette.'

'Leave her,' Henry said. 'Toussaint will care for her. Come with me.'

She hesitated, looked down at herself. Henry smiled at her. 'I like you better this way. Always, you wore too many clothes.'

She got up, followed him from the back door of the dispensary, and into the trees; although it was nearly dark he would not risk taking her through the village. This must be a dream, she thought. The strangest nightmare I have ever known, that I should be walking naked through a wood behind a black man, who held me on a bed and raped me, scarcely twelve hours ago.

But this was Henry Christopher, her twin. And he had saved her life. When everyone else was dead. Everyone else in her entire family . . . save only for Annette, and Kit. And Etienne, who had run away.

'Henry?' she asked. 'Is it true that all the plantations have risen?'

'We believe so,' he said.

'But . . . how?'

'Boukman knew. Boukman fixed the day. Boukman has spoken of the day for a long time. When the prophecy was true.'

'The prophecy,' she said. 'Was I part of the prophecy, Henry?'

He checked, looked down at her. 'I believe so,' he said.

'And now Boukman is dead. Did he prophecy his own death?'

'No,' Henry said. 'But I think he knew he would die. Richilde . . . you know I had to do it. If it hadn't been me, it would have been somebody else. More than one, maybe. And after . . . they would have killed you.'

Now it was her turn to walk away from him. 'Yes,' she

said.

'But I would have done it anyway,' he said. 'I wanted to mount you, for too long.'

'Yes,' she said, staring at the beach and the Atlantic rollers, just coming into sight beyond the trees.

'You hate me bad?'

She ran away from him, toes digging into the sand, stumbling through the shallows, throwing herself into the first of the rollers, feeling herself being smothered in the waves, feeling the water fill every nook and cranny of her body, every crevice. She had not done this since her marriage. That was too long ago.

She regained the surface, stood up to her neck, shaking water from her hair, watched him standing on the edge of the beach. 'It cools the blood,' she said.

He hesitated, then waded towards her.

'You ain't saying,' he said.

You have murdered my family, she thought. It was you, because you led the attack, so bravely, and without you the chateau would not have fallen. It was you, Henry Christopher, risen out of the dark mists of slavery and savagery that people like me and my ancestors have inflicted upon you for a hundred years; you who seized the whole rotten edifice and brought it tumbling down, in squealing, terrified agony. It was you that your people saw as Damballah Oueddo, brought to life to lead them . . . where? But as they all recognised, there could be no going back now.

'No,' she said. 'I can't hate you bad, Henry. You are my twin.'

When she awoke, it was broad daylight, and more, noon; the sun seemed to hang immediately above her head. And she was hungry, and so thirsty . . . but while she had been sleeping Henry had returned to the plantation, and had brought food, and water – and even a gown for her to wear. It was a slave gown, and had no doubt belonged to a black woman. But it was his gift to her.

And she was rested. And different. For the first time she realised that she no longer wore any of her rings. She could not remember them being torn from her fingers, but it must have been one of the women. Amelia? Yet she felt no resentment. The rings had been symbols of what had been, but what she had always felt to be a sham. Now she lived in a real world. And in the strangest of fashions, all the horrors had receded, and only lurked at the back of her mind. It was the present which mattered. And the future.

'Annette?' she asked.

'She is all right,' Henry said. 'Toussaint is caring for her.' He smiled. 'He is keeping Jean François too busy.'

She went down to the sea, to bathe, came slowly back up the beach towards him; he sat with his back against a coconut tree to watch her. She had never felt like this before. Always, when she had approached Philippe, it had been with apprehension, uncertainty, an awareness that there was no telling his mood, or his manhood. That she was taking part in a lottery, which she *must* win, every time. There had been no time for her to feel pleasure herself, or even remotely relaxed. Her life had been a constant chase, from one aspect of Philippe to the next. A constant worry, about the next time.

She did not think Henry had changed, in any way, from the boy who had played at soldiers with her beyond the orchard at Marigot. Even the hero who had led the charge so recklessly was the same Henry.

She sat beside him, water dripping from her hair. 'What is going to happen?'

His face was sombre. 'We got ten, twelve thousand people in Vergée d'Or,' he said. 'They coming all the time. There can't be a black man in St Domingue not fighting with us, or wanting to fight with us.'

'But you are not sure you can win,' she said.

'Those white men have discipline,' he said. 'And plans. I have seen the white men fight. I saw them in America. And they have uniforms,' he added, darkly.

'And you know you will not beat them by merely

charging,' Richilde said.

'Maybe not. But Jean François don't know any other way. And he is the general.'

'He has not sufficient intelligence to be your general,' she said. 'Why do you not make Toussaint your general?'

He frowned at her. 'Toussaint? He is old, and he has a short leg.'

'Does that matter? Do you suppose Frederick the Great personally led his men into battle? Or that he was the biggest and strongest of them? If that were the criterion, *you* should be the general, Henry. But a general must direct. He must work out strategy, and tactics. Make those plans of which you spoke. Toussaint can do those things.'

His frown deepened. 'You wish us to win?'

She sighed, and lay down. 'I do not wish you to be killed. Leading mad charges.'

'Well . . .' he smiled. 'Maybe two are enough. But the white men have ships, too. They can bring more men. We have no ships. I do not know that we can beat them. But I don't think they can beat us, either.'

'So you will just fight, and fight, for the rest of your lives? Is that what you want to do, Henry? Do you suppose Frederick just fought, and fought? He also built cities, and fine palaces, cared for his people, made them work to achieve prosperity, entertained writers and poets, and thinkers. That is what life is all about, Henry. Not just fighting and killing.'

'You must have peace for that,' Henry said.

She shook her head. 'He did it while almost continually at war. You must remember that those are the things you are fighting for, even in the midst of battle. If you could do that, the white men might be willing to treat with you as equals.'

'After what happened here?' He sighed, and lay down beside her, and suddenly laughed. 'You just want to see Vergée d'Or rebuilt.'

'It is my home,' she agreed. 'But it will never be a chateau again.'

'Not even if I build it for you?' He saw the expression on

her face, and looked away. 'Yeah,' he said. 'Now ain't the time for dreaming. I have to get you out of here,' he said. 'As soon as it is dark. It is a long walk to Cap François, but you cannot stay here.'

'I cannot leave Annette, either,' she said.

'I know that. We will fetch her too.'

She raised herself on her elbow. 'Henry, those things that happened at the house . . . did you wish them to happen?'

His eyes opened. 'I don't know, and that is a fact. But I wanted you.'

'And now you want to send me away,' she said.

His fingers sliding up and down her back, hurt her wound. But she refused to cry out, because to cry out might make him feel she did not wish what was happening. She had never lain on a man before – Philippe had never been able to sustain that kind of an erection. But it was magnificent, because she was able to control her movements to her own satisfaction. The wildest of thoughts tore through her mind as her passion grew, and for the first time in her life too she had some inkling of the power of lust, of the grip of the sexual passion which would drive a man into a frenzy. Or a woman.

But it was not the first time, she remembered, as she lay on his chest, and gasped. She had known it the night she had first seen Boukman. And had repressed it, because she was a white lady, and the mistress of Vergée d'or. How long ago that seemed.

'Nobody must know,' he said, stroking her hair.

'Annette will know.'

'That I have taken you,' he smiled. 'Not that you have taken me. None of your people would understand that. Now come.'

She put on the slave gown. He wanted her to go into Cap François, where she would be an object of universal pity, and universal curiosity, too. And where she would be alone, even when in Annette's company, because no one would ever understand what she had truly experienced. And from where she would never see him again, unless he was brought in to be hanged, or broken on the wheel.

'Henry,' she said. 'if you came with us, escorted us into Cap François, you would be a hero to the white people as well.'

He gazed at her.

'I would see to that,' she promised.

'I am returning you to your people,' he said. 'How can you ask me to leave mine?'

'Then let me leave mine,' she said. 'Why cannot I stay with you?'

'Because this is going to be a terrible war,' he said. 'And my people will do many terrible things, and if you stay, you will become a savage, like me.'

She followed him into the trees, back towards the plantation, a humming glow of a plantation, where there were a thousand camp fires, as the slaves who had been gathering from every part of the colony cooked their meals and sharpened their swords – and who the white soldiers in Cap François were apparently afraid to attack, or even reconnoitre.

They met a group of black men, marching through the trees. 'We seek Boukman,' their leader said. He was a squat heavy shouldered man, not tall, but suggesting the immense strength of a rampant bull.

'Boukman is dead,' Henry said. 'Now you seek Jean François. What is your name?'

'Jean Jacques . . .' the big man hesitated, then shrugged. 'Dessalines.'

'Why not?' Henry asked. 'And Dessalines?'

The big man grinned. 'We sawed Dessalines in half.'

Henry pointed. 'You will find Jean François through there.'

The black men hurried off; they had ignored Richilde – in the gloom she was just another woman. She clutched Henry's arm. 'I remember him. He was landed from the slave ship on that day last year . . .' she bit her lip.

'The day I was flogged,' Henry said.

'What would you have done, had you taken Etienne, when

246

the chateau fell?'

Henry turned away from her. 'I would have killed him slowly, Richilde. That is why you must leave here.'

More people. Amazingly, these were horsemen, perhaps a hundred of them, well dressed, and armed with swords and pistols. White people? She stared into the darkness. But their skins were brown.

'We seek Jean François,' their leader said, drawing rein. 'We have heard he commands, since Boukman's death.'

'You will find him at the plantation,' Henry said. 'But what do you seek with us, monsieur?'

'A common cause, my friend,' the man said. He was in his middle thirties, Richilde estimated, wore a little moustache. At his side rode a young man, hardly more than a boy, handsome in an excited fashion. 'I am André Rigaud.' The man indicated the boy. 'This is my lieutenant, Alexandre Petion. We have many men, who wish to fight the white people. With you.'

'Who comes?'

Richilde looked up at the walls of the city, the gate rising above the roadway. She had not noticed them before. They had walked through the night, and now it was all but dawn. Her feet were swollen. Agonisingly painful.

'Annette,' she said. 'We have reached Cap François.'

Annette fell to her knees. She had fallen several times during the night, and always Richilde had helped her to her feet. This time she let her stay, kneeling.

'It is two women,' the sergeant of the guard said, and she watched the gate slowly swinging open.

'Two white women, by God,' the officer said, hurrying forward. And stopping when within a few feet of Richilde. 'Madame de *Mortmain*? My God.' He peered at Annette. 'Mademoiselle?'

Richilde started to cry, and she had not actually wept throughout the entire holocaust. But as Henry had said, these were her people. She was finished with murder and revenge, surely. She could close her eyes, and know that she would awaken, safe and warm ... She was surrounded by people, men as well as women, half carrying her. There were carriages, and there were stairs, and there was a bedchamber. Then there were only women, undressing her and sponging her, whispering to themselves, exclaiming at the great weal across her back, at the sun reddened skin and the bruised toes, muttering, smothering her in eau de cologne ... and then most of the women were gone, and there was Dr Laval, apologising as he peered at her, and clucking his tongue.

There were glasses of cooling sangaree, and broth for her to drink. She had never felt so exhausted in her life. She wanted only to sleep, and hopefully not to dream, for weeks on end. But first of all there were questions to be answered.

Etienne stood by her bed. 'Richilde,' he said. 'My God, Richilde. But what *happened*?'

'You did not come back,' she said, hating him as she had never hated anyone in her life before. 'You did not come back.'

He licked his lips, looked across the bed at the Governor-General. 'There were less than a thousand soldiers fit for duty in Cap François,' he said. 'Monsieur Peynier decided his first duty was to defend the city. I cannot blame him for that decision. No one can.'

'You did not come back,' she whispered. 'You left us, to die.'

'I ... what good could I have done? By myself?'

She raised herself on her elbow. 'You could have *died*,' she shouted. 'Like Philippe. You could have died with your wife and children. You could have died like a *man*.'

'Madame, madame,' Dr Laval gently eased her back on to the pillows. 'You must not excite yourself.'

She sighed, and closed her eyes. She did not wish to have to look at her cousin.

'Richilde,' Peynier said, his voice close as he leaned across her. 'It was my decision. It was a painful one, believe me. The most painful decision I have ever had to make in my life. But I have several thousand French people here. Can you imagine what would have happened to them had my soldiers been defeated by the blacks in the open? Or even had been outmanoeuvred? My task must be to end this revolt as quickly as possible.'

She opened her eyes. 'You intend to do that by sitting behind a wall, monsieur?'

'I will do that by accumulating sufficient men to defeat the blacks in battle,' he said. 'I have already sent for reinforcements. And I will do that by learning of their dispositions. I must ask you, madame. Will you answer me?'

He was a stranger to her. As Etienne was a hateful stranger to her. Had Henry allowed her, she would have stayed with him. When he had refused to let her stay, as she had known he would and must, because it was the only sensible decision he could make, for her, she had determined to abide by it, to remember that the white people were her folk, and that she had no substance away from them. She had come here in that mood, to find strangers.

And yet she must help them, as much as she could, to destroy Henry, and all he stood for. Because they were her folk? Or because she knew that, for all his admirable qualities, he stood for nothing, save destruction, and savage grandeur?

She sighed. 'There are upwards of twelve thousand blacks encamped on Vergée d'Or, monsieur. And more are joining them all the time. And they have also been joined by some mulattos. Led by a man called Rigaud.'

'The devil,' Peynier said. 'He is the one we failed to catch after Ogé's revolt. He has some military experience. But what of the mood of the blacks? I believe we may have taken their holy man.'

'Yes,' Richilde said. 'Boukman. What have you done with him?'

'We have hanged him,' Etienne said. 'High above the battlements. He will stay there until he rots. Or until the revolt is over.'

Richilde turned her head away from him.

Peynier sighed. 'Have the blacks another such as he?

Who will lead them now?'

'A man called Jean François.'

'Jean François?' Etienne cried. 'But . . .'

'Yes,' Richilde said. 'He was Philippe's coachman.'

'Would he be the one who led the assault on the city?' Peynier asked. 'A very big man? But young.'

'No,' she said, 'that was my other coachman, Henry Christopher.'

'Henry,' Etienne said. 'By God, Henry. I should have hanged him long ago. When I get my hands on him . . .'

'You had better pray, cousin,' she said. 'That he does not get his hands on *you*.'

Peynier frowned at her. 'You have spoken with this man?'

'How else do you suppose I am here, monsieur?'

'But . . . will you tell us what happened? Exactly?'

'There is nothing to tell,' she shouted. 'They overran the chateau, just as they overran Rio Negro, or Monsieur Dessalines' plantation, or any of the other plantations. They tortured and they killed and they burned the place down. They fed my husband through his own cane mill. They destroyed us. They . . . they avenged their wrongs.'

'And then they let you go?' He was incredulous. 'And Mademoiselle Annette?'

She gazed at him. 'Yes, monsieur. We happened to survive the fire, and then passions died. And so they let us go.' She turned her gaze on Etienne. 'Henry let us go.'

'Unharmed,' Peynier said, and scratched his head, displacing his wig. 'There was a miracle.'

'Unharmed, monsieur?' she asked. 'Unharmed. Why do you not ask Annette if she is unharmed? She was raped by twelve men, one after the other. Ask her, if she is unharmed.'

Peynier flushed. 'And . . .'

'Oh, yes, monsieur,' she said. 'Me too.' For is that not what you really wanted to discover, she thought?

'Kit!' Etienne de Mortmain was on the dock to greet his cousin as he stepped from the boat, shook hands and then kissed him on each cheek. 'I came as soon as your ship was signalled.'

Kit Hamilton looked left and right at the evidences of siege which clung even to the harbour of Cap François, at the absence of Negroes working on the docks, and at the row of gallows, every one carrying a ghastly dark burden, which lined the sea front. He inhaled the sour stench of untreated sewage, gazed at the unswept streets. Cap François had suddenly become a dirty, frightened place – he could almost smell the fear.

Tall, and wind bronzed, carefully dressed in his blue jacket and wearing a new tricorne, exuding the confidence of the professional seaman, he seemed to dominate the nervous Frenchmen who surrounded him. 'I have heard the wildest rumours,' he said.

Etienne showed him to the waiting gig, which he would drive himself. 'All true, I am afraid. The blacks control the entire country. Save for the towns, of course. The coastal towns, anyway.'

'And no campaign has been launched against them?'

'There are perhaps a hundred thousand Negroes under arms out there,' Etienne explained. 'We await reinforcements from France.'

Kit sat beside him, looked up at the tricolour, drooping on the flagpole. 'Republican France? You, Etienne?'

'It is still France,' he grinned. 'The blacks, poor fools, because we fly that flag, march beneath the fleur de lys. They are convinced the King will intercede on their behalf, after they are defeated. After our reinforcements arrive.'

'Do you really suppose you will obtain any? France does not know what she is.'

'Then we shall have to wait until she finds out. We will hold the city. But to think of all that wealth, all that sugar, trampled by the blacks . . .'

'Yes.' Kit gazed at ι ⸱ houses they were passing, the shuttered windows and d⸱ ⸱s, the closed shops.

Etienne sighed. 'Of course there have been those who have simply packed up and fled.'

'I have spoken with them, in Jamaica,' Kit said. 'It was they who first told me what had happened. Now tell me of Richilde.'

'She is far better than could be expected. As I told you in my letter, she is pregnant. This is in my opinion the saving of her sanity. Annette . . .' he sighed.

'Yes?' Kit's voice was sharp.

'She had not the . . . well, the experience of marriage.' He glanced at Kit. 'You understand me?'

'I should like to see her,' Kit said

Etienne shrugged. 'Of course.'

'What are you going to do?' Kit asked.

'I have told you,' Etienne said. 'When the reinforcements arrive from France . . .'

'I meant you, personally. Where are you going to go? My ship is at your disposal.'

Etienne frowned at him. 'Go? I am not going anywhere, Kit. St Domingue is my home. Vergée d'Or is mine, now that poor Philippe is dead. Well, it is actually Richilde's child's. But she will need me to manage it for her, for very many years. I am not going anywhere.'

'And the girls?'

'This is their home, too. I have written to Madeleine, asking her to come and help me, at least with Annette. But this is their home, too, Kit. To run away would be to abandon Vergée d'Or. We cannot possibly do that.'

The carriage was stopping, and Kit was shown into a house in the very centre of the city. It was not a large house, by the standards of the Mortmains, but it looked comfortable enough. 'Madame Ramile has very kindly offered us accommodation, for the time being,' Etienne said. 'Her husband owns the dry goods store by the harbour. Madame,' he said. 'This is my cousin, Christopher, from America.'

Kit kissed her hand. She wore a distinct moustache.

'And this is Louise.'

The girl, she was only a child, although a pretty one, gave a simpering smile at Etienne patted her bottom. It occurred to Kit that his cousin had managed to recover from the

252

terrible tragedy of his family, and his wife and children, with amazing rapidity.

'You will wish to see your sister, Monsieur Hamilton,' Madame Ramlie said, and led him up the stairs. 'She is as well as we could possibly expect. A strong woman, Madame de Mortmain. A strong woman.'

She knocked on the bedroom door. 'Madame? Your brother is here.'

'Kit? Oh, Kit.' Richilde hurried to the door to greet him. A strange Richilde, both because of the poor quality and cut of her gown, and because the slender, elegant creature he recalled was swollen with her pregnancy. 'Oh, Kit.' She was in his arms. He heard the door close, but realised that Etienne was still in the room. 'Do you suppose we could be alone, 'Tienne?' Richilde asked. Her voice was cold.

'Of course,' Etienne hesitated. 'I will wait for you outside, Kit. And remember, Richilde has suffered a great deal.'

Kit held her away from him, to look at her, while the door closed again.

'He is afraid I will tell you how he ran away and left us all to die,' she said.

'Did he do that?'

'Yes.' She released him, sat down her hands on her lap. 'Have you seen Annette yet?'

He shook his head, sat beside her.

'Poor Annette,' she said. 'She suffered far more than I. I . . .' she glanced at him, her cheeks pink. 'I suffered only Henry.'

'Henry Christopher? The black bastard. And he always swore he would look after you.'

'He saved my life,' she said, softly. 'It was the only way he could do it.'

'And he did not enjoy it,' Kit said bitterly.

'He enjoyed it.' She seemed as if she would have said something more, but changed her mind. 'Will you take me away from here, Kit?'

'Away? Away from St Domingue?'

'Yes,' she said.

'But . . . what of Vergée d'Or? Etienne is sure the blacks are going to be defeated, eventually, and you will be able to regain the plantation.'

'Perhaps he is right. Everyone here thinks like that.' She gave a twisted smile. 'Madame Ramlie permits us to live off her charity, because she is sure it will all be repaid, with interest, in due course. But that is a long time in the future. I wish to leave now. I cannot remain here. Don't you understand, Kit? I cannot have my child in Cap François.'

His brows slowly drew together into a frown. 'You can't be serious? You cannot know.'

'I was married to Philippe for eight years, Kit. Eight years. In which time I never even had a miscarriage, did not miss a single menstruation. How can I not know? But I cannot have Henry's child, here in Cap François. These people hate, and fear. They are rabid with fear.'

'And you do not hate, and fear? You *want* this child?'

She met his gaze. 'Yes,' she said. 'I want this child.'

'They held her down,' Annette said, staring out of the window. 'They held her arms and legs, Kit, and they tore off her clothes, and they cut into her, so slowly. They laughed while they cut, and she screamed, oh, how she screamed.'

Kit gazed over her head at Etienne, who lifted his eyebrows.

He squeezed her hand. 'Annette, would you like to leave here? To go to Madeleine in St Kitts?'

Annette seemed to awake from a deep sleep. 'Leave Cap François? Leave St Domingue? It is my home.'

'Yes, but . . .'

'I cannot leave here, Kit.' She might have been speaking to a rather backward child. 'Don't you understand? I want to see them hang. I want to see every black person in St Domingue, hanging.'

Etienne sighed, as they walked down the stairs together. 'I suppose, in many ways, she is mad. We must hope she will get over it, in time. But you cannot blame her. She saw these terrible things happen, while things almost as terrible were happening to herself. And it is my wife she is talking about. My wife, and my daughter. My God, Kit, I sometimes think I am going mad myself.'

'Yes,' Kit said.

'Richilde condemns me,' Etienne said. 'For not staying, and dying. I did what I thought was best. I swear it to you, Kit. I did not know the Governor-General would decide not to send out the troops. I did what I thought was best.'

'I am sure you did,' Kit said. They walked the empty streets, and he had instinctively led them down the lane towards Monsieur Chavannes' haberdashery. But the shop was empty, its windows broken, the interior gutted. Mulattos were no more popular in Cap François than blacks.

But why had he come down here? Because the continuous tales of rape and mayhem had made him want a woman, and the only woman he knew who might accommodate him was Jacqueline Chavannes? Or because he needed help, desperately, and it was only from her wisdom that he was likely to obtain that help? The second was the more noble motive, however it might not be the most honest one.

'What happened to Jacqueline?'

Etienne shrugged. 'I have no idea. No one knows where most people are, nowadays, unless they are here in Cap François. She is probably dead. Kit, it is your decision, whether Richilde leaves or stays. I feel that her duty is here, as the mistress of Vergée d'Or, to show an example, a determination to remain, and eventually conquer. But if you feel . . .'

Kit walked away from him. Etienne was afraid to let Richilde out of his sight, because her son, or daughter, was his passport to wealth and power – when the blacks were crushed. It did not seem to have occurred to him that there was a possibility the child might not be Philippe's.

Or *had* that occurred to him, and were his thoughts and plans even more tortuous than normal?

And what am I to do, Kit thought? Is Richilde any less demented at this moment than Annette? She too was held down and raped, and by a man she must have trusted. She had managed to convince herself that he had actually been trying to help her. But did that not have to be merely an aspect of her madness? She had seen the same horrible sights as Annette, and heard the same nightmare sounds. So she was far stronger, far more able to subdue her nightmares, to pretend they were not there. But did they not *have* to be there?

Her madness was exemplified by her decision to have this child, even knowing, as she supposed, that it must be Henry's. How could any sane woman possibly contemplate such a step? For the Madame de Mortmain to produce a mulatto child, anywhere in the world, would be to damn her to total social obliteration. To have it here in St Domingue, where the only acceptable emotions were hatred and fear of anyone whose skin was even a sunburned shade darker than your own . . . except that there, in St Domingue, they would know what to do.

What a terrible thought. What a terrible decision to have to make. But how could he made any other? He would never be able to do away with his sister's child. By his own weakness he would be damning her to a lifetime of infamy. Kit Hamilton, he thought bitterly . . . a coward at the end of the day. Certainly a moral one.

Or would it not be true moral courage, to take that decision, knowing that it had to be in Richilde's best interest . . . and knowing too the horror that nothing could be done until after the delivery, just in case by some happy miracle, the child *was* Philippe's.

'Kit?' Etienne stood at her shoulder.

Kit gazed into his cousin's eyes. 'I think you are probably right. 'Tienne,' he said. 'But I make you this charge. Her life, her health, and her sanity, are in your hands. Fail me in that, 'Tienne, and by God I will kill you.'

Is he not come? Look again, Madame Ramlie, I beg of you. He said he would be here.' For all of her bulk, Richilde attempted to push herself up the bed, to look out of the window.

256

'I will certainly check again, madame,' Madame Ramlie said, gazing across the bed at Madeleine Jarrold.

'A sailor, at the mercy of the wind and the sea . . .' Madeleine sighed, and smoothed the sweat damp hair from Richilde's brow. 'He will come, if he can. But you are in good hands, here. Annette, fetch some lemonade for Richilde.'

She exuded calm. She was, Richilde calculated, well past thirty-five, and had seen a lot of life. But not enough. There had never been a slave revolt in St Kitts. However Madeleine must have wept at the news of the murder of her family, it had been no more than news. She had not seen and heard it happen.

Yet her calmness had proved a boon. She had even managed to draw Annette out of the nightmare in which she had lived for so long, had her at least accepting that life must go on. And in her somewhat aloof attitude to the hatred and fear that still, nine months after the revolt, convulsed the white people of Cap François, she had even encouraged Richilde to believe that she might prove a true friend, rather than merely an elder cousin.

Because Kit had failed her. She had suspected that he would, from the beginning, when he had visited her bedroom last November, and said that unfortunately he could not take her with him then, but that he would return for her, before the delivery was expected. It had not made sense, despite his story about a dangerous voyage he had still to undertake. She had wept and she had begged, but he had been adamant. So, he had to be ranked with those who would not and could not understand.

Which included everyone in Cap François, from Etienne and Madame Ramlie, to Monsieur Peynier himself. Coming here had been a terrible mistake. Her heart remained out there in the bush, with Henry Christopher, and through him, with his people. They had murdered, and tortured, and burned, and raped, and they had attempted to flog her. But she now knew, having listened to the unceasing drum roll and the shrill shouts of excited pleasure as each captured

257

Negro, or Negress, was ceremonially executed, that these people, *her* people, were no different. Except that where the Negroes had acted with delirious frenzy, the whites had done so with cold-blooded hatred.

There was not a single redeeming facet to their rule, she now knew. They had seized St Domingue by force, a hundred years before, and they had retained it, by force. They possessed no one with the gentle wisdom of Toussaint, no one with the religious fervour of Boukman, and no one with the heroic stature of Henry Christopher.

She knew she could not stay here. But she knew too that she could never leave St Domingue, and Henry, and Toussaint. And yet the alternative was equally unthinkable. Almost. It was something to be discussed, considered, with a friend. If she could find one. An older, wiser friend, who would understand.

Would Madeleine understand? Richilde had never discussed her true feelings with her cousin. Time enough for that after the baby was born. But Madeleine was divorced from the realities of the situation. Richilde could certainly appreciate why the people of Cap François felt as they did. For nine months now the black armies had held control of the colony, save only for the seaports of Cap François and Port-au-Prince in the south. No help had arrived from France, daily sinking deeper into a revolution of her own, and no one knew for sure what was happening out there in the bush. Certainly the cities were invested, as any reconnoitring parties soon discovered to their cost if they ventured more than a mile from the walls. But the blacks seldom wasted either men or powder any longer in attacking fortified positions. And meanwhile the whole of the richest colony in the entire West Indies was theirs, to plunder to their hearts' content, to turn back into primeval jungle, as it had been when Columbus had first landed here, almost exactly three centuries before.

She wondered what Henry Christopher thought of it all. Or Toussaint. Men who had dreamed, and who knew there was more to life than murder and robbery. But who were dominated by their leaders, like Jean François. How her heart went out to them, and how she wished she could help them. But she could not even help herself, save through the agency of Madeleine. Who was now frowning at her.

'Richilde? Is it time? Your face twisted.'

'I was thinking. I was . . .' but suddenly she *was* aware of cramps in her belly. 'Yes,' she said. 'Oh, my God, yes. Kit.'

'We will take care of you,' Madeleine said. 'Kit will be here for the christening.'

Certainly she was a marvellous midwife – as she should be, Richilde thought, having had five of her own – and with Annette fussing excitedly, and Madame Ramlie returned to help, and an hysterical Louise Ramlie rushing up and down the stairs with water, and Dr Laval coming in to stroke her forehead and approve of what the women were doing . . . the whole event passed off with only a fraction of the pain and discomfort she had anticipated. She was very hot, and Annette bathed her forehead while Madeleine massaged her belly and encouraged her, and suddenly it was over, and a child was wailing its delight at being born.

Richilde closed her eyes, listening only vaguely to the anxious whispers about her. She was exhausted, wanted only to lie there and sleep . . . and then remembered that she dared not sleep. She opened her eyes, stared at Madeleine. 'My child,' she said. 'Let me see my child.'

'My darling Richilde,' Madeleine said, putting both arms round her to kiss her and hug her. '*You* are well. That is all that is important.'

'But my child. I want to hold him.'

'Dear, dear Richilde,' Madeleine said. 'I know you will grieve . . . but God moves in a mysterious way. Your child was born dead.'

Etienne de Mortmain wiped his brow, tugged at his moustache, looked to his sister for support.

'It cannot be considered Etienne's fault,' Madeleine said quietly, staring at Kit. 'No one, no one, Kit, could possibly have supposed Richilde would behave . . . well, she had to have been more demented than we supposed.'

'She had the cunning of a mad woman,' Etienne declared. 'It was uncanny. She did not even weep, when we told her the child had died . . .'

'I do not think she believed me,' Madeleine said. 'I think she had heard it cry, and knew it lived. But Kit . . . I *had* to have it destroyed. You do understand that?'

She spoke, he thought, as if she were talking of a kitten, or a puppy. Not a human being. And yet, it was what he had decreed should happen, by leaving Richilde here in the first place. 'Yes,' he said.

'Then she was even more cunning,' Etienne said. 'She lay there, and said not a word. She lay there, Kit, for three weeks, just waiting, as we now know, for her strength to come back. And then she just got up . . . and left the city.'

'How?' Kit asked. 'That is what I cannot understand.'

'Apparently she let herself out of the house in the middle of the night,' Madeleine said. 'Then she went down to the harbour, took off her clothes, and either waded or swam round to the beach beyond the walls. Then she just walked into the forest.'

'We thought at first she had committed suicide, by drowning,' Etienne said. 'We were beside ourselves with worry, until a patrol found her footprints on the sand where she had come ashore.'

'And then you ceased to worry,' Kit said.

Etienne flushed, and glanced hopefully at his sister.

'You must accept the fact, Kit,' Madeleine said severely, 'that she *is* quite mad. To return to those savages at all . . . but to return to them, naked, just walking through the forest . . . it makes my skin crawl.'

Kit got up, went into the garden. He did not suppose there was any point in being angry. He had failed her, in not taking charge himself. Because he had been afraid of earning her hatred and her loathing. Which was now probably extended to the whole human race. Or at least all of it with white skins.

He could not believe it. And yet, why should he not believe it? He remembered the day of her wedding to Philippe, nine years ago now, when he had suddenly realised that Henry Christopher loved her, as a man should love a woman, and that that was the true reason he would never leave St Domingue. Why, then should he automatically suppose it was impossible for her to love Henry, as a woman should love a man? Because Henry had helped in the destruction of her family? She had never truly considered the Mortmains her family, had always felt an outsider, as had he. Because Henry's skin was black, his standards necessarily so much lower than her own? But whatever crimes he might have committed, could they equal murdering a child merely because its hair had been crinkly? *Destroying* it, as not fit to live.

No, he thought, the real point is that while she might have thought she was returning to Henry Christopher, who was to say she had ever got to him? He was nothing in the Negro army. Just a man. As she was just a woman. A white woman, walking naked through the forest.

'I am sorry, Kit.' Annette stood beside him. 'I am so very sorry. But . . . she seemed to understand them. Even when they were torturing her, she seemed to understand them.'

He frowned at her. Was this some quite unexpected lucidity? Or an utter condemnation?

'If she went back to them,' Annette said. 'If she could do that, of her own free will then there is nothing, nothing at all, that any of us can do about it. At least, not right now.' She sighed, and sat on the garden seat. 'Do you know, I sometimes feel that last August . . . my God, do you realise that it is more than a year ago? . . . the entire world came to an end. That we're just existing, waiting to be sent our allotted ways by God. Do you ever believe that, Kit?'

She was looking up at him. She was twenty-six years of age, and her hair was already streaked with grey. And yet, the touch of false maturity added beauty to the rather pert, youthful features. And she was right, as regards herself. Her world had come to an end. As his was threatening to do.

He acted instinctively, lowered his head, kissed her parted lips. For a moment she hesitated, then her hands closed on his arm, and she drew him down to sit beside her, while she clung to him.

'Kit,' she whispered. 'Oh, Kit. I have been *raped*. By twelve men. Twelve black men.'

'I love you,' he said.

'I have been raped, Kit. And we are first cousins.'

'I love you,' he said again.

'And they call me mad,' she said.

He held her away from him, the better to look at her. 'I love you,' he said a third time. 'We cannot marry, Annette. Not legally. But when I return to Cap François, will you come away with me?'

She frowned at him, through her tears.

'It will mean turning our backs on propriety, even on law,' he said. 'It may mean a quarrel, with Etienne and Madeleine. But it will also mean that we have found something, each other, worthwhile out of all of this hatred and horror. I do not care what has happened to you in the past, Annette. Give me the chance to care for your future.'

'Oh, Kit, my darling Kit. To be yours . . . to forget . . . will you help me to forget, Claudette and Felicité?'

'Yes,' he promised. 'I will help you to forget.'

'And will you help me hang all the black people, when the troops have defeated them?'

Neither her tone nor her expression had changed. Yet that she was deadly serious could not be doubted for a moment. Oh, Christ, he thought, what have you done, Kit Hamilton? But it *had* been done. The invitation had been extended and accepted. So, to set beside a demented sister, he would spend the rest of his life with a demented wife. The alternative would be to watch her sink even deeper into madness.

And promises cost nothing. He had made too many of them before.

'I will stand at your side, always, Annette,' he promised.

'Oh, Kit . . .' she brought him close, and then pushed him

away again. 'When you *return* to Cap François? But ...
where are you going?'

'I must go and find Richilde,' he said. 'When I come back,
from there.'

It was dawn when Richilde left the clinging mud of the
unharvested canefields behind her, and stepped into the
trees. This she had done before. She remembered following
the drums, so long ago. And she remembered walking
through these trees more recently than that. Yet she could
not doubt that this was what she had always been intended
to do, by her own will no less than by Fate.

Her feet and ankles were splashed with mud and dust, and
insects whirred at her body; she brushed them aside with
careless impatience. She did not fear them. She could no
longer afford to fear any inhabitant of this forest, not even
the human ones. And they were here, all around her. She
felt their presence, long before they let her see them.

They were amazed, and uncertain. 'Eh-eh,' someone said.
'But is a white woman.'

'No, man,' said another. 'Is *the* white woman. Is
Christophe's woman.'

They gathered around her, staring at her, leaning on their
swords and muskets. She was not embarrassed. She
remembered none of their faces, but they certainly
remembered her. Thus they had seen her before, exactly as
she now was. Only now she was not afraid of them, either.

'I seek Christophe,' she said.

'You think she is a spy?' someone asked.

'Maybe we should kill her now,' said another.

'Man, she can't be no spy. Not coming naked so. Maybe
she a jumbi.'

'I am neither a ghost nor a spy,' Richilde said. 'I am
Christophe's woman. You know this. I have come to be with
him. To be with you all. Will you not take me to him?'

They scratched their heads and then began to walk, with
her in their midst. She knew where they were going; they
had not changed encampments, by all accounts. But it was at

least reassuring that they maintained an outpost on the edge of the canefields; if Peynier ever found both the men and the courage to launch a counter assault, he would not take them by surprise. Yet the camp came as a surprise; she had not remembered it being so close to the boundaries of Vergée d'Or. And someone had run ahead, because now she could make out, in the bright and hot morning sunlight, the people gathering to receive her, dominated by the towering figures of Jean François and Henry Christopher; beside them Toussaint seemed a midget.

'She mad,' Jean François declared. 'I said that, this one is mad. I said you were a fool, Henry, to send she off so. And now she has come back. She mad. Well, this time . . .'

'Why you don't be quiet,' Henry said to his commander, and stepped forward. Jean François gave a snort of surprise, but stopped speaking.

'Richilde?' Henry asked. 'Mistress Richilde? What do you want with us?'

Richilde drew a long breath. 'I have come home, Henry.'

'You have come from the white people?' Toussaint asked.

'Yes,' Richilde said.

'Why?'

'They killed my child,' she answered, simply, and looked at Henry Christopher. 'Our child. They killed our child.'

Henry's eyes gloomed at her. 'You have had a child? My child?'

'Yes,' Richilde said. 'But he is dead.'

Henry's hands curled into fists.

'White people,' Jean François growled.

'They are no worse than you,' Richilde told him. 'They merely hate. Do you not hate?'

Jean François did not reply. But Toussaint asked her, 'And do you not hate, us, madame?'

'Yes,' she said. 'But I only hate those who would come between me and my man.'

Jean François would have spoken again, but Toussaint touched his arm, and led him back towards the huts. The other people also melted away, leaving only Richilde, facing

Henry.

'You had a child,' he said. 'My child. I did not wish that on you, Mistress Richilde. But I am proud. Even if I wish to avenge his death. Is that what you wish?'

Richilde hesitated, drew a long breath. 'If you mean, did I come here to be avenged, Henry, the answer is no. I came here because I believe that you have a cause, a right to be free, to stand face to face with any white man as an equal. I know *you* are the equal of any white man, Henry. I would have all your people feel the same. But I would also hope to help you.'

'You will tell us how many soldiers Peynier has? What he intends? How many are coming from France?' His voice was eager.

Richilde took his hand. 'I cannot tell you those things, Henry. Because I do not know them. But I do know that they are afraid of you, in Cap François. That you can defeat them, if you are brave, and resourceful, and fight them as your ancestors fought. But I think I can help your people to learn how to use their victory, after they have fought, and won.'

He frowned. 'You mean you would beg for the lives of the white people?'

'Yes,' she said. 'As I am prepared to beg for the lives of the black. But there is more to life than fighting. If you succeed, and I believe you will, you will have to build a nation, here in St Domingue. You and Jean François, and Toussaint. You are the leaders. You must teach your people how to be one, a nation, or they will become nothing more than savages. You must remember Frederick the Great, who built great palaces and cared for his people even while he was fighting nearly all of Europe. You must forge your people into a nation, Henry. For the sake of our dead son, for the sake of all those who have died, all of those who will yet die, that you may be free. You must do this thing.'

He walked beside her, towards the huts. 'Me? Jean François is our general. He tells us what to do. And you know what, Miss Richilde? Toussaint is always saying things like that to Jean François, and it just makes him angry. I think Jean François may kill Toussaint one of these days. Or Toussaint will flee for his life. He and Jean François hate each other. But me . . .'

'You will lead these people, one day, Henry,' Richilde said.

He stopped walking to look at her.

'I know it,' she said. 'I know it in my heart. When Jean François and Toussaint have both been swept away, you will rule St Domingue. Does not the prophecy say this?'

'The prophecy? You believe in that, Mistress Richilde? If you believe in that, then you must believe you are going to stand at my side when the time comes.'

She looked into his eyes. 'Am I not standing here now, Henry?'

Once again the frown of uncertainty.

'I will be standing there, then,' she promised. 'As I am standing here now. But Henry, you must learn to call me Richilde, and not mistress. Because you no longer belong to me; I belong to you.'

She held his hand tightly, as they walked into the village together.

PART THREE

The General

[Toussaint] persuaded his Negroes to go back to work, and in a short space of time had restored a measure of prosperity to the island. This was as well, because the European War came to a [temporary] end sooner than he could have anticipated, and the French government was left in the hands of a revolutionary dictator like himself. At the start of his career as ruler of France, Bonaparte was very much interested in the Western Hemisphere.

Chapter 1

THE VICTORY

In the southern half of the country, the mulatto General Rigaud also held his own, and the British gradually came to the realisation that to conquer Hispaniola was beyond their power. Of the two native commanders they preferred to open negotiations with Toussaint, and it was from Cap François that General Maitland sailed with the last British soldiers in April 1798, having secured from his Negro adversary a promise that the lives and properties of those whites remaining in the island would be respected.

Only the mulattos still questioned the right of the Negroes to decide their own future, but a brief campaign forced Generals Rigaud and Petion to flee the island. However reluctant Toussaint might have been to thrust himself forward, he knew when to take advantage of circumstances. He now turned his attention to the Spanish half of the island, with equal success. Suddenly St Domingue was one country, a black country, ruled by a black general.

'Sail ho,' came the shout from the main top. Christopher Hamilton ran to the larboard rail of the brig to gaze at the vessel approaching them out of the Atlantic.

Tall, powerfully built, sun-browned and wind-burned, Kit Hamilton looked every inch of what he was, a sea captain whose trading routes lay through the magical islands of the West Indian chain and across the warm waters of the Caribbean Sea. At thirty years of age he possessed all the confidence of health and strength, allied to a mastery of his profession; his blue eyes could be as warm as his ready smile. Yet, in repose, his face, handsome enough, too often settled into the deep-etched lines of a man who had looked on too much tragedy for a single brief lifetime – and on this voyage, the firm lips had been turned down more often than they had flared with amusement.

Rogers, the first mate, and Ducros, the Frenchman, stood at his shoulder, as the captain levelled his telescope. '*The White Ensign*,' he said. 'A Britisher. And signalling us to heave to.'

'She'll be after men,' Rogers growled, looking over his shoulder at the fluttering Stars and Stripes. For in this year of 1792 the Royal Navy was reluctant to recognise that the infant United States merchant marine had any rights at all, and often impressed men from the very decks of American vessels, claiming that they were merely rebellious Englishmen, in reality.

'Great Britain is at peace, at the moment,' Kit said. 'And we've no choice, Mr Rogers. Heave her to, and break open the gangway.' His helplessness made him boil with anger. But, when confronted with the guns of a frigate, there was nothing a trading brig could do. He preferred to turn back and study the shore to the south of him, the unbroken line of trees, with the backdrop of the mountains . . . and the yellow sand beach, on which the rollers ceaselessly pounded.

'Boat approaching,' Rogers said.

'Well,' Kit said, 'give him a whistle, Mr Rogers. We'll show our manners.'

'But will he show his?' muttered Ducros, retreating against the far rail. The Frenchman had all of his nation's antagonism towards the British. But he was a courageous man, or he would not be here at all. He had been an overseer on Vergée d'Or, and he could have no doubt that any blacks who were surely hidden in those trees would remember his face.

The boatswain cooeed, and the crew gathered in the waist as the naval officer came on board. To Kit's consternation he realised that it was the captain of the frigate himself. Now the small, slight figure in the splendid white and blue uniform saluted. 'I seek Captain Hamilton.'

Kit hurried forward. 'I am he, sir.'

The Britisher frowned. 'You? By God! I had heard there was youth here, but you . . .'

'I have powerful and prosperous friends, sir,' Kit said. 'And I have sailed these waters for better than ten years.'

'My apologies, sir. My tongue ran away with me. Edward Pellew.'

They shook hands.

'I would have a word with you, sir,' Pellew said. 'In confidence.'

Clearly this was no press-ganging operation. Kit showed his guest down into the small aft cabin, placed the decanter of brandy and two glasses on the table, raised his eyebrows to Rogers as the door was closed upon them.

'Your health.' Pellew drank.

'And yours. I am interested to discover how you knew my ship.'

Pellew smiled. 'We keep a list of all vessels regularly trading in these waters. I know something of your history, Mr Hamilton. You seek your sister?'

Kit leaned forward. 'You have news of her?'

'No, sir. Save that she is reputed to be held by the blacks.'

Kit studied him. 'You claim to know something of my history, Captain Pellew. Therefore you must know something of hers as well.'

'It is not my business to pry, Mr Hamilton.'

'Yet you must be aware that after my sister escaped

270

the blacks, last August, together with her cousin, Annette de Mortmain, my betrothed . . .' he would not have this man be unaware of a single aspect of the situation, even if he also no doubt knew of Annette's affliction, '. . . and gained the security of Cap François, she was discovered to be pregnant. It was naturally assumed that the child was by her husband, Philippe de Mortmain, who had been murdered in the revolt. When the babe was born, it was discovered that was not the case.'

Pellew gave a delicate cough, and drank some more brandy.

'The child,' Kit said evenly, 'was therefore allowed to perish. I was not there at the time, so I do not know what my sister felt or said. I do know that a few nights later, when she had regained her strength, she disappeared from Cap François. It was supposed that she might have taken her own life, but it was later discovered that she had swum along the coast until she was beyond the perimeter established by the French troops, and then come ashore and walked into the forest, apparently wishing to be re-united with her . . . with the blacks.'

'She sounds an intensely strong young lady, of both mind and body,' Pellew observed. 'May I be so bold, Mr Hamilton . . . you say you were not in Cap François when this tragedy occurred. But the way you say it suggests that, had you been there, you might have insisted the babe should live.'

'I would have insisted that, sir, yes.'

'The child of a rape? A mulatto bastard? At a time when everyone with even heavy colour from the sun is suspect and hated?'

'Times like this will pass, Captain Pellew. The babe would have been my nephew.'

'I see,' Pellew said, clearly not seeing at all. 'This is not a point of view held by a large percentage of your own countrymen,' he remarked. 'Much less the French

271

here in St Domingue. I am sorry to press this point, sir, and I trust you will not take offence, but as I will explain in a moment, it is very necessary for me to be sure of your motives. Dare I suggest that the fact of your sister's return to the forest, and indeed every other fact about this case, raises two rather . . . well, unpleasant possibilities? One, that she has, after all, chosen a rather unfortunate way of committing suicide, and has already been torn to pieces by the blacks; two, that the rape was not a rape at all, and your sister has merely sought to rejoin her . . . ah, lover. The father of her child.'

'There is a third possibility, Captain Pellew,' Kit said, evenly. 'That my sister might actually have chosen to live with a people who have been ill-used for too long, and now have sought only their freedom, rather than conceding to their oppressors, who seek only to return them to slavery.'

They stared at each other, and Pellew flushed. 'Would you agree with that point of view?' he asked.

'Very probably,' Kit said. 'In fact, sir, I believe your second conjecture to be right, and that my sister does have a Negro lover, but . . .'

'And you can sit there?' Pellew demanded.

'I was going to say, sir, that fact does not necessarily mean that my point is not also correct. As for my sister's private affairs, if I am right in thinking that I know the man to whom she has returned, he is, or was, my friend, regardless of his colour. I hope that one day he will again be my friend.'

'I see,' Pellew said again. And half shrugged, as if to indicate that clearly the Hamiltons were totally beyond his understanding. But he was looking quite contented with the situation. 'Then would I be right in assuming that this expedition has not been mounted with the intention of regaining your sister by force?'

'Look around my ship, sir,' Kit suggested. 'Do we look armed and equipped for a military campaign?'

'No, indeed. And that relieves me greatly,' Pellew confessed. 'So, you go to speak with your sister, and discover if she is well, and what her intentions are.'

'That is correct.'

'And you anticipate being welcomed by the black leaders?'

'I believe they will treat me fairly,' Kit said. 'Because I have always treated them fairly.'

'That is splendid,' Pellew said, apparently having done a complete volte face. 'I wonder, sir, if His Majesty's Government could make a request of you?'

Kit frowned at him.

'I also would speak with these people,' Pellew said. 'But I have as yet been unable to do so. You will understand, sir, that over the past year my ship has been on patrol on this coast, and we have of course endeavoured to rescue such planters and their families as we might. This has no doubt encouraged the blacks to consider us their enemies, though we were simply playing a humanitarian role. The result is that whenever I land, St Domingue could be a desert island.'

'And *you* wish to speak with the black leaders?' Kit was incredulous. 'May I ask why?'

Pellew looked into his brandy glass. 'St Domingue is too great and fertile a country to be permitted to become an empty jungle, Captain Hamilton. Do you not agree? And France, sir, well, it is the opinion of most neutral observers that France is daily slipping further into chaos. You have heard the news from Paris?'

'Some of it, sir.'

'Yes,' Pellew said. 'Well, sir, I can tell you that since the mad French declaration of war on Austria and Prussia, things have deteriorated. On the approach of the Duke of Brunswick's army, last month, Paris seems to have gone wild. I have heard terrible stories of what happened here last year, but I can assure you, sir, that they do no more than match the tales of what happened

273

in Paris last month. And there was no colour or slavery question involved there. The whole world seems to be entering a prolonged period of anarchy and brutality.' He sighed. 'But we were discussing St Domingue.'

'Which Great Britain would like to annex, if it can be done without provoking a war,' Kit said thoughtfully. 'I have heard it said that England has always coveted Hispaniola, that Cromwell, indeed, sent his commanders to the Tower of London because they took Jamaica instead, in 1655.'

'I implement my country's policies, Captain Hamilton. I do not make them. But, as I have said, here is a great and fertile land, daily descending further down the scale of human savagery. France no longer controls it. As for the blacks, well . . .'

'But you wish to speak with them, and enlist their support, perhaps. May I ask what you will say to them? You can hardly offer them freedom, when Great Britain herself is the mistress of a dozen slave-holding islands.'

'I have heard that some of the black leaders are quite intelligent,' Pellew remarked. 'I may not be able to offer them freedom, but I can offer them a better life than the existence they now maintain. I can offer them, too, a final solution to their hatred for the French.'

Kit's head came up. 'You seem to forget, sir, that I am half French myself.'

'And half English, by birth. The whole having become American. That is where your loyalties should lie, sir. Does the United States have designs upon St Domingue?'

'Of course not,' Kit said.

'Well, then . . . I do promise you, Captain Hamilton, that my government means no ill towards those French who remain in Cap François and Port-au-Prince. They will be evacuated, to wherever they wish to go. There is even talk of compensation, for the loss of their plantations, should Great Britain become mistress of the colony. Now, sir, what could be fairer than that? When compared with the miserable existence they are presently forced to tolerate?'

'And of course,' Kit said, 'the Royal Navy would supply the one weapon the blacks need to force the French to surrender Port-au-Prince and Cap François – a naval blockade to prevent supplies from entering those ports.'

'Indeed, sir. But I would beg you to remember that it would be the Royal Navy seizing Port-au-Prince and Cap François upon a French surrender, not the slaves. And would not *that* be more preferable than to have those cities, and their inhabitants, forced to surrender to Jean François? I think I am correct in stating that he claims to be the blacks' general?'

'You are correct,' Kit said.

'Well, sir, that may well happen – and soon. If things in France are as bad as they seem, Cap François and Port-au-Prince may run out of food and munitions even without a blockade.'

Kit got up, walked to the stern windows to look out at the coastline, as his ship bobbed gently on the calm sea. The man spoke sense, of course. There *was* no future for any Frenchman, in St Domingue, ever again. Hanging on, as Etienne Mortmain was doing, waiting for a counter-revolution to re-establish him, as Philippe de Mortmain's heir, in control of the vast wealth of Vergée d'Or, was merely to perpetuate the madness. And Richilde, her black lover suddenly again reduced to the status of a slave? But that was something she would have to resolve for herself, if she would not return with him now. For could he, personally, care whether the colony belonged to the British or the French? He was an American, and he knew one of the two alternatives had to happen – he had no faith in the ability of someone like Jean François, who was a brutal savage, being able to create an independent nation here, even with the patience and intelligence of someone like Toussaint ever available.

'And of course, Captain Hamilton,' Pellew said, gently, 'should the blacks be recalcitrant, and refuse to release your sister, for example, well, once we have discovered her whereabouts, I can promise you the assistance of my ship, and my men, in returning Madame de Mortmain to safety and comfort. Supposing that is what she wishes.'

'The man you need to speak to is Pierre Toussaint, not Jean François,' Kit said sombrely. He went to the doorway. 'I think it is best we use my longboat, and fly the American flag.'

'There, Mr Hamilton,' Ducros said. 'You should see the chateau through the trees. If it still stands.'

The brig hardly did more than drift before the light breeze; the frigate remained three miles farther out to sea, waiting to be signalled. It was early morning, and although there were heavy clouds over the mountains, they had not yet descended towards the shore. It was a beautiful day, with the sun just gaining in heat as it soared into the eastern sky, and the sky itself matching the blue of the sea in calm serenity. And yet, Kit knew as he levelled his telescope, horror was their business this day. Horror was what they anticipated, what they knew they must expect.

'I can see the chateau,' he said. Through the trees, the sun glinted on blackened timbers.

Pellew was inspecting the beach. 'And, as usual, no blacks.'

'Yet they are there, sir,' Rogers suggested. 'We know they are there.'

'What do you think, Ducros?' Kit asked.

The Frenchman hesitated, chewing his lip. 'It is hard to say, monsieur. We understood in Cap François that Vergée d'Or was their headquarters. But we have had no positive information for some time. Since the failure of their last attempt to storm the city, they may have retreated into the mountains. Or may have not.'

'Then we accomplish nothing by standing here,' Kit decided. 'You'll prepare the boat, Mr Rogers. Make sure the Stars and Stripes are prominently displayed, and also a white flag. Captain Pellew, may I ask you to leave your sword behind?'

'Eh?'

'I do not propose to expose any of my people to murder, sir,' Kit said. 'Therefore I am going ashore with Ducros alone. You have expressed a wish to accompany me, and you are welcome. But the three of us certainly can never fight the entire black army. We succeed here today by talk, and by proving from the outset that we *mean* to talk.'

Pellew hesitated, then unbuckled his sword belt and handed the weapons to Rogers. Kit wondered if he was afraid. If he was, he was too well disciplined to show it. Ducros most certainly was, crossing himself as he climbed down the ladder into the boat, and was clearly regretting his offer to accompany this mad American.

And am I afraid? Kit asked himself. Amazingly, he wasn't. Because he trusted Toussaint, and Henry Christopher. As Richilde had done.

The boat approached the beach, perhaps a hundred yards from where the pale-watered stream debouched into the sand, forming a miniature estuary of drying banks and flooded waterways, before losing itself against the gentle surf. But the water remained clear, and almost white.

On that beach he had become a man, in the arms of his cousin's mistress, Jacqueline Chavannes. He wondered what had happened to that tall, proud, beautiful mulatto, in the turmoil of the last year.

Beyond the beach there was a fringe of trees, empty and silent.

The keel grounded, the three men climbed over the bow, and stamped on the sand to empty water from their shoes.

'Keep your place in deep water,' Kit commanded the coxswain. 'But be alert. We may return in some haste.'

'I'll be here, Captain Hamilton,' the coxswain promised.

Kit led the way up the beach, the two others behind him. He pushed his way through the trees, to emerge on to the lawn, and face the patio, where Philippe de Mortmain had condemned a man to be torn to pieces by dogs, on the Hamiltons' first night in St Domingue. But there was no grass here now, only trampled earth. And the first skeletons, a cluster of three, black men he thought from the remnants of their clothing. And a crow, still investigating the meal he must have completed over a year ago, casting a disgusted glance at the living men who approached him, and then flapping his wings as he rose from the ground.

They gazed at the burned-out shell of the house. The walls had fallen outwards as the roof had fallen in, and yet the remains of the great staircase still jutted upwards out of the huge hall. Here the main work of execution had been conducted. They looked at skeletons, of men, and women, and children, many of the bones blackened by the fire, others torn and twisted and chopped away from their fellows, to suggest some of the dreadful things that must have taken place, while skeins of golden hair still clung to shattered skulls – and the white ants lived and roamed in their dreadful habitat.

'These were not men,' Ducros muttered. 'These were beasts.'

Kit said nothing, turned and walked back on to the drive, looked at the scattered skeletons there. Here he felt he could breathe again, as he watched the clouds sweeping lower, occasionally obliterating the sun, bringing the promise of a noontime rain shower. He walked down the drive, looked at the white township. This too had been burned. But the slave village beyond was undamaged. And so, amazingly, was the factory.

He began to hurry, away from his companions, ran into the shade of the great chimney and the huge vats, guided by instinct, and by what Annette had told him. He climbed the ladder to the first of the rollers, and paused, and lost his balance for a moment in sheer horror. Only Philippe de Mortmain's skull remained, clinging to the top of a shattered spinal column. The rest of his body had been fed through the rotating iron drums. But even the skull's expression seemed twisted in the torment he must have experienced before death.

He climbed down the ladder, slowly, regained the ground. Pellew and Ducros waited for him. And the rain began to fall, a gentle patter on the factory roof, a gentle thudding on the dry ground outside.

'You would treat with these people, Captain Pellew?' Ducros asked.

Pellew waited for Kit to speak. But Kit had nothing to say.

'I think we should leave this place, messieurs,' Ducros said. 'It is a charnel house, and there are no blacks. Thank God! They have gone to the mountains, as I said. Let us return to the ship.'

He made his way up the drive, and after a moment Kit followed. He felt the rain splashing on his hat, dampening his shoulders. In time the rain would wash all these bones away, even as it would wash away Vergée d'Or itself.

He checked, because Ducros, fifty yards in front of him and just approaching the trees which lined the stream, had also checked. He felt a sudden lurch of his heart, a constriction of his belly. There, standing in the trees, was Henry Christopher.

He was exactly as Kit remembered him, from the last time they had met, which was several years ago, on the occasion of Richilde's wedding to Philippe de Mortmain. He was better than six feet tall, and had a strong, gaunt face, handsome but reserved. Only his clothes had changed. Then he had been a coachman, wearing the Mortmain livery and white stockings. Now he wore a blue uniform jacket, straining across his shoulders, and ragged white trousers, and a blue tricorne, obviously taken from some dead French soldier. And he carried a sword, and had two pistols thrust into his leather belt. Henry, Kit recalled, had always wanted to be a soldier, and wear a uniform.

'By God,' Pellew murmured. 'By God.'

Kit advanced, slowly.

'Do you not recognise me, Kit?' Henry asked. 'I recognised you, the moment you landed from your ship.'

'You were here, then?'

'My people have watched your ship, sailing along the coast. We knew whose ship it was. We knew you would come to Vergée d'Or.'

'And you let us walk into your trap,' Ducros muttered. 'My God . . .' he turned, slowly looked at the black men, who now stood all around them.

'You have come for Richilde?' Henry asked.

Kit licked his lips. 'We have come to talk.'

'Then come to the General,' Christopher said.

He led them past the village, and the wood beyond, through the deserted and overgrown canefields, towards the distant forest. Now there were more black men, and women, gazing at them. Ducros crossed himself again, and had clearly committed his soul to the Almighty.

The Negro encampment was on the edge of the trees. Here was surprising industry, men sharpening weapons, others even attempting a form of drill, women cooking over the open fires, children playing, dogs growling at one another. Wooden huts gave it a suggestion of permanence.

And here too was Jean François, standing in the doorway of the largest of the huts, surrounded by his bodyguard, who were in turn dominated by the squat, bull-like man, who gazed at the whites with hungry eyes. All wore the suggestions of a uniform, like Henry. But Jean François had also made epaulettes for himself, and, playing the general, wore no weapons.

'Kit Hamilton,' Henry said.

'Do you remember me, Jean François?' Kit asked.

'I remember you,' Jean François said. 'You will address me as "Your Excellency". You have come for your sister?'

'I have come to see my sister,' Kit agreed. 'But this gentleman is an English sea captain, and he has come to talk. With you. And with Toussaint, Your Excellency.'

'Toussaint?' Jean François gave a bellow of laughter.

'He's not dead?' Kit asked in alarm.

'He is gone,' Henry said, quietly. 'He has fled to the Spanish side of the island.'

'But why?'

'He sought to dispute my orders,' Jean François said. 'Just as Rigaud and his brown skins sought to dispute my orders. No one disputes my orders, white man. You . . .' he pointed at Pellew. 'You have something to say to me? Say it.'

Pellew hesitated, and then went forward.

'While they speak, I will take you to see Richilde,' Henry offered. 'Come.'

He led Kit through the growing crowd of black people, who stared at the white man with dull interest.

'I am sorry Toussaint has gone,' Kit said.

'So am I,' Henry agreed, without turning his head.

'And Jean François . . .'

'He is my General,' Henry reminded him and halted.

Kit lowered his head and entered another hut, another large hut, almost as large as Jean François's headquarters. Inside, he gazed at the bodies lying on the floor, several of them bandaged against wounds, but the majority ill, he estimated, of fever and festering sores. Kneeling beside one of the sick people was Olivier, the Vergée d'Or dispenser. Richilde knelt at his elbow.

She wore a shapeless white gown, and her head was concealed beneath the bandanna of the Negress. The bandanna completely obscured the rich, curling brown hair which had always been one of Richilde's peculiar treasures, but on the other hand it left another of her treasures, the softly beautiful face, exposed. The face was not as soft as Kit remembered it. The chin had always pointed, the nose had always been a delightful retroussé; in between, the mouth had flattened from the perfect rosebud of her youth, and he suspected that the green eyes would now suggest marzipan icing rather than lush tropical foliage. Yet the beauty remained, and of body as well, for the gown was pulled tight as she knelt, and outlined shoulder and breast and thigh, strong and muscular, but voluptuous and appealing as well.

Above anything else, both face and body gave an impression of strength. Richilde had always been strong, in body and mind. She had needed that strength to survive marriage to Philippe de Mortmain, and she had needed it even more to survive the revolt, the horrors to which she had been exposed, and which had driven her cousin Annette mad. Those had perhaps been passive strengths. Her true strength had been demonstrated in her decision to return, where, despite all, both her love and her sympathies lay.

She looked up as the two men came in, gave Henry a quick smile, and then frowned incredulously as she saw her brother, hastily stood up, drying her hands on her skirt. 'Kit? But . . .'

'He has come under a flag of truce, as an American,' Henry explained. 'And with an English officer. He wishes to speak with you.'

She licked her lips, waited.

'I think you should go outside with him,' Henry said.

Richilde walked to the door, ducked her head, stepped into the open air. She hesitated for a moment, and then walked into the trees. Kit glanced at Henry, who nodded. Then he followed his sister. But what a strange, upsidedown world this is, he thought, that I should need a black man's permission to speak with my own sister.

'Is that what they make you do?' he asked. 'Tend their sick?'

She turned to face him. 'It is what I *wish* to do. It was what I did even before the revolt. Nobody has made me.'

He made a gesture, at their surroundings. 'You left Cap François, to come back to *this*?'

She raised her head. 'I came back to Henry.'

'The man who raped you? Who murdered your family?'

'He did not rape me,' she said. 'In the sense that Annette was raped. And he never touched any of our family.'

'He led the assault, I have been told. His people followed him. I have just come from the chateau. I have just seen Philippe.' He drew a long breath. 'Now I also will have nightmares. Could you not have had him buried? Have had them all buried?'

'It was Jean François's command that Vergée d'Or should be left exactly as it is. We did not bury the black men, either.'

'And you can live here, with such barbarous savages?'

She met his gaze. 'You say you have seen Philippe. Did you also see my child? Henry's child?'

'Richilde . . .'

'These people acted out of revenge,' she said. 'Out of excitement. Out of a whipped-up religious mania. That was the only way they could risk what they did. But over the centuries, whenever our people, Kit, our white people, have inflicted no less dreadful injuries upon them, it has been done in cold blood. As my child was murdered, in cold blood.'

He sighed. 'I have no wish to defend the planters. I have always loathed the whole idea. But Richilde, for better or for worse, the white people are *your* people. You belong in beautiful gowns and wearing rich jewellery, riding in a carriage and sleeping between linen sheets, eating good food and drinking the best wine. You are Madame de Mortmain. Not some white Negress scrubbing about for roots in a jungle.'

She shook her head. 'I am not coming back with you, Kit.'

'You mean you are *happy*, here?'

She thought for a moment. 'No,' she said. 'I am not happy here. I am happy with Henry. He can make me happy.' A faint flush. 'I have never been happy with a man before. Philippe was a purgatory of nine years. And I think that Henry is happy with me. But *we* are not happy, yet. That remains to be accomplished.'

'Do you know how disgusting that is?' he asked. 'You seek physical pleasure, from a black man? A black . . .'

'Man,' she said. 'With whom I have grown up. A man I know, and who knows me. Do not think Henry a savage, Kit. He is as intelligent as you or I, even if he cannot write his name. That is why he is unhappy. He knows as well as I that this revolt has become dissipated in a senseless civil war. Perhaps that had to happen. It was not planned that way. But then, it was never expected to be so successful. We know that it is a tragedy that we should control so much of St Domingue, and yet be making no effort to form a government, or even any social order. Toussaint might

284

have done those things. But Jean François drove him out. He had driven him out before I returned. When I realised Toussaint was no longer here, I nearly went back to Cap François. But I didn't. And I'm glad I didn't. I don't know who will do it. Henry is too young, and is still too uncertain to put himself forward. Rigaud might have done it, but Jean François drove him out too, and now he lives like a bandit down in the south. But someone must make these people into a nation. Make them realise that they are fighting *for* something, instead of just fighting. Make them realise that freedom has to be organised. I believe Henry may yet be the man to accomplish that. If I stay at his side. And if we can both stay alive long enough. I think that is a more worthwhile thing to do with my life than attempting to play the great lady. Than pretending to be part of a society and a people that I hate.'

'As you say, if you stay alive. You returned to these people, a lone white woman, and . . .'

'No one has touched me,' she said. 'Not even Jean François. Because I came to them. And because, once the frenzy was over, they understood that I had always tried to help them.'

'And if I tell you that everything you have just said is a senseless dream? Do you really suppose France, or England, is going to allow St Domingue to become some kind of a Negro kingdom, here in the West Indies? France is experiencing a revolution, so she can't do anything about these people, at the moment. But the British mean to. That's why Pellew is here.' He caught her hand. 'Richilde, this absurd revolt is only a revolt. These blacks are merely lucky that circumstances have allowed them to remain free for over a year. Circumstances won't allow that much longer. And then they are going to be blown apart by cannon, shot down and hung up. That is as inevitable as night must follow day. There will be nothing you can do about it. Except die with them. Or be returned to some kind of everlasting notoriety, as the white woman who lived with the blacks, of her own free will. Is that what you want?'

'I'm sorry, Kit,' she said. 'I do not expect you to understand. Sometimes I do not understand myself. I think perhaps I died, the night the chateau fell. Certainly I expected to. And next day, I discovered I was still alive. And with Henry. And I suddenly realised that was all I had ever truly wanted, that all my life, certainly since my marriage to Philippe, I had been living nothing more than a sham. I wanted to stay. Even after everything that had happened, everything that had been done to *me*, I wanted to stay. Henry made me go to Cap François. We didn't know I was pregnant, then. And I believe he was right. Of course I did. I'd been brought up to feel that. Perhaps if you'd taken me away with you, last Christmas, I'd have always felt that way. I'm not blaming you. I'm glad you didn't, now. I came back, because I love Henry. There, I've said it. I love him, and I've always loved him.'

'And you think he loves you?'

'Yes,' she said. 'Yes, I think he does love me. But there is more than that, Kit. As I said, I came back, because I thought I could help these people, to stop being savages, to create something. Even to win their war, and their freedom. So Toussaint has gone. And Rigaud has gone. Even Boukman, who at least gave it the sanctity of religion, is gone. But Henry is still alive. And however long he remains, however long he is prepared to put up with Jean François, then I am going to stay with him.'

They stood in a group, to watch the white men receding through the trees.

'A British colony,' Jean François sneered. 'The man must think we are fools.'

'We should have killed them all,' Jean-Jacques

286

Dessalines growled. 'They are white people. We should kill every white person we find, as they kill every black person.' His eyes gloomed at Richilde, and she made herself stand still with an effort – he was the only black man she truly feared, now. She had braced herself for an ordeal, with Jean François, on her return, had feared then, to provoke a confrontation between himself and Henry, had indeed resolved to prevent it by accepting the older man, if she had to. But Jean François had grown, as a man, in her ten months' absence. He was still no more than a coachman. He still had no concept of strategy or tactics, of leadership, other than by browbeating anyone who stood against him. But he had also realised that he *was* the General, that he could not dissipate his energies in either women or wine, as did so many of his followers – and also perhaps that Henry Christopher was his most loyal aide, of whom it would be ridiculous to make an enemy. Thus he had merely scowled at her, and said, 'You ain't tired suffering, Richilde?'

But Dessalines . . . his eyes followed her wherever she went, as much because of her white skin as because she was a woman, she thought. Yet Dessalines had a brain, was well aware that he was the newcomer here, even more than she. If he destroyed her, if he could ever attain that ambition, it would have to be part of a fresh wave of hatred and lust. And it would have to be inspired by the General.

Who scowled at her again. 'They came for you, Richilde,' he said. 'Why did you not go with them?'

'Because I preferred to stay here, Your Excellency,' she said.

'Because you are a fool. All white people must be fools. A British colony. Bah.'

'Yet the British will seek to implement their plan, whether you agree to it or not,' Richilde said.

His frown deepened. 'How they going do that?'

'Suppose they were to take Cap François, and Port-au-Prince? Because they can do that, Your Excellency. The reason you have not been able to drive away the French is because they are being supplied with food and munitions, from the sea. The British have the ships to put a stop to that, and force them to surrender. Then you will be fighting the British. And they have great armies as well as great navies.'

'She is right,' Henry said. 'If we cannot beat the French, it might be better for us to make peace with the British, rather than have to fight *them* as well.'

'Bah,' Jean François said. 'You keep telling us you are English yourself, Henry. And she is English too. So you are afraid of them. But these English are not gods.'

'They are men who live by fighting,' Henry said.

Jean François glared at him, then he snapped his enormous fingers. 'Then we will prevent them. Summon the army. We march on Cap François.'

'Again?' Dessalines asked.

'Again,' Jean François roared. 'And this time we will take it, you black-faced nigger. Summon the army.'

'I did not mean to send you back to war,' Richilde said, when Henry came to say goodbye. 'My God, I did not mean that, Kit will be returning there.'

'Well, like you said,' Henry said, 'we can't fight ships. He will be all right. Maybe this time they will all take to the ships. That is what we want them to do.'

'And if they don't?'

He shrugged. 'We will hurl ourselves against the walls, as usual.'

'As you did before. And you will be killed. Henry, if you were to be killed . . .' her shoulders slumped.

'If I were to be killed, Richilde,' he said, 'then you would go back to your people. Promise me that.'

'Don't you understand that that is impossible?' she asked. 'If you were to be killed, Henry, I should have to die too. I have no people, white or black. I have only you. So come back to me, Henry. Come back to me.'

Even from the sea, the vast column of marching Negroes could be discerned. And long before the brig made the harbour, the afternoon was torn apart by the explosion of the cannon, the rattle of the musketry, the screams of the dead and dying. While now the watchers from the ship could see the clouds of black smoke rolling above the town.

'Christ give us a breeze,' Kit growled, as they almost drifted towards the harbour. 'I wonder if Pellew realised he would stir them up to another assault?'

'Englishmen,' Ducros grumbled, and looked out to sea. But the frigate had disappeared, making for Jamaica, no doubt, Kit thought. To report the failure of his mission.

It was dusk before they dropped anchor, and he could get ashore. By now the firing had died down, although it continued in a desultory fashion, and there were still fires burning by the walls. He encountered Etienne, smoke stained and elated, as he hurried towards Madame Ramlie's house. 'Kit!' his cousin shouted. 'Another victory. We have beaten them again. Why, we must have killed hundreds. Thousands of them. Let them throw themselves against our walls. That is the surest way to end the revolt. By killing every nigger in St Domingue. But you . . . did you get ashore?'

'I got ashore,' Kit said.

'And Richilde?'

Kit went up the stairs, knocked, opened Annette's door. She stood by the window, looking out, but turned, her face lighting up as she saw him. 'Kit,' she cried. 'Oh, Kit. Madeleine has just been in. Have you heard . . ?'

'Etienne has told me. You have repulsed another onslaught.'

'We have won a great victory,' she insisted. And looked past him. 'Richilde? Oh, Kit . . .' tears filled her eyes. 'How did it happen? Tell me. It is better to speak of these things.'

'Richilde is not dead.' He took her in his arms, kissed her on the lips.

She pushed him away. 'Not dead? But . . .'

'She wishes to stay with them.'

'With the *blacks*?' She was incredulous. 'She is demented. Quite mad.'

Kit sighed, and sat down. 'Her reasoning was fairly cogent. And there was no way I could force her.'

'I hope she rots in hell,' Annette said, speaking in a low, hate-filled voice.

'Well . . .' Kit said. 'Annette, there are going to be other attacks. This war is not going to end soon. My ship is waiting in the harbour. I am leaving tomorrow for Savannah. If you will pack your boxes, we can go aboard tonight. I will talk with Madeleine and Etienne, of course, but if our minds are made up . . .'

'Savannah?' she asked. 'I cannot leave here, Kit.'

'But . . .'

'Not now, when we have won a great victory. And you have not heard all of it. There is news from France. Reinforcements are on their way. A commissioner, to settle with the blacks. Now we'll see. Now we'll have them all hanging. You said you'd stay with me, to make sure that happened, Kit.'

'Annette,' he said. 'You cannot spend your entire life hating. I know what happened to you is the most terrible thing that can happen to any woman. But it is in the past. You must try, like Richilde, to forget it, and look to the future.'

'Like Richilde?' she asked. 'Like Richilde? She's a white nigger. When they hang, she'll hang with them. That's what I'm staying to see, Kit. Her and Henry Christopher, hanging together.'

*

290

Richilde waited, sitting beside Olivier. They were again friends. In a different way to ever before. His desire for her was unceasing and unquenchable. If she stopped with her back to him he was immediately pinching her bottom or trying to get his hands beneath her skirt. When she slapped him he merely grinned, and waited for his next opportunity. But he would never attempt to take her by force – he was too afraid of Henry Christopher.

And he was intelligent enough to share many of her anxieties, even if for entirely different reasons.

'They going get beat,' he said. 'They must be going get beat. And we going have too much work to do, Richilde.'

Too much work. She sighed.

'If that Henry does be kill,' Olivier said, 'you would lie with me?'

'No,' she said.

He considered her reply, without offence. 'You have to lie with somebody,' he pointed out, speaking very reasonably. 'Woman must belong to somebody. If it ain't me, you know who it going be? That Dessalines. Man, you ever watch his stick? It big like a tree. He would split you ass to tit.'

'Then I won't lie with him, either,' she said. 'Listen.'

The Negro army was returned. The army. Henry had said he would send a messenger if Cap François fell. Had she wanted it to happen? Presumably Annette and Etienne and Madeleine were still there. She did not want them to be killed, and she could not doubt that the Negroes would kill every white person they found, in the heat of storming the walls. Even Henry would take part in that – he hated Etienne more than he hated anything else in the world. No, she had not wanted Cap François to fall to an assault. And yet she wanted the Negroes to win their struggle. If only the French had sailed away.

And here they were, straggling back through the trees, shoulders bowed, helping such of the wounded as could walk. Dessalines marched at their head, bull face angry, nostrils twitching as if he sought some new enemy to charge.

Dessalines?

Heart pounding, she ran towards them. 'Jean-Jacques?' she shouted. 'Jean-Jacques? Where is . . .' she bit her lip.

'I am here.' Henry was supporting two wounded men, one on each arm. 'I have brought you much work.'

'But . . . Jean-François?'

'He is dead,' Dessalines said. 'Dead,' he bellowed, raising his fists to shake them at the mountains. 'Dead,' he screamed.

She looked at Henry. 'The attack failed?'

'Of course it failed,' he said bitterly. 'They had cannon. We have no cannon.' He dropped the two wounded men outside the door of the hospital, sat with them. 'It was a cannonball blew Jean François apart.'

She could not believe it. Jean François? He had been there, since the day of her arrival on Vergée d'Or. He had been Henry's mentor, and his friend. And she had thought he was her friend as well. Until *that* night, when he had castrated Philippe and then sought her with an angry lust. But that had passed, and in many ways they had become friends again. She had even been able to sympathise with his uncertain gropings towards leadership. And now he was blown to pieces by a cannonball. The first of the triumvirate she would always associate with each other to die.

But was that not the inevitable fate of the other two, as well? Certainly of Henry, if he kept on being sent against cannon, and stone walls.

Toussaint would never have ordered so futile an assault. But Toussaint had quarrelled with Jean François . . . Her heart began to pound again.

'We must have a new general,' Dessalines said, putting into words her thoughts.

Henry Christopher raised his head, and Dessalines stared at him. 'It must be,' he said.

He was claiming the post for himself. And she knew Henry would not oppose him. Henry had too great a respect for those older than himself.

'Toussaint,' she cried.

They looked at her.

'Toussaint,' she said again. 'He only left you because of Jean François. But Jean François is dead. Send for Toussaint. He will lead you. He will teach you how to beat the French. And the English. And he will teach you more than that.'

The little figure limped through the crowd of Negroes. But it was a small crowd. A much smaller crowd than when he had gone away.

'This, is your army?' he asked.

Dessalines shrugged. 'They have eat up all the food around here. They can't stay.'

'They do not want to stay,' Henry Christopher said.

Toussaint looked at the triangles, the half dozen suspended figures. 'You are a planter now?' he asked.

Dessalines grinned. 'They talked of surrender, to the white people.'

'They came from Cap François,' Henry explained. 'With a flag of truce. But . . .'

'We ain't recognising no more flag of truce,' Dessalines said. 'They getting twenty-five lashes a day, and they hanging there, until they die. Black men should fight, for black men. Not talk, for white men.'

'Cut them down,' Toussaint said.

'Eh?'

Toussaint met his angry gaze. 'If I am to be General,' he said, 'I will be General. Otherwise I will leave again.'

Dessalines snorted.

293

'Cut them down,' Henry commanded. 'You are the General, Toussaint. That is what we wish.'

'Tell me when they can speak.' Toussaint walked away from them, towards Richilde. 'Well, madame, I could not believe what I was told. But I see it is true. Because of Henry?'

'Mainly,' she said.

'But not entirely?' He sat beside her. 'Do you know how much you will be hated, by your people?'

'How much I *am* hated,' Richilde said.

'And this does not frighten you?'

'Will you make these people a nation, Toussaint?'

'I do not know that is possible.'

'Those messengers, the ones Dessalines has been flogging, they came from Cap François.'

'So I have heard.'

'From a man called Santhonax. He is from France, and he represents the National Convention. The new government in Paris. He asks to speak with the Negro General.'

Toussaint frowned. 'Why?'

'I do not know. Those men do not know. But . . . what is to be lost by listening to what he has to say?'

'And suppose he offers peace, madame? Or is that an unthinkable thought, for a white man?'

'If he wishes to speak with you, he must be going to offer something.'

'If we could have peace,' Toussaint said wistfully. 'Peace to make something of ourselves . . .'

'A people,' she said.

He glanced at her. 'Something, madame. Something. I do not know what a nation is. Neither do any of these people. They know only tribal law, and the white man's lash. But as they have fought together, and died together, it should be possible to make *something*.'

Léger Felicité Santhonax was not a tall man; indeed, he was no more than medium height. But he carried himself like a big man, and in his clothes, which were those of a Republican general, with the red sash around his waist to separate his red and white striped breeches from his blue coat, and his plumed bicorne hat, no less than his cavalry sabre and his large paunch, he presented the picture of a *successful* man. And a courageous one, Richilde thought. Where his staff, which included several officers who had been stationed in Cap François before the revolt, seemed to huddle against each other as they stared at the huge mass of Negroes, the Commissioner walked forward, smiling, hands on hips, apparently as unconcerned by the armed black people as he was uninterested in his surroundings, either the sparkling blue of the sea to his left, the looming overgrown canefields to his right, or the tumbled ruin of Vergée d'Or, just visible through the trees in the distance.

A man to be trusted? A man with whom it would be possible to make an honest peace? Richilde thought that his eyes were too small, his mouth too slack. But he was all the hope they had.

He paused, looked at the Negro commanders. She could almost read his thoughts. Contempt, for the raggedness of their makeshift uniforms, perhaps for the idea of slaves wearing uniforms at all. But also a watchful recognition that their swords were bright and sharp, and that now, after eighteen months of trial and error, they handled their muskets with careless ease – he would know that their only powder and ball nowadays came from dead French soldiers.

'Monsieur Toussaint,' he said, and gave a low bow.

Toussaint replied in kind. 'Commissioner.'

Santhonax glanced at the two huge black men standing beside Toussaint.

'My army commanders,' Toussaint said. 'General Dessalines, and General Christophe.'

Henry looked at his idol in surprise. A general? For that rank he was even willing to overlook the French pronunciation of his name. Richilde wanted to clap her hands for him.

But Santhonax was now looking at her. 'Madame de Mortmain? I have heard a great deal about you, madame.'

She inclined her head. Today, for the first time in six months, she had taken pains with her hair, and cleaned her nails. But he would still be able to see that she wore but a single garment, and her feet were bare.

'I look forward to talking with you,' Santhonax said, eyes drifting up and down her body as he invested the word *talk* with an entirely new significance. Because, of course, as she had elected to live with the blacks, in his opinion she had to be a whore.

His gaze returned to Toussaint. 'Is there somewhere we can sit?'

Toussaint lowered himself to the ground, and after a moment Santhonax did the same, carefully folding the tails of his coat over his thighs. Henry and Dessalines remained standing, as did everyone else, including Richilde. She supposed she must get used to this, for the rest of her life. She was the inferior being in this very masculine world she had chosen for her own.

'I cannot offer you peace,' Santhonax said. 'Save you win it for yourselves. But I can offer you honour, and freedom.'

Toussaint waited.

'France, the new France, the France of the tricolour,' Santhonax said, 'would have all men free. But no other country would have it so. Thus France is at war, with all the world. We are at war with Great Britain. Because we too have had to execute our landlords. We have executed the greatest landlord of all, monsieur. The king. So we offer you your place as Frenchmen.'

'To fight for you, against the British,' Toussaint said.

'This is your country, Toussaint,' Santhonax said. 'And the British are certainly coming. A vast armament fits out in Kingston. The British have long wanted

St Domingue. And do not suppose *they* mean to free any slaves.'

'But you would set us free,' Toussaint said.

'I have the power to do so the moment you agree to my terms.'

'Then speak.'

'They are that you swear allegiance to France, to the National Convention. That you will restore St Domingue to her rightful place as the brightest jewel in the French overseas empire. You will appoint your own commanders, choose your own tactics, be answerable only to me. And I ask only your success.'

'And the white people, in Cap François and Port-au-Prince, they will agree to this?' Toussaint asked.

Santhonax smiled. 'Those white people are royalist by instinct. They will have to do as they are told.'

Toussaint gazed at him. 'You will open the gates of Cap François, to my people?'

'Once you have taken the oath of allegiance.'

Toussaint looked left and right. 'And afterwards?'

'When the war is won?' Santhonax shrugged. 'There will have to be a . . . re-organisation, of St Domingue. But your people will be free, Toussaint. That is guaranteed by my government. Free, as Frenchmen.'

'I do not trust him,' Richilde said, as Henry came to take her in his arms. 'I do not trust him, or his government.'

'They need us,' Henry said. 'They need us, and we must make sure they go on needing us. Besides, Richilde, how else could we ever get inside Cap François?'

'Look,' Kit Hamilton pointed, past the volcanic crater of Saba, rising sheer out of the Caribbean Sea. 'Mount Misery.'

They had sailed through the Anegada Passage, leaving San Martin to port, the Virgins to starboard; St Kitts was only a few hours away, if the breeze held.

And there, Madeleine Jarrold would be reunited with her husband and her family. She at the least should have been happy at that prospect, after so long a separation. But she remained as gloomily silent as her brother.

Who now sighed. 'Do you know, I had not thought to see St Kitts again, ever? But then, there are so many sights I had not supposed I would ever see at all. Those black scoundrels marching through the streets of Cap François . . . I was told poor Peynier's hair turned white when he heard what Santhonax had agreed. And those are the men who would rule France.'

'How Richilde must have crowed,' Madeleine said, bitterly. 'Did you see her, Kit?'

'I said goodbye,' Kit said.

'I do not see how you could bear even to speak with her,' Madeleine said. 'Was she triumphant?'

'Quite the contrary,' Kit said. 'She views the future with much concern. She knows it is going to be a long, hard war with the British.'

'The British,' Etienne sneered. 'She will have to worry when *we* return.' He met Kit's gaze, and flushed. 'We will return, Kit. France. The real France. We will return, and when we do there will have to be an accounting. And Richilde will be one of those brought to book. You must accept that, Kit. She is a traitor. Not only to her family, but to her race, her very sex.'

Kit turned away, went down the companion ladder to the cabin. Not that he expected any joy from Annette. But she was his responsibility. He did not know if she had discussed his proposition with her brother and sister, but they had tacitly accepted that it had happened. They had too much to do with their lives, hating and dreaming of revenge, to be saddled with a mad sister.

And did he not have something to do with his life?

She sat by the stern window, looking out at the bubbling wake stretching across the blue of the ocean. When she sat like this, her face in repose, she was again the pretty, quiet girl with whom he had fallen in love ten years before. Almost he feared to speak, to disturb the picture.

'St Kitts is in sight,' he said. 'Old Mount Misery,' pointing his finger at the sky. 'Remember him?'

'I think so.' She turned her head, gave a quick, shy smile. 'Will we stay there long?'

He shook his head, sat beside her. She had screamed and wept when told she would have to leave Cap François – or live there under black dominion. Yet he thought that the voyage, away from the sights and sounds which evoked such powerful memories, had done her good. Dare he believe that she might work her way out of her dementia, then he could be a happy man.

'We shall stay there not a moment longer than we need, to offload Madeleine and Etienne,' he promised, and smiled at her. 'I've a business to attend to, cargoes to be shipped. And I've America to show you.'

She held his hand. 'Will I like America, Kit? Will I?'

'You'll love America,' he said. 'And America will love you.'

She sighed, and rested her head on his shoulder, while he held her close. And wondered. That he loved her, that he *could* love her, he never doubted for a moment. Therefore, that he *would* love her. And yet he had never done more than kiss her lips. Because that he desired her was also undoubted – it was an essential part of his love.

'You will be happy there,' he said, putting his arm round her shoulders to turn her against him, kissing her hair as he did so.

'Oh, I so want to be happy,' she breathed. 'So very much, Kit.'

'It shall be my charge,' he said, and allowed his hand to stroke from her shoulder and across her breast. Immediately he felt her body grow rigid, and then she leapt away from him.

'They cut her,' she shouted. 'Here.' She held her own breasts, one in each hand. 'They cut her. I watched them. I watched the blood. They cut her,' she screamed.

The cabin door opened, and he gazed at Madeleine. She took in the situation at a glance, stared at him in turn. Her eyes were the saddest he had ever seen.

But could they possibly be more sad than his own?

'Get up off your knees,' Henry Christopher said. 'That ain't no work for you, Richilde.'

Richilde let her scrubbing brush lie in the welter of soapsuds on the parquet floor, sat on her heels, used her wrist to push water from her eyes. 'It is work for someone, Henry. If we are going to live in a house, then it must be a clean house.'

He held her shoulders, raised her from the floor. He wore a new uniform, blue coat and white breeches, tan boots and a red sash. He had at any rate achieved the first of his ambitions. Or was it the second, she thought, as he bent his head to kiss her?

And did she really care whether or not the house they had appropriated for their own was a filthy wreck? She was happy. Wildly, irrelevantly happy. She knew that it was a purely physical, irresponsible happiness, sometimes found it difficult to believe that she had really abandoned position and race and even family to be the mistress of a Negro general who had no idea where he was leading his army. But he made her happy.

Thus she made herself work, where everyone about her, men and women, in the euphoria of being masters and mistresses of this once lovely city, had abandoned themselves to eating and drinking and sleeping in soft beds. It had only been with great difficulty that Toussaint had managed to get them to bury the dead bodies hanging from the gallows. She laboured not so much to remind herself that she was different to them, as to remind herself that this had to be a transient phase, that at the very least all the food in Cap François would soon be eaten, all the wine be drunk, and then they would *have* to work.

Toussaint was aware of this too. As he confided most of his thoughts to her, ever interested in her opinions, she understood many of the reasons for his indulgency. He loved his people too much to wish to drive them back to work. He was prepared to allow them this holiday, knowing like her that it must end, that they would have to follow him eventually – and hoping they would do so voluntarily.

Santhonax did not seem interested, as long as *he* also had food to eat and wine to drink, and utterly amoral Negro girls to take to his bed – and the white woman to watch, with his little pig eyes.

So she also worked to stop herself from thinking, of either yesterday or tomorrow. Of what she had been or what she might yet become. Of the family she had lost and the position she had abandoned.

'Well,' Henry said. 'I don't know for how much longer we going to be living here, and that is a fact. The British are here.'

She frowned at him, then ran to the window, as if expecting to see redcoats on the streets. No redcoats, but a great many people, shrugging away their languor as they hurried towards those ramparts overlooking the sea.

There she and Henry joined them, to stare at the myriad ships, perhaps as many as fifty of them, she estimated, standing slowly towards the land, an immense spread of white canvas. Great Britain was called the 'Mistress of the Seas' – with reason, as long as she could command fleets like that.

She glanced at Henry, watched him biting his lip. He must know that he had never encountered any force as formidable as this before.

'A magnificent sight, eh, madame?' Toussaint also wore the uniform of a French officer, had Santhonax beside him as usual. 'But they are your people, are

301

they not?' He smiled, slapped Henry on the shoulder. 'And yours, too.'

'What are we going to do?' Richilde asked. She knew how scarce was their supply of powder and ball, even had they possessed any trained gunners.

'Do?' Santhonax shouted. He was as usual the worse for wine. 'Why, madame, we shall fight them.'

'In due course,' Toussaint agreed. 'But on ground of our own choosing, monsieur. For the time being, we will evacuate the town. General Christophe, you will give the necessary orders.'

Henry hesitated, while Santhonax stared at his army commander.

'Evacuate the town? Evacuate Cap François? Surrender it?'

'Better to surrender it, than die in it, monsieur,' Toussaint said. 'That fleet is quite capable of blowing this town into little pieces. And when they have done that, they will land several thousand men, disciplined and well trained soldiers. There is no way we can oppose them, successfully, on open ground.'

'But . . . do you not mean to fight them at all? By God . . .'

'We will fight them, monsieur,' Toussaint said quietly. 'But we must make them come to us, and fight on our terms.'

'And you suppose they will do that?' Santhonax sneered. 'Come to you?'

'They will do that, monsieur. Those are neither frightened planters nor garrison troops, content to hold a fortified position. They are fighting soldiers, and they have come to conquer St Domingue for their king. They know they cannot do that until they have first conquered us. They will come.' He pointed at the puff of smoke rising from the foredeck of the first warship, at the plume of water where the ball entered the sea, only a couple of hundred yards away from the wall on which they stood. 'Let us make haste.'

His calm certainty left even Santhonax dumb.

But . . . abandon Cap François? Richilde asked herself. Back to the forest and the huts and the rain? Back to living like animals? They had been going to build. Or was that just another of their dreams?

She gazed at Henry with wide eyes, but Henry was thinking like a soldier. 'If we are not going to defend the city, Toussaint,' he said, 'let us then burn it, so that the British will not have the use of it.'

Toussaint smiled, and shook his head. 'But they must have the use of the city, Henry. To evacuate their men from, when they realise that they cannot defeat us.'

Redcoats. A very large number of them. Richilde sat her horse on the edge of the rising ground at the rear of the plantation to watch them. Beside her were Toussaint and Santhonax, and Dessalines. But not Henry. General Christophe, as he was now known and as he had accepted the title, was down there amongst the overgrown jungle that was all that remained of Vergée d'Or, seeking to oppose his tactical skill and Toussaint's strategical genius to these most formidable of soldiers. Risking his life, as he had constantly risked his life from the day the revolution had begun.

And thus also risking her happiness, her sole reason for living.

Toussaint handed her his telescope, and she gazed at the British. There were two columns of them, both alike, and yet utterly dissimilar. The first column wore trousers, and tall shakos. They might have been on a parade ground, in the way they marched, ever watched by their sergeants and their mounted officers, with every musket at the same angle on every shoulder, every red jacket buttoned to the neck – almost, she thought, she could see the sweat dribbling down their cheeks, darkening arm pit and between shoulder blade. The second column also wore carefully buttoned red jackets, with the same white cross belts, and maintained the same perfect order, but they were slightly more comfortable, she estimated – they wore kilts instead of

303

trousers, which left their red knees bare, and huge bonnets instead of shakos. The Negroes were inclined to smile as they pointed at the Scots – Richilde remembered sufficient military history to know they were more dangerous than any foe Toussaint's army had yet faced.

Puffs of white smoke rose from the scrub, several seconds before the reports of the muskets reached the watchers. The British skirmishers immediately returned fire, the columns behind them formed square. But the anticipated attack never came, as Henry withdrew his men, slipping silently through the tangled, unharvested canestalks. After several moments the square formed column again, as the British marched for the factory, which stood out like a beacon amidst the surrounding devastation. But this march took them close by the old plantation farm, which in two years' neglect had become almost a forest. Richilde's heart pounded as she watched the black men, wielding machetes, rise from the grass where they had lain concealed until almost trodden on by the marching soldiers. She did not doubt that Henry was down there with them.

All was confusion for several minutes. The British had marched with fixed bayonets, but had not had time to form line abreast before the black men were amongst them, cutting and slashing, yelling and screaming. Orders were shouted, mounted officers rode into the centre of the melee with total disregard for their own safety – and half a mile to the rear the Scots began to run, bringing their bayonets to the charge as they did so.

'Enough, Henry,' Toussaint muttered. 'Enough.'

Henry might have been able to hear him. The black men were suddenly hurrying, back towards the slave village, pursued by the enraged redcoats, but, when those had been brought under control by bugle calls and shouted orders, by volleys of musketry, ineffectual as Henry's men were out of range.

Toussaint watched through his telescope, grunted his

satisfaction. 'It is your turn, Jean-Jacques,' he said to Dessalines. 'Remember my instructions, now. Do not get involved with them too closely.'

Dessalines nodded, hurried off to lead his men.

'We will withdraw,' Toussaint said.

'Where now?' Santhonax had been drinking wine.

'Into the bush,' Toussaint said.

'The bush?' Richilde asked, her heart sinking.

Toussaint smiled at her. 'Do not worry, Richilde. Henry will follow.'

'The bush?' Santhonax bellowed. 'But you've given those lobsters a bloody nose. Now's the time to close, to chase them back to Cap François.'

Toussaint shook his head. 'No, no, monsieur. Now is the time for them to chase *us*, into the jungle.' He slapped a mosquito which had settled on his wrist; dead, it left a splodge of fresh blood which it had just drawn from his veins. 'We will find allies, in the jungle.'

The jungle! How often had she looked at the densely matted slopes from her window on Vergée d'Or? Richilde wondered. That forest had attracted her, as the mountain peaks which rose out of the trees had attracted her. They had been something to explore. To investigate. One day. That had been another dream.

But this dream, like the dream of revolution, had come true. And like the dream of revolution, the reality was too grim to be considered. Here was a world she did not suppose had been invaded by man since the Spaniards had first come here, led by Columbus himself, three hundred years before, to destroy the Indians, Caribs and Arawaks, who had lived here. And fleeing Indians could hardly be described as invaders. This was a world in which the vine and the bush and the insect held sway, in which mankind was totally alien. Even men like Jean-Jacques Dessalines, to whom the West Africa jungles were still a living memory, knew nothing like this.

At least the growth, and the ground, were together too formidable for animal or even reptile life, on any scale larger than a lizard. Only the men, and their women, and children, and dogs, floundered onwards. They cut their way through clinging vines, flogged by low slung branches, tripping through poisonous leaves and bushes which brought their flesh up in agonising blisters, assailed by downpours of tropical rain which pounded on their heads like pebbles – and never knowing when the ground over which they made their way would simply not be there, and their scouts find themselves tumbling down a hundred feet and more over a precipitous slope into a fast running river, or come face to face with an equally unclimbable escarpment, rising sheer above them. They walked on beds of dead leaves which without warning would give way to outcroppings of razor sharp rock to tear at their bare feet. Whenever they halted they were immediately assailed by a host of insects, many of which they could hardly see, but which burrowed beneath their flesh to leave itching, festering sores – these they called *bêtes rouge*, the red beasts. And day or night their skins were smothered in mosquitoes, whirring and humming, pouncing in clusters on the sudden feast of unprotected human flesh which was being presented to them.

Soon it was difficult for Richilde to recall that she had ever had a daily bath, or used perfume, or brushed her hair, or slept in a bed, or protected her body, either from the sun or from prying eyes. Toussaint and Henry obviously worried for her, because she was the madame. But the Negroes suffered equally, especially their women, and even more especially elderly women like Clotilde Toussaint, who was just as used as Richilde to a sedentary life around the plantation, and who worried ceaselessly about her two sons, both just teenagers – she had only been allowed to become Toussaint's wife late in life, in a sudden spurt of generosity by old Thérèse de Milot – but who were both determined to fight alongside their father.

Because the Negroes also fought, as the British followed them. The redcoats knew that where Toussaint went, there was the main source of resistance to them, and sweating and cursing, they too hacked and pushed and forced their way through the forest, checked every so often by a fierce rearguard action, allowed, every so often, to catch a sight of their prey, as they staggered onwards, subjected, every so often, to a savage counter attack, planned and devised by Toussaint, and executed by his two faithful Generals, Christophe and Dessalines, who crept past the British outposts to wreak havoc amongst the supply trains before once again disappearing into the forests.

'L'Ouverture,' the Negroes called Toussaint. 'L'Ouverture,' they shouted, whenever he passed by. He was the man who opened the British ranks, for them to enter. And Toussaint was obviously delighted by the nickname, as delighted as he was with the success of his hit and run strategy.

Even if it did not apparently please Santhonax. The fat Frenchman indeed suffered more than any of them, cursed and swore and slapped at mosquitoes, grumbled as his supply of wine ran out, and as he had to live on water and what food could be gathered in the forest, like the rest of them.

'My instructions were to regain control of the colony for France,' he would say. 'Not abandon it to the British.'

'And we will do that for you, monsieur,' Toussaint would reply, with endless patience. 'When we are ready. And when the time is ripe.'

For he was not only waiting for the climate to take effect. He was also working at training his army, firstly in the use of European weapons – many of his counter strokes were intended less to check the British columns than to secure British muskets and ammunition from the dead – and secondly to accustom them to receiving commands, just as he taught his officers to understand

307

the elements of strategy. All based entirely upon the books he had studied, the considerations upon which he had obviously reflected during long hours driving his coach, or sitting on the box in Cap François waiting for his mistress to return from a social call or a shopping expedition.

Richilde was prepared to concede that he was probably as great a natural genius as the world had ever known – and yet, like Santhonax, she could not stop herself from occasionally feeling utter despair. It was not so much the hardships of her new life, the poor quality and often limited quantity of food, the visible deterioration of the milky white complexion she had so carefully cultivated and protected for twenty-six years into a sunbrowned hardness which made her appear almost a mulatto. These things were acceptable and even exciting, as she shared them with Henry, determined never to become a burden to him in any way, equally determined to prove to the black women that even a pampered white *mâitresse* could survive the jungle. And succeeding, she thought, in that they no longer regarded her with frank wonder or cold suspicion, but accepted her as one of themselves, whatever her colour, a development led and controlled by Clotilde Toussaint. The women like Amelia who had tormented her the day after the revolt had begun had long abandoned the army, either in surrender to the British, or to live in some remote jungle clearing, just as such a *mamaloi* as Céleste had also disappeared in the tumultuous days following the revolt, understanding that it was a time for men to do, rather than women to prophesy. If the army, and perhaps even Toussaint himself, continued to pray to Damballah Oueddo and Ogone Badagris, there was no time for any large voodoo ceremonies in this hurried, gypsy existence.

But it was this last point caused her concern. For was the army not also living like a tribe of savages as it conducted a savage campaign?

She would, she knew, have been here anyway, because of Henry. She could now be amazed at the power of an upbringing and an ideology which had kept her living in close proximity with him for twenty-six years, increasingly aware of his love for her, but only able to accept it as her due as his mistress rather than as a cause for pride, and quite unable to suppose that she might be able to reciprocate. She recognised that what had so nearly happened on the night of the voodoo ceremony had been a pure explosion of emotional lust, immediately regretted. Once the scales of prejudice had been ripped from her eyes she knew that there could be no other man for her, under any circumstances. That she dared not have another child for him in these conditions, had to resort to the very effective Negro methods of post sex contraception, was a principal source of her unhappiness.

But beyond Henry, her interest in the blacks, and her sympathy for them, had been aroused by the growing awareness that they were not, as she had always been taught to believe, an inferior race to the whites, but merely a less civilised one, and by her belief that, given equal opportunities of education and freedom, they would be just as capable of creating a nation and a culture equal to any. She had, she supposed, quite neglected to consider the endless centuries during which *her* ancestors had clawed their way out of the primeval swamp, had supposed that in some miraculous fashion the revolution would be followed by a long period of peace, to enable Toussaint to instruct his people in the cohesion and industry they had to display if they were ever to become a nation.

Instead she daily watched them revert more and more to savagery. Living in a jungle, fighting and killing, were impulses that lay too close to the surface of their consciousness. What disturbed her most was that Toussaint himself did not appear to share her concern. That he did dream of a future for his people, as a civilised nation, was certain, and from his conversations with her she was equally certain that he even had well laid plans to be implemented when the time came. But beating the British came first, in his estimation. She understood this, even as she understood that they had to be beaten not because they were *there* – or he might have been prepared to sue for peace – but because he was fighting for France, in a partnership which he hoped and believed would bestow great benefits on his people once victory was achieved. Thus, to gain that victory he was prepared to practice the most formidable patience, confident that no matter how long it took, his people would follow him in peace as they were following him in war.

Perhaps, she thought, it is that sublime confidence which most terrifies me. Because there was only one Toussaint, and he was already past sixty. When she looked at his Generals, at Jean-Jacques Dessalines, the most savage of men, or even at Henry Christopher, still uncertain of what he really wanted in life, and still, above all else, the soldier pure and simple, she could not but shudder at what might lie ahead.

But Henry, at least, was hers to control. She hoped and thought. He sat on the banks of the stream along which the army was camped, and watched her kneeling in the shallows to wash her hair. It was evening, and they were high in the mountains, higher than she had ever been in her life before – although the peaks still towered above them – and thus it was delightfully cool, with the rushing water cold enough to bring her flesh up in goosepimples, while even the mosquitoes seemed to find it difficult to struggle up to this altitude.

Her hair rinsed, and squeezed as dry as she could, she commenced to launder her tattered gown – her only garment – using the Negro method of pounding it between stones, as were several other women further down the stream. This worked very well as regards cleanliness, but it played havoc with the material.

'Do you suppose we will ever be able to get some new clothes?' she asked.

'Some day,' Henry said: his uniform was equally tattered.

She sighed. He was a man of very few words. And yet she could feel his gaze on her back, which was worth ∙ more than a speech.

'I wouldn't mind if we could stay here for a while,' she remarked. 'It really is a delightful spot. Do you think we could stay here, Henry? Surely the British aren't going to climb this high after us?'

'They coming,' he said.

She raised her head, somewhat chagrined to realise that he had not been watching her after all, but was instead looking past her down the tumbled slopes, at the forest, and at the soldiers who could just be seen, like a line of red ants, toiling up a sharp escarpment. They were several miles away, and several hundred feet beneath them, but, as he said, they were coming.

'So where do we go now?' she asked, turning to look at him.

He smiled. 'These mountains have to slope back down again some time. But you know what I am thinking? It is time we should fight a battle.'

She frowned at him; it was the first time she had ever heard him make a criticism of Toussaint, even implicitly. 'You mean here?'

'It could be here,' he agreed. 'But when they get up here, they done the worst. Down there would be better.' He pointed at the very escarpment over which the British were clambering, with increasing difficulty as the slopes grew steeper and more strewn with boulders. Certainly they did not look in much shape to fight after such a climb.

Yet they were British soldiers. 'Do you think your men are capable of meeting the soldiers, in a pitched battle, yet?' she asked.

Another smile, this time a trifle wry. 'Yet? Or ever?'

She crawled to sit beside him, rest her head on his shoulder. 'Well, then . . .'

'They would fight, behind a wall,' he said.

She raised her head. 'A wall?'

'I saw those men fighting behind walls, in America,' he said. 'Ten men behind a wall can beat twenty outside.' He thought for a moment. 'And if it was a big wall . . . '

'You are thinking of a castle,' she said.

'A castle?'

'Like the fort in Cap François. Or Brimstone Hill in St Kitts.'

'They were both captured,' he said, half to himself.

'By bombardment from the sea,' she said. 'But there is no castle anywhere in the world which can stand up to siege guns.'

'Yes.' Suddenly he was enthusiastic: 'But they must be able to reach. If we could build a castle down there, where those soldiers are now, nobody could drag guns close enough. And no ships could reach us, either.' He snapped his fingers. 'And yet we could watch the ships.'

Which was perfectly true. From where they sat they looked, not only over the forested slopes beneath them, but all the way down to the coast, could even make out the scarred ruin of Vergée d'Or, huddled against the trees fringing the white sand beach, and beyond, the surging blue of the Atlantic. The view from a few hundred feet lower down would be no less dramatically beautiful.

But he was dreaming again. 'It would be quite impossible to build a castle, down there in the jungle, Henry,' she said. 'It would be . . . well, like building the pyramids. It would take years, and thousands of people.'

'The pyramids?' he asked.

'I will tell you about them,' she offered. And saw his preoccupation and perhaps disappointment, at her lack of enthusiasm. 'Anyway,' she said. 'If you *could* build

312

such a fortress, Henry, it would be so impregnable no one would ever dare attack it.'

He smiled at her. 'And *you* don't think that would be a good thing, Richilde?'

Toussaint had noted the British vulnerability, and ordered an attack for dawn. A more determined attack than usual, for he intended to accompany his men and direct them from the immediate vicinity of the battle. But it was still to be a hit and run affair. He instructed Louis-Pierre, the tall serious Negro who was his third General, to break camp at sun-up and move along the ridge – not up towards the mountains any longer – with a view once again to descending to the plains. 'If we cross the mountain,' he said with a smile, 'we shall be fighting Rigaud's mulattos as well as the British.

'Bah,' Santhonax grumbled. 'Are they not also against the British? Have we not sent them messengers inviting them to unite with us in the common cause?'

'Indeed we have, monsieur,' Toussaint agreed with his invariable patience. 'And they have not replied. Until they do, it would be best for us to proceed with caution.'

'Caution,' Santhonax said, standing beside Richilde to watch the army filing down the hillside towards the trees, while the sun plunged into the peaks behind them – it would take them all night to reach their assault positions. 'I have never met a man who set so much store by caution. Is it not true, Madame de Mortmain, that he sought no part in the actual slave revolt, wished only to restrain it?'

Richilde could no longer make Henry out. She turned, to walk back to where she would sleep, her still damp gown clinging to her legs and shoulders. 'That is true, monsieur.'

'Then I cannot understand how he has achieved such authority,' Santhonax said, following her. 'What is needed here are men of spirit. Men like your Henri, eh, madame?'

'Toussaint commands because he is the most capable of command, monsieur.' She knelt, waited for him to go. '*Henry* might win a battle for you, but Toussaint will win the war.

'That is no way to speak of your lover.' He knelt beside her, an absurd series of jerky and uncomfortable movements in so bulky a man. 'He *is* your lover, is he not, Richilde?'

She met his gaze. 'He is my lover, monsieur.'

'A Negro, who was once your coachman.' He grinned at her. 'Or did you enjoy his black stick more than your husband's, even then?'

'Does it matter, monsieur?'

'Of course it matters.' He cast quick glances, left and right, to estimate just how thoroughly they were shrouded in the gloom. Richilde sighed. She knew exactly what was going to happen next – could not decide how firmly he should be repelled. He was, after all, the Commissioner.

'Richilde . . .' He took her hand. 'Believe me, I know much of what you have suffered. I have heard a great deal of this Philippe de Mortmain, a true aristocrat, the sort of man who so nearly brought France to her knees. I can understand how difficult it must have been, your life with him.' A sly smile. 'I have also heard much about the . . . the perquisites of you great ladies. In France it was the pages. Here it was the blacks, eh?' He chuckled. 'Or in your case, it is still the blacks, eh?'

Still she gazed at him, as his fingers began to slide up her arm, and his gaze dropped to her nipples, clearly visible through the thin, damp material of her gown.

'But now, to surrender yourself entirely to a black embrace . . . of course I realise that you are in their power. But it will not always be so, Richilde. When the British are beaten, when I am able to take my proper place as Governor General of St Domingue, and reduce these savages to *their* proper places, then if you wished you could sit at my side. Would you not like that, Richilde?'

314

'My dear monsieur,' she said. 'How could you possibly consider taking me to your bed, when, as you say, I have been impaled upon a black stick, time and again?'

He frowned at her, unsure whether or not she was laughing at him.

'How could you be sure,' she asked, 'that I am not riddled with some hideous disease?'

His frown deepened. 'You are not, madame? Say that you are not. There would be a waste.'

His arrogance was hardly less incredible than his lack of humour.

'Or worse, monsieur,' she said. 'How could you be sure I would not be continually comparing you with the manhoods I have known?'

'Bah,' he declared. 'I fear comparison with no man. I have eight inches. Did you know that, madame? I am renowned throughout Paris. Here, I will show you . . .' he began to release his trousers and she realised that she was dealing with neither a gentleman nor an intelligent savage. He would have to be crushed.

'Spare me, monsieur, I beg of you,' she said. 'I have no desire to investigate your manhood. Or to experience it.'

'You would spend the rest of your life in these conditions? You wish to do that?'

'No, monsieur, I do not *wish* to do that. But I am prepared to do that, if such is the decree of fate. Nor am I a prostitute, merely because I share a black man's bed.'

'And you suppose a savage can know anything of love? Will he not throw you aside the moment he tires of you?'

It was time to end such a ridiculous conversation. 'Henry and I share more than our bodies, monsieur,' she said. 'Certainly we share more than would ever be possible with any other *man*, much less a puffed-up bullfrog from the Parisian gutters.'

He stared at her for a moment, then swung his fist,

rising as he did so. She fell away from him, rolled over to reach her knees again, saw him on his feet above her.

'Bitch,' he snarled. 'Whore. White nigger.'

His boot was carving through the air, and she could only roll again, desperately seeking some weapon to defend herself.

But the sounds of the scuffle had alerted the encampment, and Santhonax was surrounded by black men, led by Louis-Pierre, who gripped his arms.

'Release me,' he bawled. 'I am Monsieur Santhonax. I am the Commissioner. Release me.'

'You have attempted to assault Madame Richilde,' Louis-Pierre said. 'Say the word, madame, and I will have him flogged.'

'Flogged?' Santhonax bellowed. But now he was afraid, and his voice trembled. 'Flogged?'

Richilde reached her feet. She was aware of anger combined with an understanding that this was a situation which had to be faced, or it could become a festering sore running through the black army. And he deserved far worse than a flogging, not so much for insulting her, as for revealing so clearly his true attitude towards the people he pretended to govern.

'Do not flog him,' she said. 'We will put the matter to General Christophe, when he returns.'

Santhonax glared at her. 'Christophe?' he shouted. 'Do you suppose I am afraid of a black savage?'

'That, monsieur,' she said, 'we shall discover tomorrow.'

It was midday before the column of women and children was rejoined by the army, elated with another considerable, if limited, success. Santhonax was there to greet them.

'There has been a mutiny,' he told Toussaint. 'These niggers of yours have dared to place me under arrest.

Me, Léger Santhonax. You must make an example of them, Toussaint.'

But Toussaint had already spoken with Louis-Pierre. 'You have insulted Madame de Mortmain,' he said.

'Bah,' Santhonax said. 'How may the Commissioner insult a mere woman? How may he insult anyone?'

'You may insult whoever you choose, monsieur,' Toussaint agreed. 'Providing you are prepared to answer for it. But you are fortunate. General Christophe is prepared to regard the incident as a personal matter, between you and him.'

Santhonax gazed at the huge young man, licked his lips.

'You have choice of weapons, monsieur,' Henry said, speaking very quietly.

Richilde held her breath. She could have no fears for Henry were he able to come to grips with any adversary, but he knew very little of accuracy with a pistol, or skill with a sword.

Santhonax was still chewing his lip, looking from Henry to Toussaint to Jean-Jacques Dessalines, grinning at him, and then at the black faces which surrounded him.

'I do not fight with savages,' he said, and walked away.

Dessalines gave a bellow of laughter, which was taken up by the watching soldiers. The camp echoed with their mirth. Santhonax checked, and almost turned, as if he would come back to face them, then walked into the trees.

'You have killed him more surely than with a sword thrust,' Toussaint said.

'I did not mean it this way,' Richilde said.

'He insulted you, madame,' Toussaint said. 'He deserved his shame.'

'But he is the Commissioner, appointed by France,' she said.

'Yes,' Toussaint agreed, thoughtfully.

317

She sat beside Henry in the cool of the afternoon. 'I seem to attract misfortune.'

'You are a beautiful woman.'

'There's a profound thought,' she said. 'But Henry, to have Santhonax hating us . . .'

'Santhonax is nothing,' he said. 'He was useful, because he got rid of the French for us. When we have beaten the English, we shall have no more need of him. We have no need of him now.'

'He has similar plans for you.'

Henry grinned. 'Then we are even. But we are the stronger, would you not say?'

'Men are coming.' Louis-Pierre stood above them. 'Mulattos. General Toussaint wishes your presence.'

It was the young man, Alexandre Petion, accompanied by an even younger man, with handsome, liquid brown features and alert dark eyes, which flickered over the black faces before coming to rest on Richilde, standing with Clotilde Toussaint and several other women.

'My aide,' Petion said. 'Jean Boyer.'

The young man gravely shook hands, but still stared at Richilde.

'We have sought you this fortnight,' Petion said. 'But you never stay in one place long enough to be found.'

'Thus the British cannot find us either,' Toussaint said.

'You run away,' Petion said. 'We stand and fight.'

'And get beat,' Dessalines said, with a shout of laughter.

'And could you meet the redcoats on an open field, black man?' Boyer asked, speaking quietly.

Dessalines's smile faded into an angry frown, and he reached for his sword.

'We need to co-ordinate our strategy,' Toussaint said, resting his hand on Dessalines's arm. 'That is why we have sought this meeting.'

'General Rigaud feels our cause is hopeless,' Petion

said. 'The British have offered good terms for our surrender. It is better to accept the inevitable than to spend the rest of our lives fighting a war we cannot win.'

'Those terms do not include freedom for black people,' Henry said.

'Would you rather be dead, than alive as a slave?' Petion asked. 'Things are different in England. There is a great anti-slavery movement there. Certain it is that no English planter dare abuse his slaves like a Mortmain or a Milot. There is even talk of emancipation, one day.'

'One day,' Henry said.

'We would rather be dead, than return to slavery,' Toussaint said.

'General Rigaud wishes the matter laid before Monsieur Santhonax,' Petion said. 'It is for him to decide.'

'Santhonax is a fool,' Dessalines growled.

'I have sent to tell him you are here,' Toussaint said. 'But I do not think he will agree to surrender to the British.'

'They would chop off his head when he went back to France,' Dessalines said. 'That is what they do to those who surrender.'

'It does not matter what Santhonax would do,' Henry said. 'We shall never surrender. We shall not be slaves again.' He looked at Richilde, followed her gaze towards Boyer.

'There is no need to surrender, or even to consider it,' Toussaint said. 'We will beat the British.'

'What with?' Petion sneered.

'With what we have,' Toussaint said. 'We have sufficient.'

Petion stared at him, then decided there was no point in arguing with such confidence. 'My message is for Monsieur Santhonax,' he said again.

'I have sent for him,' Toussaint repeated.

'But he will not come,' Louis-Pierre said, standing above them. 'He is dead.'

'Dead?' Toussaint asked.

'Dead?' Richilde cried, starting forward. 'But how?'

'I found him, madame,' Louis-Pierre said. 'Hanging from a tree. By his own belt.'

In all the violence and bloodshed with which she had been surrounded for the last four years, this was the first time Richilde had actually ever felt complete responsibility for a man's death.

'That is nonsense,' Henry insisted. 'He killed himself because of his guilt. And his shame. He deserved to die.'

'But what of the future?' she asked – even she could feel no real sympathy for such a man. 'He was France's representative.'

Toussaint smiled. 'I will have to be France's representative, until they send someone else.' He watched Petion and Boyer riding away to the south. 'Even if *they* will not willingly acknowledge the fact.'

'France,' Dessalines growled. 'Mulattos. Why do we not settle with them all?'

'Because we must beat the British first,' Toussaint said, with his usual patience.

If only, Richilde thought, she could convince herself that was possible. Her emotions were naturally totally confused. The British were her own kith and kin, by birth and background, even if both her father and her brother had been forced to change their nationality and however she had been brought up as a Frenchwoman. And besides, the soldiers themselves were not slave owners. She doubted if they even hated and feared the Negroes, the way the planters had done. They were merely helpless young men called to do a distasteful job of work in unfamiliar surroundings and for the profit of their masters in England.

Yet it was a job they were doing well. Like the mulattos, she found it difficult to understand Toussaint's certainty of victory. Certainly his hit and run tactics were brilliantly successful, but every such raid cost him as many men as the British, and as the months became years his army also dwindled because of desertions and sickness, usually a variety of fevers which caused men, and women, to waste away as they shivered and groaned. The future became impossible to consider. Even Henry had no idea of how long this desperate, primeval existence might continue. Undoubtedly he enjoyed it. It was a part of his dream, and if she was sure that his dream had encompassed other things as well, even in a very general sense, such as commanding huge armies of brilliantly uniformed men, of building palaces, and even a vast fortress to overlook all of St Domingue, he was young enough to enjoy the excitement of the present while remaining sure the future would arrive, eventually.

She wished she could share his optimism. She was no older – they celebrated their joint thirtieth birthdays after three years in the forest – and allowing for the fact that she was a woman, she was just as strong and, miraculously, just as healthy. When she did come down with a feverish attack, he took her into the forest, cradled in his arms, like a babe, found a clear, cool rushing stream, and sat her in it, up to her neck holding her there for an entire night. Next morning she was half frozen, and as weak as a babe, but the fever was gone.

Then he had made love to her, to restore her body warmth. It was the most tumultuously delicious hour she had ever spent, so much so she had wondered if she might not be delirious. But in fact she found all the physical pleasure she could possibly dream of in any of his embraces, adored his explorations of her which he still carried out in a sort of fascinated wonder. To him she was the greatest treasure in all the world, and even had she not found in him everything she could ever wish or respect in a man, she would have had to respond to such adoration.

She was by now utterly attuned to life in the forest,

321

with feet so hard not even burrowing insects like chiggers could find a home for their eggs in her flesh, and with sunbrowned skin so similarly toughened as to repel even the fiercest of mosquitoes. Her muscles were so firm that she could walk for hours over uneven ground without feeling fatigue, and her digestion was similarly trained to exist sometimes for thirty-six hours without food before being able to indulge in a stupefying meal. She had allowed her hair to grow until it stretched past her thighs, and could be used as an extra garment, which was useful, as she had been forced to do as the other women, and retain nothing more than a piece of cloth wrapped round and between her thighs and secured round her waist, thus leaving both her torso and her legs utterly exposed. But in fact since Santhonax's death she was unaware of any necessity for prurient modesty. She was surrounded by black girls with figures better than her own, and she was General Christophe's woman. He certainly saw her only as a woman, and no longer considered her either as white or as an ex-mistress. And this acceptance she thought extended throughout the entire army, with the possible exception of Jean-Jacques Dessalines. But she was not alone in fearing Dessalines. Sometimes she thought even Toussaint gave a shudder when he considered the savage instincts of his chief lieutenant, who was only restrained from an orgy of mutilation and slaughter, whenever prisoners were taken, by the calm composure of his commander. Richilde could only comfort herself with the reflection that even Dessalines had a most healthy respect for Henry's giant muscles.

But he remained a symbol of everything she feared about the future, everything that prevented her achieving the happiness she could not help but feel was there, dared she reach out and take it. She had no regrets for the past, for either the vanished mistress of Vergée d'Or or the equally lost excited girl who had been surrounded by anxiously eager relatives and seamstresses on her wedding day. If she sometimes missed her family, she would remind herself that she no longer had a family. Etienne and Madeleine and Annette undoubtedly regarded her as the most despicable sort of traitor to her race and to them, and even Kit had revealed a total lack of ability to understand any aspect of her feelings. Besides, she knew that even if in some miraculous way they could all be reunited, *she* would never be able to forgive *them* for murdering her child, whatever their motives.

But it was the memory of them, not less than her fear of Dessalines, which made her so desperate to see an end to the war, and a beginning of a new and better life for the black people. However physically enjoyable they might find their surroundings, she could not allow herself, or Henry, to sink into pure primitiveness. The dream would not dissolve into a perpetual hunger, whether it be for food, or shelter, or sex. On that she was utterly determined.

Thus she knew the depths of fear every time he led his men away to carry out a raid on a British patrol or encampment. And when he was not the first to return . . . She gazed at Louis-Pierre, striding towards her, and her heart constricted.

'The General sends for you, madame,' Louis-Pierre said.

'General Christophe?' she asked.

'All the Generals, madame.'

She hurried, in the midst of a crowd of women and children, all aware that something tremendous had happened. The British had at last realised they were accomplishing nothing by the endless pursuit of an always elusive foe. Thus they had changed their strategy, and instead of flying columns of exhausted men, had established fortified posts at selected places. They were well aware that the Negroes had, from time to time, to descend from their mountain fasts to find and slaughter the wild cattle of the central plains, and accumulate whatever other food they could discover, just as they had always relied upon successful ambushes for their powder and ball. Cut off from all those sources of life, the redcoats had concluded, Toussaint's army must disintegrate. As he could not allow that to happen, he would thus be forced to issue forth from his hideaways and fight a battle on open ground, which was the only favour the invaders asked of providence.

And they had been proved right. The Negro army had waited, and suffered, for two weeks, while the last of their food was consumed, glowering at the Union flag flying above the closest British camp, a large fort containing, Dessalines's scouts had said, not less than an entire regiment, sitting in the woods behind Rio Negro Plantation, daring the blacks to attempt to reach either the canefields or the fishing on the coast. And after two weeks, Toussaint had been forced to order an assault, knowing full well that to have his irregulars charge the disciplined volley fire and glittering bayonets of the soldiers had to be the dream of every British commander.

But now . . . those waiting in the trees had heard no gunfire. Could the British have withdrawn? That was impossible – the Union flag still fluttered in the breeze above the orderly row of huts, behind the sheltering earthworks. She ran towards Henry, who stood, with Toussaint and Dessalines in the open, under the very guns of the fort. Their men stood around them, apparently as bemused as she was.

'Use this.' Henry gave her a piece of cloth to hold across her nose and mouth. Stomach rolling, she walked beside him up to the gateway, recoiled from the stench, stared at the fully uniformed guards who lay at their post.

She clutched Henry's arm. 'Plague?' she whispered.

Henry pointed at the white men's complexions, all tinted a dreadful shade of yellow. 'Fever,' he said. 'Yellow fever. An entire regiment. Dead.'

She turned to look at Toussaint in horror. His face was equally grim, but his eyes were dancing. 'As I promised, madame,' he said. 'We have found allies, in the forest.'

One of the terms on which Toussaint insisted was clothes for his women. Richilde was almost disconcerted to feel the material of a gown on her shoulders, the gentle tug of it across her breasts. Suddenly she was afraid of the future indicated by the restraining garment – the future she had anticipated for so long – as much as by the thought of having to face white men again, even if from a distance.

There were a great number of them, redcoats and blue coats, gleaming buttons and braid, bristling bayonets rising out of a forest of muskets, shakos proudly erect. Certainly they were undefeated, by any human adversaries, still looked a sufficient force to gain any victory.

'But they have lost the will to fight,' Henry said. 'I watched them do that at Yorktown, in 1781. Were Toussaint so minded, we could destroy them all.'

But Toussaint had better things to do, for which Richilde thanked God. His first priority had been the expulsion of the British from St Domingue, not their annihilation, or even their surrender. He sought the fact of victory, not the glory.

And now he had achieved it.

General Maitland saluted the flag, and gave a grim smile. 'You could fly your own, General Toussaint,' he said. 'Or do you look for support from the Directory in Paris?'

'I agreed to fight for them, monsieur,' Toussaint said.

'And you are a man of your word,' Maitland agreed. 'L'Ouverture! You have at the least opened a new world for the black man in Hispaniola. I can only hope, for your sake and the sake of your people, that your French masters understand that.'

'Masters?' Dessalines growled. 'We have no masters.'

'Every man has a master, General,' Maitland remarked. He held out his hand. 'I congratulate you, General Toussaint. I know you will honour the terms of our agreement.'

'Your people will be allowed to embark, unmolested,' Toussaint said.

'And the lives and properties of such French citizens as choose to remain behind will be respected?'

'As long as they do not take up arms against us, monsieur.'

Maitland nodded, looked up at the tricolour and again along the row of black faces waiting by the trees, gazed at Richilde.

'I have with me an American sea captain,' he said. 'Who would like to speak with his sister.'

She waited, suddenly exposed, feeling the breeze fluttering her hem and her hair, feeling too the eyes of several thousand people on her, white as well as black, feeling the immense weight of their thoughts, their imaginations, of what she might be like, of what she might have experienced these last six years, of what she might have suffered. Or enjoyed?

Kit was thirty-four, she recalled, and had become a serious, perhaps somewhat pessimistic man. This much was evident from the cast of his still handsome features. But also an exceedingly prosperous one, as could be told, not only from the cut of his clothes, but from his manner, which denoted more confidence, more aware-ness of who and what he was than even she remem-bered.

Now he shook hands with Toussaint. 'I will add my congratulations, General,' he said. 'I must confess I never supposed you would succeed.'

Toussaint smiled. 'And I will confess, monsieur, that there were times I never supposed I would succeed, either.'

Kit looked up at the flag, obviously thinking much as General Maitland had done, glanced at Dessalines, shook hands with Henry.

'So after all you have become a soldier,' he said. 'And a famous one.'

'It is what I wanted, Kit,' Henry said, simply.

'And is it the summit of your ambitions?'

Henry gazed at him. 'That is for Toussaint to say.'

Kit nodded, held Richilde's hands, kissed her on each cheek. 'You are looking well.'

'I have been living a healthy life.'

'Not all white people have found it so, or I would not be here,' he reminded her.

'But you will have observed that my skin is now brown,' she pointed out.

'It becomes you. Richilde . . .' He hesitated.

She shook her head. 'I will stay here in St Domingue, Kit.'

'With Henry?'

'With Henry. This moment, the ending of the war, is what I have been waiting for, for six years. Now Toussaint and Henry can start to build, and I wish to be here to help them.'

'Will you have another child, for Henry?'

She met his gaze. 'If I can.'

He nodded, and sighed. 'Well, then . . .'

'How is Annette?'

His face seemed to close. 'She is well.'

Her turn to hesitate. 'Kit . . . will you continue to trade with Cap François, after the British have left?'

'If your people wish it.'

'We wish it,' Henry said. 'Like Richilde has said, we need to build.'

'Yes,' Kit said. For a second time he looked at Dessalines, then turned and rejoined the British forces.

'He is an unhappy man,' Henry remarked. 'Because you will not go with him.'

She shook her head. 'Because of Annette,' she said.

Toussaint stood beside them. 'General Christophe,' he said. 'You will take your regiment and prepare to occupy Cap François the moment the British evacuate. I put you in command of the entire north coast.'

Henry saluted. 'And you?'

'The main army will march south. We must finish with Rigaud and Petion.'

'But . . . you mean the war will go on?' Richilde was aghast.

'For a little while, madame. A divided country is no country at all.' He smiled. 'But I promise you, it will be only for a *little* while.'

Chapter 2

THE INVADERS

Even before the conclusion of [the] peace [of Amiens, with England, in 1802] an expeditionary force had been assembled, comprising twenty thousand of those veterans who had played havoc with the military reputations of Europe. But as they were only intended to subdue a parcel of rebellious blacks, no Lannes, no Massena, was sent to command them. Instead the First Consul gave this perquisite to his brother-in-law, Charles Victor Emmanuel LeClerc, a veteran of the Egyptian campaign. Pauline LeClerc accompanied her husband – a fine chance this, to see the world – and possibly the only men in the French armada who had any doubts as to the eventual outcome of the campaign were the Generals Rigaud, Petion and Boyer, included for the sake of their local knowledge. On 3 February 1802 the French fleet, under the command of Admiral Villaret-Joyeuse, dropped anchor off Cap François.

Christopher Hamilton dismounted, handed his reins to the groom, a white boy. As the maid who opened the front door of the house for him was a white woman. It was just as easy to obtain white servants in New York, if one was prosperous, as black.

Which was why he lived here. Besides, New York was where Alexander had made his headquarters. Officially he practiced law, but in fact he was steadfastly pursuing his political career. Since completing his most successful term as Secretary of the Treasury, in which he had managed to place the finances of the infant republic on a firm footing, he had spent a brief spell as Inspector General of the Army, before turning his attention to his real goal, the Presidency itself. In the last election he had been unsuccessful, but his intervention had secured the position for his old friend Thomas Jefferson, to the exclusion of Aaron Burr. Now there could be no doubt that the two men would clash again, when the position of Governor of New York State came up, in 1804. That that was still two years away was irrelevant; the battle lines were being drawn. Thus Alexander needed the support of all his friends and relations, just as he needed the financial backing provided by his interest in the shipping firm, even if he no longer took any active part in that business.

But Kit Hamilton was also a social asset, a romantic if slightly notorious character, rendered more so by the stark tragedy of his domestic life.

'Is the mistress at home?' he asked.

'She is in the garden, Captain.'

Kit nodded, went through the house, and into the rose garden at the rear. It was a small garden, hardly more than a lawn surrounded by flowerbeds, but it was Annette's favourite place. Even on a brisk autumn day she sat here, reading her book, looking up with a quick, shy smile.

'Kit!' She turned up her face for a kiss, on the forehead, squeezed his hand. She loved him. No one could doubt that for a moment. As a brother. Ten years might have passed since that August night in 1791, yet there was still no way of telling when her mind might be engulfed by terrified loathing. But he had assumed the burden of that shattered mind, in the optimism of ignorance, he was prepared to admit to himself, certain that the lively and loving girl he remembered must recover, at least when under his care.

Now he sat next to a thirty-six year old crone, with hair as white as snow, with movements matchingly slow, and yet with a demeanour utterly proprietorial. He was her cousin, her protector, and her man. They lived in conditions of complete intimacy, even shared the same bedchamber – yet he had never touched her body below the neck. That he might still wish to do so apparently never crossed her mind, nowadays, just as that he had once in the past tried to do so had been easily relegated to the level of the nightmares from which she continuously suffered. What agonies of desire he might experience when confronted with her ample figure, what doubtful company he might from time to time be forced to seek to preserve his own sanity, was no concern of hers – he did not suppose she was even aware of such emotions. She concentrated on simpler things.

'I'm so glad you're back,' she said. 'It looks like a storm.'

He nodded. 'Wind's freshening all the time.'

'Did you visit them?' she asked.

'We're unloading a cargo of prime sugar,' he said. 'Some of it from Vergée d'Or, believe it or not.'

She gazed at him, face cold. But he could not cease trying to break through the cocoon of hatred in which she limited her life.

'It is quite remarkable what Toussaint has managed to accomplish,' he said. 'They are actually growing cane again. Not on the old scale, of course. Not yet, anyway. But now that he has expelled the Spaniards from the west, as well as the mulattos from the south, and rules the whole island, they've a lot more space to play with.'

'Does Richilde still walk around with nothing on?'

He smiled. 'Richilde is again the grand lady. She is the head of Cap François society.'

'Living with a black man?'

'They love each other.'

'That is impossible, except in a diseased brain. Presumably she is again a mother?'

He shook his head. 'Although I think she would like to be. Annette . . .' he drew a long breath. 'Why do you not come on a voyage with me, to Cap François? To see it again, to see how peaceful it is, even how prosperous it is again becoming. I know Richilde would be so pleased to see you. She asks after you every time I visit.'

Annette stared at him.

He sighed, got up. 'It was just an idea. A sea voyage would do you good.'

He had turned to go inside before she spoke.

'I will go back to St Domingue,' she said. 'When the French send an army to reconquer it, and hang all the blacks. That is when I will go back. With Etienne.'

'That is not going to happen, my dear,' he said patiently. 'France is at war with all Europe. She has no fleets and no armies to spare for colonial adventures. Besides, why should she? St Domingue is as French as it ever was. Toussaint makes no claim for independence. He is Governor General. He rules beneath the tricolour. He has been recognised by the First Consul. Believe me, Bonaparte must be happy to have at least one of his dominions in such secure hands.'

'It will happen,' Annette said, quietly. 'My family will be avenged. No matter how long it takes, it will happen. And then I will go back.'

'Sail ho, bearing due north,' came the call from the main top.

Kit levelled his glass, Rogers at his elbow, gazing across the sparkling blue waters. February was one of the good months of the year, below Cuba – the winter gales through which they had battled on their way south from New York and down the Gulf Stream were nothing more than unpleasant memories. Now their one concern was the possibility of encountering a British man of war on the hunt for men – it was a situation which daily grew more aggravating to American seamen, and yet which seemed insoluble, while Great

Britain so arrogantly, and so effectively, ruled the oceans.

But this was an unusual place for a British frigate to be. The *Stormy Petrel* had just rounded Cap-à-Foux at the western extremity of St Domingue, and the green of the land was only ten miles away to starboard, while already just looming above the horizon, he could make out the craggy low peaks of the island of Tortuga, where once the buccaneers had held sway, and where now only a few French planters remained, eking out a precarious existence, cut off, despite Toussaint's blandishments, from the mainland of the colony. His course lay between the island and St Domingue itself, with Cap François only a day's sail beyond that. Since their evacuation of the city and hinterland nearly four years before, the British had hardly shown a flag in these waters.

Yet bearing down on them now was undoubtedly a frigate.

And more than one. 'Look there,' Rogers said, pointing.

Kit counted two more sails, and then several others.

'That is a fleet,' he muttered.

'An expeditionary force,' Rogers said, as suddenly the entire northern horizon was filled with white canvas.

'And signalling us to heave to,' Kit said, as he watched a puff of smoke rising from the foredeck of the leading frigate.

'They'll have foul bottoms, if they've just crossed the Atlantic,' Rogers observed. 'If we run for it, they'll never catch us.'

Kit continued to stare through his telescope, his heart commencing to quicken its beat as he realised that he was not staring at the white or red ensigns of the Royal Navy, but at the tricolour.

'Heave her to, Mr Rogers,' he said quietly. 'It can do no harm to discover what they are about.'

A French fleet, he thought. More, as Rogers had accurately determined, a French expeditionary force, launched across the Atlantic in the middle of a life and death struggle with Great Britain. His memory went back all of twenty-three years, when as a boy of fifteen he had watched de Grasse's fleet drop their anchors off Cap François. He gazed up at the yellow varnished hulls, the closed black gunports, the masts towering towards the sky as his jolly boat, Stars and Stripes proudly flying from its stern, threaded its way between the slow moving hulls, on its way to the flagship, as he had been directed. De Grasse had come to secure the independence of the Thirteen Colonies, and also to tweak the lion's tail. What could this immense armament, crowded with soldiers – they thronged the bulwarks to look down at him – and even with women, he observed with surprise, be seeking? It could only be either Jamaica or Canada. And in these latitudes, Jamaica was more likely.

The jolly boat came into the side of the huge three-decker which was named *Bucentaure*. Kit stared at her in total admiration – he had never in his life seen so enormous a ship. Certainly a hasty count of her gunports, taken in conjunction with the huge carronades mounted on her bow and in her stern, convinced him that she could not carry less than a hundred guns. Another calculation, made as he climbed the ladder and stepped through the opened gangway on to the snow-white deck, to the 'cooee' of the boatswain's whistle, and surveyed the cluster of red-pompommed sailors, the two lines of blue coated soldiers drawn up beyond, the crimson sashed officers waiting to welcome him, convinced him that her complement could hardly be less than two thousand men. And again, women, for both forward and on the poop there was the flutter of skirts.

'Citizen.' His salute was returned. 'Captain Duguay, at your service. Welcome on board.'

'Captain Hamilton, brig *Stormy Petrel*, out of New York.'

'And bound for Cap François?' Duguay inquired.

'That is my destination, monsieur,' Kit agreed.

'Do you trade regularly with Cap François, Captain Hamilton?'

'I do, monsieur.'

'Then my Admiral would speak with you.' Duguay led him aft, and up the ladder to the poop. At the top a short, powerfully built, and surprisingly young, man waited for them. Duguay saluted. 'This is Captain Hamilton, of New York, Citizen Admiral,' he said. 'Admiral Villaret-Joyeuse.'

Kit clasped the proffered fingers.

'And bound for Cap François?' the Admiral inquired.

'Yes, Your Excellency.'

'Good. Good. I would talk with you, Citizen Captain. We all would talk with you.' He turned, led Kit to the group of men wearing military uniforms who waited further aft. 'General LeClerc, here is a man who may be able to give us information as to our destination. Captain Hamilton, may I present Citizen General LeClerc, in command of the army.'

Again Kit shook hands, again impressed by the youth of the man – he doubted LeClerc was yet thirty. But he was preoccupied with what he had just heard. 'Your destination is Cap François?'

'Kit, by God!'

He turned, gazed at Etienne de Mortmain, more floridly stout than ever, hurrying across the deck towards him, arms outstretched.

''Tienne? But you were in Jamaica.'

'What nonsense,' Etienne said. 'I have spent these last three years in Paris. Preparing for this occasion.' He turned to LeClerc. 'This is the man of whom I have spoken, Citizen General. My cousin. He will be invaluable to us.'

Kit glanced from him to Villaret-Joyeuse, and then LeClerc, and then at the ships which composed this immense armament. 'And now you go to Cap François?' he asked, incredulously. 'To recruit blacks?'

LeClerc smiled, deprecatingly. Etienne gave a shout of laughter. 'Not to recruit the blacks, Kit. Never that. To hang Toussaint, and return the rest to slavery.'

Kit could only stare at his cousin in total consternation. 'Hang Toussaint? But . . . he too flies the tricolour.'

LeClerc once again gave a deprecating smile. 'A man may fly any flag he chooses. It is his intentions that are important.'

'And you doubt Toussaint's intentions? He has now ruled for four years, in the name of France. I should have thought that if he intended anything different he would have made it plain by now.'

LeClerc shrugged. 'Who can tell the workings of a black devil's mind, Captain Hamilton? Certain it is that the First Consul, my brother-in-law,' he said with a squaring of the shoulders so that Kit could be in no doubt of his importance, 'intends to restore St Domingue to its proper status. If the blacks resist us, then we shall destroy them.'

Kit allowed himself another glance at the fleet. 'The British tried that, with respect, Your Excellency,' he remarked. 'For five years.'

'The British!' This time LeClerc's smile was frankly contemptuous.

'With whom you are at war,' Kit reminded him. 'Is your entire fleet not a hostage to fortune?'

'You are short of information, Captain Hamilton. Peace has been agreed, between France and England. It waits only to be formally signed, at Amiens. We have naught to fear from the Royal Navy. As for the British adventures in St Domingue, we have them much in mind, believe me, Captain. And have no intention of repeating them. I would have you meet these gentlemen.' He gestured to the other officers. 'Or perhaps you know them already. General Rigaud.'

Kit shook hands with the mulatto, grey and somewhat weary in appearance.

'General Petion.'

A bundle of nervous energy, Kit estimated.

'And Colonel Boyer.'

Incredibly young. But then, so was LeClerc, Kit reminded himself. And of the pair, the mulatto was far the more purposeful man, in his firm lips and hard mouth.

'These gentlemen were born and bred in St Domingue,' LeClerc explained. 'They know the forests and the mountains. What is more, they know Toussaint, and his savage Generals, Dessalines and Christophe. You will observe that I do not treat this campaign lightly. Then there is your cousin, who also knows both the men and the country.'

Kit put up his hand to scratch his head, lowered it again. 'The campaign? With respect, Your Excellency, there is no *need* for a campaign. Toussaint will welcome you with open arms.'

LeClerc glanced at the mulatto officers, then at Etienne, then at the Admiral. 'If you are right, Captain, and my advisers are wrong, why, then, as you say, there will be no campaign.'

Villaret-Joyeuse clapped Kit on the shoulder. 'You'll dine on board, Captain Hamilton, and we will discuss the matter further.'

'But first, the ladies,' LeClerc said. 'Pauline, my dear, this gentleman is an American sea captain, related to Citizen Mortmain.'

Kit was drawn forward, checked in consternation Pauline LeClerc was by no means a beautiful woman – her features too closely resembled those of her brother Napoleon – but she had an extremely well developed figure, as he could tell at a glance, for she was dressed unlike any white woman he had ever seen in his life before, in what appeared to be a single utterly diaphanous garment, which had no shape to it other than an embroidered gather just beneath the breasts, themselves to all practical purposes quite uncovered, and which, in the gentle breeze propelling the ship onwards, snuggled at groin and buttock, wrapped itself round thigh and calf.

As if in a dream he kissed the offered fingers, and listened to the somewhat abrasive Corsican tones. 'Why, Captain Hamilton,' she said. 'You are quite handsome. All the Americans I met in Paris were old, and ugly. But they were ministers, not sea captains.'

He endeavoured to concentrate on the pert features, the careful ringlets of yellow hair.

'You should visit America, madame. Most of the men there are young.'

She glanced at her husband. 'Perhaps we shall visit America, in due course, Captain. But now, let me see, you know Citizeness Mortmain?'

'Citizeness . . ?' He gazed at the plump young woman, with the faintly familiar, doe-like features.

She giggled. 'You will remember me as Louise Ramlie, Captain. We met, oh, ten years ago, in Cap François, when my poor mama was caring for your sister.'

'And now . . .' he glanced at Etienne, who was puffing out his chest in pride. 'I must congratulate you.'

'And this is Citizeness Palourdes. Colonel Palourdes is General LeClerc's aide-de-camp.'

The girl, and she was certainly no older than Louise de Mortmain, gave him her hand with grave expression. She was in fact by some way the most attractive of the women, in her demeanour, which was quietly modest, and in looks, with a perfect heart-shaped face, around which long black hair made a delightful shroud, and which contained a straight nose and a wide mouth, perfectly set off by the pointed chin and the serious dark eyes. Her figure, too, like the others distinctly delineated by the transparent gown she wore, was at once slender – she was above average height – and full, both at breast and thigh. With a spasm of disloyalty to Annette, he realised she was the most beautiful woman he had met in a long time.

'And this, is Citizeness Jacqueline Chavannes,' Pauline LeClerc was saying.

Jacqueline, Kit realised, had to be more than forty years of age, and he had not seen her since two days before Richilde's wedding, which was now nineteen years in the past. Nineteen years during which she had certainly, if apparently temporarily, been sucked into the horror and passion of the slave rebellion.

Yet it might have been nineteen days. Her hair remained the same impenetrable mat of glossy blackness, her face and eyes possessed the same hard glittering beauty, and her figure – she was at once taller and more powerfully built than any of the Frenchwomen around her – was as voluptuously attractive as ever. If she suffered by comparison with Seraphine Palourdes, it was only because of the French girl's obvious youth and innocence.

Nor had her liquid voice changed in any way, either. 'Captain Hamilton is an old friend,' she said. 'We *knew* each other, as children.'

Pauline LeClerc glanced from man to woman, and gave a peculiar smile; it made Kit think of a lizard, about to swallow a fly. 'I forgot,' she said, 'that you are all going home, in a manner of speaking. And now, Citizen Admiral, shall we dine?'

Kit found himself next to Jacqueline, as they slowly descended the companion ladder to the great cabin. 'Perhaps you can explain to me what is truly happening,' he suggested. 'I see you, standing next to Louise de Mortmain, dealing with Etienne as an equal . . .'

'Necessity makes for strange bedfellows,' she agreed. 'We are all people with wrongs to avenge. Possessions to regain.'

'But ... did your people not fight alongside the blacks?'

'Once,' she smiled. 'Does Richilde still sleep with the niggers?' She smiled at him. 'Because that is what Etienne seeks, you know. To regain Vergée d'Or.'

He was seated on Pauline LeClerc's right. 'My husband intends to make Cap François his headquarters,' she remarked. 'And you trade there regularly. So I will hope to see a lot more of you.' She accompanied her words with a slow gaze, up and down his body, to leave no doubt that she meant exactly what she had said. But such febrile sexuality, such implicit amorality, was too strange for him, certainly with her husband seated beside him – he could feel himself flushing, and looked away in embarrassment. Besides, as the sister of the greatest man in France, she had to be merely amusing herself at his expense.

He found himself staring across the table at Seraphine Palourdes, who met his eyes for several seconds before turning her head to talk with Boyer, seated beside her.

Pauline LeClerc gave a low laugh. 'Believe me, Captain Hamilton, should you enlist my support, all things are possible.'

It was necessary to say something. 'I suspect your husband means to employ me,' he said. 'And will no doubt keep me busy.'

'I do indeed,' LeClerc said, indicating that he had been listening all the while, which merely increased Kit's embarrassment. 'If you are agreeable, citizen, I would have you act as a go-between for us. Will you do that?'

'If it can avert bloodshed, General, and lead to an honourable peace, I will be happy to do so.'

'You know the Negro who commands in Cap François?'

'Henry Christopher? Yes. I know him well.' Kit gazed at Etienne.

'Ah, yes, Christophe,' LeClerc said. 'We have been told of him. I understand he is by way of being your brother-in-law.'

'By way of, General,' Kit said, refusing to take offence.

'Thus you trust him, as no doubt he trusts you,' LeClerc said, giving not the slightest indication that he might be treading on delicate ground. 'But you will understand that I must have guarantees of the blacks' willingness to submit themselves to French rule. Thus my message to this Christophe, which he may relate to Toussaint, is that he should evacuate Cap François with all his force, leaving their weapons behind them.'

Kit looked at him in dismay. 'Do you really suppose Christophe would agree to such a capitulation?'

'It is not a capitulation, Captain. It is a command, issued by the new Governor General of St Domingue, myself. A command which, if these people are as anxious to be ruled by France as you claim, they will be happy to obey. After all, Captain, now that I have arrived, and with an army to protect them, there is no longer any necessity for them to bear arms. Is there?'

Kit sighed. 'I doubt they will agree, until they have some evidence of your intentions towards them.'

LeClerc's eyes were opaque. 'Any Negro found with arms in his hands or on his person, after I land, Captain Hamilton, will be considered as being in rebellion against France, and be hanged. You may tell this brother-in-law of yours that *those* are my intentions.'

Saturday was market day, as it had always been market day, in the past. Thus it was a page from the past, with the differences those of degree. The houses of Cap François might be dilapidated, their gardens neglected, but the city, because of its situation, curving round its land-locked bay, was still beautiful, and in the good-natured hubbub set up by its inhabitants was again *alive*. The soldiers on the ramparts might have black

341

faces, but they wore French uniforms and paraded beneath the tricolour. And Richilde de Mortmain proceeded from stall to stall, followed by her maid, as ever in the past. That this girl was named Aimee, rather than Amelia, that she was free rather than a slave, and that she was utterly delighted at being in the employ of General Christophe's woman rather than resentful at her lowly station in life was again a matter of degree. But what a delightful degree.

The truly apparent change was in the market itself; the goods on display. For while Toussaint had recognised that if he was ever going to restore St Domingue to its old position of being the wealthiest island in the Caribbean it was necessary to re-establish the sugar industry, he was still reluctant to use force to drive his people back to work, and any man prepared to farm had been granted his acre of land. Thus the market was no longer a huge junk stall, but instead displayed produce in every variety, from goats and chickens to baskets of mangoes and pomegranates. A selection from which Richilde made a careful, if wide, choice to the delight of the various traders. She was the best known woman in Cap François, at once because she was white and because she belonged to the commanding general, which meant that she was plentifully supplied with the *assignats* which Toussaint had issued to act as money, basically worthless, but eagerly sought by the uneducated Negroes, to whom money had always been a tangible suggestion of white omnipotence.

But more than her wealth or position, the very fact of her presence reassured them that their new found freedom was not such an impermanent uncertainty as they sometimes feared. They sought a return to normality, even if it was to be an utterly different normality to any they had ever known, and she was the symbol of their goal.

Just as she also sought a return to normality. A ship had been sighted, making its way slowly along the coast towards the port, and had been identified as the *Stormy Petrel*. She had in fact become used to Kit's visits, and treasured them as her only link with the world she had abandoned. That he came at all showed that he was reaching towards an understanding. That he came so regularly when the trade available hardly justified it, indicated he was accomplishing his intention. And that he could come, and take part, however warily and however briefly, in this unique social experiment, encapsulated all of her hopes for the future. Her personality would not permit her to hate on a timeless and unyielding scale. Whatever he had done, he had acted as he had thought best – and he was her brother.

Thus, as he would be here by this afternoon, she planned this night to have a supper party, for Henry's principal officers, and their wives. For part of Toussaint's attempts to restore that all important normality had been a restoration of the civil law as decreed by the new French republic, just as he had sought to diminish the part played by voodoo in his people's lives. He regarded, rightly in her opinion, the West African gods as the products of despair, and as such they were no longer necessary. He himself was a practising Catholic, and if he had attended voodoo ceremonies often enough in the past, as she knew so well, he was now anxious to put that behind him. Indeed, one of his principal sources of concern was that nearly all the ordained priesthood, necessarily white, had fled the country. Nor was he likely to replace them, with France itself sunk into atheism.

His rejection of voodoo had not been universally popular. Many of his aides, and notably Jean-Jacques Dessalines, were genuine believers in the Snake God, and at once feared and resented his derogation. It was an emotion Richilde was herself afraid to consider too deeply; Ogone Badagris touched too powerful a chord of primeval sympathy in her own personality. She was merely happy that Henry was a sceptic in either direction. He was, in fact, the most individualistic man she had ever met, far more so than Philippe, who had had the individuality of wealth, which merely encourages outrageous behaviour. Henry pursued entirely his own path through life, preceded any action with hours or even days of profound and silent thought; deeply personal moods which were disturbing to behold, and which might have frightened her had she not known him so well. For if, knowing him as she did, she could no longer doubt that he had foreseen the Negro revolt for many years – his true reason for never accepting Kit's offer and leaving St Domingue – she also could no longer doubt that obtaining possession of her, as a product of that revolt, had always been his goal, as he had pursued it with such single-minded purpose on that terrible August night.

Nor, in ten years, had his love for her seemed to diminish in any way. Hers for him had certainly grown as she had come to understand him, to *know* him, better than she had ever known anyone in her life. Yet they alone of all the military hierarchy created by Toussaint were not married. Because he had never asked her. The subject had never been raised between them; she did not know if it had ever been raised by Toussaint. Sometimes she supposed it was because she had not had another child for him – and as she was now approaching her thirty-fifth year it was unlikely she would ever do so. And thus she had to suppose that eventually he would – as Santhonax had warned – throw her over for another woman.

But as he had never done that either, and clearly loved her as much as ever, she had to reassure herself that it was simply because he knew, or feared, it would pose her an insoluble problem.

As if it truly mattered. They lived together as man and wife, were so regarded by the society they ruled, and she had as much pride in her Cap François home as she had ever had in Vergée d'Or. It was a large house, and had once belonged to Monsieur Peynier; she had visited it often enough in the past as Philippe's wife. It was thus entirely fitting that the military governor of the city, as appointed by General Toussaint, should have taken Peynier's place. With his lady. And his retinue of servants. Because it was within these walls that the past was most convincingly recreated. Again, these liveried footmen and white gowned maidservants were not slaves, and again they were delighted to have the opportunity to work for their great hero and his beautiful white mistress.

In fact, Henry was a stern master. He was a soldier, with a soldier's outlook, and Richilde often wondered if her servants' lot had in any way been improved. But they were free. There was the vital thing. Even if not one of them would ever have dared look Henry in the face and tell him that he or she was leaving for another employer. There could be no better employer than General Christophe, save possibly General Toussaint himself, and *he* preferred to live in absolute simplicity, out in the country. But he never criticised his protégé's arrangements, or his style.

Certainly she was not prepared to do so. After her years in the jungle, despairing that she would ever again be able to live like a lady, to sleep between linen sheets, to wear proper clothes, to soak in a hot bath and eat with silver cutlery off china crockery, was to make all that had gone before merely a long nightmare. And to share these things with Henry was a source of continual wonderment. With his serious thoughtful approach to life he had undertaken the mastery of those civilised arts as a challenge to be surmounted. His patience was inexhaustible, as his good humour, at least where she was concerned, never appeared to fade, however often she had gently to remove the meat from his fingers and spear it with his fork, or endeavoured to prevent him from blowing his nose on his serviette. But for her it was an unending joy to sleep with him in the enormous tester bed they shared, to reach out and touch him in the middle of the night, to feel that tremendous strength and purpose living quiescent at her side, just as it was for her to interpret the pictures in the books of Peynier's library. Henry was insatiable in his search for knowledge, of people and houses, ships and fortifications, weapons and military history – yet he seemed quite unable to grasp the elements of reading and writing himself. This she put down to male perversity, for that he possessed the intelligence and the application to master so simple an art could not be questioned. Yet it was not something she truly wished to change. Because of it he needed her.

She supposed she had never been so happy in her life. All that had gone before, all the uncertainty of her youth, the groping after some reality in the totally unreal world of Vergée d'Or as created and maintained by Philippe de Mortmain, the horrors of that August night in 1791, of her virtual imprisonment here in this very city, the murder of her only child, the grim years in the forest, had all come together in this utterly unique situation. That it had as yet no permanency, that any progress had to depend upon some return of material prosperity, that such prosperity would in turn depend upon a degree of application lacking in the average Negro, and certainly one who had only recently earned his release from a lifetime of horrifying servitude, were worrying considerations. Even more worrying was the realisation that the entire young nation lived, worked, and played at the behest of the personality of Toussaint, and Toussaint was an old man. But this was one subject on which Henry, usually so willing to consider every aspect of any situation, was totally unresponsive. For all his hard commonsense, his considerable intellectual powers, he regarded Toussaint almost as a god, could not envisage life without his reassuring presence.

In which he was utterly representative of the people he commanded. And of her? She had at least learned to live for the present. And this present *was* utterly happy. Especially when it would contain, however briefly, both of her favourite men. She waited for them at the top of the grand staircase, her heart pounding with pleasure, but slowing in concern as she watched their hurry, their animated and unsmiling conversation.

'Kit!' She embraced her brother, kissed him on each cheek. 'Annette?'

She always asked this, knowing the answer would always be the same.

'Well,' Kit said. 'Well.' He glanced at Christophe.

Who gave Richilde's hand a tight squeeze – he had never been able to make himself kiss her in public, even on the cheek. 'Kit has brought us an ultimatum,' he said.

'A command,' Kit suggested.

'That is better?'

Richilde looked from one to the other, her slowly gathering frown matching her slowly constricting heart. 'An ultimatum? A command? From whom?'

Christophe snorted, flung out his right arm in the direction of the sea. 'There is a French fleet, out there.'

'Anchored off Tortuga,' Kit said.

'But . . . isn't that what we expected?' she asked. 'What Toussaint has wanted?'

Henry chewed his lip, walked past her, threw himself into a chair, long booted legs thrust in front of him.

'I don't understand,' Richilde said to Kit.

'This is a fleet of war, Richilde,' he said. 'An immense fleet of war. Far bigger than de Grasse's in 1780. And it carries an army. Twenty thousand men. It is an expeditionary force. Intended for here.'

'But . . .' She felt like scratching her head. 'We fly the French flag. Toussaint governs in the name of France.'

'They are aware of that,' Kit said. 'But claim to distrust his motives.'

'Distrust Toussaint,' Henry growled.

'They have never met him,' Kit explained. 'When he and this LeClerc come face to face . . .'

'All will be well,' Richilde said. 'I'm sure it will.'

'Before they can meet,' Henry said, 'I am required to surrender Cap François. To disarm my men and withdraw them from the city.'

Richilde glanced at Kit. 'Because the French General is suspicious. But will that matter? It is surely what Toussaint wishes, peace with the French.'

'But is it what the *French* want, Richilde?' Henry asked. 'They do not trust us, but they expect us to trust them. And they will allow me no time to send to Toussaint. My answer must be returned by tomorrow.'

She gazed at his huge, strong face. 'What else can you *do*?' she cried. 'Start another war?'

He chewed his lip, and she felt a pang of real fear.

'You will find it difficult to defend Cap François,' Kit pointed out. 'That is the biggest fleet I have ever seen. And those soldiers have beaten all Europe.'

Henry gazed at him.

'I'm sure Toussaint would wish to make peace, to have peace,' Richilde said. 'He doesn't want another war. No one wants another war.'

'He will trust them,' Henry said, thoughtfully. 'I know he will.'

'Well, then . . .'

'He is too eager to trust people,' Henry said, even more thoughtfully. 'He is too eager to be ruled by the French. You have not heard who is on that fleet.'

Richilde looked at Kit.

'Etienne, and his new wife. And all the mulatto generals.'

'Those men are our enemies,' Henry said. 'Your cousin is my sworn enemy. You expect me to trust *him*?'

'But . . .' she could hardly frame the words. 'Then you do mean to fight, for Cap François?'

He shook his head. 'As Kit says, I do not think we can defend Cap François against a fleet and an army of French regulars. We could not defend it against the British, remember?'

How she remembered. But somehow this was different. The British had planned a straightforward war of conquest, horrible enough, to be sure, but not to be compared with the prospect of a war of *re*-conquest, inspired by men like Etienne.

'We will evacuate the city, like we did then,' Henry decided.

'Which is what this LeClerc is asking you to do, anyway,' Richilde said. 'Can you not then negotiate?'

'I will not negotiate,' Henry said. 'He has come to return us to slavery. I know that. We will withdraw into the bush. But LeClerc will not have Cap François to use as a base. When we withdraw, we will burn the town.'

'Burn the town?' General LeClerc stared at Kit in disbelief. 'That is absurd.'

For reply Kit pointed. An immense pall of smoke hung on the western horizon, only slowly breaking up as the wind struck at it.

'The man is a savage,' Etienne de Mortmain observed. 'An utter savage.'

'A savage would hardly reason so clearly, act so decisively,' Admiral Villaret-Joyeuse remarked. 'He means to fight, and he knows the city is indefensible. Is that not so, Captain Hamilton?'

'He knows Cap François is indefensible from the sea, certainly. Your approach, General, as I suggested, was a little too uncompromising.'

LeClerc stared at the smoke, his fingers curled into fists. 'If he wishes to fight, he will find that we too wish to fight. I promise you that, Captain. And we will not fight these savages in any Christian spirit, I promise you that too.'

Kit sighed. 'It is still possible to avert a war, General. If you can make contact with Toussaint . . .'

'Will he not act as his General has indicated?' asked Major Palourdes.

'He has a mind of his own.'

'Bah,' Etienne said. 'You speak of coachmen, slaves, niggers. You speak of them as if they were men like ourselves. Negotiate with savages? What an absurdity.'

They stared at him.

'Toussaint is no savage, monsieur,' Alexander Petion said, quietly.

'Well,' Kit said, 'the decision must be yours, General. I have apparently failed in my mission.' He smiled, 'I have even failed in my personal mission, which was to trade. If you will excuse me, I will rejoin my ship and make for Havana.'

'Not so fast,' LeClerc said. 'You tell me I must seek a meeting with this Toussaint. He is an acquaintance of yours?'

'I have met him,' Kit said, cautiously.

'Then I would have you act as my negotiator, again.' He gave a brief smile. 'You can hardly be less successful a second time, Captain.'

'I doubt negotiation is really my forte, General,' Kit said. 'Besides, I have a living to earn.'

'You will be well paid,' LeClerc promised. 'And I need you.'

Kit frowned at him. 'You would keep me here against my will, General? I am an American citizen.'

'Who once fought for France, I am told. Come, come, monsieur, is this not a great cause we pursue here? Peace, and the restoration of St Domingue to her proper prosperity? Of your cousin to his estates?'

'In which Richilde shall have her proper share, I give you my word,' Etienne was quick to add.

'Believe me, Captain, we will make it worth your while,' LeClerc said, and looked at his wife.

Remarkably, he wished to stay, at least for a while. He wished to see the outcome of this new struggle, if it were possible to do so. And he felt the necessity to remain at Etienne's shoulder, should the French be victorious, to attempt to restrain his cousin from the excesses of which he was certainly capable. 'Tienne's words on board the *Stormy Petrel*, as they had sailed down to St Kitts, nine years before, kept coming back to him; the thought of Richilde in these people's hands was unthinkable – and it could happen.

But he knew too that he was staying for another, and far less admirable reason: he had nothing to go home to New York for, and a great deal to remain here for. Over ten years he had played the nursemaid, emotionally and even physically, to a demented woman, had restricted his private life and all the demands of his powerfully masculine nature, because of a careless vow, carelessly accepted. Now suddenly the past had caught up with him, and it was possible to lose himself for a very brief season in a world at which he had only just nibbled in his youth, a world typified by the outrageous garments of the French women, the provocativeness of their conversation and the gaiety of their careless approach to life. They were the outpourings of revolution. They were not constrained by centuries of privilege and power and position, but sought only to enjoy each day, each hour, each moment, as it came, and with whoever it might bring.

And it was a world, for him, represented and made sure by the presence of Jacqueline Chavannes.

He watched her on the quarterdeck of the flagship as he conned the huge vessel towards the harbour. By now most of the flames had died down, and yet the smoke pall still hung above the destroyed city, still drifted inland towards the mountains to illustrate Christophe's determined act of defiance. Had it been *his* decision, Kit would have remained at Tortuga, pending the outcome of the negotiations with Toussaint; but LeClerc was determined to take possession of the city, even if it was a burned-out shell.

'You can see the deep water clearly now, Admiral,' he said. 'It is the area of dark blue which stretches in that semi-circle round the bay. Your ships may safely lie at anchor there, providing there is no storm.'

'It is not yet the season,' Villaret-Joyeuse said, perhaps to reassure himself. 'And there are no isolated coral heads?'

Kit shook his head. He left the group of officers, walked to the rail, stood behind her, watched her single transparent garment being flattened against her flesh by the gentle breeze, and knew the most powerful passion he had experienced for many years.

'You are a most capable seaman, Kit,' she said, without turning her head.

'It is my profession,' he reminded her. 'I am not so capable a man, alas. At least when it comes to controlling my heart.'

Now she did turn her head, and he moved to stand beside her.

'I have been told,' she said. 'that your treatment of Annette was gallant in the extreme. Has she not recovered at all?'

'Rather has she dwindled.' But his brain was immediately running off at a tangent. She could only have been told about Annette by Etienne. A man who once would not have deigned to speak with a mulatto at all, much less discussed his family. 'Truly,' he remarked, 'this catastrophe has brought about some strange alliances, as you say. Did you see much of my cousin, in France?'

She gazed at him. 'I an not *his* mistress, if that is what you mean, Kit.'

He flushed. 'I had not considered that. I wondered . . . if you knew his plans. Does he really hope to regain Vergée d'Or? To recreate Philippe's plantation? Philippe's spendour?'

'You must ask *him* that,' she said, quietly. 'I had supposed you sought something different from me.'

'I . . .' He could feel his cheeks burning.

She smiled at him. 'And to he who seeks, it shall be given. Is that not a quotation? I understand the General means to disembark his army this very day, but we ladies are to remain on board, until the land is secured and made safe for us. I am sure you will find more duties to occupy you afloat than on land. LeClerc can hardly mean to commence negotiating with Toussaint before tomorrow.' She blew him a gentle kiss with her lips as she turned away. 'You are invited to dine, with the ladies.'

He watched her glide towards the companion hatch. Too late he remembered that he had not discovered whose mistress she actually was.

Toussaint gazed at the slowly dispersing smoke cloud. His face was expressionless, but that he was angry could not be doubted.

'Is this how you treat the city I gave you?' he asked Henry Christophe. And turned to Richilde. 'I had supposed, madame, that you loved Cap François. That you would prove a restraining influence on this . . . savage.'

Never before had he spoken to Henry in such terms. Richilde caught her breath, could think of nothing to say.

'Cap François is indefensible from the sea.' Henry would not lower his gaze. 'You know that as well as I.'

'And why should we talk in terms of defence?' Toussaint demanded. 'By your own account this LeClerc wished only to treat. He is the representative of the country on whose account we hold this land.'

'He does not wish to treat,' Henry said. 'He has come to conquer. By deceit, if possible. By force of arms, if he must. Etienne de Mortmain will see to that.'

Toussaint gazed at him. 'It is a mistake, it is a catastrophe, for those who hope to attain high office to be influenced by personal hatreds,' he said. 'So the man once had you flogged. That is long ago, in the past. He has suffered more than you for it.'

'He is my enemy,' Henry said. 'He also murdered my son. He is Richilde's enemy as well. I tell you, he has not come to treat.'

'Henry is right,' Dessalines growled. 'Why should we

353

treat with them? We beat the British. We will beat these as well. Let us start now. The sooner the better.'

Toussaint stared at him in turn, then at the other officers, gathered in a semi-circle round the Generals. 'Is that all you know how to do, fight, and kill, and destroy?' he asked. 'Is that what you would make my memory?' He turned, walked to his horse, mounted. 'Were I to have no more hope of the future,' he said, 'I would blow out my brains, here and now.'

Chapter 3

THE WAR

The French victories, in a country such as St Domingue, were largely worthless, as the British had discovered, but they were impressive – some of the Negro commanders surrendered without firing a shot.

There were seven for supper: Pauline LeClerc, Louise de Mortmain, Jacqueline Chavannes and Seraphine Palourdes, two officers of the ship, and Kit. The Admiral and the Captain had both gone ashore with the soldiers and the Generals, and the returning colonists. Leaving their wives to play.

Because that was undoubtedly their purpose. The chattering conversation swirled about Kit's head, as the wine swirled about his mouth before slipping down his throat. He was surrounded by bare shoulders and flowing hair, by scantily covered bosoms and outrageous conversation, concerned entirely with anatomy and past exploits, all overseen and controlled by the glittering personality of Madame LeClerc.

Kit had been seated at her right hand, where she could lean over occasionally to kiss him on the cheek. 'You have no idea what a new face, a new *man*, does to me,' she said. 'Especially after all those weary days on the ocean. I had thought to go mad, more than once. But now, having arrived, it is all worthwhile. That is one of life's great compensations, do you not think, Kit: in time everything is worthwhile.'

'A very comforting philosophy, madame,' he agreed. 'It would enable you to endure a great deal.'

She leaned away to gaze at him, chin resting on her forefinger. 'Why, yes,' she said. 'I suppose it would.'

'Is it a philosophy shared by your husband?' he asked, determined to remind her of her situation, no matter how drunk she might have become. As if she was drunk at all, he thought, no matter how much wine might have slipped down *her* throat.

She made a moue. 'Charles is not a philosopher, alas. He is a soldier, and he dreams. Of great deeds.'

'You mean he has not yet accomplished any?' Kit asked, politely.

For a moment her eyes hardened, as if wondering whether he was poking fun at her, through her husband. Then she appeared to decide that the question had been genuine.

'Alas, no,' she said. 'He accompanied my brother to Egypt, four years ago, and has fought with him in several campaigns since, but always on the staff. This is his first independent command, which is why he is so anxious to bring it to a victorious conclusion.'

'But he is still very young,' Kit suggested.

'They are all very young, monsieur,' she said. 'Lannes, Ney, Bernadotte, Soult, Victor, Junot, even Massena, they are all young. Because Napoleon is himself young. France has suddenly become a young country again, after too many years of being *old*.' She made the word sound almost obscene. 'Thus Charles is old, not to have gained a reputation. But you know, Kit, I did not invite you to an *intimate* supper to discuss my husband. That is the height of bad taste.'

'I suppose I am feeling guilty,' he said. 'That the soldiers should be on shore, preparing to be attacked, while I sit here in comfort.'

'What nonsense,' she said. 'You have played your part. Now let them play theirs. And if you are distressed, Kit, you may be pleased to know that Charles is aware I am having this little party, and who will be attending, and what games we will play. His sole concern is to keep me happy.' She smiled. 'Should he not keep me happy, why, he would not even have an *opportunity* for greatness. Napoleon would see to that.'

For a moment she looked almost vicious. Because, Kit had no doubt, she *was* vicious. But he was more concerned with what she had said, as the stewards were clearing the table, leaving only the cheese and the wine.

And Louise de Mortmain was producing a pack of cards, and handing them to Pauline, who gave them a perfunctory shuffle.

'Are we then to gamble?' Kit asked, a trifle anxiously – he had no doubt that everyone here was far wealthier than himself – but also in some disappointment that the evening should end so prosaically.

Louise giggled, and Pauline smiled. 'In a manner of speaking, Kit.' She dealt the first card, face up, to the officer on her left. 'We are taking our chances on what the evening might hold for us.' The card was the two of Hearts. She now dealt the four of Diamonds to Louise, the seven of Spades to the second officer, the Jack of Hearts to Seraphine Palourdes, which brought an 'Oooh!' from Louise, and then the two of Clubs to Jacqueline.

'A pair,' Louise cried. 'A pair.'

'Of deuces,' Pauline said in disgust. 'Ah, well, the night is young.' She smiled at the officer holding the first deuce, who was licking his lips in anticipation. 'We play aces high, Lieutenant Pinet. So the deuce is the lowest card in the pack. It calls for nothing more than a kiss. A five minute kiss, with no other part of your body touching. Go to her.'

Louise clapped her hands in delight. Pinet hesitated, flushing, then got up and walked round the table. Jacqueline leaned back, her head tilted, and he lowered his mouth to hers.

'I will tell you when to stop,' Pauline said, tapping her fingers on the table.

The two mouths seemed almost to melt. Jacqueline of course had clearly played this game before, Kit realised; her hands remained on the table, lying flaccid. But Pinet, under the influence of that masterful tongue, could not keep his still. They kept moving forward, as he wished to touch her arms or shoulders, only to have them slapped by Seraphine Palourdes, to remind him to keep them behind his back. Kit studied the girl – she was by some distance the youngest person present. But as old as any of her female companions in vice? The evidence of his eyes suggested that. And yet that perfect heart of a face was so innocent, so angelic; indeed, it was almost obscene to suppose she could be the least corrupt.

'Enough,' Pauline remarked. 'Your breeches will not be able to stand any more strain, Pinet.'

The officer straightened, face crimson with passion and embarrassment. Jacqueline's expression had not altered at all

'Well,' Pauline said, picking up the pack of cards again. 'I suppose that will have to do as an *hors d'oeuvre*.' She smiled at Kit. 'Let us hope the evening provides some better entertainment as it goes on.' She dealt him the King of Spades.

'A King,' Louise screamed with excitement. 'A King.'

'Well, well, Kit,' Pauline said. 'Now let us see who will be your Queen.'

She turned over her own card, hesitantly, frowned at the nine of Spades. 'Damnation. But wouldn't it be amusing if it turned out to be you, Pinet?'

That possibility had not occurred to Kit, and he felt distinctly alarmed as she dealt the next card – he had no idea what a King involved, but if the two had been a kiss . . . the card was again a two, this time of Diamonds.

Louise gave a shriek, and Pauline slowly shook her head. 'I do not think it is going to be your night, Pinet.'

Louise herself was dealt the six of Hearts, the second officer the seven of Clubs . . .

'Now there is bad luck,' Pauline said. 'But you can hardly spank yourself, I suppose. Or should we try?'

'They fell on top of each other,' Jacqueline insisted. 'Only the top card showing counts.' She glanced at Kit, and flushed. Clearly she was anxious to discover who would be the next person to be dealt a King. Undoubtedly she hoped it would be herself. Had she not invited him to the supper party? Or had she merely been acting on instructions from Pauline? But had he not accepted, entirely in the anticipation of being able to sleep with her? With her, after the party. Now he was not so sure that that was what he wanted. His excitement began to grow, even as his instincts, lurching through the wine fog which was obstructing his brain, kept shrieking warnings. Warnings which would have to go unheeded, this night, and in this company.

And perhaps, warnings that he had heeded too often in the past.

Still unlucky, Pinet this time received the three of Clubs, while Louise got the eight of Hearts.

'I have a suspicion that you and Montcere *are* going to get together eventually,' Pauline said. 'Even if it is only at the end of a stick.'

Her deliberateness, the way she commented on almost every card, only served to heighten the slowly growing tension in the cabin. Kit reached for his glass, and discovered that it was empty. And the wine bottles had been removed.

Because to become actually drunk would make him incapable?

Montcere had received the Queen of Hearts, to a shout from Louise, and then Pauline was turning over the King of Clubs, in front of Seraphine.

'Oh!' the girl said, and raised her head, to gaze at Kit; little pink spots appeared in her cheeks.

But he could feel a hot flush in his own.

'A fuck,' Louise was shouting, clapping her hands. 'A fuck.'

Kit's head jerked up, as he gazed at the smiling Pauline.

'Well,' she said. 'There is a start. Although *I* am bitterly disappointed, dear Kit. Nevertheless, for this evening I shall have to enjoy you by proxy.'

Seraphine pushed back her chair and got up. Kit also pushed back his chair, uncertain where they were going. Or even what he was supposed to do. Louise could not have been serious. 'What *does* the King mean?' he asked.

'Louise has told you,' Pauline said. 'But it is a free fuck, you see. All the face cards are fucks. But whereas the Knave is designated a rear entry, and the Queen a front entry, the King leaves the first holder, that is you, free to make his choice. Come along, Kit.'

He gazed at Seraphine, who was slowly removing her gown. As he had suspected, it had been her only garment in any event, and now she shrugged it past her shoulders, Jacqueline having obligingly released the ties, and he watched the large, almost perfectly shaped white breasts slowly coming into view, crowned with magnificent, and erect, pink nipples. He thought of Venus rising from the ocean.

'*She's* ready,' Pinet remarked.

Kit tugged at his cravat. But it was more to allow himself to breathe. He felt that he must speak, must appear, at the least, as nonchalant as everyone else. 'You said you play aces high,' he said. 'What can *that* signify?'

Pauline laughed. 'An ace gives absolute rights, except that of permanent injury, on the partner. I love drawing aces. Or even being drawn against one. There is sport. Shall I help you?' She signalled Louise, and between them they pulled off Kit's coat and unbuttoned his shirt. Louise was busy with his shoes, as Pauline unfastened his breeches. Certainly he was ready. He had never been so ready in his life. All his thirty-eight years of repression and self discipline seemed to have exploded in the gigantic rush of desire, and now Seraphine was naked, her belly and her legs as perfectly shaped as the rest of her, her groin a curling mass of black delight . . . he realised that she was the most perfect creature he had ever beheld in his life. And the most innocent? That at the least could not be.

His own breeches were about his ankles, and Louise was shrieking her enjoyment. 'He wears drawers!' she screamed. 'He wears drawers.'

'All Americans wear drawers,' Pauline said, knowledgeably. 'They are all prudes.' Gently she eased the cotton underpants down his thighs. 'Oh, you *are* ready.'

He stood up. Suddenly he was desperate to have it over. And desperate, too, to enjoy this girl, as she seemed to wish it, in one unforgettable embrace. 'Which cabin?' he asked.

Louise gave another shriek of laughter, and to his total consternation he watched Pinet and Montcere pushing back the candles and the cutlery, and watched too, Seraphine climbing on to the table, every movement a picture.

'Now, Kit,' Pauline chided him, gently. 'You'd not rob us of our sport? But it is for you to tell her how to lie.'

And that, Kit thought, is the society which would impose itself on the stately ruins left by the Mortmains and the Milots. Or even on the primitive ambitions of Toussaint and Christophe.

But he had been a part of it. The drumming in his head, seeming to keep time to every movement of his horse's hooves, would alone have reminded him of that. If only other memories could be clearer. But perhaps he did not wish to remember. It had been magnificent, as he had crawled on to the table, between her spread legs, as she had reached for him, her expression serious, and yet sufficiently passionate. As she had kissed him, with opened mouth and wet tongue, to make sure he sustained the necessary erection, as that glorious body had moved against and beneath him, legs half in and out of bowls and dishes.

But actual sensation, that of entering her, that of climaxing, that of knowing whether or not she had climaxed with him, was lacking, lost in the drink fog, in the awareness of the people around him, in the hands smacking his shoulders and buttocks, in the laughter . . . and in the growing sense of shame and humiliation, of self disgust. He had made love to the most beautiful girl he had ever known . . . in the most debasing circumstances he had ever known. That other and similar events had followed, as Louise had finally drawn a seven to match Jacqueline's, and had had to submit to a caning on her bare buttocks, and as Pauline had produced a Queen for Montcere's, to end the evening in a riotous, doggy style romp on the deck, had merely confirmed his self contempt. And his confusion, as he had raised his head and seen those splendid black eyes gazing at him, so seriously.

He would no longer be a part of that society. On that he was determined. The question he had to answer was whether he wished any longer to help that society become the ruling society in St Domingue.

'You look terrible,' Etienne remarked, riding beside him. 'You must have had a heavy night. Which one of them did you get?'

He asked the question in a perfectly matter of fact tone – and his wife had been amongst the participants.

'I was drunk,' Kit said, truthfully enough.

'Anyone can tell that.' He watched the horseman galloping towards them. 'Well?' he shouted.

The hussar drew rein in a flurry of dust and sweat and swinging blue sabretache. 'We have seen no blacks, monsieur.'

Etienne peered at the trees, the fields of waving cane. He and Kit had ridden in advance of the main body, which marched behind them, a reconnaissance in force commanded by the General himself; 'Tienne had been impatient to see his old – and as he hoped, his future – home. 'Then we shall go on,' he decided.

He kicked his horse, and cantered forward, and after a moment Kit rode behind him, the hussar at his side. How familiar it all was, even after ten years. But ten years ago he had approached Vergée d'Or from the beach, not this well beaten road. He wondered where Christophe was today. He had no doubt they were being watched, even if no shot had yet been fired on this campaign.

And where Christophe was, there would be Richilde. How his stomach revolted as he imagined Richilde being forced to endure an orgy like that of last night. And they were the women who affected to regard her as a savage.

He looked for the crows, but the crows were gone. As were the bleached bones. The civilising hand of Toussaint had passed over the plantation, and he knew that the factory had recently been used for grinding. But the bones of the house still stood, gauntly waiting.

Etienne dismounted, let the reins lie, walked on to the cracked stone of the front patio, stood with hands on hips. 'Do you know,' he said. 'It is not as bad as I had supposed. There is quite a lot that can be saved. I shall not rebuild on quite such a lavish scale, of course. We have lost ten years' revenue. But still, I can promise you a fine house. And it is good that the blacks have recultivated so much of the cane. We shall be a profit making concern from the start.'

Kit also dismounted. 'Do you really suppose they have been cultivating that cane for your benefit?'

Etienne chuckled. 'Possibly not. But it *has* turned out for my benefit, has it not? I certainly mean to reap it. As I mean to get started on rebuilding Vergée d'Or just as quickly as possible. And living here. I have already written to Madeleine, asking her to find a passage for

Cap François. In fact, Kit, I thought that if you were going in that direction after leaving here, you might give her a berth on your ship.'

'Supposing I am ever allowed to leave here,' Kit remarked. 'And do you suppose Madeleine will wish to come? She does have a husband and children of her own, you know. Besides, what will Louise say? Won't *she* wish to be the new mistress of Vergée d'Or? Supposing Richilde isn't interested.'

Etienne frowned at him. 'I don't think Richilde enters into the matter, Kit. She has chosen to live with a black man, and I understand that she is unlikely to change her mind. As for Louise, well, she is a dear thing, but I will confess to you that I married her during a period of despair, when I doubted I should ever see Vergée d'Or again. Besides, that dragon of a mother of hers . . . but that is in the past. The fact is that she is not really the right material to be the mistress of Vergée d'Or. Madeleine will be happy to come. I have told her that she can bring the children, and I can tell you that she is virtually estranged from that English boor of a husband she has. It is my ambition, Kit, as far as it can be done, to restore Vergée d'Or as it was in our childhood, when we first came here. I meant to discuss the matter with you, in fact. I should also like Annette to return here.'

'Annette?' But what was so absurd about that? Had he not suggested she return often enough? But Annette, part of a society ruled by Pauline LeClerc and Louise de Mortmain?

'I do not see it could do her any harm,' Etienne said. 'This is, after all, her home. And if the chateau is rebuilt on somewhat different lines then there will be nothing in the building to remind her of that night. She is my sister, Kit, and although I am eternally grateful to you for looking after her all of these years, yet the ultimate responsibility must be mine.' He turned his head as another hussar appeared, then half a dozen more, guiding their mounts with some urgency through the tangled rubble and stone. 'What news?'

'Blacks approach,' said the lieutenant in command.

'Armed?'

The boy nodded, led his men towards the approaching troops.

'We'd best rejoin the military,' Etienne decided.

Kit followed him back along the road, wondering if Etienne intended to have a regiment of soldiers stationed permanently on the plantation to protect him. But LeClerc had also taken the news seriously enough, had formed his men into two squares, with the field guns between, and had taken himself and his small cavalry force within the lines of bayonets. Here Etienne and Kit joined him.

'You know these people,' LeClerc said. 'Will they charge, or engage in musketry?'

Kit pointed. 'I do not think they mean either.' For the approaching column of blacks, and it was several hundred strong, was carrying a white flag.

'Well, well,' LeClerc said. 'A pleasant surprise. You'll accompany me, Captain Hamilton.' The square opened, and he walked his horse forward, his aide-de-camp and Kit behind him, together with a trumpeter; Etienne preferred to remain within the safety of the French ranks.

Kit could not help but glance curiously at Palourdes, who would know as well as anyone about last night. But the man's thin features were expressionless as he concentrated on the coming encounter. Presumably, such ability to separate work from play in the mind was an asset for any man. But Kit realised he was discovering a powerful dislike for the unsuspecting soldier, who had the use of Seraphine whenever he chose, games apart.

The black soldiers advanced to within fifty feet of the little group of horsemen, then their leader came forward, accompanied by a single aide, bearing the white flag. The Negro was vaguely familiar – he was tall and thin and sad of expression – but Kit could not remember his name.

'We seek the French commander,' he said, in good French.

'I am he,' LeClerc said. 'Your name?'

'I am Louis-Pierre, General in the army of General Toussaint L'Ouverture.'

'L'Ouverture?'

'It is a title given to the General, monsieur,' Louis-Pierre said. 'Following his victories against the British.'

'I see. And your purpose?'

'We acknowledge the flag of France, monsieur. We will not fight against it. We have come to place ourselves under your command.'

'Indeed? General Toussaint has sent you?'

Louis-Pierre shook his head. 'It is our decision, monsieur.'

'Ah. Well, it has been a wise decision. Tell your men to pile their arms, Louis-Pierre.'

Louis-Pierre hesitated. 'We have come to serve, Your Excellency. Not to surrender.'

'If you will serve me, Louis-Pierre, you must first learn to obey me. Now tell your people to pile their arms.'

Another hesitation, then Louis-Pierre turned and gave the necessary orders to his men.

'Call up the guards,' LeClerc said to his trumpeter, who immediately gave a blast on his bugle. The French soldiers formed column and marched forward, one regiment to either side of the blacks, who watched them with interest. But by now all their muskets and swords and spears had been piled, and they had resumed their ranks.

'We await your orders, Your Excellency,' Louis-Pierre said.

'Yes,' LeClerc said. He turned to Palourdes. 'Every tenth man will be hanged,' he said. 'Starting with this insolent fellow.'

'You cannot do that,' Kit protested. 'These people came of their own free will, to serve with you.'

'They came to me as a result of my proclamation, Captain Hamilton,' LeClerc said. 'A proclamation which also pronounced that any black man bearing arms would be treated as an enemy. These men came bearing arms.' He gave a brief smile. 'But I am being generous. I am not hanging them all. The rest will be put to work, on rebuilding Cap François.'

Kit stared at him in horror, then at Louis-Pierre, whose hands were being tied behind his back while he gazed at his captors in consternation. He suddenly realised that this was, indeed, Annette's home.

'Louis-Pierre?' Toussaint asked. 'Can it be true?'

Suddenly, Richilde thought, he looked old. He had always *been* old, in relation to those he commanded, in his outlook on life. But it had been the age of wisdom, and authority. No suggestion of debility had ever entered into it. Even his short leg had never seemed anything more serious than a characteristic. But now his shoulders were hunched, and that brilliant brain seemed to have gone, if not dull, into retreat.

But then, she thought, are we not all dull, and tired, and old? I am old. I am thirty-four years old. I seek peace and domestic bliss, with my common-law husband, not another long season of trekking through the jungle. And even six and seven years ago, when she had crawled these treacherous paths, and had known the happiness of superb health and total optimism, she had yet dreamed of an end to it all, of the building period which would follow the expulsion of the British. The building period! Their greatest achievement had been the total destruction of Cap François.

Did Henry regret that? She did not think so, however he might have regretted her tears. But they had not affected his resolve. She was beginning to realise that nothing, save his own will, would ever affect Henry's resolve. But, as she watched him standing beside Toussaint and Dessalines, in a forest clearing as he had done so often in the past, even he looked tired. It was difficult to suppose that giant frame, those magnificent muscles, ever ageing. But he, too, was thirty-four. And he too had dreamed of building.

Unlike Dessalines. The bull-man was the only one of them who appeared utterly happy. *He* had been the one left adrift by the British evacuation, the speedy termination of the war with the mulattos in the south, with the Spaniards in the east. Fighting, murder, and destruction were the only arts he understood. They were his gods. She had a sudden, frightful sensation that in his arrival in St Domingue, only months before the rebellion had commenced, and on the very day that James Ogé had stepped off the ship on to the giddy path to destruction, he was perhaps an incarnation of Damballah Oueddo himself, come to exhort his people to fight, and fight, because he was the god of war.

'Bah,' he now said. 'Louis-Pierre is a fool. He always was a fool. Surrendering. How could he do that? Why did you not command him, Toussaint?'

'How could I command him otherwise?' Toussaint asked. 'Him, or any of them? Any of you? For ten years I have told them we fought for France. Now France has come to us. And we have rejected her.' His eyes, so full of sadness, rested on Henry Christophe.

'And you still think I was wrong?' Henry asked. 'After Louis-Pierre?'

'Henry was right,' Dessalines shouted. 'There can be no peace between us and the white people. I say, let us kill all the white people.' As usual when in his most declamatory style, his gaze rested on Richilde. 'Lead your people, Toussaint. Command us to war. We wait only the word.'

'What people?' Toussaint asked. He looked around the clearing, at the four hundred or so blue coated men who waited there. They were well armed, carried muskets and bayonets and filled cartridge belts; they were his personal bodyguard. There were perhaps another two thousand men, the regiments commanded by Dessalines and the garrison who had followed Henry from Cap François, scattered about the forest in various encampments. But there was only a handful of them, and they had no cannon. And a week in this forest would rip those smart jackets and breeches to rags, as Richilde well knew.

'Then make peace with the French,' she said.

Their heads turned.

'Spoken like a white woman,' Dessalines sneered. 'You wish to see us all hanged.'

'Why should LeClerc negotiate a peace with me now, madame?' Toussaint asked. 'He must know my forces are scattered, my people divided against themselves, between those who wish peace, and those who would fight.' Once again he looked at his men.

'Why must he *know* that?' Richilde demanded. 'He has not been a month in St Domingue. What can he have learned in that time? He has learned that Henry, your military governor of Cap François, Toussaint, preferred to burn the city and withdraw his men into the forest rather than surrender. And he has learned that another, small, body of your people *has* surrendered, and he has hanged a tenth of them. He must know that you are angry about that, and he must now be awaiting your attack. And he must expect that you can still muster ten, twenty, thirty thousand men to lead against him. He has Rigaud and Petion with him. They will have told him all about your defeat of the British. Dare he risk a campaign such as that?'

Toussaint stroked his chin.

'If you were to negotiate from strength,' she said.

'*Pretend* to negotiate from strength, at the least. Make him believe that you command a vast army out here, that the reason you have not yet attacked him is because you have been waiting for all your troops to assemble, that you are offering him one chance to make an honourable peace, or you will launch a war against him even more terrible than you launched against the British . . . he must agree to negotiate then.'

'She wishes us to surrender,' Dessalines growled.

'I am trying to save lives,' Richilde said. 'All of our lives.'

'And you are speaking sound sense,' Toussaint said. 'In any event, it is our only hope. I will go to this LeClerc, this brother-in-law of the great Bonaparte, and . . .'

'Never,' Henry said.

Toussaint looked at him.

'He would seize you and hang you, on the spot,' Henry said. 'If you are determined to negotiate, then I am the man to do it. I burned Cap François. I am the one with whom he first negotiated. He can resume negotiations, with me.'

'And do you not suppose he will hang *you*, on the spot?'

Henry shrugged. 'I am a soldier,' he said. 'I am *a* general, not *the* General. I expect to die, one day, in your service.'

'Neither of you will go,' Richilde said.

Once again the heads turned as they looked at her.

'*I* will go,' she said. 'They certainly will not hang me. And both my brother and my cousin are with the French. I will go, and speak with them on your, on our, behalves. I will be able to secure the best terms, and I will know whether or not they are to be trusted.'

'You?' Toussaint asked. 'But madame, those white people hate you more than they hate us.'

'I will go,' she said. 'And bring you peace.'

370

Henry had allowed her to pack a box before leaving Cap François, and thus she was able to dress herself with some elegance, but there was little she could do about her toilette save brush her hair very carefully – it remained very long, contained only the slightest wave – wash her face, clean her nails, and shelter the whole beneath a broad-brimmed straw hat. Shoes were obviously impractical for the journey she had to make, but she did not think she could approach the French army barefoot – so she wore her boots. If they made an incongruous adjunct to her gown, she supposed they could expect her to look incongruous. And she rode astride; it was too long since she had ridden side saddle.

Henry himself accompanied her and Aimee to the forest fringe, inside Vergée d'Or, whence they could see the white tents of the French encampment, even distantly hear the bugle calls. The young Negress had insisted on going with her. 'You are the General's woman,' she had said. 'You can't walk before them white folk without a maid.'

'If anything should happen to you,' Henry said, 'I will slaughter every Frenchman I can find, for the rest of my life. I swear this. You may tell them.'

She squeezed his hand. 'Nothing will happen to me, Henry. I will bring you peace.'

Yet her heart pounded as she rode out of the trees and on to the so well remembered road leading towards the destroyed city. Memory went back all of eleven years, to the day she and Annette had walked into Cap François, the only survivors of the Vergée d'Or massacre. Then they had been welcomed – but on the white people's terms. Now she was a self professed enemy of the French, Christophe's woman.

'Halt there,' came a shout, and she reined her horse, watched the blue-clad infantrymen starting up from their stand beside the road. She waited, as they approached her, in the beginning looking past her for any sign of blacks, and only slowly taking her and her servant in.

'My God, a white woman,' someone said.

'No, a mulatto,' said another. 'White women don't have brown skins.'

The sergeant stood before her, frowning at her, appreciating her grey eyes. 'My God,' he said. 'It *is* a white woman. It is . ... you are the white nigger,' he accused.

'I am Madame Richilde de Mortmain,' she said carefully. 'I have come to speak with General LeClerc.'

'You have come to surrender,' he said.

'I have come to speak with General LeClerc,' she repeated, keeping her voice even.

'You'll get down,' he commanded.

She hesitated, then dismounted, covering her legs as well as she could. But not well enough. His eyes gleamed, and he licked his lips.

'She's the white nigger, lads,' he said to his men. 'She lies with the blacks. What do you think? Shall we see what she offers?'

Richilde stepped back, tension flooding her body in a deluge of sweat. 'I am an emissary from General Toussaint,' she gasped. 'If you touch me . . .'

They surged forward, two seizing her arms, the others reaching for her thighs to lift her from the ground, while the sergeant unbuttoned his breeches. Behind her she heard Aimee scream as she was dragged from the saddle. She wanted to scream herself, and could find no breath. This was August 1791 all over again – but these were white men.

'Stop there! Attention!' The voice was brisk, and hard . . . and most magnificently familiar. The hands grasping Richilde let her go, and she struck the earth with a thud which left her for a moment incapable of movement. But Colonel Boyer had already dismounted, and was reaching for her hand, while his escort glared at the abashed guard. 'Madame de Mortmain,' he said, and gently pulled her to her feet.

She gasped for breath. 'Colonel,' she said, 'you have my utmost gratitude.'

'You took a grave risk,' he said. Then the hard, strong, handsome features suddenly smiled. 'You are a woman who likes risks. You have come to surrender?'

She shook her head. 'I have come to see General LeClerc, with a message from General Toussaint.'

He frowned at her. 'Toussaint sent *you*, to do his work? Christophe permitted this?'

Her chin came up. 'We are all one, in Toussaint's army, Colonel. And I am best suited for such a mission.'

'Even at risk of rape?'

Her turn to smile. 'At least I was sure I would not be hanged.' She looked round in alarm. 'My maid!'

Two of the soldiers still held Aimee's arms, but now they released her beneath Boyer's glare, allowed her to scramble back into the saddle, endeavour to straighten at once her bonnet and her gown. One of the men grinned at her as he handed her up her parasol.

Boyer's face remained sombre, as he assisted Richilde into the saddle, carefully looked away as she swung her leg across. 'I would not count on your sex, madame, to preserve you from *that*. Not in this army.' He remounted himself. 'Make way there,' he commanded.

The guard stood to attention, staring at Richilde, with hungry, unsatisfied eyes, while Boyer's staff fell in behind him.

'I had counted on the presence of my brother, and my cousin,' she explained, as they walked their horses down the road. 'Are they not here?'

'Your cousin is, certainly, madame. Your brother has departed.' His mouth twisted. 'He quarrelled with our commanding General. He could not stomach the hanging of men who had surrendered in good faith. Well, neither can most of us. But we have taken an oath. Captain Hamilton had not. He also . . .' Another twist of the lips. 'Did not find General LeClerc's society to the best of taste. I am sorry, madame.'

Not half so sorry as I am, she thought, as they approached the camp. She had counted on Kit's presence, as a stabilising, non-emotional factor. Now she would have to rely on Etienne. Etienne, of all people.

But she had volunteered to carry out this mission, and it was her duty, whether she succeeded in it or not, to obtain as much information as she could for Toussaint. Thus she looked at the encamped army with interest: the orderly rows of tents, the men drilling, the horsemen practising charging and reassembling in the open space under the city walls. This was an immense, and well disciplined force, she realised. And an utterly confident one. It was certainly larger than the army the British had attempted their conquest with – and they had come uncomfortably close to success.

And supporting them, as with the British, was a fleet of war. She looked out at the three deckers and the frigates and the transports, riding quietly at anchor. At least a hundred of them, altogether. They would not be able to remain there once the storm season started. But that was not until June, and it was only March.

Closer at hand, she looked at the beach, and two armed sentries patrolling there, and the half dozen people swimming, and playing in the shallows, the morning sun gleaming from their crystal white bodies. Only black people had ever swum on that beach in the past. But these were . . . Her head jerked.

'The General's lady is very fond of sea bathing,' Boyer observed. 'Early in the morning, before the sun becomes hot enough to scorch her complexion.'

'The General's lady?' She stared. Because she realised that all of the six women were white, or at least pale-skinned mulattos, and that all of them were quite naked, and apparently unashamed – certainly they

374

could be in no doubt that from the road, however the sentries might prevent intruders approaching, every aspect of their femininity was clearly visible. 'My God!'

'Indeed,' he agreed. 'Should you choose to look closely, madame, you will also discover your cousin-in-law, the new Citizeness Mortmain, as well as several other wives of our officers. And mistresses, of course,' he added. 'As I said, your brother found this new French society distasteful.'

She looked at him as they rode past the swimmers and into the camp itself, immediately attracting stares, and gathering groups of men, and a great deal of comment. 'And do you not find it distasteful, Colonel Boyer?'

Boyer returned her gaze. 'St Domingue is my home, madame. I would sit down with the devil himself, or his succubus, to regain my place in it.'

They approached a cluster of tents, set apart from the main army, and very heavily guarded. Here Boyer dismounted, and assisted Richilde down also, before in turn giving his hand to Aimee. 'You'll remain here,' he said, and walked away from her, towards a cluster of officers seated or standing a few yards away.

'Man, but I am frightened,' Aimee confessed. 'You know that I am frightened, madame? You think they going hang us?'

'No,' Richilde said. 'Is my hat straight?'

'Well . . .' Aimee held the brim to tilt it back. 'That is better. But madame . . . you ain't afraid?'

I am terrified, Richilde thought. Terrified at the thought that I belong to such a race, such a nation — even half of me. 'Of course I am not afraid,' she said. 'They are human beings, like us.'

She looked up as Boyer returned, now accompanied by a tall, saturnine looking young man, who wore a moustache. 'You are Christophe's woman?'

'I am Madame de Mortmain,' Richilde said.

'This is Major Palourdes,' Boyer explained. 'The commanding General's aide-de-camp.'

Richilde inclined her head. She did not see any point in embarrassing them both by offering him her hand.

Palourdes looked her up and down, slowly. 'By God,' he said. 'I have heard much about you, citizeness. But perhaps none of the tales do you justice. The General will receive you.'

He turned to lead her. She glanced at Boyer.

'I will remain with your servant, madame,' Boyer said.

For which she supposed she must be grateful; she would have been happier had he remained at *her* side.

'I understand that my cousin, Monsieur de Mortmain, is with your army,' she said conversationally, hurrying to keep pace with Palourdes's long strides, terribly aware of the officers emerging from their tents to stare at her, and once again of the comments with which she was surrounded.

'Citizen Mortmain is out visiting the ruins of his old plantation,' Palourdes said.

'*His* old plantation?'

They had halted before the largest of all the tents, before which there were two guards, and a staff bearing the tricolour. 'You will wait here, citizeness,' Palourdes said, and ducked his head to enter the doorway.

Richilde reached into her reticule for a fan, became increasingly aware of the heat as the sun rose behind her.

'There's a handsome one,' the first guard remarked. 'Do you suppose she's for the General?'

'Wouldn't surprise me,' said the second. 'He never gets tired, does he?'

She flushed, and bit her lip, and turned away, to watch Generals Rigaud and Petion hurrying towards her.

'Madame de Mortmain.' Rigaud raised her hand to

376

his lips. 'A happier meeting than our last, I would hope.'

'So would I, General,' she agreed.

'Madame.' Petion also kissed her hand.

'Citizens.' Palourdes stood in the doorway of the tent.

Rigaud nodded, and Richilde went forward, having to duck her own head to enter, pausing just inside the doorway to look at LeClerc, who was seated behind a trestle table piled high with plans, mostly of streets and houses and churches – clearly he was already contemplating rebuilding Cap François.

She was immediately struck by his youth, and also by the coldness of his face, as he raised his head to look at her in turn. 'Christophe's woman,' he remarked.

Richilde decided against offering him her hand, either; besides, she was too afraid he might notice it was shaking. She stood before the desk. 'I am Richilde de Mortmain.'

LeClerc glanced at the two mulatto officers. 'I have summoned you,' he said, 'to give me your opinions on what this woman has to say. Have either of you ever met her before?'

'We have met Madame de Mortmain,' Rigaud said.

'And you have no doubt that this woman *is* Citizeness Mortmain?' LeClerc asked.

'Of course not,' Petion said, adding, 'sir,' as an afterthought.

LeClerc stared at him for a moment, then looked at Richilde again. 'I am informed that you have a message for me,' he said. 'From the black rebels.'

Richilde met his gaze; she was well aware that only boldness would serve her here – he must never even suspect the butterflies in her stomach. 'I have a message, General, from the Governor General of St Domingue.'

His head came up, and he frowned at her.

'General Toussaint,' she said, 'holds a commission as

Commander-in-chief of St Domingue, given him by Monsieur Santhonax, in the name of the National Convention in Paris.'

'The National Convention,' LeClerc said contemptuously. 'History has passed you by, citizeness.'

'Perhaps you would be good enough to let me finish, uninterrupted,' Richilde suggested. 'Or I had best return to my people.'

'*Your* people?' LeClerc commented. But as she would not lower her gaze, he shrugged. 'Continue.'

'Acting on that commission,' Richilde said, 'General Toussaint waged war on the British, and drove them from St Domingue. He then . . .' she glanced at the two mulattos, 'completed the reduction of those who would not recognise the authority of the Convention, and then evicted the Spaniards from the eastern half of the island, to complete the conquest of the entire area of St Domingue, for France. He then despatched letters to Paris, informing the government of what he had accomplished, and, as Monsieur Santhonax had died, further informing the government that he proposed to remain in command of St Domingue, as Governor General, until other arrangements could be made. The then government, to which I understand the First Consul was already a party, confirmed these arrangements.'

'The First Consul has now changed his plans,' LeClerc said. But he spoke more quietly, was obviously interested in what she had to say. She felt an almost exhilarating surge of confidence.

'As he is entitled to do, General,' she said. 'Although it would have been wisest, as well as more polite, to inform General Toussaint by letter rather than by presenting him with a series of ultimata, or by hanging his people.'

LeClerc leaned forward again. 'The so-called General Christophe, your *lover*, citizeness, began hostilities, by burning Cap François.'

She did not even flush, any more. 'General Christophe conceived your demand of him as an act of war. So does General Toussaint, just as he considers your hanging of General Louis-Pierre and sixty-four of his men as an act of aggression. The General is constrained, however, by his honour. He swore on oath to Commissioner Santhonax to uphold the government of France, and he considers himself bound by that oath. He therefore would be most reluctant to take up arms against you. If he were forced to do that, General, then be sure the entire country would rally to him. In case you are unaware of it, General Toussaint is regarded almost as a god by his people. Certainly as their hero. You may ask these gentlemen if that is not true.'

LeClerc glanced at Rigaud.

'That is certainly so, General,' the mulatto said.

'He also,' Richilde said, 'commands an army of fifty thousand well armed men.'

'*Fifty* thousand? That is impossible. How does he feed such a number, in those forests?'

Richilde shrugged. 'If you would care to mount your horses, General, and accompany me back to our encampment, I will show you.'

LeClerc glared at her, then again looked at Rigaud.

'There are certainly at least fifty thousand blacks capable of bearing arms, General,' Rigaud said. 'Logistics for such a force, in St Domingue, would be difficult, certainly. But by no means impossible. These people need very little to survive.'

LeClerc's stare returned to Richilde.

'General Toussaint,' she went on, beginning now to sense victory, 'has been assembling his people these last two weeks. But as you say, General Rigaud, feeding such an army is a difficult business. Therefore General Toussaint must present you with the following choices: one, that you recognise him as Governor General of St Domingue, his officers as appointed by the French government, through him, and his people as loyal subjects of the Consulate. This is all he asks. He will then be willing to retire from his position, handing it over to you, and his Generals will also retire, as will his people surrender their arms and return to their peaceful pursuits. It follows of course that you will give a guarantee for the lives and safety of the black people of St Domingue.'

'You mentioned two alternatives, madame.'

Another victory. She smiled at him. 'That you refuse the above terms, and therefore will have to be regarded as an enemy, and destroyed, as were the British destroyed.'

LeClerc gazed at her for several seconds, and then allowed his eyes to wander up and down her body. 'And suppose,' he said at last, 'that I make no reply at all, but merely hand you over to my men for their amusement, before I hang you?'

The crude threat did not even make her sweat. 'If I am not back at General Toussaint's encampment by this evening, with your reply, he will assume that you *have* replied, by a declaration of war.'

LeClerc continued to study her for several more seconds. 'You are a courageous woman,' he said at last.

Richilde waited. Now that she had won, her knees suddenly felt weak.

'Well,' LeClerc said. 'My mission is to pacify St Domingue, and return it to French control. Clearly if that can be done without waging a major campaign, the First Consul will be well pleased. Your General Toussaint may have his titles, as may his officers.'

'And his people will have their freedom.' Richilde insisted.

'May I point out that there is a great deal of reconstruction necessary, Citizeness?' He smiled. 'Rebuilding Cap François, for a start.'

'You have but to *employ* the Negroes, General.'

He nodded. 'As you say. They shall be free.'

It had all been so very simple, she thought. Too simple by far.

'Then you will draw up a treaty of peace, to this effect, General?'

'What, can this black fellow read?'

Richilde refused to lose her temper. 'Yes, monsieur,' she said. 'He can read. I would like to take the treaty with me, when I leave.'

LeClerc shrugged. 'You shall have your treaty. Major Palourdes, you'll summon my clerks.'

'I should also like the treaty, when it has been written out and I have had a chance to study it,' Richilde said, 'read aloud to all your people.'

LeClerc frowned at her. 'Citizeness? One would almost suppose that you do not trust me.'

'General LeClerc,' Richilde said, at last allowing her face to relax into the semblance of a smile. 'I do not trust you.'

Chapter 4

THE BETRAYAL

Toussaint agreed to an armistice, having secured for himself and his generals the preservation of their military ranks and privileges. He then handed over the administration to LeClerc and retired to his home on the west coast. French diplomacy and commonsense had accomplished what several European armies had been unable to do – except that it was never Napoleonic policy to rely on diplomacy alone. Commonsense, certainly; in the dead of night, hardly a month after the capitulation, Toussaint and his family were arrested by French soldiers and taken on board a waiting warship. They were carried direct to France, where the Negro leader was not even granted the privilege of an interview with the man who had outwitted him. He was confined in a prison in the French Alps, left a winter in an unheated, insanitary cell, encouraged to die.

'His Excellency, Citizen General Pierre Toussaint, and Citizeness Toussaint,' bellowed the major-domo.

Toussaint limped forward, Clotilde, several inches taller at his side. The huge meadow, which had so rapidly been converted into a lawn, was packed with French officers and their ladies, and with French soldiers, too, standing guard around the edges – for beyond the fencing there was a huge crowd of black people, gawking at the whites, and at their leaders, waiting to mingle on equal terms with these people from across the ocean. Almost they seemed to steam, for it was a very hot afternoon – and promised eventually to be a wet one, as enormous black clouds drifted in from the sea.

Richilde, standing next to Henry, felt her fingers sweating inside her gloves. She had naturally put on her very best gown – but it was in a fashion several years out of date, and had been run up by Negro seamstresses during her sojourn in Cap François as the Military Governor's lady. Just as her hair was loose. Now she was about to meet high society straight from Paris, dressed in the very latest creations, with their hair a mass of ringlets and oddly shaped chignons – and at their head would be the sister of the First Consul himself.

She kept her gaze fixed on the enormous back of Dessalines, immediately in front of her. But Dessalines was now moving forward.

'His Excellency Citizen General Jean-Jacques Dessalines,' the major-demo bellowed.

Richilde watched the bull-man facing LeClerc. Pauline LeClerc was just beyond her husband, and could not be clearly seen as yet. But Richilde wondered what she made of the grim figure in front of her – and what he, with his oft repeated chant to destroy all the whites, made of her.

'His Excellency Citizen General Henri Christophe,' the major-domo shouted. 'And Citizeness Mortmain.'

The field became an immense *rustle*, as heads turned and people, mainly women, crowded forward. This was the moment for which they had been waiting, their first sighting of the woman who had spent ten years living with the blacks. Richilde's knees felt weak, and she could only move by being carried along on Henry's arm.

LeClerc smiled at her as he bent over her hand.

'Well, citizeness,' he said. 'Your moment of triumph. I would have you meet my wife.'

Richilde was completely taken aback by the utter indecency of Pauline LeClerc's gown, for a moment could find no words. While the Frenchwoman looked Henry up and down before turning her glittering gaze on Richilde. 'The white Negress,' she remarked. 'But you are not *such* a fool, are you, Citizeness.' Another glance at Henry's giant frame. 'I look forward to having a conversation with you, Citizeness. And with your paramour, to be sure.' She smiled. 'I have already met your brother.'

'She has insulted you,' Henry muttered, in English. 'I should like to wring her neck.'

'I doubt she converses with anyone any differently,' Richilde pointed out, determined to have nothing spoil this afternoon. And now they were before Admiral Villaret-Joyeuse, who in the strongest contrast to the LeClercs was clearly a gentleman, before she was shaking hands again with Rigaud and Petion, and finding herself face to face with Major Palourdes.

'You'll take a glass of champagne, General, citizeness?' He ushered a girl forward. 'My wife wishes to meet you.'

Amazingly, Seraphine Palourdes gave a brief curtsey. Richilde was once again taken aback by the shapeless gown, as well as its transparency, which left nothing to the imagination, and revealed that Seraphine Palourdes was a remarkably beautiful young woman.

'It is my pleasure, Citizeness Palourdes,' Richilde said. 'And have you also an acquaintance with my brother?'

To her surprise, Seraphine shot her a quick glance, and a trace of colour appeared in those pale cheeks.

While Palourdes gave one of his sardonic smiles. 'My wife is acquainted with Captain Hamilton, citizeness. During his brief sojourn with our army, he made himself popular with the ladies.'

384

Richilde raised her eyebrows. She could not imagine Kit playing the gallant. But Madame Palourdes's flush certainly suggested that something had happened. And why not, she thought, she is a most delicious creature.

'Well, madame. General Christophe, I am sure we have met before, on Vergée d'Or.'

'Jacqueline!' Richilde cried. 'But how good to see you.' Her reaction was instinctive, for all the studied insult her old friend had just attempted to offer Henry. And the mulatto had clearly prospered; she was dressed after the fashion of her new white friends. 'How splendid you look.'

'As do you, Richilde,' Jacqueline acknowledged. 'The very picture of strength and health. When you begin to dress more fashionably, you will be the toast of St Domingue.'

'More fashionably? Oh . . .' she glanced at Henry. 'I do not think these modern gowns would become me.'

'What nonsense.' Jacqueline said. 'I am sure General Christophe would appreciate it.'

Henry merely stared at her. But her gaze was drifting past his left shoulder.

'Richilde! My dear Richilde.' Richilde turned, heart pounding, gazed at Etienne. An Etienne as florid and as prosperously dressed as she had ever known him, from snowy cravat to polished black boots, and with a plump giggle of a woman on his arm. 'Have you no kiss for me?' he asked.

Richilde realised that her right arm had been released. She looked over her shoulder, but Henry had already turned his back, and was walking into the throng.

'I observe that merely being called 'General' does not necessarily give a man manners,' Etienne remarked.

'For which you should be thankful, 'Tienne,', Richilde said. 'He has left, undoubtedly, to prevent himself from strangling you on the spot.'

'Eh? Eh?' Etienne lost some of his rich colour. 'Does

he still bear a grudge for a whipping? Are not those days gone forever, Richilde?'

'He mourns his only child,' Richilde said evenly. 'As do I. You have not introduced me to *Citizeness* Mortmain.'

'Because you already know her, my dear,' Etienne said. 'Louise, you remember my cousin Richilde?'

'Of course I do, 'Tienne,' Louise giggled. 'I was but twelve when you last saw me, madame. Citizeness,' she hastily added.

Richilde frowned at her. 'Not the child with the hot water?'

Louise gave another giggle.

'We have a great deal to talk about,' Etienne said. 'Of course it cannot be done here. But as soon as Madeleine arrives, and Annette . . .'

'Madeleine? Annette? Annette is returning to St Domingue?'

'On Kit's next voyage. He promised me. It is my intention to reunite the family, rebuild Vergée d'Or, recommence living, if you will. And of course, my dear, there is always a place for you there, if . . .' he paused, deliberately.

She gazed into his eyes, coldly calculating, as they had always been. 'If I divest myself of Henry,' she said. 'But I regard myself as married to him, 'Tienne. As you say, it is something we shall have to discuss.'

'Now, you listen to me,' Etienne began, and checked as a large drop of water fell on his hand. 'My God!'

The black cloud had arrived overhead, and a moment later the rain was cascading down, only less heavy than the storm which had overturned her coach on that ride to Rio Negro, so many years ago. Richilde gathered her skirts and ran for the few trees at the edge of the meadow, was rescued by Henry, who had taken off his uniform jacket to hold over her. She looked back, at Louise de Mortmain jumping up and down as her gown seemed to dissolve, and then beyond, at Pauline

LeClerc, gazing up at the heavens with a bemused expression, while rouge ran down her cheeks like a pink stream. Then the Commanding General's wife gave a peal of laughter, and with a single movement tore off her gown, to go dancing through the rain. Immediately she was joined by several of her ladies.

Richilde looked up at Henry, who held her closer; water dripped from his chin on to her face. 'Those,' he said, 'are the people who would rule us.'

'Cap François,' Annette de Mortmain cried. 'Oh, Cap François. How I have dreamed of returning here. How I have wondered if I ever should.' Tears rolled down her cheeks.

Kit had to leave her side to con his ship into the harbour, and find a berth amidst the French fleet which clustered at anchor. It seemed like only yesterday that he had left here, in a rage, to sail north. Because, in seafaring terms, it was only yesterday. Had he been in that much of a hurry to divest himself of the woman to whom he had volunteered his life? And in exchange for what? If he dreamed, it was of a whore, to whom all men were but playthings. In affairs of the heart he was surely the most unfortunate of men.

Yet he knew that he would be also the most relieved man on earth when Annette was finally returned to her brother's care. And there could be no conscience involved here; she had been overjoyed at the idea. That the French would eventually regain control of St Domingue had been *her* dream for eleven years; now that it had happened she had been almost sane on the voyage. He had feared, of course, her reactions as she had approached her homeland once again, but in fact she merely seemed delighted, and if he watched her carefully as they rowed ashore, she continued to gaze at the new city with rapt interest. And in truth LeClerc had done wonders in hardly more than a month rebuilding the city. Everywhere there were black labourers scurrying to and fro, supervised by French architects and overseen by French soldiers. Here was the past coming back to control the present. Annette clapped her hands in delight. 'Of course,' she reassured herself, 'we could not hang them *all*, Kit. They are needed for labour.'

But LeClerc had done wonders in more than mere architecture. He had succeeded in his mission. How, Kit found it difficult to understand. Yet Etienne had been quite definite in his letter. Toussaint had accepted honourable terms of capitulation, and St Domingue was once again a peaceful French colony. Kit supposed that had to be one of the most extraordinary coups that history would ever record.

He found them a carriage for hire, and hurried Annette out of town. He had no wish to encounter either Pauline LeClerc or any of her minions, or any of his black friends. Not with Annette on his arm.

She peered out of the window as the coach rumbled towards Vergée d'Or. 'I did not expect ever to see it again,' she said, tears still rolling down her cheeks. 'Oh, how fortunate I am.'

Madeleine was there to greet them, as statuesquely and blondely beautiful as ever in her mid forties, embracing Annette tenderly as she gazed above her head at Kit, who could only shrug optimistically. While Etienne and Louise fussed.

'You will find it all rather primitive at the moment,' Etienne explained. 'We have only this wooden cottage, for the time being, and that is all. But it is quite comfortable.' He showed them up the steps and on to the shallow verandah; behind there was a living area from which extended a corridor to the three bedrooms. 'But of course our first priority is to harvest a crop and have it ground, to earn some income. Do you know, Kit, I have ridden over the plantation, and I think it is going to be a good crop. You've no desire to abandon the sea, and return to planting?'

Kit stood at the rail, hands on hips, looking out at the site of the chateau. Because it was no more than a site, now; Etienne had been busy here, too, and all the stone had been accumulated into a huge dump some yards away, while the skeleton of the grand staircase had been pulled down. Now only the foundations remained, and the cellars, like huge caves in the ground. And the work proceeded; even as he watched, a gang of labourers under the supervision of a white overseer were picking away at the loose stone on the patio. And the overseer carried a whip. Indeed had the past returned, except that surely . . . he turned to his cousin. 'How much do you have to pay these people to work for you?'

'Ah,' Etienne said with a grin. 'I am not actually paying them anything. They are a labour battalion lent to me by LeClerc.'

'You mean the government is paying them?'

'In kind. The government supplies them with food, and clothing where it is absolutely necessary.'

'But not money?'

'Now really, Kit, what would be the point in giving these people money? They would only buy strong spirits with it.'

'And they can leave this work whenever they choose?'

'Of course not. They have been conscripted as a labour battalion, as I said. To desert the battalion would be mutiny, and in the French army that is punishable by death.'

Kit stroked his chin. 'Then they are as much slaves as they ever were.'

'Well . . .' Etienne smiled. 'They know no other existence. And it is the only way to get them to work. The only way we are going to get the colony back on its feet.'

'What do the black leaders think about this?'

'I shouldn't think they think very much about anything.'

'The General did say that this Toussaint person made some remonstrances to him,' Madeleine said. 'But he was sent off with a flea in his ear.'

'Yes,' Kit said. 'And Richilde?'

Etienne and Madeleine exchanged glances.

'We have seen nothing of Richilde,' Madeleine said. 'She has not even come to call.'

'Perhaps she feels you should have called on her,' Kit suggested. 'And invited her to join you here. This is her home.'

'That is a debatable point,' Etienne said. 'I am Philippe's heir.'

'With a responsibility to care for his widow,' Kit said. 'I should have supposed it your duty to seek her out and offer her a home.'

'I'm afraid I take a different view. My responsibility towards Philippe's widow exists only as long as she remains a widow. Richilde considers herself married to this scoundrel Christophe, although they have certainly never entered a church together, except perhaps to loot it. There is no question of my having any legal responsibility towards her. But having made that clear, she is, of course, welcome here whenever she wishes, provided she comes alone.'

'I see,' Kit said again. 'Well, things seem to be working out for you very well, 'Tienne. I wish you success. But I do not think I wish to return to St Domingue to live. My home is in New York, my future is in America. Now I must leave you.'

'You'll not stay to supper, Kit?' Madeleine asked.

He shook his head. 'I have a deal to do.'

'Kit.' Annette held out both her hands. 'You are saying goodbye. How can I ever thank you.' But he was already an item in her past. What he might once have felt for her, what he might still feel for her, was irrelevant. He had kept her and fed her and clothed her for eleven years, against the moment she could resume her proper station. And that moment had arrived.

'But I should prefer you not to try,' Kit said.

'But you'll come to see me? Whenever you are in Cap François?'

'Whenever,' Kit agreed.

Etienne walked with him down the steps to the waiting gig. 'You are going to see Richilde?'

'She *is* my sister, 'Tienne.'

'Of course. I understand entirely. And I am glad of it. Kit . . .' he hesitated. 'I would not discuss this before the girls, but Richilde *is* more than welcome to make Vergée d'Or her home again.'

'On your terms,' Kit said.

'On the terms of the new colony of St Domingue,' Etienne said, gazing at him. 'It would be best if you could convince her of this, and convince her too that there is not too much time. Now is her last chance to make her choice. Either resume her proper station in life, or be condemned forever as a white nigger, doomed to suffer whatever . . . well, whatever vicissitudes of fortune lie ahead.'

Kit frowned. 'What are you saying, exactly?'

'What I have said.' He shook Kit's hand. 'As you value your sister, Kit, persuade her to come here, at the very earliest possible moment.'

Kit drew rein where the road – it was hardly more substantial than a cart track – sloped down to the little bay. He could hardly imagine anything so peaceful, the curving arms of white sand, built up against the ages old coral of the inner reef beyond, the swiftly changing colours of the sea, from white to a deepening shade of green before the blue was reached beyond the reef, the palisade of palm trees which separated the beach from the scrub behind, the breeze filtering off the ocean, and the little cottage nestling in the midst of the trees. Here he had left the hustle and bustle of the rest of the coast, that part nearest to Cap François, and thus more firmly under French control.

It was a scene entirely in keeping with his own mood.

He had only realised, these past few weeks, perhaps as late as last night, how all his life he had been straining, to be something or to escape something, or to possess something. Annette had been the end of that strain, as she had been the longest part of it, as her presence had dominated his life for ten years, as his love for her had slowly turned into bitter ashes in his throat. Now he, too, felt at peace.

As if he, or anyone in St Domingue, apparently, could ever truly feel at peace. What *had* Etienne been trying to hint?

A dog barked, and then showed itself from the far side of the hut, a large, shaggy mongrel. It kept its distance, but maintained its baying warning to its owners. Kit cupped his hands. 'Anyone home?' he shouted.

Richilde appeared on the little porch, drying her hands on the skirt of her gown. The true Richilde, he thought, wearing but a single garment, so that the morning sunlight outlined her legs, and with her hair loose and fluttering in the breeze – he had forgotten how long she had allowed it to grow. Just as he was inclined to forget with what strength and purpose she moved, what, indeed, strength and purpose flowed from her very being. He wondered what the reaction in New York or Boston would be were he to recommend to the good matrons that their daughters should all be sent into the woods in their early womanhood to survive as best they could, as a guarantee of future health and strength.

'Kit? Is it really you?' She hurried from the house. 'Down Beast. Away with you.'

Beast subsided, panting, and Kit dismounted to take his sister in his arms.

'Etienne told me you would be coming back,' Richilde said. 'Bringing Annette. I didn't believe him. I *couldn't* believe that Annette would really wish to come back here.'

He tethered his horse, walked beside her, hand in

392

hand, back to the porch. 'She wanted that more than anything else in the world.'

'So now at last you are rid of her.'

'Yes. I feel a strange sense, half of relief and half of, well . . . loneliness, I suppose. But also of distress, at what I see here.'

There was a hammock suspended from the porch uprights. Richilde sat down in it, began to swing, gently; Kit sat in the one straight chair. 'It is my fault,' she said.

'Your fault?'

'Well . . .' she shrugged. 'Henry wanted to fight them from the beginning, remember? I recommended peace. And I negotiated it for Pierre. I thought I was doing the right thing. Our people did not really wish to fight any more. Most important, Pierre did not wish to fight any more. And without him these people are nothing.' She sighed. 'But LeClerc outwitted me. All of us. Can you believe, that when he told us he intended to recruit a Negro force, we actually encouraged our people to volunteer? To be driven by whips to carry stones and plant cane.'

'And there is nothing you can do about it?'

'We have surrendered our weapons.'

'You did what you thought was best,' Kit said. 'You can have nothing to reproach yourself with. And you have at least stopped the killing. What does Henry think of it all?'

Again she shrugged. 'He fishes. He has built himself a boat, and goes fishing.'

'And leaves you here, alone?'

'What have I got to be afraid of, Kit? My notoriety does have some advantages. No one will ever lift a finger against the woman of General Christophe. But Henry . . .' she sighed. 'We had such dreams, Kit. Such dreams.'

'Of great armies, and splendid uniforms.'

'Of much more than that. Of making St Domingue

into a new country. Of showing the world what we could do, given the chance.'

'You identify yourself with these people?'

'They are *my* people, Kit.'

'Yet must you from time to time consider your own future. As you say, you had dreams. They were never practical, real prospects.'

'They were,' she said fiercely. 'They could have happened. If Toussaint had been ten years younger, perhaps. He is tired now, too tired. Or if Henry had somehow had some sort of an education.' She gave a twisted smile. 'That is our fault; he was our slave. If only one could have some glimpses, into the future.'

'It is not so opaque as all that,' he said. 'All the upheaval, the turmoil of the past few years, is now over and done with. Even in France it is done with. They may not have a king, any more, but they have a First Consul for life, who is more powerful than any king. And he has secured recognition by all the European powers, has ended the war ... Europe has reverted entirely to how it was twenty years ago, save that the old French aristocracy has been destroyed. A new one has already arisen. It is composed of people like LeClerc and his Pauline, but are they any more vulgar or indecent than the Mortmains or the Richelieus, or even the Bourbons themselves? So here on St Domingue too, it is over. The past has returned, and you may be sure its grip will be tightened, with every passing week.'

'Then that is a tragedy,' she said.

'All life is a tragedy, Richilde. We can only endeavour to make our way in its midst. It is your way that I want you to consider.'

'My way is Henry's way.'

'Sitting on an empty beach? You are not yet thirty-five years old. You have lived but half your life. You will spend the rest of it, here? Etienne offers you a home, and your proper place in society.'

'Etienne? I would rather be dead.'

He chewed his lip. 'Well, then . . . New York? I have a fine house there, Richilde. An empty house, now. And a fine, free life. An expanding one, too. Alexander is going to be Governor of the State, in a couple of years' time. And then, who knows. I think he even has the presidency in mind. He is handicapped, of course, by being born in Nevis, but I do not think that is an insuperable obstacle. Certainly he is well thought of. America is the country of the future, Richilde.' He held her hand. 'I sail at dusk. If you were to come with me, when you awake tomorrow morning St Domingue will be nothing more than a cloudbank on the horizon.'

'And Henry?'

Kit sighed. 'It will make things difficult. It will be difficult for him, as well, now he has had a taste of power, of being a general. But he is welcome, if he wishes to come.'

'He will never leave St Domingue,' she said. 'Or his people. The people he has led into battle, time and again. That is *too* difficult, Kit.'

'Well, then . . .'

'My place is at his side. He is my man, and where he goes, there will I go too.'

Yet she knew that Henry could not spend the rest of his life fishing. She waited on the beach to help him drag his pirogue up the sand. 'Kit was here today.'

Henry lifted a grouper from the bottom of the boat, walked towards the hut. 'A big one, eh? Food for two days. Kit? I'm sorry to have missed him.'

She walked behind him, bare toes sinking into the sand. He wore nothing but a pair of drawers; his uniform, carefully washed and pressed, hung on a hook inside their tiny bedroom. It was a memory of things past, of dreams once shared.

'As he was to miss you. He takes a gloomy look of the future.'

Henry sat in the hammock with a sigh. 'Don't we?'

'Well . . .' she sat beside him. 'Kit, as usual, is full of solutions.'

'He wants us to go to America?'

'Well . . . yes. Yes, he does. He does not trust the French. He feels we aren't safe, here. There is no slavery in New York, Henry. He will find you a place on board his ships, and we can be properly married, and . . .' she bit her lip as he looked at her. 'But St Domingue is your home.'

'I must stay,' he said. 'Because I too do not trust the French. I must stay, in case Toussaint once again has to call on me, and my soldiers.'

'And if he never does?'

He grinned. 'Then I will go fishing. And come back to you, to make love.'

But when they were finished, he looked deeply into her eyes. 'But if you wish to go, to America, Richilde, I will not stand in your way.'

'Do you wish me to go?' she asked.

'Half of my life would go with you.'

'Then I shall stay. And clean your fish. And make love. In any event, Kit has already left.'

Because what more, she wondered as she lay with her head on his arm, could a woman really want? A strong, resolute, utterly loving man, a quiet bay, no sound to disturb the evening save the ever present whisper of the surf, the rasp of the cicadas, the faint jingle of harnesses . . . she sat up, heart pounding, a tremendous gush of sweat pouring from her neck and shoulders, even as Beast barked.

Henry was also awake. 'Horsemen,' he said.

She got out of bed, ran to the window, peered into the night, saw the gleam of swords and muskets through the trees. 'Oh, my God,' she said. 'Oh, my God. Those are French soldiers.'

Henry was priming his pistols. 'I will drop two, at any rate.' By dint of constant practice he had made himself into a good shot.

She held his arm. 'No,' she said. 'They would kill you, eventually.'

'Have they not come to do that, anyway?'

'And you will give them what they want? Get out the back. Make the sea, and swim round to the next headland. Quickly.'

He hesitated, while Beast's barking grew more urgent, and the sound of men filled the night. Then he nodded. 'It is a slim chance. But the only one. Come.'

She shook her head. 'It is no chance at all, Henry, for both of us. They are at the door. I will talk with them.'

'You? But . . .'

'It is *you* they have come for,' she said. 'They have no cause to fear me, therefore they have no cause to wish my life. It is you they mean to destroy. I will come to you the moment they have left. Wait in the woods. You will know when I am there.'

Another hesitation. 'You would have me play the coward.'

'I would have you play the *man*,' she said. 'Don't you understand, if the French are moving against you, secretly, in the dead of night, they will be moving against Toussaint too, and Dessalines? Against every black man of any importance in St Domingue? Toussaint will have need of you, now.'

Henry hesitated, for a last long moment, then he kissed her on the lips. 'I will wait for you, in the woods,' he said, and ran for the back of the house.

'Christophe,' a man called. 'We know you are in there. Come out with your hands in the air.'

Richilde moved slowly towards the door. It was of course possible that they might open fire the very moment anyone appeared. But so many things were possible. She grasped the handle, drew a long breath, and threw the door wide. Instantly Beast brushed past her, leaping into the yard before the little house, feet spread, glaring at the men and the horses.

'Come forward,' the officer said.

Richilde blinked into the gloom, could make him out,

still mounted, although several of his men were on foot. But she was accomplishing her objective. They were all looking at her, rather than the beach or the sea. She moved forward, stood beside the dog.

'Citizeness Mortmain,' the officer said. 'Is your paramour hiding under the bed?'

'General Christophe is not here,' she said.

'Bah,' the officer said. 'Search the place,' he commanded.

Four of the dragoons came forward. Beast gave a low growl and leapt at the first one. There was the flash of a musket and an explosion, and the dog gave a howl, rolled over three times, and lay on its side, tongue lolling. Richilde restrained a scream with an effort. For suddenly she knew that all the years had rolled away and she was back in the hall of Vergée d'Or chateau, on 23 August 1791. Only then she had been twenty-four years old, had not truly believed it was possible for her to die.

'That was not necessary,' she said, forcing herself to speak quietly, to maintain the legend that she had become. 'Be sure I will report it to your commanding General.'

'Bah,' he said, and himself dismounted. Behind her she heard the sound of her house being torn apart. Well, she thought, this is not the first house of mine that has been destroyed. Will it be the last?

'He is not here, Captain,' the sergeant said.

The Captain stood before Richilde. 'Where is he? Do not play games with me, citizeness. We are not here to play games.'

'I do not know where he is,' she said. 'He went fishing, and has not yet returned.' She bit her lip, aware that she had betrayed herself.

The Captain smiled; she saw the gleam of his teeth. 'He went fishing, but his bateau is on the sand? So, you do wish to play games. This is your last chance, citizeness. Tell me where I can find Christophe.'

She became aware that the men who had searched

the house were standing immediately behind her, that the rest of the command, reassured that the dreaded Christophe was not about, had also dismounted and were crowding forward. An immense weakness seemed to fill her stomach, to seep upwards into her chest, making breathing difficult.

'If you do not tell me, citizeness,' the Captain said. 'I will give you to my men.'

Richilde inhaled. 'I do not know where General Christophe is,' she said. 'I have not seen him in days.'

The Captain stared at her, then he jerked his head, and she felt fingers close to her arm.

She walked, or rather was dragged, behind their horses, her wrists tied in front of her, and then secured to the sergeant's saddle. They had not allowed her to regain her gown, as if, torn to shreds as it was, it could possibly have provided any protection. And after a while it did not matter. She fell, and was dragged over the dusty earth, and was coated in mud to join the blood and the sweat ... and the semen; her hair seemed stuck together in a solid mass on her back.

And she suffered agonies of fear, that Henry, who would certainly have watched what was happening from the trees, would attempt to rescue her, and be killed. But the trees remained silent; he was after all, a *man*, who knew where his primary duty lay. For that she was grateful, and yet, perversely, she wished that he could, in some way, have managed to raise sufficient force to attack her captors – or at least be able to let her know he was *there*.

So, am I a girl, an Annette, to go mad? she asked herself. Because a dozen men had rammed their evil selves into me, and even worse, have torn at my most private parts with their filthy fingers? I am Richilde de Mortmain, Christophe's woman. I have but to survive, to be avenged. And if I do not survive, then will I still be avenged.

Thus the woman, who had survived the past, who could keep the future in perspective. But beside her, always, was the woman who had to endure the present. The pain, some of it dull from the punches she had received, the tremendous pressure on her shoulders and back as she was dragged forward, some of it sharp, as each time she fell some new cut was ripped across the flesh, the agony of her bruised and bleeding toes, and all of it hideous as she inhaled dust, and worse, from the horses in front of her, as she listened to the laughter of the men. Occasionally one would lean from the saddle to poke her with his whip, and, as they had not actually tortured her as yet, and she had not told them where Christophe was, as yet, she dared not consider what might be going to happen to her in the next couple of hours.

She allowed herself the luxury of tears, but mostly they were tears of anger, and outrage. And she had not screamed once, nor had she begged for mercy. That had angered the sergeant. 'Scream, you nigger whore,' he had shouted, slapping her face to and fro, even as he had knelt between her legs. 'Scream.'

She could afford to weep, now.

Dimly she became aware that she was surrounded by increasing dust, and increasing noise, and thus increasing people. More horsemen, and foot soldiers as well, herding large numbers of black people towards the French encampment. It seemed as if all the Negroes in St Domingue had been arrested at the same time. All who *could* be arrested, anyway. All who had not escaped to the forest. LeClerc's way of honouring his promises. A treachery Kit had feared, because he knew these people. A treachery she had discounted, because they were white, like herself.

Not all the black people were bound. Most were just being herded along by the whips and the gun butts of their captors. Several saw her, and recognised her, and called out her name, and one man attempted to help her back to her feet the next time she fell, only to be driven away by the sergeant's whip. But they had noticed one immense fact about her.

'Man,' they called to each other. 'That is Christophe's woman. But they ain't got Christophe.'

'They ain't got Christophe.' The whisper went across the huge throng of prisoners. 'Christophe gone.'

'And Christophe going get *them*.'

Christophe would get their enemies. There was all the hope they needed. All the hope she needed. She could even smile at the sergeant, as they finally halted, and she sank to her knees while he dismounted. 'Christophe is gone,' she whispered.

'And you will hang,' he said. 'And when you are dangling, I will poke my bayonet up your cunt.'

'Christophe will get *you*,' she said, and did not even turn her head away from his swinging fist.

She was dragged to her feet again, released from the saddle now, to be pushed and prodded with the other captives towards a vast wire enclosure which had been prepared, again apparently very recently – but it was at least a month since Richilde had last been near to Cap François. Now it was already half filled with blacks. But she was not going to be allowed to claim the anonymity of the mob. As she was led towards the pen, she heard a familiar voice.

'Citizeness Mortmain.'

Instantly she was jerked to a halt, pulled out of the line. She raised her head, looked at Palourdes, lowered it again. For the first time she was truly aware of her nakedness.

'Where is your paramour, citizeness?'

'In the forest by now,' she mumbled through her parched and bruised lips. 'Raising an army to strike at you.'

'She is a devil, Major,' the Captain said. 'She fought us like a she-wolf, in order that Christophe might escape.'

'I can see that, from her condition,' Palourdes commented, drily. 'But the Commanding General would wish a word with her, I am sure. Bring her along.'

Richilde was pulled away from the other prisoners, and sent stumbling towards the officers' encampment, terribly aware that Palourdes was walking at her shoulder, and watching her, and now that other men were also gathering to stare at her, to congratulate the Captain, and to make the coarsest and lewdest of suggestions. But could anything they wished to do, or have done, to her be any worse than what she had already suffered?

LeClerc breakfasted outside his tent. Suddenly brought to a halt by the sergeant, Richilde's knees gave way and she sank to the ground, to her chagrin, while even more to her shame she was unable to keep from staring at the jug of iced water on the General's table.

'It seems that Christophe has escaped, Citizen General,' Palourdes said.

'The devil,' LeClerc said, delicately slicing a piece of bread, and conveying it to his lips. His gaze roamed over Richilde. 'Why was she not killed in resisting arrest?'

Richilde caught her breath. Up to this moment she had not believed she was actually in any danger of her life.

The Captain stood to attention. 'I supposed you would wish to question her further, Citizen General.'

'If Christophe has escaped, he has escaped,' LeClerc said. 'She will have no more idea where he is at this moment than do we. You were sent to arrest him, and you failed. No doubt through . . .' once again his gaze scorched Richilde's flesh. 'Dallying with this woman. You are reduced to the rank of sergeant.'

'Sergeant?' cried the Captain. 'But Citizen General—'

'And are dismissed my presence.' LeClerc finished chewing, swallowed, leaned back. 'Well, citizeness, it seems you and I are always encountering one another. Have you anything to say?'

'Yes,' Richilde said. 'I would like to ask why? In the

name of God, *why*? You had outwitted me, you had outwitted all of us, you held all of St Domingue in your hand, and now this. You must be mad.'

He shrugged, seeming to indicate that it did not matter how she insulted him. 'As neither you nor your friends are very intelligent, citizeness. Has it escaped your notice that we are now in June? The hurricane season, citizeness. Admiral Villaret-Joyeuse has informed me that he must take his fleet, the mainspring of my strength, back to France to be safe from these winds, and that he will not be returning until November. It thus became necessary to close that hand, and grasp St Domingue even more tightly, until a new fleet, with reinforcements, arrives. And this I have done.'

'By arresting me?' she asked contemptuously. 'And a few hundred, even a few thousand, blacks? What you have done, Citizen General, is convince even the most peaceful of our people that you are not to be trusted. That you *have* to be destroyed. And you *will* be destroyed, General. Because you will even have convinced Toussaint, and he above us all wished to give you a chance to make this peace into a permanency. But now . . .'

LeClerc smiled. 'I am sure you are right, and that I have convinced the slave Toussaint of my true intentions, citizeness. Look there.'

He pointed, and she turned to follow the direction he was indicating, to see a ship, standing out of the harbour, her sails filling beneath the offshore breeze as she made for the open Atlantic.

'Do you suppose he stands on deck, taking a last look at his homeland?' LeClerc asked. 'No, he will not be doing that, citizeness. He will be in the hold, weighed down by his chains, with his sons beside him. And he will remain chained until he reaches France, when no doubt the First Consul will know what to do with him.'

'You . . .' She could not believe it.

403

LeClerc smiled. 'So you see, citizeness, Toussaint did not escape. And without Toussaint, as you yourself will agree, we have to deal with nothing more than a slave mob. Believe me, I have my plans already made for destroying *them*.' His smile faded. 'And I will commence by demonstrating how I will deal with anyone, white, black or brown, male or female, adult or child, who seeks to defy my orders, who seeks to give aid or support to any rebellious slave.' He glanced at Palourdes. 'Take her away and hang her. Hoist her high above the battlements of Cap François that she may be seen for a good distance. Let the niggers understand that I will deal with them, no less harshly, if any one of them raises his hand against me.'

Richilde's knees gave way, and she would have fallen if Palourdes had not caught her arm. Despite everything that had happened, she had never seriously supposed that the French would ever seek to kill *her*. Desperately she licked her lips; her throat was suddenly more parched than ever before.

'I wish to protest against that order, Citizen General,' Palourdes said. 'Citizeness Mortmain is no traitor. She has made her loyalties clear from the beginning.'

'You wish to protest,' LeClerc sneered. 'But you wished to protest against this entire coup, Palourdes. What, are you afraid of upsetting a few blackamoors? My orders stand, and *you* will carry them out. Have *you* anything to say?' he asked Richilde.

'I . . .' But she was Richilde de Mortmain. And she was Christophe's woman. She could not beg this upstarted guttersnipe. At least, not for her life. 'I request the privilege of a gown, *Citizen* General,' she said, both surprised and delighted by the steadiness of her voice. 'In common decency.'

He allowed his gaze to roam up and down her body. 'Why should you wear a gown, citizeness?' he inquired. 'As you have appeared before *your* people often enough, I have heard, in your natural state. But I will have my men give you a *bath*, eh? So that you will be more easily recognisable.'

'You . . . you are surely not a *man*, monsieur,' she said. 'Are you not afraid that by the time you regain your hole, it will become blocked, by the filth which emanates from your mind?'

He stood up, his face suffused, and for a moment she thought he would strike her. Then he sat down again. 'Have it done,' he said to Palourdes.

The Major held her arm, turned her round. Her eyes were filled with a haze of tears, which she knew were about to start rolling down her cheeks. But surely a woman could weep, as the rope tightened about her neck?

'My God! The white nigger. And looking more like a nigger than usual. What are you doing with her, Palourdes?'

Richilde blinked her vision clear, experienced the greatest humiliation of the day, as she gazed at Pauline LeClerc, her scantily clad body shaded by an enormous parasol carried by an attentive Negro boy, and accompanied as usual by her two disciples, Seraphine Palourdes and Jacqueline Chavannes.

'She is to be washed clean, and then hanged, citizeness,' Palourdes explained.

'Hanged?' Pauline demanded. 'Oh, really, Palourdes.'

'Orders from the Commanding General, citizeness.'

'An example,' LeClerc said, having overseen the arrival of his wife, and left his table. 'Besides, she deserves it for her consistent defiance of us.'

'You are absurd, LeClerc,' Pauline remarked. 'And wasteful. I do not think hanging a naked white woman will advance our cause in the slightest. Hang some of the blacks. I will take Citizeness Mortmain off your hands.'

'You?' LeClerc stared at her. 'May I ask with what intention?'

You, Richilde thought, keeping her feet with an effort. Now waves of exhaustion were sweeping over her in company to the pain. But waves too of hope. And these she both hated and distrusted. She had not intended to allow herself to hope, ever again.

Pauline LeClerc was smiling. 'I wish to . . . observe her. I think she is a very interesting specimen. Do you not think she is an interesting specimen, Jacqueline?'

'Oh, indeed, citizeness,' Jacqueline said. Her face was expressionless. Could *she* really be meaning to save my life, Richilde wondered?

'It is impossible,' LeClerc said. 'My orders have been given.'

'Impossible? My dear Charles, I would have said that my brother the First Consul might well consider it impossible to hang a white woman.'

He bit his lip. 'And do you not realise, citizeness, that this man Christophe, once he understands that she is still alive, will wish to regain possession of her? She will be a constant encouragement to the Negroes to attack.'

Pauline gave a peal of laughter. 'And do *you* not realise, my dear General, that they are going to attack you anyway? In any event, could you wish for anything better than to lure Christophe into Cap François, looking for his mistress? I should have thought such a plan was obvious.'

Which was absolutely true, Richilde realised, with a pang of real horror. Henry would undoubtedly launch one of those all out and futile frontal assaults on the French position, once he knew she was alive. And he would lead the assault himself.

LeClerc was chewing his lip.

'So I will take care of her for you,' Pauline said. 'You may release her, Palourdes.'

Palourdes looked at his commander, and LeClerc shrugged and nodded. His fingers released Richilde's arm. Once again she nearly fell, had to transmit strength to her knees by a conscious act of will.

'She needs assistance,' Pauline said. 'You will help her, Jacqueline. She is an old friend of yours, is she not?'

'An old friend,' Jacqueline said, and took Richilde's arm. Seraphine Palourdes took the other.

'Do not worry, citizeness.' Pauline said, 'We will soon have you clean, and fed, and watered.' She gave a shrill laugh. 'And even housed.'

'I . . .' Now the tears were coming very fast. She had to force herself to speak, in view of what she had to say. 'I *am* a traitor, to France,' she said. 'You do wrong to interfere with your husband's sentence, citizeness. I will not thank you for it. I will hate you. And I will harm you, if I can.'

Pauline gazed at her from beneath arched eyebrows. She gave another of her shrill laughs. 'The poor woman is overwhelmed. She does not know how to thank.'

Jacqueline smiled at Richilde. 'There is nothing to thank *me* for, Richilde. I am but obeying Citizeness LeClerc.'

'As for me, my dear,' Pauline said. 'You will thank me by *amusing* me.' She looked over her shoulder at the scowling LeClerc. 'I will let her amuse you too, my dear Charles. From time to time.'

Chapter 5

THE KING

Unlike Toussaint and Christophe, Dessalines had been born in Africa, and knew all the horrors of the Middle Passage. Dark-skinned and dark-visaged, squat and repulsive, talented and terrible, he assumed command of what was now openly a war of extermination.

Kit Hamilton leaned on the rail of his ship, watched the bananas being hoisted on board. Here in Port Royal, in Jamaica, he was almost entirely surrounded by land, as the long sandspit of Los Palisadoes curved round from the mainland to enclose the bay. On the end of Los Palisadoes, close indeed to where the *Stormy Petrel* now rode to anchor, there had once been the town of Port Royal, the capital of Jamaica, and also of Henry Morgan's buccaneers, the City of Sin. Strange to suppose that the first Mortmain, who had certainly been with Morgan at the sack of Panama, must have trodden those long disappeared streets. Because on the morning of 7 June 1692, just a hundred and ten years ago, he realised, Port Royal had disappeared into the sea. The earth had opened up and swallowed the capital of every vice in the New World. Now it was only possible, by peering down through the translucent green water, to make out the rubbled remains of the buildings where once the pirates had roistered.

He wondered what history would say of St Domingue, of Cap François, in a hundred and ten years' time?

No earthquake there. But a man-made convulsion which in its pitiless intensity was far more vicious than any act of nature, however primeval. And which was still happening. He could not doubt that. The uneasy truce which existed between LeClerc and Toussaint could not endure, however honourable the intentions of the Negro leader.

He sighed, strolled across the poop deck to watch a ship standing round the end of the sandspit. He recognised her, of course; there were not that many trading vessels out of New York making the West Indian circuit. She was called the *Golden Star*, and he had left her anchored in Cap François when he had sailed from there, four days before. Like him, she would now be seeking a cargo in haste, in order to run back north to the safety of New England before the first of the hurricanes which ranged across these sunlit waters from June to October came tearing through the sky.

'Ahoy, the *Stormy Petrel*,' came the hail across the water. 'You've heard the news?'

'What news?' Kit shouted. Not another war, he thought.

Further conversation was rendered impossible for serveral minutes as the *Golden Star* dropped her anchor, the rasp of the chain through the hawsepipe sending the sea birds screaming around the bay. But the moment she was secure a boat was lowered and pulling towards the *Stormy Petrel*, Captain Lowery himself at the tiller. 'Toussaint has been arrested,' he called.

'Toussaint? But . . . whatever for?' Of all the men in St Domingue, Kit would have thought Toussaint the least likely to break the treaty.

Lowery came up the ladder, a small, swarthy, Nantucket Islander with a drooping moustache. 'It was a bit of skullduggery on the part of the French, if you ask me.' He shook hands. 'Must have happened the night you sailed, Hamilton. Seems his home was surrounded, and he and his two sons placed under arrest while they were at table. That same night they were put on a ship for France.'

'Good God.' Kit led his friend into the cabin, set out a bottle of rum and two glasses. 'But what is LeClerc hoping to achieve?'

'A return of the colony to slavery, I would say.' Lowery drank deeply.

'He supposes arresting Toussaint will accomplish that?'

'Not just Toussaint. All the Negro leaders were arrested. Or at any rate, that was the French plan. Kit . . .' he leaned across the table. 'Your sister was certainly taken.'

'Richilde? But . . . she is not a Negro leader.'

Lowery flushed. 'She lives with one. Or she did. The word is that Christophe escaped, but that Richilde was taken. Dragged into Cap François with a lot of blacks, naked and beaten.' He bit his lip. 'That is what I heard.'

Kit gazed at him. 'Would not her cousin have looked to her protection?'

'I can but repeat what I have been told. I supposed you would wish to hear of it.'

'Aye,' Kit said. 'I thank you.' He gazed into his glass for several seconds. So once again he was being summoned back to that tortured island. And once again he had to attempt to rescue Richilde from the grave she had dug for herself. But there was nothing else he could do; certainly she could not be abandoned in a French prison.

Besides, if LeClerc had declared war on the blacks, as his action in arresting Toussaint would most certainly be considered . . . it was impossible to imagine what might be going to happen next.

He drained the drink, got up. 'There's a cargo of bananas, contracted for, and waiting for you, Lowery,' he said. 'I'm for Cap François.'

410

'Citizens. Citizenesses. I am sure you all know Citizeness Richilde Mortmain.' Pauline LeClerc smiled at her guests. 'At least by reputation.'

Richilde feared she knew them all too well. She had expected nothing like this. But then, the entire three days since her capture had been totally confusing. She had been kept a prisoner, certainly, but in the most luxurious of confinements, attended only by Jacqueline and Seraphine Palourdes, and by Pauline herself. Her cuts and bruises had been smoothed and ointmented, until they had all but disappeared, she had been fed the best of food and given the best of wine to drink. She had been kept in bed on a feather mattress and between linen sheets. In the beginning she had momently expected some sudden reversal of fortune, or at the least some obscene assault from these creatures whom she knew to be utterly amoral. Nor could she doubt that they loathed her. Jacqueline certainly – and she in addition sought revenge – and Pauline also, she thought. She could not be sure about the young one, Seraphine, who said little, and who went about whatever duties Pauline appointed her to with the same sad, resigned expression. Presumably, Richilde thought, she should be grateful to her in view of the way her husband had endeavoured to save her life. But then, should she not be grateful to all of them?

But today had been the greatest surprise of all, as she had been taken from bed, and bathed and perfumed, and had her hair dressed, in the fashionable chignon which all the French women wore, and then given this gown to wear, one of the transparently indecent garments which again seemed to form the main part of her new friends' wardrobes – because they were dressed hardly different.

'In France, my dear Citizeness Mortmain,' Pauline had explained with her invariable glittering smile, 'they wear flesh coloured tights beneath their gowns, because of the cold and the damp. Here, in this delightful climate, we have no need for such subterfuge.'

Yet Richilde could hardly feel less than utterly exposed, as she gazed at the faces of the other people who were attending this 'intimate' little supper party, in the great dining room of the Governor General's old residence, where Monsieur Peynier had once entertained, as had Henry and herself more recently. A fact which, mercifully, seemed unknown to the LeClercs. In any event, the burned out building had been rebuilt in so different a style as to be almost unrecognisable.

Present tonight there was LeClerc himself, of course, together with two other of his senior officers from the garrison, and their wives, and naturally, Palourdes. These she could have stood, and she was heartily relieved to discover that Etienne and Louise were *not* here. But to make up for the slight blessing, she found herself gazing at the mulatto General, Alexander Petion, and even more disturbing, at his aide-de-camp, Jean Boyer.

Boyer, indeed, was placed on her right during supper, while the wine flowed and the conversation became animated. And horrifying.

'How many did you dispose of today?' inquired General Morel.

'How many did we *marry*, you mean,' LeClerc said, with a shout of laughter. 'Oh, I suppose about a thousand. The difficulty is not the marriages themselves, my friend, but disposing of the bodies when they start returning to the surface.'

Richilde glanced at Boyer, saw that his face was rigid with distaste, and indeed with anger. As Pauline LeClerc, predatory eyes ever restlessly roaming the table, observed, just as she had observed Richilde's look.

'You do not know of it, of course, my dear Citizeness Mortmain,' she smiled. 'But Charles has devised a new method of dealing with blacks. Well . . . it is not new, I suppose. Did not Fouché practice it at Nantes, in '93?'

'There is nothing *new*, when you come down to it,' LeClerc grumbled.

'These blacks, you see,' Pauline said. 'These people

who were brought in with you, are told that they are going to be returned to Africa. Which presumably is what they wish. Thus they are yoked together, a man with a woman, the republican marriages, Fouché used to call them, when he did the same with the aristocrats in Nantes, and thus yoked, are marched on board the waiting ship, which is alongside the quay, you understand. A long line of couples, happily embarking. And once on board, would you believe it . . .' she gave one of her shrill peals of laughter. 'They are told to keep on marching, as they do, right across the ship, only to find that a port has been opened on the far side. Yet must they keep on marching.'

'Oh, my God!' Richilde clasped both hands round her throat.

'And so in they go, plop, plop, plop. While all the time the bands are playing on the quay for their embarkation on the other side, so their screams are not heard by the others waiting to embark. It is so droll.'

'It is mass murder,' Richilde said.

The LeClercs gazed at her.

'It is mass *execution*, citizeness,' the General said at last. 'And you may believe me when I tell you that when I lay hands upon that devil Christophe, I shall have the greatest pleasure in dispatching him, whether or not you accompany him. It is no simple matter, you know,' he complained at large. 'To dispose of so many people so quickly. Fouché at least had the Loire, which runs fast, and carried the bodies out to sea. Here there is not even any tide.'

'I cannot help but agree with the citizeness,' Major Palourdes said. 'The methods you are employing, Citizen General, not less than your attitude to these unfortunate people, is barbaric, and utterly unworthy of a civilised nation. It is indeed but lowering us to the level of the blacks.'

LeClerc turned his glare upon his aide. 'You oppose,' he said. 'You *oppose*. You are always opposing, Citizen

Major. You are not a soldier at all. You are some whimpering choirboy.'

Palourdes's face paled in anger, and he made to rise, but was restrained by Jacqueline's hand on his arm.

'Well, I am sick to death of your *opposing*,' LeClerc said. 'I need an aide-de-camp who supports me, not opposes me in everything. As of this minute you are relieved of your rank and your post. And of any post in this army. Consider yourself under arrest. You will take passage on the next ship bound for France, and there you may *oppose* the First Consul, and see how you fare with him.'

Palourdes hesitated, then threw off Jacqueline's hand and stood up, bowed to Pauline. 'You will excuse me, citizeness,' he said, and left the room.

Seraphine Palourdes promptly stood up as well.

'Oh, sit down, Seraphine,' Pauline shouted. 'Let the men do the quarrelling. It is the heat.'

'Yet might not Citizen Palourdes be right, Citizen General?' asked Petion.

LeClerc glared at him in turn.

'I had assumed your action in attempting to arrest all the black leaders was to make sure of your grip on the colony during the absence of your fleet.' Petion went on, refusing to lower his gaze. 'I cannot say that I approved of such treachery . . .'

'Treachery?' LeClerc shouted, jumping to his feet.

'That is certainly how it must seem, General, to the blacks. What word would *you* rather use?'

'It was a military necessity,' LeClerc declared.

'As you wish, citizen. As I was saying, I cannot truly approve of such military necessity, but I can understand its . . .' he smiled. 'Necessity. And it may well have succeeded. But to continue executing every black you can lay hands on, and in what is, after all, a barbaric fashion . . .'

'Barbaric?' LeClerc shouted. 'You talk to me of barbarism? What of that patrol of mine ambushed yesterday? Every man castrated while still alive, and several with their buttocks cut off as well, as if they were intended for some cannibal feast.'

Richilde caught her breath. Could it be true? Could Henry have permitted such a thing, however great his rage and his grief?

'Yes,' Petion mused. 'I suppose it comes down to the chicken and the egg.'

'And now this fever,' LeClerc grumbled, sitting down again. 'Which strikes down my men, leaves them with ghastly yellow faces, and leaves even those who survive quite unfit for duty. You know of this fever, Citizen Petion?'

Petion looked at Richilde.

'It is called yellow fever, Citizen General,' Richilde said. 'Given time, it will kill all your men. Perhaps even you.'

He glared at her, then turned to his wife. 'You invited me to an entertainment, madame. I did not come to be plagued by insubordinate officers and insolent prisoners.'

'Dear Charles,' Pauline said. 'I apologise. But I did invite you to an entertainment, and an entertainment you shall have. May I suggest we all withdraw to those chairs over there?' The chairs had been arranged in a row, at the far end of the room. 'Oh, not you, Citizeness Mortmain,' Pauline said. 'You must remain at table.'

Richilde gazed at her, heartbeat suddenly quickening, then at Jacqueline – who smiled.

The guests walked away from her, sat down.

'Now,' Pauline said. 'We are going to watch a little play. There are no words, except those which will come naturally and involuntarily to the actors, and there is no scenario. Because we are going to re-enact the fall of the Chateau of Vergée d'Or.'

Richilde stood up.

'Stay there, citizeness, or I shall have you tied to your chair,' Pauline said. 'Although it would be better for you to co-operate. Because, my friends,' she said to her guests. 'We are fortunate to have with us one of the very few survivors of that historic occasion. It has often been asked, *how* did Citizeness Mortmain survive? When all around her, her own husband, were being killed in the most horrible fashion. We know the facts, yet find them difficult to relate to what our imaginations tell us must have been the situation. So tonight we shall carry out a scientific investigation. There you have the citizeness. Her chateau has fallen, but she has managed to retreat to her boudoir, the most private apartment in the house. She knows what has happened outside, in general, but she does not know who is already dead, who may be suffering untold tortures; all their screams are merged in the general cacophony. See her there, pale of cheek, hands clasped about her throat, facing the door through which she knows her fate must come . . .' she clapped her hands, and the door burst open; six black men stood there. 'Now,' Pauline said. 'We must sit back and let events take their course.'

Colonel Boyer stood up. 'You cannot be serious,' he said.

'I assure you that whatever is going to happen will be entirely authentic, Citizen Colonel,' Pauline said. 'These fellows are under sentence of death. But I have promised them their freedom, if they successfully conquer Citizeness Mortmain. And of course entertain us into the bargain. They are thus in exactly the same position as the men who did burst into her boudoir on that unforgettable night eleven years ago. Where men, and women, are placed in exactly the same positions, it has long been my belief that they will act in exactly the same ways. Do not be afraid for her. They have my absolute command that no matter what they may choose to do to her, she must neither be killed nor mutilated, at least on this occasion.'

The Negroes were hesitating, looking from Pauline

to the mulatto officer, uncertain what might happen next. Richilde was aware of a feeling of rising horror, as if she was about to be sick – but it was a mental rather than a physical sickness. She would not vomit, but she would lie on the floor and shriek her brains into madness. Save that suddenly she was too exhausted even to do that.

'It is obscene, citizeness,' Boyer said. 'But then . . .' he might have been going to say. 'You are obscene.' But he controlled himself, bowed. 'You will excuse me.' He looked at Richilde. 'Will you accompany me, Madame de Mortmain?'

'Accompany you?' Pauline demanded. 'Accompany you where?'

Boyer stepped away from the chairs and the other guests, rested his hand on the pocket of his jacket, which was now seen to be sagging as if carrying a heavy weight. 'I have decided to resign my command in your army, Citizen General,' he said to LeClerc. 'I can no longer fight for a man who practices treachery and murder on so vast a scale. I cannot believe that the First Consul, your *brother-in-law*,' he said with heavy irony, 'commanded or indeed would authorise such uncivilised behaviour. You are driven, Citizen General, by an insensate ambition to equal the achievements of others greater than yourself. Well, you will do so without my aid.'

LeClerc stood up. 'You are mad,' he declared. 'I shall have you arrested. You *are* arrested.'

Boyer drew his pistol, presented it at Pauline. 'If anyone makes a move to stop me, I shall shoot Citizeness LeClerc.' He allowed himself a grim smile. 'Through the breast.'

LeClerc stared at him.

Pauline stifled a scream. 'Charles . . .'

'Come here, citizeness,' Boyer said.

Pauline looked left and right. 'Charles . . .'

417

'You had best stop that fellow,' LeClerc said to Petion.

Petion stood up. 'On the contrary, Citizen General. I think I shall accompany him.' He also drew a pistol.

'You came here tonight, armed, intending some treachery . . .'

'We came on our guard against *your* treachery, Citizen General,' Petion said.

'Yet are you committing treason, in time of war. I will have you shot.'

'When you may,' Petion agreed. 'Citizeness LeClerc, you will accompany us to the main gate. And we *will* shoot you, if we are taken. So my advice to you, General LeClerc, is to remain in this room . . .' he glanced at Jacqueline and the other ladies, 'amusing yourself, until your wife returns to you. She *will* be returned to you, I give you my word.' He smiled. 'And *we* are accustomed to keeping our bargains.'

'You cannot let them take me,' Pauline shrilled. 'Charles, you cannot. You cannot let them hand me over to Dessalines and Christophe.'

'I imagine you would enjoy that very much, citizeness,' Petion said. 'At least for a while. But I am not going to do that. Come.'

Boyer reached for Pauline's arm, pulled her against him. 'Now remember, citizeness, we are all going for a moonlight bathe. One of your favourite pastimes. Attempt to play us false, and we shall kill you without a moment's hesitation.' He looked at Jacqueline Chavannes. 'Are you coming?'

Jacqueline drew a sharp breath, glanced at LeClerc. 'No,' she said.

'It is your last chance,' he warned. 'If you stay, you are an enemy, from now.'

'I will stay,' she said. 'To see you hanged.'

'As you wish.' Boyer backed to the door, still holding Pauline's arm, while the other people in the room, including the black men, stared at him as if mesmerised.

Petion beckoned Richilde, who went to him, also feeling as if she were in a dream, that she must awaken, and find herself still Pauline's prisoner, confined to her bedroom.

Or had the whole last week been only a nightmare, and was she really sleeping securely, her head on Henry's arm?'

'Now remember,' Petion said. 'No one is to leave this room until Citizeness LeClerc returns. If you ever wish to see her again.'

'Wait,' Seraphine Palourdes said. 'I should like to accompany you.'

'You, citizeness?'

'If you will permit me to fetch my husband.'

'You would not be considering attempting to betray us, citizeness?'

She met his gaze. 'My husband has just been cashiered, *monsieur*. And is probably destined for at least prison. If he remains in Cap François.'

'Very well,' Petion agreed. 'You may go and fetch him. Meet us in the yard. But haste, citizeness. If you are not at the gate when we reach there, you must fend for yourself.' He bowed to LeClerc. 'If you will take my advice, Citizen General, when your wife is returned to you, contract your defences, call in your garrisons, and sit tight within the perimeter of Cap François. When your fleet returns in November, sail for France. You have not the talent, even at treachery, to win this country, much less hold it.'

'It is unwise to go too far from the city, citizeness,' said the captain of the guard. 'We do not know where the blacks are, but it is believed they are very close.'

'Yes,' Pauline LeClerc said. 'Yes, you are right. We had best turn back.'

'We are not going far, Captain,' Petion pointed out. 'Only to that beach down there. We are three men.

Three soldiers, as you can see. And believe me, we are armed.' He smiled at the Captain. 'We wish to bath. And you, you rogue, wish to oversee the ladies. Come along, citizens, citizenesses.'

The little cavalcade walked their horses past the guard. Boyer had found a shawl for Richilde, and this she kept wrapped around her hair and face, so that there was no risk of her being recognised; the Captain was confused enough by the presence of the three senior officers, together with the Commanding General's lady – dressed for the dining room but sitting astride horses.

'When you hang,' Pauline said, 'I am going to sit and watch you die. Every movement, every wriggle. I shall clap my hands in time to your writhings.' She looked at Seraphine. 'As for you, you treacherous little toad, I am going personally to flay you alive, and paint you in salt.'

Seraphine kept her eyes fixed on the road they followed, as she had done since leaving the gate. Like her husband, she had said nothing throughout the escape; both were overwhelmed by the magnitude of the disaster which had overtaken them.

'You are entitled to be angry, citizeness,' Petion agreed. 'But let me repeat the advice I gave your husband. Return to France, while you may. Or you may be the one to find yourself hanging, and I doubt it will be by the neck.' He drew rein, looked over his shoulder. 'Far enough. You may return, citizeness. Comrades, let us make haste.'

'Ride, madame,' Boyer shouted.

Richilde kicked her horse, sent it forward, and the five of them galloped down the road.

'To me,' Pauline was shouting back at the guard. 'Come to me. After them. Bring them down. Oh, bring them down.'

'I know not how to thank you. How can I ever thank you?' Richilde gasped, as they slowed their horses, now well beyond musket range. 'To risk so much . . .'

Petion smiled at her. 'Our decision to abandon the French cause was taken before tonight, madame. Almost the moment that LeClerc began practising his "military necessities". St Domingue is our country, and if we do not always see eye to eye with the blacks, we must oppose murder, as well. So it was merely a matter of when. It was Boyer's idea that we wait the opportunity to take you with us.'

'Colonel Boyer?' Her head turned.

'You are our passport to safety, Madame de Mortmain,' the Colonel said, gravely. 'To Christophe, we are renegades who fight for the French. He might well decide to treat us as enemies, before we could explain our change of allegiance. He is hardly likely to do so if we come under your protection.'

'I see,' she said, unsure whether to be relieved or chagrined. But she did not suppose he was telling the whole truth; she could remember how he had always looked at her, from the moment of their first meeting, that day in the forest that Santhonax had died.

'Then I think,' Major Palourdes said. 'That Madame de Mortmain had best commence protecting us.'

Petion drew rein, realising that they were surrounded by armed men.

'French soldiers,' someone said. 'Pull them from their horses.'

'And women,' said someone else.

'Pull *them* from their horses too.'

'Wait,' Richilde said, urging her horse forward. 'I am Richilde de Mortmain. My friends and I seek General Christophe. Would you risk his displeasure?' But as she spoke her heart gave a distinct pitter patter; she, and her companions, all supposed Christophe to be in command here. But they did not even know for certain if he was alive.

The black man came closer, put his hand on her bridle as he peered at her. He wore blue uniform and a cocked hat, and she saw to her inexpressible relief that he displayed the badges of Henry's personal guard. She even recognised his face.

'Good evening to you, Captain Gounod,' she said.

He frowned at her. 'Madame de Mortmain? We heard you had been executed.'

'Well, I have not, as you can see. Thanks to my friends here. You will provide us with an escort to General Christophe's headquarters.'

'Of course, madame. Of course.'

This time her heart lurched in relief, so much so that she felt sick, physically sick this time. She had not dared ask a direct question. But he was there, even if he thought *her* dead. And only two hours later she was slipping from the saddle to be in his arms. 'Richilde,' he said. 'Richilde! They told me you had been hanged.'

'White people,' Dessalines bellowed. 'Mulattos. You know what to do with the men.' He drove his fingers into Seraphine Palourdes's hair, pulled her against him. 'I will take the woman first.'

Seraphine gave a little gasp as the brutal fingers tore at her bodice, but her expression never changed as she gazed at Richilde.

'These are my friends, Jean-Jacques,' Richilde said. 'They saved my life. I promised them a welcome here.'

'No doubt you remember me, General Dessalines, General Christophe,' Petion said, ignoring the black soldiers who had seized his arms.

'We remember you,' Henry said. 'You fight for LeClerc.'

'Not any longer,' Petion said. 'I fight for St Domingue. I can tell you the French dispositions. There are also several thousand mulattos living in the south, who will follow my lead.' He looked around him at the black men. There were only a few hundred of them, gathered in the jungle clearing – always a jungle clearing for Jean-Jacques Dessalines, Richilde thought, it was his true metier. And for Henry?

'My men will be a valuable augmentation of your

army,' Petion was saying. 'Where *is* your army, General Dessalines?'

'Army?' Dessalines bellowed. 'Army?'

'It is assembling,' Henry said, quietly, his arm still round Richilde's waist. 'This treachery of LeClerc's has taken us by surprise.' Richilde felt his arm tighten. 'They still hold Toussaint.'

'Toussaint has gone,' Petion said. 'He has been sent to France.'

'To France?' Henry asked in dismay.

'He will not be coming back,' Boyer said. 'It is up to us, now.'

Henry looked at Dessalines.

Who gave a roar. 'Well, was he a god? He was a man. A man who did not believe in gods. And a man who was weak. Weak,' he shouted. 'He trusted people.' He stared at Palourdes. 'He trusted white people. Believe me, I will not make the same mistake.'

Richilde clutched Henry's arm. She dared not speak, dared not utter what was certain everyone, including the blacks, was thinking. But only Henry could say the words, because only Henry could offer himself as an alternative.

'*I* will lead you,' Dessalines shouted. 'I will drive out the French. I will make us free, as Toussaint never tried to do.' Now he too was staring at Henry, anticipating a challenge. 'I will beat the French,' he said. 'I will avenge Toussaint.' His gaze turned on Richilde. 'And all our other wrongs. I will make the French hate the day they ever landed here. I swear these things, or may Ogone Badagris strike me dead.'

Henry drew a long breath. 'Long live General Dessalines,' he shouted.

Richilde's stomach seemed to fill with lead.

'Shoal water ahead,' came the call from the maintopmast.

'Starboard your helm. Trim those braces,' bawled Mr Rogers.

Kit hurried from the cabin, where he had been completing his papers for landing, as Cap François was only a few miles away, ran up the companion ladder. 'What's the trouble, Mr Rogers?'

'Shoals, sir, dead ahead,' said the mate.

'That's not possible.' Kit took the telescope. He had sailed this course too often to believe a reef could suddenly have surged to the surface where his ship had passed but a fortnight earlier. He stood at the rail, levelled the glass, stared at what was undoubtedly broken water, spurts of white, leaping around what was equally undoubtedly a brown mass on the surface. Slowly he focused, his stomach rolling, his brain refusing to accept what his eyes were seeing. 'By Christ,' he said.

'I have altered course to give it a wide berth, sir.' Rogers said.

'Well, alter your course back again, and make haste.'

'Captain?'

'Those are dead bodies, Mr Rogers. Men and women. Being attacked by the sharks.'

The brigantine resumed her former course, every man on deck now to stare in horror at the huge mass of bodies, pushed together by the slow moving tide, which bobbed in the low swell, while the black fins, unable to believe their good fortune, carved through them like upturned knives, scattering blood equally with the foam of their darting movements.

'They're tied together, in pairs,' someone whispered.

Someone else, a seaman of ten years' experience, vomited over the side.

'The devils,' Rogers muttered. 'The black devils.'

Kit glanced at him. 'Do you suppose black men did this, Mr Rogers?' he asked. 'To their own?'

'Then who . . . you do not suppose the *French*?'

'It is certainly a method of execution used by the French before,' Kit said. 'I have read of it.' They were close now, and he stared into the seething brown horror. He sought white limbs, trailing brown hair, while his entire body seemed to contract into an angry vice.

He did not see her. But that did not mean she was not there.

Four hours later they were entering the harbour. It was like stepping back in time. When he had left here, only ten days before, Cap François had been the busy, bustling place he remembered from his childhood, more bustling indeed, *than* he remembered, as it had still been being rebuilt. There had been black people everywhere, as well as white, as well as ships, for the fleet of Admiral Villaret-Joyeuse had still been at anchor. Now the harbour was empty, save for two trading vessels, and the blacks were gone, just as the building had ceased and the bustle had disappeared. Now there were only French soldiers to be seen, patrolling the battlements, dragging guns into place. Moving slowly, and dispiritedly, and when he went ashore, the men who greeted him on the dock and demanded his papers were yellow-faced and trembling.

'Do you suppose, Citizen Hamilton, that General LeClerc has the time to speak with every sea captain who comes here?' inquired the captain of the port. 'We are in a state of war, as you should be able to see. Besides . . .'

'He will see me,' Kit said, and regained his papers, strode through the city towards the military headquarters, which had now been brought inside the walls. 1791, he thought, all over again, the shops shuttered and the houses too, with only frightened faces to peer at him through the cracks.

'Kit! Kit Hamilton!'

'Madeleine? Well, there is one relief, at the least. But what is happening here?'

Madeleine shrugged. 'The blacks, your friends, have broken the treaty and risen against us. They are in arms everywhere, and now we are told the mulattos have joined them. The whole country is in a state of war, all over again. It is quite terrible.'

Kit peered at her. She looked tired, but neither frightened nor deprived of any of the comforts of life; her clothes were new and recently laundered, and she smelt of perfume – her parasol was also new.

'And Vergée d'Or? Annette?'

'Well, we have had to abandon the plantation again, at least for the time being. We are using the house which used to belong to Louise's mother. You remember it, Kit. You will come to see us there? Annette . . . well, it would be idle to pretend she has not been upset by what has happened. She wept when we left Vergée d'Or. But we are all upset. You *will* come to visit?'

'As soon as I may. I seek some information about Richilde.'

'Richilde?' Her brows drew together.

'I was told she had been brought here, a captive.'

'I believe she was arrested,' Madeline said. 'As part of the general counter revolutionary precautions. But of course the General released her, sent her back to her . . . her paramour.' She pointed, long finger at the end of an outflung arm. 'She is out there. In the jungle. With her cannibal cousins.'

'They seek to defy me. They massacre my men. They *mutilate* them.' Charles LeClerc stood in front of his desk, waved his arms.

'As you drown them, by the thousand?' Kit asked.

LeClerc glared at him. 'You come here, with your foolish American ideas, having no concept of the true situation . . .'

'I am trying to *discover* the true situation, Citizen General,' Kit said, patiently. 'I have been told it was you broke the treaty, by arresting Toussaint. By attempting to arrest Christophe and Dessalines. By arresting my sister.'

'Your sister is as much a nigger traitor as any of them,' LeClerc said. 'She should have been hanged. By God, I was weak there.'

'And Toussaint?'

'Toussaint will shortly be where he belongs. Behind bars. Where they all belong. And where I intend to see that they all go, by God. By . . .'

'With your permission, Citizen General, I should like to have a word with General Petion. Or Colonel Boyer.'

LeClerc's head came up. 'What for?'

'I but seek the truth of this matter.'

'You . . . a damned American, come here, trying to badger me, a general of France. Be careful I do not have you locked up as well. Or hanged.'

'Will you then resume war with the United States?' Kit demanded. For only a few years before French attempts to bribe American envoys had actually led to an abortive conflict, carried on entirely at sea. Peace had only been signed on 30 September 1800.

'Ah, bah! You are not worth the trouble. As for the mulattos, you are welcome to talk with them, if you can find them. Ha ha. Yes, indeed. They have run off as well. They are all niggers. They are all . . .' he was overcome with a sudden spasm of shivering, despite the heat, turned away from Kit, and fell to his knees. Instantly his aides hurried forward, attempted to raise him up. LeClerc waved them away, used his desk to drag himself to a standing position. 'Brandy,' he gasped. 'A glass of brandy.'

A servant hurried forward with a tray.

'You, General, had best go to bed,' Kit said. 'And pray.'

'Pray? A French soldier does not pray. I have work to do. Bed, what nonsense. I . . .' Another spasm seemed to tear through his system. The brandy glass dropped from his fingers and crashed to the floor, shattering into a thousand crystals.

'You,' Kit said, pointing at the servant. 'Put your master to bed.'

'But . . . what is the matter with him?' asked General Morel, hurrying into the room.

'He has yellow fever,' Kit said.

'What will you do?' Kit asked.

'Do?' Etienne stood in the middle of the small drawing room, hands tucked beneath the lapels of his coat. 'Why, wait for the position to be stabilised, of course, so that we may return to Vergée d'Or. My dear Kit, the illness of the Commanding General is of no real consequence. There are other generals.'

'But . . .' Kit looked at Annette, who sat as ever, with her interminable needlework, but now raised her head to smile at him.

'It cannot take long, Kit,' she explained. 'They are only blacks. General Morel will hang them all, soon enough.'

Kit looked at Madeleine, who refilled his glass with wine.

'I'm afraid I agree with Annette,' she said. 'About the length of time it will take. These people are only savages. I know you have a quite absurd regard for their potential, Kit, but you must confess it has never been realised. Not even Toussaint succeeded in making anything of them, and now he is gone . . . well, who is left? Not that absurd little boy Henry Christopher.'

Kit drew a very long breath. But there was absolutely no point in losing his temper with these people. They lived in a world of their own. A world which, he supposed, had lasted too long for them ever to regain touch with reality.

'And suppose the French decide to evacuate?' he asked, quietly.

'Oh, come now. Do you really suppose the French are going to walk away from their richest possession? Can you really see Bonaparte accepting such a blow to his prestige? Of course, I forget,' Etienne said. 'You

428

have never met him. I have, you know. He gave me an audience, when this expedition was first mooted. "My dear Citizen Mortmain," he said to me. "It is to people like you that we look to sustain the greatness of the French colonial empire. Do not fail me." And do you know what I said back to him? I said, "I shall not fail you, Your Excellency. Providing you do not fail me." Do you know, there was an absolute silence? I do believe everyone else in the room was terrified. This little Corsican is not used to being answered in kind. But he merely looked at me for several seconds, and then said, "I never fail, Citizen Mortmain. I sometimes change direction, but I never *fail*."'

'Yes,' Kit said. 'Well . . .'

'And having despatched such a force, thirty thousand of his best troops, his entire fleet, this is one direction he will not change. I do assure you of that, Kit. Far more likely . . .' he chuckled, 'that if LeClec does not end the matter quickly enough, Bonaparte will appear here himself, with the Imperial Guard at his back. That would show these blacks what warfare is all about, I can promise you that. He is a remarkable man, Kit. Of course, he is no gentleman. You can see that at a glance. And it is confirmed when he speaks. But still, a remarkable man. And who knows? The age of gentlemen may well be passing.'

'Yes,' Kit said, again, and equally sceptically. 'Well, my offer stands, of course. I sail tomorrow. You are welcome to berths if you should change your mind.'

'America,' Etienne said. 'What has America got to offer us, that St Domingue has not?'

It does not contain a few thousand black men all thirsting for your blood, for a start, Kit thought. But he did not say it.

Madeleine came to the door with him. 'And Richilde?'

He sighed, and shrugged. 'Like you, she regards St Domingue as her home. She has gone back to Henry.

She will not leave him. Believe me, I have tried often enough to persuade her in the past.'

She held his arm. 'You do understand, Kit, that it is now war to the bone?'

He nodded. 'I have seen some of the evidence of it. It sickens me, which is why I am leaving.'

'And you therefore understand that when the blacks are smashed, she will suffer with them? There will be nothing we can do to save her?'

He gazed at her. 'Would you even try, Madeleine?'

She did not lower her eyes. 'No,' she said. 'Not now. I think she would be better off dead. She is diseased.'

'Then, dear cousin,' he said. 'We can only hope and pray that she does not feel the same way about you.'

Kit adjusted his tricorne hat, looked up at the sky. The moon was just rising; in another hour it would be bright as day. Then why did he not leave Cap François tonight? There was nothing to remain here for, now. The colony was inextricably caught up in a downward spiral, which would probably, so far as he could see, leave it once again deserted. Save that it had never been deserted, in the past. Not even the labour hungry Spaniards had been able to kill off all the aboriginal Indians; at least, not before replacing them with Negro slaves.

He sighed, walked towards the dock. And yet, Hispaniola exerted the most powerful charm. There was no wind – one reason for waiting for the dawn breeze to spring up before attempting to leave – and thus there was endless sound, shrouding the occasional challenge of a sentry, voices drifting across the empty rooftops; he listened to bull frogs croaking in the ditches, to the rasp of cicadas, the shrill cries of the nightbirds, even to the loud buzz of one of the strange insects called 'singers' by the black people, usually silent during the hours of darkness. While the air was filled with the fragrance of oleander and night blooming jasmine,

430

where it should have contained only the stench of decaying corpses.

'Kit,' Jacqueline Chavannes said.

He turned, sharply, his hand dropping to the pistol he carried in his pocket. But she was alone, in the shadows, her head shrouded in a shawl. But for her voice he would not have known her.

'My . . . my mistress would speak with you.' she said.

'I am leaving Cap François,' he said. 'Nor am I in the mood for after supper parties.

'And do you suppose we are?' She came closer. 'You can spare her a few minutes of your time. It is most urgent.'

He hesitated, his brain calling out to him to shun these people, and flee their company. But his every male instinct was equally begging him again to weaken, just for a few minutes. Because here in St Domingue was every feminine charm he had ever loved, or desired. As he had learned on his last trip home, there was naught but an empty house in New York. And once he went this time, he would not be coming back. Quite apart from Richilde, he would never again see Annette, to whom he had devoted so much of his life, in such futility. And he would never again see this woman, who had first introduced him to the desires and the mysteries of her sex. He doubted he would truly miss either of them. But he would also never again see Seraphine Palourdes. There was a strange admission. He had *seen* her but once in his life, but as every single occasion he had held a woman in his arms had been equally attended with an overwhelming guilt, he could at least remember that night as the most memorable of such adventures. Since then he had avoided her. And to her, he had obviously been nothing more than an itinerant penis, one of her mistress's toys.

Yet now he was leaving St Domingue forever, he thought he would like to see her for one last time.

'A few minutes,' he agreed, and walked beside her.

431

'You will return to New York?' Jacqueline asked.

'That is my home.'

'You will not try to see Richilde again?'

'There does not seem much point, now.'

'But you will return here?'

He shook his head. 'There does not seem much point in that either, Jacqueline. Perhaps, when the war is over, it may be possible to re-open trade with Cap François. But I see nothing ahead but savagery and barbarism. It is difficult to trade with barbarism.'

They had reached the Governor General's palace, and were challenged by the guard. Jacqueline gave the password, and they were allowed up the steps. 'And have you no thoughts, no regrets, for anyone you may leave behind?' She gave an almost nervous smile, strange in so self-possessed a woman. 'I mean, apart from your sister?'

She had paused, in the upstairs hall. Such servants as they had passed had hastily turned and scurried away. No one was obviously allowed to overlook Madame Chavannes escorting a man to her mistress's pleasure. Even when her husband lay dying, no doubt in this very house.

Jacqueline opened the bedroom door, showed him in. It was a room he had never entered before, but he realised with something of a shock that Richilde and Henry must have slept in here, during those brief summers when their revolution had seemed to have succeeded, when their horizons had been bright with promise.

'Captain Hamilton! Kit!' Pauline LeClerc sat in the centre of the huge tester bed, arms outstretched. She was, he observed, entirely nude – and possessed a figure, superbly delineated by the flickering candlelight, which put even Seraphine Palourdes to shame.

'Citizeness.' He remained standing by the door, became aware that it had softly closed, as Jacqueline had left them alone.

'Will you not come closer?' Pauline asked. 'I can hardly see you, over there.'

He approached the bed, and she held her hand towards him. Cautiously he took the white fingers, kissed the knuckles.

'It is good of you to come,' she said. 'So good.'

'Madame Chavannes said you wished to discuss an important matter.'

She withdrew her hand. 'Am I not an important matter?' She gave a twisted smile. 'I had intended us to know each other better, long before this. That Palourdes bitch was merely to be an appetiser. I had not realised she would upset you.'

'She did not upset me,' he lied. 'May I ask where she is?'

Pauline uttered a peal of laughter. 'What, do you still hanker after that cunt? She is gone, Kit. Gone to the blacks.'

'To the . . .'

'She accompanied your sister.'

'Good God,' he said.

Pauline realised she might have made a mistake. 'She went with her husband, of course. He is a traitor, like Petion and Boyer. They are all scoundrels.'

'Or patriots and honest men, citizeness. It is all a point of view.'

She gazed at him for several seconds. 'I did not invite you here to talk politics.' She cupped her breasts, one in each hand, held them up. 'Can you truly stand there, as if turned to stone? Or do you have to be *told* what I am offering you?'

'Citizeness,' he said. 'Your husband is dying.'

Once again the stare. 'Do you not suppose I know that?'

'But it does not interest you?'

'He was Napoleon's choice. My brother has this habit of dictating other people's lives for them. But *I* do not intend to die.' She moved, suddenly, rising to her knees to seize his hand. 'You are leaving Cap François. Take me with you.'

'Eh?'

'Kit,' she said. 'I hate this place. I loathe and abhor it. It is nothing but disease and death. If I stay here I shall die. I know it. No fleet will return for us until the autumn, and it is only June. I cannot stay here. Take me with you. I will pay you. I will pay you in gold coin, and I will pay you with my body. I will be *your* slave, Kit. Just take me with you.'

Her plea was so desperate he nearly softened. He reflected that she was but a woman, young and beautiful and full of life. There was no reason to condemn her as he condemned her husband and his people.

But there was every reason. He had seen enough of her to know that she was possessed of a heart as cold as a block of ice, that her own desires and her own ambitions were the driving force behind LeClerc's absurdities, that she was probably the most vicious person in Cap François.

As she was proving by attempting to desert her dying husband, whether she loved him or not.

She frowned at his expression, understanding her fate. 'I saved your sister's life,' she said. 'Don't you understand that? I saved her life. LeClerc would have hanged her, publicly. He had already commanded her execution. And I intervened.'

Kit frowned at her in turn. 'Is that true?'

'How do you suppose she managed to leave the city? She is Christophe's woman. She was an invaluable hostage. But I stepped in, because she was a woman, like myself, and because she was your sister.'

Kit hesitated, his brain swirling.

As she saw. She squeezed his fingers. 'You owe me a debt. You, owe me. But yet will I surrender myself to you. I will be your slave, Kit. Just take me from this

434

living hell. Listen to me. Come to bed, now. And I will make you the happiest man in all the world. Then we can leave this place.'

'If you are coming with me,' he said. 'You had best come now. I sail at dawn.' He turned away to avoid looking at her, stared out of the window at the sleeping city. He certainly could not refuse to take her, if she had indeed saved Richilde's life. Her desertion of her husband must be between her and her conscience. He would never have believed her tale, but for the simple fact that Richilde *had* been arrested, and had been let go again. Because Pauline had certainly been right about her value as a hostage.

But what tangled path was he now allowing his feet to explore?

Pauline got out of bed, began to dress.

'I will put some things in a satchel for you,' Jacqueline Chavannes said.

Pauline and Kit turned together; she had re-entered the room by another door, so quietly they had been unaware of her presence – and she already carried a satchel.

'I can manage, thank you, Chavannes,' Pauline said.

'But I must play my part,' Jacqueline said.

'Your part? Your part is to remain here, with my husband. Your lover. Keep his brow cool,' Pauline said contemptuously.

'Stay here? While you go off to safety with Kit? You must suppose me demented.'

'Do you seek to defy me?' Pauline demanded.

'I seek my rights, Citizeness LeClerc. Do you suppose I have any more desire than you to remain in this pit? Do you suppose I wish to be hauled before Dessalines, and subjected to his lust? And do you suppose I intend to let you take Kit? I have a greater claim on him than you, citizeness. I was the first woman he ever knew.'

Pauline gazed at Kit with her mouth open.

'Which is perfectly true,' he agreed. And shrugged. 'So you both come. But make haste. And do not suppose I intend either of you as my mistress in the future. I am repaying a debt. Nothing more.'

But oh, to be sure he would keep that resolve, when exposed to nothing but their company.

'No,' Pauline said. 'I will not share my exile with this . . . this creature. I know her for what she is, Kit. A crawling thing. A nigger. I am her mistress. I have commanded her to stay, and she will stay. I think you had best tie her up.'

'You listen to *her*?' Jacqueline cried. 'You believe *her*? You are a fool, Kit Hamilton. You have always been a fool. You believe that she saved your sister's life? Oh, she stopped her from being hanged, but only to keep her as a plaything. She would have had her raped, time and again, by twelve black men, just to amuse her after dinner guests. Until eventually she would have had her murdered, for the same sport.'

Pauline drew a sharp breath as Kit's head turned. 'That is a lie,' she said. 'That is a *lie*.'

'You have but to ask the Captain of the guard,' Jacqueline said. 'If, a week ago, this *citizeness* did not go riding one night after supper, with General Petion and Colonel Boyer, and Major Palourdes and his wife, and Richilde. Even the Palourdes fled her miserable company. And they took this *thing* as a hostage, to secure their escape. You have but to ask the guards, Kit. It was to them she went wailing for assistance when she was finally released.'

'Why, you . . .' Pauline hurled herself at the quadroon. Although she was considerably the smaller woman, she was also much the younger and at least as strong, and far more vigorous. The force of her attack sent Jacqueline sprawling, and Pauline knelt on her chest, tearing at her face with her nails. 'Wretch,' Pauline snarled. 'Foul thing from the pit of hell. I shall have you whipped, from one end of Cap François to the

436

other. No, better than that. I will have you bound and delivered to Dessalines, as a present from me. That is what I shall do. I shall . . .'

Carefully Kit opened the bedroom door and stepped through it, closed it behind himself, and hurried down the corridor towards the street.

'Gone,' Jean-Jacques Dessalines said. 'Gone,' he shouted. He raised both hands high in the air. 'Gone,' he bellowed, his voice reverberating.

'Gone,' the black soldiers, and their women, and their children, shrieked in unison. They crowded the beach outside of Cap François, roamed the empty battlements, stared in disbelieving joy at the French fleet, already hull down on the horizon.

That fleet had re-appeared a week ago, after a long, hot summer of vicious warfare, surely bringing, the Negroes had supposed, fresh troops to prosecute the war. But instead it had only remained anchored off Cap François just long enough to embark those fever-ridden survivors of LeClerc's expeditionary force.

'Gone,' Henry Christophe said. 'We have won, again.'

'Gone,' Alexander Petion said, and looked at Jean Boyer.

'Gone,' Richilde de Mortmain whispered, and looked at Seraphine Palourdes. They had become friends, by force of circumstances, and yet she knew the young Frenchwoman very little better now than during her three days as Pauline LeClerc's prisoner. Seraphine spoke little, moved through life with a cautious suspicion, as if attempting to discover in advance from whence the next blow would be delivered. She had reason for her scepticism, this much at least Richilde had learned, from her husband. Both her mother and father had perished in the Terror, her father on the guillotine, her mother torn to pieces by the mob on that dreadful August night in 1792 when the Parisians had supposed themselves about to be conquered by the Prussians.

Just a year after our own holocaust, Richilde thought. Thus tainted as a royalist, or at least an enemy of the state, for all that she had only been nine years old, and although her father had been a reputable merchant rather than an aristocrat, Seraphine had been destined for at best a Parisian brothel. From that fate she had been rescued by Palourdes, but only on account of her beauty and innocence. Albert Palourdes was, in his own way, an honest and even an honourable man – Richilde had good cause to thank him for being those things. But he was also a revolutionary, who hated all hereditary wealth or privilege, and as a career soldier, a harsh and grim and loveless man. Certainly he was so to his wife, his harshness increased by his inability to discover what went on behind that lovely mask.

The orbit of the LeClercs into which they had drifted had not improved their relationship. As a soldier Palourdes had considered it necessary to be loyal and subservient to his appointed chief, as his wife had been commanded to adopt the same attitude to that chief's wife. But Palourdes must have found Pauline's excesses difficult to stomach from the very beginning. It was less easy to be sure, about Seraphine. She had been in the prison whence her mother had been dragged by the mob, and undoubtedly she had been forced to watch her die. No one could say what else she had been forced to endure before encountering Palourdes. In many ways, Richilde thought, her life had been very like Annette's, save that she had been half Annette's age when the catastrophe had occurred. And save that she had twice Annette's strength of mind, in that she had not gone mad. Or was her quietness, her constant self communion, but a form of madness?

But certainly she was sane enough to understand what had happened. The French had sailed away, like the British, after eight futile months of murder and bloodshed, and yellow fever. They had left their Commanding General behind them, and more than a third of his original invading army. For the second time in five years St Domingue had proved only a burial ground for a European army. So once again the black people were going to be granted an opportunity to make something of themselves. To become a nation. Or were they? Seraphine Palourdes, now even more of a renegade white than Richilde de Mortmain, must doubt that more than anyone.

Jean-Jacques Dessalines was also looking around him. 'They have gone,' he said, speaking loudly, so that he could be widely overheard. 'We have driven them out. We have driven them out because I, Jean-Jacques Dessalines, determined that they should be opposed, that they should be driven out. Where Toussaint wished only to deal with the white people, to remain subservient to them, I said, death to all white people. That is the only language they understand. And that is the language of victory. Was I not right?'

The Negro soldiers had crowded round to hear him. Now they shouted, 'Yes,' with a great voice.

'So now I tell you this,' Dessalines shouted. 'There will be no more white people. No more colony. From today we are free of that. We are independent. We are a nation of free men.'

'Yes,' they shouted.

'General Dessalines has spoken well,' Petion said. 'And truly. We will show the world how we can live, as free and equal people. We shall be the Republic of St Domingue, and we shall have a president, as they do in the United States . . .'

'President?' Dessalines roared. 'President? A president is the white man's way. We are black men. We are not ruled by presidents, who are elected and then discarded. Who sway people by oratory. Why, Monsieur Petion, the people might even choose *you*, as president.'

Richilde clutched Henry's arm, but Petion decided not take up the insult.

'You have a better suggestion, General?' he asked, speaking quietly.

'We are black people,' Dessalines shouted again. 'We wish to be ruled by strength, that we too may be strong. We seek a king. The strongest, the most able man amongst us shall be king.' His gaze swept them, and he jerked his head at one of his aides, who had obviously been previously coached.

'Long live King Jean-Jacques,' the man shouted.

'King Jean-Jacques,' the cry was taken up.

'Long live King Jean-Jacques.'

'Monsieur?' Dessalines inquired of Petion.

Who looked at the men surrounding him, and shrugged. 'Long live King Jean-Jacques the First, of St Domingue.'

Dessalines looked at Henry, Richilde at his side. But she could say or do nothing. Henry remained what he had always been at heart, a soldier, faithful to the ideals that Toussaint, and perhaps even herself, she realised, had instilled in him. And Dessalines was his superior officer. Toussaint had made that clear.

'Long live King Jean-Jacques the First,' he shouted, and now the cheers became general – Richilde realised that there had been a considerable number of the blacks waiting on Henry's response.

But it was too late now. Jean-Jacques was beaming on his people, and preparing himself for his new role. 'Now let us see what the French have left behind them,' he said.

'This woman,' they shouted, and Richilde's heart constricted as she saw Jacqueline Chavannes, naked and with her hands bound behind her, her glorious hair a dishevelled mass clouding across her face, her body showing the marks of mistreatment and the emaciation of starvation, being dragged forward.

'Who is this?' Dessalines demanded.

'We found her beneath the palace,' they said.

'She is, or was, General LeClerc's mistress,' Boyer said.

'I have been a French prisoner,' Jacqueline said, her voice as strong as ever. 'For four months they have kept me locked up in a cell. They are fiends. I hate them. I have prayed for your coming, Great King.'

'You are a traitor,' Dessalines said. 'Where is the General?'

'He is buried,' one of the captains said. 'We have found his grave.'

'Then open it up,' Dessalines said. 'Let us gaze upon his corpse.'

Jacqueline looked at Richilde, her face seeming to collapse as she realised what was going to happen to her. 'Mercy,' she said. 'For the love of God, Richilde, *help* me,' she screamed.

Richilde made to step forward, and was restrained by Henry; now was not the time to challenge the new king.

'And then we will bury him again,' Dessalines said, with a roar of laughter. 'With his mistress in his arms.'

Chapter 6

THE TYRANT

Dessalines was a grotesque misfit as emperor of a nation. He thundered forth pronunciamentoes, mostly intended to inflame his countrymen against white people in general and the French in particular; he complained bitterly about the tiresome aspects of government; he spent long hours changing from one magnificent uniform to another and attempting to learn how to dance the minuet. His brutalities indicted every Negro in the West Indies; his absurdities made a black skin an object of ridicule.

The surgeon raised his head. 'He is dead.' The men seemed to take a step forward together, but Kit was in front of them all, looking down on the body of his cousin. The most brilliant man in America, Alexander Hamilton had been considered. Shot to death.

He raised his head, looked across the bed at Aaron Burr. The dapper little man, Vice President of the United States – and he could, Kit remembered, have achieved the Presidency itself had he not disclaimed his rights to a fresh vote after tying with Thomas Jefferson in the election of 1801 – flushed, but would not lower his eyes. 'You were there, Captain Hamilton,' he said. 'It was a fair fight.'

'Between a good shot and a poor one,' Kit said. 'Oh, aye. It was a fair fight.'

He left the room, was followed by the President himself. 'It *was* a fair fight, Kit. God knows we would all have wished Aaron to fire in the air once your cousin missed. But he was not obliged to.'

'Because they hated each other.'

'Had they loved each other, would they have fought in the first place?'

Kit sighed, his shoulders slumped.

Jefferson embraced him. 'I have been told he was your only living relative.'

Kit shook his head. 'I have other relatives.'

'But none so dear?'

'I have a sister,' Kit said.

'A sister? Now that I never knew.'

'And cousins. Although where they are I have no idea.'

'But you know where to find this sister of yours?'

'Oh, aye, Mr President. I know where to find her.'

Jefferson hesitated for a moment. 'It might be best for you to take a holiday, Kit,' he said. 'You are angry, and that is no proper state for a man to conduct business. You are also a better shot than Aaron . . .' he smiled. 'I cannot afford to have another member of my administration brought down. Not even if, perhaps, he deserves it. In a few months' time, things will look different.'

Kit went down the stairs to his horse. A holiday. But was that not what he wanted to do more than anything else in the world? Where he wanted to go, more than anywhere else in the world?

It was two years since he had sailed from Cap François, leaving Pauline LeClerc and Jacqueline Chavannes wrestling on the bedroom floor. Two years in which he had heard nothing precise of what happened to all those people who had played so large a part in his life. He knew merely what was common knowledge. That the French had been evacuated by their fleet the moment it could return to their rescue, and that the

Negroes had declared their independence, and chosen the bull-man, Jean-Jacques Dessalines, as their first king. He knew too that Bonaparte, in offering to sell the entire vast hinterland of Louisiana to the United States, had definitely turned his back on the New World as a goal of French expansion, and that therefore St Domingue should be left in peace to pursue its own salvation – the British, having had their fingers so badly burned in the nineties, were not likely to interfere again.

Just as he knew that Pauline LeClerc, pursuing her self-interested way through life, and having after all survived the yellow fever, had remarried, an Italian prince named Camillo Borghese, and was now no doubt indulging her doubtful pleasures to the total scandalisation of Rome.

And he knew too that Toussaint l'Ouverture was dead, technically of lung disease following a winter confined in a damp Alpine cell, but more truly of a broken heart. Had he been allowed to remain in St Domingue, then indeed would his people have pursued their salvation. But he had been succeeded by an altogether different man. With whom Henry and Richilde, and Seraphine Palourdes, would have to make their way as best they could. If they had even survived to try.

And he no longer had anything to keep him in New York. As Jefferson had said, things would look different in a few months' time.

'It doesn't seem to have changed a great deal,' Rogers the mate said, peering through his telescope at the houses of Cap François. 'Do you suppose we'll find a cargo worth shipping?'

For Kit had not told the mate that he might be in command on the way back. It was not a decision he had yet taken himself. Nor could they suspect his motives in any way. During the last two years he had confined his West Indian trading to Kingston and San Juan and

444

Havana, but those routes had necessitated sailing past Hispaniola often enough, and he had never failed to peer at those green clad peaks through his glass. It had been his childhood home, and his crew knew that. What could be more reasonable than that he should wish to revisit it at the first opportunity?

'If they wish to trade,' he said. 'But you'll keep the guns loaded, Mr Rogers, just in case.'

The anchor plunged into the still blue water, clean now, at least of corpses, he supposed. The jollyboat was lowered, and he was rowed ashore, happy to recognise the blue uniformed officer who commanded the guard. 'Captain Gounod,' he said.

'Captain Hamilton,' the Negro acknowledged. 'We had not expected you. You'll salute His Majesty.'

'Eh?' Kit turned, sharply, half expecting to see Dessalines standing behind him, looked at the wooden carving resting on a stone plinth at the end of the dock. There had been a stone statue there once, of Louis the Fifteenth, as he remembered. This had been torn down • and replaced by the wooden sculpture, like all West African art a strange melange of the grotesque and the exquisite, purporting to represent a man wearing European uniform and carrying a sword, but with heavily Negroid features.

Gounod saluted, waited for Kit to do the same. 'There will be a proper statue in due course,' he explained. 'When we can find a stonemason to carve it. You are visiting General Christophe and Madame de Mortmain?'

'Why, yes,' Kit said, feeling the tension oozing from his mind as he learned that they at least had survived the storm.

'Then I will give you an escort.' Gounod snapped his fingers, and one of his men hurried forward, to lead Kit through the streets, in the direction, he realised, of the old Governor General's palace. Where he had left Jacqueline and Pauline to wrestle. But as Pauline had fallen so thoroughly on her feet he supposed Jacqueline had also prospered; she had risen from the ashes before.

It was reassuring, however, to learn that Henry was once more military commander of the port, and indeed the entire north coast, and that Dessalines had not apparently turned out to be quite the mad tyrant he had expected. But yet, things were very different to when he had visited here during Toussaint's brief reign. He looked at groups of Negroes still employed in rebuilding the partially destroyed town, and at others being marched off, clearly to do some field work, as it was still early in the morning. They were marshalled like any slave gang, and were driven by the whips and shouts of overseers, like any slave gang – but the overseers were black men wearing army uniforms. He glanced at his companion, but the soldier did not seem disturbed by the sight, or even interested in it, so he decided against asking any questions.

He climbed the steps of the palace, heart pounding, remembering the occasions he had visited here in the past, and indeed, the occasions on which he had fled here, his heart fit to burst. But there was Richilde . . . and Seraphine Palourdes? He stopped, quite unable to proceed.

'Kit!' Richilde hurried down the steps to embrace him. He had seen her in so many guises he never knew quite what to expect of her. Today she was in what he might disparagingly have called, had he wished, her white Negress role, wearing a very simple housegown, her feet bare, and with her hair concealed beneath a bandanna; she had obviously been engaged in her domestic chores. Yet was she, in her tall vigour, the health of her delighted flush, the clarity of her eyes, the firmness of her grasp, the same intensely healthy woman as he had ever known, even at the age of thirty-eight.

But his gaze kept drifting to Seraphine Palourdes.

446

As Richilde saw. 'I think you have already met Seraphine,' she said.

Kit gave her a quick glance, but she was clearly innocent of any double meaning. He kissed Seraphine's hand. 'I had heard you had elected to remain in St Domingue, madame,' he said, inhaling her scent, once again enjoying the velvety texture of her flesh, remembering so much. 'And yet had not expected to meet you, so soon. Your husband . . .'

'Is adjutant to General Christophe, monsieur,' she said, quietly as ever.

'But Kit . . . to have you back . . .' Richilde linked arms with him as they went inside, past black servants who stood respectfully to attention. 'I would have written, but . . . is all well with you?'

'Alexander is dead,' he told her.

She stopped, her face aghast. 'Alexander? He was hardly older than you.'

'He did not die of a disease, Richilde. He was shot to death in a duel. By a man called Aaron Burr.'

'Oh, Kit.' Her distress was clearly genuine, although she had never laid eyes on Alexander, that she could remember. 'I am so sorry.'

'But Henry is well?'

'Henry is always well. Even if he works too hard. There is so much to be done.'

'I had observed.'

She gave him a quick glance. 'It is His Majesty's determination, Kit, to restore the prosperity of St Domingue.'

'With whips?' Kit inquired. 'You approve of this? Henry approves of this?'

'In St Domingue, Captain Hamilton,' Seraphine Palourdes observed. 'It pays to approve of what His Majesty decrees.'

Kit looked from her to his sister.

Who shrugged. 'He is at least ruling. We see little of him, thank God. He has made a capital for himself, in the forest. We hear rumours, but he leaves Henry much to himself, to get on with the task of restoring Cap François, and restoring the sugar crop, too. He will be so pleased to see you. Shipping is hard to come by, since the French left.'

'There is so much that I wish to know,' he said. 'So much I have to understand, obviously. Etienne? And Annette?'

'They left with the French army, so far as we know. Certainly they are no longer here. Vergée d'Or is a government sugar plantation.'

'Poor Annette,' he said. 'How she must have hated leaving again. Jacqueline Chavannes? Did she also leave with the French? I had gained the impression that she and Madame LeClerc were no longer exactly friends.'

The two women exchanged glances, and then Richilde looked at the door in relief. 'Here's Henry,' she said. 'He will be so pleased to see you.'

'Alive?' Kit asked. 'They buried her *alive*?'

'It was terrible,' Seraphine Palourdes whispered. 'How she screamed, and begged. But she was bound, and placed in his arms. Can you believe it? He had already mouldered to a skeleton.'

Kit looked at Richilde. There was so much to be remembered, about the three of them. More than either of them knew.

More than Henry knew, certainly. But he also could remember. 'She was a tragic figure,' he said. 'All of her family were doomed, it seemed almost from birth. But yet . . . do you remember your first night in St Domingue, Kit? How your cousin . . .' His sombre gaze rested on Richilde for a moment. 'Had a man torn to pieces by dogs? To impress you, I think, with his terrible power.'

'I remember,' Kit said.

'Well, I think His Majesty had some such idea in mind, as he had just been elected king.' Henry half smiled, a rare lightening of his grim features. 'You must also remember, Kit, that my people are for the main part simple and uneducated. They believe what they see, and can remember. Hence this.' He shrugged his shoulders. Because his jacket was certainly one of the most gorgeous Kit had seen: blue, faced with red, but with gold braid at every button hole and also composing his epaulettes, and with a white cross belt to support a silver hilted sword. Henry's eyes twinkled. 'I can promise you that His Majesty's uniforms are far more brilliant. But you will have the opportunity to see for yourself, soon enough. I will have to report your arrival, and he will certainly wish to see you. He is greedy for news from the outside world, as he is, indeed, for trade with the outside world. And there are few traders who come to St Domingue, now. They think we have reverted to savagery.'

Kit looked down the sweep of the dining table, at the crystal and the silver cutlery. And then thought of the work gangs outside. 'I would say you have reverted entirely to the St Domingue of twenty years ago. As you say, your king is but a reincarnation of Philippe de Mortmain.'

Henry frowned, and indicated the door with his head, to suggest that not all the footmen were necessarily loyal to *him*.

'But can you seriously support such methods, Henry?' Kit persisted. 'You?'

Henry sighed. 'His Majesty is right, in that our people must work, Kit. We must restore St Domingue to prosperity. Then perhaps it may be possible to allow them more leisure, more choice. We do not imagine the path ahead of us will be an easy one, or a brief one. There is, as you may suppose, much discontent, which means we must sometimes deal harshly with men and women who have fought for us, and supported us, faithfully and long. Yet must the work be done. If you have any better suggestions, then believe me, I will be happy to listen to you, and to present them to His Majesty. Or indeed, as I say, you may present them yourself.'

Kit looked at Richilde, and then back at Henry again. 'But you support him, and will continue to do so.'

'He is my king,' Henry said simply. 'Chosen by my people.'

They rode through a jungle roadway, a squad of hussars first, brightly clad in new crimson uniforms with yellow braid on their breeches and across their chests, then the General's party, with his ladies, then their wagon, for it was a two-day journey and there was no food to be had on the way, and then a rear guard of more hussars.

'By whom do we expect to be attacked?' Kit asked.

'It is His Majesty's orders that we always travel well protected,' Henry explained. 'It is his opinion that the more people see of the army the better. Besides, if we are prepared to be attacked, by anyone, then we stand less risk of being attacked, by anyone.'

Warfare, bloodshed, the necessity to be constantly on the alert, had clearly entered his blood. And perhaps Richilde's as well, Kit thought, watching his sister, wearing a sky blue habit, riding sidesaddle as she might have done as Philippe de Mortmain's wife, followed by her maids and even one of her cooks. She looked from left to right, at the trees which clustered close, certainly watchfully, but equally certainly without apprehension at anything which might be about to happen. She and Henry were the new aristocrats of this savage, unstable world, and they moved through it with the utmost certainty.

And what of Seraphine Palourdes? She rode just behind Richilde, as was her place. She was doomed, it seemed, always to be the inferior. But could she so quickly have become accustomed to this new life? He felt *she* was more nervous than she pretended, kept casting anxious glances into the trees on either side. How the sight of her, the knowledge of her presence, made him remember that night on board the *Bucentaure*, and then remember so much more. Jacqueline, being interred alive in the arms of a corpse. Was it possible to imagine a more horrible fate? And it had been at the whim of a man who could so command the execution of any person in his kingdom, and who had never made any secret of his hatred of white people.

And who was supported faithfully by Henry, and therefore by all those who supported Henry, because that was his nature.

He longed to ride beside the French girl, to engage her in conversation, to discover if she also remembered that night, or anything particular about it. To discover, in fact, if it might be possible to seduce her again? Because suddenly he was aware of desire, where he had almost supposed it dead.

But that way led both to madness and dishonour. So instead he rode beside Albert Palourdes; he had last done that, he remembered, the day after the French had landed, three years before. The day LeClerc had made his intentions so terribly clear.

'Will you make your home here now?' he asked. 'I mean, in St Domingue?' he added, as the soldier's sombre face turned towards him.

'I cannot return to France, monsieur,' Palourdes pointed out. 'Not as long as Bonaparte rules. And now that he too is an emperor, that may be for a very long time. Besides, I will prosper here. This brother-in-law of yours, this Christophe, is a man of many parts. But he is to be trusted.'

'And the King?'

Palourdes's face seemed to close. 'I do not know His Majesty as well as I know General Christophe,' he said. 'I serve General Christophe.'

Kit would have continued the conversation, probed further, but his nostrils were assailed by a dreadful stench. He looked at the ladies, saw that each of them was holding a perfumed handkerchief to her nose. They rode round a bend in the track and sighted the imperial citadel. But before the gate there was a row of gallows, to either side of the road, and from each cross bar there hung the naked body of a man, or a woman, some freshly dead, others already decomposing, all surrounded by a cloud of red headed crows, who cawed angrily and flapped their wings as they flew away from the intruders.

'His Majesty guards himself with the bodies of his enemies,' Palourdes observed. 'Or his suspected enemies.'

Kit urged his horse forward beside Richilde's. But there was nothing he could say to her, and nothing, apparently, that she wished to say to him. He studied the approaching village, for it certainly could not be described as a town, was reminded of the drawings he had seen of African kraals. Here was the same circle of wooden palisades, with a single gate, and inside, the same accumulation of huts. The roofs were of troolie palms rather than more securely thatched, and the guards wore brilliant uniforms and carried muskets and bayonets rather than spears and bows, but the differences were of degree rather than fact. Dessalines was clearly reaching all the way back into his West African heritage, in creating this refuge in the jungle after the only pattern he knew. But he was carrying his people with him, backwards.

General Christophe's party was allowed through the gate, but once within the hussars were relieved of their weapons and their horses, and led away to barracks apparently reserved for visiting soldiery. The main party then had to submit to a search, which included even the women, while the men also were disarmed. Richilde stood very straight, and with her eyes closed as the Negro captain slid his hands over her body, raised her skirts to make sure there were no poignards strapped to her thighs or calves. Seraphine Palourdes, submitting to the same humiliation, breathed deeply and could not prevent her cheeks from glowing.

Kit looked at Henry, who shrugged. 'His Majesty does not yet feel secure, Kit.'

But it was easy to see that he did not enjoy watching his womanfolk manhandled.

They were given no chance to discuss the matter further, however, being immediately escorted, almost as if they were prisoners, up the central walk towards the largest of the thatched houses. To either side there were gaily uniformed soldiers, and their women and children, all clad in the most splendid new clothes: the little boys with satin knee breeches in a variety of colours and white stockings with buckled shoes, their sisters also a mass of satin and silk, with brightly coloured bonnets and parasols and a rustle of frilly underskirts. But they remained, just simple children, picking their noses and gawking at the white skins, just as they were also obviously sadly undernourished.

At the palace, for such it was obviously intended to be, they were admitted through a small door into an ante-chamber, which was crowded with men, and women, all wearing the very best, jostling about to obtain a position nearest the inner door, protected by two enormous green-jacketed hussars, each carrying a drawn sabre, and beyond which there came the most peculiar of sounds, certainly intended, Kit supposed, to be musical, but hardly recognisable as any tune or rhythm he had ever heard before.

He went forward, with Henry and Richilde, to look past the guards into the reception room, and at King Jean-Jacques the First who, together with half a dozen men and an equal number of women, was dancing what was obviously intended to be a minuet, guided and instructed by an elderly mulatto woman, while on the far side of the room half a dozen musicians scraped at unfamiliar fiddles. All of the people in the room were elegantly uniformed or gowned, with Dessalines himself, in a pale green frock coat over white knee breeches, quite the most spectacular person present. But there was something irresistibly amusing about that huge, bull-like figure being so dressed in any event, much less cavorting about the floor in the centre of what was really nothing better than a large hut. Kit could only suppress a smile with an effort.

And just in time, for Dessalines had looked across the room and seen the new arrivals. Instantly he clapped his hands, and the music ceased. 'Henry,' he said, beckoning him in. 'It is good to see you. Richilde!'

Henry bowed, and Richilde sank into a deep curtsey.

'Major Palourdes. Madame.' Dessalines's eyes lingered on Seraphine, also curtseying, then he looked at Kit. 'The American sea captain.'

'Your Majesty.' Kit followed Henry's example, and bowed.

'By God, but I am hot. Hot,' Dessalines shouted, his voice rising into a bellow. 'Fetch me something to wear.'

Two valets immediately hurried into the room to remove his green jacket; Kit saw with surprise that he wore nothing underneath; another valet stood by with a towel to dry that mighty torso. And two more were waiting with a fresh uniform jacket, this one in crimson with black facings.

'You,' Dessalines said, pointing at Kit. 'May be useful to us. Has Petion come yet?' he demanded of the major-domo.

'Not as yet, Your Majesty,' the official replied, in a deep bow.

'Ha! Trust him to be late. Out,' the King shouted. 'Out!'

The ladies and the courtiers hurried for the door.

'That mulatto whore does not know anything about dancing,' Dessalines announced. 'And she used to teach it, mind. She is a cheat and a swindler and I will

454

have her flogged. You, Richilde, you will teach me to dance.'

Richilde gave a quick glance at Henry. 'If you wish it, Your Majesty.'

'I wish it. You, and Madame Palourdes. You will teach me. Tomorrow. But now ... Henry, I have received no money from you this last month.'

'There is none to be had, Your Majesty,' Henry said.

'That is nonsense. There is always money to be had. People must have money. There is a consignment of clothes and uniforms arriving at Port-au-Prince from Jamaica, next month, and I must have money. The confounded Englishman will not even enter the harbour. I have to send the money out to him. If I had a navy ... even a sloop of war. But I am surrounded by cheats and traitors. You, Captain Hamilton. You will bring clothes for me from New York? I will show you what I wish.'

'They will also have to be paid for, Your Majesty,' Kit pointed out.

'I know that. That is why I have summoned you here, Henry. And Petion. Where the devil is Petion? I will have him flogged. He thinks generals cannot be flogged. I will show him how wrong he is. Damned mulatto scoundrel. All mulattos are scoundrels. They are only one degree better than white people ...' He stared at Seraphine Palourdes. 'Scoundrels. But black people are scoundrels, too. They will not work. Henry, you do not make them work enough.'

'They are working very hard, Your Majesty,' Henry said, patiently. 'Too hard. Perhaps if you were to give them something more worthwhile to work for ...'

'Bah. They will not work. And I will tell you why they will not work.' His enormous forefinger stabbed through the air. 'It is because they do not understand that I am their King. Too many of them remember me, as they remember you, as mere slaves. We must correct that, Henry.'

He paused, but no one said anything.

'Because I *am* King,' Dessalines insisted. 'And if I am King, then I am chosen by Ogone Badagris himself.' He glared at them. 'Do you deny that?'

'I am sure that is true, Your Majesty,' Richilde agreed.

'Then I *am* Ogone Badagris. His spirit has entered my spirit, and we are as one. Is that not right?'

Richilde hesitated, but how often had that very thought occurred to her? 'It is certainly possible, Your Majesty.'

'Well, I shall prove it to these scum. I shall prove it,' he shouted, and Kit almost expected to see him beat his chest. 'I am the lord of the voodoo. I am the *hougan* of all *hougans*. Summon my people from all over the country, Henry. Call them here. Their *hougan* would demonstrate his power to them.'

'Voodoo,' Alexander Petion said in disgust. 'A nation, governed by voodoo. Is that not the very edge of madness?'

But, like everyone else, he stood in the vast crowd in the clearing outside the royal kraal, watching King Jean-Jacques. And his aides. Richilde was taken back all of the twenty years and more to that night outside Vergée d'Or, perhaps the most important night of her life. But not one she had ever expected to repeat. She glanced at Kit, standing beside her, and at the Palourdes, standing just beyond him. They were the only white people present. And they had no idea that she had ever stood in the darkness and the wind before, just as they had no idea what was about to happen. They stared at the tethered, frantic cockerels, listened to the beat of the rada drums, with fascinated attention, watched a young man, tall and strong, but sweating with apprehension, who was being led forward to sit cross legged on the earth, his handmaidens waiting attentively at his side.

And stared at their King, shrouded in the red robe of

his sacerdotal office, who now waved at the drummers to lower their cadence, while he stopped forward.

Madness, she thought, But is that not what has overtaken this country, this people . . . this woman? She had grown to love the Negroes, as she had fought with them and laughed with them and lived with them and cried with them, and all but died with them. Besides, they were Henry's people. But she was always aware that she was living in the midst of an uncontrolable emotional force, which would somehow have to be harnessed before any real progress could be made. She still thought that Henry possessed the strength to do that, still dreamed, of the day which had to come, when Henry would rule St Domingue with her at his side to guide and advise him, and had been foretold in the prophecy. Without her dreams she was nothing. But in reality she often found the future quite impossible to contemplate. These last few weeks she had for the first time really appreciated having Kit at her side. Because they were all growing older, even Henry, while they obeyed a madman.

Because Dessalines did not *wish* to harness the unstable power he pretended to rule. He sought to release it.

'Hear me, oh mighty one, Ogone Badagris, Lord of the skies and the earth, of fire and water, and of the souls of men,' he shouted, his voice echoing over the trees. 'Hear me, oh Damballah Oueddo, oh Dreadful One, master of the passions that make us men. We are your people, chosen by you, and led by you to victory. I am your King, chosen by you. Guide me so that I may lead my people to greatness and prosperity. Inspire me that I may know what must be done and that I shall do it. Show my people the way, that lies through me, that they may be humble in their hearts, and obedient in their actions. These things we ask of you, oh mighty ones, as we live and work in your sight and at your bidding.'

He paused, his mighty chest rising and falling, while the drums swelled in noise, booming their message across the forest, undoubtedly taking hold of the minds of those who heard them, as once they had taken hold of her own mind. Once again she stole a quick glance at the people beside her. Seraphine's eyes were almost closed, and she breathed slowly and regularly. Palourdes and Kit were both staring at the King, certainly caught up in the mood of the moment. Henry also stared at Dessalines, his face hard. But like her, he was not affected this time. He felt her glance, and returned it, then gave her hand a quick squeeze of reassurance.

The ceremonial sabre was brought forward, gleaming in the flickering light. Dessalines held it high, while the drumbeat rose into a tremendous roar of sound, and then he uttered a great shriek and swung it around his head, slicing cleanly through bone and muscle and arteries, throwing away the sword and grasping the head between his hands as he did so, expertly, holding it high, while the two girls fanned the blood spouting neck. Seraphine gave a gasp and sank to her knees – but she still watched, as Dessalines replaced the head, as the blood red cloth was thrown over the young man, as the cadence of the drums changed to the rhythm of the dance.

And as the young man slowly toppled forward to sprawl on the earth, his severed head rolling away from his dead body.

'He *is* mad,' Petion said. He walked with Kit and Boyer and Henry, in the garden of the palace, listened to the music emanating from the reception room. 'You must admit that, Christophe. To execute one of your own people, without reason . . .'

'He had his reasons,' Henry said. 'He explained them to you. He did not expect that boy to die.'

'Now, Christophe, you know and I know that these

458

voodoo ceremonies where the dead are brought back to life are all illusions. Dessalines merely has no knowledge of how it is done. Possibly he believes in it himself. That only confirms his madness.'

'Then you are condemning our entire nation to madness,' Henry said.

Petion stopped walking, stared at him. 'You do not believe in this nonsense yourself, surely?'

'What I believe is my business,' Henry said. 'And you are talking treason.' He gave one of his rare, grim smiles. 'That is not a very sensible thing to do, when actually inside the palace, and without even a sword at your side.'

'I am saying what I must because we are all here. You must realise where his madness is leading us. Where it will certainly lead us in the future. We have had people at Port-au-Prince, visitors from the United States, and from England, and France, and Germany, good people who wish us well, who have come all this way to see what the black man and the brown have made of their independence, only to be repelled by the poverty of the people, by the primitive conditions under which most of them are forced to exist, by the death sentences which are handed out as freely as the planters used to inflict the lash . . . God knows what the world would say of us were it to know this charnel house, where the stink of rotting flesh is never absent, much less attend one of His Majesty's voodoo ceremonies.'

'There is no hope for our economy,' Boyer put in, on a less emotional level, 'while His Majesty spends every cent he can scrape together on uniforms for himself and his soldiers. Why does he need to keep so many men under arms? Who are we going to fight?'

'The French will come back,' Henry said. 'Bonaparte does not forget. The very presence of a Negro nation where once was a French colony will bring him back. It is a mortal affront to his prestige.'

459

'If Bonaparte ever intended to return to St Domingue, he would not have sold Lousiana to the Americans,' Petion said. 'Is that not true, Captain Hamilton?'

'I cannot say,' Kit said. 'He is well on the way to becoming absolute master of Europe. And with Pitt and Nelson both dead, it is difficult to see who is going to oppose him. He certainly has the *power* to return here.'

'It is not practical,' Boyer said, 'while the British navy rules the oceans.'

'Nor does it alter the fact that we are living, if that is a reasonable word to use, at the mercy of a grotesque tyrant,' Petion said. He cocked his head to listen to the music. 'A man who dances the minuet one minute, and cuts off the heads of his subjects the next.'

'What are you proposing?' Henry asked, quietly.

'That he be deposed. That we collect our forces and put an end to this farce. Your people from the north will follow you, Christophe. Certainly mine in the south will follow me.'

'And His Majesty's will follow him,' Henry said. 'And we will start a war all over again. A war which will be fought to the last man. There is no fleet going to evacuate any of *us* who decide we have had enough.'

'Dessalines's men can hardly follow him, if he is not there,' Boyer said, also speaking very quietly.

'You are proposing to assassinate your King,' Henry told him.

'For God's sake,' Petion exclaimed. 'The man was a slave but fifteen years ago. And since then he has been nothing more than a soldier. *We* chose him King. Well, it is time we realised our mistake.'

'Yet is he the King,' Henry said. 'I will not rebel against my King.' He gave another grim smile as the two mulattos exchanged glances. 'I shall not betray you, either, gentlemen. I believe you have nothing but the good of St Domingue at heart. But I will tell you this: if you raise the standard of revolt in the south, I will fight beside His Majesty against you, and you will bring upon your peoples the most dreadful calamity.'

'And you will stand there and do nothing, the next time *His Majesty* decides to attempt a voodoo ceremony?' Petion demanded. 'Suppose he were to choose as his victim someone dear to you? Even Richilde, perhaps?'

Henry stared at him, brows drawing together. 'You may consider His Majesty to be mad, General Petion. I certainly do not consider him to be a fool.'

He walked away from them.

'What is this?' the King bellowed. 'Papers? Papers? I have no time to read papers. Tell me what they say.'

Richilde and Seraphine exchanged glances; they were well aware that Dessalines, like Henry, could not read.

The manservant bowed low. 'It is a petition from the people of Morne Rouge, Your Majesty,' he said. 'They beg to be excused from next month's tax collection, because of a rain storm they have suffered. Rain such as no man has ever seen before, Your Majesty, which has washed away all of their crops, and flooded their homes, causing great damage.'

'Rain storms? Rain storms? What do I care about rain storms? I *send* rain storms,' Dessalines shouted. 'To remind my people of my power. For am I not Ogone Badagris, come to life to rule over them? They have been punished, for thinking evil thoughts of their King. Their taxes next month will be doubled. Tell them that. And if they are not paid, I will personally go and collect them. With my soldiers. Tell them that.'

The secretary bowed, and withdrew. Richilde patted a bead of sweat from her temple. As it was still early in the afternoon it was extremely hot, and she was also overheated by the endless dancing. She was also worried. Because Henry was not here. She always worried when separated from Henry, but never before had she been forced to remain in the royal palace while he had been despatched on some entirely unnecessary investigation of a reported uprising in the east. Only the presence of Kit, who had been invited to remain a while longer, in order to discuss trading projects with the King's ministers, was the least reassuring. But Kit was not Henry. He had no faithful regiments at his back. Had even Petion and Boyer remained, she would have been reassured, but they had returned to Port-au-Prince in the south. And Albert Palourdes was a negligible quality in the affairs of state.

So she remained, with Seraphine, to entertain a madman, and teach him to dance. There could be no doubting the fact of Dessalines's madness, now. When he had cut off that unfortunate boy's head, and been unable to restore him to life, he had gazed at the corpse in utter disbelief for several seconds, then he had thrown back his head and given an almost animal like howl of anguished dismay. He had, of course, very rapidly recovered himself. Whatever the twisted mental processes he endured, his was a sharp and active brain. He had laughed at the horror around him, taken the credit for the disaster as his own decision, to reveal to them his power. It was difficult to be sure whether or not anyone had been convinced, as they had dispersed to their villages to repeat what they had seen. What was certain was that Dessalines himself had been severely shaken. He now pronounced himself a reincarnation of the god on every possible occasion, almost as if he was trying to convince himself.

But what would happen when he attempted the feat again?

And indeed, what would happen before then, as his brain sought some other remedial action? There could be no doubt, for instance, that he had always desired her, had been restrained from reaching out for her only because he feared Henry.

There could also be no doubt that he desired Seraphine. And now he had them both, with Henry sent away. Being Henry, he had obeyed without question, saying only, 'I leave Richilde in your care, Your Majesty, until my return.'

But he had gone. And suddenly, for the first time since the early days of the revolution, she was afraid he might not return.

The door had closed behind the secretary, the ladies and gentlemen were taking their places again, Richilde and an equally perspiring Seraphine at their head, while the musicians struck up their tune . . .

'Stop that noise,' Dessalines bellowed. 'Stop it. Do you think I wish to be driven deaf with your scrapings? Out. Out. Get out. All of you. Get out.'

The musicians ran for the door. The ladies and gentlemen curtsied and bowed, and followed them.

'Not you, Richilde,' Dessalines said. 'You will stay. And you, Seraphine.'

They hesitated, again exchanging glances. But the door had already closed upon the others, and they were alone, with the King.

'I am wearied,' he said. 'With all of this dancing. All of this business. I should not be wearied. I am Ogone Badagris.' His huge forefinger stabbed the air. 'Do you not believe me, Richilde? Speak, woman.'

Certainly lies cost nothing. 'I believe that, Your Majesty,' she said.

'Well, you are wrong,' he shouted. 'If I were truly Ogone Badagris, I would not be weary. I would be able to dance. I would have restored that boy to life. Can you deny that?'

'No man, Your Majesty, can understand the intentions of the gods.'

'Ah, but they can,' Dessalines said. 'The gods make their intentions plain enough. It is the blindness of men which leads them into error. I have been a fool, all of these years. Can you deny that?'

Richilde drew a long breath. 'Your people would not agree with you, Your Majesty,' she said. They would not dare, any more than I would dare, she thought.

'Well, I can tell you that I have. Is it not true that many years ago there was a prophecy, made by the great *mamaloi*, Céléste, on Vergée d'Or?'

Richilde stared at him, her heart beginning to slow. Seraphine looked from one to the other, in bewildered apprehension, aware that there were forces swirling about her which she did not understand, but which might well encompass her destruction.

'I know of no prophecies, Your Majesty,' Richilde said.

'Do not lie to me, Richilde,' Dessalines shouted. 'I know all about this prophecy, and so do you. It has been a beacon, guiding Henry and yourself for twenty years. Can you deny this?'

'Your Majesty . . .'

'Black he shall be,' Dessalines intoned. 'Black as the night from whence he comes, and into which he will sweep the whites. And big he will be, a man of greatness apparent to all. Yet will his might be surrounded by beauty, and his blackness surrounded by light. By this beauty, by this light, shall you know him.' He threw out his right arm, finger pointing. 'You always supposed that it referred to Henry, and yourself. Do not deny it. Many people have spoken to me of it, have shown me how Henry, alone of the leaders of the first revolt, alone of Toussaint, and Boukman, and Jean François, has survived, unharmed. But I have also survived unharmed, Richilde. And I am as mighty a man as Henry.' He grinned. 'And as black. Why should the prophecy not apply to me? Have I not stumbled all these years through the darkness, waiting only for the white beauty to come to me?' He held out his hand to Seraphine Palourdes.

Seraphine took a step backwards, licked her lips, looked from Dessalines to Richilde in stark fear.

'I will make you my queen, pretty Frenchwoman,' Dessalines said. 'I will let your white beauty surround my black strength. I will do it now.' He unbuttoned his jacket.

'Oh God, oh God,' Seraphine gasped. 'Help me, Richilde. *Please!*'

'Your Majesty,' Richilde said urgently, realising that the moment she had for so long feared had finally arrived. 'You cannot take Madame Palourdes to wife. She is already married.'

'Ha,' Dessalines shouted, throwing his jacket on the floor and releasing his breeches in turn to show them a hugely erected penis. 'What do I care for marriages? I will make you a widow, eh?' He gave a bellow of laughter. 'And then a wife.' He reached for her, and when she tried to duck away, drove his fingers into her hair, dragging her towards him. 'Now,' he said. 'Now, I will make you a goddess. I . . .' his other hand was peeling down her bodice, ripping away the layers of material as if they had been paper, to bare her from the waist up. Seraphine's reaction was perhaps instinctive. She swung her hand, and Dessalines gave a howl of rage and pain and released her as he jumped backwards, blood streaming down his cheek where her nails had torn the flesh.

'Oh, my God,' Richilde said. Her legs seemed to have turned to stone. She simply could not move.

Seraphine stared at the King, and saw him staring back, saw too the enraged anger in his eyes, knew that she was about to die. She threw back her head and screamed, a high pitched wail which reverberated through the palace and took even Dessalines by surprise. He tossed his head like the angry bull he was, about to charge, and the door burst open, to admit several of his aides, but also Kit and Albert Palourdes, who stared from the women to the King, understanding in a moment what had happened, and what more had been about to happen.

'You have assaulted my wife,' Palourdes cried. 'You

black savage. You . . .' his voice trailed into a wheeze and blood frothed through his teeth as he fell to his knees and then forward on to his face. One of the guards withdrew his sword from the dead man's back.

'Albert,' Seraphine whispered, and slowly sank to her knees in turn, beside her husband. Everyone else in the room seemed to have been struck dumb by the suddenness and finality of the execution. Kit was first to recollect himself, sprang forward, knocked the guard sideways with a single sweep of his fist, catching the sword which fell from the man's fingers, and seizing Seraphine by the arm to jerk her to her feet and push her towards the inner doorway.

'Richilde,' he snapped. 'Haste!'

Richilde found that she was panting, her mind clouded with the certainty of the catastrophe which was about to overtake them all. She made herself move forward, and had her arms seized by two of the guards. Kit, already at the door, and still half carrying Seraphine, hesitated, facing the crowded room.

'Ha,' Dessalines roared, having recovered himself. 'A plot, by God. You would assassinate your King. But you have failed, as all will fail who dare to pit themselves against Ogone Badagris. Throw down your sword, white man, or I will cut your sister's throat.'

'Run,' Richilde shouted. 'Leave Kit, leave. He will not harm me. He fears Henry.'

'Not even Henry will protect a traitor against her King,' Dessalines said, and himself took a sword from the other guard. He stood beside Richilde, dug his fingers into the hair to pull her head back, presented the blade to that pulsing white throat. 'I will do it now, and mount her head on a stick.'

Kit gazed at his sister, breast heaving as she gasped for breath, body sagging as she was supported by two of Dessalines's aides. Then he looked at Seraphine, whose eyes were shut as she seemed to have fainted. Then he threw his sword on the floor.

Richilde's hands were bound behind her back, and she was marched outside into the sunlight, down the ceremonial walk, surrounded now by almost everyone in the kraal, whispering their excited comments. She was taken through the gate, and on to the road, to look at the hanging bodies; here men were already erecting a large new gallows, a simple affair of two uprights with a cross beam some eight feet from the ground.

Up to this moment she had been so shocked by the rapidity with which catastrophe had followed catastrophe she had not been able to think. Now she realised that she was about to be hanged, her heart seemed to slow and she wanted to vomit. She had lived for so long in danger of her life, had experienced so much, had seen so much death and destruction, it was not the thought of actually dying herself that frightened her. But she had never anticipated such an end, far from Henry . . . and with Kit as company. She turned her head, and looked at him, as he had been marched out beside her. She opened her mouth, but could frame no words. Neither, it seemed, could he.

The guards stripped her by the simple method of ripping the cloth from her shoulders down. They looked embarrassed, preferred not to meet her eyes. Many of them had campaigned with her, and Henry, in the forests, against the British. And all of them knew there would have to be a reckoning, for this day's work.

As did she. If only she could survive to see it. But that was an impossible hope. The sunlight played on her flesh as she was pushed forward, to stand beneath the gallows, and a rope was thrown over the cross bar. She realised that it was too long since she had prayed, because she had not been sure, in twenty years, to whom she *should* pray. And now it was too late. The rope came down and struck her in the face, and the Captain of the guard stepped forward . . . but to release her wrists. She stared at him in horror. He could not mean to leave her dangling, and strangling, slowly, able to use her hands to hold herself up on the rope until her strength gave way?

And then she realised that he did not even mean to hang her, at this minute. He retied her wrists, in front of her, then raised her arms and secured them to the drooping rope. Four of his men pulled on the standing part, and she rose to her tiptoes, and then from the ground altogether, to hang from her wrists, swinging several inches above the earth.

The pain in her arms was excruciating, but she was alive. And for every second she remained alive, no matter what torments Dessalines had in mind for her, there was hope. She looked at Kit, who had been similarly suspended opposite her, and even attempted a smile. But there was no response, as he watched the other preparations being made.

For the soldiers now produced the cut down branch of a casuarina tree, stripped of its leaves and bark to become a long, powerful stake. This stake they shaved down at one end, to make a sharp point, then the blunt end was embedded in the earth, beneath the cross bar of the gallows, and exactly equidistant between Kit and Richilde. Above it another rope was looped over the bar. Then they waited, while the afternoon sun began to decline, and the mosquitoes rose in their thousands from the forest, to nip and tear and bite at their defenceless bodies as they gazed at the hideous weapon of destruction which was waiting, for its victim.

Who was at last dragged from the gate of the kraal by two soldiers, each holding a wrist, naked white body bumping and writhing on the earth. It was impossible to decide whether or not she could have walked had she been given the chance; there were welts and bruises, cuts and bite marks, scattered all over her flesh. And behind her walked the King, wearing only a pair of drawers, his face still twisted with angry venom.

Behind him was dragged the body of Albert Palourdes.

Richilde found herself nearly choking from a combination of pain and horror as she watched Seraphine being pulled to her feet beneath the gallows. Her eyes were closed and she hardly breathed as her wrists were bound and carried above her head, and a moment later she was swinging, long hair brushing her thighs, and opening her eyes as her hips touched the sharp point of the stake, which kept seeking to get between her legs.

'Ha, ha,' Dessalines said. 'Raise her higher.'

Two soldiers pulled on the rope, and she was raised another inch.

'That will do,' Dessalines decided. 'Hang there the night, pretty Frenchwoman, and reflect on the fate of those who defy their King.' He stood immediately in front of her, and spat in her face. Her head jerked, and her eyes opened again. Dessalines smiled at her. 'Tomorrow,' he said. 'We will *lower* the rope. Just an inch or so. But you will feel it, stroking your pretty slit, as you swing. And the day after that, my little chick, we shall *insert* it, and lower you another inch. Then you will beg for death. You will beg and scream and pray for death. But you will not die. Not for at least a week, as we lower the rope, just a little every day. Think about that, pretty Frenchwoman.'

Seraphine said nothing, Obviously, if she opened her mouth, it could only be to scream her misery.

And now her husband's body was laid at her feet, beside the stake.

'Is that how a mighty King behaves, Jean-Jacques?' Kit asked. 'To a defenceless woman?'

Dessalines grinned at him. 'And defenceless men. Ha ha. You plotted against me. Do not worry. Your turn will come. You will hang there, and watch her die. Then you will watch your sister die, slowly, the same way. Then you will die yourself, the same way. Sleep well, white man.'

He walked away from them, followed by his people, and they were alone, in the darkness, with the dead, and the mosquitoes.

There was no sound, above the humming of the insects, the gentle soughing of the breeze. Richilde thought the girl's courage almost superhuman, in that she did not even appear to weep, much less howl her agony, her apprehension of the quite unimaginable torture which would be hers tomorrow. Yet she too was hanging silently, in the darkness. But she had lived in this atmosphere of vicious violence for too long, was too used to it.

To be reconciled to being impaled, slowly, for day after day? There was madness lurking at the edges of her consciousness.

Would it ever end? Would it end, when Henry returned, and found her corpse, spitted on a stake? Henry's anger would be frightful, of that she had no doubt. But she could also now have no doubt that Dessalines anticipated this, had deliberately provoked the entire episode in order to force a showdown with Henry. And the King retained sufficient sense to know that the first overt act must come from the General. Well, he could be sure of that, when Henry found her.

But Dessalines had sufficient supporters, and there would once again be war, and destruction . . . and even after he had won his war, for she did not doubt he would, could Henry accomplish any of the things of which he dreamed, without her at his side, to guide and encourage him?

Would he even wish to?

'Kit,' she said. 'I am terribly sorry.'

'You did your best for these people,' he said. 'Your very best.'

Almost she thought he was about to say something more, about Seraphine perhaps, or even to the French girl. But he did not, and speech was difficult in any event, because of the pain. If her wrists had now become numbed, the pain stretched down into her arms and forearms, and she could not stop herself giving a convulsive twist or jerk every so often as a mosquito sucked her blood. She wished there was something she *could* say or do to Seraphine, to relieve what must be the girl's much greater agony, just as she wished she could have conveyed more to Kit, of her sense of the horror and injustice of *his* fate, that in merely returning to see her and reassure himself as to her welfare, he should have come to such an end. But she could think of nothing, so she hung in silence, and in time, remarkably, even seemed to sleep, a sort of coma, out of which she awoke to the coming of daylight, and the sound of jingling harnesses, and opened her eyes to look at the dawn, and the red jacketed hussars who formed the escort of Henry Christopher.

'Dessalines,' Henry said, his voice only a little more than a whisper.

'As I foretold, Christophe.'

Richilde blinked past Henry, saw Petion. And a whole host of soldiers, waiting on the forest road. And Jean Boyer? She hoped not. Somehow, to dangle naked before Petion, before an entire army, seemed unimportant beside the shame of dangling naked before Boyer.

'Take them down,' Henry commanded. 'Take them all down. And be careful the Frenchwoman does not fall on the stake.'

He himself held Richilde in his arms while his men cut the bonds holding her wrists, and she could lean against his great chest, weeping with pain as the blood slowly felt its way back up her tortured arms, yet able to allow herself to relax, until her head jerked in terror as she heard the bellow of the bull man.

'Christophe? You dare to interfere with my justice? These people ... these white people ... conspired against me.'

'Oh, my God.' Richilde whispered. 'Do not let him take us alive, Henry. Please.'

Henry squeezed her a last time, then handed her to Petion. He stepped past her, faced his King, who was accompanied by most of his guards, and most of his courtiers, too, come to see Seraphine's impalement.

'I left Richilde in your care,' Henry said.

'Ha. And she conspired against me. Be careful, Christophe, that I do not include you in that conspiracy.'

'You have already done so,' Henry said, and took off his uniform jacket to throw it on the ground, and stand before Dessalines, naked from the waist up, huge torso swelling in the morning sunlight as he breathed.

'Are you mad?' Dessalines demanded. 'You seek to defy *me*? Over a woman? A *white* woman? An *old* white woman? Here, take your pick from amongst any of my girls. They are young, and strong, and know how to make a man happy. They will give you *children*, Christophe.'

Henry pointed, turning his head from left to right to look at his men, and Petion's, and Dessalines's. 'This man is unfit to rule,' he shouted. 'He is unfit to live. He is unfit.'

'I will hang you beside them,' Dessalines bawled. 'You, seek to defy me? I, who am the incarnation of Ogone Badagris? I will crush you like a nut. I will impale you before I impale the white people. Seize him and string him up.'

The guards moved, restlessly, aware of the mass of Henry's troops, and of the waiting mulattos.

'If you are Ogone Badagris,' Henry said. 'Then I am Damballah Oueddo. Come, oh mighty one. Come and pit your strength against me.' He drew his sword, threw away the scabbard. 'Come and cross swords with me, oh Lord of the Tempest.' He threw the sword away as well, and placed his hands on his hips, huge muscles rippling. 'Or come, and wrestle with me, bull-man, that I may break your neck in ten places.'

Dessalines stared at him, tongue slowly circling his lips.

'Come,' Henry shouted, his voice reverberating like a peal of thunder. 'Or crawl away forever into your burrow like the snake you are.'

Richilde's breath was almost painful to draw, and she

wanted to close her eyes. But she could not. So she watched, as Dessalines gave a tremendous roar and charged forward, drawing his sword as he did so. And Henry had thrown away his weapon. But, almost like a trained matador, he swayed his body to one side as Dessalines reached him, avoiding the sword thrust, and then bringing his hands together to club Dessalines on the back and send him sprawling in the dust.

'Come,' Henry shouted. 'On your feet, oh Great King. On your feet.'

Dessalines seemed to be gathering his wits and his strength, while the watching people were so silent they might have been turned to stone. Then with a bound he reached his feet again, and ran, not towards Henry, but to the nearest hussar. He swept the man to the ground with a stroke of the sword which he still held, vaulted into the saddle, wrenched the animal round, and rode for the trees, swinging his sword left and right.

Christophe's hussars watched him go. Even Christophe watched him go. But his way took him past the mulatto escort of Alexander Petion.

'Bring him down,' shouted Colonel Boyer, his voice crisp and clear.

The muskets exploded. Dessalines reeled in the saddle, almost regained his balance, and then tumbled over the horse's head, to hit the ground and lie still.

PART FOUR

The Emperor

Dessalines's successor had obviously to be Henry Christophe, but because of mulatto opposition he was elected president for a four-year term only. The youngest of the three great revolutionary leaders had for too long lived in the shadow of the other two. He was known and loved in his own, northern half of the island, but not elsewhere. In the south Petion held sway, and in 1810 Christophe was forced to acknowledge that a separate and independent regime existed there. Meanwhile, the Spaniards had regained control of the eastern half of the island. Christophe was left with the north; soon he followed the example of his predecessor, and became the Emperor, Henri I.

Chapter 1

HENRI I

Haiti, under [Christophe's] rule, was a surprising phenomenon. To the east the Spanish colony of Santo Domingo basked lazily in the sun; to the south the light brown followers of Petion groped in search of an ideal social structure and slid perilously from corruption to national bankruptcy; in the north there was unceasing activity as the Emperor stormed around his kingdom exhorting, demanding, encouraging, driving his people to work as they had never worked before, even as slaves and above all, building.

Could it really be over? All of the years of striving and agony, of hopes and disappointments?

Richilde stood beside Kit, with Henry on her other side. She and her brother were the only white people present in the crowded reception hall of the late King's kraal; Seraphine was in bed, suffering from shock as well as her injuries. She was going to be a problem for the future. But now, Richilde knew, all the problems were going to be solved.

Alexander Petion addressed the assembly. He stood next to Jean Boyer, smiled at the black men and the brown. 'As General Christophe said,' he declared, 'Jean-Jacques Dessalines was unfit to rule us, unfit to have authority, unfit as a man, but also, my friends, as an institution. Free men do not have kings. The very word is indicative of a subservient nation. But we *are* free men, my friends, my comrades. We will model ourselves upon that other republic which has declared its freedom, here in the Americas: the United States of North America. We shall be the United Peoples of St Domingue. No, as of this moment St Domingue no longer exists. We are the United Peoples of Hispaniola. We shall be ruled by a president, who will be responsible to his people, and will rule for four years, and four years only, and then peacefully step down from his power, and acknowledge the rule of his chosen successor.'

He paused, to glance at Henry. But Henry's face remained expressionless.

'To have a president,' Petion continued, 'we need to have an election, to choose one. We must have an election in which every adult man in Hispaniola has his say. But that will take time, and until it can be done, we must be governed. I have therefore a proposal to make to you all. My proposal is that we here today elect ourselves a provisional president, who will rule us until the plebiscite can be held. We shall hope that the plebiscite confirms our choice here today as the first President of Hispaniola. But if it does not, then whoever it is we choose will step aside, and hand over power to his successor. I pledge myself should I be elected to abide by the result of the election, whenever it can be held.' He looked at Henry.

'I will abide by the election results,' Henry said.

'Well, then, it but requires us to choose our provisional President,' Petion said, and looked at the men. That he claimed the position for himself could not be doubted. Just as that he had the necessary qualifications could not be doubted, more qualifications indeed than anyone in the room, save perhaps his own aide, Boyer. He had fought since the very commencement of the revolution, for his mulattos in the beginning, but at the end for all the coloured peoples, and he was educated, well travelled, knew Europe as well as America, and was most certainly a civilised man, with no trace of the savage in his character.

But also no trace of the magic power that Henry exuded, no great deeds of daring in his past. And above all, no connection with the prophecy. And yet, Henry, secure, as Richilde now understood, in his faith in that prophecy, would step aside again, prepared to wait, for his day to come. Uncaring that too many days had already passed him by.

Desperately she squeezed Kit's hand. He glanced at her, and understood.

'Long live President Henry Christophe,' he shouted.

The cry was taken up. 'Long live President Henry Christophe.' The black men outnumbered the mulattos in the room by two to one. Petion hesitated, looked at Boyer, and then shrugged.

'Long live President Henry Christophe,' he cried.

'Long live President Henry Christophe,' Richilde said. 'Oh, long live President Henry Christophe.'

He looked down at her, and half smiled. His face remained solemn, however, there was not even a gleam of triumph in his eyes. He walked away from her, to stand in the centre of the room, and wait there, for the tumult to die. He made an immense, dominating figure, in his red hussar uniform, with his sword dangling almost like a dagger at his side. Now he took off his busby, held it under his arm, looked around him.

'I thank you,' he said. 'I thank you all. You have placed much confidence in me, and I will do my best to honour that confidence. But do not suppose I can promise you any easy life. We are an infant people, and we are beset with troubles. Our men and women are starving. The Spanish seek to re-establish themselves in the west. The French await only the opportunity to launch themselves once again at our throats. And . . .' he glanced at Petion. 'There will undoubtedly be other problems. So, if you will have me as your leader, then you must be prepared to work, as I will be prepared to work, to bring peace and prosperity to this great country of ours. Will you give me that promise?'

'We will follow you, President Christophe,' they shouted.

Petion said nothing.

'Well, then,' Henry said. 'I will make you a promise back. I will promise you that I will not fail you, and that I will deal justice to all, and injustice to none. Now listen to what I would have you do. In the first instance, I wish those dead bodies out there taken down from their gallows, and buried. Then I wish a state funeral arranged for King Jean-Jacques . . .' He held up his hand as there was a mutter of objection. 'He was our King, and he must be buried as a king deserves. And then . . .' he drew a long breath. 'Then I would have you burn this place. Burn it until no trace of it remains, until its ashes can be stamped into the dust.'

'Burn the King's palace?' Even Petion was amazed. 'But . . . where will you live?'

'Not in the jungle, and that is certain,' Christophe said. 'I will live at Cap François, where I have always lived, until I can think of somewhere more suitable. And it is to Cap François that we must all repair as soon as the King has been buried. I wish a meeting, of all our leaders, all our generals and all our mayors. This is necessary, to tell them of the election you wish to hold. It is also necessary to tell them what they must do, what *we* must do, to make our country great.'

'As you must tell me,' he said to Richilde, as they lay together that night, under the canvas roof of their tent, deep in the forest, with the flames of the royal kraal still lighting up the western sky.

'Me?' She sat up, tried to see his face in the darkness.

'You have waited long for this moment,' he said, with a half smile. 'Do not pretend that you have not. Well, so have I, Richilde. But I am a soldier, and I was a slave. I know nothing but fighting.'

'And now you have no one left to fight,' she said.

This time his smile was grim. 'There are always people to fight,' he said. 'The French will be back, soon enough. They will have to be fought.'

'I do not think the French will ever come back, Henry.'

'Well, I think they will. Or if not them, some other European power. This is too great and fertile a land to be ignored by the white people. The Spaniards have already returned to the west, because Dessalines would not immediately march against them.'

'And will you now march against them? Have you not more important things to do here? Send one of your generals. Send Petion to deal with the Spaniards.'

'Before I have to fight him as well, you mean? But I am waiting for you to tell me of these more important things I must do.'

There were so many, she was not at all sure where to begin. So she temporised. 'You must allow me time. I had supposed I would be advising a king, who could command. Not a president, who must persuade.'

'You will be advising a king,' he said.

She frowned into the darkness. 'But you have just been chosen President.'

'Petion dreams these dreams of his. But republics will only work, real republics, with peaceful elections every four years as he wishes to happen, will only work where every man in that country can read and write and understand what his betters are talking about. Where there is total illiteracy, or even part illiteracy, men cannot understand the issues and the principles their leaders are concerned with. Thus they cannot choose. And indeed I do not believe that my people wish to have to choose. They wish only to be led.'

The simple profundity of what he had just said left

479

her speechless for a moment. Then she said, 'But will Petion ever agree to another monarchy?'

'Do I have to wait for Petion's agreement?' he asked. 'I *will* wait to be elected President. Then you will be able to work out what proportion of my people wish me as their master. If it is a sufficiently large number, as I think it will be, then I will take the opportunity as it comes, to declare myself King.' He waited for her comment, and receiving none, hugged her against him. 'There is so much that needs to be done,' he said. 'So much that cannot be accomplished in four years. You know this.'

'I know this,' she said.

'So tell me of them, these things that have to be done.'

'Your people must be adequately fed,' she said. 'That is the most important thing. For that you must make them clear land to plant corn, and you must tame some of the wild cattle in the interior and make them breed, and give milk, and you must set up organised fleets to bring fish in from the sea. You must also arrange some means of distribution. I do not think you should give food away, because your people are by nature indolent, and if they are *given* food they will not work at all. I think you must set up a succession of great markets, as Toussaint did, but on a larger scale. I know there is no money in Hispaniola, but you must encourage your people to barter, one man's vegetables for another man's fish, and so on, and you must appoint inspectors to supervise the markets and make sure that every man deals fairly with his neighbour. The inspectors should have the power to set a price on all goods. But they too will have to be carefully watched by your ministers, to prevent corruption.'

'What you have just said is the strongest of all arguments for a monarchy,' he pointed out. 'I must *make* them cultivate land. I do not take issue with that,

480

Richilde. I know I will have to make them. But I must have the eternal, the everlasting, the unceasing authority to do that. Just as I must have the unopposable authority to appoint these inspectors, and to punish them when, as you say, they are found to be corrupt.'

'Yes,' she said. 'I think you are right.' Because he was right, and in more ways then he knew. Henry understood nothing of the arts of dissimilation or persuasion. He *could* only command.

'Now let us speak of the palaces we shall build,' he said. 'The fortresses. The fleet.'

She sighed. 'Such things cost money, Henry.'

'Then we must get money. I told you and them that the road would be hard. Only one third of the people, less the army, of course, can be set to food production. Another third must be set to re-cultivating the canefields, that we may have an export crop. I will invite Kit to charter his vessel to us, as the nucleus of our merchant fleet. I shall also ask Kit to act as our agent in America, and attract other ships to come here to trade. He may give whatever guarantees for their safety or their eventual payment he chooses. I will support him. Will he accept such a task, do you think?'

She hardly heard his proposition beneath the enormous impact of what he had just said, apparently without realising it. The scale on which his thoughts roamed. Hispaniola was to be divided into the army, and the workers for domestic consumption, and the workers for export. And the rest? Because that he had plans for them as well could not be doubted.

'Yes,' she said. 'Yes, I am sure he would wish to help us. You have only spoken of part of your people.'

'The last third will build,' Henry said. 'A palace. A palace worthy of you.' He smiled in the darkness. 'And of me.'

'Henry,' she said. 'I do not wish a palace. There are more important things to do first.'

'There can never be a more important thing than building a palace. Did not Frederick the Great build a palace?'

She sighed. 'Yes.'

'What was it called?'

'Sans Souci. But Henry . . .'

'What does that mean, Sans Souci?'

'It means what it says, without care. But Henry, Frederick came of a long line of kings, and he ruled a country which was already peaceful and wealthy. You are starting from the very bottom.'

'Which is all the more reason why I must have a palace,' he explained. 'Because that is where Dessalines made his mistake. He was quite right when he said that the people did not properly respect him. But it was not merely because they remembered him as a slave, like themselves. It was because, having been chosen to rule them, he did not sufficiently rise above them in stature and prowess. He lived in a kraal. A kraal is the biggest house they have, in Africa. But these people here can remember Vergée d'Or chateau, and Rio Negro chateau and even the Governor General's house in Cap François. How can they ever look up to a man who calls himself their King, but lives in a house inferior to those?' He thought for a moment. 'And there is another thing. A king must live *with* his people, where he can be seen and his greatness understood, every day. He must not bury himself away in the jungle, as if he was afraid of them.'

'Then let us live in the Governor General's palace, in Cap François,' she said. 'I was happy there.'

'We shall live there, while Sans Souci is being built.'

'Sans Souci? You mean to call your palace Sans Souci?'

'Why not?' he asked. 'Frederick the Great is dead. He will not mind if we borrow the name of his house. It has a ring to it. Sans Souci! We cannot remain in Cap

François, Richilde. We have seen too often that Cap François is indefensible. We must remove ourselves from the coast, and we must be close to the citadel.'

'The citadel? You will build a fortress, and call it Sans Souci?'

He laughed. 'No, Sans Souci will be the palace. The fortress will be something else again. When the French come back, I intend to meet them with a fortress not even *they* can conquer.'

He paused, as if expecting her to comment, but she could no longer argue against his fixation.

'Do you remember?' he asked. 'That day in the forest, so many years ago, when we saw the redcoats climbing up towards us? I said then I would build an impregnable fortress, where they were climbing. This I shall do. It will be the greatest fortress ever built. The fame of it will reverberate around the world.'

'A fortress? In the jungle? But Henry, that will be too expensive . . . it will cost lives, as well as money. It is just *impossible*.'

'Nothing can be impossible, to the man who would rule Hispaniola,' he said. And frowned into the gloom. 'Hispaniola. That is a Spanish word. How can I be King of a country named by the Spaniards?'

'It is its name, Henry.'

'Well, then, we will change the name. We will call the country . . . Freedom. What do you think of that?'

'Henry . . .'

'Yes,' he said. 'The white people will laugh at the King of Freedom. But we must have a name, Richilde. A name which has nothing to do with the white people, whether they be Spanish or French or English. A name we can call our very own. Tell me of such a name, Richilde.'

Her brain seemed to have gone blank. Then she remembered . . . 'I have read,' she said. 'That the Indians who lived here before the Spaniards came, called this land, Haiti, the High Place.'

'Haiti?' demanded Alexander Petion. 'That is barbaric. No one will ever know how to pronounce it.'

'Then they will have to learn,' Henry said. 'I wish a flag designed for the country of Haiti. It must have black in it, and red, for the blood that has been shed to bring this miracle about, and gold, to represent the light and the glory that lies ahead of us.' He gazed around the group of officers, gathered in the old gubernatorial council chamber in Cap François. 'Now, here are my first orders as President of Haiti. I will give every man in the country a choice, up to a point. I am told there are approximately five hundred thousand men, in Haiti.'

'You are told,' Petion said. 'By whom?'

His gaze drifted to Richilde, seated with several other women, in the far corner of the huge room; but the other women were clearly intended to make the fact of her presence less obvious.

'Five hundred thousand men,' Henry repeated, refusing to lose his urbanity. 'Between the ages of twelve and sixty. They will all have to go to work. We have fifty thousand men under arms. That still leaves four hundred and fifty thousand. These I wish divided into three groups. One third will cultivate the land and catch the fish and in general provide for our domestic needs. One third will grow sugar cane, under the supervision of appointed officers, and thus create an export crop. And one third will build. I wish you all to return to your respective towns and villages and districts, and seek out all of these men. You may ask them, in the first instance, to volunteer for one of those three services. But as soon as we reach the required number in any one of the three, then we will have to appoint men, to whichever of the three is short handed.'

They stared at him, unable for a moment to take in the immensity of the manner in which he was summoning the nation to work.

Petion, as usual, was first to recover. 'You need one

hundred and fifty thousand men, to build?' he demanded. 'To build what, President Christophe?'

'To build a palace,' Henry said. 'The palace of Sans Souci. I have already chosen the site. It will be by the village of Millot, that is at the foot of the mountains, and yet not far from Cap François. It is close, too, to Vergée d'Or, where our revolution began.' He smiled at them. 'My palace will make Vergée d'Or chateau look like a village hut.'

'*Your* palace?' Petion inquired.

'The Presidential Palace,' Henry said. 'But I will build it. And I will turn Millot itself into a great city. A city worthy of the capital of Haiti.'

'I see,' Petion said. And looked at Richilde again. 'This also has been recommended to you. Told to you, perhaps?'

'This has been decided,' Henry said, still retaining his smile. 'And when the palace and the city are built, then my workers will build a citadel, up in the mountains. They will build the most impregnable citadel the world has ever known, that the world may know that Haiti will never again be conquered, not even by the French.'

Petion stared at him, then looked at Boyer, then seemed inclined to tear his hair out by the roots. 'And in pursuance of these fantastic schemes you would devote the labour of one third of your people? I should have thought it was the duty of the army to build your fortresses. They have precious little else to do, and there are far too many of them. How can we have one man in ten under arms? Who have we to fight? Who *can* we fight?'

'The army is going to fight the Spaniards, to begin with,' Henry declared. 'I will make that your task, General Petion. The Spaniards must be expelled from the west of the island. Haiti must be re-united.'

Petion shook his head. 'I decline your invitation, Mr President.'

At last Henry frowned. 'You refuse to lead my armies into battle?'

'I refuse to lead them because there will *be* no battle. We shall be commencing yet another interminable bush war. And with what? Are you aware, Mr President, that your fifty thousand soldiers muster hardly a hundred thousand cartridges between them? Two bullets for every man, and they are going to fight a battle? You have perhaps fifty cannon balls, for all of your artillery. King Jean-Jacques spent all his money equipping his soldiers with uniforms, not with bullets. Or do you now propose to arm your men with bows and arrows? Because if you do, Mr President, then you must take command of them yourself. I know naught of prehistoric fighting.'

Christophe stared at him for some seconds, then looked at Richilde, then he got up and left the room.

Henry walked up and down the floor of his private office. 'That man is my enemy,' he stormed. 'He has always been our enemy. The mulattos are not for Haiti. They are for the mulattos. I should have him . . .'

'No, Henry,' Richilde said.

He paused in his perambulation, to glare at her.

'You swore on oath, to your people,' she said. 'To deal justice to every man. Even Alexander Petion.'

Henry's huge fingers curled into fists. 'So I must be opposed,' he growled. 'Constantly. You . . .' he pointed at Captain Gounod, waiting with Kit by the door. 'You knew of this state of affairs? Why was I not informed sooner?'

'I did not know that it applied to the entire army, President Christophe,' Gounod protested. 'I knew that *our* people were short of shot, but I supposed it was part of King Jean-Jacques's policy, to prevent us from opposing him.'

'Ha,' Henry said. 'Who is that?' he shouted, as there came a rap on the door.

The door opened, to admit Colonel Boyer, who stood stiffly to attention.

'Well?' Henry demanded. 'You have brought a message from General Petion?'

'No, sir, Mr President,' Boyer said. 'I wish you to know, sir, that General Petion's attitude does not reflect the opinions of the majority of his officers. If you wish to repeat your command, sir, I will willingly lead my men against the Spaniards. I hold the opinion that every moment they remain in possession of their old colony will be disastrous for our hopes of regaining it.'

Henry stared at him. 'This is some trick?'

'Henry,' Richilde protested, and flushed as Boyer glanced at her.

'It is no trick, Mr President,' the mulatto said. 'You have but to issue the command.'

Henry regarded him for several more seconds. Then he said, in a quieter tone, 'I thank you, Colonel Boyer. Be sure-that when I am ready to march against the Spaniards, you will have a command. But your General did me no disservice by bringing to my attention the condition of the armed forces. This I propose to remedy before undertaking any offensive action at all. I thank you.'

Boyer hesitated, then saluted, gave Richilde a brief bow, and withdrew.

'That man,' Henry said, 'is far more dangerous than Petion could ever be. He has a resolution that Petion entirely lacks.'

'A resolution which could be a great asset to you, Henry,' Richilde said.

'To you, perhaps,' Henry said. 'Not to me. Never to me.' He beckoned Kit. 'Can you get me ammunition for my men, Kit?'

'I can try, Henry,' Kit said. 'But it will be difficult, without money.'

'And I have none, until after the next sugar crop,' Henry mused. 'But can we not pledge the crop?'

Kit hesitated, glanced at Richilde.

'Yes,' Henry said. 'They will not take the word of a black man. But you must try for us, Kit. Invite them to come here and see for themselves what we are trying to do. Pledge the crop. Pledge whatever is necessary. But return to me in haste with a shipload of guns and ammunition. Can you do that?'

'I will try,' Kit said.

'Then leave, immediately. The matter is most urgent. And bring back as many ships as you can, too. And people. We are not afraid to receive people. Not now. You will be well rewarded, Kit. You may have anything you wish, that is in my power to give.' He grinned. 'You may have Madame Palourdes.'

Kit's head jerked.

·Henry gave a roar of laughter, and slapped him on the shoulder. 'Do you suppose I have not seen how you look at her? You desire her. And so you should. She is a fine looking woman.'

'What makes you suppose that she will desire me?' Kit asked.

'That is important? She is a lonely widow woman, in a strange land. She cannot spend the rest of her days just staring out of a window. She must have a man, and it is better that she should have a white man, one of her own kind, than a black. I am the only black man who can be allowed to have a white woman, eh? Or someone else may suppose he is the hero of the prophecy. But you are afraid, that she will have gone mad, like Annette de Mortmain. I do not think she has gone mad, Kit. She is not a Mortmain. She is made of sterner stuff. Do you not think so, Richilde?'

'I do not think she is mad, Henry,' Richilde agreed, and gazed at her brother.

'Then go to her, Kit,' Henry said. 'I allow you this night with her, and tomorrow you will sail for New York. She will be here for you when you get back. But for this night, why, you may discover what you can look forward to. Go to her, Kit. Your President commands you.'

Kit hesitated at the bedroom door. Richilde had offered to come here before him, and prepare her. But he had declined. He wished to know her true reactions, not those she would present after she had had the time to consider her situation.

Was he excited? He supposed he was, in a subdued, almost subconscious fashion. He had certainly wanted her, for several years. He wanted her more than ever now, knowing what she had suffered, what more she had so nearly suffered. And it was exciting to know that she was to be his. Yet he also knew that he would never force her, *could* never force her. And whatever his feelings, she had never revealed the slightest indication of any affection for him. So once they had been forced to make a public display of love, a display which haunted him, as much for his shadowy memory of the woman as for the humiliation of it. But she had never suggested any memory of it at all, as it must have been only one of many.

He drew a long breath, and knocked.

'Yes,' she said, her voice as quiet as ever.

He opened the door. She had been sitting by the window, looking down at the city. This was the room she and Palourdes had shared when Pauline LeClerc had lived in this palace. He had thought it a mistake to return her to such familiar surroundings, where every object must remind her of happier times. Richilde had thought that such familiarity was essential. Besides, she had pointed out, there had *been* no happier times. Seraphine Palourdes had never been happy in her life, certainly not since her childhood.

That must be his first objective. Her happiness.

She had turned her head to discover the identity of her visitor. Now she stood up, little patches of colour

489

filling the pale cheeks. Copying Richilde, she wore a simple housegown, in green. It was made of thick material, Richilde having absolutely forbidden any of the current French fashions in Cap François, but it was simple to decide that she was wearing nothing underneath. And her feet were bare. While her magnificent black hair hung in a straight shawl past her shoulders.

'Captain Hamilton,' she said. 'You have come to say goodbye?'

He wondered how she had known that. And if it bothered her.

'Only for a season,' he said. 'President Christophe wishes me to return to New York, and do some business for him.'

'Of course,' she said, and sat down again. She looked away from him, out of the window. 'I do not suppose . . .' she hesitated, biting her lip.

'I cannot offer you a passage, madame,' he said. 'Much as I would like to. President Christophe would not permit me. And I must return here.'

'Of course,' she said. 'President Christophe is your friend, and Richilde is your sister.' She forced a smile. 'It is merely that I cannot help but wonder what his plans are for me.' Her head turned to give him a quick look. 'To anticipate them, perhaps. I . . . I cannot contemplate the future without a shudder. I have not the fortitude of your sister.'

'Richilde loves,' he said. 'And thus does not need fortitude.'

'And I cannot love,' she said. 'At least, a black skin. But I have never loved a white skin, either. I have never loved.' Now she looked directly at him. 'And yet I must *belong*, it seems. Because I have a woman's attributes.'

Perhaps a cue? 'Is there no one you *could* love?' he asked.

'No one I have ever met,' she said. And gave a half smile. 'I do not think I have been very lucky in the men I have met.'

He bit his lip in turn, and her smile became genuine, if sad.

'You must not take that as a reflection upon yourself, monsieur. Circumstances . . . I should rephrase what I said. Circumstances have never been fortunate, in my encounters with your sex.' She held out her hand. 'It is good of you to come, to say adieu. I am sure I will prosper here, with Richilde's friendship to sustain me.'

Kit drew a long breath. But she was so lovely, so desirable, if he did not speak he thought he would burst.

'President Christophe has already selected the man,' he said. 'To whom you must belong, as you put it.'

Her head came up, pink spots flaring in her cheek. 'So soon? And you know who it is?'

'It is I.'

She stared at him, while the colour deepened, and then faded. 'You?' She spoke in hardly more than a whisper.

'Yes.'

'And you agreed to this? You, who know me for what I am? Who have seen what I have had done to me?'

'I, who know you as the most desirable woman I have ever met.'

Seraphine sat down. Kit had the impression that her knees had simply given way. 'You,' she said. 'Desire me?' She raised her head again. 'I am flattered, monsieur. Even if you mean merely to amuse yourself with me. Shall I undress now, or will you take a glass of wine, first?'

He could not be angry with her. She knew only such treatment, could envisage nothing better.

'I will marry you,' he said. 'As soon as I may. As soon as I can discover a priest.'

A faint frown gathered between her eyes. 'What has marriage to do with desire, monsieur?'

'In our cases, surely, a great deal. I will love you,

491

Seraphine. I am sure of that. I would like to feel that one day you will love me back.'

'Love,' she muttered. 'I know nothing of love.' Then her head raised again. 'But if you love me, if you desire me, if you will marry me, then you will take me away from here. Take me to America with you.'

He shook his head. 'I cannot.'

'I see.' Her head bowed again, her shoulders sagged.

'I cannot, because President Christophe wishes you to stay here,' Kit explained again. 'He is my friend. He is virtually the husband of my sister. And he is the man I have sworn to help as far as I can. He trusts me, I think, and yet he has known so much treachery, white treachery, in his life, he cannot bring himself wholly to trust anyone, save Richilde. I must prove to him that I, too, am wholly trustworthy.'

'So I am to remain here, as a prize, for when you return,' she said.

'You will not be harmed, or insulted. As you say, you are Richilde's friend, and you may be sure that she will care for you. And I will not be gone a moment longer than I have to.'

'Should that consideration make me happy, monsieur? In view of my fate when you return?'

Her coldness, her rejection of him, was inspired more by a resentment at the way she was being treated, as if she were a slave herself, rather than any absolute dislike of himself. Of this he was certain.

'I would hope the idea would grow upon you, madame,' he said. 'As you consider it.'

'And I shall consider it,' she promised. 'As I have nothing else to consider.' She stood up again. 'As he sent you to me, no doubt President Christophe commanded you to take at least a memory with you on your voyage. To discover if I have changed, perhaps, from our last . . . meeting. I would but ask you to be gentle with me.' Her mouth twisted. 'The King left me bleeding in many ways.'

'When I take you, Seraphine,' Kit said. 'You will be smiling. I will see you, in two months' time. Think of me, if you can.'

'Heave,' came the command.

'Heave,' shouted the work gang.

'Heave,' bellowed the soldiers standing behind them, in a tremendous roar which went up to the skies.

'Heave,' said Henry Christophe.

There was a sound like that of a whistling wind, and the huge tree came crashing to the ground, slicing through other, smaller trees, leaving a swathe of destruction behind it. Instantly the men with axes swarmed over the fallen monster to hack it into manageable pieces, while others went on to the next tree, where the ropes were already being secured – the immense taptap of the axe-blades sounded like an entire forest of woodpeckers, Richilde thought.

She sat in a tent, before a trestle table, overlooking the site, but more concerned with the pile of returns and the mass of figures before her. Henry had chosen already to take up residence under canvas at Millot, regardless of heat and rain and mosquitoes, to drive his men onwards, day after day after day, to the completion of his palace – even if they had not yet completed clearing the site. His energy was insatiable. And Richilde knew, whatever Petion might think, that this was no mere vanity, the fulfilment of a lifelong dream. It was an act of deliberate statecraft. Henry, not less than Dessalines, was aware of the importance of outward show to his people; he merely, as he said and as she hoped and believed, intended to put more substance behind the show than had ever occurred to Dessalines the bull-man. And he was thinking not only of impressing his own people. He looked forward to receiving foreign ambassadors, and even more, foreign financiers, and to meeting them in circumstances as splendid as ever they might have known in London or Paris or Berlin.

But Petion did not only think. He also spoke, ranging the country to raise his voice in criticism of the wasteful extravagance of the President. This he was entitled to do, as he also was a candidate for the Presidency, but Richilde knew that Henry, for all his promises, had no intention of laying down his authority were he defeated at the election; the only hope of avoiding another outbreak of civil war was for him to win, and win overwhelmingly. Thus the returns which were now being laid on her desk were of vital importance to the whole nation.

And they were exactly what she was looking for. She raised her head to smile at Captain Gounod as he laid another pile of papers on her makeshift desk.

'These are the last, madame,' Gounod said.

'Have copies of all these returns been sent to Port-au-Prince?'

'Indeed, madame,' Gounod said. 'With instructions for General Petion to attend us here in the north.'

'And with absolute guarantees for his safety?'

Gounod's eyes were hooded. 'Of course, madame.'

She gazed at him for a moment, and then returned to her sums. She checked and re-checked. But there could be no doubt of the verdict of the people of Haiti. The black people, at any rate, and they outnumbered the mulattos by some eight to one. She did not suppose every black man would have wished to vote for Henry Christophe, left to himself. Henry had lived all of his life in the northern half of the country, had never even visited Port-au-Prince, and did not appear to have any wish to do so. When she had suggested it might be politic for him to make a tour of the country he had shaken his great head, and pointed out that he had too much to do here. But with Gounod riding from town to town, with a regiment of hussars at his back, and summoning the people into the market square and telling them that they must vote, there and then, for either President Christophe, the hero of the revolutionary war, or General Petion the mulatto renegade, who had once fought for France against them, it would have had to be an exceptionally bold or foolhardy man who would have dared raise his hand for Petion.

Hardly an election, she supposed, as it would be regarded in England or America. But necessary, for Haiti, as Henry had explained to her on the night of Dessalines's death. And she did not suppose there truly was any large number of black men who would have preferred a mulatto president to Henry.

She assembled her papers, put on her straw hat – it was very hot – and went outside. Her grooms held her stirrups for her as she mounted, riding side-saddle because that was how Henry liked to see her ride, and trotted over to where Henry and his officers over-looked the work of clearing the forest. 'All the election returns are in,' she said.

Henry turned his head.

'You have received over four hundred thousand votes, President Christophe,' she said.

'And Petion?'

'Just under a hundred thousand.'

'Long live President Christophe,' Gounod shouted, and threw his bicorne in the air.

'Long live President Christophe.' The shout was taken up. The workers laid down their tools to cheer.

'A hundred thousand men voted for Petion?' Henry demanded. 'You told me there were no more than fifty thousand mulattos in all Haiti.'

'I do not think there are many more than that,' Richilde said.

'Then I have been betrayed, by my people.'

'That is not so,' Richilde insisted. 'Perhaps those black men in the south who voted for Petion were forced to do so. In any event, your people have not betrayed you, Your Excellency. They have voted for you by a margin of more than four to one. There can be no doubt of the choice of the majority, the vast majority, of the people of Haiti. The future is yours, Henry. To do with as you please. But Henry, you must remember your promises, of justice to all men, black or brown. You must rule, not merely bully.'

Henry looked at her for several seconds, then he smiled. 'I shall rule,' he said. 'I shall rule, my Richilde.'

'Kit!' Henry Christophe stood on the terrace of the Governor General's palace in Cap François to welcome his friend, arms outstretched. 'Oh, welcome back.' He gazed out at the harbour, the *Stormy Petrel* riding to her anchor, the lighters already swarming around her to unload her cargo. 'You outsailed the others, eh? That is good. That is what I like to see.'

Kit glanced at Richilde. 'There are no other ships, President Christophe.'

'Eh? No other ships? How can that be?'

'May we go inside? I would speak with you in private,' Kit said.

Henry frowned at him, then turned and walked into his study. Richilde followed the two men. 'You have failed me,' Henry said.

'I'm afraid I have. In New York they regard you, well . . .' he hesitated.

'As a savage,' Henry said. 'Why are you afraid to speak the truth?'

'They are businessmen,' Kit explained. 'They will not advance money on a sugar crop which may never be reaped because of some new civil war. They have the opinion that the wars of the past twenty years have completely destroyed everything of value in the country. I could not persuade them otherwise.'

Henry gazed at him. 'Then you have brought me nothing?'

'I have brought you a ship filled with arms and ammunition, with powder and with ball, as you requested me to do.'

Henry's face lit up. 'Your ship is filled with arms? For me? But . . . if you had no money . . .'

'I sold my house, everything I possessed,' Kit said. 'And thus paid for them.'

Henry got up, slowly, while Richilde's eyes were filled with tears.

'You did that, for Haiti?'

'I did that, for you, Henry,' Kit said. He gave a twisted smile. 'You are my President now, as well.'

'You did it, for Haiti,' Henry said. 'Yours will be a forever honoured place amongst my people. I will make you rich, and famous.' He smiled. 'Whenever that can be done. But first, you shall have your reward.' He pointed. 'I am told you spent but half an hour with Madame Palourdes, before departing for New York, and that you did not share her bed.'

'I did not consider the time was right, Your Excelency,' Kit said.

'You do not desire her?'

'Of course I desire her. But . . .'

Henry turned to Richilde. 'Fetch her here.'

Richilde left the room.

'Guns, and ammunition. Powder and ball,' Henry said. 'That is splendid. Yet it is but a start. What must I do, Kit, to find more money? To make people understand, that I am no savage, but a king.'

'A king?' Kit asked.

Henry glanced at him. 'That is my intention. It is a secret, and you will not repeat it. But now I know what my people want. Yet if I am going to do everything I must, for Haiti, and my people, I must have money, and recognition. What must I do, Kit? What must I do?'

His anguish, his determination to achieve his ambitions and his dreams, was almost frightening to behold. Kit sighed. 'You, we, must practice patience, to begin with,' he said. 'We shall reap a crop of sugar, in only a few months, and I will ship it for you to the United States. When they see that we can deliver, then they will change their attitudes.'

'You cannot ship the crop we will produce in a single ship, Kit,' Henry pointed out.

'I know that. I will return to the mainland, and endeavour to interest other shipmasters in our business. I but felt I had to return here as soon as possible, to deliver the munitions, and to acquaint you with the situation.'

'Yes,' Henry said. 'Yes, you are a good and faithful friend, Kit. But I never doubted that. And the munitions are important. Now I can carry forward at least the first part of my plans.'

'There are other things you can do,' Kit said. 'You must prove to the world that you are *not* a savage, but a leader of your people. You must prove that you can be trusted, and that you will deal with white people as well as with black.'

'Have I ever done otherwise?' Henry demanded.

'You must be positive. Petion knows this. That is why he is inviting the French émigrés back to the south. To Port-au-Prince. This is the best way . . .'

Henry's brows drew together. 'Petion is bringing the French back to Haiti?'

'Did you not know? He has his agents in Jamaica, and in Savannah and Charleston, attempting to convince the blancs that with Dessalines dead and Haiti now a constitutional republic, it is safe for them to return.'

'No,' Henry said. 'No, I did not know of this. How can he do this, without referring to me, his President?'

'I am sure he means to inform you,' Kit said. 'But I consider it a good move. Nothing will more speedily restore international confidence in you and your government, than a spirit of letting bygones by bygones; of encouraging the planters, who are, after all, mostly Haitians themselves, by birth, to return. And I may say, Henry, that they are the people to give you the very best sugar crop.'

'French people?' Henry asked. 'Planters?' he

shouted. 'People who supported the French invasion, and who will certainly support the next French invasion as well? You expect me to allow such brutes and traitors back into my country?'

'You are the President of Haiti,' Kit said. 'You must inspire confidence. You must not carry personal hatreds forward into the affairs of government. You must rise above such things. I know that you hate Etienne, for instance. But Etienne is a capable planter. If you were to restore him to Vergée d'Or, he would soon have a crop . . .'

'Etienne?' Henry asked, his voice again low. 'Etienne de Mortmain is in Haiti?'

'He has written to me to say he is going to Port-au-Prince,' Kit said. 'At the invitation of General Petion, governor of the city.'

'Oh, my God,' Richilde said. She stood just inside the doorway, holding Seraphine Palourdes by the hand.

'Etienne de Mortmain,' Henry growled. 'Is invited back to Haiti, by that mulatto swine? By God . . .' His huge fingers curled into fists.

Kit looked at his sister in bewilderment.

'Etienne had Henry flogged, once,' she explained. 'After you had left.'

'I heard of it,' Kit said. 'But that was a very long time ago, Henry. Twenty years ago. And he will return here as your inferior. As your subject.'

'He also murdered my son,' Henry said.

'I doubt he really had anything to do with that,' Kit said. 'That decision was undoubtedly taken by his sister Madeleine.' He bit his lip, and looked at Richilde again, realising that he might have said too much. 'And that was a time when fears and passions were running high. Nothing would more thoroughly convince the world of your stature were you to bury that particular hatchet.'

'*I* will convince the world,' Henry said. 'I will convince them by my deeds, by my strength, by my power. But I cannot convince the world if I cannot convince my own people. If I cannot convince myself. I have sworn that no Frenchman shall ever set foot in the land again. And I have sworn that if I ever set eyes upon Etienne de Mortmain again, I shall kill him with my own hands. These oaths I shall keep, and if the world does not like it, then the world will have to put up with it. I will not rule to please the world. I will rule, for Haiti, as I am its King.' He glared at the three white people, and then suddenly allowed his face to dissolve into a smile. 'But we are not here to quarrel. We are not here even to discuss affairs of state. We are here for a much happier occasion. For a marriage. Come here, Madame Palourdes.'

Seraphine approached him, slowly, face flushed, breathing heavily.

'And you, Kit,' Henry commanded.

Kit also went forward, had his hand seized, and placed on top of Seraphine's.

'By the authority I possess as President of Haiti,' Henry said. 'I now pronounce you man and wife.'

'You do not look happy,' Henry said. 'Why do you not look happy? Do you not wish to be married to her, Kit?'

Kit glanced at the woman. 'We had thought to be married in a church, and by a priest.'

'Bah. The vault of heaven is your church, or should be. As for a priest, we have none. None in your religion, anyway. But, as President and King of Haiti, I am a priest, a *hougan*.' He smiled at their expressions. 'Do not worry, I am not going to chop anyone's head off to prove it. Yet do I have that authority. As for the priests of your religion, we will have them back, soon enough. But will it not be me who will appoint them? Therefore any authority that they can have, must come from me. Therefore anything they can do, I must be able to do better. Richilde, let us have some wine, to toast the happy couple.'

Richilde filled four goblets with red wine, offered Kit and Seraphine one each.

Henry raised his glass. 'I drink to your future happiness. And to yours, Madame Hamilton.'

'As do I,' Richilde said, and kissed Seraphine on the cheek. 'Kit will make you happy, my dear. I know he will.'

They gazed at each other.

'And now, a feast,' Henry said. 'Tell the cooks, Richilde. Tell them we wish a banquet, and send for Gounod and his wife, and Labalastierre and his wife, and Foucans and his wife. We shall have a party. We have much to celebrate. Kit has a wife, Seraphine has a husband, and I have powder and ball for my soldiers.'

Kit did not doubt that this last was the real cause for the celebration. It was, indeed, unusual to see Henry so thoroughly determined to enjoy himself, just as it was unusual to see him take more than a single glass of wine. But this evening he laughed, and joked with his officers, and even kissed Richilde before them, and allowed the huge power of his personality to flow over them.

'Because it will happen,' he said. 'It is *there*. We have the power, now. The power to do what we wish, what we seek. The power to rule.' He brooded down the table. 'The power to punish.' His head turned, as he could feel Richilde's eyes. 'I swore an oath. To destroy that man. If a man breaks his oath, if a man does not avenge his dead son, then he has no right to call himself a man.'

Richilde said nothing. Kit could only marvel at her obvious adoration of this man. So why had Henry never married her? Why did he not marry her now, as he was in a marrying mood? Could it be, that after all of these years, something of the relationship between slave and mistress still remained? It was difficult to doubt that he loved her.

But, married or not, aware or not, as Richilde

501

undoubtedly was, of the immense angry power her patient love so barely restrained, they were happy. She was happy. He looked at the woman seated beside him. She had eaten almost nothing, and had just allowed the wine to brush her lips.

As Henry had noticed. 'Your bride is impatient,' he said. 'And we are showing no manners, in keeping her waiting here. Do you retire, Kit, to the reward you have earned so well.' He pointed. 'And do not fail to accomplish your duty this night, eh? I will personally have the situation investigated tomorrow morning. See to it.'

Seraphine stood up. Kit hesitated but a moment, and then followed her from the room, pausing only in the doorway to bow to the party.

She walked in front of him down the corridor, black hair swaying; this night she had been given no time to prepare herself, even by dressing her hair.

She opened the bedroom door, went inside. The covers on the bed had already been turned down.

Kit closed the door. 'He means well,' he said. 'Henry. It is just that he is impatient of custom and habit, of tradition and manners. You cannot blame him for being those things. He was born and lived a slave for the first twenty years of his life.'

'And you support him, because you knew him then.' She did not look at him, even removed herself from the line of the mirror, so that she could not see herself, as she released her gown, shrugged it from her shoulders.

'I knew him from the moment of his birth,' Kit said. 'But I do not support him for that reason. Sometimes I do not *know* why I support him. Save that I believe he is a great man, in his instincts, his ambitions, what he would do, and that he is the leader these people want, and need, and must have, if they are not to revert to savagery.'

He watched the beauty unveiling itself before him. He had, in fact, not remembered her with any accuracy, he discovered. He had not been able to see her prop-

502

erly, as she had hung in the darkness outside Dessalines's kraal, even had he wished to look. But now he wished to look. The too thin girl had become the most perfect woman. The breasts were larger than he had remembered, and the thighs more perfectly shaped, as the legs remained long and slender, delicately muscled at thigh and calf, muscles which revealed themselves as waves of tension swept through her body.

And through his own. He had not touched a woman in too long. But she was not smiling. Her mouth was tight, as if she was holding back an immense desire to scream. Memories of Annette swept through his mind.

'He will not really investigate us tomorrow morning,' he said. 'There is a bolster on that bed, if you wish to place it between us.'

At last she turned, inhaling. 'I am not afraid of you, monsieur,' she said. 'If I am anxious, it is a fear of being hurt. Albert often hurt me. And Dessalines ... Dessalines savaged me.'

'I will not hurt you,' Kit said.

'Then take me now, monsieur, and love me. Show me that it is possible to love, and not to hurt.'

He swept her from the floor, laid her on the bed, undressed, took her in his arms. His own desire was swelling, overwhelming, unquenchable. Yet he would have prepared her, loved her, made her desire him as much as he desired her. But her lips remained closed to his kiss, her body made no response to his fingers. So in the end he could only take her as she had feared, and as he had done once before. Even that was a joy, just to feel her body against his while he surged into her in a paroxysm of passion. But it was a selfish joy, which faded the moment he was spent, and he could raise his head, and look at her, and watch the tears rolling down her cheeks.

'We offer our congratulations to the President on the ratification of his election by the people of Haiti,' Alexander Petion said. 'We speak on behalf of all our people in the south.' He stood before his delegation of half a dozen officers, headed as usual by Jean Boyer, facing Henry, who was seated at the head of the council table in the gubernatorial palace, surrounded by *his* officers; but he had some thirty men around him. Richilde sat with the wives, on the right of the room.

'I thank you, General Petion,' Henry said, his face hard.

'We wish you a happy and prosperous, and successful, four years in office,' Petion went on, and turned his head, as if looking for someone. 'May we inquire, Mr President, if the American sea captain has yet returned? We observed no ships in the harbour.'

'He has been, and he has left again,' Henry said. 'His business is trade. The trade of Haiti.'

Petion allowed himself a slight smile. 'But there is no trade here in Cap François, Your Excellency.'

'There is trade in Port-au-Prince?'

'We are visited by ships,' Petion said. 'And people. There are people would do business with us, can we but promise them a profit.'

'French people,' Henry said, his voice deceptively quiet.

'People of French descent, certainly,' Petion said. 'As they speak the same language as ourselves, they find it most convenient to represent · their less fortunate countrymen. They are largely from New Orleans. That is a city in the American territory of Louisiana, Your Excellency, and like Haiti, belonged to France but a few years ago.'

Henry refused to rise to the bait of becoming angry at the implied slight on his knowledge of the outside world. 'I know where New Orleans is,' he said, quietly. 'But you are also receiving back Frenchmen from Haiti. Planters and the like.'

Petion inclined his head. 'I am negotiating with them for their return, on behalf of your administration, to be sure. We need their skills, as I am sure you appreciate,

Your Excellency. You are finding difficulty in attracting American resources, even with an American to negotiate for you. But they will be more prepared to trade with us when they know that we are making a multiracial society here, that white people, even those who . . .' his gaze drifted to Richilde, 'are not especially privileged, may yet live at peace and in prosperity in our midst.'

Henry pointed. 'No white people, unless, General Petion, they are especially privileged by reason of their services to the state, are welcome here. Or will ever be welcome here. I am displeased that you should have undertaken such a course of action without reference to me. That is tantamount to an act of treason.'

Petion's head came up. 'A president rules with the aid and advice of his cabinet, and ultimately, with the consent of his people, Your Excellency,' he said. 'I am not aware that you have yet formed a cabinet.'

'What do you suppose this is?' Henry asked.

Petion gave a contemptuous shrug. 'This is some sort of a council. To which you read lectures. This has no aspect of democracy in it. This is an absurdity. I have put forward a serious proposition which in my opinion, and in the opinion of my advisers, is for the good of the state. Of Haiti.' His lips curled as if he still found the name distasteful. 'It is not to be turned aside merely because of personal hatreds felt by you and a few others. Nor am I to be lectured as if I were some clerk. I am Vice President of Haiti.'

'I doubt you will remain Vice President of Haiti very much longer, if you continue to defy me,' Henry remarked, his voice a low growl. And Richilde suddenly realised that he was choosing this moment for his coup d'etat. Without confiding his intention to anyone. Not even to her. Her heart began to pound, and she was aware of a rush of sweat on her neck and shoulders. But no fear. It was impossible to fear, when Henry decided to act.

Petion stared at him. 'Do you suppose you can dismiss me, Christophe?' he demanded. 'I have been elected by the people.'

'By less than a quarter of the people.'

'Nonetheless, I have been constitutionally elected. I have rights. I have the right to put forward certain policies, and have them debated by the entire council, not dismissed out of hand, as if you were some monarch, and I some puling courtier.'

Henry stood up. He had donned his red hussar uniform for this occasion, and now his immense presence seemed to fill the room. 'I am a monarch,' he said. 'As of this moment. I declare myself to be a monarch. My people have chosen me. I declare myself to be Henry, King of Haiti. No! this is a great land, and will be greater. I declare myself Henry, *Emperor* of Haiti.'

Even the black officers seemed taken entirely by surprise, while the mulattos seemed to move insensibly closer together, except for Boyer, who, Richilde discovered to her embarrassment, was looking at her. He well knew the influence she possessed.

Petion continued to stare at the huge figure in front of him in total consternation. 'That is not legal,' he said at last.

'What do I care for legality?' Henry thundered. 'I make the laws, as of now. I *am* the law.'

'You ... you are another Dessalines,' Petion shouted. 'A tyrant and a murderer.'

'I am your King,' Henry said. 'Chosen by his people.'

'Not a single mulatto cast his vote for you, Your Excellency,' Boyer said, quietly. And Richilde caught her breath. Somehow she did not really care what happened to Petion. But Boyer, so courageous and so courteous, and so reliable, she thought, as a man ...

'No doubt they were confused,' Henry said, also now speaking quietly again. 'Or coerced. But you gentlemen have the opportunity to make amends for the shortcomings of your people, here and now. On your knees, to swear allegiance to your Emperor.'

'You . . . you . . . ' Petion seemed temporarily to have lost the power of speech. But he recovered himself quickly enough. 'Swear allegiance to you? *Henry*. You are supposed to be ruling a French speaking nation, not an English speaking one. You do not even have the right name.'

Henry considered the point, without either haste or anger, without even the confusion which might have been expected. 'You are quite right,' he said at last. 'I will change my name, for the sake of my people. I am the Emperor Henri, of Haiti. On your knees.'

'I'll be damned if I will,' Petion shouted.

'You'll be hanged if you don't,' Henry said.

Petion gazed at him. 'You . . . do you suppose my people will stand idly by and watch this happen? Do you suppose your savages have any chance against my trained soldiers? Your *hussars*, with their two cartridges a man.'

'You are mistaken,' Henry said. 'Captain Hamilton did not *altogether* fail in his attempts to bring me supply. He brought me powder and ball, General Petion. I have fifty thousand men under arms, and I can raise many more. And arm them, and give them bullets to shoot with. This is your last chance to save your people from destruction. On your knees.'

Petion struck a pose, hand thrust into his coat. He had, Richilde remembered, been in Paris during the Convention and the Terror, had no doubt witnessed the deaths of Robespierre and Danton. Yet there *was* something heroic about the little man, defying the might and power of Henri Christophe. 'Never,' he shouted.

Henry's brows drew together. Then his hand came up, again pointing. 'Take that man outside and hang him,' he commanded. 'And all of his people with him.'

Petion gasped, and looked right and left as the red uniformed guards moved forward. Richilde drew a long breath, and stood up.

'Your Majesty,' she said.

Henry's head turned, sharply. It was the first time he had actually been addressed in such terms.

'I would but remind Your Majesty,' Richilde said. 'That General Petion and his officers came here under a guarantee of safe conduct, issued by yourself. A guarantee you must honour, if you are truly to prove yourself worthy of leading your people to peace and prosperity, and international recognition.'

Henry glared at her for several seconds, while again she held her breath. Indeed, everyone in the huge room might have been holding their breaths.

'And will these scoundrels not conspire against me, the moment they are safely back in Port-au-Prince?' he demanded at last.

'Then you may arrest them, and execute them, Your Majesty,' she said. 'Without in any way contravening your honour. Their future existence is in their own hands, once they leave Cap François on this occasion.'

Henry turned away from her, 'Madame de Mortmain has interceded for you,' he said. 'And reminded me of my honour. So be it. But as of this moment you are dismissed from your privileges and prerogatives, either as Governor of the south . . .' he looked at Petion. 'Or as officers in the army.' This time he looked at Boyer. 'Captain Gounod will accompany you to Port-au-Prince and disband your puerile militia. And my advice to you, General Petion, and your people, is to think very carefully. Those who do not serve their Emperor are his enemies, and the enemies of Haiti. They will be exterminated. And you can tell your French friends that every one of them that sets foot in Haiti will be shot.' He leaned forward, resting on his hands. 'And Etienne de Mortmain, should *he* ever dare to return here, will be flayed alive. Tell him that. Now get out. Crawl back to your holes, and stay there, lest I tread on your necks.'

Petion gazed at him for a moment, and then turned and left the room. His officers followed him. Boyer alone hesitated to salute, before bringing up the rear.

And the council chamber was silent. But that Henry was deeply angry could not be doubted. His entire torso seemed to swell as he breathed. He had been challenged, and as ever when challenged, his instincts had been to seize his antagonist and squeeze the life from his lungs. Now his frustration was plain to see.

But he had taken the most important step of his life. Could he but be reminded of it. Richilde stepped away from the women. 'Long live the Emperor,' she shouted. 'Henri, of Haiti. Now is the prophecy fulfilled. Long live the Emperor.'

Chapter 2

SANS SOUCI

Christophe's palace of Sans Souci outside his capital city of Millot was unashamedly a copy of its European namesake, a fabulous accumulation of halls and marble pillars, of ballrooms and reception rooms, built around a staircase which even when surrounded by a hundred and fifty years of decay takes away the breath.

Richilde sketched the crown, taking her inspiration from the several pictures of crowns to be found in the few books which had survived the destruction of the library when Henry had burned Cap François in 1802, but keeping the design as simple as possible, merely a circlet with six prongs. A blacksmith made it out of iron, polished the metal to a brilliant shine, and then Henry faced his people in the main square of the city.

They had come from far and wide, abandoning farms and villages and fishing boats to converge on Cap François, until Richilde estimated there must have been well over a hundred thousand people jammed into the square and the approach streets, restrained by the soldiers in their reds and blues and whites, steaming and chattering in the midday sun. In the centre of the square, facing the site of the old Hotel de Ville, a platform had been erected. It stood close by the gaol, and brought back a flood of memories, at least to her, of the night Ferrand de Beaudierre had been torn to pieces by the mob, that night, she had no doubt, when the

510

sequence of events which had led to this revolution had truly started.

And the night of the day when Henry Christopher, for the first and only time in his life, had been suspended from the triangle and flogged. And now, not quite twenty years later, he stood alone on the dais, surrounded by the people who had chosen him to be their Emperor. It had been his decision to mount the platform by himself. His Generals formed a cluster at the foot of the steps. Their women, and his, stood together, just in front of the main crowd, Seraphine Hamilton, as sad faced and resigned as ever, shoulder to shoulder with Richilde. There was no point in feeling disappointed, however, Richilde knew. However much she might have dreamed of standing beside him when he achieved the greatest moment of his life, as she had stood beside him on so many other occasions, tragic as well as happy, horrific as well as famous, she understood that this had to be *his* moment. The people of Haiti wished to observe no human weakness in their Emperor. And how could they, she asked herself, when Henry had no human weaknesses?

That he was their choice, and that he was carrying out their will, however subconsciously it might be expressed, could not be doubted. They laughed and they cheered, and they called his name, and the roar when he mounted the dais sent the birds scurrying out to sea and into the jungle.

'Henri,' they roared. 'Henri,' as if they had been waiting for twenty years to call him by his, to them, proper name.

He made a magnificent figure, for over his red hussar uniform, surmounted by its black busby, and with his gold hilted sword hanging by his side, he had thrown the red cloak of the *hougan*, which swirled about him as he climbed the steps, and turned to face the crowd. His face was solemn, even hard, but his eyes glinted with triumph. Of them all, who had dreamed, and fought, and died, out of Toussaint and Jean François, Céléste and Boukman, James Ogé and Jacques Chavannes, Louis-Pierre and Dessalines, he alone had bestrode the revolution from its beginning, and still survived, to reap the rewards of victory.

He raised his arms, and silence slowly crept across the square. 'My people,' he shouted. 'I come before you, as your Emperor. Tell me straight, would you have me as your ruler, to be henceforth obeyed without question?'

'Yes,' they bellowed with a tremendous shout.

'Then be it so,' Henry said, and pointed, down at General Labalastierre, who now came slowly up the steps, bearing the iron crown on a red velvet cushion. Henry took off the busby, handed it to the General, then grasped the crown and raised it above his head.

'Kneel,' he commanded.

The entire concourse settled themselves on their knees. The square rustled and thumped and sighed, and then sank into an immense silence.

'In the name of Ogone Badagris,' Henry shouted. 'And of Damballah Oueddo, great lords of the heavens, and of the lords Loco and Agone, and the great mistress of the skies, Ezilee the gentle, and of the Prophets Jesus Christ and Mohammed, and of all those who claim to speak in the name of the eternal ruler of heaven and earth, wind and water, men and beasts, but most of all, in the name of the people of Haiti, whose chosen king I am, I proclaim myself, Henri, Emperor of Haiti.'

'A staircase,' Henry said. 'I wish a central staircase. It shall be of iron, and it shall reach up and up, to the very roof of the palace. It will be wide, and yet it will curve, and spiral. It will make the grand staircase at Vergée d'Or look like a ladder. Design me such a staircase, Richilde.'

An entire bedchamber of the palace in Cap François

had been cleared of furniture, and covered with sheets of paper. In their midst Richilde crawled, or sprawled, with ruler and pencil. With her were several black draughtsmen. But none of them truly knew anything of the principles of architecture. Richilde was reaching back into her memory, of pictures of Frederick the Great's palace of Sans Souci at Potsdam, and forward into her imagination, to create a fitting home for an emperor.

Who stood above her, looking down at the drawings.

'You will have a grand staircase, Your Majesty,' Richilde promised. 'It will go here . . .' she marked the plan. 'And it will ascend for four stories.'

'Four stories?' Henry demanded. 'That does not seem a very large palace.'

'Vergée d'Or chateau was only three stories high,' she reminded him. 'We shall have great galleries extending from it, on four sides. It will be the focal point of the entire house. Now here, on the ground floor, will be the reception rooms. One for receiving foreign ambassadors. Not large, you see, Your Majesty, but sufficient.'

'Foreign ambassadors,' Henry said, gloomily.

'They will come,' Richilde promised him. 'And then, on the other side, will be the great ballroom, for when you wish to have a Court occasion. Behind that will be the kitchens and the wine stores.'

'There is no dining room,' Henry protested. 'We must have a dining room.'

'The dining room is here, on the first floor.' Richilde showed him another piece of paper.

'It does not look very large,' he grumbled.

'I have deliberately not made it very large,' she explained. 'I think that dining with the Emperor should be a great privilege, and should be confined to small groups of people at a time. That is the way to get to know your people, to understand what they are thinking, what they are trying to attain. During small and intimate dinner parties.'

'Should *they* not be trying to attain what *I* am trying to attain?' he demanded.

'They will hold opinions of their own,' she said. 'You must always allow them to do that, and to tell you those opinions. You do not have to do everything they suggest. Or anything they suggest, for that matter. But it must be for the good of the nation that you sift the ideas of other men, and choose the best.'

'Ha,' he said. 'Where do I make the grand entry? I wish there to be a grand entry.'

'Down the staircase, Your Majesty.' She indicated the plan again. 'This hall extends the entire width of the building and reaches as high as the ceiling also. It is a vast vault, down the very centre of which will flow the staircase. Thus, when you leave your apartments on the top floor, and begin to descend, you will be seen coming down, by everyone gathered in the great hall. I would suggest that you leave your apartments attended only by . . .' she glanced at him, but his face was expressionless, 'your lady, and a few attendants, and that your lords and their ladies should be waiting to join you on each level, so that when you start upon the final spiral of the staircase, you will be leading an assembly of all your most eminent men and women.'

'Lords and ladies,' he said, thoughtfully. 'I have no lords and ladies.'

'You must create them, Your Majesty. You are Emperor of Haiti. You must have a nobility. Napoleon created his own nobility, out of his Generals.'

'A nobility.' He walked to the window, looked out at the city. 'A nobility. Yes, I shall have to consider that.' He turned, and gave a shout of laughter. 'You! Richilde de Mortmain! Rise! I will commence my nobility with you. As of this moment . . .' he frowned. 'What is the highest rank I can give you?'

Richilde drew a long breath. 'The highest female rank in the land is obviously that of Empress, Your Majesty.' She hesitated, but he merely gazed at her. 'The next below that would be Duchess, I would think.'

514

'Duchess. Yes. That is a fine sounding title. As of this moment you are Duchess.'

'I must be Duchess of Something, Your Majesty.'

'Of course. You are the Duchess of Sans Souci. Come here and embrace your Emperor, as the first Duchess of the realm.'

She went forward, and was squeezed in that giant embrace, while the draughtsmen stood with bowed head.

'And are you happy, my Henry?' she whispered against his chest. 'Now that you can make all of your dreams come true?'

'Happy,' he said. 'How can an emperor be happy, my Richilde? How can I be happy, until I hear from Petion?'

General Gounod stood with bowed head. Behind him in the square in front of the palace his men also waited, dishevelled and undisciplined, many without even their weapons, their uniforms torn and tarnished.

The Emperor stood before them, his hands on his hips, his head seeming to toss with anger as he looked at them. 'Independence?' he inquired. 'They have declared independence?' he roared. 'And you let them? You let yourself be defeated?'

'We were outnumbered, Majesty,' Gounod protested. 'And they were led by Boyer. A skilful commander, Majesty. It was all we could do to fight our way clear, and make our retreat into the mountains. There I left a strong force, to guard the passes and protect the plains, before returning here. But they did not march in pursuit. They themselves were busy fortifying the passes, against us.'

'To guard the passes, and protect the plains,' Henry said contemptuously. 'You are a failure, Gounod. I should have your head. No doubt I *will* have your head, soon enough. Protect the passes.' He turned away, stamped into the palace. 'General Labalastierre, you will order a general mobilisation. Every man who can carry arms, and for whom we can find a weapon. Send a messenger to General Faucans in the west. Tell him I wish his troops to concentrate, south of Millot, in one week's time. Tell them we go to war, and that this time we shall exterminate these half breed scum.'

'Yes, my Emperor,' Labalastierre said, and left the room.

Henry looked at Richilde, waiting at the top of the stairs. 'You have done me an ill service, madame,' he said. 'In begging lenience for Petion and Boyer and their crew. No doubt you consider that you owe them your life. I understand that, and I forgive you, this time. But do not beg for their necks when they are dragged here before me.'

Richilde came down the steps. 'I sought the preservation of your honour, Your Majesty,' she said. 'Rather than the settlement of any debts of mine. And again I must beg Your Majesty to practice patience, and forbearance.'

He frowned at her. 'What are you saying?'

'And even commonsense,' she said. 'Your Majesty, Henry, I beg of you, where is the sense in going to war against a handful of mulattos? They hold one city, and a small strip of land beyond the mountains. The south is a place in which you have never even been sufficiently interested to visit. They have not attempted to capitalise on their victory over Gounod. They know their weaknesses. Yet will they be difficult to conquer. Boyer and Petion know how to fight this kind of a war. They have practised the art, often enough, at your side, my Emperor. So you will launch this tortured land once again into ten years of conflict, and destroy everything you have set out to achieve. Has not Kit been here, and with seven ships, to load our sugar? Is it not the finest crop we have had since the revolution? That is because your people have been at peace, instead of war. And because of that, have you not been promised credits, and even recognition? Have you not Sans Souci to complete, and your nation to raise to prosperity? Have you not the Citadel of La Ferriere to build? Would you squander all of those achievements in the pursuit of some bush feud against a totally unimportant group of men?'

'You would have me do nothing?' he roared. 'Those people, those mulattos, set upon my army and my governor, and defeated them, drove them out. They have killed my soldiers. And now they declare themselves an independent republic. And you would have me do *nothing*? That is honour? That is how an emperor behaves? That is how Napoleon would behave?'

'Napoleon's mistakes have only arisen when he has allowed his heart to rule his head, Your Majesty,' Richilde said. 'You must never make that mistake yourself. I am not saying that you should never settle with Petion, that you should never reclaim the Spanish half of the island. I am begging you to arrange your tasks in a proper order of priority. Here, in the north, you have the heart of Haiti. Here you have the richest canefields, the most cattle, and the most people. And here you are absolutely certain of the love and respect of your people. This is your base, your rock, upon which you must build. I am but begging you to make this part of Haiti, the true Haiti, an impregnable fortress, before you undertake the reconquest of its outer fringes. And it must be impregnable not merely in the size of its army, in its castles and its guns, but it must be impregnable in the wealth and prosperity of its people, the respect in which they are held by the rest of the world. Accomplish that, Your Majesty, because that is the greatest task before you, and let Petion and his friends wriggle away to themselves, and I will make you a prophecy: when Haiti is so strong that dealing with Petion will be but the work of a week, then will you no longer have to deal with him at all, because he will no longer be able to stand against you.'

Henry stared at her for several seconds, then looked

at Gounod, still waiting in the doorway. The Emperor chewed his lip, the savage in him still wrestling with the would-be statesman. Then he pointed at one of his aides. 'You,' he said. 'Recall General Labalastierre.'

'It will be quite a building.' Kit Hamilton sat his horse beside his sister, gazed at the walls of Sans Souci, gleaming white in the afternoon sunlight, rising out of the huge park which had been cleared by Henry's workmen. '*They* are certainly impressed.'

Together they looked at the group of white men, American merchants and bankers, whom Kit had at last persuaded to accompany him on an all expenses paid visit to Haiti, to view for themselves the potential and also the orderliness of the new country, and who were now being taken on a guided tour by the Emperor himself, Generals Labalastierre and Gounod at his side, their height and breadth and brilliant uniforms dominating the sombre browns and blacks worn by the white men.

'What will he do next?' Kit asked, as they turned away.

'He plans a city, around the palace. And of course, after that he plans his citadel up in the mountains. He has had that dream for so long I do not know if I will be able to dissuade him of it. But at least it is several years in the future, and I would not have you suppose he deals only in grandeur. He is already implementing a tremendous cattle ranching programme in the plains, rounding up the wild animals there and domesticating them. He is projecting a great extension of acreage under cane, here on the coast. And he has created a huge fishing fleet.'

'But he still dreams of going to war.'

'Well . . .' she glanced at him. 'He *is* a soldier, by instinct.'

'It is quite a source of wonder, in New York, that he has not yet fought it out with Petion. Some say it is because he knows his own weakness.'

'Now you know that cannot be true, Kit,' she protested. 'In cold terms. But he understands that it will be a long and bitter war. That Petion and Boyer will fight the sort of defensive campaigns against him that he and Toussaint and Dessalines fought so successfully against the British. And he understands more that it will cost all the money he is so hardly accumulating, and mean the end of his plans for the country. So he is content to wait.'

'You persuaded him to understand these things?'

She flushed. 'He sometimes gets so *angry* he just cannot see the wood for trees.'

'Why, do you help him so?' Kit asked.

She frowned. 'Should I not? He needs my help. And he is my . . .' she hesitated.

'Quite,' Kit said.

'I love him,' she said, defiantly. 'And through him, I love the people of Haiti. They have the capacity to be a good people. Even more important, they have the capacity to show black people the way to go, the way to take their proper place in a white man's world. Can you deny that more and more of them will soon be given the chance? Great Britain has abolished the slave trade. So have most of the countries in Europe, save for Spain and Portugal. And that will follow. Even the United States will follow. And the next logical step after the abolition of the trade is the abolition of slavery itself. And that too will follow.'

'I don't doubt that you are right, Richilde,' he said. 'There is already a strong movement towards that in England. When the war with France ends, if it ever does, I think Abolition may well come about. And I think this is a splendid experiment, if you like, even if I doubt that either Britain or France will follow Emancipation by allowing any other black kingdoms, or mulatto republics, to spawn, here in the West Indies. But I cannot think of a better man than Henry to make it happen, here. With you at his side. In fact I can think of no other man who *could* make it happen. Not even

Toussaint, because Toussaint was too broad-minded, too willing to see the other man's point of view. He lacked the iron that Henry commands in his mind and his will. But he, even he, could not do it without you. You have stood at his shoulder for twenty years. And what is your reward? To be made the Duchess of Sans Souci. Hardly a compliment when you consider some of the other titles he has bestowed.'

'He has an imagination,' she said, 'which is wholly uninstructed, uninformed. He is not truly aware of what may be considered ridiculous. You brought him some marmalade, which he happened to enjoy. But he liked the word better. It rippled off his tongue. Marmalade. So he made Gounod the Duke of Marmalade. Is that any more ridiculous than having the Duke of some little island or county in England? And he knows and values sunshine. If he recognises anything in heaven or earth as being actually greater than himself, it is the sun. So he has named Labalastierre the Prince of Sunshine. These things do not seem absurd to him.'

'Yet do they tell the world that he is nothing but an unlettered savage.'

'Let the world of *lettered* men equal anything that he has accomplished before they jeer,' she said, angrily.

'And you are content, to remain his mistress, because you love him.'

'Because he makes me happy,' she said. 'As I make him happy. Are you happy, Kit?'

His head turned away, and she instantly regretted her words.

'I am sorry,' she said. 'I did not mean . . .' she sighed. 'Is there nothing you can do?'

'Do?' he asked bitterly. 'I sometimes wonder if she is actually aware of my presence, even when I lie on her. I am cursed, in my relations with women, and there it is.' His fingers curled into fists. 'I sometimes think that perhaps I am wrong, to be gentle with her. Perhaps I should flog her, or kick her. It would at least awaken some reaction. With Annette, one was at least aware of hatred. With Seraphine there is nothing. She could be a painting hanging on the wall, save that she moves and breathes.'

'Perhaps she is afraid to feel,' Richilde said. 'Because whenever she has felt in the past it has meant pain, either mental or physical.'

'Then, as I have said, she is just as mad as ever Annette is, and I am the most misbegotten of men.' He sighed, glanced at her as their horses picked their own way down the road towards Cap François. 'Did you know they are all back in Haiti?'

She frowned at him. 'Etienne?'

'And Annette, and Louise, and even Madeleine.'

'My God. But . . .'

'Aye. I wrote to him, and warned him of Henry's implacable hatred, and he returned a cold answer. He has been given a plantation, by Petion, and dreams of rebuilding the family name and the family fortune. As he has always dreamed.'

'But to bring them back here,' she said. 'Madeleine . . . does she not wish to be with her own?'

'Her children have grown up, and are too English for her, I think. Certainly they find her too French for them. But do not suppose Madeleine is the cold fish she pretends, beneath that composed exterior of hers. She hates, just as strongly as Etienne or Annette. She remembers the destruction of her family, and looks to see the Negroes restored to their proper servitude. Nor do they doubt for a moment that it will happen, that the blacks are so incapable of enjoying freedom or of managing their own affairs that Henry's kingdom must collapse in civil war, and soon. That is why I think you were wrong to restrain him from immediately invading the south, and settling the matter once and for all. There can never be peace in Haiti, while people like Etienne and Madeleine and Annette are whispering in Petion's ear.'

'There is peace now,' she said. 'And that is what Haiti needs. And would you have had them destroyed? Your own cousins? Together with countless others? I would rather let nature take its course. Etienne, Madeleine, Annette, they will not live forever. All the generation which remember August 1791, and which hates, will fade away in time.'

'As will Henry, you know. How old is he now?'

She gazed at him. 'He will be forty-eight years old this December,' she said. 'As will I. I know we are growing old.' Even if she found it an impossible fact to accept. But she was still thinking of Kit and his problems . . . and remembering her own, as a girl. What had been done for her could surely also be done for Seraphine.

'Would you have me help you?' she asked. 'To make your wife respond to you?'

It was not difficult, through the good offices of Anjelica, the wife of General Labalastierre, and thus the Princess of Sunshine, to discover a *mamaloi* of repute. For however much the Emperor might appear as a sceptic, in the absence of Christianity as imposed for so many years by the French, voodoo was fast becoming the sole religion of the superstititous black people. But was it not, Richilde thought, a religion that in many ways she believed in herself? It reached back into the human subconscious, could not be so very different to the old European beliefs in Pan and Dionysius, Aphrodite and Artemis, which appealed perhaps to the baser instincts of humanity, but were none the less valid for that.

Of its power, there could be no doubt at all. And undoubtedly it could be used for good as well as ill, for white equally with black magic.

Anjelica Labalastierre had prepared the way, told her when the time was ripe. Up to that moment Richilde had kept her own counsel, but this night she

522

visited Kit and Seraphine, found them sitting silently and sadly in the house given them by the Emperor, Kit checking the accounts of his last voyage, Seraphine's fingers entangled with her endless and pointless needle-work.

'I have come to take you for a short journey,' Richilde said, wrapping her cloak in a cowl over her head.

They stared at her in amazement, much as she, she remembered, must have stared at Jacqueline Chavannes, so many, many years ago. But Kit at the least had an inkling of what she had in mind. He stood up. 'I have just returned from a long voyage, Richilde. I doubt we feel like society this evening.'

'I do not offer society,' Richilde said. 'And you will soon be away on another lengthy voyage, will you not? But as you are here, I have come to offer you a glimpse of happiness. Should you not come, then you are a fool, and you are both damned forever.'

Seraphine glanced from one to the other, in bewilderment.

Kit hesitated, then shrugged. 'Fetch your cloak, Seraphine,' he said.

Richilde had had the horses saddled and brought to the door, and the three of them rode out of the city, challenged on the gate, but allowed to pass the moment it was established that it was the Duchess of Sans Souci, and her brother, wishing to ride abroad, however much the commander of the guard might shake his head at the absurdities of the white people.

Richilde led them along the coast road, and then followed a fork into the interior, skirting the back of Vergée d'Or as she plunged into the jungle, following the directions given her by the Princess. Soon the track became hardly more than a path, and branches and forest creepers threatened to sweep them from their saddles. It was here she had come, again with Seraphine, but also with Petion and Boyer and Albert Palourdes, that night in 1802 when they had fled the

Cap François of the LeClercs, in search of Henry, and safety. Now she searched for something far less honourable, aware that her heart was pounding and her flesh was clammy with sweat. Here she was dabbling in things she had sought to put behind her. No, she realised, that was not true. She had never sought to put voodoo behind her. She had wanted to know more of it, to understand it, perhaps even to use it. And had never been allowed the opportunity. How strange that she had never realised that as the mistress of Henry Christophe, even when he had been no more than the General in command of Cap François, all the mysteries of obeah and the worship of the Snake God were hers for the asking.

And tonight she was going to ask. But not for herself. She would not dare that, any more, because she dared not risk knowing the answer. She could only observe, and remember.

The little hut suddenly loomed in front of them, and Richilde drew rein. 'We have arrived.'

'Here?' Seraphine had not lived in Haiti for ten years without understanding something of the society in which she moved. 'That is the house of a *mamaloi*.'

'Who is expecting us.'

'Voodoo is unspeakable,' Seraphine declared.

'I had not supposed you would sink to black magic,' Kit said. 'I doubt we can benefit from that.'

'And I promise you that you can,' Richilde said, and dismounted.

'Who comes to visit Elaine?' came the whisper.

'The Duchess of Sans Souci. And Captain Hamilton and his wife,' Richilde said.

'You are expected.'

'I do not believe in voodoo, Highness,' Seraphine said. 'Therefore it can have no effect on me, either for good or for evil.'

Richilde held the curtain for her. 'Enter,' she commanded.

Seraphine hesitated, then stepped past her into the

gloom, paused to inhale, the incense, the other smells, attractive and repulsive, which filled the room, and to stare at the *mamaloi*, crouching on the far side of the fire. Richilde's heart nearly stopped beating. It could have been Céléste, all over again. But that was the red robe, and the gnarled features, the age of the woman.

'Welcome, Madame Hamilton,' Elaine said. 'I have long waited for you to visit me.'

'I am not visiting you,' Seraphine said. 'I was brought by the Duchess.'

Elaine smiled, and stood up. 'It is still a visit, madame, and you are welcome. Come.'

Another curtain, at the back of the room, was swept aside, and Elaine led them into an inner chamber. Here it was utterly dark, save for the inevitable fire glowing in the centre of the floor, doubling the heat. Richilde felt sweat trickling down her face. Because now memory was surging through her mind, awakening her body, her every sense, making her feel every urge of her womanhood, making her dream of the tumbling ocean rollers which had finally sated her surging desire, that night thirty-three years ago.

Elaine stooped, a taper in her hand. When it glowed, she straightened, handed it to Richilde. 'Light the candles, Your Highness,' she instructed.

Richilde could see them now, set into the wall. She stepped away from Kit's side, lit each wick in turn. The room glowed; the candles were scented. She could hear Seraphine breathing. Perhaps she had anticipated a bedchamber. But it was not. It was a *love* chamber. Against the centre of the far wall – the room revealed by the flickering light was larger than it had appeared – there was a mattress, laid on the earthen floor, reaching almost as far as the fire. In the wall, above the mattress, were two rings, to which were attached buckskin thongs. At the foot of the mattress, beyond each corner, were two stakes, to which were also attached buckskin thongs. Seraphine gave a gasp, and turned, but Elaine had remained behind her.

'You practise witchcraft,' Seraphine whispered.

'In this case, white magic, madame,' Elaine said. 'Undress.'

'I will not.'

'Then you will be stripped.' Elaine stretched out her hand, stroked the material of Seraphine's collar. 'It will be a pity, to destroy a beautiful garment. And you will be humiliated. We may need to call others. Undress, Madame Hamilton. Then your secrets will belong only to this room.'

Her voice seeped around the chamber.

'My secrets?'

'You will have secrets, madame. I promise you. What, are you afraid to be naked before your husband, who would also be your lover? Before the Duchess of Sans' Souci, the most famous woman in the realm? Before me? I am an old woman, Seraphine. I have seen many naked woman, many naked men. Many more beautiful even than you.'

Her quiet voice filled the room, yet seemed to echo. It made thought difficult, when combined with the heat, and the incense. Seraphine's fingers were already at the buttons of her gown.

But she looked at Richilde. 'I will not be bewitched, Highness,' she insisted. 'You have no right to make me suffer this.'

'We do not seek to bewitch you, Seraphine,' Richilde said. 'We seek to help you.'

'We would release you from your prison,' Elaine said.

'My prison?' Perhaps without her being aware of it, Seraphine's gown was sliding past her thighs, and to the ground. She wore no stays, in the informal society that Richilde had established in Cap François. A moment later her shift joined her gown. She wore no stockings, either. Only her soft skinned riding boots.

'The prison of your mind,' Elaine said. 'Now lie down.'

Again Seraphine hesitated, glanced at Kit, and for

the first time that he could remember since their wedding night, flushed with embarrassment. Or was it only the firelight, flickering in her cheeks?

She lay down.

'Arms above your head,' Elaine said, reassuringly, and gently secured the young woman's wrists to the buckskin thongs. 'Will you not remove your wife's boots, monsieur?'

Kit knelt, unlaced Seraphine's boots. She gave an involuntary little kick, and then lay still.

'If you intend me no harm, madam,' she asked, 'why bind me?'

Elaine smiled at her. 'To keep you *from* harm, child.' She secured each ankle in turn, leaving the girl spread-eagled on the mattress. Then she rose, slowly, with the faintest rustle of material. 'You must also undress, monsieur, and stand at the foot of the bed,' she said. 'Your woman must gaze upon you, throughout the ceremony.'

Kit obeyed; the heat of the fire scorched his back, made his blood run the more quickly. But no doubt this was what the *mamaloi* intended. He glanced at Richilde, but Richilde was almost invisible in the darkness, pressed against the far wall. Now memory was almost painful in its intensity.

Elaine removed her red robe; she wore nothing underneath, possessed a younger and more heavily muscled body than her withered features had suggested might be possible. She left the bedside, stooped by a chest in the corner of the room, turned and straightened, suddenly, and rose at the same time, throwing both arms outwards, fingers extended. Drops of liquid scattered through the flickering light, brushed Kit's cheeks, fell on Seraphine's belly. The scent was at once erotic and intoxicating, sending Richilde's mind, and no doubt Kit's and Seraphine's as well, she thought, whirling into space.

Elaine began to dance, a slow movement, of belly

and thighs and groin and stomping feet, accompanying herself with clapping hands in time to the tune she sang. She moved around them, and her sex, her song, served to envelope them, to fill the room. Kit felt himself panting, felt he would explode long before he could enter the woman.

Elaine swept round the room, pausing by the chest to seize a bottle. Her movements stopped, and it seemed the entire night had stopped with them. The only sound was their breathing.

Elaine knelt before Seraphine's feet, her back touching Kit's penis, brushing it from time to time. She uncorked the bottle, poured a little into the palm of her hand, and commenced to massage the woman's toes, slowly and gently, humming the same little tune. The scent, vaguely sweet, the tune, mind-consuming in its erotic cadence, kept his mind swimming, and obviously Seraphine's as well. Richilde wished to escape the room and the enormous power of suggestion which was present here, but she could not move. She watched Seraphine staring at Kit, her breathing, which had been heavy with distaste and anticipation of discomfort when she had first lain down, subsiding until her breasts did no more than flutter.

Slowly Elaine worked, from time to time pouring more fluid into the palm of her hand. She came up Seraphine's body, from calf to thigh, from thigh to groin. Now Seraphine scarcely breathed at all, and her mouth sagged open; she was so still she might have been asleep. But her eyes remained wide, staring at Kit. And as Elaine reached her belly, her breathing began again, slowly, building up, as was his own.

Elaine's song grew louder, as she worked. Up from the belly to caress the ribs, to seek the breasts, to leave them and stroke neck and armpit, before returning, once again to stimulate the nipples into erection. Now Seraphine panted, and her ankles strained at the buckskin cords as she attempted to bend her knees. And still she stared at Kit, mouth wide, tongue circling her opened lips.

Elaine stopped, sitting astride Seraphine's thighs, picked up a fowl feather which had lain unnoticed at the side of the mattress, and very gently drew it across Seraphine's right nipple. Seraphine's body jerked, and she uttered a huge sigh, while Elaine threw back her head and gave a gigantic shout, and then leapt up, as if she were a girl.

'Now,' she screamed. 'Now, now, now.'

Kit obeyed. Could this be different to any of the others? Seraphine had never once attempted to resist him. She had always lain beneath him, in perfect submission. She could not possibly be any more submissive merely because she was secured. The difference had to be in him, that he was kneeling between her legs, before a strange woman and his sister, without feeling any embarrassment or reluctance, concerned only with the pulsing white flesh beneath him.

And Seraphine was no longer secured. Even as he reached his own climax her legs came free, to wrap themselves around his body, as a second later her arms came free, the cords loosened by Elaine, to allow her fingers to close on his back, to eat into his flesh. Jacqueline Chavannes had screamed her ecstasy. Seraphine Palourdes reached hers in silence, but her entire body tightened on his, seeming to suck him against her.

Elaine touched Richilde on the arm, and jerked her head. The two woman stepped through the curtain, into the front room of the hut, gazed in consternation at Henry Christophe.

'Did you not suppose I would know where you had gone?' he asked. 'Did you not know I would be told, immediately, that you had left the city?'

Richilde looked past him, at the hussars waiting in the doorway. 'I had no wish to deceive you, Your

Majesty,' she said, aware of a curiously empty feeling in her belly. It was the first time that he had ever appeared truly angry with her. 'I did not suppose that you would be interested.'

'I should not be interested, when you visit a *mamaloi*, to seek spells to cast across my bed and my person?'

'That is not why I came, Henry,' Richilde said, and looked at Elaine, who seemed quite undisturbed by her Emperor's anger. Quietly she drew the curtain again, and allowed Henry to look into the inner chamber, before closing it.

'The Duchess sought love for her brother, Christophe,' she said. 'That can be no crime.'

'You should have confided in me,' Henry grumbled, somewhat embarrassed.

'As she says, she did not suppose you would be interested,' Elaine said. 'But I am pleased that she has brought you to visit me, Great King, however inadvertently. I am pleased to be able to look upon your face, and into your eyes. I am pleased to be able to warn you.'

'Warn me?' Henry demanded. 'Of what can you warn me, if there is no conspiracy?' He looked left and right, into the shadows, as if expecting to discover Petion and Boyer, lurking with drawn swords.

'I would warn you of yourself, Great King,' Elaine said. She stepped forward, until she stood immediately in front of him, and reached up to stroke his cheek, tracing her finger right down his face and then across the pulsing arteries of his throat. 'You ask too much, of yourself, Christophe,' she said. 'You are killing yourself, with effort, with overwork, with endeavour. And sometimes, with anger.'

'You speak nonsense, old woman,' Henry said. 'How can I be working too hard, when I am taller, and stronger, and more able than any man in my kingdom?'

'Thus your heart has more work to do than most,' Elaine said, quietly. 'You must allow it to rest, from time to time, to beat more slowly. To enjoy some of the peacefully pleasurable things in life, and not be constantly seeking things to do, and people to fight, and ideas to excite. Hear my words, Great King, or you will not see your allotted span, and there will be a sad day for your people.'

Henry looked from her to Richilde, waiting in the shadows, scarce daring to breathe.

'You are talking nonsense,' he repeated. 'I have much to do. Time enough to rest, when I have accomplished all I must.'

Elaine sighed, and shrugged. 'You are the Emperor. You must do as you see fit. But at least let me help you to survive the envy and the hatred of mortal men.'

Henry frowned at her. 'You can do this?' he asked.

'I have that power,' she said. 'If you will believe in it.'

'Show me,' he commanded.

Elaine knelt before another of her chests, in a corner of the room, opened it, and reached into the interior. When she rose, she carried a shining object in her hand. 'Take this, Great King.'

Henry peered at it. 'A bullet? Why does it gleam?'

'Because it is a very special bullet, Great King. It is made entirely of silver.' She raised it by the cord which had been passed through its base to turn it into a pendant, allowed it to swing, gently, to and fro before him. 'I took it from the body of a French officer, during the war,' she said.

'Ha ha,' Henry remarked. 'A *dead* French officer.'

'But he died of yellow fever, Great King, despite having been in the forefront of several battles. Not a single shot could harm him while he wore this talisman.' She smiled, for Henry had involuntarily stepped backwards. 'It carries no disease, now. Take it, Great King, and wear it, and believe in it.'

Henry hesitated, then slowly stretched out his hand, and took the bullet from her fingers.

'If I believe in this, I can never be killed by mortal man?'

'If you believe in that bullet, Great King, then only that piece of silver can ever harm you, from the outside. So wear it always. Never let it from your sight, and you may enter battle without fear.'

'I have never feared, before,' Henry said, and slowly hung the silver bullet around his neck. 'What payment do you require?'

'Merely the satisfaction of knowing that I have pleased my Emperor,' she said. 'But you will remember, Great King, that that bullet only protects you from the weapons of mortal men. It will not help you against the harm that you do yourself, every minute of every day, by your unceasing labour.'

'Bah,' Henry said. 'I am the strongest man in Haiti. Only an assassin's bullet can bring me low, old woman. But I am grateful for your charm. I will wear it, as you suggest.' He held out his hand. 'Come, Richilde. You may let Kit find his own way back to Cap François. When he is ready!'

A vast crowd waited outside the palace of Sans Souci, stamping and shuffling, coughing and spitting, causing little dust storms to eddy upwards into the still air. There were farmers and their wives and children, and their chickens and their goats and their dogs, come in from the surrounding country; there were sailors from the coast; there were merchants from Cap François, together with their wives; there were soldiers, in variegated uniforms, and there were the members of the new nobility, wearing even more gaudy uniforms, with cocked hats and masses of feathers, with their ladies in silks and satins. And there was even a handful of white traders, Americans, who had come to Haiti at the invitation of Kit Hamilton, and who had remained to manage their factories. But there were no mulattos in the crowd.

Everyone present was aware that he or she was witnessing a famous occasion, as Emperor Henri solemnly cut the blue ribbon draped across the huge wooden doors, and the major domos threw them open.

Few people truly knew what to expect, whatever the rumours which had flown from mouth to ear throughout the land these past two years. Now there was a gigantic gasp, as the watchers gazed at the entry hall, the largest expanse of polished stone they had ever seen, and then at the huge curving staircase, which rose out of the centre of the hall, and then clung to the balustrades of the galleries on each floor as it slowly and gracefully mounted upwards.

This was all that the peasants were allowed to see, as they were restrained by the soliders. The nobles, and the white people, were permitted inside the building itself, to gape at the marble pillars supporting the upper floors, at the great wide galleries stretching away in every direction, at the high ceilings, and most of all, at the great dome of a roof rising sixty feet above their heads. Perhaps there was as yet insufficient furniture, and perhaps not all the pieces, garnered far and wide, from the length and breadth of the land, from the ruins of every great house which had not been entirely destroyed during the years of the revolt, truly matched. This was not a point to disturb the black people. It was the size of the palace that took away their breaths, and even that of the Americans.

'It is quite splendid, Kit,' Seraphine said, and squeezed his arm, as she so often squeezed his arm nowadays – they seemed to be perpetually honeymooning.

While the Emperor, having mounted to the very top of the staircase, could look down on the concourse, and smile. 'Is it as it should be, my Richilde?' he asked.

'Not yet,' Richilde said, seriously. 'It will be more complete when the drapes arrive from New York, and the rest of the furniture. And the walls are too bare. We must have paintings on the walls.'

'Can they not be bought in New York, also?'

'Indeed they can, Your Majesty,' she said. 'But I doubt pictures obtained in New York would be appropriate for Sans Souci. Should this palace not contain scenes of Haiti, and portraits of you and your people?'

'Of course you are right,' he agreed. 'We will have Kit find us an artist in America.'

She shook her head. 'Let you and me find us an artist, from amongst your own people, Henry. I am sure there will be some who have a natural gift with a brush. That I think would be more fitting.'

'I marvel at the scope of your mind, my dear, dear Richilde,' he said, and held her hand, to draw her from the stairs on to the gallery, and thence along a wide corridor, from off which, as she well knew, the doors opened into his own apartments. And *they* were most certainly fully furnished; the palace in Cap François had been looted for that purpose.

'Henry,' she protested, looking back at the amused black people. 'Not now. And here. We have guests.'

'I have something to show you,' he said, leading her the length of the corridor, to open another pair of double doors, and take her into a magnificent apartment, hall, reception room, bedchamber, with a pantry and kitchen secluded to the side, the whole facing the mountains and receiving a glorious fresh breeze through its opened windows. Richilde ran on to the balcony, and looked down at the grounds below, cleared for the laying out of the imperial gardens, although as yet little had been done.

'It is magnificent,' she said.

'It is yours,' Henry said.

'Mine? Oh, but . . .' she bit her lip. It had not occurred to her that she would not be sharing the imperial bedchamber, as she had always shared Henry's bedchamber. 'It is magnificent,' she said again. 'I will be able to see out over the city. Because we can commence that now, Henry. I have drawn up plans, for streets, and sewers, and . . .' She was talking, wildly, anxiously, to prevent him from uttering the words she had always feared to hear.

'We cannot commence the city now,' he said. 'Which

is not to say it cannot be built. I have given instructions that anyone who wishes may build in Millot. Providing he keeps to your street plans, of course. It will be something for you to occupy yourself with.'

'Something to . . . Henry, why cannot we build Millot, ourselves? Now? It was what we always planned to do next, once the palace was completed.'

'We start work on the citadel, tomorrow,' he said.

'The citadel?' She looked up at the mountains, rising above the palace.

'That has become necessary, now,' Henry said. 'Urgent. I should have built that before, even before this palace.'

'But why?' she cried. 'Why is it urgent now, when it was not so urgent, two years ago?'

'Great Britain has gone to war,' he said sombrely. 'With the United States. The news arrived yesterday.'

'England? And America? But why? England is still fighting Napoleon.'

'Great Britain is very powerful,' he said. 'You have told me so, time and again. As to the war with America, that appears to be a nonsense. It is apparently about the British right, which they claim, to seize ships on the high seas, and to impress some of their crews. This is what Kit has told me. But that has to be nothing more than an excuse. It is but a pretext, to launch fleets and armies once again into the West Indies. Against Haiti.'

She shook her head. 'That cannot be, Henry. I am sure of it. The British will never return here. Certainly not until they have beaten the French. Or been beaten by them.'

'You will see,' he promised. 'They will invade us again. I know exactly how they will go about it. They will treat with Petion, and he will happily treat with them, the scoundrel. Thus they will have a secure port and even allies when they begin their march to the north. Thus the citadel must be built, and in a hurry. Did I not tell you, in the forest, years ago, that I would build the most impregnable fortress the world has ever seen? A fortress to which we could always retreat, when we were attacked? And did you not reply, that if I built such a fortress, then no one would ever dare attack us? If it were there now, then we would have nothing to fear. The work commences tomorrow.'

She sighed. 'Yes, Henry.' She sat on the bed.

He stood above her. 'Do not be sad. Millot will still be built. Everything we have set out to do will still be done. We have just had to alter our priorities, that is all.' He smiled at her. 'You do not believe any of that nonsense that *mamaloi* spoke of me?'

She raised her head to gaze at him. 'Of course not, Henry.' How can I, she wondered, when you are so tall and strong and dominant, and so obviously as healthy as you have ever been in your life?

But then she thought, why *should* I not believe her, as you so obviously believe in that silver bullet?

Henry turned away from her, walked to the window, looked out at the afternoon. 'There are so many plans I have had to alter, since I became Emperor. It is sometimes hard to remain true to one's real interests, one's real path. I love you, Richilde.' He half turned, and then changed his mind, continued looking out of the window. 'I have always loved you. Have you ever doubted that?'

'No, Henry,' she said, scarce daring to breathe.

'Ever since we were children together,' he said, as if she had not spoken. 'I have loved you. I would have been content to live the rest of my life, with just you, in that little hut on the coast, fishing, and lying with you. But the French would not let us do that simple thing. And now I cannot go back. I love you, but I can never marry you. I, the black Emperor of Haiti, would betray his people were he to marry a white woman. Can you understand that?'

'I have always understood that,' she said.

'Yet must I marry. The Emperor must have an

Empress, to sit at his side on great occasions, and that he may have children, to continue his line.' Now at last he turned.

Richilde gazed at him. 'I understand that, Henry,' she said.

'Do not doubt,' he said. 'That I shall continue to love you above all other women, above life itself. These apartments are yours, and I swear that I will visit you at least once a day. I will still rely upon you, utterly, for help in the many things I must do. But I must have an Empress.'

'I understand that, Henry,' she said again, and wished he would leave before the tears came.

'You will not attempt to flee Haiti?' he asked. 'I would not allow that.'

Because the prophecy required her presence.

'I will not attempt to leave Haiti,' she said, and stood up.

He gazed at her. 'I feel this more than you,' he said. 'Were I not the Emperor . . .' he sighed, and his right hand clutched the breast of his jacket, beneath which, she knew, the silver bullet lay against his chest. Because he most certainly had come to believe in the efficacy of the talisman, even if he had never been engaged in battle since receiving it.

But it was his talisman. Not hers.

'Well, then,' he said, attempting to smile. 'I have commanded all my Generals, and all my senior citizens, to bring their daughters to the reception this evening, that I may choose one, as my Empress. They will be waiting for me, now.' He held out his hand. 'Will you come with me, and help me choose, the Empress of Haiti?'

Richilde looked at him for several seconds. Then she shook her head. 'No, Henry,' she said. 'This is one decision you must make for yourself.'

Chapter 3

THE COURT

Haiti became a showpiece of what could be accomplished by the Negro. Like the ministers of Catherine the Great's Russia, Christophe could present to the world a reasonable façade of power and prosperity provided he could keep his visitors in the halls of Sans Souci or beneath the rising shadow of La Ferriere. Many were impressed; many more came only to sneer at Negroes wearing caricatures of European uniforms and mincing about a ballroom with European airs and graces, at upstart noblemen with titles such as the Duke of Marmalade.

'Kit should have returned by now,' Seraphine said, anxiously, standing on the balcony of Richilde's apartment in the palace of Sans Souci, from whence it was possible to see the rooftops of Cap Françis in the distance, and beyond, even the ocean. 'Something has happened to him. The British . . .'

'Now, Seraphine,' Richilde said. 'The war with the British ended months ago. And the weather has been fine all year. There is nothing can have happened to Kit. He has just been delayed, that is all.' Gently she removed her finger from the babe's mouth, the chubby little hand having seized her flesh and inserted it before she had really noticed, in order to give her a hearty bite. 'I do believe little Alexander has cut another tooth.'

'No doubt.' Seraphine returned into the room,

scooped the child from her sister-in-law's lap, gave him a kiss, and then brought him against the breast exposed by the unfastened nursing bodice. 'He is always cutting teeth. One day I swear he will remove a nipple.'

'Then we should find you a wet nurse,' Richilde said.

Seraphine shot her a glance. 'No,' she said. 'No, I should prefer to continue feeding him myself.'

Richilde made no reply, picked up her needlework. Seraphine had now lived in Haiti for a dozen years and more, and for most of that time as a part of the people, rather than as an alien. Yet she would never overcome her repulsion for black skins, would not allow her child to feed from a black breast. Whereas I, she thought, would give half of my life to have a brown skinned babe at *my* breast, were such a thing possible for a near fifty-year-old.

She looked out of her window, and up into the mountains, at the towering scar which represented the citadel, rising out of the forest and the craggy escarpments. Henry was up here, superintending the building of his monument. He spent most of his time up there, left affairs of state largely to Gounod and Labalastierre, busily pursuing his dream. In fact, she knew, he had so organised his kingdom that his presence here was hardly needed. All of his people knew what he required of them, and they knew too that he *was* there, huge and terrible, if ever opposed, gigantically reassuring and rewarding, when they carried out his wishes. Undoubtedly they grumbled. Perhaps they even remembered the less hectic lives they had lived under Dessalines, or even under the French – certainly they worshipped the memory of the comparatively lazy days under Toussaint l'Ouverture. But then, they worshipped Toussaint himself, and were encouraged to do so, by the Emperor. He could explain, to her, that this was an act of policy. A nation had to have heroes, and dead heroes were safer and more reliable than live ones. But it was also, she knew, because he himself worshipped Toussaint, more than a little. The lame old coachman, whose life had been such a triumph and a tragedy, was one of the only three creatures he had ever loved in *his* life.

His mother had been the second. And she was undoubtedly the third. She might have felt more pride in belonging to such an elect group had she not always been aware of it, and had she not known that just as his worship of Toussaint had not prevented him from burning Cap François, in defiance of what he had known would be Toussaint's wish, or that his love for his mother, who had always believed it was right and proper for the black people to work for the white, had not prevented him from leading a slave revolt, so his love for her had not been allowed to interfere with his triumphant march onwards, in search of his destiny.

In many ways, she thought, not having to share his bed nightly was a considerable relief. It was not that, at forty-eight, she felt any less of a woman, that her sexual urges had in any way diminished. In fact, now that the transition to infertility had been completed, she was able to enjoy sex more than ever before, and she sought no other man but Henry. But inevitably their old intimacy had vanished. She did not think he ever repeated anything they said, or related anything they did together to the Empress Honeybelle. But he certainly related to *her* the conversations of the imperial bed, as usual seeking her comments, her ideas. As if she could possibly comment on his marriage, with any honesty. He did not love Honeybelle, she knew. Honeybelle was an extraordinarily lovely girl, tall and slender, with all the exquisite grace of her people. She had a bright and sunny disposition, and if she seemed quite unable, at eighteen, to understand the dignity that should accompany her exalted position, this unawareness certainly increased the attractiveness of her personality. She remained on the best of terms with Richilde. Like everyone else in Haiti, she knew that the Duchess of Sans Souci had been Henry's woman since the revolution, twenty-four years ago, and thus long before she had been born. And again like everyone else in Haiti, she was happy to accept the situation. Besides, Richilde sometimes thought, as she found the girl staring at her with enormous brown eyes, Honeybelle clearly found it quite impossible ever to be jealous of a woman very nearly three times her age.

Just as she found it impossible to be jealous of a girl young enough to have been her own granddaughter. Rather did she fear for her. For after more than two years of marriage, Honeybelle had not yet become pregnant. The fault was undoubtedly with the Emperor. But not even the Duchess of Sans Souci would dare tell the Emperor Henri that fact. Yet would he seek to remedy the situation soon enough, she was sure of that.

But for herself, life had settled into a very even tenor. Sometimes she managed to recall the tensions of being Philippe de Mortmain's child bride, the deluge of the revolution itself, the long days and nights in the forest, the nausea of LeClerc's administration, the constant awareness of the looming and irrational fury of Jean-Jacques Dessalines, with something like nostalgia. But on the whole she wanted only peace, and the feeling that her life had not been entirely wasted. Certainly it was not being wasted at the moment. She remained in charge of the growing township of Millot. This was, in fact, not a happy duty. There were many people who wished to live in the shadow of the palace, as Henry had prophesied, and there was no one in Haiti prepared to argue with her dispositions, with the streets she had laid out, the simple rules of sanitation that she imposed. But there was also no one in Haiti with the resources of Henri the Emperor, or even one tenth of them. So where she had dreamed of a city of marble and statues, of fountains and perhaps a flowing stream, of gardens and shade trees – a recreation, perhaps, of Cap François as she remembered it from her first morning in this strange, passionate land – she looked down on nothing more than an overgrown village of mud huts, with troolie palm thatched roofs, only occasionally enhanced by a building made of wood. But even the wooden buildings, as they reflected the whims of their owners, and particularly in regard to paint, were but garish excrescences, hurling the sunlight skywards from a variety of pinks, and pale blues and browns, and favourite of all, bright yellow walls.

The Emperor had said, let them build, and the Emperor's word was law. The most disturbing thought was that, when he had completed his fortress, he would certainly then turn all his mighty energy on his capital city of Millot, and carelessly order the destruction of all these houses, which, however poor, were still the loved possessions of a man and a woman, and have them replaced with stone according to the original plan.

But, as La Ferriere remained no more than a scar in the trees, a costly, bloody scar, the rebuilding of Millot had to be some years in the future. If it were ever to happen at all.

She listened to trumpets blaring, the thudding of hooves, laid down her work. Seraphine was already on her feet, her son clutched in her arms, staring at the door as she always did whenever there was a disturbance. She could never overcome the fears which still lurked at the back of her memory.

Richilde also gazed at the door, knowing that if Henry had returned in haste from the citadel – he had not been due at Sans Souci for another week – then some crisis was at hand, and his visit to her would not be long delayed. In fact, she realised, listening to the boots hitting the stairs and the corridors, swelling closer, he was coming to her before anyone else.

Her heart began to pound. She could think of no occurrence quite so urgent – save perhaps that something *had* happened to Kit. She glanced at Seraphine, but the Frenchwoman might have been turned to stone, scarce seemed to breathe; she had even neglected to refasten her bodice.

The double doors burst open, and Henry strode across the hall, blue uniform jacket stained with sweat, and brow as well, fingers of his left hand nervously clutching the hilt of his sword, white gowned maids scurrying to get out of his way, anxious aides remaining in a huddle on the gallery. Yet he did not look unhappy. Merely thunderstruck. 'Richilde!' he shouted. 'Richilde! There is an English ship in the harbour. Kit has brought it in.'

'Kit?' Seraphine shouted, and bit her lip as Henry glanced at her. Little Alexander began to cry.

'Kit?' Richilde asked. 'A prize, you mean? But there is no war between us.'

Henry waved his hand. 'No prize. A great warship. A ship of the line. Seventy-four guns, it has; he has seen them. And it has an admiral on board. It has come from the English King, King Regent, to present credentials at the court of the Emperor Henri. An ambassador, Richilde. An ambassador, at last. And from England.' He strode across the room, held her in his arms. 'An ambassador, at last.' Then he released her, and stood back, whole body seeming to droop. 'What must I do, Richilde? Tell me what I must do?'

From her balcony, Richilde could look down on the procession as it slowly approached Sans Souci. It was incongruous to see the naval officers mounted on horses, their legs encased in flawless white stockings rather than boots. But there could be no denying the glowing hilts of their swords, or the shine of their leather shoes, the perfect cut of their blue jackets, the jaunty angles of their tricorne hats. They were the representatives of the greatest navy in the world, a navy which ruled unchallenged over the seas, despite the gallant efforts of a few Yankee frigates.

And at their head rode Vice-Admiral Sir Home

Popham, Knight Commander of the Bath, Fellow of the Royal Society, probably the most talented if one of the least famous of all the remarkable group of officers who had come to maturity under Jervis and Nelson. His features, as seen through her glass, were curiously soft and open, for a sea captain who all his life had possessed absolute power of life and death over those who sailed beneath his command. And that he was interested in what he saw could not be doubted; his head turned from left to right, looking at the houses of Millot, asking questions of Kit, riding at his side, and then gazing up at the palace itself, before which, as she knew although she could not see them, Henry and his nobles would be waiting; once again she had declined to take her place with the ladies. She was not one of the sights to be gawked at, any longer.

Beneath her, the band struck up, as best it could, but she almost thought the Admiral, used to his own superb musicians, winced as he disappeared from her sight. She wondered what he would make of the guard of honour. At her recommendation, Henry had dismissed all of his soldiers save for his own regiment of hussars. They were the best disciplined of his men – it was possible to say they were the *only* Haitian soldiers who had the least concept of timing or orderliness in their manoeuvres – but even they were not greatly better than an armed rabble, for all their brilliant red uniforms. As Popham would very readily discern, she had no doubt at all.

Then she could only wait, for Kit and Seraphine, who had attended the official banquet, to join her.

'Oh, it was grand,' Seraphine said. 'Barbaric, but grand. If only the Empress hadn't eaten that fish with her fingers.'

'I think Popham carried it off very well,' Kit said. 'He immediately followed her example.'

'But His Majesty was displeased,' Seraphine pointed out. 'He was frowning most severely.'

'Did he remember to say King George?' Richilde asked, anxiously. 'And not King Regent?'

'He did,' Kit said. 'He was very good. And he spoke with Popham in English, which impressed the British no end. Popham is apparently this new Commander-in-Chief in Jamaica. That means he commands the entire West Indies. I think we may have a good friend there. And you'll never guess what news he's brought.'

'Not another war?'

'The end of one,' Kit said. 'After all of these years. The end of the war with the French.'

'Oh, my God,' Richilde said. 'That will set Henry to preparing to resist a French invasion, all over again.'

Kit laughed. He laughed so readily nowadays. His transparent happiness, and that of Seraphine, was perhaps her greatest achievement, Richilde thought. 'Not any more. It has ended not in a truce, but in the total defeat of the French. Napoleon has been abdicated and been sent off to some remote island. There is a Louis back on the throne, the Eighteenth, I think. Henry can at last stop worrying about the French.'

'If Bonaparte has finally been driven from power,' Seraphine said wistfully, 'perhaps we could go back. I should love to go back, at least for a visit.'

'Well, it may be possible,' Kit said. 'We shall have to persuade the Emperor to spare us for a season. Certainly I have never seen him looking so pleased. He has even accepted an invitation to dine on board the warship, tomorrow. I am to accompany him. There will be a famous occasion.'

Richilde awoke to the sound of her doors opening, sat up. Her maids had turned down the candles, and the apartments were dark, save for the moonlight streaming in the opened windows and across the floors; four stories up, and in the cool period of the year, she suffered little from mosquitoes or sandflies. And despite the gloom, there was no doubting the giant figure who stood beside her bed.

Midnight passion was unusual, between them, after so many years. 'Henry?' she asked. 'What is the matter?'

He sighed, and sat on the bed. 'I have come from the warship,' he said.

She waited.

'I never knew,' he said. 'That there could be anything so perfect in the world. I have never seen such clean decks. And the guns . . . my God, Richilde, if I had even half of those guns I could wipe Petion off the face of the map, tomorrow, And the men. They call them marines. Have you ever seen marines on parade, Richilde?'

'No, Henry,' she said.

'They wear red jackets, with silver braid, and tall hats, and white pants, and black shoes, and they carry muskets and long bayonets. And they stand, like statues, not even a wink, staring straight to their front. They are the finest men I have ever seen. How may I match such men?'

'You matched them once, do you not remember? You and Toussaint matched them, and beat them. You have naught to fear from them.'

'Fear from them?' he asked. 'You do not understand. I do not fear them. But I must *match* them. I looked at these men, these magnificent creatures, and this Admiral Popham could see that I was impressed, and he said, "My master, the Prince Regent of England, commands regiment upon regiment of men such as these. It is the finest army in the world, Your Majesty." And then he waited, for my reply. I had to reply, Richilde, as best I could, without you at my side. And so I said, "As he is a prince, Admiral, he should command many men. And he should be proud of them. But I, I am an emperor. My soldiers are as the sands of the sea. Their discipline is that of black men, severe, to be sure, but more concerned with ardour and courage, than with the stoic virtues. And their weapons are the finest in the world." I boasted to him, Richilde. I could not be rendered inferior to a mere prince.'

'What did he say?' Richilde asked.

'He thought for several moments, and then he said, "I should like to see your army, Your Majesty. I have heard much about it. I should like to see it very much." And do you know what else he said? He said, "I should also like the privilege of meeting the Duchess of Sans Souci, of whom also I have heard so much."'

'And what did you reply?' Richilde asked, softly.

'What could I reply? I said, "Then you shall see them both, Admiral. Tomorrow afternoon, you and I shall hold a grand review of my soldiers, and at that grand review, the Duchess of Sans Souci shall be present, and you may talk with her." Oh, Richilde, my Richilde, what am I to do? I have but five thousand men here in Millot. And of those, four thousand have no discipline, and their weapons are old and rusty. This Popham, he will look at them, and he will sneer at their numbers, and he will laugh at them as they march past. All the world will laugh. All the world will laugh at me, and my puny army.'

Richilde got out of bed, and stood beside him. His arms went round her waist, and he kissed her breasts. 'What am I to do, my Richilde?'

'You have in store in Cap François,' she said, 'all of the uniforms accumulated by Dessalines for the army he never had.'

'That is true,' he said. 'But I have no men to put in them. This Popham is not a fool, Richilde. He will know the difference between a soldier and a farmer dressed up in uniform. The only men I have who I can possibly set against those marines are the Imperial Guard, and they are scarce a thousand strong. I have promised him untold legions.'

'I am sure Admiral Popham is not a fool,' Richilde said. 'But he is certainly a white man, and I have heard it said that to a white man, all black faces look alike. Send to Cap François for those uniforms, Henry. And then summon the Prince of Sunshine to meet us, to discuss our plans for tomorrow. For what you have promised, you must deliver. The Duchess of Sans Souci, and the finest army in all America.'

She wore a white lawn gown, and a feather boa, tucked her hair out of sight beneath a huge straw hat, decorated with hibiscus blossoms. She was well aware that her clothes, and the style of them, were considerably out of date, but at least she would appear like no white savage. She came down the great staircase, behind Henry and the Empress to be sure, but accompanied by Seraphine and Kit, also dressed in their best, and very well aware that she was the cynosure of all eyes, and not merely those of the British officers – the black courtiers were sufficiently unused to seeing the Duchess of Sans Souci attending a state occasion.

'Your Grace,' Sir Home Popham bent low over her fingers, and spoke in English. 'I have waited for this moment with the most keen anticipation.'

'I wonder why, Sir Home,' she said. 'I am but a woman.'

'A very famous one,' he pointed out.

'Am I, famous? Outside of Haiti?'

'Indeed you are. They have written about you, poems and even a novel. But I am afraid those gentlemen scribblers knew very little about what they described.'

She smiled, 'No doubt I am depicted as a naked savage.'

'Very much so,' Popham agreed. 'With your hair down to your ankles and a bow and arrow ever at your side.'

'Well, sir,' she said. 'I do have hair which stretches a long way, when loosed. And there have been occasions when I have longed for a bow and arrow readily to hand. But I think that at my age running naked through the forest would be tiresome. I should like to read one of these stories. Would that be possible?'

'I shall obtain one for you, and send it to you, you have my word,' Popham promised.

'The parade is about begin,' Henry said, also speaking English. 'The Duchess will sit with you, Sir Popham, and you may continue your conversation.'

He was anxious, and would indeed have preferred Richilde to be able to engage the Admiral in conversation throughout the review. But Popham, although the soul of politeness, and alertness, quick to reply to any of her remarks, was also an acute and interested observer, of the troops which now began to pass before him.

'You will understand, Sir Home,' Richilde explained, 'that His Majesty has ordered but one company of each regiment to appear today. To review the entire army would be most tedious, and besides, as you will know, we are in a state of war with the south, which could erupt into actual fighting at any moment, thus a considerable proportion of our troops are already deployed in the mountains.'

'Indeed I understand that,' Popham agreed. 'And it is very good of His Majesty to take so much time to show me his strength. But you know what humanity is, Your Highness. Our politicians and so-called diplomats back in England are inclined to rate the value of an ally, or the importance of an enemy, entirely by the size and capability of the army he can put into the field. Now these fine fellows, these are the Imperial Guard, am I right?'

Richilde nodded, as the red coated hussars rode by, emerging from beyond the left wing of the palace, walking their horses in review order past the dais, and then disappearing round the right hand palace wing.

'Those are, as you say, the Imperial Horse Guards,' she explained. 'These are the Imperial Foot Guards.'

Bright yellow jackets, smartly sloped muskets and gleaming bayonets, impeccable discipline.

'Fine fellows. Oh, fine fellows,' Popham commented.

'The Imperial Marines,' Richilde said.

Popham gazed at the sky blue jackets, the tall shakos. 'Bless my soul,' he said. 'I had no idea Haiti possessed a navy.'

'It doesn't,' Richilde said with a smile. 'Except for coastal protection. But that is no reason not to have a regiment of marines, is it, Sir Home?'

'Why no,' he agreed. 'I suppose not.'

He looked back at the parade, but after the Marines had passed there was a hiatus. Richilde was aware of beads of anxious perspiration rolling down her back and filling her gloves. 'Now we will have the first of the regiments of the line,' she said, hopefully. 'Oh, there they are.'

Dark blue jackets, these, white breeches, gaiters, gleaming muskets, tall shakos, led by their drummer-boys, who wore red sashes and beat time as they tramped past, dust eddying from their feet. There were three companies of these.

'All from the same regiment?' Popham asked.

'Oh, good heavens, no,' Richilde said. 'Those are the first three regiments of the line. You will observe that although they all wear the same uniforms, their regimental banners are different. There are twenty-seven regiments of the line altogether, arranged in brigades of three regiments each.' For once again, the three companies having disappeared round the right wing of the palace, there was a break in the procession.

'Each regiment is eight hundred men. You are, as I said, just seeing the lead companies here. So each brigade is approximately two thousand four hundred foot soldiers. His Majesty combines these with two regiments of cavalry, of three hundred men each, and a battery of artillery, to make a division. I know these are smaller divisions than in your European armies, but His Majesty has discovered that such small tactical units are best suited for jungle warfare.'

Popham scratched his ear in astonishment, as much at her detailed knowledge of such military matters as at the implied size of the army being displayed for him. He watched the next company appearing from the left. As Richilde had prophesied, these wore the same blue uniforms as their compatriots, but carried different banners. And behind them came two more. And then more and more, in groups of three companies, until all twenty-seven has passed, and Richilde could listen to the excited murmurings of the junior British officers who stood behind the Admiral, and were clearly most impressed.

'Now we have the cavalry,' she said, and with an effort had to prevent herself from twisting her fingers together. Sir Home Popham might not know the difference between one black man and another, but as an English gentleman he would surely be an excellent judge of horseflesh. Yet had everyone remembered her instructions. As company after company of horse rode by, each company in different uniform jackets and flying different banners, there could be no doubt that the horses on the inside rank, and therefore the only ones which could be accurately inspected by the Britishers, were entirely different beasts.

'Twenty-seven regiments of the line, twenty regiments of horse, plus the Imperial Guard,' Popham remarked, half to himself. 'And such splendid fellows. Why, Your Grace, your Emperor could hope to do battle with the best of European armies, and on an open field. If he were as well served with artillery.'

'It is approaching now,' Richilde said, as the first battery of six guns came round the corner. 'We have thirty of such batteries, as you will see.'

Popham removed his tricorne to wipe his brow; he had been seated in the hot sun for three hours already.

But it was a case of maintaining his composure, as cannon after cannon rumbled by, sending dust swirling upwards to be flicked into their faces by the afternoon sea breeze, and at last sighing with relief as the final caisson disappeared around the side of the palace. He got up, saluted, and then held out his hand to Henry. 'Your Majesty, I congratulate you. That is the finest army I have seen in a long time. Truly, sir, I am impressed.'

Henry smiled at Richilde. 'It is time for tea,' he said. 'The Duchess will entertain us all to tea.'

The meal was served in the ballroom, where a hundred officers, and their ladies, could be comfortably accommodated, and where the palace had already reached perfection, in its huge crystal chandeliers, its monogrammed silk drapes, and in the paintings which adorned the walls: portraits of Henry and his principal generals, in most cases grotesque caricatures, but filled with the colour and the exuberance of the African.

It was a buffet meal, so that the throng could keep moving as they talked, an ever changing kaleidoscope of colour and animation. Popham stayed very much at Richilde's shoulder, throughout the afternoon, allowing her to introduce him to the Negro Generals and their wives, and in turn introducing her to his flag captain and lieutenants. And eventually managing to stand beside her at one of the south facing windows, with Christophe temporarily stranded on the far side of the room and the crowd.

'Is that La Ferriere?' He pointed at the white scar high in the mountains.

'Yes,' she said. 'Would you like to visit there?'

'Indeed I would. But unfortunately I must get on to Jamaica, and write my despatches.' He smiled at her. 'May I ask what those walls are made of?'

'They are made of stone, Sir Home,' she said. 'And they rise one hundred feet out of the rock, and are more than thirty feet thick at the base. It is the most marvellous thing ever built by human hand. And it has, literally, been built by human hand. And human blood.'

He glanced at her. 'You disapprove of this?'

'I disapprove of the shedding of human blood, Sir Home, whatever the reason. I have seen too much of it.'

'Indeed you must have, Your Grace. But I have been told that the Emperor relies upon your advice in all things. Yet you do not approve of the citadel?'

'I do not approve of the citadel, Sir Home. I do not think it is necessary, and I think the cost is far too high. As for relying upon me, His Majesty follows his own council, and relies on no one.'

Popham was still smiling. 'Yet he is not above drawing upon your wits and your imagination, I think. Your very fertile wits and imagination.'

She shot him a glance. 'La Ferriere is real, Admiral. I would suggest that if you doubt that, you make the time to look at it.'

'I believe that it is real, Your Grace,' he said. 'And I beg of you not to take offence. As I have not taken offence at the . . . shall we say, the masquerade, which was presented for my entertainment, this afternoon.'

She frowned at him, while her heart gave a great lurch. 'I do not understand you.'

'There is a sergeant in the Imperial Guard, who I noticed at the very beginning of the review,' he said. 'Because he has a scar on his right cheek. But of course I am mistaken; in *every* regiment, certainly in every third company in His Majesty's army, there is a sergeant with a scar on his cheek. I have no doubt that it is the result of some initiatory duel, as in Germany.'

She stared at him. 'What will you do?'

'Do, Your Grace? Why, I shall write my report.'

'And say?'

'That His Majesty, the Emperor Henri, is one of the most resourceful men I have ever encountered. And Your Grace, in war, resourcefulness of the sort I have witnessed this afternoon often does make up for lack of numbers.' His eyes twinkled. 'However, purely for the gratification of my own curiosity, and with the word of an officer and a gentleman that what you tell me will go no further ... how many men *does* His Majesty command?'

Richilde met his gaze. 'His Majesty commands all of the thirty thousand odd that were represented here today, Sir Home. Unfortunately, not all of them have the discipline or the bearing of your marines, whom he wished to match. But I will tell you this: in their own jungles, and led by a general with Henry's genius, they are the finest troops in the world. As both the British and the French have discovered.'

'Indeed, Your Grace,' Popham said. 'I do not for one moment dispute what you are saying. Believe me, ma'am, I regard Haiti as full of promise for the future, and with you at His Majesty's elbow I am even more confident than I was before.'

'You are monopolising the Duchess, Admiral,' Henry said, joining them. He was in a tremendous good humour since the success of the review.

'I am but attempting to convince her how much I admire what I have seen here,' Popham said. 'I look forward, on my next visit, to inspecting your fortress, in the hills.'

'You will do that,' Henry said. 'And I will have more to show you than that. I will have a united country to show you, when next you come here, Sir Popham. Tomorrow I lead my armies south, to settle with Petion.'

'But *why*?' Richilde cried. 'Why now?'

'Because now is the time,' Henry said. 'I know it. I feel it in my bones.'

He stood in the centre of her private drawing room rather like a defiant schoolboy hauled before the headmistress.

'Henry,' she begged. 'Nothing has changed. The citadel is still not completed. You have no more men or guns than yesterday. What we showed Popham was a sham. Don't you understand that? It was the same thousand men, again and again and again, only changing their uniforms at every circuit of the palace. Why . . .' she bit her lip. She dared not tell Henry that the British Admiral had seen through their subterfuge.

'I know that, Richilde,' he said, with gentle patience. 'But a great deal has, in fact, changed. Bonaparte has been defeated. The power of France is in the dust. We do not know for how long it will remain there, but we must take advantage of it while we can. Popham has told me that there is a great revolt going on against the Spaniards in South America. Spain has no men to interfere with us here in Haiti. This is another factor we must take into account. And he has reassured me that at the present, at any rate, the British have no desire to extend their possessions in America. They have sufficient, for the time being. These are all factors we must consider. And of which we must take advantage. For the first time since August 1791 we have absolutely no fear of a foreign invasion. But these things will change. Other kings will come to power, other policies will prevail. Of course I had not intended to move against Petion until La Ferriere was completed. But that was when I had European intervention to fear. Now that is no longer a problem. Now we *must* move against him, and complete the unification of Haiti, while we may.' He threw his arm round her shoulders and gave her a squeeze. 'As for the citadel, work will of course continue on that, for the sooner it is completed the happier I shall be. I am placing it in your care.'

'My care?' she cried. 'That is impossible.'

'Why is it impossible? You know my requirements.'

'I also know that I could never drive men to their deaths the way you have been doing.'

He held her shoulders. 'You can, and you will. This is the backbone of Haiti that we are creating. You will do it, my Richilde, as you have done so many things in the past. Because I have asked you to. Because I need you to. Because it must done.'

Her resolution was leaking away like water from a holed bucket. 'But why me?' she asked. 'Why *me*?'

'Because in all Haiti,' he said. 'There is no one else I can trust, as I trust you.'

Chapter 4

LA FERRIERE

On a mountain top towering above his country,
[Christophe] erected La Ferriere, the Citadel, the
eighth wonder of the world and the architectural
marvel of the Western Hemisphere, an impregnable
bastion with walls several feet thick and rising a
hundred feet and more from base to battlement,
guarded by three hundred and sixty-five cannon, an
engineering phenomenon, for each block of
masonry, each cannon, each ball and each sack of
food had to be carried by man muscles up the pre-
cipitous face of a mountain.

'There, Highness,' said Colonel Laborde. 'You can
see it now.'

All the previous day they had walked their horses
through the forest, along a cleared roadway, to be sure,
a track trampled by the feet of thousands of men, with
their horses, and the enormous weights they had carried, marked in an almost continuous row beside the
road – and already becoming overgrown by the venge-
ful jungle – by the graves of those who had fallen.

But all the time they had been climbing, too, and now
suddenly there was a break in the trees, and she could
follow the direction of Laborde's pointing finger, and
gape at what appeared, from below, as the sharply
pointed bow of an enormous ship, jutting out of the
mountainside several hundred feet above her. A ship
made of stone, and greater than any vessel ever
launched.

Seraphine was equally amazed. As Kit spent so much time at sea, ceaselessly ferrying Haitian sugar to America, and guns and ammunition back to Haiti, she had refused to remain by herself at Sans Souci, had opted instead for the ride through the forest and into the mountains, her son in her arms. It was the first time she had undertaken such an expedition, and everything was a source of wonder, or a source of fear. For Richilde, everything was a source of memory. Because at the end of it, after twenty years, nothing had truly changed. She was again making her way into the heart of the island, and Henry was again away campaigning. Only that immense stone monstrosity, looming above her, was a symbol of the years that had rolled away, the dreams that had faded, and the men who had died.

Another night camp, with the mosquitoes whirring about them, and the horses moving restlessly in the picket line. And then another dawn, the brilliant red sunlight scorching out of the Atlantic Ocean, far beneath them now, and immediately glinting from the walls of the fortress. But now they were coming closer, and it was a matter of arching the back and the neck, and staring straight upwards, at the bicorned heads peering down at them, and at the gaping mouths of the cannon, glaring over the forest. Henry's plan called for three hundred and sixty five cannon, one for each day of the year, just as his supply requirements called for sufficient food for one thousand men a year. The final, impregnable bastion.

A wooden drawbridge was lowered, and their horses' hooves clattered over a ravine some hundred feet deep, out of which the immense walls rose sheer. Then they were in a courtyard, as large as a village in itself, all hewn out of the living rock. At the rear were the barracks and living quarters, to the right the stables, to the left the storerooms. Richilde was taken to see the well, which stretched down through the rock for several hundred feet, to tap the resources of an inexhaustible jungle stream. She had not been up here since the work had first commenced, and her blood had curdled as she had watched men and women being flogged like any slaves she remembered, as they had carried and dragged the huge blocks of masonry upwards. It had been nauseating and hateful – but she could not help but marvel at the results that had been achieved. She had been born and bred and lived all her life in the West Indies, where the works of man are meaningless compared with the immense and creative architecture of nature; she had only ever read of the Pyramids or the Hanging Gardens of Babylon, the Colossus of Rhodes or the Temple of Diana, but she could not believe that the Pharaohs or the monarchs of Chaldea, the Greeks or the Persians, had ever built anything to equal the Citadel of La Ferriere.

Which she was charged with completing. There was actually little left to be done to the fortress itself. Henry was more concerned to use her brains to establish the storerooms and the interior arrangements. He saw his fortress as the last retreat of himself and his people, or at least a selected few of them, where they would retire were they ever assailed by overwhelming force, and in which they would live, as in a town but with complete security, while yellow fever and hurricane winds gradually destroyed the invading army, as had happened twice before.

But the remainder of the cannon still had to be dragged up from the coast and hoisted into place along the immense battlements. The work continued as soon as Kit returned, and all along the coast from Cap François and through the forest the sweating labourers dragged and tugged and cursed and fell, and were crushed beneath the unceasing wheels and were buried by the roadside with so many others. While the cannon were slowly emplaced, each with fifty twenty-pound iron balls stacked beside it.

And *I* am doing this, she realised. Me, Richilde

Hamilton, daughter of a colonial shipping agent, sometime wife of the last of the Mortmains, and now mistress of the Emperor of Haiti. I am driving people to their deaths because Henry would have it so. While he fought and killed and hacked his way into the mulatto stronghold of the south. And yet found the time to continue government. Thus they received a messenger a week, with news of the campaigns, which were necessarily inconclusive, as she had always known they would be, with queries as to the progress of the citadel, with demands for more men and munitions, and with odd pronunciamentoes, as they occurred to him to make. Thus there was suddenly no more Cap François, but instead Cap Haitien, which Henry had decided was far more suitable. And with that there were orders for changing the uniform of the Imperial Marines, who alone had been left to guard Sans Souci, from pale blue to deep green, orders which Kit had patiently to carry out, and orders to change the imperial monogram to HC, and orders to seek the offices of a suitable *mamaloi* to discover why the Empress had not yet become pregnant, and inquiries as to why the food supplied by the north-west area was down a few per cent this year, and instructions for Richilde to take care as the hurricane season approached. Henry's energy bubbled out of the forests and drove everything before it, as if he were some gigantic volcano, rumbling away in subterranean splendour.

Yet it was a curiously happy time. However much Richilde hated having to drive the labourers to the very limits of exhaustion, she knew that she was creating a monument which would stand as long as time itself. And however much she waited with anxious dread to hear the reports of the unceasing campaigns in the forest, there could be no doubt that Henry *was* slowly squeezing the life out of Petion's small armies, slowly gaining the victory of which he had dreamed, and that he was happy too, happier campaigning than he was

560

doing anything else. Nor could she truly feel apprehensive for his safety, as long as he continued to wear and trust the silver talisman. He had never been seriously wounded in his entire life.

There were domestic joys, too, as Seraphine gave birth to her second child, and as Kit came up to La Ferriere to spend Christmas with them, while the winds howled around the battlements and far below they could see the seething whitecaps of the ocean. It was a stormy winter, normally the best time of the year, and with the spring there was no lack of those who muttered that this coming summer would bring a hurricane. Richilde had never actually experienced a hurricane. The storms roamed the West Indies every year, but there were so many islands that it was possible to spend a lifetime, as indeed she had done, without ever encountering anything more severe than a gale. But this year she at last knew that the real thing was coming close, as she watched the great banks of cloud building to the south and east. It was a time for Kit to locate a land-locked 'hurricane hole' in which to hide his ship until the worst was over, and then to arrange berths ashore for his crews, which suited them well enough. And then it was a time for waiting and watching, as the cloud formations built and dispersed, and then immediately rebuilt again. But the storm had not yet arrived when the Emperor returned from the wars, and with him, his prisoners.

Richilde was down in the huge subterranean vaults, like everything else in La Ferriere hewed out of the solid rock by man muscles, supervising the rotation of the sacks of grain which were always stored here, when she was summoned by Colonel Laborde, who commanded the garrison.

'Haste, Your Highness,' came the call. 'The Emperor approaches.'

Henry! She had not seen him in more than a year.

And she wore an old gown and was dripping sweat and coated with dust. She gathered her skirts and ran up the stone steps, emerged into the courtyard as the drawbridge went rumbling down, and listened to the horses' hooves clattering on to the wood. She pushed hair from her eyes, moved away from where Seraphine and the other women waited, stood by herself as Henry came into the courtyard. He had clearly not bathed or changed his clothes in several days, but she had seen him returning from a campaign often enough in the past. What struck her now were the deep lines of fatigue which were etched in his face, the unutterable weariness with which he slipped from the saddle and threw his reins to the waiting groom.

'Your Majesty.' She sank into a deep curtsey. 'We had no prior warning of your coming, or I should have prepared myself. And the fortress.'

He raised her and embraced her. 'I like you well enough with honest sweat on your brow, Richilde,' he said. 'And the fortress is always prepared, is it not?' His gaze swept the battlements. He could not count beyond ten, but he could see where additional cannon had been emplaced.

While Richilde waited, aware that there had been a distinct lack of real warmth in his greeting.

'The campaign goes well?' she asked.

'The campaign is over, for a season,' he said. 'We have had a great triumph, and taken one of Petion's fortified towns.' At last the grim face broke into a smile. 'He does not have very many of those. But my men need to rest, and the storm season is upon us. I wished to see the citadel again, and you. And besides, I have a task to perform. A duty to complete.' He turned, and Richilde's heart gave a great leap before seeming to slide all the way down into her stomach, as she watched the prisoners being pushed forward, staggering, falling to their knees as they tripped. They had clearly been forced to walk, all the way from the battlefield, after having been stripped of their clothing and their boots, so that their feet were a mass of blood and sores, and their flesh was lacerated, as much from thorns and swinging branches as from the whips of their captors.

Their white skins.

Richilde found herself on her knees as well, gazing at the man before her, head drooping, white hair and beard a tangled, matted mass. Etienne would be, she realised, sixty-four years of age, and had not worn well. Even the last time she had met him, fifteen years ago at Charles LeClerc's garden party, she had noticed that he had put on a great deal of weight. Now the rolls of flesh hung uneasily, and he shivered, despite the afternoon heat.

'Richilde,' he whispered. 'For God's sake, help me, Richilde. Help us all.'

She had to bite her lip to stop herself from crying out as she looked past her cousin, at Louise, also on her knees, plump white flesh discoloured with blood and bruises, and then beyond her, at Madeleine, who had remained on her feet. Madeleine was but two years younger than Etienne, and was therefore sixty-two. But she was still tall, and slender, and upright, her beautiful features a mask of cold reserve, for all the whip marks on her shoulders and buttocks. Beside her there was a girl, perhaps twelve or thirteen years old, Richilde thought, with the soft Ramlie features of her mother curiously juxtaposed with the big nose of the Mortmains. The *very* last of the Mortmains. She had not even been aware that Louise had had a child.

But there was no Annette. Thank God, she thought. Annette would have been more than she could bear.

'Stand, Duchess,' Henry said. 'It is for them to kneel before you.'

Slowly Richilde rose to her feet.

'Your other cousin, the woman of whom Kit was fond, took poison when we entered the town,' Henry said. 'These lacked her courage. They begged for their lives. *He* . . .' he thrust out his riding crop and tapped Etienne under the chin to make his head jerk, 'begged for his life. His life, not theirs.'

'And you have granted them that, Your Majesty,' she whispered, scarce daring to hope.

Henry's smile was terrible. 'No,' he said. 'I will keep my oath. I have brought them back to die, here at La Ferriere, where the whole world will hear their screams.'

Richilde gazed through the window at the huge black storm clouds building out to sea, slowly filling the afternoon sky. They seemed no more than a complement to the mood that hung over La Ferriere. She wished that Kit were here. He had experienced hurricane force winds before. He knew how to cope with storms.

But Kit was in Cap François. Correction, she thought; Kit was in Cap Haitien.

'The storm will be upon us by dawn,' Henry said. 'I am glad to be here, and not in the forest. Will Sans Souci withstand the storm? Is it strongly enough built?'

His Empress was down there. But he was more interested in the palace itself.

'Yes, Your Majesty,' Richilde said. 'The palace is strongly enough built to withstand a storm. But they should remember to shutter the windows, or there may be some damage.' She turned away from the evening, looked at him. He sat in his hip bath, soaking, while the maids scurried to and fro, bringing fresh pitchers of warm water to pour over his back and head. His face was starting to relax as some of the exhaustion left his muscles.

'Would it do any good for me to beg?' Richilde asked, speaking English. 'For me to throw myself on the floor at your feet?'

'I will not have you beg,' he said. 'I swore an oath,

and you knew of this. They knew of it, too. Yet have they come back, time and again, always with my enemies, with the enemies of Haiti. They must die, that the world will understand how the Emperor Henri deals with his enemies.'

She sighed. 'Even the little girl? She has never harmed you.'

'She has Mortmain blood in her veins. She has Etienne's blood in her veins. That is a measure of her guilt.'

'Then let it be quick,' Richilde asked. 'Please, Henry. That they should all die is terrible enough. But let it be quick. Behead them, and have done with it. There is surely revenge enough.'

'No,' he said, and stood up, water rolling from his shoulders and down his legs. The girls hastily wrapped him in towels.

'Henry . . .' her shoulders sagged. 'What will you do with them?'

'Etienne will be flogged. Slowly. One stroke of the whip every five minutes, from dawn until dusk, until he dies. I think it will take several days. Perhaps a week. And while he hangs and suffers, and screams, his women will be spreadeagled before him and raped by my men, one after the other, until *they* die. It will be the last memory, the last sight his eyes will carry, as he goes down to hell.'

Richilde clasped both hands about her throat. 'You cannot be *serious*.'

'My people are erecting a triangle now, with a bed before it.'

'You . . . I had supposed you a man, not a beast, like Dessalines.'

His head came up, and then his hand, pointing. 'Beware, woman. You are not so far removed from a Mortmain yourself.'

'I *am* a Mortmain,' she shouted. 'The same blood runs in my veins, through my mother, as in any of theirs.

And I am white. And I was married to a man who ill used your people, and allowed you to be flogged. Because that is what you are avenging here. Your flogging. Not the death of your child or the enslavement of your people. You are avenging your flogging. Well, why do you not send me down with Madeleine and Louise and the girl. My God, she is my cousin and she is about to die and I do not even know her name. Why do you not execute me as well? Are you afraid that I will not scream? Do not be afraid of that, Henry. I will scream. I will scream more loudly than any of them. Because I will not only know pain, and fear, and humiliation, I will know the horror of failure, the horror of knowing that a man to whom I have devoted my life, to whom I have given almost every minute of my life, is at the end of it nothing more than a savage monster. Dessalines at least acted in rage. But you . . . your hatred is something cold, and malignant. It is the hatred of a snake, lurking in the weeds, waiting, year after year, to accomplish its . . .' His huge hand slashed through the air, and although she saw it coming and jerked her head, she could not avoid the blow. For a moment she lost her senses, and then she discovered herself sprawled on the floor, her scalp seeming to be made of steel and constantly rising and then slamming back again on her brain.

She gazed at his feet, as he stood above her. 'I did not wish to hurt you,' he said. 'I have never wished to hurt you, my Richilde. You are more precious to me than life itself. But you would make me into a woman, or a priest. I am a man and an emperor. There are things I have to do, for the sake of my people, of my fame, of my immortal memory. You have known this, always. You will not turn me aside now.'

He walked away from her, and she sat up. She had to hold her jaw between her hands to speak. 'Then do not ever approach my bed again,' she said. 'Or I will scratch out your eyes.'

He stopped, and turned, while the maids, huddled in the corner of the room, stared from one to the other in utter terror. Once again the Emperor pointed. 'Go,' he said to Richilde. 'And bid your cousins farewell.'

Outside in the courtyard, the wind had already risen. It came in squalls, accompanied by teeming rain, which pounded on the beaten earth, splattered from the battlements, drove the soldiers from their labours; the triangle stood only half completed, awaiting its victim, as the mattress awaited its occupants, slowly turning into a soggy mass.

The guards stood to attention, but did not query her as she went past them, opened the door to the cell, stood at the top of the stone steps and looked down at the huddled figures beneath her. They had not been secured in any way, sat on the cold earth floor, starting to their feet as they saw her.

'Richilde,' Etienne shouted. 'You have saved us.' He ran forward, reached for her as she descended the steps. 'I knew you would. I told them . . . did I not tell you, Louise? Richilde will save us. Henry but means to frighten us, and humiliate us. But if he is taking us to see Richilde, we will be saved.'

She said nothing, resisted his embrace, and his face slowly changed.

'Why should *she* save us?' Madeleine demanded. 'Is she not the white nigger herself?'

To speak, to unclench her jaw, was to send rivers of pain gushing through her head. 'I would save you if I could,' Richilde said. 'I have begged for your lives. But he is adamant.'

'You have begged for us?' Madeleine sneered. 'Have you any concept, any idea, of what we have suffered?'

'I know what you have suffered,' Richilde said. 'I have suffered it myself. I suffered it because Etienne ran away, when he could have stayed and fought with us, and perhaps shown us how to win. But I suffered. And I survived.'

'Because you are a white nigger,' Madeleine spat. 'You were always a white nigger.'

'Because my crimes were not so great as yours,' Richilde said. 'I had never murdered a child.'

Madeleine refused to lower her eyes. 'A mulatto bastard,' she said. '*Your* mulatto bastard. Christophe's spawn. The only mistake I made was is not strangling you with it. My God, there was another. I held you in my arms, within ten minutes of your birth, and I let you live.'

Richilde gazed at her. 'I begged for your life,' she said. 'But I regret that. Henry has made the right decision, after all.'

'But me, Richilde,' Louise cried. 'I have never harmed you. Marguerite here was not even born when all that happened. Are we to die, too?'

'Henry hates everything named Mortmain,' Richilde said. 'I am sorry.'

'But can he not let us live?' Etienne begged, kneeling at her feet, fingers entwined in her gown. 'He hates me, that I know. Let him flog me. For God's sake, Richilde, let him castrate me, but just let him be merciful, and allow me to live, as his slave.'

He was a despicable object, she thought. But then, he had always been a despicable object, even before the night he had galloped away and left her to die, with his mother and father, his wife and his children, his brother and his sisters.

'You are going to be flogged,' she said. 'To death.'

He stared at her, his mouth slowly drooping open.

'So you had best prepare yourself,' she recommended. 'As you must die, I beg of you to do so like a man.'

Still he stared at her, and then he burst into tears, and fell to the floor at her feet.

'And us?' Madeleine asked. 'Are we also to be flogged to death?'

'No,' Richilde said. 'You will be . . . the army will have you, until you die.'

568

Madeleine's head jerked. Louise gave a shriek of horror. The girl Marguerite, so like her grandmother in looks, just stared at her with wide opened mouth.

'And you will stand aside and watch this?' Madeleine asked in a low voice.

'I have no say in the matter,' Richilde said.

'Yet have you more say than you suppose, Richilde,' Henry said.

Their heads turned, to look at him, standing at the top of the steps, wearing his red hussar uniform.

'Mercy,' Etienne screamed. 'Mercy, Great King, oh mercy. Grant us our lives and we shall be your willing slaves forever more.'

'You must die,' Henry said. 'I have sworn this. And you.' He pointed at Madeleine. 'As I have sworn to avenge the death of my son.'

Madeleine said nothing, just stared at him. Etienne gave a tremendous shriek of agony, and once again collapsed to the floor.

'You . . .' Henry again pointed, this time at Louise. 'You are but an accident. You will leave this place, with your daughter.' He turned to Laborde, who waited at the top of the steps with several soldiers. 'You will provide Madame de Mortmain and her daughter with an escort into Cap Haitien. Give them clothes to wear, and make sure that the captain of their escort understands that they are not to be molested or harmed in any way. In Cap Haitien, they are to be kept under guard until a ship can be found to take them away. Captain Hamilton will attend to it. He is in Cap Haitien.'

Laborde saluted.

'Thank you, Henry,' Richilde said. 'Oh, thank you.'

'You . . . are sending us out into a storm?' Louise shrilled. 'You are sending us to our deaths.'

'For God's sake, Louise,' Richilde snapped.

'Take them away,' Henry commanded. 'They turn my stomach.'

The guards came down the steps, pulled Louise and her daughter to their feet, pushed them up towards the door. Madeleine remained standing against the wall, face rigid. Etienne was on his knees, whimpering and weeping, but raising his head as his wife reached the top of the stairs.

'Louise,' he cried. 'Have you nothing to say to me?'

Louise looked over her shoulder, briefly, and was then pushed out into the night.

'Your cousin has begged for you,' Henry said. 'At great personal risk. You should know this, and remember it, as you die. And I am listening to her prayers. I am being as merciful as I may. Bring the woman,' he told Laborde. 'And the man. He will watch.'

The door was opened again, and the wind leapt inside, swirling around the cell, causing Madeleine's hair to flutter. The guards came towards her, and a tremor seemed to run from her neck down to her toes.

'Henry,' Richilde said.

'Be quiet,' Henry said. 'Have I not promised to be merciful?'

The soldiers came towards them, half carrying Madeleine between them. She gazed at Richilde as she drew abreast. There were no tears in her eyes.

The rain was now falling heavily, and the thunder was rumbling, following the savage streaks of lightning which cut across the sky. The drawbridge was just being raised again, after the departure of Louise and Marguerite. And the entire garrison, with their wives and their children, and even their dogs, seemed to have been paraded for the occasion, crowding the courtyard, lining the battlements. No doubt, Richilde thought, Seraphine was somewhere in the crowd.

Madeleine looked left and right, at the black people, and gave another shudder, and then her head jerked with real interest as she realised that she was being pushed and dragged, not towards the soaking mattress set beneath the gallows, but towards a flight of steps leading to the east facing battlements, from where the drop was sheer for a hundred and fifty feet.

'Oh, my God,' Etienne wailed. 'Spare us, oh Great King. Spare us.'

'I will remain down here,' Richilde said.

'You will accompany me,' Henry said. 'You will stand at my side throughout. Or the original sentence stands.'

Richilde drew a long breath, walked at his side across the courtyard, aware that the rain had plastered her hair to her scalp and her gown to her back, and was thudding on to her skin as if she were being stoned. She watched Madeleine's white body being pulled up the last of the steps, and pushed across the firewalk, to the first of the huge embrasures, where a cannon protruded its long barrel into the night.

'Go out there, Madeleine de Mortmain,' Henry said. 'And jump.'

Madeleine realised that her arms had been released. She turned, to look at him, to look at Richilde. Her hair, too, the gold heavily streaked with grey, lay plastered on her shoulders. She watched the crowd surging up the various stairs to crowd the battlements, and stare down into the blackness. Richilde wondered what she thought, as she stood there. Did she remember her English husband and her estranged children, the long, lazy days in St Kitts? Or her girlhood, when she had been the toast of that small island, when with her name and her beauty and her French charm she had lived and laughed and loved like a queen?

Did she wish she had never abandoned that small but secure niche to follow her brother in his insensate search for revenge and reinstatement? Or did she hate too much ever to regret?

Madeleine turned away from them again, held on to the stone of the embrasure, and stepped into the opening, leaning against the cannon. She looked down, into the darkness, and made the sign of the cross. She turned again, standing straight now, swaying as the wind struck at her. She pointed. 'I will see you, in hell, Henry Christophe,' she said, and seemed to fall backwards. Her misery tore a despairing wail from her mouth as she realised she was lost, and then that too was swallowed up by the wind and the darkness.

Madeleine's scream was echoed by Etienne, now grovelling on the soaking stone as he realised that his own moment had finally arrived.

'Bring him,' Henry said, and went back down the steps. He led them across the courtyard to the far end, where although the battlements had been completed, the powder store beneath was still being worked. Here torches were lit and set in the walls, to send their light flaring into the darkness. Richilde stood at Henry's side, feeling the water rolling down her legs to gather in a pool between her feet, listening to the whine of the wind and the growl of the thunder, watched Etienne being carried in; he could not even walk, such was his terror; watched too, against the farthest wall, soldiers who had already embedded iron rings into the stone – clearly acting on orders given more than a few hours previously – now fixing them with mortar.

Etienne was dragged across the rubbled floor and set against the wall, each wrist secured by an iron cuff to keep him from falling. His eyes were tight shut, but yet the tears seeped out and rolled down his cheeks, and now, as his feet touched the earth, he could not stop himself from opening his eyes, and looking around him in bewildered terror.

'Are you in pain?' Henry demanded. 'Are you in agony?'

Etienne stared at him, lips trembling; his whole face seemed to have been reduced to a jelly by his fear.

'Richilde begged for you as well,' Henry said. 'And

so I struck her. Now I grant her wish. You will suffer no pain, Etienne de Mortmain. You will merely have the time to think, of all the evil you have done, of all the sunshine you will no longer see, of the pit of hell which awaits you, with so many souls eager to lay their hands on your body.'

Etienne looked at him, mouth agape, then he looked at Richilde. Such was his fear he still did not understand what was about to happen.

'Commence,' Henry said.

The stonemasons came forward from the gloom at the back of the room, set the first bricks in place. The mortar had already been mixed, and waited in buckets for their use.

Etienne stared at the men for a moment, then raised his head again. 'No,' he shouted. 'No,' he screamed, and commenced to writhe against the wall, a terrible sight.

'What, would you *rather* be flogged to death?' Henry demanded. 'Would you like to be castrated by my women? Would you prefer to be fed to the ants? Be quiet, man, and try to die like a human being, and not an animal.'

Etienne wept and screamed and attempted to kick at the wall, but he could not reach it. And it was already two feet high.

'Perhaps, in a thousand years,' Henry said, 'someone will knock down that wall, and find your skeleton, and wonder what crime you had committed to have been so executed. Perhaps they will know, Etienne.'

The wall had reached three feet.

'Richilde,' Etienne begged. 'Sweet Richilde. Help me, Richilde, help me, for God's sake.'

'I would like to leave,' Richilde said, in a low voice.

Henry glanced at her.

'I am cold, and wet,' she said. 'And my head aches. I would like to lie down, Your Majesty.'

'You will lie down, when we are finished here,'

Henry said. 'You will wait, until the last brick is in place. It will not take long.'

It took, she supposed, several hours for the wall to be completed. Several hours in which Etienne screamed and howled and begged, and thrashed against the wall. When the last brick was in place, his screams could still be heard.

Richilde threw herself across her bed, soaked as she was, shivering as she was. The wind howled, and the lightning sent vivid flashes across the sky, each accompanied by unending peals of thunder. Almost it was possible to imagine the citadel was shaking, as perhaps the entire mountain, or all of Haiti, was shaking.

Equally was it possible to imagine that Madeleine was still falling, white body twisting through space, falling forever, into a bottomless cavern of hatred and despair.

Her door opened, and then closed, and a candle flared. She hugged the mattress closer, suddenly feeling the pain in her jaw where before it had been fading.

'You will catch cold,' Henry said. 'Lying there like that.'

'I will not die,' she said.

'No,' he said. 'You will not die, Richilde. You and I will never die. We will live forever. We are immortals, you and I. We are the favoured creatures of the gods.'

She preferred not to reply.

He waited, for several seconds, then he said, 'But you will not share your bed with me, ever again.'

'I will not share my bed tonight,' she said. 'I am in too much pain.' She did not specify whether the ache was in her heart, or her belly, or her jaw.

Another brief silence, and then she heard the door close again. That was Henry Christopher. A gentle, thoughtful giant, capable of remorse and sadness, of regret and even compassion. But where did Henry Christopher leave off, and the Emperor Henri of Haiti begin? There was a boundary which was becoming more uncertain with every year.

Eventually she slept, and was awakened by a sort of moaning sound, which cut across even the howl of the wind. And then by another noise, a shouting, a fierce, angry bellowing.

It was still dark, although she supposed that it must be near dawn, and the wind still howled as the rain still cascaded over the stone of the fortress, as the lightning still cut across the sky with its accompanying booms of thunder. Her clothes were almost dry, her flesh clammily damp and her muscles stiff. She opened the door, went outside, reached the courtyard. This was as packed as it had been last night, when Madeleine had been hurled to her death. The entire garrison was here, with their women, and their children. Seraphine was here, holding her babe in her arms, while little Alexander clutched her skirts and screamed his terror.

But he was afraid of the storm. The watchers were afraid of the man, who wore the red robe of the *hougan*, and strode the battlements above them, clenched fists waved at the heavens as he defied its anger.

'Come to me,' Henry shouted. 'I am Henri Christophe, Lord of this land. Come to me, if you dare. Come hither, Ogone Badagris, and match me, god to man. Dare your muscles against mine, great Damballah. Face me, if you can. Come to me!'

Richilde found she was holding her breath, as he strode up and down, seeming to shrug away the bolts of lightning, tossing his head to defy the rain.

'He is mad,' Seraphine whispered. 'Like Dessalines, he has gone mad.'

'No,' Richilde said. 'No, he is not mad. He is guilty, and miserable.' She left the shelter of the doorway, once again walked through the rain to the foot of the steps, then slowly climbed them, *feeling* the thousand and more eyes which were staring at her. She reached the top of the steps. 'Henry,' she said.

He turned, fiercely.

She held out her arms. 'Come downstairs, Henry. Come to bed.'

He took a step towards her, and then suddenly every muscle in his body seemed to collapse, and he fell headlong at her feet.

A great wail arose from the watchers, as Richilde knelt beside their Emperor. Feet pounded on the steps, and General Labalastierre and Colonel Laborde reached her.

'He has been hit by a thunderbolt,' Labalastierre shouted. 'He has been struck down by the gods.'

'No,' she said. 'He has been struck down by exhaustion. Carry him to bed.'

Soldiers were summoned, and tenderly six of them raised the huge body of their King from the ground, carried him down the steps.

'He does not breathe,' Laborde whispered. 'He is dead. What is to be done?'

'He is not dead,' Richilde said, watching the mighty chest flutter. But a great lump of lead seemed to be forming in her stomach, as she remembered the *mamaloi's* words, remembered too the utter exhaustion which had been etched in his face yesterday afternoon.

They carried him into his bedchamber, laid him on the bed. 'Leave us,' Richilde commanded.

Labalastierre hesitated, glanced at Laborde. They both feared witchcraft.

'He will be well, once he has rested,' Richilde told them. 'I will stay here with him, and watch.'

'His Majesty is ill,' Labalastierre said. 'We must send for the Empress.'

'By all means send for her,' Richilde agreed. 'By the time she gets here he will be well. But only if he is left, to rest. Help me get his uniform off.'

Between them they stripped that massive, inert frame, and then they wrapped him in a blanket.

'Now go,' Richilde said. 'Go, and His Majesty will be well.'

They hesitated a last time, and then left the room. Richilde closed and locked the door, and then stood above him, looking down on him. She held the fingers of his right hand, found they could move quite easily. But the fingers of his left hand were stiff, and his mouth was twisted, the left side rigid.

She sat on the bed, and stared at him. Her knowledge of medicine was inadequate, but she could tell that he had had some sort of a seizure, as Elaine had foretold. The question was knowing how long it was likely to last, and what he would be like afterwards, and what might be done to prevent it happening again. Only rest would do that. But would Henry ever rest?

And for the moment, she realised, she was in command, of him and of the fortress. Labalastierre and Laborde would obey her, if she acted in the Emperor's name. She stood up, biting her lip in a sudden irresoluteness.

'You will leave him,' Henry said. His voice was hardly more than a whisper.

Richilde stared at him.

'You will leave him because he deserves to die,' Henry said. 'And because he will not again secure so easy a death as starvation.'

She knelt beside him. 'Thank God,' she said.

'That I should condemn your cousin, twice?'

'That you are speaking, so soon,' she said. 'I had feared . . . so much.'

'Who struck me down?' Henry asked. 'I felt no pain, and I saw no one. Who struck me down?'

'No one struck you down, Henry,' she said. 'You have had what the surgeons call a stroke. It is . . . I do not know for sure, but it is to do with the heart, when it becomes overtired.'

'A stroke?' he asked. 'I cannot move my arm.'

'Raise your right hand,' she commanded.

Slowly his right arm came up.

'That is the important one,' she said. 'The other will soon be well again.'

The right arm fell, across his chest, the fingers seizing the silver bullet which lay there.

Richilde smiled. 'You still have your bullet, Henry. All will be well. Now you must rest. Just rest. And all will be well.'

'You will not leave me,' he begged.

She hesitated, then nodded, and lay down beside him. 'I will not leave you,' she said. Because as you have said, Henry, she thought, Etienne does not deserve to live, and he will not again find so pleasant a death.

When Richilde awoke, the rain had stopped, and the wind had dropped. It still soughed, and when she went to the window, set high in the wall of the citadel, and looked down at the forest, she saw that the trees still swayed and bent. She saw too that several had been uprooted, and that great swathes had been cut through the bushes. But the storm itself had gone, and Haiti could resume its normal life. As if Haiti would ever have a normal life.

'What do my people say of me?' Henry asked.

She returned to the bedside, looked down at him. Much of the tightness had left his face.

'That you were struck by a thunderbolt, from heaven,' she said.

He smiled. 'A thunderbolt, from heaven. That is good. Yes, I was defying the gods, and Ogone Badagris struck me down. They will understand that. You will not deny this tale, Richilde. You will confirm it.'

'If that is what you wish, Henry.' She sat beside him. 'They have sent for the Empress. She will be with you in a few days.'

He frowned at her. 'She must not come here.'

'Not come here? But Henry, she is your wife.'

'My Empress,' he corrected. 'She must not see me like this. She must not. Send her back.' He rolled on his side, away from her, faced the wall.

Richilde rested her hand on his shoulder. 'By the time Honeybelle reaches La Ferriere, Henry, you will be nearly as healthy and as strong as ever before in your life.'

He rolled on his back again. 'Nearly?'

'You have just rolled over,' she said. 'Last night you could hardly move your arm. You are recovering moment by moment.'

'Nearly?' he asked again. 'Will I not regain *all* of my strength?'

Richilde sighed. 'You will regain all of your strength, that any man can know, Henry. But your heart, your mind, has given you a warning, that you are overtired, that you can no longer work as hard as you do, and fight as hard as you do, and demand so much of your body. You are over fifty years of age, Henry. I am over fifty years of age. We are not children any more. We must recognise that fact.'

'Bah,' he said. 'My heart gave me no warning. My heart obeys me, not I it. I was struck down by a thunderbolt, sent by Ogone Badagris. Do you not understand that?'

Richilde would not lower her gaze. 'If you do not heed me, Henry, you will have another stroke, and from that you may not recover at all. Why do you not spend a month here, with me, and Honeybelle? Or better yet, let us all go back down to Sans Souci. There you can rest, and go fishing, as you did before you came to power. Surely you can spare the time to do that?'

'No,' he said. 'Because I *have* come to power. If I rest, the whole country will rest. If I rest, Petion will recover from his defeats, and regain the territory he has lost. He may even invade the north.' He smiled, and picked up her hand. 'Believe me, Richilde, my dear,

dear Richilde, there is nothing I would like better than to remain here with you and go fishing. But I cannot.'

She sighed, and left the bed, and stood by the window.

'Have you forgiven me?' he asked. 'For executing Etienne and Madeleine?'

'No,' she said. 'No, I have not forgiven you. Not for executing them. But for acting the savage. But I understand what you did, and why you did it.'

'Understanding,' he said. 'That is your greatest gift, Richilde. The gift of understanding. My people do not have that gift. You must teach it to them, before we die.'

She turned back to smile at him, through her tears. 'I shall at least endeavour to teach it to you, Henry. Before we die.'

By the time the Empress arrived, three days later, Henry was, as Richilde had promised him, as well as ever before in his life. And by then, too, the legend of how he had challenged the gods, and been struck down by them, had spread beyond the fortress, to add to the legend of Christophe himself. And, as he had foreseen, he gained only credit from it. Because the gods had been unable to kill him. They had done nothing more than knock him senseless, as one man might do to another. He had survived the thunderbolt, and now, as he displayed to his people by himself hefting cannon balls, two in each arm, and carrying them up to the battlements, he was stronger than ever before. When next he sought to oppose Ogone Badagris, the god would not find it so easy to gain even so limited a victory.

Richilde knew that it was useless to attempt to restrain him. She could only wait, and watch, and try to get him to bed for a rest from time to time. But even that was difficult, for Honeybelle had a tale of her own to tell, of the great waves which had pounded the beaches, and driven across the coast road into the forest; of a tidal wave running through the streets of Millot, sweeping away houses and people, and even pounding at the doors of Sans Souci itself.

'My palace?' Henry shouted, in real alarm. 'What has happened to my palace?'

'It still stands, Your Majesty,' Honeybelle said. 'There has been a little damage. But Millot . . .'

'And Millot belongs to your people, Your Majesty,' Richilde reminded him. 'They are *your* people.'

'Yes,' he said. 'Yes, you are right. We must get down there, right away, and discover what has happened, and what must be done.'

So once again, a trek through the shattered forest. But for Richilde, a happy escape from the gloomy terrors of La Ferriere, where she could still hear Etienne's screams. As he had only been walled up for six days when they left, he could indeed still be screaming.

And I have acquiesced in this, she thought. As I stood by and watched Madeleine being hurled from the battlements. They had been guilty of everything Henry had accused them of. Yet had they also been her cousins. But Henry was her man, whatever his growing loss of any sense of reality, or proportion. And these were her people. Where he, and they, went, so must she.

Certainly there was enough to be done, down on the coast. Millot was indeed shattered, but now at last she could persuade Henry to give the orders to rebuild the town, and create the city of which she had always dreamed. In that sense the hurricane had turned out to be a blessing. Just as the destruction of Vergée d'Or, further along the coast, was a blessing. She rode out there, with Seraphine, and looked at the beach, almost totally gone, now, gouged out by the huge Atlantic rollers to leave only rock, even the little stream diverted and buried. Just as the foundations of the chateau itself had been ripped and torn, and the factory chimney had finally fallen, to wreck the remainder of the building and the machinery. Henry was furious. It would take a great deal of time, and money, to re-create Vergée d'Or as a prospering plantation. Richilde was content, that this strongest of all links with her past should finally be nothing more than a scar on the earth. The beach would return, she knew; the chateau with its lawns and terraces, its staircases and its portraits, its galleries and huge rooms, where so many people had died, would never rise again. It was a sobering reflection on the irrelevance of man when compared with the might of nature, that even had there been no revolution, Vergée d'Or might still have been wiped off the face of the map, by the hurricane. The chateau had been at least as strongly built as that of Sans Souci, but had been so much nearer the beach. Certainly it would have taken a terrible pounding.

But what then had happened to Cap François? Seraphine was naturally concerned about Kit, so they obtained permission from Henry to go into the city. But Cap François had withstood hurricanes before. Several of the wooden docks had been severely damaged, and the seas had risen far enough to wash right across the road and into the town, yet their force had been absorbed by the shoals lying off the beach, and the damage itself had been slight. Kit had put the necessary repairs in hand, and was on the point of setting off with Rogers and the crew to discover what had happened with the *Stormy Petrel*, but he already knew that all of the merchant ships which had been in the harbour at the approach of the storm, and had been securely tucked away in a shallow lagoon protected by a bank of mangroves a hundred years thick, were perfectly secure.

He was also able to reassure Richilde that Louise and Marguerite had arrived, safely. He had placed them in a house, under guard, and would despatch them to Jamaica as soon as the weather improved. Richilde decided against visiting them. She had nothing to say to them, and they would only have hate to express to her. The Mortmains were finished; their bloodstained saga at an end. She was content that it should be so; it was time also for Louise and Marguerite to find their way back to France, and their Ramlie relatives, and forget the tumultuous years during which they had followed Etienne blindly to destruction.

And it was time for her to return to Sans Souci, and Henry. Kit would be joining them in a few days. Somehow, knowing that Henry had at last expiated his hatred and his desire for vengeance, even knowing that he had been struck down, and recovered, made her feel more relaxed than she had been in a long while. Because he *had* recovered. And he was, however reluctantly, obeying her and taking life somewhat more easily. They had, she realised, suddenly entered upon the second half of their lives together. A time for coasting gently downhill, rather than constantly making the effort to mount the slope that lay ahead of them.

But as she saw the cavalcade approaching them on the road from the palace, her heart lurched, and then sank. Because Henry was there, with Labalastierre and Gounod, and his hussars, clattering towards her, bristling with warlike determination.

'Richilde!' Henry shouted, catching sight of her party and giving rein, and then remembering his dignity. 'Duchess! Great news! The very best. Petion is dead.'

She could only stare at him. 'Petion? But how?'

Henry shrugged. 'Heart failure, or some such thing. He must have been struck down the very same moment as I. But I recovered, and he died. There is a measure, eh?'

'What will you do?' As if she did not already know, what he would do.

'Do? Why, recommence the war. With Petion dead . . . there is only that boy, Boyer, to command the mulattos now. Now we shall wipe them from the face of the earth. Now the victory will be ours.'

Chapter 5

THE SILVER BULLET

Christophe, the magnificent warrior, had no claims to power beyond his physical stature and the living memory of his accomplishments against the French. When age had begun to sap the strength of those giant muscles, and the memories of his followers, Christophe had no promises, no development plans with which to revive their loyalty. The ex-slave could only become a tyrant, and stand whip in hand over a resentful people.

Richilde stood on the battlements of La Ferriere, and listened. She did this every morning, at dawn, had done it, every morning at dawn, for the past year and more. At dawn the land breeze swept down from the mountains, brought with it the sounds of the mountains, and even, perhaps, the noises of the plains beyond. Sometimes it was possible to hear, or imagine she heard, the roar of cannon, and the cries of dying men.

The Emperor continued his war, now to the exclusion of all else. But he fought with no greater success against Boyer than he had ever fought Petion. Haiti was an offensive general's nightmare, as had been proved so often in the past. Pitched battles could only ever be fought by mutual consent. Retreating armies could never be overtaken and routed by fast riding cavalry, where they could melt into a jungle so thick that a man on horseback was forced to travel even more slowly than one on foot. And defensive positions could not be surrounded or flanked, where they were situated above impregnable precipices, from which uncrossable ravines stretched in every direction. Henry's victories against Petion had been gained where victories *could* be gained, by the capturing of towns and villages and sugar plantations. Boyer, who had lived and fought in these conditions all of his adult life, knew better than to offer such hostages to fortune, and long before the Negro host could reach his civilised outposts they had been burned and evacuated. And he kept on fighting, kept on campaigning. He had a soldier's ruthlessness, beneath the charm she remembered so well. And besides, he had an educated man's vision of the present and the future. He calculated that no matter how many skirmishes he might lose, no matter how many villages he might be forced to burn, he would still eventually win the war. Because Henry just fought. It was what he liked doing best. To campaign, in the midst of his soldiers, to expose himself to enemy fire, glorying in the immunity from harm granted him by his precious silver bullet, to plan and then to execute, the kill and to savour the glory of triumph, these were the true delights of life, to Henry. She realised that they always had been.

He expected his people, all of his people, to feel the same. All Haiti, every man, woman and child in the country, was in his opinion born with but a single simple purpose in mind: to support and sustain their Emperor in his determination to conquer the entire vast island. That each of his people might have an ambition of his or her own, that most of those ambitions were simply to till an acre of land and catch a net of fish, and raise a family, was incomprehensible to him. To express such a wish was an act of treachery. And, tucked away in his forest as he was, in the midst of his faithful soldiers, he was unaware of the deep resentments, the deep discontents, which were seeping through the life of his nation.

Richilde herself was not entirely aware of them. She spent most of the time, nowadays, at La Ferriere, protected by the cannon and the walls and Laborde's garrison, and by the immensity of the forest as well. The fortress, so high and so impregnable, so free from mosquitoes and from heat, had ceased to frighten and depress, was her own little sanctuary; its mood suited hers. That it contained the bones of Etienne, and that somewhere at the bottom of the east facing ravine there lay the bones of Madeleine, was no longer a disturbing factor; all sugar plantations, for example, had possessed their own cemeteries, and these usually very near to the house. She had been brought up to live close to her ancestors – and not very many of those had died peacefully in their beds. And besides, to leave La Ferriere, and go down to the coast, *was* to become aware of the gathering discontent. It meant watching the, as yet, unfinished city of Millot, suspended between drama and achievement by the requirements of the Emperor's war. It meant listening to the grumbles of the labourers and the farmers and the fishermen, a tithe of whose meagre earnings were gathered by the tax collectors, to pay for the Emperor's war. And it meant visiting Sans Souci, where the paint peeled and the wood rotted, and the Empress Honeybelle danced and played her way through life, uncaring of the misery beyond her front door.

La Ferriere was the place to be, until Henry came home. If he came home. Because she remained obsessed by a nameless dread, a certainty that that paralytic attack *had* been but a warning of what the future would hold for him, should he not be capable of slowing down, and accepting life more as it came, instead of perpetually attempting to mould it to his own pattern.

And today, at last, she knew he was coming. As the

dawn breeze whispered across the morning, she could hear the clank of wagon wheels, the rattle of accoutrements, drifting towards her. Others heard it too. Both Seraphine and Laborde heard it, and came to join her on the battlements.

'The army returns,' Laborde said. 'That is strange, Your Highness. We have had no messengers to tell of the victory.'

Good, honest, faithful Laborde, she thought. He cannot conceive of Henry ever returning, unless he has gained a victory. But now she could see the red uniforms of the hussars, winding their way along the forest track beneath her. And now too, she could see the horse litter, on which there lay the body of the Emperor.

Desperately Richilde looked for blood and bandages. Blood and bandages, evidences of a physical wound, were things she could cope with, and if he had survived them so far, he would survive them always.

But there was no blood, and no bandages.

She stood in the doorway as the Emperor was carried into his quarters and laid on the bed. His eyes were open. That was the most terrible thing she had ever seen. His eyes, so intelligent, so evident of his will and his determination, glared at her as if he would communicate his thoughts, for he had no other means of expression. His lips were rigid, and his entire face twisted. And he could barely twitch the fingers of his right hand.

'He just fell from his horse,' Labalastierre explained. 'As we were going into battle, His Majesty just fell from his horse. There was no thunder, Duchess. He just fell from his horse.'

'The battle?' Richilde asked. 'What happened?'

Labalastierre sighed. He looked exhausted, and his uniform was caked with sweat and dust. But so were all their uniforms. 'We lost the battle, Duchess. When our soldiers saw what had happened to the Emperor, they fled '

Richilde discovered she was holding her breath. Christophe had never lost a battle. It was impossible to suppose that he could ever do so.

'Our men scattered,' Labalastierre went on. 'Shouting that the Emperor was dead. I knew he was not, and I sent messengers after them, but they would not return. So I brought His Majesty here, with the Imperial Guard. But Duchess, the soldiers will come back, as soon as they know His Majesty is not dead, that he is again well and strong. Duchess, you restored him to health the last time. You must do so now, again.'

Richilde chewed her lip, and stared into Henry's eyes.

'You must do this, Duchess,' Labalastierre said. 'And quickly. Boyer will not wait for long, when he learns what has happened.'

'Yes,' she agreed. 'I must do this, and quickly.'

He waited, but she did not continue. 'Shall I send for the Empress?' he asked.

She shook her head. 'No, not this time. It were best no one sees him like this.'

Labalastierre groaned. 'The whole army has seen him, like this, Duchess.'

'And they will see him again,' she said. 'When he is well.' But would he ever be well again? Could he?

Labalastierre hesitated, then turned for the door. 'You must tell me what you wish done. It will be done.'

Richilde's shoulders sagged. And then she squared them again. Were she to despair, then there was truly nothing left. 'Yes,' she said. 'I wish you to summon Captain Hamilton, the moment he returns to Cap Haitien. And I wish you to find a *mamaloi*, named Elaine. Your wife knows of her, Prince. Find her, and bring her here. Those are the people I need.'

Kit arrived a week later, to Richilde's very great relief. Because by then she knew that Henry would be a long time recovering, if he ever would. She spent her days massaging his arms and legs, and had achieved a measure of success, in that he could move the fingers of his right hand. His brain was also certainly unaffected. He understood everything that had happened, everything that was happening, everything that she said to him. And she wished he couldn't. The agony in his eyes was horrible to watch.

And Elaine had vanished into the jungle, her hut deserted. She had prophesied the illness of the Emperor. She had not waited to be arrested by his angry soldiers.

'How long?' Richilde asked Kit. 'You must have seen seizures like this before.'

She asked the question in a corner of her own bedchamber, where they could not be overheard.

Kit's face was grim. 'It is a very complete paralysis. He may regain the partial use of his limbs. But he will never sit a horse again, or draw a sword.'

She stared at him in stark horror.

'Will you tell him?' he asked.

'No,' she said. 'That would be to kill him. We shall tell no one. We cannot tell *anyone*.'

'Are you sure you know what you do?'

'Yes,' she said fiercely. 'As far as his people, as far as the world is concerned, he is recovering. He is getting better, every day. Do not fail me, in this, Kit.'

'Because they will turn against him, when they know,' Kit said. 'And you, and Seraphine, and myself and the boys. Richilde, that is bound to happen. You cannot stop time. You cannot pretend, forever. Listen to me. You have done everything for Henry that you can. All of your life you have done that. Now you can do no more. Surely now is the time to think of yourself, just for once? I am due to sail again in a week. Come with me. It need only be a journey to Cap François, as far as anyone knows. You and Seraphine have been to Cap François before. There will be nothing unusual in that. In Cap François you will come on board to say farewell, and we shall sail away. It will be as simple as that.'

She gazed at him for several seconds, then she turned away. 'You will be sailing from Cap *Haitien*, Kit. And I would like you to come to me, and wish me goodbye, before you leave. I doubt we shall meet again.'

Now she never left Henry's bedroom at all, had her meals served in there, tended to his needs, continued her massaging of his limbs, forced his mouth open to pour soup down his throat, waited for him to be able to move his lips. If he could but utter a word, then she would know he was recovering. But his lips could not even twitch.

The Empress arrived. She had been told nothing but rumours. Now she stood in the doorway of the bed-chamber, and gazed at her husband, who gazed at her. She did not advance to the bedside.

'It was his wish we did not send for you immediately, Your Majesty,' Richilde said. 'He wished you to wait until he is well again. But as you are here, I know he will be grateful for your comfort and support. It will not be long now. He will soon be well.'

Honeybelle's nostrils dilated. 'I will return to the coast,' she said. 'His Majesty is right, and I should not have come. I will see him in Sans Souci, when he can travel.'

The door closed, but Labalastierre had remained on the inside.

'How much longer, Duchess?' he asked.

'Soon,' she said. 'Soon, all will be well. Every day, his strength returns. I can feel it, and see it. Soon.'

'How soon?' he insisted. 'Tomorrow? Next week? We have heard that Boyer is on the march, Duchess. We must know, how soon.'

Richilde bit her lip, and Labalastierre gazed at her

for several seconds. Then he turned and left the room.

She slept, in the bed beside him, listened to his breathing. She doubted *he* slept. She doubted he had truly slept since his return, on the litter. And awoke, with a start, unable to decide for a moment what had disturbed her. Then she realised that it was the absence of the sentry's boots, hitting the stone firewalk above her head.

She sat up, looked left and right. Nothing had changed inside the room, and it was just dawn. But there was sound outside, an immense rustle. She dropped her gown over her head, ran to the door. Here too there was no sentry. She ran along the corridor, stood in the doorway, gazed at the courtyard. It was full, of people, soldiers, and their women, and their horses, and their dogs, and their children, and their bundles of precious belongings. And the drawbridge was slowly being lowered.

Richilde ran forward, found Labalastierre, at the head of the garrison, Laborde at his side. 'You cannot leave him now,' she said. 'You cannot desert him. He is recovering. Every minute, he is recovering.'

'You have said that every day, for the past month, Duchess,' Labalastierre pointed out.

'Perhaps I have been optimistic. But it will happen. It *is* happening,' Richilde insisted. 'I will swear to it.'

'It is happening too slowly, Duchess,' Labalastierre said. 'We have received a message from General Boyer, summoning us to surrender. He has taken possession of Cap Haitien, Duchess. The entire island is in his power, save only for this fortress.'

She stared at him, unable to believe what she had just been told. But they had to stay. They *had* to.

'And is that not what this fortress was built for?' she cried. 'As a retreat for our people, after invasion? It is stocked with food, and munition, for a thousand men for a year.' She pointed, at the cattle and the chickens, which had been taken from their pens. 'There is more livestock than on the entire coast. Boyer cannot hope to carry the citadel by assault. And he cannot besiege us here, either, for a year, without food. We must win in the end, if we defend the citadel.'

Labalastierre's face was stony. 'General Boyer has offered us our lives, and our ranks, if we surrender,' he said. 'He has promised us death if we continue to fight. We have agreed to surrender. You would do well to accompany us, Duchess. He has stated that he will execute *every* human being he discovered inside La Ferriere.'

'Are you men?' she shouted. 'Or cowards? Who do you think made you what you are? Who made you a prince, General Labalastierre? It was Henri Christophe, not Jean Boyer. Would you desert him now, when for the first time in his life he needs you, instead of you needing him?'

Labalastierre kicked his horse, and the animal moved forward. Richilde had to jump out of the way to avoid being trodden on. But she threw herself forward again to grasp Laborde's bridle.

'You at the least, Colonel Laborde,' she begged. 'Will stay and defend the citadel. You were placed in command. It is your fortress. Colonel . . .'

He wrenched her fingers free, threw her hands away. 'I must obey General Labalastierre,' he said.

She stood, hands hanging at her sides, as the garrison slowly marched out. They would not look at her, gazed in front of themselves as the dust eddied from their hooves and their feet, hung on the still morning air. Even when the last had gone through the gateway, she continued to stand there, unable to believe that it had happened, unable to believe they would not turn round and come back, to man these battlements, from which no shot had ever been fired in anger, against which all the muskets and cannon in the world could be fired, could they ever be brought to bear, without result. It was only when the sounds of their progress down the hillside began to fade, that she turned, to look at the houses – and at Kit and Seraphine, standing there, with their children.

'Have you not gone too?' she demanded. 'Did you not hear what Labalastierre said? Boyer will execute everyone who remains in the fortress.'

'Are you leaving?' Kit asked.

She stared at him. 'No,' she said. 'No, I will stay with Henry.'

'Then we will stay with you,' Kit said.

Her mouth opened, and then closed again, as tears sprang to her eyes. And then her head jerked, as from within the Emperor's apartments there came a crash.

Richilde ran into the house, gasping for breath, pulled open the door of the bedchamber, half fell beneath the enormous weight of Henry's body, leaning against it. Kit, at her shoulder, grasped the Emperor's arms, pulled him upright.

Richilde gazed at Henry, unable to believe the evidence of her eyes. His face remained rigidly twisted, his left arm hung useless, it was apparent there was little strength in his legs – but he had got out of bed and crossed the room.

'Easy, now,' Kit said. 'Easy now, old fellow. Let's get you back to bed.'

He half pushed, half carried Henry across the room, laid him on the mattress.

'My soldiers,' Henry whispered, his voice seeming to issue from the very pit of the grave. 'Where are my soldiers?'

'Kit!' she cried. 'To horse. Ride after them. Bring them back. Bring but one back. Just Labalastierre will do. Let him see for himself. Let him hear the Emperor speak. Let him know that all will be well. Oh, bring them back, Kit. Bring them back.'

Kit ran from the room.

Richilde knelt beside the bed, held Henry's head in her arms. 'Oh, Henry,' she said. 'Oh, *Henry*. How I have prayed. Oh, Henry.'

'My people have deserted me,' he said.

'They were afraid. How could they not be afraid, with you lying here, so stricken?'

'But you were not afraid, my Richilde.'

She smiled. 'No, I was not afraid, Henry,' she lied. 'And neither will they be, when they come back.'

He said nothing. but his eyes closed, almost for the first time since he had returned to the fortress. Then they opened again. 'It is good of Kit to have remained. My two old, faithful friends. It is good.'

'You have other friends, Henry,' she said. 'You will see.'

He sighed. 'I have no friends. Only followers. Who will follow me no longer.' Almost his lips smiled. 'I equipped this fortress, for a thousand men, for a year. How many years may two men defend it, my Richilde?'

'Five hundred years, Henry. But there are also two women. We will defend La Ferriere for two hundred and fifty years.'

Now he did smile, then his face grew solemn again. 'But one of the men is a cripple. Tell me straight, Richilde . . . will I ever sit a horse again?'

She hesitated. 'Yes,' she said. 'Of course you will, Henry. All you need is time.'

But the hesitation had been fatal. His face closed again, and his eyes remained open.

She fed him. Then she said, 'Kit will be on his way back, by now, with Labalastierre. I must go and look for them.'

'Load a pistol for me,' Henry said.

She frowned at him.

He smiled. 'I am lying here, helpless. I can but use my right arm. I have never been like this before, incapable of defending myself. Fetch me a pistol, Richilde. Just the feel of it will make me stronger.'

She chewed her lip, tempted to remind him that there was no one in the fortress for him to defend himself against. And that she knew too the despair which was lapping at his mind. But it was essential to keep him from becoming agitated – and she need take no risks. She went to the guardroom, primed a pistol, but removed the ball. She gave it to him, watched his huge fingers curl around the butt.

'Now I will grow stronger,' he said. 'By the minute. You watch.'

Richilde raised her head, gazed at Seraphine, who stood in the doorway.

'Kit has returned,' Seraphine said. Her features were once again the calm, composed mask Richilde first remembered of her. The same features which had hung beneath the gallows outside Dessaline's kraal, waiting for death.

Richilde ran outside, and into the courtyard, watched Kit dismounting, looked past him at the empty gateway, the empty forest.

'They would not come?'

'They *could* not come,' Kit said. 'They had already encountered Boyer. Can you not hear?'

She listened, to the sounds of an army on the march. She gathered her skirts and ran up the steps to the battlements, looked down on the forest, saw the gleam of swords and bayonets amidst the trees.

'They will be here in half an hour,' Kit said.

Seraphine stood at his side, waiting.

'We must raise the drawbridge,' Richilde said. 'The three of us can do it. Then we will defy them. No man can take this fortress, if but a single cannon is mounted. And we can do that too.'

Kit looked at Seraphine.

'We must,' Richilde shouted. 'We must. Come on.' She ran for the steps, checked at the sound of an explosion. Her heart lurched all the way down to her belly, and then rose as rapidly. The gun was unloaded. He would be lying there in total mental anguish. She raced down the steps and into the house, opened the bed-chamber door, and gazed at Henry Christopher, his right hand, holding the pistol, still slowly sliding away from his opened mouth.

She sank to her knees, aware that Kit and Seraphine were standing beside her.

'The silver bullet,' she whispered. 'I forgot the silver bullet.'

Jean Boyer stood above the body of the Emperor, slowly removed his cocked hat. 'He had greatness,' he said. 'The greatness of strength, and determination, and ambition. Had he also possessed the ability to harness those things, the education to understand what had gone before, to conceive what might come after, who knows what he might have accomplished?' He raised his head. 'No tears, Duchess?'

'I think I have shed them all,' Richilde said. 'Your Majesty.'

'But you stayed with him, to the end. With Captain Hamilton. There is faithfulness.' His lips twisted into the ghost of a smile. 'I am not a majesty, Madame de Mortmain. I think Haiti has had its fill of emperors, and dukes, and princesses. I promise you that His Majesty will have an emperor's funeral, however.

Richilde scarce dared breathe. 'And me, General Boyer?'

'Captain Hamilton's ship waits in Cap Haitien. I would suggest you accompany him to the United States, madame. I would invite you to stay, and grace our society as you have done for so long, but . . .' Once again he looked at Henry Christopher's shattered face. 'You will not look upon his like again, and you, madame, above us all, have too much to remember. I give you, those memories, of the greatest black man the world has yet known'.